Cynthia Harrod-Eagles is the author of the contemporary Bill Slider Mystery series as well as the Morland Dynasty novels. Her passions are music, wine, horses, architecture and the English countryside.

Visit the author's website at
www.cynthiaharrodeagles.com

Also in the *Dynasty* series:

DYNASTY

15

The Reckoning

Cynthia Harrod-Eagles

sphere

SPHERE

First published in Great Britain in 1992
by Macdonald and Co (Publishers) Ltd
This edition published by Warner Books in 1993
Reprinted 1996, 2000
Reprinted by Sphere in 2007, 2009, 2011, 2012, 2013

A CIP catalogue record for this book
is available from the British Library.

ISBN 978-0-7515-0058-5

Printed and bound in Great Britain by
Clays Ltd, St Ives plc

Papers used by Sphere are from well-managed forests
and other responsible sources.

MIX
Paper from
responsible sources
FSC® C104740
www.fsc.org

FT
Pbk

Sphere
An imprint of
Little, Brown Book Group
100 Victoria Embankment
London EC4Y 0DY

An Hachette UK Company
www.hachette.co.uk

www.littlebrown.co.uk

Every author should have a Julia Martin.
This book is dedicated to mine.

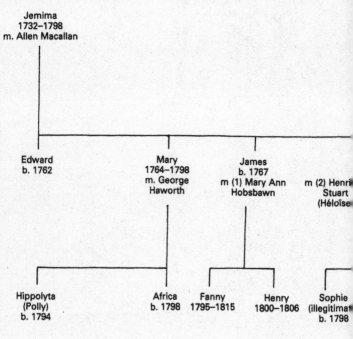

Jemima
1732–1798
m. Allen Macallan

Edward
b. 1762

Mary
1764–1798
m. George
Haworth

James
b. 1767
m (1) Mary Ann
Hobsbawn

m (2) Henri
Stuart
(Héloïse)

Hippolyta
(Polly)
b. 1794

Africa
b. 1798

Fanny
1795–1815

Henry
1800–1806

Sophie
(illegitimate)
b. 1798

THE MORLANDS OF
MORLAND PLACE

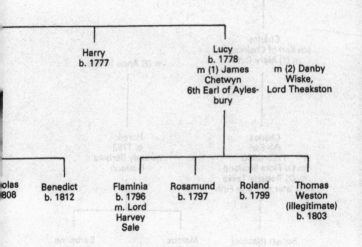

Harry
b. 1777

Lucy
b. 1778
m (1) James
Chetwyn
6th Earl of Ayles-
bury

m (2) Danby
Wiske,
Lord Theakston

...olas
...808

Benedict
b. 1812

Flaminia
b. 1796
m. Lord
Harvey
Sale

Rosamund
b. 1797

Roland
b. 1799

Thomas
Weston
(illegitimate)
b. 1803

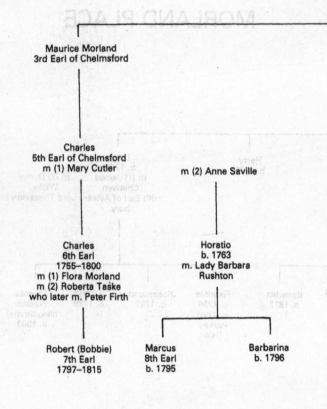

Maurice Morland
3rd Earl of Chelmsford

Charles
5th Earl of Chelmsford
m (1) Mary Cutler

m (2) Anne Saville

Henry
b.
m (1) James ... m (2) Henry
Chatwyn
5th Earl of Aylesbury
Lord Theakston-
bury

Charles
6th Earl
1755–1800
m (1) Flora Morland
m (2) Roberta Taske
who later m. Peter Firth

Horatio
b. 1763
m. Lady Barbara
Rushton

Rosamund
b. 1792

Flaminia
b. 1798

... d. 1817

... Thomas
... Paston
(illegitimate)
d. 1803

Robert (Bobbie)
7th Earl
1797–1815

Marcus
8th Earl
b. 1795

Harvey
1806

Barbarina
b. 1796

THE CHELMSFORD COUSINS

Aliena

Marie-Louise

Henri de Stuart
Comte de Strathord

Henrietta
(Héloïse)
b. 1777
m. 1806
James Morland
(q.v.)

SELECT BIBLIOGRAPHY

E. Baines	*History of the Cotton Manufacture of Great Britain*
A. Briggs	*The Age of Improvement*
C.C. Brinton	*English Political Thought in the Nineteenth Century*
J.R.M. Butler	*The Passing of the Great Reform Bill*
S.G. Checkland	*The Rise of Industrial Society in England*
J.H. Clapham	*An Economic History of Modern Britain*
F.O. Darvall	*Popular Disturbances in Regency England*
A.V. Dicey	*Law and Opinion in England*
H. Finer	*English Local Government*
W.T. Jackman	*The Development of Transportation in Modern England*
H. Martineau	*History of the Thirty Years' Peace*
J. Neal	*The Pentrich Revolution*
R.H. Prothero	*English Farming Past and Present*
J.F. Stephens	*History of Criminal Law*
N.W. Thomas	*The Early Factory Legislation*
R.K. Webb	*Modern England*
S.B. Webb	*English Local Government*
R.J. White	*Waterloo to Peterloo*
L. Woodward	*The Age of Reform*

BOOK ONE

Acts of Men

When I have born in memory what has tamed
Great Nations, now ennobling thoughts depart
When men change swords for ledgers, and desert
The student's bower for gold, some fears unnamed
I had, my Country – am I to be blamed?

William Wordsworth: *England 1802*

CHAPTER ONE

A cold and steady rain had been falling since dawn, but by nine o'clock the wind had gone round and it had eased to a drizzle. Lord Theakston, waiting for his lady to appear for breakfast, stood at the window of the morning-room looking down into the street. The spring of 1816 had been the wettest in memory, and London was never at its best in the rain. The wind gusted in unpleasant flurries which caught under umbrellas and hurried their owners forward for an undignified pace or two. Pavements glistened; puddles collected in ruts and potholes to trap the unwary; trees dripped and gutters overflowed.

The sweeping-boys were much in demand. It was a thankless sort of job, Theakston reflected, watching a skinny boy shove accumulated dung and mud – the consistency of uncooked pudding – off the crossing at the corner of Park Street. A moment later the wheels of a carrier's cart dragged it all straight back again, as the horses clopped on down Upper Grosvenor Street soaked and rat-tailed, flattening their ears against the rain.

Theakston craned his neck and looked the other way down the street. In Hyde Park the glorious blossom candles of the great horse-chestnuts were now no more than a dismal carpet of brown, scattered petals. Rotten Row was deserted. He sighed. It didn't seem a bit like May, the poets' smiling month.

The door opened at last and Lucy came in, her hay-coloured, curly head bent as she buttoned the cuff of her primrose muslin. His heart lifted simply at the sight of her. He wondered if he'd ever get used to being married to her. It seemed such an improbable, exotic sort of privilege – like having a lioness for a pet.

'Still raining?' she said. 'I wonder if it ever means to let up?'

3

'Startin' to grow webs,' Theakston said, spreading his fingers, and was rewarded by a flash of blue as Lucy looked up for an instant from her troublesome button to smile at him. Hicks, the butler, walked in bearing the coffee-pot and newspapers, followed by Ollett with the heavily-loaded tray. Her ladyship, much to the servants' approval, liked an old-fashioned, hearty breakfast. They had no patience with the fashionable notion of toying with a mere slice of toast or half a sweet roll.

Lucy took her place at the table and Theakston sat opposite her. 'Well, I must say, it isn't a bit the way I expected Peace to be,' she remarked as Hicks filled her cup. She glanced at the *Times*, lying folded beside her husband's plate, and the *Chronicle* beside her own. 'Nothing but gloomy news, until one hardly likes to open the papers. And everyone complaining about being hard-up. If this is what we get for winning the war, I wonder why we bothered to fight the French at all.'

'Habit,' suggested her husband. He smiled at her. 'I suppose after twenty-three years, one does sort of miss it.'

Lucy grinned. 'My soldier hero!'

Last year, in glorious June sunshine, Lord Wellington had led his rag-bag Allied army to victory at Waterloo, and the Corsican Tyrant had been defeated at last. Theakston had been there – Colonel Lord Theakston, gallantly leading his regiment of light cavalry to the charge, and making Lucy realise precisely how much she'd miss him if he were killed.

Stripped of his regal titles, 'General Bonaparte' was now a prisoner on a tiny island in the middle of the Atlantic Ocean, from which, it was hoped, he would find it impossible to escape again. But after the euphoria of the victory, peace had brought no plenty to the victors. Already 1816 was a year of bankruptcies, of unemployment, of soaring prices.

'What did you think Peace would be like?' Theakston asked, watching the dishes being placed in their meticulous order. Buttered eggs *here*, cold beef *there*, the truckle of Cheddar *just so*, the mutton ham from Devon adjusted *exactly thus*. Hicks considered the arrangement, and tweaked a chafing-dish round three degrees to the south-west. A butler had his pride, after all.

'I don't know,' said Lucy, frowning. 'That everything

4

would be jolly, I suppose.' She peered into a dish. 'What's this, Hicks?'

'Lobster cutlets, my lady. Jacques was of the opinion the lobsters would not hold until tomorrow. The damp weather, my lady.'

'Oh,' said Lucy. She helped herself largely to sausages, added a handsome wedge of cheese, and after a moment's thought, some pickles. 'All these breakdowns, for instance,' she reverted to the conversation. 'I don't understand why suddenly nobody's got any money.'

'Wars are expensive things to run,' Theakston said, carving mutton ham to go with his eggs – each fragrant slice so thin he could have read the *Times* through it, if he'd been wanton enough to try.

'Exactly. So now we don't have one to run, we ought to be better off, oughtn't we?' Lucy said.

Theakston shook his head, having very little understanding of the matter himself, too little to be able to enlighten her. 'I don't know. Better ask John Anstey,' he suggested. 'He understands these financial mysteries. Probably see him at the sale today.'

'Oh, did he say he was going?'

'He's after George's Mantons.'

Lucy's face sharpened with distress as she remembered the last time she had seen one of those guns, tucked under George 'Beau' Brummell's arm as he strolled, immaculately attired, in the wake of the Duke of York at the Christmas shoot at Oatlands. Now they were just another item on another sale list: 'three capital double-barrelled Fowling Pieces by Manton', part of the 'genuine property of a Man of Fashion, gone to the Continent'.

'I still can't believe it,' she said, putting down her knife. 'George, of all people! It's like – it's like the end of the world.'

Theakston sympathised with her. It was the end of the world in a sense – the world of their youth, which had seemed to them unchanging and unchangeable. He and Brummell had been at school together at Eton, and had joined the same regiment – the 10th Dragoons, the Prince of Wales's Own. As dashing young subalterns of nineteen they had met Lucy at a dinner party at Chelmsford House, when she was the new bride of the Earl of Aylesbury, and out to set the Town by the ears.

The three of them had been friends ever since, for twenty years dominating, and to an extent, shaping London Society – Brummell most of all, of course. And now the Beau – the ultimate arbiter of fashion, the original Dandy, the founder of the Bow Window Set, and Perpetual President of Watier's Club, the 'Great Go' itself – had cut and run. Last Thursday he had been obliged to flee the country to escape his creditors. It was a devastating blow to them all, and especially to Theakston, who had no dearer friend except Lucy. Things would never be the same again: with Brummell had departed a large piece of their lives.

Theakston sought to distract her a little. 'Meant to say to you – I think we ought to go to the sale in the carriage.'

Lucy was a Morland of Morland Place by birth, and therefore not only a bruising rider but a tireless walker. She stared at her husband. 'Really, Danby! Chapel Street's only a step away. I'm not going to have the horses put-to for that short distance. Parslow would think I'd gone mad. A little rain won't hurt us, but it would mean hours of grooming and tack-cleaning for him.'

'I've spoken to him already. He entirely approves. It isn't the rain, my love,' he hurried on as Lucy's brows drew down alarmingly, 'it's the crowds. Bound to be unpleasant. You've no idea. I went to Codrington's sale last month, remember. You don't want to have to push through that sort of mêlée.'

Lucy sighed, picked up her knife, and returned her attention to the sausages. 'Yes, poor Codrington! I'd forgotten. And there was Henry Mildmay last year. It seems as though we're to lose all our friends.'

Round-faced, sweet-voiced Mildmay had fled the country after £15,000 damages were awarded against him by the courts for 'Criminal Conversation' with Lord Rosebery's wife. He had no means of paying such a sum, and he and Harriet Rosebery, who were deeply in love, had run to Stuttgart to avoid Sir Henry's being arrested. They would never be able to return to England.

'It makes you wonder who'll be next,' Lucy said. 'I wish there was something we could have done to save George.'

'Nothing for it. Gone altogether too far,' Theakston said. He forbore to remind her that lately Brummell had worn out the affection of all but his closest friends by borrowing money

6

he had no hope of repaying. Only three weeks ago Lucy had made a sharp comment when Theakston had admitted parting with yet another two hundred pounds, to cover the Beau's losses one evening at Gordon's, a disreputable gambling-hell in Jermyn Street.

Meyler, one of Brummell's creditors, had finally denounced him publicly in White's as a swindler, and with the prospect of having all his many debts called in at once, the Beau had been forced to flee abroad to avoid arrest.

Brummell had confided only in Theakston and Tom Raikes, who had helped him with his plan of escape. He had slipped away from a performance of the opera and hurried to an appointed spot where Raikes was waiting with a hired chaise. In this they had driven out to Eltham Common, where Theakston had earlier taken Brummell's own carriage, packed with a few of his most precious possessions.

It was a strange place for three middle-aged, town-bred Dandies to find themselves, an unpromising site for an emotional farewell. In rain and darkness, with the soaked grass of the common under their thin-soled, city boots, and nothing of comfort anywhere but the small familiar sounds of the horses, they clasped hands briefly.

'Good luck, old fellow,' Raikes said gruffly. 'It's a damned shame.'

'Tom. Danby. My dear friends. Thank you for everything! Can never repay you –'

'God bless you, George,' Theakston said unsteadily. He thrust his purse into Brummell's departing grip. 'For the journey. Hush! Better hurry.'

A moment later Brummell was gone. The carriage lights shewed briefly, swaying through the murk, and then the rain came on more heavily and blotted out sight and sound. Raikes and Theakston travelled back to London in the hired chaise and a gloomy silence.

After that there remained only the outcry and scandal, the speculation and condemnation, and finally the announcement on the back page of the *Times* that by order of the Sheriff of Middlesex, Mr Christie would hold an auction on Wednesday the 22nd of May at 13 Chapel Street of the entire contents of the premises. The proceeds would be distrained for Brummell's creditors.

That was where they were bound today – a sort of last rite for their departed friend. Lucy looked past her husband's shoulder at the dreary swathes of rain blowing past the window. 'I hate this Peace,' she said with passionate illogic.

He sought to comfort her. 'It's the start of a new era,' he said. 'A new world, I suppose. It'll take some getting used to.'

'I don't want a new world,' said Lucy, reaching for the lobster cutlets. 'I want the old one back.'

Despite Danby's warning, the scene in Chapel Street still took Lucy by surprise, and she looked a little pale as their carriage drew up outside number thirteen just after ten o'clock. It wasn't so much the size as the style of the crowd which brought home to her forcibly that their friend had really gone, and gone for ever. The neat little house had its windows stuck all over with sale bills advertising the more important items of furniture; and the once-white steps were muddy from the passage of the kind of boots which never would have been tolerated there a week ago.

'Oh, Danby, it's awful!' she said as the footman came round to open the carriage door. 'All those horrible people staring – and the upstairs windows left open! George would never have allowed that, on a day like this. He hated fresh air.'

'You don't have to come in,' Danby said. 'Let Parslow take you straight home again.'

The mere suggestion stiffened her resolve. 'I'm not a funk,' she said. 'And I must have something to remember him by.'

Theakston stepped out and turned to hand her down. The crowd, gathered in spite of the rain simply for the pleasure of seeing which famous people would turn up, parted to let them through, and a murmur of recognition rippled back through the ranks. They mounted the steps and passed through the open front door, to be besieged by a crowd of shabbily-dressed 'agents', thrusting out their business-cards and offering to save the lady and gentleman the disagreeable labour of bidding for themselves.

'I'm your man, my lord!' 'Anything at all that you fancy, my lord – I'll get the best price.' 'You want to be sure of securing what you're after, my lord – don't risk losing it to another!'

8

Danby thrust them all away good-naturedly, and led Lucy through into the booklined parlour, where in the past callers who were *not* intimates of the Beau had been kept drumming their heels until a suitable realisation of their inferiority had overtaken them. Here there was a press of people of various ranks, uneasily jostled together in the quest for a bargain or a keepsake; and here, almost immediately, they were accosted by Marcus Morland, who looked extremely relieved to see them.

'Oh, thank heaven, a friendly face at last!' he cried, making his bow to Lucy. 'How do you do, ma'am – sir?'

'Hullo, Marcus,' Lucy said. He was a distant relative of hers, who had become Earl of Chelmsford last year on the unexpected death of his cousin Bobbie. 'I didn't know you were in Town. I thought you were house-hunting with your mother.'

'We were – we came back yesterday.' The new earl's pale hair was ruffled and he looked hot. 'I say, there are some very queer people here today! I was up in the bedroom just now, and there were two of the most vulgar cits you can imagine, not at all the thing! There they sat on the dressing table smoking tuppenny cigars and talking about Trade, while their wives gave the mattress and bolster a most tremendous *shampo*-ing!'

'I'll give you *shampo*, young Chelmsford,' Theakston smiled. 'None of your Peninsula slang here, if you please!'

'Ah yes,' Lucy eyed him critically, 'you've shaved off your whiskers. I couldn't think why you looked so different.'

'Mama didn't think they were becoming to an Earl,' Marcus said, embarrassed. 'I don't think she likes to be reminded of the army – you know, Papa being killed and everything. But I say, this is an awful business, isn't it? Mr Brummell of all people! I hate to think of all his things going to strangers.'

If he had hoped to ingratiate himself by sympathising he had chosen his words unwisely. Lucy didn't like being reminded of the horrid reality.

'And have you come to acquire some of his "things" – or is it mere idle curiosity that brings you here?' she asked coolly.

Marcus flushed. 'Mama asked me to come. She's after the Beau's dinner-service – I mean, she thought it might go cheap

9

– that is, she said if it should be a bargain –' he stumbled.

'I should stop before you get yourself even more involved,' Lucy said unkindly. She glanced around her. 'Every corpse has its carrion-eaters, I suppose.'

With that she moved away. Danby lingered a moment to comfort the stricken young man. 'Don't mind it. Her ladyship's upset.'

'Yes, sir, of course, she's bound to be,' Marcus said gratefully. He eyed the older man hungrily. 'Have you heard from Lady Rosamund lately?'

'Not since last week.'

'I suppose she'll be coming home from Morland Place soon?'

Theakston shook his head. 'There's no date set for it. Sophie hasn't been quite well, and I suppose Rosamund will stay until she sees her improve. I think there's some talk of a visit to the seaside.'

Marcus liked Sophie Morland very much, and was sorry to hear that she was unwell, but he had hardly seen Rosamund since Christmas. 'Surely she doesn't mean to miss the whole Season?' he asked wistfully.

'I don't think she cares much about the Season,' said Lord Theakston. 'She was never fond of balls and squeezes, you know.'

'But she was so gay in Brussels last year,' Marcus said. 'She danced every dance.'

'Things were very different in Brussels. We shouldn't judge anything by Brussels, you know.'

'I suppose not,' Marcus said hesitantly. 'And of course it must have been a shock for her when poor Tantony was killed, just after they'd become engaged. But she ought to be over it by now,' he went on with faint indignation. 'It isn't as if it was a love-match, after all.'

Theakston hesitated, thinking of his enigmatical stepdaughter. Marcus had been her childhood champion. When she was still in pigtails, 'Marcus says' and 'Marcus thinks' had punctuated all Rosamund's conversation – none the less after he had gone away, like a story-book hero, to the war, and she hadn't seen him for two years.

Last year Lucy had taken her and her cousin Sophie to Brussels for their come-out. Marcus had been there too: a dashing staff officer at Headquarters, and making a fool of himself over that practised siren, Lady Annabel Robb. So Rosamund had dedicated herself to becoming the toast of the Season: feverishly gay, she had danced every dance, flirted with all the officers, and finally become engaged to handsome Philip Tantony, at the same time as Sophie had accepted a Major Larosse.

Well, poor Tantony, like Larosse, had died a hero at Waterloo. Bel Robb had dropped Marcus callously and married elsewhere, and Marcus, his eyes opened, was now not only free and eligible, but as eager to marry Rosamund as she could ever have wanted. Yet Rosamund seemed curiously unwilling to come to the point. No-one had thought her particularly attached to Tantony; assumed she had accepted him because she couldn't have Marcus; but Theakston wondered whether perhaps they had all mistaken the situation. He had a notion that Marcus was deceiving himself, perhaps wilfully.

So now he diverted Marcus's attention by asking, 'How did you get on with your house-hunting?'

'Not very well. We looked at half a dozen places, all very splendid, I thought, but Mama's awfully particular, and nothing seems to be just exactly what she's looking for. For myself,' he added in a burst of confidentiality, 'I'd as soon live in Town all the time, but Mama says we have to have a Seat. She wonders that none of the previous Earls have purchased before now.'

'You've chosen the right time to buy: everybody else is selling. But you have Shawes, in any case,' said Danby – unguardedly, since it was next door to Morland Place where Rosamund had been staying. 'It's small, but very handsome.'

'Yes, but it won't do for Mama. Yorkshire's so far away,' Marcus said wistfully. 'I say, sir –'

Theakston cut him off hastily. 'I must go to her ladyship. Good luck with your commission – the dinner-service is very fine. I should get Abrams to bid for you – he's the best of 'em,' he added with a nod towards the throng in the hall.

'Oh no, sir, I mean to bid for myself,' Marcus said proudly, and Theakston shrugged and left him to it. Lady Barbara was unlikely to get her dinner-service that way, he thought; but he had no brief for Lady Barbara, who was very nearly the most unpleasant woman he knew.

11

He caught up with Lucy in the dining-room next door, talking to Lord John Anstey of York, a family friend of her childhood, and patriarch of the vast Anstey coal empire.

'I really am surprised at Brummell – running off like this and leaving Alvanley and Worcester to stand the row,' Anstey was saying. 'I hear they're damnably compromised – joined with him to raise a loan, which is bound to be called in now. And then there's the Manners brothers. He was involved in some sort of annuity scheme with them, so I hear – all very shaky. Tipping the double to the duns is one thing, but to leave your friends –'

Lucy was looking ready to explode.

'No, no – nothing else he could do,' Danby said quickly. 'If he hadn't run, he'd have been taken up, and that'd be the end of that. He'd never be able to pay anyone back from inside the King's Bench, now would he?'

Anstey looked doubtful. 'But surely he's all to pieces? I hear his debts are frightful. What can he hope to do – even from France?'

'It's much cheaper to live in France. He has some capital left – not much, but with the strictest economy, he might live on the interest and pay back a little here and there,' Danby said, aware of how futile it sounded. Brummell practise economy? As well expect water to run uphill. 'And then there's a considerable sum still held up in Chancery, which must become his sooner or later.'

'In Chancery? Then it'll be later rather than sooner. Men have grown old and died waiting for legacies to be released from Chancery.'

'I know. But it's the best hope there is,' Theakston said with a shrug.

Anstey looked at Lucy and sighed. 'Well, I suppose he must feel the disgrace as heartily as anyone. He owed you quite a sum, didn't he?'

Lucy frowned. 'Danby gave him a trifle from time to time, but he knows we'd never press him for repayment, not like that dreadful Meyler creature. It's all *his* fault George has had to run. He was the one who started all the fuss.'

'I'm afraid it had to come sooner or later, Lucy,' Anstey said gently. 'Even Hobhouse was saying –'

12

'Oh, Hobhouse! All his friends conveniently forget now that if positions had been reversed, he'd have given them anything,' Lucy burst out. 'He was the most generous man in the world.'

'Well, he won't be the last to come to grief, I'm afraid,' Anstey said. 'There are breakdowns everywhere, and bankruptcies, and any number of small banks failing. That's half the trouble, you know – this damned paper money! There's no end to the bills banks can issue, and with trade stagnant that can only lead to inflation. We must get back to gold currency, but we daren't do it too quickly, especially with prices rising so fast.'

Lucy understood nothing of such matters, but gold currency was a feature of her youth and it had a solid, reassuring sound in a world suddenly grown unfamiliar. 'Quite right,' she said. 'We should never have got away from gold. This paper money was the start of all our troubles.'

Anstey almost smiled. 'You may be right. But we can't do it for a year or two – especially with the landowners pressing us to abolish the income tax.'

'Oh, income tax – I hate the very sound of it! As well be in the paws of the cent-per-cents, as pay income tax, I always say!' Lucy exclaimed.

Anstey met Theakston's eye and both burst out laughing. 'Oh Lucy, what do you know about money-lenders?' Anstey said.

'Enough to know you might as well be dead,' she retorted. 'So will things be getting back to normal soon?' she went on, looking up at Anstey hopefully.

'Not soon. I'm afraid it will get worse before it's better.'

'But why, John? What's gone wrong? Now the war's over –'

'It's very complicated,' Anstey said patiently. 'It's not just us, you see, but all the rest of Europe, too. No-one can afford to buy our goods, so the manufactories and workshops have to stop producing. They lay off the hands, and men out of work can't afford to buy the food the farms produce, so farmhands are laid off too. There's unemployment everywhere.'

'Even in the coal mines? I thought you were doing so well?'

'We were, a couple of years ago. The increase in steam-engine machinery meant every machine needed coal. But now the manufactories are idle, so I've had to turn off men as well. Everything's connected, you see, Lucy. We're all involved. I dare say even your returns have fallen.'

'I wouldn't know about that,' Lucy said blankly. 'My agent sees to all that. But in any case, we've always lived in a pretty small way, so I daresay we keep ahead with the world.'

Anstey boggled at the idea of Lucy living 'in a small way', and even Danby coughed a little and hid a smile with his hand.

Lucy didn't notice, pursuing thoughts of her own. 'Are you in trouble, then, John?'

'Good Lord no,' he said quickly. 'Things aren't come to that pass yet.'

'Well, I'm glad to hear it. Only so many people are going to the wall, it makes one nervous.'

'Oh, I'm not completely to pieces yet,' Anstey smiled. 'I've enough to spare, at any rate, to bid for Brummell's Mantons. I've always coveted them.'

Theakston nodded. 'They're capital pieces; but Hobhouse is after 'em too, so be sure you don't just bid each other up.'

'Thanks for the warning. Are you after anything in particular?'

'George's cellar,' Danby admitted. 'Ten dozen of port, and sixteen dozen of burgundy, claret and champagne. I helped him lay 'em down, in happier days. Know he'd sooner I drank 'em than one of your Russell Square types.'

Anstey sighed. 'It's a bad business, but it can't be helped. Ah, there's Mr Christie going into the dining-room now. I think we must be about to begin. Shall we go in? May I offer you my arm, Lucy? Hullo, isn't that Harriette Wilson? Everyone seems to be here, don't they? And there's Tom Raikes. And young Scrope Davies – I hear he's almost as far up the River Tick as poor Brummell was.'

By the hour of Promenade the rain had stopped, leaving the afternoon grey, cold and gusty. It was enough for Lucy, having been confined indoors all day. She put on her driving-coat and, in memory of the departed Beau, one of her more dashing hats, and went out for a drive in the Park.

The dreadful weather so far that year had evidently lowered many people's expectations, for there was far more of a crowd than might have been expected, most of them driving or riding. Lucy's progress was slow, for everyone seemed to want to discuss Brummell's downfall, who had guessed it was coming, what it would mean for Society, and who had got what at the auction.

Lucy bore with the remarks of the genuinely concerned as patiently as possible; the merely impertinent got short shrift; but at last she had had enough of it, and with the justification that her horses were getting cold, drove on at too smart a trot for anyone else to accost her.

They were almost round at the Stanhope Gate again, when Parslow murmured discreetly, 'Lady Greyshott, my lady, on your right, if you should want to look the other way.'

'No, it's all right – Lady Greyshott I don't mind,' Lucy said, slowing her team.

Helena Greyshott was a distant cousin, and an exact contemporary of Lucy's. Her career through Society had been even more exciting and scandalous than Lucy's, and many had been the duels fought over her, both before and after her marriage. Her husband, a lazy and cynical dilettante considerably her senior, had made it known from the beginning that he did not mean ever to go out on his wife's behalf. The meetings had therefore taken place between rivals for her affections, which, coupled with the fact that Lady Greyshott herself liked to be present, caused a number of the stickier hostesses to strike her from their visiting-lists.

Helena Greyshott cared not a whit; though of late she had grown comparatively staid, having found true happiness at last, it seemed, in the affections of a single lover, a Captain of the Blues who had enjoyed her favours for the last two years. She came striding towards Lucy now, her little feet heedless of the puddles which splashed the smart black galoshing of her boots, or the mud which decorated the flounce of her gown and the hem of her pelisse.

She had with her her thirteen-year-old daughter Thalia, an extremely pretty girl who was popularly supposed to have been fathered by Sir Henry Mildmay. In fact she was Greyshott's child, but neither parent bothered to deny the rumours. The Honourable Thalia Hampton was looking far less pleased with the mud and puddles than her mother, and was trailing a pace or two behind, her heavenly violet eyes stormy.

15

Lucy halted her blacks and Parslow jumped down to go to their heads.

'Lucy! Thank heaven for someone sensible to talk to at last,' Helena said. 'I came out for a walk to get away from callers. Nobody has anything to say but how bad the weather is and who is the latest bankrupt.'

'How are you, Helena? How's Captain Twombley?'

Lady Greyshott laughed. 'Oh dear, poor Harry! But I really can't help it – every single time I hear his ridiculous name ...! I keep begging him to change it, but he says he likes to surprise people: Twombley by name but not at all by nature! He's away at the moment, in Vienna, which accounts for my foul temper. The rain accounts for Thalia's. Do stand up straight, my darling. You look like an old woman.'

Thalia scowled fearfully, and Lucy took pity on her. 'Perhaps you'd like to take a turn round the Park with me?'

'Not I!' Helena said quickly. 'You get down and walk with me, Lucy. You know I can't bear to be driven by anyone else – not even you.'

Lucy caught Parslow's eye and read the slight flick of his head. 'Very well,' she said. 'I'll walk with you, and Parslow can take Thalia round. Would you like that?'

'Oh yes please, Lady Theakston,' Thalia said quickly. To drive behind Lucy's famous blacks – and with Parslow, who was a legend with her generation – and most of all not to have to be walking in the mud – was a delightful prospect. The exchange was quickly made, and Parslow drove off with the slight figure tense with excitement beside him, while Lucy and Helena linked arms and walked off in his wake.

'Poor Thalia hates the rain,' Helena remarked. 'She's getting as vain as a monkey. I dread to think what she'll be like in four years' time.' Lucy looked a question. 'Ceddie doesn't want her brought out until she's eighteen, but I've told him we won't be able to hold her back so long. I wanted sixteen, so we've compromised.'

'Seventeen's a good enough age.'

'Rosamund was seventeen, wasn't she? How is she now? Has she got over that awful business in Brussels?'

'Oh, I think so. Tantony was a nice enough man, but I don't think she was violently in love with him.'

'I didn't mean that,' Helena said. 'I was thinking of her

helping you tend the wounded. Harry told me what Brussels was like after the battle. And then watching poor Bobbie Chelmsford die. It must have been a terrible shock to her nerves.'

Lucy pondered the idea. 'I suppose it may have been. I'd never thought of Rosamund's having nerves. She didn't seem to be particularly upset.'

'But didn't she go out of Town to recover? I'd heard that she was rusticating.'

'She's staying with her cousin Sophie, but that's more for Sophie's sake. Now that *was* a tragedy. Sophie was quite nutty on her Major Larosse – and with her disadvantages she's not likely soon to replace him.'

'Hmm. Whereas Rosamund's already got another suitor, from what I hear. They say Marcus Chelmsford means to make an offer for her. Or has he spoken already?'

'He's made his intentions pretty clear,' Lucy said. 'I've no objections. If she wants him, she shall have him. I've grown to like her a lot since Brussels, and I wouldn't stand in her way. She's always liked Marcus, and I want her to marry someone she'll be happy with.'

'I feel the same way about Thalia. Lord! If only our mothers had been as understanding! Not that I've been unhappy with Ceddie, of course. He and I rub along together well enough. Still, I think it would have been nice to have been married to someone I loved, the way I love Harry. But things were different in our day, of course.'

'They certainly were. I was only fifteen when I was married for the first time.'

'Girls today are lucky. Except, I suppose, a good many of them may never marry at all, with so many of our young men falling at Waterloo ... You'd better encourage Rosamund to snap Marcus up as soon as possible. There'll be plenty of others after him.'

'I suppose so. I shall miss her, though. She's become quite good company.'

'That's the trouble with daughters. Just when they've got past the tiresome stage, they're married and gone. Boys you keep. You must miss your boys now?'

'Yes,' Lucy said, though the truth was she had never really got to know her son Roland. The three children of her first marriage – Flaminia, Rosamund and Roland – had been brought up wholly by tutor and governess, until Minnie was married straight out of the schoolroom, and Roland sent to school so that he could mix with others of his own age. Far more of a loss to Lucy was Thomas Weston, her love-child, whom she adored. The boys had refused to be parted, so when Roland went to Eton, Thomas went too.

'I hear great things of Thomas,' Helena said. 'Little Maurice hero-worships him, you know.' Her son, Maurice Hampton, was in the same lodgings with Thomas and Roland. 'He says Thomas is known as Old Tough, of all things, which I gather is a great compliment.' Lucy smiled. 'He tells me – let me see if I have it right – that he is handy with his *fives*, is something of a *scud*, and has a growing renown as a *swipe*! And all this at the age of thirteen!'

Lucy laughed. 'Boys are the strangest creatures, aren't they? Roland is four years his senior, but it's always Thomas who leads. I don't quite know what's going to happen next year. Roland has already said he doesn't want to leave school if Tom is still there.'

'Let Thomas leave too.'

'But Thomas needs the advantage,' Lucy frowned. 'Roland's place is assured, but Tom has to make his own way in the world.'

'You could send them on a Grand Tour together. That would be education for them both.'

The idea struck Lucy. 'That may be the very thing,' she said. 'It never occurred to me – I'm not used yet to thinking of Europe as accessible.'

'Ceddie says it's a wonderful experience, and a great educator. He had his Tour before the war, of course – Lord, how different things must have been then! Still, he's determined Little Maurice shall go when he's eighteen – especially as it looks now as though he'll inherit both titles.'

'What, your brother's as well?' Lucy asked in surprise. 'But surely Ballincrea will marry again? He's young enough.'

Helena shook her head. 'Maurice was devoted to Mary. I don't think any of us realised how deeply. He never cared for another woman, you know; and now she's dead he says he won't marry again, and that he's quite happy for the title to come to Little Maurice. He was always fond of him. Little

18

Maurice was named for him, of course.'

'Well, it's early days yet,' Lucy said. 'Mary only died in January, didn't she? When he's over the shock of it, he may think differently.'

'Perhaps,' Helena said without conviction. 'I don't care for Little Maurice's sake – he'll have Ceddie's title anyway – but I wish Maurice weren't so very unhappy. We were very close when we were children, and I care about him.'

'It's been a sickly winter,' Lucy said. 'There've been so many deaths. Old Lord Penrith went in February –'

'Yes, and now that oaf Georgie Sale is Marquess of Penrith – how it suits him! Ceddie saw him in the Great Go the other day, eating his way towards an apoplexy. Said he looked as stuffed as a Christmas goose! What does Minnie think about being the marchioness at last?'

Lucy's elder daughter, Flaminia, had married the younger of the late Marquess's sons, Lord Harvey Sale, but since George Sale was a confirmed bachelor, Harvey was likely to inherit the title after him.

'I really don't know,' Lucy said indifferently. She had never cared much for her elder daughter, whom she thought dull. 'Minnie is the world's worst correspondent, and now that she has the twins, she never leaves Stainton.' Lucy thoroughly disliked the very idea of being a grandmother, and in fact had managed to see her granddaughters only once so far, at their Christening last September. 'And I never go there, of course – quite the wrong part of the country. It seems to suit Minnie, though.'

But Helena Greyshott was looking rather puzzled. 'Surely you've seen her lately? I mean, she must have visited you while she was in London?'

'Visited me? No. Why should you think she was in London?'

'Because I saw Polly Haworth recently in Brook Street. Polly does still live with Minnie, doesn't she?'

'Yes, of course.' Lucy was a little puzzled too. Polly Haworth was her niece, whom Lucy had brought up in her own household with her daughters. Minnie had always been devoted to Polly, and when she married, begged Polly – who had no fortune – to make her home with her. Minnie was very dependent on her cousin, and hated to let her out of her sight for a moment. Still, Polly was a thousand times cleverer than dull Minnie, and must sometimes want to escape the monotony of her company.

'I expect she came up to Town on her own for some reason – to have a tooth pulled, or something of the sort,' Lucy suggested. 'Though I'm a little surprised she didn't at least leave her card. It's not like Polly to be remiss about such things.'

Helena looked at Lucy rather strangely. 'No, I'm sure not.' She hesitated, and then said, 'I expect there's some simple reason. If she had the toothache, she might well put off formal calls until she'd had it seen to. I had the toothache once, and I know I didn't want to see anybody or go anywhere.'

She linked arms with Lucy again and walked on, her mind working busily. She had not had an opportunity to speak to Miss Haworth, for she had been driving by in her chaise, and Polly had been standing on the flagway deep in conversation with somebody. The Somebody had been male, and since he'd had his back to Helena, she hadn't been able to recognise him; but she'd had a good view of Polly's face, and Polly didn't look in the least as though she had the toothache, or any other kind of ache.

But she decided against saying any of that to Lucy. She also decided against mentioning that Harvey Sale was also in London: Cedric had mentioned seeing him coming out of Gordon's late one night and turning off down Well Street towards Bab Mae's Street. It might be nothing at all, and it was certainly none of her business, but she couldn't think of a good reason why Polly Haworth and Harvey Sale should both be in London, either together or separately, without Flaminia, and without calling on Lady Theakston.

CHAPTER TWO

In the hall at Morland Place, Héloïse was drawing on her gloves, about to go out. James came in from the yard. 'You look killingly fine today, Marmoset,' he said cheerfully. 'I like that bonnet – is it your new go-calling hat?'

She gave her husband a pitying shake of the head. 'Really, now, you must know better than that! Does one go calling at this time of the morning? And you must have seen this bonnet fifty times at least, my James. Am I so poor a shab-rag that you cannot tell any longer what I wear?'

'*Au contraire*, my wife, you are so very beautiful that it would be an insult to notice your clothes,' he said smartly.

She put herself into his arms. '*Mon doux menteur*,' she smiled.

'It's no lie,' he said seriously, his blue eyes very dark as he looked down into her face. The strength of his emotion – the fact that small and plain and thin as she was, she was beautiful in his eyes – made her feel weak with gladness and gratitude. The pains and troubles of last year were behind them, and they were closer than ever before. God had been very good to her, she thought humbly, and she didn't at all deserve it.

'So where are you going?' James asked when he released her.

'To the village, to visit the misfortunates,' she explained, brushing her gown straight. 'There is White, who has sickness, and Batty, who has sickness *and* a new baby, and of course Cobbey and his wife, who are just old and poor. I shall take them food, and medicine.'

'And good advice, I'm sure.'

'But of course,' she assented, smiling. 'Man does not live by bread alone. One must always take the opportunity to improve the state of mind.'

'Yes, and since we no longer have a priest to undertake that part of it ...' James said darkly.

Father Aislaby, the family chaplain, had left them suddenly in February, almost without notice, to undertake missionary work in India. His going had been a great inconvenience to everyone. As well as tutoring the male children of the house, he had educated the six choristers of the chapel school, who had had to be sent back to their parents with apologies. He had also performed quite a number of secretarial duties for the family and estate, which now had to be shared out amongst people who already had too much to do.

Héloïse missed him in his priestly capacity. In a sense he had never been 'her' priest – he had been chosen and appointed by her predecessor, and was too reserved a man for her ever to feel she really knew him, or, more importantly perhaps, that he knew her – but she was used to regular confession and to daily celebration of the mass. The silent chapel and unserved altar were a yawning chasm in her life. Though she kept the sanctuary lamp burning, and attended herself to the flowers and candles, the living feeling of a chapel that was used was gradually seeping away, as the heat leaves the earth after sunset. She had been, as yet, unable to replace him: a household chaplain, it seemed, was an anachronism in 1816.

However, she said mildly, 'He did not do it to annoy, James. He had the call, and when one has the call, one cannot ignore it.'

'He had the call, all right – to get away from our wretched cold, wet winter. He didn't go off to do missionary work in Ireland or Manchester, you notice!'

'That is not even worth a protest,' Héloïse smiled, turning away. 'But I must get on. There is so much to do today.'

James opened the door for her. 'Who goes with you?'

'No-one,' she said, faintly surprised. Then, thinking she had his trouble, 'I do not stay long in each house, and the ponies stand very well.'

James shook his head. 'It's not that. I just don't want you driving about alone. There are too many rough customers on the roads these days – men on the tramp, discharged soldiers – and Ned says there are quite a few Irish beggars passing through, too. You had better take Stephen with you.'

Stephen had his own work to do – but she scanned her

22

husband's face and saw that he was sincerely worried for her safety, so she said meekly, 'Very well.'

He looked relieved. 'I'll go and find him for you,' he said, following her out onto the step.

But there was no need – Stephen was already there, holding the heads of the bay ponies harnessed to the little park phaeton. James had had that carriage made for her when they first became betrothed, more than twenty years ago. The life-span of a carriage, of course, was only eight or ten years at the most, and the parts of the phaeton had been repaired and renewed so often that there probably wasn't a single splinter left of the original. But the design was so pleasing, light and graceful, and the ponies were so well schooled, that even an indifferent whip like Héloïse could enjoy driving it. Besides, it spoke of James to her, and she wouldn't have changed it for the most expensive new carriage in York.

'Ah, Stephen,' James said, 'I want you to go with my lady to the village this morning.'

He met Stephen's eye with a grave and admonitory look, which Stephen returned intelligently. Héloïse observed the exchange with a small smile, but said nothing.

'Certainly, sir,' said Stephen. 'I was going to suggest it myself. The roads are very poached, my lady, and if a wheel was to go into a rut, you'd need someone to push you out.'

'So I would,' she said, kindly going along with his fiction. James helped her up into the carriage and she took up the reins and nodded to Stephen to let go of the horses' heads.

He climbed up beside her. 'Would you wish me to drive, my lady?'

'No thank you, Stephen. You will have quite enough to do keeping lookout and manning the guns.'

'I beg your pardon, my lady?'

'Never mind it. *Au revoir*, husband.'

'*Bon voyage*, wife. Give my love to Tharshish. Bring me back ivory and apes and peacocks.'

'And spices, horses and mules,' she agreed. She shook the reins. '*Allons, enfants*,' she suggested to the ponies.

The cottages of White and Cobbey were close by each other, low, single-storey oblongs of daub and timber, with thatched roofs and tiny, tightly-closed windows, like most of the houses in the village. They were in Back Lane, which curved round the churchyard and the bell-field, in the centre of which was still the deep hollow where Great Paul, the tenor bell, had been cast some four hundred years ago – the gift of a long-ago Morland. It was good, Héloïse thought as she drove past, to live in the heart of your own history like this.

Inside the cottages were dark and rather damp. The earthen floor was a foot or so below the level of the road, and there was a large fireplace in which a fire was kept going all year, on which the cooking was done. Furniture was sparse and functional – a table for all purposes, with a bench and a couple of stools, a bed in the corner, and perhaps a cupboard. Where there were children, they slept on mattresses in the half-attic.

The labouring poor lived in a plain enough manner, and their diet was monotonous in the extreme: bread, potatoes and beer for the most part, enlivened now and then with an onion, a bit of cheese, perhaps a little bacon on Sunday, occasionally tea, and in the summer cabbage and beans when they could be had.

That was when times were good. Hunger was a reality they were all accustomed to, and when times were bad, starvation shuffled up to the door, and sometimes stepped in over the threshold. Sickness, injury, unemployment, old age – these were the crises which beckoned the Spectre closer. 'Misfortunes', they were called, with the wry understatement Héloïse had come to expect from the English common man. Visiting the 'misfortunates' was one of her duties as Mistress of Morland Place; seeing them in happier times was one of her pleasures.

For stark their lives were, but not entirely bleak. Even the Cobbeys, tottering on the very brink of starvation, had a few possessions of which they were proud – a patchwork quilt, a set of pewter plates, an embroidered cushion given them on their wedding-day by Jemima Morland, whom they called 'the old mistress'. They set a stool at the best place before the fire for Héloïse when she called. They had worked for the Morlands all their lives, and had wonderful stories to tell her. Mrs Cobbey remembered the day they had all gone up to the Big House to have Jemima presented to them as the heiress,

24

after her older brothers had died 'of the plague'.

'She were ten year old, my lady – I were just a year and a month younger. I remember my Da lifted me up so I could see over the crowd, and he said to me, "One day tha'll work for her, Molly – she'll be tha mistress,"' Mrs Cobbey smiled and shook her head at the memory. 'I thought she were the Queen of England, my lady. It were years before I got that sorted in ma mind!'

And Cobbey remembered when Morland men had gone off to fight for the Young Chevalier. 'Ah, they were better days then, my lady, when men spoke out, like, for what they believed in. We brought up our bairns to stand up straight and fight for what was right. But now – well, my lady, I don't know what the world's coming too, straight I don't. Young men today – why, it's all soft collars and trousers and slang, my lady. It were never like that in ma day.'

That was the plaint of all the older people; but Héloïse supposed that every generation found the succeeding one ill-disciplined and incomprehensible. Either the world had been steadily going to rack since the beginning of time, or else human memory was faulty. It was hard to say which, since to her own certain knowledge, girls nowadays had much more freedom than she did in her youth.

The Whites in the next cottage had a great many children, of whom they were very fond – much tumbled-over and slapped though they were in that confined space. Mrs White found time, between spinning and housekeeping, to teach them to read and to cipher; and White, a wool-comber by trade, took time from his labours to take the children to prize-fights, public hangings and country fairs, and to the Church festivals the common people thought of as particularly their own – Plough Monday, Easter Day, and Harvest Home.

In this the Whites were not exceptions, from Héloïse's experience. So many children still died in infancy or child-hood, and the survivors were put to work, in the house or the neighbouring fields, as soon as they were old enough to understand. But most parents contrived to send their little ones to the dame-school for a time, or to teach them the very minimum at home. They gave them their religion, fed them first in time of famine, kissed them when they hurt them-selves, and cried dreadfully when they died. Knowing this,

Héloïse wondered how Parson Malthus could bring himself even to suggest that the ills of the world would be cured if only the poor would refrain from having children.

The last call, on the Battys, presented a different kind of domestic scene. The cottage itself was much bigger, for Batty was a journeyman weaver, and weavers were the élite of the wool-workers. As well as the living-quarters, his two-storey cottage housed his loom-shop, which comprised the whole upper floor. He had two looms and a hand-jenny, and everyone in the house did their part. Mrs Batty – his second wife, and much younger than he – did the spinning; the children scribbled and wound wool from the time they were old enough to grip; and the eldest boy, who was thirteen and a cripple, did a little weaving on the second loom.

Mrs Batty had lately been confined, however, of their ninth, and had almost simultaneously caught the feverish cold which was going round the village. When Héloïse called, the house was full of snivels and unwashed children. Mrs Batty was in bed, dismally croaking at her five-year-old – a sturdy little fellow who had just discovered the twin delights of roaring and kicking his smaller sisters – and trying to be heard over the din of the new baby. She looked startled when Héloïse came in, but was obviously feeling too miserable to make more than a token struggle to get up.

'Oh m'lady! I wasn't expecting anyone! I'm right sorry you've caught me like this. It's not fitting. Stop that, our Jacky, do! Leave Martha be! Oh m'lady, just let me get up and make maself decent –'

'No, no – lie still, Mrs Batty, and don't upset yourself. I came to see how you are, that's all.'

'Oh, that's right kind of your ladyship! But the place is such a mess, and the bairns so fractious – !'

'Never mind, poor little souls. They all have such dreadful colds, don't they, and that would make anyone feel cross,' Héloïse said soothingly, eyeing with deep misgiving the noses of the two little girls. Master Jack, at least, had been startled into silence by her appearance, and was staring at her with his mouth open. She hastened to consolidate her advantage. 'Now then, Jackie, just you run outside to the wood-pile and bring in some more wood for the fire. It's burned down very low, I see.'

26

'Do as her ladyship says, our Jacky – quick now!' Mrs Batty whispered violently. The child stared one moment more, then scuttled away importantly through the back door.

'A better fire will make you feel more cheerful,' Héloïse promised, approaching the bed. 'Just you give me the baby for a moment while you see to your little girls. Their noses need wiping.'

'Oh no, miss – m'lady – it isn't fitting!' Mrs Batty cried, clutching the wailing bundle more tightly.

'Nonsense, do you think I've never held a baby before?' Héloïse said cheerfully. Howling and damp it may be, she thought, but it was at least a better prospect than those noses. She took the infant from the mother, and at once it stopped crying. The silence was blissful. A moment later Héloïse realised that the muted, heavy double thump of the loom above their heads was missing. Normally, Batty worked at his loom from five in the morning until eight at night: that noise was like the heartbeat of the house.

'Is your husband out?' she asked in surprise.

Mrs Batty reddened. 'Oh – why, yes, m'lady. Yes, he is out.'

'Work is short, then, is it?' Héloïse said sympathetically. Times were bad everywhere, and she knew from what Edward had said that they had been giving out less work than usual, for they could not sell the finished cloth. The warehouse on King's Staith was filling up.

Mrs Batty hesitated, and looked away to either side as if seeking inspiration. 'Yes, m'lady,' she said at last.

'I'm sorry. I wish there was something I could do, but you know that business is bad everywhere. But look, I have brought you some calves-foot jelly, which I want you to promise to keep for yourself, for you must keep up your strength while you are feeding the baby. And here is some of Mrs Thomson's special elixir, which you can all take. Everyone says it is very good, you know, for sore throats and coughs. Do the children cough at night? Well, then, this will help you all sleep more soundly.'

'It's very kind of you, m'lady,' Mrs Batty said feebly, getting on with the nose-wiping at last. Just then, little Jack came back in with an armful of wood and an air of importance.

'Me dad's comin'!' he announced, jerking his head towards the back door. The news seemed for some reason to agitate Mrs Batty.

'Oh, quick, our Jacky, run out and tell Dad her ladyship's here! Go on, now, quick!'

But before Jack could obey, the door was flung open and Weaver Batty walked in. He stopped dead at the sight of Héloïse, and another man coming in behind him bumped into him and cursed, and then stepped back quickly into the shadow of the doorway. From somewhere between them a paper slithered and dropped with a soft, flat sound to the floor.

Héloïse looked at Batty curiously. 'I'm sorry if I startled you,' she said. 'I have just come to visit your wife and see how she does. Everyone has this dreadful cold, it seems.'

Batty looked disconcerted, but at Héloïse's words he made an obvious effort and said, 'Oh, that's right kind of you, my lady. I know it bucks our Annie up wonderful to have your ladyship call. I'm main sorry I wasn't here to greet your ladyship, only –' He stopped, not seeming to know how to finish the sentence.

Héloïse moved round the bed to return the infant, now asleep and disagreeably damp, to its mother, but without taking her eyes from Batty's face. Something was wrong, she felt: he seemed more than naturally put out at her presence, and the atmosphere in the room was briny with tension.

'I'm afraid you haven't much work at the moment,' she said smoothly. 'I'm sorry for it, but we have none to give out, you know.'

'Oh – yes, well – that's all right, my lady,' Batty said awkwardly. 'It can't be helped.'

But there was a definite movement in the doorway behind him, and Héloïse smiled and said, 'Don't let me keep you out of your own house, Batty. Please come in – and bring your friend in too.'

Batty hesitated, and then with what was almost a shrug stepped aside and turned his head to the other man behind him. 'It's me brother Tom, my lady. Come in, Tom. Aye, aye, it's all right. Come on in.'

The man who stepped in behind Batty was not unlike him, but younger, darker, and thinner, with a sharpness in his face and a brightness in his eyes that spoke some unusual zeal, or perhaps some past suffering. There was an alertness about him which you never saw in a man like Batty, whose life was lived in familiar surroundings and accustomed routines. He seemed recently to have been involved in a fight, for he had a bruise on the side of his face which just missed being a black eye, and a cut on his lip. As he came reluctantly forward, Héloïse saw that one of his hands was roughly bandaged, too, across the knuckles.

She made no comment on these things, however. What intrigued her most was the increase of tension in the room. She said conversationally, 'I had no idea you had a brother, Batty. Is he a weaver too?'

'Yes, my lady.'

'Ah, it runs in the family, then. I dare say little Jacky here will be a weaver too, one day! But I have never seen your brother here before, I think.'

'Well, no, my lady. He doesn't live around these parts. He's from Loughborough –'

There was a slight hiss of escaping breath, and Batty stopped short on the last word and reddened. The dark eyes of Tom Batty glittered a little more brightly.

It meant nothing to Héloïse. 'That is a long way away,' she said gravely. 'Well, I shall not intrude any longer on your family reunion. I hope you enjoy your visit to York, Mr Thomas Batty. But you have dropped your newspaper, I think.'

He looked, but she moved, scooping it up dextrously and glancing at it before holding it out to him. 'Ah, Cobbett's *Political Register*,' she said. 'Yes, I have heard of this. So you are interested in politics, are you?'

Tom Batty spoke for the first time, in an unwilling sort of growl. 'Every man should be', was all he said, but it contained an amazing amount of emotion for a short sentence. It was accompanied by a quick, hard look at the back of his brother's neck, as though there were some cause of conflict here between them.

'You are a Reformist?' Héloïse said, not as if she were very interested in the answer. 'But I should have thought there were other things that would be closer to a weaver's heart, especially in these hard times.'

29

'Aye, that's what I –' Batty began eagerly, but his cadet broke in sharply.

'Without Reform, nothing else will ever come right. Reform is the beginning of it, and all else will follow.'

'Nay, Tom, Parliament's not for the likes of us,' Batty began pleadingly. They had obviously had this argument before. 'We've enough to do without –'

'Why should we pay taxes for other men to spend? Why should others spend our taxes without consulting us what to spend it on?'

An orator, Héloïse thought. Such men can be dangerous. But she said, smilingly, 'Come, now, do you consult your wife or your children before you spend the money they earn? You know what's best for the family, and you make decisions on their behalf. So does the Government, on our behalf.'

The orator looked angry. 'Aye, but we aren't children, are we? Except some folk want to treat us like children – but they may find out differently one day.'

Héloïse's smile vanished. She said gravely, 'Such talk, you know, is unwise. It may stir up discontent, and discontent so often leads to trouble and bloodshed.'

The orator's eyes brightened and his lip curled a little with contempt, as though he were thinking *What do you know about bloodshed, my fine lady?* But his voice was even as he said, 'Sometimes there has to be bloodshed. There's a new world waiting to be born, and labour's always painful.'

Batty intervened, shocked. 'Tom! Not in front of her ladyship! It's not proper!'

But Tom seemed to have been riled beyond common prudence. 'Not proper? I'll tell thee what isn't proper, Will – you having no work, with all these brats to feed, that's what's not proper!'

Héloïse felt the tension like a knot inside her chest. 'If there were any work to give out, Batty would have it, I assure you. He is a good weaver. But there is none.'

'See, Tom, I told you,' Batty said anxiously. 'And her ladyship came here special out of the kindness of her heart to see my Annie, hearing she wasn't well.'

'Oh, yes Tom,' Annie croaked from the bed, as eager as her husband to make amends. 'So kind –'

'Kind, is it?' Tom said harshly, turning back to Héloïse.

30

'Then can you tell me, my lady, why there are folk starving on the road all the way from Leicester to York, while others live in big houses and have plenty to eat?'

'*Tom!*'

'Yes, I can tell you,' Héloïse said calmly, holding down the anger inside. 'It is because it has pleased God to call them to different stations in life, to work for His glory in different ways. It is not our business to question the ways of God.'

'Oh, *God!*' cried Tom. 'I don't believe in your *God!* God doesn't exist. There's only Man.'

There was a shocked silence. Héloïse reddened as though she had been struck, and Batty and his wife both looked at Tom with wide eyes and open mouths, as though he had just sprouted a second head. The frozen tableau lasted only a second or two. Héloïse turned to Batty, gave him a brisk, 'Good day to you', and walked out. She moved so fast that she had reached her phaeton before Batty caught her up.

He was almost weeping. 'Oh my lady – please!' She paused and looked at him coldly. 'Oh please, my lady, please don't be angry. Tom doesn't really mean it. Only he's had a bit of an accident, a knock on the head, like, and it's shaken up his wits. When he's himself again, he'll feel that badly! He doesn't mean any of it, truly, my lady!'

Héloïse studied his anxious face for a moment, and then said, 'I think you should persuade him to go back to Loughborough as soon as possible.'

'I will, my lady, I will! Thank you, my lady!'

She climbed up onto the seat, took the reins from Stephen, and drove away, leaving Batty standing beside the road looking frightened.

The bays knew they were going home, and trotted smartly, their slender black muzzles leaning together as if they were whispering secrets. The phaeton bowled along the road, and the little harness-bells tinkled sweetly on the cool, damp, grey air.

'Stephen,' she said after a while, 'are there many political meetings in the area?'

Stephen didn't seem to find the question surprising. He had been her eyes and ears on many past occasions. 'Well, my lady, there's the Debating Society meetings upstairs at Lunt's

Coffee-house. That's the second Monday of the month.'

'Yes, but those are for gentlemen. What about – amongst the common people? Working men – do they have political meetings?'

Stephen thought for a moment or two. 'Not here-abouts, not as a regular thing, my lady. In the Hare and Heather there's a bit of an argle-bargle sometimes, and since the Peace, it's often about change and such-like. And in the barber's shop – well, every Saturday afternoon there's someone laying down the law, and someone else disagreeing with him – but that's barber's shops, my lady. It's always like that. It's where they go to read the newspapers and pamphlets, my lady – the barber gets 'em all.'

'Do they talk about Reform?'

'Everyone's got his own idea about how to save the world, my lady. Some of 'em talk about Reform.' He looked sideways at her. 'But there won't be any trouble here-abouts. Everyone knows everyone else. It's where there's a lot of manufactories, that's where the trouble will be.'

'How do you know?' she asked sharply. She looked at him. 'Has there been trouble already?'

'In Nottingham, mainly, my lady,' Stephen admitted. 'And Leicester. The stockingers, my lady – like the last time, back in the year 12, you remember?'

'Yes, I remember. Frame-breaking. They talked about King Ludd living in Sherwood Forest.'

'That's right, my lady. Well, there's been something of that going on lately. I think it's the unemployment, and the high price of bread. Just the night before last, Heathcote and Boden's mill at Loughborough was broken into, and all the machines broken – fifty or more, they're saying. Thousands of pounds' worth of damage – my lady? Are you all right?'

'Take the reins,' Héloïse said. 'Drive home as quickly as you can.'

As Edward was hurrying out, Héloïse stopped him. 'Ned – you won't arrest Batty?' He looked at her questioningly, surprised. 'Our weaver Batty. He hasn't done anything wrong.'

'He knew about it. He should have reported him.'

'But he's his brother,' she protested.

'He should have given him up.'

James stood beside her. 'Would you give me up?'

Edward looked from her to him and back again. Then he grunted and turned away. 'Don't wait dinner for me.'

When he was gone, James looked at his wife's troubled face, and put his arm round her shoulders. 'Don't worry, he knows his own people.' She didn't appear comforted, and he drew her with him to a chair, to sit down and take her on his lap. 'Come, come here, that's right. What is it, Marmoset? You don't mind so very much about Batty, do you? I expect Ned will let him off with a caution.'

'Oh no, James, it isn't that.' She was silent for a while, and he waited, seeing that she was marshalling her words. At times of deep emotion, she sometimes had difficulty thinking in English. 'It was the things he said – they took me back. Reminded me of Olivier – my first husband. I've heard it all before, you see – this talk of a new world.'

She had lived through the Revolution in Paris. She had seen it grow from its earliest days, from the salons of her father's mistress, where the *philosophes* had talked about the Condition of Man – as though there were only one man, and one condition!

'They played with words, you know, like children tossing a glittering ball back and forth. That's how it starts, always, with words.'

But words were dangerous, words had power – they were the progenitors of deeds. They broke down barriers, accustomed men to thinking the unthinkable. You could make even the most beastly crime sound noble if you were clever with words. And if you spoke of it often enough, it ceased to be something no decent man would contemplate.

'I've heard them before, all the fine, resounding phrases, the clichés, the rhetoric, the promise of better days to come. But first there must always be suffering – that's always part of the plan! Suffering and bloodshed, so that a new and better world might be born. He didn't say much, but I could see it in his eyes, James, that black passion.'

'Yes,' James said, holding her.

'The gutters of Paris ran with blood – literally ran with blood. Thousands of ordinary people were butchered – bewildered, you know, like cattle. And Olivier and his friends –

they said it didn't matter! People must die so that the new world could be born. But if the people didn't matter, what was the new world for? Who did they do it for, if not for people?'

'I don't know,' James said.

She held him tighter. Her mind was full of images, pictures burned into her brain that would never leave her, no matter how long she lived in peace and safety. 'He had my best friend arrested – Mathilde's mother. She was executed. Poor Lotti, who knew nothing of politics, who never thought about anything but horses. And my father ... So many people died, James, but there was no new world.'

'There never is, my love. Just the same old one, a little more battered than before. Yet change does happen.'

'Yes, but not like that. When it comes, it comes gradually, so that you hardly notice. You look back, only, and see that it has come, like the growth of a tree. Women know that – why don't men? Why do they delude themselves, generation after generation?'

'I don't know, my darling. But don't be afraid, it won't happen here. There won't be a revolution here. This is England.' He smiled. 'More than that, this is Yorkshire.'

She could not smile. 'James, that man, Tom Batty – he spoke to me in such a way – he looked at me – as if there were no difference between us. As if we were the same. No-one has ever spoken so to me.'

He didn't understand. 'We are all equal before God,' he tried.

'I don't mean that. We are all made equal in God's sight, but He puts us in different places, with different tasks to perform, and different duties and responsibilities. If we don't fulfil them, it makes trouble for everyone. And I've met men who were out of their place – but I've never met a man before who didn't seem to know he had one.' She looked at him, troubled, afraid. 'What will happen if there are others like him? How can we go on, if all the world becomes like that?'

'It won't happen. You've said yourself that things don't change that much. It's just the time we're living in – everything's upside down, but it won't stay that way. Things will get back to normal again – it's just a matter of time.'

*

34

The servants had their dinner at noon, and the nursery dinner was served at the same time. When it was finished, Héloïse went up to the day nursery to see her younger son, Benedict. She felt uneasy, afraid. No news had yet come back from Ned, and her mind had been dwelling so on the past that she caught herself listening, jumpily, for the sound of tramping feet outside. In the nursery, with Benedict, she hoped to find distraction for her thoughts.

One of the problems that had arisen on Father Aislaby's departure was what to do with Benedict and Nicholas, whom he had taught along with the choir boys. A family debate back in February had brought forth the suggestion, from Miss Rosedale, Sophie's former governess, that Nicholas should go to school.

Héloïse had been instant in her opposition. 'Send him away? Oh no, how could you think it? He's too young!'

'Surely he isn't strong enough?' Sophie said.

Edward, who had been to Eton, concurred. 'It is a hard life, you know. There's a good deal of bullying, and Spartan conditions – essential for toughening up the normal lad, I grant you, but Nicholas has never been robust, and he's, well, what I'd call *sensitive*.' He sounded embarrassed at using the word, but everyone knew he was thinking of Nicholas's attacks of asthma, and the occasional skin rashes, which Dr Ross said were of a nervous origin.

'In any case,' James said, 'it's far better for the heir to Morland Place to be brought up at home, and learn about his duties from the earliest possible moment.'

Miss Rosedale waited patiently until they had finished, and then said, 'I didn't mean to Eton. I agree that the regimen there would be too harsh for him. I only meant that he might benefit from going to St Edward's, as a day-boy. He would still be under the proper influence of home, but it would give him a chance to mix with other boys of his own age.'

'Yes, that would knock a few of the corners off,' Edward said approvingly. 'Oh, very gently, of course,' he added, catching Héloïse's eye.

She smiled. 'I am not such a foolish, protecting mother as you may think, dear Ned, and I have sometimes thought it a pity he should not have friends of his own age.'

'Well, at St Edward's he'll meet all sorts,' James said. 'The sons of tenants as well as the sons of neighbours, Yes, I think it's a good idea, Rosey. Let him learn amongst the people he'll command one day – if you think his health is up to it.'

'As long as he's living at home, we can keep an eye on him.'

'But what about Benedict?' Héloïse said. 'He is too young to go to St Edward's.'

Miss Rosedale looked around the circle of faces. 'I can teach him here for a year or two, until he's old enough to join his brother – or at least, until you get another chaplain. If you will entrust him to me, that is.'

'Entrust him to you?' Héloïse said. 'Of course we will! But will you have time, with all the other things you do?'

Miss Rosedale laughed. 'Time? My dear ma'am, anyone else would have dismissed me a year ago, when Sophie ceased to need a governess! I have been racked with guilt ever since, taking such a great salary from you and doing nothing to deserve it. This is my cunning plan, don't you see, to have you keep me on a little longer.'

'But indeed, I could not do without you,' Héloïse exclaimed. 'I have been in fear that you would grow bored and decide you wanted to leave, and then what should I do? First Mathilde married her John and went away, and then my dear Marie accepted her Mr Kexby, who has been asking her for so long – and of course I am very, very happy for her to have an establishment at last – but I could not at all do without you, and for my own sake, I hope you will stay for ever.'

'If you managed my poor Fanny,' James put in, 'I'm sure you can manage Benedict, imp though he is.'

'Thank you,' Miss Rosedale smiled. 'I'm sure he will plague me just as much as Fanny did, but my experience being greater now, I hope to survive it. Is it decided then?'

'Yes – if Nicholas likes it,' Héloïse said. 'I should not wish to send him to school against his will.'

But Nicholas had been delighted with the idea. He saw it as an adventure: exciting, different – a change of scene, new faces. Now the choristers had gone, there was only his little brother at home to lord it over; at St Edward's, he would be king of a whole new court. Master Morland of Morland Place – the heir to the whole estate – the most important person in the area – he would lead, and others would follow.

Benedict, who was four, condemned to stay at home under Miss Rosedale's charge, sulked furiously for the first week, the more so because Nicholas came home every day full of stories – many of them wildly exaggerated – about the wonderful times he was having. But they had settled down at last, and Benedict had benefited from the close personal attention Miss Rosedale was now able to give him, and from the more liberal regime she favoured. Under Father Aislaby, there had been rather too much sitting still for a very young boy full of natural energy, which had meant that when he was let out of the schoolroom and into the charge of the nursery-maids, he had run amok. Miss Rosedale wisely incorporated a sensible amount of physical activity into the lessons, and kept him on a much more even keel.

At the moment Miss Rosedale was away in Scarborough, chaperoning Sophie and Rosamund. It had been thought necessary for Sophie's health and spirits that she should have a change of scene and the benefit of sea air, and Scarborough was the nearest genteel watering-place. Héloïse would by no means countenance the girls' going even to such a respectable place chaperoned only by Rosamund's maid. Either she or Miss Rosedale must accompany the young ladies; but Héloïse had a strong aversion to Scarborough. It was a place she didn't like even to think about, much less visit.

'It won't hurt Benedict to miss his lessons for a week or two,' Héloïse had said. 'The maids can look after him, and I can spend a few hours with him every day. I can teach him French,' she added on an inspiration. She was only too aware that her education was infinitely inferior to Miss Rosedale's. With such a teacher, her son may well have surpassed her already in every other subject.

Benedict didn't much want to learn French, or anything else, from his mother, but he was always glad to see her, and was happy to play with her, or to be taken out for a drive or a walk. Héloïse was glad simply to have the opportunity to romp with him, and enjoy his affection.

He was a happy little boy, quite ready to take pleasure and love wherever he found them. He had recently come out of dresses and into trousers – always a shock to the maternal system. The cropping of his baby curls had made Héloïse feel suddenly old, for she would never have another baby now.

37

On James the transition had the opposite effect. A baby was the property of the distaff side, but once a boy went into trousers, his father might legitimately take an interest in him. He might show him how to fish and shoot and play cricket, teach him how to whistle, to use his fives, to whittle a stick – all the essential knowledge of manhood. Nicholas had always been too frail, and James too otherwise occupied, for them to have been close in that way; but since Father Aislaby had gone and Bendy had shed his frocks, James had been exhibiting a proper fatherly interest in his younger son.

'He needs a man's influence, you know,' he would say sometimes in the evenings. 'Miss Rosedale is an excellent woman, but she is only a woman, after all.'

'Yes, my James,' Héloïse would reply serenely. 'As soon as I can find a chaplain-tutor –'

'Oh, no hurry, my love! No hurry at all. Miss Rosedale's doing an excellent job – and I can take the lad out with me now and then.'

This afternoon Benedict found his mother in thoughtful mood, and not much inclined to romp, so he went back to the battle he was fighting all over the day-nursery floor with his lead soldiers. They were a splendid and extensive set. The English soldiers were red, and the French soldiers blue – that much Bendy knew. He was too young to know anything about the war which had gone on for most of his mother's life, but he knew that opposite sides in any game were always French and English. He also knew, both from his brother and the servants, that the French general on the white horse for whom the worst fates were always reserved was Boney, and that Boney was The Bad Man.

So while Héloïse sat nearby, deep in thought, watching him without really seeing him, he went back to his private game. He crawled about the floor on his stomach, moving the pieces and murmuring the commentary to himself. 'And then he goes down here and round here and they come round here and he goes BOOM! You're dead! Like that. And they all fall down. Hurrah! And then they come over the hill – dum-de-dum-de-dum – like that, and down here, and they go BOOM BOOM – and then old Boney comes – dum-de-dum-de-dum – and BOOM! He's dead!' He flung the battered horseman up in the air, and as it fell with a clatter he chanted the foolish nursery song, 'Silly old Boney sat on his pony . . .'

The battle of Waterloo, Héloïse thought, thus reduced to its essence. She thought of all the young men who had died, of the terrible wounds she had witnessed as the survivors crawled back into Brussels. The battle of Waterloo, the culmination of everything that had happened since the calling of the Estates General in 1789 had set the creaking wheels of the Revolution in motion. Could it happen here? Had it started already? How would they know, until they were in the middle of it and it was too late to stop?

'Oh Bendy!' she said. He looked up, but it was not at her. The door had opened, and Mathilde looked in.

'Madame! They said you were in here. Am I intruding?'

'TILDA!' Benedict bellowed, scrambling to his feet and rushing at her.

'How's my friend Bendy?' she said, fielding him just in time to save her dress.

'I'm playing French and English. Come and play,' he commanded, tugging at her hand. 'You can be French,' he offered generously.

'Kiss me hello first,' Mathilde said, stooping.

'Soldiers don't kiss,' he informed her sternly, pulling himself free. 'Never-never-never.'

'Oh, don't they? I'm sorry. I'll try to remember that.' Disgusted with womanhood, he stumped back to his game. Mathilde turned to Héloïse. 'You're looking thoughtful.'

'You look blooming,' Héloïse said, rousing herself. Since Mathilde's soured and difficult mother-in-law, Mary Skelwith, had died last winter, she seemed to have gained in confidence, and was now a happy, contented young matron. 'What a smart pelisse. And a new bonnet, I see.'

'The pelisse is my wedding one made over – don't you see? I took the fur off, and put on the braid and the frogging and new buttons.'

'So you did. How clever!'

'And John chose the bonnet. I think he had very good taste, don't you? I wasn't sure at first if perhaps there weren't too many feathers, but he says it suits me. You don't think it's too fine, do you?'

'I think it's charming. A new bride has every right to be fine.'

'Not such a new bride now,' Mathilde said seriously. 'It's a year and two months and thirteen days ... But I didn't come to talk about me. I came to see how you were. I heard there'd been some trouble in the village. Are you all right? You do look rather pale.'

'Oh no, I am quite well. What did you hear?'

'I was at the Somersets', and they said you'd discovered a runaway frame-breaker at one of the village houses, and that Edward had gone to arrest him with half-a-dozen constables. Only when they got there, of course, he'd rubbed off.'

'I did not know he had escaped. Your information is later than mine.'

'All the Somersets are chattering away like disturbed starlings about it.' Mathilde studied her. 'It's upset you, too, I can see that. There wasn't any – unpleasantness, was there?'

'Not in the way you mean. But it has worried me.' She looked at Mathilde's healthy, happy face under the smart, exceedingly over-trimmed bonnet, and her next words died in her throat. Mathilde remembered nothing of the France she had fled as a child not much older than Benedict, nor of the mother who had died under the guillotine's knife; and if she had, it would only have made it even more impossible to talk to her of such hideous fears. Mathilde was just starting out on the adventure of married life, and no shadows should be cast over that.

'I'm merely being silly, however,' Héloïse said firmly. 'Tell me, how is your new house coming along?'

Mathilde was easily distracted on that subject. The house had been building since the second month of her marriage. 'Oh, very well. It's beginning to look like a house at last. In fact, it would be finished by now,' she laughed, 'if John didn't keep thinking of new things to add. He's decided to have a sort of turret room now, on the side – like a French castle, you know. It will have splendid views over the moors. John says he'll use it as his study. I expect he'll get even more and better ideas, up in the clouds like that.'

She was silent a moment, looking at some agreeable internal landscape. Benedict slaughtered some more French infantry, and resurrected Boney to meet his fate again. Mathilde came to the end of a train of thought and sighed, and looked at Héloïse.

'There is something particular I wanted to talk to you about, if you don't mind.'

'Of course not,' Héloïse said. 'I hope you will always feel you can bring your problems to me.'

'Oh, it isn't a problem. Well, yes, it is in a way, but it's good news – the best news. I wonder if you've guessed already?' She blushed, and Héloïse looked at her blankly, but it was enough for Mathilde. 'You have guessed. I can see.'

Enlightenment crept in slowly. 'Mathilde – *ma chère petite* – can you mean –?'

'Yes! I'm expecting a child! John and I are to have a child!'

'Oh my dear! I am so very happy for you! When does it come?'

'Oh, not for ages yet. Not until January. I wish it could be sooner. January seems such a long way away, and I want it to be here now.'

'It will pass soon enough,' Héloïse smiled. 'Oh, but this is wonderful news! You are so like a daughter to me, dear Mathilde, that it will be like being a grandmother, and I have long wanted to be a grandmother!'

Mathilde blushed more deeply. 'Well, that's rather what I wanted to talk to you about. I mean – well, in a sense, you will be the grandmother, won't you?'

Héloïse's attention sharpened. She looked at Mathilde carefully, but said nothing.

'So I wondered if you could advise me how – or rather what, exactly – we should tell James.' Héloïse was too surprised to speak, and Mathilde's eyes clouded. 'You do know about it, don't you?' she said anxiously. 'I haven't said the wrong thing? She swore you knew all along.'

This was painful. 'Who swore?'

'Mrs Skelwith. It was she who told me. Last Christmas.' She paused, and her mouth quivered. 'I think she did it to spoil things for me. She didn't like me, you know. Only it didn't, of course, because I like James very much. How could I not? Only, you see, I don't really know who knows what, or who's supposed to know what, and –'

'Mathilde, let us be clear about this at once. What was it that Mrs Skelwith told you?'

Mathilde looked frightened. 'That James is really my John's father,' she said in a small voice. 'You did know, didn't you? Oh please, say you did! If I've said the wrong thing I shall never forgive myself!'

Héloïse let out a long breath. 'Yes, my dear, I knew. I just didn't know that you did.'

'Oh, thank heaven! Well, that's all right, then,' Mathilde said with a shaky laugh. 'Only John's mother was such an *odd* person, you see –'

'Yes,' Héloïse said. 'And she may well have told you only to upset you, as you suspected.'

'It did upset me at first, because I didn't know whether it was true or not, and whether I was supposed to admit I knew. But in the end, after Mrs Skelwith died, I decided to speak to John about it, and we had a long talk and brought it all out into the open, which was such a relief! He said he'd known about it for a long time, but that it was supposed to be a secret. So I said, surely it didn't matter any more, now that his mother was dead, and he said that there might still be a scandal if it became public knowledge. He said there was no sense in opening old wounds, and that we'd better simply forget about it. As if,' she added in a burst of feminine reason, 'you *could* forget about something like that!'

No, Héloïse thought, it was not something you could just forget.

'But now there's a baby coming,' Mathilde went on, 'it does change things, doesn't it? Because James will be the baby's grandfather, won't he? And the poor little thing won't have any other grandparents – or any other relatives at all, come to that, with both of us being orphans. So I thought I'd ask you what's best to be done.'

She stopped, and looked at Héloïse so hopefully that Héloïse wanted to laugh. An absurd spring of laughter was bubbling up inside her over the whole nonsensical, incongruous, painful business. All the secrecy and deceit, the jealousy and suffering and bitterness that had marred the thirty years of John Skelwith's innocent life, were wiped away in an instant by the open-hearted innocence of this young woman, who saw with a mother's single-mindedness only that her baby ought to have a family. Perhaps Mary Skelwith's death had finally purged the evil. Perhaps they might all live in the sunlight from now on.

'I think,' she said, a little unsteadily, 'that honesty is always the best policy, and that secrets are dangerous, disagreeable things. I think I had best talk to James about it.'

Mathilde looked relieved, and then faintly doubtful. 'You – you are still pleased, aren't you, Madame? About the baby?'

Héloïse took her hands and reached up on tiptoe to kiss the rosy cheek. 'More pleased than I can tell you. Now I can be a real grandmother.'

CHAPTER THREE

Scarborough was enjoying a rare fine day that wet summer. Inland, indeed, a band of heavy grey clouds could be seen, raining away over the rest of Yorkshire as if it never meant to stop; but here along the coast there was a thin, blue sky high above, and a breezy sunshine chasing across the sparkling, white-capped sea.

Sophie and Rosamund had gone out early for their walk. They both had early habits – Sophie from living in the country, and Rosamund from riding with her mother before the Park grew crowded – and when the weather allowed they liked to get out and have the town and the sands as much as possible to themselves.

'I think this is the best sort of day at Scarborough,' Sophie said, watching the waves come bounding in, glittering and foaming, to dash half-way up the sand in the vain effort to reach the Promenade wall. The breeze tugged at the poke of her bonnet and fluttered the ribbons under her chin. 'It feels so fresh and glad, as though it might really blow everything inside your head away, and leave it all clean and empty and new.'

'I don't think I want my furniture blown away. I've arranged it the way I like it, and I don't want it interfered with,' Rosamund said firmly.

Miss Rosedale, walking a little behind them to pursue her own solitary thoughts, heard the exchange and smiled to herself. Yes, that would always be the difference between them, she thought. Rosamund liked to take hold of the stuff of her life and wrestle it into submission; Sophie survived by enduring.

The curve of the bay was marked by high cliffs, dazzling-white in the early sun, topped with lush green folds of hill, and circled this morning by whimpering grey gulls. Below lay the crescent of the sands, still smooth and firm from the high water – the tide was going out now. Sophie turned an eager face back.

'May we walk on the sand, Rosey? It will be lovely to make the very first marks.'

Miss Rosedale thought of the fury of Rosamund's maid, Moss, if she were presented with two pairs of sandy, water-marked boots to put to rights. On the other hand, who could resist that virgin expanse? Certainly no woman of spirit.

'If you aren't afraid of the horses,' she said. 'They'll be arriving at any minute.'

'No, of course not,' Sophie said at once, and then, 'They won't run us down, will they?'

'Of course they won't,' Rosamund said impatiently. 'Do you think grooms are blind? Come on, foolish.'

They descended the steps, crossed the band of dry sand above the tide-mark, still rough from yesterday's footprints, and gained the firm, sleek dark-golden strand, unmarked except for the tiny airholes of whatever secret beasts lived below. Then they turned and walked along parallel to the sea, examining their own footmarks and exclaiming like children over them.

Looking at the two straight young backs in front of her, Miss Rosedale felt that the time here had been well-spent. Sophie was definitely feeling more cheerful and at peace with herself. The sadness of loss was finding its own level inside her, settling into the shape it would probably bear for the rest of her life. Growing tolerable, it would eventually become unnoticed, she hoped.

Rosamund had not been her pupil and in any case had a less transparent character, and so it was harder to judge how she felt. Outwardly she seemed calm and contented. It was only when she didn't know she was being watched, and relaxed her guard, that Miss Rosedale could see evidence in her face of the shock and grief she had suffered last year. Pleasure was now a conscious, rather than an unconscious thing: to that extent she had grown up.

But Rosamund had enjoyed her time here, too. Like Sophie, she had bathed in the sea for the first time in her life, made a formidable collection of shells and interesting pebbles, and sketched the foreshore from every possible angle. And in her own inimitable manner, she had made friends with the

45

man who hired out the donkey-carts, heard the life-history of every servant in their lodgings, and learned the name of every gentleman's groom in Scarborough.

The first of these were coming onto the sands now, bringing their masters' horses for exercise, riding one and leading one or two others. The glossy animals, beautiful in their nakedness, lifted their heads enquiringly to snuff the strange, exhilarating air, and whickered softly in excitement. It was good, Miss Rosedale thought, to see them enjoying themselves, their eyes shining with pleasure as they went down the beach, trotting to the end, and then cantering, pulling a little and tossing their heads playfully, back the other way.

One groom came down on foot, leading a carriage-horse that was slightly lame, taking it down to bathe its legs in the healing salt water. As he passed them, Rosamund called out to him. He stopped and knuckled his forehead, and he and Rosamund had a very satisfactory discussion of the condition and its progress, while the horse, a friendly soul, blew into Rosamund's ear and nibbled tentatively at the rim of her straw hat.

'Shall we move on, young ladies,' Miss Rosedale said at last, having an eye to Sophie's boredom and the increasing activity on the sands. Behind them, two water-carts had come down to collect sea-water for the baths up in the town, and at the top of the strand the first horses were already being harnessed up to the bathing-machines. Sunshine had been in such short supply this summer that everyone was making the most of the bright morning with an early start.

They walked on, and the girls' conversation reverted to the fascinating topic of the letter Sophie had received the day before from her cousin Africa Haworth, with whom she had gone to school for a time. Africa was the sister of Polly Haworth, with whom Rosamund had been brought up. Rosamund had a keen interest in Africa's doings, for she lived a life of such stunning adventure and excitement that even Rosamund's mother's history paled by comparison.

Africa had been born in the middle of the Battle of the Nile, on board her father's ship, after which she had been named. Except for her brief period at school in Bath with Sophie, she had lived on ship-board all her life, travelling

46

with her father wherever he went. She had been with him on the epic voyage twice across the Atlantic in pursuit of Ville-neuve's fleet; she had been present at the Battle of Trafalgar.

When she was younger, Rosamund had listened open-mouthed to the stories of Africa's adventures. She had been wild with envy at the mere thought of living in a ship's cabin and romping about the rigging with the jolly sailors; but of recent years her interest in the life-style had been more acad-emic. For one thing, there were no horses at sea; and for another, she liked comfort and luxury, and disliked dirt and disorder. Sleeping on damp sheets and having your clothes always sticky with salt did not appeal to her at all; and when she thought of what the food must be like ...!

Captain Haworth had lately been raised to flag rank, and Africa's letter came from Jamestown in St Helena, where he had been appointed port admiral and station commander, taking over from Admiral Cockburn. St Helena was a small, rocky island in the middle of the South Atlantic, a regular port-of-call on the Cape route, where ships took on water and fresh fruit and vegetables. Fifty or more naval and merchant ships might be expected to be at anchor in Jamestown at any one time; and there was also a small permanent squadron of naval vessels guarding the island – which was the real reason for the presence of a young and resourceful admiral. For it was on St Helena that Bonaparte was imprisoned.

'I haven't met him yet,' Africa said in her letter, which had been written in great excitement soon after their arrival, 'but I saw him at a distance going by in his coach. He makes his coachman drive hell-for-leather – I suppose to give him some excitement in his life, for he must have very little to do now he is a prisoner.

'Admiral Cockburn promises he will introduce us to The Prisoner. He lives up on the top of the island in a house called Longwood with his servants. He was down here in Jamestown at first, but it was thought it would be too easy for him to escape and slip on board an American ship – of which there are always several here – so after a few weeks they converted the farmhouse for him. I'm told it's very comfortable, but also very well guarded – a hundred and twenty-five sentries by day, and seventy-two by night. You see how they fear his resourcefulness! It makes me quite nervous about meeting him.

47

'Of course, Papa won't have direct care of The Prisoner – that's the job of the new Governor, Hudson Lowe – but the naval defences are his responsibility. Papa says it's even more nerve-racking than the blockade at Brest during the war, for at least then you knew which were the enemy ships. The inshore squadron has orders to fire a signal gun at the approach of any ship, which means in clear weather when they are still fifty miles off. As soon as the signal gun is heard, the shore battery is manned as a precaution – five hundred guns, enough to blow anyone out of the water.

'Admiral Cockburn says that General Bonaparte can be charming, but he's very temperamental. His moods change quickly, and he takes offence easily, sometimes at the strangest things. Papa says that's because he's quite mad. He says all emperors are mad, and that if they don't start off that way, being emperor makes them so. However, I am still looking forward to speaking to the great man, and I shall write and tell you All as soon as it has happened.'

The question of the incompatibility of imperial sovereignty and mental health was being so warmly debated that none of the three of them noticed the approach across the sands of two tall gentlemen. They were brought up short with surprise when their way was blocked, a tall hat was swept off, and a voice said,

'Miss Sophie Morland – how very pleasant! Lady Rosamund, if I don't mistake? And the good Miss Rosedale! How do you all do? How charming to meet you here like this.'

Even Miss Rosedale was too taken aback for a moment to know quite how to reply; and it was Rosamund, the least acquainted of the three – for she had not been 'out' when he was around – who responded.

'Mr Hawker, is it not? How do you do?' she said with cool friendliness, holding out her hand. 'We have never been introduced, but you are a sort of cousin of mine, by marriage at least.'

'Indeed, ma'am, and of course I knew your mama very well in Vienna at the time of my honeymoon. How is Lady Theakston?'

'Just the same,' Rosamund said shortly. She looked at Sophie, who was blushing with a variety of consciousnesses. Sophie had not been made a party to all the secrets, but of

48

course she knew there had been something strange about Fitzherbert Hawker's marriage to her half-sister Fanny. His name was never spoken except with revilement by Papa and Uncle Ned, and so she didn't know whether she ought to acknowledge him.

Hawker was smiling at her now. 'Come, sister Sophie, won't you know me? You were at my wedding, you know.'

That was true. Sophie felt she could not do otherwise than offer her hand, and he pressed it so gently and smiled so kindly that she felt at once he must have been misjudged. Hawker then turned to Miss Rosedale with a grave look.

'You, ma'am, I believe, were my poor Fanny's best friend.' When she did not acknowledge his words, he added in a low voice, 'You and I share the greatest grief. I loved her, you know – no-one could have loved her more.'

His eyes, his expression, his voice were all perfectly sincere. Miss Rosedale felt the sudden pressure of tears in her throat, and found herself clasping his hand almost before she knew it. But after all, she thought, as she recovered herself, it could do no harm now. Poor little Fanny was dead; and it would be better for everyone if there were never to be a hint that her marriage was not all it should have been.

'What brings you to Scarborough, Mr Hawker?' Miss Rosedale asked evenly. 'I would not have thought it would be quite to your taste.'

He smiled disarmingly. 'Too slow, you mean – too provincial? Well, ma'am, I'm a little surprised myself to be here. It's certainly a long way from Vienna! But I came here at the urgent request of a friend, who is convalescing with the aid of Scarborough's noted air and waters.'

With a turn of his head, he brought their attention to the man standing silently beside him. 'Might I have the signal honour of presenting him to you?' Hawker went on; and seeing Miss Rosedale's quick, slight frown, he added, 'I would not, of course, have the impertinence to request it, except that he is a distant relative of Lady Rosamund's – and blood, they say, is thicker than water. Lady Rosamund, may I present to you my good friend Jesmond Farraline? He's quite respectable, you know – his brother is the Earl of Batchworth.'

Rosamund did not consult Miss Rosedale's face, afraid that she might find herself in the position of being obliged to refuse the acquaintance. She didn't want to do that. For one thing, she was growing just a little bored with Scarborough and nothing but female companionship; and for another, Farraline was the most staggeringly handsome man she had ever seen.

'Mr Farraline,' she said, extending her hand. The tall, graceful man swept off his hat, stooped, placed his own elegant hand under hers, and brushed the air just above her glove with his lips. His hair was so fair that it glittered almost silver in the sunlight; as he straightened he looked down into her eyes with a gaze so direct and so intensely blue that she felt almost faint. 'In what way,' she heard herself asking, 'are we related?'

'My mother was a Manvers before she married,' he said. His voice was light and pleasant, caressive like a warm breeze on the skin. 'In fact, I believe my grandfather and your uncle were brothers, which must make us cousins.'

'My uncle Manvers is in fact my great-uncle. But still, cousins of a sort,' Rosamund conceded. 'But if you are related to me, you must also be distantly related to my cousin Sophie.'

'Indeed, ma'am. How do you do, Miss Morland?'

Sophie merely acknowledged the introduction with a nod, overcome by so much beauty. Rosamund, a little defiantly, completed the job by presenting him to Miss Rosedale.

'You are staying up at St Nicholas Cliff, aren't you?' Farraline said.

'Where else?' Hawker murmured. It was the most expensive and exclusive part of Scarborough. 'These are ladies of fashion, Jes.'

'I'm sure I've seen you coming out of Wood's Lodgings. I'm staying almost next-door, at Hampton House, with my mother. I often see you walking along the flagway past our windows.'

'With your mother?' Miss Rosedale said, surprise, relief and approval vying in her tone. The presence of the Dowager Countess changed everything. She would be answerable to Lady Theakston if Rosamund got into bad company, but this immediately made it more respectable.

Farraline bowed his head. 'Yes, we've rented Lady Culvey's house for two months. I should be honoured if you would allow me to bring Mama to call on you, ma'am. I think she finds it rather lonely here, having no acquaintance in Scarborough, you understand.'

'Is your mother here to take the waters?'

'Oh no, ma'am – it's I who am the invalid.'

Hawker broke in. 'He's so modest, ladies, that he'll never tell you himself, but he is not recovering from measles or influenza or any other undignified civilian ailment. The fact is that Jes was most honourably wounded in the final defeat of Boney's forces outside Paris. The wound didn't heal properly, and he has had to undergo a further operation, the details of which, of course, I wouldn't mention before ladies.'

'Dear me,' Rosamund said, her eyes dancing with amusement at Hawker's style. The pronouncement had had an immediate effect on both Sophie and Miss Rosedale, she could see: Farraline was now a Soldier Hero, and Hawker a Soldier Hero's Friend. 'I hope the operation was a success, Mr Farraline?'

He bowed to her, his eyes responding to the amusement in hers. 'Thank you, Lady Rosamund, I am almost completely recovered.'

'But the sands are growing disagreeably crowded,' Hawker broke in. 'Shall we move on? Were you walking to the Spa? Will you permit us to escort you a little way? Miss Rosedale, do me the honour, ma'am, of taking my arm. This sand is very tiring for a lady to walk over. We can talk about my dear Fanny,' he added in a low voice. 'Apart from Lady Henrietta's kind letter, I know nothing about her last weeks. I have no-one in the world with whom I can talk about her.'

It was well done. Miss Rosedale, nursing only a subsiding spark of suspicion, could not refuse him, and in taking his arm implied a consent to walking a little behind the others and conducting a tête-à-tête. Jesmond Farraline, with perfectly grave courtesy, offered an arm each to Sophie and Rosamund, and as they walked along ahead, opened an unexceptionable conversation about the weather and the remarkable facilities Scarborough had to offer.

John Skelwith and Mathilde were invited to take 'family dinner' at Morland Place on Sunday. It was not the first time they had eaten there since their marriage, but the occasion

51

was bound to be marked with an unusual tension. It was the first time Skelwith had entered Morland Place as the openly acknowledged fruit of James Morland's loins.

'Openly', of course, was a relative term. Even though, after Héloïse's talk with James and Edward, they had agreed there was no purpose in further concealing from each other the knowledge that they all knew what they knew, they had also agreed that it would be foolish and unseemly to broadcast it to the neighbourhood at large. Mathilde was enough of a daughter of the house to make John's acceptance as a son unremarkable, and as for those who guessed – let them keep their guess to themselves.

Even that degree of openness, however, needed courage. When Skelwith walked in through the great door with Mathilde on his arm, to be received by the family standing formally in line in the hall, there were difficult feelings to be faced by all of them. Héloïse noted, as she always did, John's likeness to James, and felt again the complicated mixture of affection, jealousy and regret which she always felt on seeing him, ever since the truth about his parenthood had first been revealed to her. She loved him because she loved anything that was part of James; but he ought to have been her son, and the knowledge that another woman had borne a child to her man filled her each time with a futile, jealous rage.

She stepped forward, embraced Mathilde, and then took John's hands. Looking into his face, she saw that it was far more difficult for him, who was part of it, than it could ever be for her, an outsider. She was ashamed of her selfishness. 'Dear John,' she said, 'I am glad! Now I may love you openly as I have always done secretly. If I can ever be anything of a mother to you, I shall be happy.'

His eyes filled abruptly with tears. He had loved his mother, difficult as she had been. Héloïse put her arms round him and hugged him, hard, to allow him to conceal them. 'Thank you,' he said, muffled, into her hair. 'I'm glad too.'

It was enough for now. Edward watched the exchange and the embrace and struggled against the hard feelings inside him. It was not John Skelwith's fault, none of it; but still he remembered the pain Skelwith's birth had caused Edward's parents – his mother's grief, his father's shock. And old Skelwith – his misery and humiliation at being cuckolded by a careless boy of nineteen. It would have been better, far, if this young man had never existed.

And John Skelwith had married Mathilde, which was hard to bear, and had now got her with child, which was harder. Again, it was no blame on him – Edward had given her up quite freely, and acknowledged that Skelwith would make her a better husband than he ever could. But feelings had little to do with reason and logic: he had loved her, and was jealous. And Edward liked John, too, for a plain, decent, pleasant sort of chap, which was hardest of all. It would be nice simply to be able to hate him.

But no, it wouldn't, for here was his lovely, his darling Mathilde, coming to him to be embraced, all bright eyes and bright cheeks and silken, healthy skin; enceinte with his, Edward's, great-nephew. He and this child would share some little of the same blood: it was, he supposed, a kind of way of possessing her. He and Mathilde were joined, now, for ever with the bonds of kinship. He must remember, too, that but for the accident of his illegitimacy, Skelwith might even now be heir apparent to Morland Place, might have been running it himself these nine years, taking precedence over Edward as the young stag does over the failing one. Things might have been worse.

All these thoughts tumbled through Edward's mind in the time it took Mathilde to reach him. He embraced her and kissed her forehead, and she looked at him with the overspill of her love and happiness in her eyes and on her lips, and whispered, 'Dear Edward! Be happy for me!'

He said, 'Yes. I am glad you're happy, my dear.' Then he and Skelwith shook hands in a grave and manly sort of way, and nothing needed to be said between them.

Then John Skelwith approached James, and Mathilde fell a little back, seeing it was not her meeting that would be difficult. James looked at the tall young man, the first of his children, whom he had long, long ago given up in his heart; the child he had been denied the right to rear. Was that why, he wondered, he had afterwards been able to care only for his daughters? He had loved Mary passionately, had been bitterly hurt by her refusal of him, her acceptance instead of old Skelwith. He had been young then, vulnerable, and she had hurt him so badly – was that why he had hurt all the other women in his life? Great with his child, she had refused to come to him, to let him care for her and for his son. Was that why he had so signally failed afterwards in responsibility as a husband and father?

Things had gone wrong for him early in his life, and afterwards he did not seem to be able to get right again with the world. Even now, after all their sufferings, when he and Héloïse had finally reached a place of safety together, John was coming out of his past to threaten that fragile equilibrium. For despite her generous response, he *knew* that it hurt Héloïse. Oh yes, it was better by far to have the thing out in the open and acknowledged, but still his first grandchild would not be hers, and whether or not she had any right to mind it, he knew that she did.

The fruit of my loins, he thought. Six children – that he knew of – had come out of his body, and what kind of a father had he been to any of them? Had his existence made any difference to them, for better or worse? But John Skelwith was standing before him, looking at him with pained embarrassment, with apprehension, with curiosity, and something must be said, to get them over this moment and into the social haven of dinner. Should he call him *son*? No, perhaps that would not be tactful at this point.

'Welcome, my boy,' he said at last. 'We'll – we'll talk together later. For now, I'm glad there are no more secrets. I'm glad you're here.'

It was little enough to have said – the least he could say, perhaps – and John's reaction shamed him. Skelwith's eyes brightened with genuine emotion, as though James's words had been everything he wanted to hear. He said warmly, 'I'm glad to be here, sir. I'm glad to be –' But he couldn't say the word *son* either. 'I'm glad to be here,' he finished lamely.

Mathilde laughed, breaking the increasing tension. 'Oh, how solemn we all look, as though it were a funeral, instead of a happy occasion! We've come home,' she said, going up to James in her turn and putting up her face to be kissed with such confidence that he kissed her more in automatic response than spontaneous affection. 'We've come home, and I'm going to have a baby!'

And then James smiled too, irresistibly. 'So you are. It seems almost improper, now I come to think of it. It seems like only five minutes ago that we were having your birthday ball, and scratching about for young people to invite to make the numbers even.'

There was a palpitating moment in which Héloïse held her breath: it was at Mathilde's ball that Fanny first met Fitzherbert Hawker: he had been one of the extras invited to make up the numbers. Would the same memory occur to James? But Mathilde had turned to Edward, and was saying, 'Oh yes, and you powdered for the occasion, didn't you? I remember thinking how elegant you looked!'

'No need to powder now,' Edward said wryly, shaking his grey head. 'Nature has done it for me.'

Mathilde laughed with him, and they all seemed to be moving naturally towards the drawing-room, the atmosphere pleasant now, and growing easier. Edward offered his arm to Mathilde, and James walked on the other side of her. 'Come and have a glass of madeira,' he said. 'We've a new Boal I think you'll like.'

'It won't hurt the baby, will it?' from Edward.

'Sound wine never hurt anyone,' from James. 'Of course it won't.'

Left alone, John Skelwith turned to Héloïse and smiled invitingly. 'Will you, Madame?' he said, offering his cuff.

My God, she thought, he looks like James when he smiles. Each time, it was like a physical shock. He should have been mine, her heart keened. Oh, how he must have haunted his poor mother!

She laid her hand on his sleeve. 'It will take a little getting used to,' she said, for something to say.

'Yes,' he agreed. 'But that's the worst over, at least. It will be easier from now on.'

Will it? Héloïse thought; but she smiled assent at the proposition.

'What were you and Hawker talking about, Sophie? You had a very long conversation with him,' Rosamund asked. She was sitting before the mirror while Moss put her hair into its night-time braids. Sophie, already in bed, sat up, hugging her knees. With her dark curls falling from under her frilled nightcap, she looked no more than fourteen.

'We were talking about poor sister Fanny,' she said. 'He

55

really did love her, you know.'

'Oh Sophie! He married her for her fortune – everyone knows that.'

'No, Ros, I'm sure you're wrong,' Sophie said with a frown. 'The way he spoke about her was so tender and sad – it almost made me cry. I'm sure everyone's misjudged him.'

'You're such an innocent,' Rosamund said. She caught Moss's eyes in the mirror, and saw the same conviction there. 'Of course he's bound to say things like that to you. He's trying to make an impression.'

'Why should he want to impress me? He cared about her, I know he did.'

'Then why did he stay away in Vienna all those months, while she was at Morland Place, and expecting the baby? And he's never been back since, remember – not even to her memorial.'

'He explained that to me,' Sophie said eagerly. Rosamund raised an eyebrow. 'Well, he told me some of it, though he said he was in honour bound not to tell all. He was obliged to be away, but it was much against his will – he couldn't tell me why, because he'd sworn not to. And when Fanny died, and the poor little baby too, he was too grief-stricken to think or act. He said he hardly ate or slept for a week. Of course, he couldn't have got back in time for her funeral, anyway – and he wasn't asked to her memorial.'

'Wasn't asked?'

'That's what he said. Well, I know for a fact Papa and Uncle Ned both hated him, so it's probably true. He says he would like to visit Morland Place now to see her headstone, only he's afraid he wouldn't be welcome.'

'I should think he wouldn't,' Rosamund said with a hard smile. 'That will do, Moss. You may go now.'

'Yes, my lady,' Moss said, disappointed. It was obvious her ladyship was about to tell Miss a few home truths, and Moss would have liked to hear that. When the door closed behind her, however, Rosamund, thinking better of it, merely said, 'You mustn't let your sympathy run away with you. You think anyone who's had a bereavement is a saint. Not everyone feels as you felt about Larosse, you know.'

Sophie's lip trembled. 'Well I like him,' she said defiantly. 'And I know Miss Rosedale does, too. They talk about Fanny all the time, and she believes he really loved her. He told Rosey he was afraid there'd been some neglect of Fanny during her last months, otherwise she wouldn't have died, because she was so strong and healthy. But Miss Rosedale told him it was because Fanny insisted on doing too much, and wouldn't rest. She said she thought travelling to Manchester in the coach to see her grandpa may have done the mischief. He asked about the baby, too, and she told me he was almost in tears when she said it was born dead.'

Tender-hearted Sophie was almost in tears telling about it. But Rosamund had very definite ideas about Mr Fitzherbert Hawker. It seemed to her on reflection a strange coincidence that they had encountered each other on the sand quite by chance; and since that meeting, the acquaintance had got along like a chaise-and-four. Farraline had brought his mother a-calling the very next day; the return call had found Hawker sitting with them, having 'just stepped round a moment ago'. They had all met at the library tea-rooms the following day and drunk tea together; and tonight Lady Batchworth had invited them to an evening-party at Hampton House, where there had been plenty of opportunity, it seemed, for *tête-à-têtes*.

That Hawker had some plan in all this, she had no doubt. She had heard enough about him, in the days when he was courting Fanny in her first London Season, to know he was a rogue, adventurer and fortune-hunter. Rosamund had still been in the schoolroom, but in some ways there was no better vantage point for watching the game. Grown-ups sometimes said things they assumed a schoolroom miss wouldn't understand; and Rosamund had never been averse from listening at doors and talking to servants, when it was a matter of gathering useful information.

She wondered briefly if his present bout of ingratiation was aimed at her and her fortune – for he surely couldn't hope for anything more from Morland Place. He must surely be aware that Sophie wouldn't inherit – and yet, perhaps he knew more than Rosamund? Morland Place was not entailed. Could he mean to re-establish himself with Héloïse, win Sophie's heart, and take the prize that way?

No, that was too far-fetched! It must be some more immediate plan he had in mind. And she didn't want to upset

Sophie any more at this stage, so she said merely, 'Well, he certainly seems to have charmed you.'

'Yes,' Sophie said, and sighed. 'I do like him. Yet whenever I meet a man of his age, I can't help thinking "Why are you alive, and René dead?". I know it's wicked; but it does seem so unfair.'

'It is unfair, dear Sophie. But if we all got what we deserved in this life, it would be a pretty poor show for most of us.'

'Yes,' she said solemnly, 'then I should never have had René's love, for I know I didn't deserve him.'

This was not the direction in which Rosamund had meant to lead her cousin's spirits. After a moment she said, 'He was a good man, and I know how you cared for him. But one day you'll meet another man who will love you, and you'll love him, and you'll marry and be happy.'

Sophie looked up briefly, and down again. 'Oh no,' she said quietly. 'I couldn't. René is the only man I could ever –' She stopped, and then said even more quietly, her face well hidden, 'Ros, do you know – I mean, I suppose you must – about marriage? What it means? What happens – afterwards.'

'Yes,' Rosamund said briefly, her eyes bright with amusement and compassion. How protected Sophie had been all her life! Even in Brussels, when they'd all had to cope with the influx of dreadfully-wounded soldiers, Sophie had been kept apart from the worst sights, and had certainly never been allowed to bandage anything but heads and arms. Mens' bodies must be mysterious and awful to her, because utterly unknown.

'Well,' Sophie went on, what was visible of her cheeks very red, 'I know that when one marries one must – I mean, it's one's duty – but I don't think, I really don't think, I could ever do such a thing with anyone but René. I couldn't bear it. Don't you feel the same?'

'Oh Sophie!' Rosamund knew a great many more things than Sophie, amongst them that marriages like her mother's with Papa Danby, and perhaps Aunt Héloïse's with Uncle James, were far from being the norm. In polite society, or at least in the upper echelons of it, couples married for practical and family reasons, and once the desired number of children had been born, the sort of activity that so alarmed Sophie ceased. And even amongst the second circle, she imagined that it was hardly an everyday occupation. Physical passion was not an ingredient of the average marriage.

Rosamund had loved Philip Tantony, and her senses had been excited by him. After her schoolroom infatuation with Marcus, it had been a new experience to feel that physical attraction – new and vivid and heady. Sometimes even in memory it made her quiver: she could recall sometimes exactly what it had been like to touch his hand and look into his eyes. She had looked forward to the life of intimacy with him; she didn't suppose she would ever feel that way again about anyone.

But she knew she must marry: to remain single would be to place herself outside society, to endure restrictions on her freedom, to be regarded as an eccentric, eventually to be an object of pity. She didn't want to live like that. Any sort of marriage would be better than such isolation.

Sophie had looked up for an answer. Rosamund said, 'I think I could bear it, provided it was someone I liked reasonably well.'

'Like Marcus?'

'Well, yes, perhaps.' She shied away from the specific. 'But one way or another, I must marry.'

'Because your mama will make you?'

'Because – because it will be expected of me. And you'll marry too, one day.'

'Oh no,' Sophie said with quiet conviction.

You will, Rosamund affirmed, but silently. You were not designed for the single life, and all men are not so blind to their own interest. You will marry – and unlike me, dear Sophie, you will marry for love.

An exhibition of art at the Assembly House was a welcome indoor diversion in the continuing wet weather; and dawdling about amongst the pictures provided plenty of opportunity for private conversation. Lady Batchworth had commanded, and Mr Hawker had arranged, and they had all gone together as a party.

The dowager had appropriated Miss Rosedale as a sort of courier-cum-private secretary, and having handed over the catalogue, was requiring Miss Rosedale to explain each picture to her, and to tell her what she must think of it.

'Your mother is very affable and condescending,' Rosamund remarked to Mr Farraline, with whom she was idling a little behind the nodding turban – the dowager's taste having been fixed about the year '98, when things 'Eastern' had been the rage. 'Not many ladies of her rank would seek out the company of a governess like that.'

'You are being entirely mischievous, Lady Rosamund,' Farraline said, surprising her. 'Mama is not in the least condescending, and hardly ever affable, as you very well know. What she does, she does for her own advantage.'

'What can you mean?'

'Mama likes to be beforehand with the world. She knows quite well that Miss Rosedale is both knowledgeable, and has excellent taste, and will provide her with just the right things to say about the paintings when next she is in company.'

Rosamund suppressed a smile. 'You really shouldn't speak of your mother like that to me, Mr Farraline.'

'Why not? Don't you like frankness?'

'Not when it embarrasses. How shall I keep my countenance in company with Lady Batchworth if you expose her to me so shamefully?'

He laughed. 'Ah, it was not the impropriety that troubled you, then, but the inconvenience? I think I begin to understand you a little better, ma'am.'

'Good God! I hope not! But since we are being frank, you may answer some questions, if you will.'

'You alarm me. I'm afraid you are going to ask me things I won't care to answer.'

'I am going to ask you about yourself, which I imagine will please you. I never met the man who didn't like talking about himself.'

'Cruel, Lady Rosamund. Isn't everyone – male or female – self-absorbed?'

'Yes, it's true,' she smiled. 'Tell me, then – how was it that you fought at Paris? Or was that a hum? For you were not in Brussels, or we should have met. You did not fight at Waterloo.'

'My regiment was in America, and we didn't arrive until several days after Waterloo. We were in time to join the pursuit, but we missed the battle – to my great regret.'

She raised an eyebrow. 'How could you regret it, an experienced soldier? In Brussels it was only the Hyde Park officers who spoke like that.' Her eyes clouded. 'I danced with them only a few days before, and all their talk was of glory and the magnificent feats of arms they were going to perform. They were so excited when they marched away, poor fellows, but so few of them came marching back.'

'Ah, but the heart of my regret, ma'am, is not the battle itself, but the opportunity of dancing with you beforehand.'

'Pho! Absurd!' Rosamund said, not entirely pleased.

'But I mean it. Long before I met you, I knew of you by repute – not only that you were the loveliest and gayest of the débutantes, but that you had not flinched from tending the wounded after the battle. Your courage and compassion were not forgotten, I assure you. Your health was drunk in the mess on many occasions, and with a serious gratitude that I think would not have displeased you.'

'If you want to praise anyone on that account, praise my mother. It was she who did the things that required courage,' Rosamund said shortly. When he did not reply, she looked up at him, suspecting him of a gross and purely social flattery; but his expression was one of intensity, and that strange directness which made her feel rather giddy. It was as if there were no barriers between them; she felt undefended against him, almost naked.

'I wish you won't flatter me,' she said abruptly. 'I don't like it.'

'You prefer frankness? Then let me tell you I was not flattering you. I do most sincerely admire you for what you did.'

She looked at him askance. 'It was unfeminine,' she said neutrally.

He smiled. 'Yes, that's been said too. But not by one whose judgement may be relied upon for impartiality.'

'Who is that?'

'I had heard you variously described as beautiful, vivacious, and a ministering angel; also as a right 'un, and a devil to go on horseback. Those were the majority opinions. But one particular person spoke of you as – let me see if I have the words right – a red-headed minx, a hoyden, and an unscrupulous schemer.' He enjoyed the shocked anger in Rosamund's face. 'Can't you guess? Dear ma'am – and you who

61

stole Bel de Ladon's lover from her!'

Rosamund's eyes opened wide. 'Good God! You don't mean – can you be acquainted with Lady Annabel Robb?'

'Oh, of course, she was Bel Robb then, wasn't she? She married de Ladon in a fit of pique to shew she didn't care about young Chelmsford's defection to your camp.'

'No, sir, you are quite wrong,' Rosamund said stiffly. 'Lady Annabel had already tired of Marcus Morland before he inherited the title. It was *she* who dropped *him*. I had nothing to do with it.'

He was clearly enjoying himself. 'But after he inherited the title, she tried to get him back. Did you not know that? No, evidently not. Her engagement to de Ladon was never meant, I fancy, to be more than an annoyance to everyone. But when Chelmsford refused her, she went through with it and married him – and has lived to regret it, I'm sure.'

Rosamund's cheeks were warm. 'Why are you telling me this?'

'I thought you might enjoy it. Few women have ever got the better of Bel. It's something of a triumph.'

'Not the kind of triumph that interests me.'

'Then I honour you the more, ma'am.'

'And you haven't told me yet how you heard it. Are you acquainted with Lady Annabel?'

'Only at arm's length, I assure you! Solely by virtue of being Fitz's best friend. We were all together in Paris, you see. De Ladon brought his lady there for the celebrations and sightseeing, as soon as Boney was safely taken; and of course Fitz came with the politicians.'

Rosamund looked up at him, and then looked at Hawker, strolling with Sophie on his arm a little in front of them.

'Do you mean that – Mr Hawker and Lady Annabel –?'

'Fitz is very popular with the ladies,' Farraline said lightly. 'I'm told he makes love very prettily.'

Rosamund was silent for a moment, and then said bluntly, 'Why do you talk to me like this?'

'Don't you like it?'

'It's the oddest conversation I ever had in my life. It isn't the way gentlemen talk to ladies. What do you mean by it?'

'To tell you the truth, I hardly know myself,' he said, looking down at her with an air of puzzlement she almost

62

believed in. 'I just felt, suddenly, that I couldn't bear to go through the usual tedious minuet of small-talk with you. I thought you might be bored with it, too. Don't you ever long to say exactly what comes into your head, and to hell with the conventions?'

She only just managed not to laugh. 'I've been told I do that already, rather too often. But, really, Mr Farraline, it won't do! What would become of us all, if we all did and said exactly what we liked?'

'You can't be too free and frank for my liking – and I don't care much about the rest of Society. Shall we make a pact, Lady Rosamund? Shall we swear that we will never say anything to each other but the honest truth? That we shall never pretend to be shocked or offended by anything the other says?'

She shook her head, in wonder rather than refusal. 'Why me? Why should you suppose I was less well brought up than any other young female?'

'I thought you looked bored,' he said. 'At Mama's card-party, I thought you looked in need of rescue. Was I right? Shall we make a pact?'

'You may yet regret it. I may still ask you things you don't care to answer.'

He met her eyes. 'And I may you.'

'You're a strange one, Mr Farraline,' she said, laughing. 'But you're right – I do find myself growing bored sometimes with drawing-room chit-chat. I agree to your pact – on condition that it's purely between ourselves. No-one else must ever know how shamefully we flout the conventions.'

'Your reputation is safe in my hands, ma'am,' he said. 'And to prove it, I shall now suggest we look at one or two of the pictures, so that we are not found shamefully at a loss when asked for our opinions.'

'I can't imagine your ever being at a loss,' Rosamund said, and it was not entirely a compliment.

CHAPTER FOUR

Edward came looking for Héloïse, and ran her to earth at last,
unexpectedly, in the steward's room. With the cuffs of her
sleeves turned back, and a harrassed expression creasing her
face, she was struggling with the household accounts.

'You seem to be having difficulties,' he said. Tiger padded
past him to push his grizzled head into her lap, and she pulled
his soft ears absently.

'It is a poor thing that I make such heavy weather of it,' she
sighed, 'but though I was taught to reckon at school, it was a
very long time ago. And I do not entirely understand Father
Aislaby's method of book keeping.'

'He was a law to himself. But why don't you leave it for
James to do?'

'James has enough to do already.'

'So have you.'

'Yes, it's true, but when James has a spare moment, he
plays with Benedict, and I do so like to see him taking an
interest in his son. I don't want to interrupt them. I must
struggle on as best I can. But what did you want me for?'

'Ah yes,' Edward said, looking conscious. 'I have some
news for you.'

'Good news, I hope?'

'I don't know whether you'll consider it good or bad. I've
just had word from Colonel Rolleston – he's one of the
Nottingham magistrates. Friend Batty has been taken up.'

'Oh?' It was impossible to tell from such a small comment
how Héloïse felt about it.

Edward went on, 'He'd gone into hiding in Sherwood
Forest – very traditional of him, in a way. I must say I had
rather suspected he'd keep running north, away from the
scene of the crime, but when we flushed him out here it seems
he just went back home. I suppose in the end he didn't know

where else to go. It isn't likely a man of his order would have friends in far-off places.'

'How was he taken?'

'They were searching the woods anyway. The Nottingham Justices – Rolleston and Mundy and Sherbrooke and the like – tend to be pretty vigorous about machine-breakers, and they suspected a lot of them were hiding out in Sherwood. They called on the militia and the yeomanry to flush the woods, and Batty was one of those they rounded up.'

'They knew him, then?'

'Oh yes. He was recognised at once. He's well-known in those parts as a trouble-maker. He and a man called Brandreth were apparently among the ringleaders of the attack on Heathcote and Boden's. They've caught the others, but this Brandreth got away, which won't make them any more likely to be lenient.'

'What will happen to Batty – to all of them?' Héloïse asked.

'If they're convicted, they'll be hanged.' Edward met her eyes steadily. 'It's important to make an example of these people, just as we did in 1812.'

'Yes, of course,' said Héloïse. She remembered the executions in York – not that she had attended them, but she remembered the occasion, one of awful solemnity and large public interest. The North Riding was not a troubled area, and the magistrates, Edward amongst them, tended to be more lenient with offenders than their colleagues in the Midlands, or even in the West Riding. Even so, there were a number of public executions every year for various crimes, ranging from murder to will-forging, and it was traditional for parents to take along their children as an essential part of their education: an object lesson, a salutary warning on the consequences of wickedness.

She understood the necessity for such punishments intellectually, and particularly in the case of machine-breaking, which could so easily turn into riot and revolution; but hangings always made her remember the mob from Marseilles who in her youth had dragged men and women from their houses and hanged them from the lamp-posts. And she remembered weaver Batty and his tear-filled eyes as he pleaded for his brother, and imagined that brother hiding, trembling, in the woods, listening to the beaters coming closer and closer. The

65

plain fact was that it always seemed different when you knew the people involved.

Edward sat on the edge of the desk, evidently thinking she needed further persuasion. 'There's a lot of concern at the Home Office at the moment about public unrest. We've all – all Justices – had a letter from Sidmouth telling us to be particularly vigilant, and to punish any trouble severely. It's all this talk about reform. Such nonsense! What have the common people to do with politics, I ask you? It makes me fume when I think of them standing around in the tap-room of the Hare arguing about Government and franchise and so on! And it can only lead to trouble. Oh, they're not revolutionary by nature, I grant you, but when they're got hold of by unscrupulous people like this Henry Hunt – Orator Hunt they call him – and Tom Batty and his kind, they can be whipped up into misguided actions.'

Héloïse nodded understanding. 'Is there danger?' she asked bluntly.

Edward frowned. 'There's no danger as long as they don't band together. On their own, they're good people, most of 'em, and they just want to be left alone to get on with their lives, like everyone else. But just now there are so many people out of work, and hungry – that's a dangerous combination. And if the harvest fails ...' He glanced out of the window at the continuing steady rain. 'It's the organisers we need to stop – the educated men who stir up the poor for their own ends.'

'It was so in Paris,' Héloïse said quietly. 'The *bourgeoises* were the real revolutionaires. The poor were only their weapon. Perhaps it is always so.'

'These Hampden Clubs, for instance,' Edward went on, broodingly, 'I'd have banned 'em, if it were up to me. Sidmouth's had reports that in some villages they're only waiting for the signal from London to rise up. They really believe there's going to be a march on the Tower, the palace surrounded and the Government overthrown. And for what? Do they really think a revolution will put more bread in their mouths?'

'James says it can't happen here – in England, in Yorkshire.'

Edward was torn between the need to reassure her and the

desire to educate her. 'He may be right,' he said shortly. 'There've been alarms before, of course, and they came to nothing. But since 1789 there's no real security anywhere. England isn't France, but everyone knows it can happen. We've got to guard against that, and stamp out any little flames before they become a forest fire.' He patted her arm and stood up. 'Don't worry, though – we're quite safe here at Morland Place. Our own people are true, thank God! You won't come to any harm in this neighbourhood.'

Tiger yawned noisily, and thrashed his tail as an encouragement to the movement. 'I must be off,' Edward recollected. 'Compton's got a brace of poachers for me – caught red-handed with their pockets full of my birds. Not local lads, however – tramping men, so I understand. Probably Irish.'

'Irish?'

'There's altogether too many of them around these days. They come over to work in the manufactories in Lancashire, and then when there's no work they wander all over the countryside making a nuisance of themselves. I shall have this pair flogged – maybe they'll spread the word to their friends to keep away.' Tiger nudged him, and he touched the dog's head thoughtfully, his mind wandering off on another track. 'You ought to have another dog,' he said. 'It was bad luck, losing both of yours like that last winter, though of course Kithra was an old dog, and Castor – well, distemper can strike any time. But you must miss having a dog at your heels. I know I'd feel naked without one. Would you like a puppy? I've got some very promising whelps coming up now. I'd be happy to start training one for you.'

Héloïse smiled. 'It's very kind of you, dear Ned, but I truly don't think I have time at the moment for a dog. It would have a very dull time of it, following me around the house. Perhaps when things get easier –'

'Yes. Very well, just as you like. I just thought you might feel lonely. You seem to be always on your own these days, with Mathilde and Marie both gone.'

The wistfulness of his voice told her it was his own loneliness that had prompted these thoughts, though in his busy life he probably had never time fully to be aware of it. The distant sensation of emptiness had translated itself in his mind to a concern for Héloïse's lack of companions.

'Of course I miss them,' she said, 'but I shall have Sophie again soon, and Miss Rosedale.'

'Yes, of course. When is Sophie coming back? She seems to have been gone for ever.'

'Soon. She'll be coming soon. Miss Rosedale writes very comfortably of her, that her spirits are much raised by her holiday.'

'Good. I miss her sweet face, and the music in the evenings,' Edward said revealingly, and went away to interview his poachers.

Left alone, Héloïse did not at once return to her books. Her mind was full of confused images, of poachers and peasants, of weavers and orators, of the savage drunken *fédérés* from Marseilles and cold-eyed 'lawyer' Robespierre, of her first dog Bluette and her last dog Castor, of her darling child Sophie and poor dead Fanny. Troubled times indeed – and yet when in her life had the times not been troubled? What an age she had lived through! From the Revolution through twenty years of war to a Peace filled with the threat of upheaval and change ... She was not yet forty, but she had been married for the first time at fourteen, and the cloistered calm of her short childhood seemed many ages away.

And now there was one other image in her mind, as disturbing in its way as any of the others – the image of a face, dark, handsome and male. Miss Rosedale, in her last letter, had told her about Fitzherbert Hawker's sudden appearance, and her conviction that he had been misjudged, at least in relation to his sentiments for Fanny. But that was not, of course, something that she would be able to speak of to Edward.

She sighed and picked up her pen again. Meanwhile, there were still the accounts to be done, and she hadn't even finished entering the heap of crumpled bills and receipts. Now where would Father Aislaby have put the income from selling surplus cheese made in the Morland Place dairy? Was that household income or estate income? The cows were estate property, but the dairy-maid was a household servant, and the cheese was made originally for consumption in the house. On the whole, she thought it was probably household income. And what about the piano-tuner? Did that come under servants' wages? He wasn't, of course, a servant, but he was a

68

regular item in the budget. But then again ... After some deliberation, and in her careful, curly, convent-taught hand, she put the piano-tuner in under *sundries*.

Miss Rosedale had succumbed to one of the tremendous colds in the head which afflicted her from time to time, and since she plainly couldn't keep the young ladies within doors for its duration, she had been obliged to let them go out with only Moss in attendance.

'Don't you worry, miss,' Judy Moss had said, torn between offence and determination, 'I can keep an eye on 'em. They won't get up to any larks with me on their heels, I can tell you.'

Miss Rosedale emerged muzzily from a handkerchief for long enough to say, 'The gentlemen –'

'Yes, miss,' Moss said stiffly. 'If I can mind Lady Rosamund and Miss Sophie in a city full of officers like Brussels, I'm sure I can take care of them in Scarborough.'

Miss Rosedale was feeling too awful to have the energy to point out that two prowling wolves were far more dangerous than a pack of noisy, frisking hounds. She must trust to her charges' instincts of self-preservation.

The wolves in question must have been on the watch, for hardly had Rosamund and Sophie set foot on the flagway than Mr Hawker and Mr Farraline appeared, exquisite from the crown of their tall hats to the tip of their glossy Hessians. Mr Hawker wore a green coat with handsome brass buttons, a wonderful foil to his dark colouring; while Mr Farraline was resplendent in saxe blue, with a red-and-white striped waistcoat which tiptoed with catlike surefootedness along the dividing line between the killingly smart and the vulgarly ostentatious.

'May we have the honour of escorting you, ladies? Where do you go this morning?' Farraline asked when they had replaced their hats.

Moss coughed slightly, and nudged Rosamund in the back with the handle of her own umbrella, an indignity which roused the devil in her ladyship.

'We thought of walking up to look at the castle,' she said airily. 'We should be glad of your company. I'm a good walker, but on such a steep road a gentleman's arm would be

69

welcome even to me; and Sophie could hardly contemplate it without.'

Moss's gasp was audible only to the young ladies, but it was enough to make Sophie demur, though mildly. 'I think it may be too windy up there today, Ros,' she murmured.

'Tush. Of course it will be windy. That's precisely the point – only think how fresh and delicious!' Rosamund turned firmly in the direction of the headland, and the gentlemen, only too happy to fall in with the scheme, offered their arms, Farraline to Rosamund and Hawker to Sophie.

'That was well done,' Farraline murmured as they walked ahead – the flagway being only wide enough for two.

'I'm an old campaigner,' Rosamund said. 'I'm used to getting my own way.'

'It's an excellent idea, though I'm afraid Miss Morland may be right about its being too windy for ladies up on the headland. I fear for your bonnets. But oh, for the freshness and the invigorating air! And the view – nothing in the way as far as the eye can see! Don't you ever feel hemmed in, Lady Rosamund? Don't you ever feel the houses crowding in on you, ready to suffocate you?'

'Yes, sometimes; but then I usually send for my horse and go out for a gallop.'

'Yes, that would do it. At home I sometimes follow the same plan –'

'I'm afraid I have no idea where home is for you.'

'The family seat is at Grasscroft, on the edge of the Pennines. We have moors all around us there. But I'm building a new house on Cheetham Hill, just outside Manchester, for the convenience of being nearer the mills.'

Rosamund looked at him in surprise. 'Nearer the mills?'

He smiled. 'Yes. Does it shock you? It shocks everyone else, including Mama!'

'I'm not shocked, but intrigued. It sounds like a story, and I love a story.'

'Then I shall make it one for you. You see, just before Papa died, he bought the Ordsall mills from old Samuel Ordsall. Over the years he'd gradually grown more and more interested in machinery – well, you can hardly live in that part of Lancashire without being aware of its influence.'

'I suppose not.'

70

'You're not convinced, I can see, but it's true! Well, Papa was very excited by everything to do with machinery and steam-power – it takes some people that way – and he came to feel strongly that the future way lay through manufacturing. So he looked for some mills to invest in, and he came upon Samuel Ordsall. Have you heard of him?'

'No, I'm afraid not,' Rosamund said politely.

'Oh, he was a grand old fellow! I met him once – one of the first of all the mill-masters, a character straight out of history! He started off as an apprentice blacksmith in a tiny village in Derbyshire. By the time he was twenty he owned the forge, and by the time he was thirty he had his own mill employing a hundred spinners. When Papa met him, he was old, but he was still looking to the future. He wanted someone to invest money so that he could expand his business – this was during the war, of course, when the demand for cotton goods was outstripping the supply.'

'Of course.'

'He offered Papa a partnership, but somehow Papa persuaded him to sell entirely. Well, Old Samuel had no heir, so perhaps it wasn't so hard. However it was, Papa became the first Earl of Batchworth to be a mill-master!'

'Tremendous.'

'Mama and Kit – my brother – thought he was mad, and I must say I did too, at first. But he took me round the mills one day – against my will at the time – and I began to see what it was that fascinated him about the machines. There's something about them when they're running –'

'And when your father died, he left the mills to you?' Rosamund hurried him along.

'Good God, no!' Farraline laughed. 'Papa would never break up the estate. Everything went to Kit, along with the title. Kit would have sold the mills if he could, but there was a clause in Papa's will preventing it – apparently he'd promised Old Samuel he'd keep them in the family, as a condition of the original purchase. So Kit did the only thing he could – he just ignored them, and left them to an agent to run.'

'Very wise.'

'I was in the army, of course, and I suppose I intended to make it my career, until I took the wound at Paris. I was invalided out, went home to Grasscroft, and one day, out of

71

boredom, had myself driven in to Ordsall to see the mills again.'

'And did they still please you?'

'More than ever – but I saw at once that they weren't being properly run. The agent was no good, and I told Kit so, but he simply wasn't interested. So I offered to run them myself, provided he would give me a free hand. Now I have shocked you, I can see.'

'No – no, not at all,' Rosamund said, more bemused than shocked. 'If it was what you wanted . . .'

'Well, a younger son must do something, you know. The army is closed to me, and I have no vocation for the church or the law.'

'But you don't actually – you don't surely go into the mills every day like a –'

He grinned. 'Exactly like a –' he mocked. 'Yes, my dear Lady Rosamund, I attend to the day-to-day running, and have even been known to take off my coat and get my hands dirty! That's why I needed the house, of course; and Kit was happy to build it for me – and to do the thing handsomely – in the hope that living in a gentlemanly manner would rub off on me, and make me give up my vulgar obsession. He and Mama find my taste for the mills appalling. They think I'm mad. But they'll see – one day you'll all see! The future belongs to the machine! The day will come when almost every task you can think of will be done by machinery.'

Rosamund shook her head. 'Your mother and brother were right. You are quite mad,' she said, but in a pleasant, friendly way. He only laughed, taking no offence. 'But what can you be doing here?' she went on. 'Idling away the working day in strolling about Scarborough like a gentleman of fashion? Won't your precious machines be going to rack without you?'

'I feel it very strongly, I assure you. But my arm was getting worse and worse, and in the end I had to go to London to consult a physician. Fitz put me onto a good man – a former army surgeon, one of the best, who'd set up his plate in Mayfair since the war ended. He recommended the operation, and –' He shrugged. 'Here I am convalescing.'

'You must be anxious to get back.'

'Yes, I am – though I have enjoyed my stay here much more lately than at the beginning.'

72

She avoided the compliment. 'You haven't seemed like a man consumed with restlessness.'

'Nor you like a lady cabined, cribbed and confined – yet you must find Scarborough slow work after London.'

'Perhaps I'm convalescing too.'

He hesitated a moment before saying, 'I knew Tantony. We served in the Peninsula together. He was a fine officer – one of the best – and a decent man. You chose well, Lady Rosamund.'

'Thank you.'

He pressed her hand against his ribs for an instant, and they walked on in silence, hearing behind them how Hawker was telling Sophie a preposterous story about one of his adventures in Paris, which was making her laugh. Rosamund listened for a moment, and then said, 'Mr Hawker – he is doing well in the diplomatic world? Is he fixed in Europe?'

'I imagine so, for the time being. There's nothing to keep him in England, and Society is much freer over there.' Farraline looked at her enquiringly. 'Are you worried for your cousin?'

'Is she his object?' she asked bluntly.

A faint smile came and went on Farraline's lips which Rosamund couldn't quite account for, but he said promptly enough, 'Oh no. She has nothing that could tempt him.'

'He pays her attention, however. He seems to want to please her.'

'Yes, but – difficult to believe though it may be – I think it is only that. He wants to please her, to give her pleasure. I think, Lady Rosamund, that he likes her.'

'*Likes* her?'

'I think she reminds him of his wife,' Farraline said gently. The word caught Rosamund up short, for though she had thought of Hawker in relation to Fanny, she had hardly ever thought of Fanny in relation to Hawker. His wife – yes, she had been *Hawker's wife*.

Farraline watched her as if he knew what was going through her mind. Then he said, 'I've known Fitz a long time. I've seen him with more women than I can count – women of all ages and all degrees. He goes through them as casually as a man riffles a pack of cards. I've seen him charm them, seduce them, amuse them, make use of them, even avoid them. I

73

never saw him with his wife – a matter of great regret to me – but I've heard him speak of her, and I've no doubt at all that for once in his life, probably for the only time in his life, he was in love.'

'Good God,' Rosamund said blankly. Farraline was plainly in earnest. And yet she couldn't believe that their meeting in the first place was accidental. She couldn't believe that Hawker had not arranged it for some purpose. 'Then what,' she asked Farraline directly, 'is his plan?'

'His plan? Ah, that!' He laughed. 'I will tell you one day.'

'I thought we had a pact, Mr Farraline.'

'We have. But we didn't agree to tell each other *everything* – only nothing that wasn't true.'

'Unscrupulous!'

'It's the coarsening effect of the manufactories. I shall soon cease to be a gentleman at all.'

'That is nothing to boast of.'

'How cruel you are, Lady Rosamund. You shouldn't have agreed with me.'

'You refuse to tell me what Mr Hawker's design is? But you admit that he has one – that our acquaintance has not been accidental?'

They reached the top of the path and he stopped and turned to face her, suddenly serious, his burning blue eyes looking directly into hers in a way that made something inside her clench in a most extraordinary fashion – frightening but exciting.

'No, it hasn't been accidental. But I have the strongest feeling that you and I must have met at last, one way or another. I don't believe that I could have gone through my life and never known you.'

He held her gaze. The damp breeze coming up over the headland pushed against her like a cold animal nudging, and she could taste the salt of it on her lips, see the tiny droplets of moisture catching and gathering on his eyelashes. Behind his head the grey sky moved fast and indifferent, hurrying the day on, as though impatient to be rid of summer altogether. She felt her feet anchoring her to the path against the pressure of time, which wanted to snatch her and Farraline away, away from this instant which was so unexpectedly important. She felt as though she had been stripped bare to

74

the soul. She felt that he and she were alone together on the brink of some momentous discovery.

And then the others arrived, catching up with them, and shook them loose from their foothold so that they slipped again into the stream of time.

'It is very windy up here,' Hawker said. 'I'm afraid your feathers will uncurl, Miss Morland.'

Moss took the cue. 'It's going to rain,' she said disapprovingly. She was a stout little person, and not designed by nature for hilly walks. 'This wasn't a good scheme of yours, my lady.'

'Well, never mind it,' Rosamund said. 'I've seen the castle now, so we can go back down again if you like. Is that what you want, Sophie?'

'I am feeling a little chilly,' Sophie said apologetically.

'It won't do to be catching a cold, Miss Sophie,' Moss said sternly. 'You wouldn't want to miss the Assembly tomorrow night, would you?'

'She certainly wouldn't,' Farraline said. 'Fitz, what are you thinking of? Take Miss Morland out of this cold wind at once.'

'Of course – sister Sophie, come on this side of me, where the path is firmer. Your feet aren't wet, I hope?'

'No, not at all. It was only the sudden breeze on the headland that chilled me. I'm quite comfortable now, Mr Hawker, thank you.'

'I'm glad. I shouldn't have wanted to miss the chance of dancing with you tomorrow. You will allow me a dance, I trust?'

He sounded quite genuinely concerned, and his tone was gentler than Rosamund had ever heard it. She walked back down the hill in silence, with plenty of things to ponder, and Farraline seemed content to do without conversation, and not to break into her thoughts.

One of the things which Nicholas liked most about going to school was that he now had a bosom friend – Henry Anstey, seventh of the eight Anstey children, and Nicholas's exact contemporary. They shared a desk at school, frequently did each other's work, and outside of lesson hours did those things together that boys do, got into mischief, and talked endlessly. Both sets of parents were more than happy with the association, and since Morland Place was so close to St Edward's School, Henry was allowed quite often to go home with Nicholas to supper, and stay the night.

In summer, school ended at six o'clock, and the walk to Morland Place was only a mile straight across Hob Moor. But today was a dark day – grey and overcast, though not actually raining – and they had lingered a long time at the crossing of Holgate Beck, seduced by the suspicion of a water-rat's hole in the bank. By the time they set off again up the track, it was growing distinctly gloomy.

The boys didn't notice, however, occupied as they were in deep and far-ranging discussion.

'What was it Mr Cook was jawing about?' Nicholas asked, slashing at the grass with a stick as he walked.

'Weren't you listening?'

'No. Fender had a beetle he'd brought in his pocket. What did he say?'

'He was warning us about something. He said it caused blindness, consumption and curvy of the spine – or something. And he said sometimes it made you go mad.'

'I heard that part. But what is it we're not supposed to do?'

'I don't know. I didn't understand that bit,' Henry said vaguely. 'I think it's something older boys do. But he said if you do it, you don't grow up properly. You stay short all your life.'

'Like Willens? Willens is short.'

They both giggled.

'And he's short-sighted. That's why he has to sit at the front. Yes, I bet Willens does it.'

'I bet old Cook knew. I bet that's why he gave us the jaw.'

'D'you think Willens'll go mad?'

'He is mad already!'

They made the joke last all the way to the crossing of the track which led back down to the post road, coming out opposite the gallows-tree. Then a new topic presented itself.

'My father saw a ghost once on this path,' Nicholas said.

'A real ghost? Truly?'

'Well, his horse did, anyway. Down there by the road. It stopped dead and wouldn't move. Papa said it must have seen the ghost of a hanging man. He says lots of horses won't pass the gibbet.'

'Do you believe in ghosts?' Henry asked.

'Oh yes. Morland Place is *full* of them,' Nicholas said proudly. 'The servants are always seeing them. I never have though,' he added sadly. 'P'raps I'm not old enough yet. But I bet I will one day.'

'If I saw a ghost, I wouldn't be scared,' Henry said firmly, feeling he was being left out.

'I bet you would,' Nicholas countered, as proprietor, so to speak, with the honour of ghosts to defend. 'Everyone's scared of ghosts.'

'*I* wouldn't be. I'd just stare straight at it, and say "Begone!", like they do in novels.'

'You've never read novels, have you?'

'My sister Louisa reads 'em, and the ladies in the novels always say "Begone!" when they want someone to go away, and they do.'

'Well, a ghost wouldn't. They moan and rattle chains and things.'

'If it started moaning and rattling at me, I'd go right up to it and I'd go like *that* and like *that!*' He squared up, Gentleman Jackson style, and delivered a left and a right to an invisible opponent, to his own entire satisfaction. 'I'd give it toco all right!'

Nicholas was impressed, in spite of himself, by his friend's style, and his objection was only half-hearted. 'I bet you wouldn't. I bet –'

He broke off. They had been wandering on all this while, and had reached the highest point of the stray, where a clump of trees and gorse-bushes gave the only cover in an otherwise bare landscape. In the uncertain light, Nicholas had seen something moving in the shadow of the trees.

'I say!' Henry breathed. He had seen it too. Both boys stopped and stared. 'Do you think it's a ghost – like the one your father saw?' Henry asked in a small voice.

'It was only his horse saw it,' Nicholas whispered. 'I don't know. I don't know what ghosts look like.'

'Aren't they white?'

'I don't know. P'raps not *always*. What shall we do?'

Henry felt his reputation was at stake. 'Let's go and see. And if it is a ghost,' he said stoutly, 'it had jolly well better not start moaning at me.'

77

'Or rattling,' Nicholas said, trying to sound as resolute as his friend; but already his breath was coming shorter, and he could feel the tightness in his chest. His old enemy, asthma, lay always in wait for him in moments of tension.

They walked towards the trees. The dark clouds pulled down closer to the earth, increasing the gloom and making everything look strange. The queer light gave a yellowish tinge to all colours, and altered perspective, so that it was hard to tell how far away things were. The Thing in the trees moved again, shapelessly, and Henry suddenly found that he was holding Nicholas's cold, damp hand. He hung onto it as they moved nearer. He could hear Nicholas's breathing now, the only sound in the still, grey dusk. Nearer, nearer . . .

And then the Thing jumped out at them. Nicholas shrieked high and shrilly, and Henry's heart seemed to stop dead, painfully, in his chest. His feet nailed themselves to the ground, and he swayed with terror. In the same instant, Nicholas tore his hand free and turned to fly, and the Thing grabbed him round the waist and heaved him up off the ground.

'Now then, young gent, just you hold on!'

The hoarse voice, the strange accent, proved it no ghost. Henry saw instantly, with a flood of an entirely different sort of fear, that it was a dirty and ragged man, a tramping man perhaps, or a footpad – dangerous, probably, but human after all, flesh and blood. He was holding Nicholas against him with one arm, and trying to shove the other hand into the various pockets of the boy's clothing. Nicholas, his feet off the ground, was thrashing like a fish, but silently now, his eyes popping as he tried to drag air into his rigid lungs.

'You must have something about you, me young covey! Stop wriggling, you little bastard, or I'll break your back!' the man panted, jerking his prey as a cat jerks a mouse. Henry felt the blood flowing through his limbs down to his feet, telling him to run. The man had Nicky, he was occupied, he'd never catch him. He could get away. Run! Run!

The instinct was so strong, the physical imperative so immediate, that his feet lifted and his limbs twitched and he had taken a step away before his mind caught up with him. And then Nicky's wildly-staring eyes caught his for an instant, and Henry thought no more, but launched himself at the man

78

with a shrill cry. He actually got a kick and a blow in before the man's free hand swung out and knocked him on the side of the head, making his teeth rattle. Henry cried out and would have fallen from the force of the blow, but the big, hard hand caught him by the hair and yanked him upright. For such a scrawny creature, the man was amazingly strong. Henry's head was so filled with pain he couldn't cry out or fight any more. Though his mind was still clear enough to tell him to struggle, he was aware that he was simply blubbing like his own little sister . . .

And then something happened. Henry didn't at once know what, but the agonising grip on his hair was released, he fell to the ground, and lay there on the cold damp grass in amazement, his head throbbing like a sore tooth. An instant later he saw that another man had appeared on the scene. Nicholas was discarded and fell to the ground like empty clothing. The two men were struggling breast to breast, silently except for their panting breath and grunts of effort. The striving feet surged nearer and Henry tried to make himself crawl away, but failed. The feet surged away again. They stumbled on Nicholas. The first man cried out, they broke apart, the second man landed a smashing blow somewhere on the first man's face. Then the first man was running away, and the second man was left victor of the field, panting and alternately shaking and sucking his injured hand.

Only for an instant, though. As soon as he saw the attacker was definitely in flight, he turned and surveyed the fallen. Henry, looking up, saw quick and noticing eyes sweeping over them both, eyes which saw and understood everything.

'Are you all right?'

Henry nodded, and glanced towards Nicholas, meaning *see to him first*. But the man was already kneeling by Nicky, the firm, square hands reaching out for the suffering boy. Henry sat up and held his throbbing head, hearing the soothing murmur of the man's voice as he lifted Nicholas and turned him over onto his hands and knees.

'That's right, my boy – you'll breathe more easily so. We may not be four-footed, like the beasts of the field, but our bodies work better that way at times of trouble. Breathe, my child, breathe. All's well. Just breathe – that's right. In – and out. In – and out.'

The accent was not quite English, Henry thought, but the voice was nice – warm and furry and sleek. You could almost feel it, like a hand stroking you. It made you want to trust him. Henry sniffed away the last of his tears. In a little while Nicholas seemed to be breathing properly again, and the man allowed him to sit down like a human boy again, and squatted between him and Henry in a way Henry had never seen a grown-up do.

'Now then, are you both all right? No injuries anywhere?'

'No, sir, I don't think so,' Henry said shakily. Nicholas shook his head, still a little blue round the lips.

The man looked at Henry. 'You were struck, my boy. I saw it. You will have a fine bruise, I think. Does it hurt?'

'A bit,' Henry admitted. 'It aches me.'

'Let me look.' The nice hands took hold of Henry's head and tilted it gently, and the fingers parted his hair. 'Nothing to see. I think you will survive.' He released him. 'Well, it was a fine, brave thing you did, to help your friend. I think tomorrow you will feel the pain was worth it.' Henry glowed inwardly at the simple praise. It seemed a thing worth having, from this man.

'And now,' the man said, 'if you are recovered enough, I had better see you to your homes.'

He stood up fluidly, revealing himself to be a wonderfully round and rubbery person, a short man, and not fat, precisely, but barrel-bodied, all smooth curves. His arms and shoulders were very big and strong-looking, his feet very small, his movements light and nimble like a dancer. He had the warmest, kindest face Henry had ever seen, and yet so ordinary-looking that if you had looked away the instant after first seeing him, you wouldn't remember at all what he looked like.

'Where do you live?' he asked.

'Nicky lives at Morland Place. That's where we were going. I'm to stay the night there. I live in York.'

'Morland Place, eh? Well, you shall guide me to it. I think it is over that way, is it not?'

'Yes, sir.'

They began to walk together, one either side of him. 'Tell me your names,' he said.

'He's Nicholas Morland. I'm Henry Anstey, sir.'

'Ah, very good. My name is Moineau.'

'Are you –' Henry didn't quite know how to put the question politely, but the smiling eyes were encouraging. 'Are you a foreigner, sir?'

'I am a foreigner in every land, and in none. I am a citizen of the world,' he said. 'Now tell me, where have you come from, and why were you walking alone in the dark? I thought in England that gentlemen's sons had always some attendant with them.'

'We've come from school, sir,' Henry said, and Nicholas, recovering under the soothing influence of that voice, joined in the explanation.

'My mother wanted me to be taken to school and back by a footman, but Papa said it would set me apart from the other boys. And in any case, he said no harm could come to me on our own land, which it mostly is here-abouts,' he added proudly. 'Only we stopped at the beck, and it got late, and then it got dark.'

'Ah, I understand. What did you stop at the beck for?'

'We thought we saw a rat,' Nicholas said.

'A rat, eh?' the man said. 'A big one?'

'Enormous!' Nicholas said.

'Did you catch it?'

The interest was so flattering, and so unexpected in a grown-up, that before they knew it, they were chattering away to him nineteen to the dozen, and he was coaxing out of them opinions they hardly knew they had. Never had the walk back to Morland Place seemed so short – though when they got there, they both felt unaccountably tired, and suddenly rather depressed.

But the stranger seemed to understand even that. 'What you need, my boys, is supper, and a hot bath, and a good story, and then bed,' he said.

This seemed to Henry and Nicholas quite perfectly to fit the bill.

'But we shall have to tell Mama and Papa,' Nicholas said waveringly. The prospect was not inviting. Exclamations, explanations, people fussing over him, probably some horrible medicine to take.

'I shall tell Mama and Papa,' said the stranger firmly. 'Don't worry about anything any more.'

It was an instruction they were glad to follow; but Henry had one last access of good manners. 'I hope you haven't gone out of your way to bring us back, sir?'

'Why no. By a strange chance it was to Morland Place I was coming when I came across you in your difficulties,' said the stranger.

It was an intriguing piece of information, and in normal circumstances Henry would have had difficulty in restraining his curiosity. But they had reached the barbican, and one of the nursery-maids, Matty, was standing there evidently looking out for them; and she set up such a female shriek at the sight of them that there was no opportunity for any more civilised, masculine conversation.

CHAPTER FIVE

The stranger's gentle authority and extraordinary presence actually curbed the outcry, which might otherwise have lasted for half an hour or more as each new person on the scene demanded the story again and made all the same exclamations. But in a few quiet words, the 'citizen of the world' told all that immediately needed to be told. In what seemed a miraculous way, he arranged for Nicholas and Henry to be whisked off upstairs away from the fuss to their supper, with a recommendation that no-one ask them any more questions tonight.

Explanation there had to be, of course, and once the boys were gone from the scene, the stranger turned to the three members of the family present and said with a charming smile, 'The full story, as I know it, you shall have, and at once. But if I might suggest – not here?'

He made a graceful but somehow authoritative gesture which had them not only escorting him towards the drawing-room, but ordering wine and biscuits to be brought at once for his refreshment.

In the brighter light of the drawing-room, his oddness was more fully apparent. He was dressed very strangely, in loose-fitting trousers, with soft leather boots on his small feet. His coat was rather old-fashioned in cut and plain blue like an army staff-officer's; he sported a curious leather waistcoat, a white stock, and a rather shapeless, broad-brimmed hat, which he had removed to reveal his close-cropped, round head. As a final oddity, he had with him a pack-bag which he wore on a strap over his shoulder, like a foot-soldier on the march. He was clearly not a labourer, though perhaps not quite a gentleman. Héloïse, gazing at him in fascination, felt there was something indeterminate about him: like a physician, perhaps – as though his status in life depended not on his rank but on his abilities.

83

In the drawing-room he looked around him enquiringly.

'My name is Moineau,' he said, as if in answer to their question.

Héloïse put her hand to her mouth to conceal a smile, for *moineau* meant sparrow, and really, this round, perky little man was very sparrow-like. He saw the movement and turned to smile at her. It was a very nice smile, she thought; made him look quite boyish. It was hard in any case to judge his age, for he had one of those smooth, neat faces which always look young, and nice blue eyes, and soft fawn hair.

'A foolish name,' he agreed, 'but my own.'

'I beg your pardon,' Héloïse said, embarrassed.

'I could not take offence from those who invite me so readily into their house. And how comfortable it is! There is a good spirit here.'

'Thank you,' Héloïse said, still rather confused. His was not the normal way of speaking. She took refuge in formality. 'I am Lady Henrietta Morland, and this is my husband James, and this my brother-in-law Edward. Won't you please sit down and tell us what happened?'

Moineau sat down with what sounded like the faintest sigh of relief. At once Tiger went to him, to lay his head in the man's lap and gaze at him adoringly. Stroking the hound's head, Moineau told the story. He was a natural story-teller, and held his audience as wrapt as if it were one of the Arabian Nights, and not the account of a mere brush with a footpad.

'Let me assure you,' he concluded, 'that your boys have come to no harm, except for a shaking-up, and a bruise to young Master Henry's face, which I think he will consider a small price to pay for the story he will have to tell all his friends tomorrow.'

'Henry is the son of an old family friend,' James said. 'And by the by, my love, we should send a message to Anstey House at once to explain what's happened. You know how news flies. It wouldn't do to have them hear a garbled version from someone else, and think poor Harry was in desperate case.'

'Of course, I will do it at once,' Héloïse said, and rang the bell. 'Won't you pour our guest some more wine,' she added as she moved to the writing-table.

James rose to do so, and there was a short silence as Héloïse wrote her note. When the butler entered, she spoke to him over her shoulder as she completed it. 'Ottershaw, I have a note here which must be taken at once to Anstey House. There, it is done. You will seal it for me, please.'

'Very good, my lady.' Ottershaw received the note from her with a grave inclination of the head. The fact that his eyes did not betray so much as a flicker towards the stranger reminded Héloïse of her duty.

'Just a moment, please – Mr Moineau, will you honour us by staying to supper?'

Moineau glanced briefly down at himself, and then smiled radiantly at her. 'The honour would be mine, Madame.'

'Then it will be one more, Ottershaw, if you please,' Héloïse concluded.

'Very good, my lady.' Ottershaw's final bow was all-inclusive. The fact that the stranger had been too well bred to apologise for his clothing had not been lost on the Lord of the Backstairs. As he remarked afterwards to the housekeeper over a comfortable glass of solera before bedtime, 'There's such a thing, Mrs Thomson, if I may so express myself, as a *natural* gentleman. It don't matter where they're from or who their parents were, they're at home in any company.'

Mrs Thomson sipped non-committally. 'Foreign, didn't you say, Mr Ottershaw?'

'A foreign name, and a trifle of a foreign accent – but a foreigner can be a gentleman, all the same.'

'Gentleman-*like*, I grant you, Mr Ottershaw,' Mrs Thomson demurred, 'but it's not the same thing.'

'I didn't mean to suggest it was, Mrs Thomson,' he said loftily, 'only that there are those who have their own kind of manners, which go anywhere and fit any occasion, be it in the company of a commoner or a king.'

The subject of this pronouncement settled himself more deeply into his chair when the butler withdrew, and looked around the company with the delightful air of being ready for anything.

'So,' he said invitingly.

'We are most indebted to you, sir,' James responded. 'You have done us a great service, for which we can never repay you.'

'No gratitude is necessary, I assure you,' Moineau said. 'But I must say I am a little puzzled that you allow your son

85

to walk to school unescorted. These are troubled times.'

James exchanged a glance with Héloïse, and said, 'So I've found out, to my cost. It was entirely my fault – my wife was full of very proper maternal fears. I didn't want the lad to be coddled, or to find himself distanced from the other children by the presence of servants. Well, I've been proved wrong. I can only say in my defence that such a thing has never happened before. Indeed, it would have been unthinkable until now. For a Morland to be attacked, virtually on Morland land!'

'I told you,' Edward said, 'that there were all sorts of bad people about these days – tramping men and discharged soldiers and Irish beggars. The times are not normal.'

'So it seems,' James said ruefully.

'From now on, Nicholas shall have a footman to take him to school and fetch him afterwards,' Héloïse said.

'Certainly,' Edward agreed. 'And I suggest also that we lock the outer gates at dusk as we used to in the old days, and loose the dogs in the yard – *and* give the gatekeeper a shot-gun, just in case.'

'Oh come – must we live in a state of siege?' James protested.

'State of siege, nonsense! Just common-sense precautions. I'm sure our visitor agrees with me.'

'Indeed I do. There are such strange people wandering the lanes nowadays,' he said with a straight face and a laughing eye. There was a moment of pause, during which they all realised they still knew nothing about him beyond his name, and then, before anyone could launch any kind of question, he said, 'I wonder what will happen to the ruffian? Will you not search for him, and bring him to justice?'

Edward shrugged. 'He'll be long gone by now, and I haven't enough constables even for regular duties. I certainly haven't enough men to conduct a search for a nameless vagrant – unless I use our own servants, and, frankly, they have enough to do already.'

'Ah, you are responsible, then, for law and order?' Moineau said, looking at him with interest.

'In this area. I'm the local Justice of the Peace.'

Moineau sat forward. 'I have often wondered how it works in England. Is it you who appoints the constables? How are they chosen?'

'Well, in theory every citizen is liable to serve as a constable, if asked,' Edward said, 'but since they're allowed to nominate a substitute, in practice we have a few regular people who do the job, and they're paid for it out of a fund provided by the better class of householder. In normal times it works pretty well. Being local people, the constables know everyone, and everyone knows them. When a crime's committed they know exactly who has done it, and how.'

'But the times, as you say, are not normal,' Moineau put in. 'What happens if there is a special need?'

'I can appoint special constables, or if necessary call in the militia, or even the army. But that's pretty much by way of a last resort, because they don't like being called, I can tell you. You remember Colonel Barker at Fulford, Jamie, back in the year twelve, when we had that spate of rick-burning?'

'Lord, yes! How he griped at having to perform what he called "police-duties". Of course, he was always saying that England should have a regular permanent body of police, paid for out of taxes – but that's the army for you! Their minds always run that way.'

'Would it not be a good idea, then?' Moineau asked.

'Good idea?' Edward exploded. 'It's bad enough having a standing army, without police as well! It'd be no better than military rule. A man couldn't call his soul his own.' He fixed Moineau with a gimlet eye. 'We in England are a liberty-loving people, sir. We don't lightly submit to a Government's tyranny, like our friends on the Continent.'

'I beg your pardon,' Moineau said meekly.

Edward thawed a little. 'You don't understand, perhaps, that the English people are self-governing and self-regulating. If a country – a *free* country, that is – has rational and humane laws, and an effective and enlightened magistracy, it needs no other police. There will always be one or two male-factors, of course; but if the vast majority of the population does not regulate itself by its own strong sense of morality, not all the standing armies and government spies in the world will control it.'

'In France they have a permanent police-force,' Héloïse said mildly, 'and it seems to work very well. Everyone says the Paris police are admirable.'

'They may be admirable, but by God, the Parisians pay for

87

it dear enough!' Edward said. 'I tell you, I'd sooner have half-a-dozen murders a year, than be subjected to domiciliary visits and spies and informers, and all the rest of the apparatus!'

'Oh, but surely –'

'And I speak for the majority in this country, I can tell you – high and low! It's too great a price to pay for a little security. No, no, there'll be no Government-paid police-force in this country. Never! A liberty-loving people will never hand the Government such a powerful instrument of oppression as that!'

'You must guard yourselves, then, by your own efforts,' Moineau suggested.

'That's every citizen's duty,' Edward said. 'Which is why, Jamie, I suggested those simple precautions of locking the outer gates at dusk –'

'Yes, yes, you're quite right,' James said hastily. 'I just don't like the idea of being shut in. I wandered freely all over these fields when I was a boy, and I don't like to think of my own children losing that liberty.'

'When we were children, you never saw a stranger from one year's end to the next,' Edward pointed out. 'People stayed put where they were born, and we all knew where we were. But nowadays, what with all these turnpikes and canals and fast travel, everyone seems to be going to the Devil at fifteen miles an hour! The old ways, the old traditions are going by the board – young people have no respect for their elders any more –'

'Ah, speaking of young people,' the visitor interrupted what was evidently, even to him, an accustomed tirade, 'I wonder if I might pay a brief visit to the nursery? Would you permit? I promised the boys I would say goodnight to them if I could.'

It was the most extraordinary thing for a stranger to ask, and yet from this stranger, somehow unexceptionable.

'Of course,' Héloïse said, with barely a blink. 'There is just time before supper. I will take you myself.' As Moineau stood up, she caught sight of his hand. 'Oh, you are injured!'

'It is nothing, Madame – merely the result of that ruffian's unwise decision to try to smash my knuckles with his nose!'

It was very hard to express concern, Héloïse discovered,

while trying not to laugh. 'Nevertheless, you will let me bathe it,' she managed to say.

'I will not allow you to be troubled. It is only a graze. It will heal very well if it is left alone,' he said pleasantly, but quite firmly. 'And I will not take you away from your fireside either, Madame. A servant can conduct me to the nursery. I shall not be above a few minutes, I promise you.'

Héloïse rang the bell, and William answered, which was a good thing, for he was too stupid to think his mission an odd one. He escorted Moineau away, presenting Tiger with a severe problem, for the hound clearly wanted to keep the newcomer in sight, but did not like to leave Edward. He solved it by going to sit at the drawing-room door and pressing his nose to the crack for the first hint of Moineau's return, his tail beating a soft, practice tattoo on the carpet.

The other three looked at each other with bemused expressions, like people waking from an exhibition of mesmerism.

'Well,' said Edward inadequately, 'what a curious fellow!'

'I'm not sure you ought to have invited him to supper like that, Marmoset. We know nothing about him,' said James with a belated fit of conventionality.

'We know he saved Nicky's life,' Héloïse reminded them.

'But who is he? Where has he come from? Jamie's right, we don't know anything about him. He's like some kind of tramping-fellow, with his hat and his pack.'

'He's not a labourer,' James said. 'Didn't you see his hands? No callouses. They're clean and soft as a gentleman's. And he speaks like an educated man.'

'But he's not a gentleman,' Edward said shortly.

'Well I like him,' Héloïse said defiantly.

'So do I, in a curious sort of way,' James said. 'He reminds me of my old tutor when I was a boy – Father Fox, you remember, Ned?'

Edward raised an eyebrow. 'He's nothing like Father Renard. Father Renard was a tall man, dark-haired –'

'I didn't say he *looks* like him, I said he reminds me of him. Anyway, how much do we need to know about him? He saved Nicky and Henry, as Héloïse points out. The least we can do is feed the poor fellow. I wish we could reward him, but somehow I don't feel we could offer him money. I think it would offend him.'

Edward looked thoughtful, 'I wonder how he's been supporting himself. He doesn't look hungry, does he? And he was very interested in the constables and law enforcement and so on.'

'What are you saying?' Héloïse frowned.

'Well, m'dear, didn't it cross your mind that he might be a housebreaker?'

'And you let him go upstairs alone?' James said, clearly amused. 'He could be stealing the silver this very minute!'

'We don't know what he's got in that pack, do we?' Edward said, annoyed.

'You shall not look in it, upon my life,' Héloïse cried, beginning to be upset, 'Housebreaker, what nonsense! He is a *good* man.'

'In any case, he's not alone upstairs,' James retracted. 'He's got William with him, and even William would think it odd if he started to rifle through drawers and stuff our priceless treasures in his pockets. Do you suppose that's why he wears such loose trousers, Ned?'

'James, stop it!'

'I'm only teasing, my love.'

'I know, but I don't like it. It is not *comme il faut* to abuse a guest behind his back.'

Both men looked a little ashamed.

'By Jove, yes, he is our guest after all,' Edward said after a moment.

'He's a queer cove, but I don't believe there's a particle of harm in him,' James said. 'There, love, will that do?'

They waited. The silence was punctuated only by the sound of the clock ticking, and the patter of rain on the windows. The grey clouds had fulfilled their threat. A log, burned through, fell in on itself with a little sigh, and the strike mechanism of the clock engaged with a clunk like a penny dropped into a bucket. Then Tiger pricked his ears and started singing; his tail beat faster and louder on the floor, and then he stood up and shuffled backwards as the door swung open and Moineau came in. The clock whirred and began to strike, and Ottershaw appeared behind him to announce that supper was served.

'The boys seemed quite recovered from their adventure,' Moineau said as they walked across the hall to the dining-room. 'They're regaling Benedict with the story. He's wild with envy!' he added with a chuckle. 'I hope I didn't keep you waiting?'

'Not at all,' Héloïse said, thinking how natural it sounded for him to be talking about her children. She wondered if he had ever had children of his own; and if so, what had happened to his wife.

In the dining-room, one end of the long mahogany table had been set, and an array of cold dishes laid out. There was a round of roast beef and a ham in cut, its moist, pink-brown face wreathed in parsley; a pork pie whose raised crust looked as though it were decorated with a golden plaited rope, and a blue Chinese bowl full of Barnard's special pickles; a moulded dish of brawn, whose jelly covering quivered and gleamed in the candle-light; a dish of spiced eggs on a bed of spinach; a plate of cherry tarts, a basket of bread rolls, and a pyramid of fruit.

'It's just a simple supper,' James apologised as they took their places. 'If we'd known we were to have a guest, I dare say there'd have been a custard or two and some other kickshaws, but I'm sure you'll take us as you find us.'

But Héloïse had noted the gleam of appetite in their visitor's eyes as they lit on the table, and she wondered briefly and guiltily how long it had been since his last meal. Yet, impolite or not, it was hard not to keep remembering that they knew nothing about him. Who was he? What was he doing here? There was something about his carriage which suggested the army to her, and by his name, at least, he was French. Was he another of those sad creatures, like poor Sophie's Major Larosse, who had fought against their own countrymen in order to destroy Bonaparte?

Edward said the grace, and at the end of it Moineau, along with Héloïse, crossed himself. The mirrored movement caused them both to look up at each other, and they both smiled.

'So, Mr Moineau,' Héloïse said as James began to carve her some ham, 'it is time I think for your story. It is very impolite of us, but very natural, you will agree, to wonder who you are and where you come from.'

'I did not suppose I could escape for ever without telling you something of myself,' he said with an engaging grin.

91

'Though I by no means flattered myself that you would want more than a very little of my story! I shall begin, Madame, and you shall stop me when you have had enough.'

Héloïse nodded, delighted with him, though she could see that James, and more particularly Edward, were still uneasy. They couldn't quite determine how to categorise him, and didn't know, therefore, how to respond to him. But men were strange, stiff creatures, she thought. Women and children and animals would love this little man unquestioningly.

'My name is Antoine Philippe Moineau,' he began, 'and I was born in a village called Nouzonville –'

'In France?' James asked, lifting another delicate slice and laying it fastidiously on Héloïse's plate.

'Of course, in France,' Héloïse answered for him. 'What sort of a question is that, my James?'

'Well, I guessed you were French from your accent, sir,' James said with a defiant look at his wife, 'and from the north of France, of course.'

'While you, madame, I can tell, are *une vraie Parisienne*,' Moineau said mischievously. 'There is a certain air, a certain –'

'But we were not speaking of me, monsieur,' Héloïse nipped the diversion in the bud. 'We were speaking of Nouzonville. That was your family's home?'

'My father was the *notaire*,' said Moineau. Héloïse flashed a quick glance of relief and triumph at the others: an attorney's son counted as gently-born. The glance was not lost on Moineau, but he continued without pause. 'He had land, too, good farm-land. I was brought up in a pleasant old house, stone-built – small, but comfortable. We were a large family, and as a younger son, I had a great deal of freedom. I spent more of my childhood playing in the woods, and helping the shepherd tend my father's sheep on the hillside, than at my lessons. But what boy would not do the same, if he could?'

James smiled at that. 'Certainly not me! Roaming abroad with the village boys was my delight. It rarely falls to the eldest son's lot,' he said with a glance at Edward.

'I suppose you were expected to follow your father into the law?' Edward asked.

'I did not wait to find out,' Moineau said. 'When I was fourteen, I entered a monastery.'

'Good Lord!'

'It is not such a strange choice in France,' Héloïse defended. 'Or it was not, in the old days.'

Moineau nodded. 'There was a monastery on the top of the next hillside, and when I was out with the sheep I used to look across at it, sitting there in the sunshine like a great white ship. I used to hear the bells ringing the divisions, and think what a good, happy, peaceful place it must be. The idea grew to be an obsession with me, and at last I broached it with my father. He was glad for me to go, and at the earliest opportunity – younger sons have to be provided for somehow.'

It answered Héloïse's question about a wife, at any rate. But as if he had heard her thought, he went on, 'I never took my vows, however. The Revolution came before I had finished my training, and in that irreligious period of our history, the monastery was closed. So I was thrown out into the world again. By then I had had enough of being shut in, and I decided to see as much of the world as I could. I took to wandering, and liked it so much I have been wandering ever since.'

'Did you never go home again?' Héloïse asked.

'To Nouzonville? Never. My father was killed in one of the purges, for attending a Mass in the old form – anti-revolutionary activity was what they called it,' he said sadly. 'My mother had been long dead, and my brothers scattered abroad. I had nothing to go back for; so I made the world my home.'

'Have you been *everywhere*?' Héloïse asked impulsively.

At the same instant, Edward asked, 'What did you do for your living?'

Moineau gathered them both in a look. 'Yes, I have been everywhere – or very near – and done a great many things. I have been a shepherd, and a groom, a carpenter and a soldier. I ran a tavern, once, in Saxony – that was amusing; and I was tutor to a prince's sons in Poland. I went to Italy for a time, and was ordained in Rome itself, the heart of our church! I held a cure there, and later one in Portugal, and again in Germany. So I have many languages, you see.'

'Then you are Father Moineau!' said Héloïse. 'But this is wonderful! We have a chapel here, but our chaplain left us some months ago, and there is no-one to say the Mass. If we

93

could prevail upon you to stay with us for a few days, and perform our Sunday celebrations, we should be so grateful!'

Edward and James exchanged alarmed looks. 'My love,' James said quickly, 'Father Moineau will not want to be delayed on his journey. He doubtless has friends expecting him. They'll be worried about him.'

Héloïse looked distracted. 'Oh, I had not thought – but tonight, Father, you will stay tonight at least? It is dark, and raining, and they surely will not look for you tonight. And then you might conduct the early service tomorrow, before you leave.'

Father Moineau smiled at her with complete satisfaction. 'I shall be happy to stay until Sunday, Madame – more than happy. I should like to see how the boys go on.'

'It will not delay you?'

'My time is entirely my own. I make it a rule never to travel anywhere in a hurry: the best adventures fall to those who allow them time and space to grow.'

'And you must have plenty of adventures,' Edward said, not entirely without irony. It had all been a little too pat for him. 'You must tell us some of them.'

'If it would amuse you, I shall be happy to oblige,' said Moineau, looking as though the irony was not lost on him. 'Perhaps, like a mediaeval minstrel, I can pay for my supper with a story.'

In bed that night, James made love with more than usual vigour. Afterwards when Héloïse was lying in his arms happy and slightly bemused, he said suddenly, 'You really like that little man, don't you?'

'Yes,' she said. Then, 'Don't you?'

The answer was a long time coming. She could almost feel the struggle going on. Then her husband's voice came, slightly grumbling in tone, out of the darkness.

'Yes, I do. But I don't see why the deuce I should.'

Since Marie had left, Alice had been acting as lady's maid to Héloïse, though she wanted very little maiding – only inaccessible hooks and buttons doing up, and her hair arranging. Alice arrived the next morning just after James had disappeared into the dressing-room with Durban to be shaved. She hardly needed Héloïse's formal question to spill over into chat about the stranger.

'Whether he slept or not, my lady, I can't say, for when Stephen went in this morning according to your instructions, he was already up and dressed. Not that he would have needed valeting, however, for Stephen says there's not a thing in his pack to change into, bar a clean shirt, stock and stockings. Though they were clean, Stephen says, my lady, and the wonder of it is how he keeps 'em clean, being a traveller as he is! But Stephen's took the worn ones away to launder, and he says Father Moineau thanked him very pretty, and said as it would be the first time they'd felt a touch of starch in many a long month. I suppose he hasn't been staying at the best inns, my lady.'

Héloïse wouldn't normally have encouraged a servant to chatter about a guest, but she was eager to know anything and everything about Moineau. So she said, 'Did Stephen do everything for him?'

'There wasn't anything to be done, my lady, for he'd already washed *and* shaved himself in the cold water, though Stephen took his can of hot in, of course. But he brushed him down, at any rate – and a very nice set of brushes he had, quite old but good, Stephen said, with horn and silver backs, all rolled up in his housewife along with his razors and such, and some books, so he must be a book-learned man, my lady. But Mrs Thomson said Ottershaw said you could tell that anyway by his speech. But all Stephen's brushing went by the board as soon as Father Moineau got to the nursery.'

'He's been to the nursery?'

'First thing, my lady. Went along there right away, and Lord, there've been such rompings! You never saw the like! He had Master Benedict in such a fit of giggles he like to be sick; and Sarah said he was crawling about the floor at one time, my lady, with his head full of spills, pretending to be some kind of giant hedgehog he'd seen on his travels and was telling the children about. What sort of a man is he, my lady?' she finished wonderingly.

'A good man, I think,' Héloïse said, concealing a smile.

'Well, he seems to know how to get round people, and that's a fact. The children worship him already. They're going to be that upset when he goes, my lady! And Sarah said he's got Jenny eating out of his hand, and you know what she's like, my lady, about anyone interfering in her nursery.'

'Where is he now?'

'In the chapel, getting ready for Mass. Does everyone have to go, my lady?'

'Everyone.'

'Well,' said Alice, 'I suppose they'd all want to go anyway, to get a look at him. It'll be the one day there'll be no-one staying in bed and claiming to have the toothache.'

It was a great comfort to Héloïse to have the daily celebration again, and Father Moineau looked very much at home, even though the vestments, made for Father Aislaby, were far too big for him. He had found his way round the chapel and vestry with no trouble, and even discovered how to ring the bell to summon the household to the service. As Alice said, everyone seemed to be there, goggling at the stranger who had brought a little excitement and variety into their routine lives.

After Mass, breakfast, where conversation was short and neutral. Edward did not normally linger over breakfast in any case, having always more things to do than time to do them. James was usually a leisurely breakfaster, but today – his fatherhood touched, perhaps, by rivalry – he hurried through his meal saying that he wanted to take the boys to school himself.

'I'll go straight on to Twelvetrees afterwards,' he said, draining his cup and standing up. 'You'll see that someone goes to fetch Nicholas at twelve o'clock, won't you, my love?' Saturday was a half-day at school. 'I shall be with a customer.'

'Yes, of course. Don't worry,' Héloïse said. A moment later, she and Moineau were alone at the table. He went on eating with the calm attention of a man who knows his priorities. The breakfast table was always particularly well spread, for Edward still liked the old-fashioned sort of meal – cold meat, cheese, bread and beer, with perhaps a veal or game pie, or a hot dish of mutton chops or beefsteak for a relish; while James, being a more modern and fashionable man, preferred the lighter breakfast dishes like boiled or buttered eggs, mushrooms, fried bacon, sausages, grilled kidneys, boiled haddock, oysters and the like, together with toast, rolls or buns, and coffee.

Father Moineau, to shew his entire impartiality, had gone a fair way to sampling everything on the table except the beer, and was now tackling a wedge of game pie topped with a slice of cheese and flanked with a spoonful of pickled red cabbage. His appetite was truly remarkable, Héloïse thought. She leaned over to refill his coffee cup, and he looked up at her with a smile.

'The squirrel, of course, buries nuts and seeds to carry him over the lean times ahead,' he remarked, 'but I have not the squirrel's memory. What very excellent coffee this is.'

'You must meet my cook,' she said. 'He is always delighted to speak to a fellow-countryman.'

'Ah, he's French, is he? I thought that must be the case. It's a long time since I had such fine cooking as this. Even the nursery supper last night looked tempting!'

Héloïse leaned her chin on her hands. 'You have certainly won the children's hearts, from what I hear. And I'm told my head nursery-maid is your willing slave.'

He cocked his head. 'But not the men of the house,' he suggested for her. 'That fine, tall fellow who came to bring me hot water this morning was very upset by my lack of baggage.'

Héloïse smiled apologetically. 'The men don't know what to make of you.'

'They're always the last to succumb. Men are suspicious of charm because it's a thing they can't explain rationally. Women – like children and animals – are more instinctive. They react first, and worry about it afterwards – if at all.'

'My husband and brother naturally wonder where you came from, and where you are going. Indeed, I do too. That was something you didn't tell us last night.'

He ate another piece of pie before answering. 'I have no objection at all to telling you what you want to know. But I wanted the story to be for you alone to begin with. Afterwards, you may tell as much of it as you wish. Of course, you may find that some of it is known already. If I am any judge, your excellent man Stephen is already abroad making enquiries, and he will come hurrying back to tell you that I arrived at the Hare and Heather on the stage-coach yesterday – you see, I am not, after all, a tramping-man! I hope it isn't a disappointment to you.'

She laughed. 'I didn't suppose you were. Though, I don't know why, I assumed you had walked a long way.'

'All the way from Dover?'

'Is that where you came from? And before that, France?'

'From Belgium. I was an army chaplain until quite lately. It was not a thing I'd care to do for a lifetime – army food is very disappointing! But that's what took me to Brussels last year.'

'You were in Brussels? You were at Waterloo?' Héloïse asked eagerly, and then caught herself up. 'But on which side?'

Moineau shrugged. 'Does it matter, for a chaplain? A soul wears no uniform. I might just as easily have joined the Allied Army, but it happened I came upon the French first.'

'Then why did you join at all?'

'There is always a shortage of chaplains, and I had a great desire to see how the story would come out. I had followed it from the beginning – from afar, of course. It was one of the best stories there will ever be, I think: the adventures of the little lawyer's son from Corsica who rose to be Emperor of half the world! Who could resist being there at the end?'

'But how could you know it would be the end?' Héloïse asked, hearing the irony in his voice, seeing the pain behind the laughter in his eyes.

He shrugged again. 'I knew. And I knew I would be needed. Souls and bodies come apart so easily on a battlefield. Ah, Madame, you were there! You saw the pitiful wrecks of men brought in from the battlefield – but you did not see those who were left out there. That was a sight beyond bearing. It is not something I shall ever forget, though I have been a soldier myself, in my youth.'

Her mind was working now, sifting out the underlying sense of his words. 'Father Moineau, how did you know I was in Brussels? Your being here – it is no coincidence, is it?'

'I came here to see you,' he said. 'I came looking for you. The coincidence was only that I came across your son in trouble, on my way from the inn to your house.'

'Then why didn't you say so at once?' she asked simply.

'Because I have something to tell you which I think you will wish to hear in private.'

98

She looked at him apprehensively. 'Go on,' she said.

He told her his story. Though he did not dwell on it, his words took her back to those terrible days during and just after the final conflict between Wellington and Napoleon, when the wounded had come in to Brussels by the cart-load, and she had done her small part to help tend them. But she had not stayed long. After the funeral of Major Larosse, she had brought Sophie home, leaving others better qualified to cope with the situation.

'When the French army retreated,' he said, 'I did not go with it. I knew that I was more urgently needed where I was. I suppose, in a way, I was a deserter – one of many. I stripped off the insignia of the army, and went out onto the battlefield to do what I could.

'The English army was busy, collecting up its own wounded and taking them into Brussels, but there was no-one to attend to the French casualties on the field – except the scavengers, of course. You know about them?' She nodded bleakly. 'I suppose they were merciful in their way – they usually killed before they robbed, and many of our countrymen must have been grateful for death. Only when all the Allies were accounted for – wounded and dead – were the working parties sent out to bury the French dead and bring in the survivors. There were not many, of course, by that time, but enough. I went with them, and offered my services to the town commandant. He was glad to accept. One cannot be a wandering priest without learning a little of medicine, and I was welcomed in both capacities.'

'Yes,' said Héloïse. She saw it all in her mind.

'A hospital had been set up for the French wounded – who were prisoners of war, of course – and I spent a great deal of my time there. One prisoner in particular needed my help. I found him an interesting case. The poor fellow was grievously wounded, and had little chance of recovery. He knew that, and was eager to make his peace with his conscience and with God.'

Héloïse sensed he had come to the heart of his story. She listened, all attention, almost without breathing.

'He told me that he had been born in Paris, the illegitimate son of a nobleman. His father perished in the Revolution, but left money for the support of his mother and himself. But as

99

he grew up, he began to resent his illegitimacy, and the obscurity it forced on him and his mother. He began to hate his father's memory, and by association, all aristocrats – who took their pleasure where they had no right, and left others to bear the cost. I'm sorry, but so he felt and spoke.'

'Yes. Go on,' Héloïse said.

'He espoused the Revolutionary cause with all an intelligent young man's passion. Napoleon became his idol. As soon as he was old enough, he joined the army, hoping to spread the new ideas about liberty and equality to the whole world.'

Héloïse nodded. 'There were many such, I expect.'

'All was well at first. The army was invincible; victory followed victory until Napoleon ruled half the world. It seemed that the Revolution had succeeded beyond all expectation. But then reaction set in. Victory did not lead to peace; war cost France dear in blood and tears, dearer every year: and Napoleon, the man who had ousted kings, crowned himself Emperor. Our friend began to wonder where it would end, and whether his hero was as flawless as he had supposed. Then he had word that his mother had died.'

'Ah! And had he seen her since he joined the army?'

'You have guessed it. No – they parted with harsh words, and he had never gone back. His revolutionary fervour, his hatred of his father's name, had broken her heart. He had never had the chance to make his peace with her, and now he began to feel it was his actions which had hastened her death. But what could he do? It was too late to tell her of his doubts, and he knew no other life but the army. So he went on marching and fighting, more doubtful every year that it was the right thing to do. And as the revolutionary fires died down, he began to wonder if his father had really been the ogre he had made him in his mind, or if, perhaps, he had been wrong about that, too.'

Héloïse nodded.

'Then came the abdication, and the restoration of the monarchy. Our friend began to make enquiries about his father's family, for it was permitted now, even laudable, to have aristocratic blood. But the restoration did not bring with it the end of the evils of the empire, and when the Emperor returned, he like so many of the veterans could not resist the call. And so his way led inevitably to Waterloo.'

'Where he was wounded. And met you.'

'Yes. As he lay near death, he wondered from the depths of his heart if his life had all been wasted. He began to think that the men he had killed must have been just like him after all, and that killing them was a terrible sin. If only he had fled France instead of joining the army, and taken his mother with him, she might still be alive. He should have taken her to England, and lived a blameless life, and seen her comfortably established in the bosom of his father's family, whom he was sure would have welcomed them.'

'In England?'

He looked into her eyes, his gaze holding her like a supporting hand. 'His mother was French, but his father was English by birth, though living in France as a French citizen. His mother had told our friend when he was a child that he had a large family in England – in Yorkshire – including a half-sister who had been his mother's dearest friend. He begged me, as he lay dying, to find that sister and tell her his story, and beg her forgiveness for his part in his mother's death.' He paused, and then said gently, 'He told me her name. Do I need to tell you his?'

Héloïse shook her head, her eyes blank. 'His name is Morland Cotoy. His mother was Marie-France Cotoy, and his father was Henri de Stuart – my father.'

'I have fulfilled my task, then. But I am sorry to bring you no better news.'

'He is dead, my brother?' Moineau nodded, and she sighed painfully. 'I searched for him. When I went to Paris during the Peace of Amiens, I searched for him and for Marie-France, but they had moved from the only direction I had, and I could not find any trace of them. Yet I always hoped that one day I would see them again. I was present at his birth.' She looked at him. 'And you were present at his death. And there's an end.'

'I'm sorry,' he said again.

She looked down at her hands. 'I should feel grateful – I found a large family here, who have loved me and made me welcome. Yet he was my only brother – my father's only son. I always wondered if he would grow up to look like Papa. And now I shall never know.'

Moineau didn't speak.

'He fought for Napoleon at Waterloo?'

'Yes.'

She was thoughtful. 'It may even have been him who killed some of our friends.'

'It does not do to think like that.'

'No, I know. I'm sorry. But he was right – it was all a waste, such a waste.'

She and Moineau faced each other across the ruins of an English breakfast-table, and mourned together, for the brother she had never had the chance to know, and for the long-lost country of their childhood. France, their France, was gone, and gone for ever.

'Now you have told me, will you go on?' she asked him later when they were walking in the rose-garden. Last night's rain had battered the petals from the full-blown flowers, but the half-opened blooms were fresh and glistening with fat diamond drops which intensified their colour and texture.

'I have done what I came to do,' he said neutrally.

'But where will you go next?'

'I don't know. I had made no plans.'

They walked on, leaving the path to make a dark trail through the silver of the wet grass. Above them the grey clouds rolled thoughtfully, as though contemplating further mischief; the air was damp and prickling with threatened rain. They went through the gap in the hedge and came out on the bank of the moat, where two of the swans were standing grooming themselves, their straight black legs somehow surprising, emerging from the smooth white hulls of their bodies. They eyed the humans speculatively for a moment, and then went on with their preening; small discarded feathers lay about them like snow-flakes on the grass.

'Beautiful!' Moineau looked at the rosy brick of the house reflected in the grey, disturbed water. 'It looks so timeless,' he said. 'It is a good place. You must be very happy here.'

'Yes,' she said. 'I still find it hard to believe that it's mine. But of course in a sense it is not – I am only the guardian, for the generations to come. What I love was taken from those who loved it in other days.'

'That is a good way to feel. I would like to know your

history, and how you came to be mistress of this fairy-tale castle. It must be a fascinating tale.'

'It is a long one,' she said, looking at him. 'I wish there were time to tell it to you. But if you have to be leaving us –'

He smiled invitingly, but said nothing.

'Do you have to leave us?' she asked. 'There is a place here which seems almost providentially designed for you to fill. Our chaplain-tutor left suddenly, as I told you, and his many duties are left undone. We might almost have been waiting for you to arrive. You are a priest, and you have been tutor to a prince's sons, so you said. The children love you already, and I –' she paused.

'Yes?' he asked teasingly.

She smiled. 'I should like to have you as my personal chaplain. Will you take the post? Will you stay?'

It seemed almost too good to be true, but she knew already what his answer would be.

'Yes,' he said.

CHAPTER SIX

Apart from her visit to Brussels the year before, Rosamund
had travelled very little in her life, and always in her mother's
carriage with either her mother or governess in command. So
her trip to Yorkshire, travelling post and accompanied by her
maid, had been a delight to her, with all the excitement of
staying at post-houses, ordering her own meals and making
her own decisions.

And even with the sadness of her holiday's being over, and
having to say goodbye to Sophie without knowing when they
might meet again, there was still the journey home to look
forward to. It was a sort of compensation, though she feared
she would not be quite as autonomous as on the way up from
Town: her mother had sent Parslow for her.

'She must really be anxious to have you back,' James
smiled, 'if she's willing to be without him for the best part of a
week. I suppose she thought no-one else could persuade you
to come back.'

'It's on account of the unrest in Nottinghamshire, and all
the strange people on the roads,' Rosamund said.

'She is very right,' Héloïse said. 'Not that I think you will be
in the least danger,' she added hastily, 'but you are very
young to travel only with a maid, especially as you will be two
nights on the road.'

James eyed his niece with amusement. 'But try not to let it
spoil your fun, all the same.'

Rosamund laughed. 'I won't. I like old Parslow – he's a
right 'un.'

The parting was sad, though Rosamund had had the satisfaction of seeing Sophie restored to the bosom of her family,
and witnessing her high glee as she rushed about the house as
though she were half her age, romping with her brothers and
the dogs and greeting every servant from the highest to the
lowest with a hug. Monsieur Barnard, who adored her second

only to Héloïse, clutched her to his apron as though she were his own child and planted floury kisses on her head; and no-one but Sophie could have got away with kissing Ottershaw, who had modelled himself on the stately Chelmsford butler, Hawkins, and had dedicated a lifetime to out-Caesaring Caesar.

Rosamund watched all this with delight, and was glad to see how Sophie had been missed, and how happy she was to be home. It was a very different household, she thought with the faintest wistfulness, from the one she was returning to; and it was possible to see how Sophie might be content, for a time at least, simply to 'stay at home with Mama and Papa and the boys' as if she had never been betrothed and on the point of marriage.

At last the boxes were all strapped onto Lucy's chaise, Parslow had inspected the post-boys and horses to his satisfaction, the farewells had all been said, and Rosamund, in her smart blue travelling-dress, a neat carriage-hat and a huge muff, stepped in and took her place. The post-boys cracked their whips, everyone waved madly, and then they were passing out under the barbican and her holiday in Yorkshire was over. Now it's back to real life, she thought with a sigh.

Parslow heard the sigh and caught her eye sympathetically. 'I hope you've had an agreeable time, my lady?'

'Yes, thank you. I'm sorry to leave.'

'Her ladyship is very anxious to have you back, however,' Parslow said encouragingly.

'I can't think what for,' Rosamund grumbled a little. There were some wonderful horses at Twelvetrees she had looked forward to trying, and Uncle James had said he could arrange for her to have a gallop round the Knavesmire race-course one day.

It wasn't for Parslow to tell her that Lucy missed her; so he said, 'Her ladyship is planning a large party at Wolvercote for the summer, and she needs you to help entertain, my lady.'

'A large party?' Rosamund said, brightening. That sounded better than just their dull selves.

'For when Lord Aylesbury comes home, my lady. Her lady-ship thinks it's time to introduce him into society.'

'Ah,' said Rosamund, seeing much more of the picture. Her brother was so painfully shy and awkward, that it would

105

obviously be better to keep him at Wolvercote and introduce selected people into his world, where he felt relatively safe, rather than to pitch him head first into the outside world and let him sink or swim on his own. Such a degree of tenderness towards Aylesbury did not seem much like her mother, however. 'Was it Papa Danby's idea?' she asked bluntly.

'I believe so, my lady,' Parslow said, straight-faced. 'I understand his lordship said he would never have got over the first fence himself at that age, if he had not been so fortunate as to be riding stirrup-to-stirrup with Mr Brummell.'

Rosamund laughed. 'That's like him! And how they must miss poor Mr Brummell, too. He was always very kind to me, despite my freckles. What else has happened since I went away?'

'His lordship's man has left, my lady, after a slight contre-temps.'

'Oh good. I never liked Deacon – sour creature! But what will Papa Danby do without him?'

'Bird is attending to his lordship's needs at present, my lady. It seems possible that he may take on the position of valet permanently, and that a new groom will be appointed.'

'Good idea. What else?'

'I believe her ladyship has had a letter from Mrs Firth in Vienna, my lady. And Mr and Mrs Robert Knaresborough are celebrating another increase to their family –'

'Another? That's five in six years!'

'And the kitchen cat's had kittens.'

'Which one?'

'The ginger tabby, my lady. The one Mrs Docwra calls Marmalade.'

'Well, that caps the globe, as she says! I thought it was a tom-cat.'

'So did Docwra,' Parslow said, unmasking for an instant. 'I think the cat was rather surprised too.'

She met Parslow's eyes, and felt a rush of affection for him. He had been there all her life, a permanent figure in her rapidly-changing background, and more of a father to her, in many ways, than anyone else had been. Yet she knew very little about him – not even where he came from, or what he had done before entering her mother's service. She didn't even know what his first name was. Perhaps, she thought with a smile, he didn't have one.

His eyes returned the smile, and then, perhaps thinking that the unmasking had gone far enough, in a closed carriage and with Judy Moss as witness, he turned his head politely to look out of the window and give her the privacy of her own thoughts.

She could have done without the courtesy, for her own thoughts were little satisfaction to her. She had enjoyed her holiday and Sophie's company, but she was not pleased to be returning home as unattached as she went away, to face the consequences. Farraline had disappointed. Oh, not in himself: the more she had seen of him, the more she liked him; his company stimulated, his ideas intrigued, and his person attracted her strongly. But though he had sought her out on every occasion, she had begun to doubt some time before she left that he meant anything serious by it.

She could not quite understand him. He talked to her with a degree of intimacy she had never experienced from a man, but his manner was not lover-like, and though he sometimes told her scandalous things to shock or amuse her, his conversation was often about his mills, about manufacturing and Parliamentary reform. These were hardly the topics of courtship.

'Do you realise that despite the huge population of Manchester, it hasn't a single Member of Parliament?' he said the last time they had danced together. 'It's the same with all the manufacturing towns – because they're new growths, they have only their historic representation, which might have been appropriate to a village, but will certainly not do in these modern times.'

Rosamund had done her best to understand his fervour and to keep the steps of the dance at the same time. 'Why do you want Manchester to have a Member?' she asked. 'What difference would it make?'

He crossed his hands to her and they swung about before he answered. 'Manufacturers need a voice. They have special requirements, special interests. They need a spokesman in Parliament.'

'Why doesn't one of them become a Member, then? He could stand for some other place, couldn't he?'

'There's still the property qualification. To be a candidate

107

for the House of Commons, a man must own, or be heir to, a rental of three hundred pounds per annum from landed property. Mills and manufactories don't count. Even old Samuel Ordsall couldn't have stood for Parliament, though he was rich enough to have bought half of Lancashire. And if he had bought himself the qualifying property, he would still have been kept out of the House by interest.'

'Interest?' Rosamund said, moving up a place and clapping.

'The votes of the voters, my dear ma'am, are all owned. There are so few of them, you see, and a rare commodity will always command a high price.'

They reached the head of the set and danced down, and at the foot Rosamund waited with an inward grimace for the tirade to be resumed. But Farraline's thoughts had moved off on another tack. As they began the long process of working back up – the traditional opportunity for conversation between young people of the opposite sex – he said in softer tones, 'And are you really leaving us tomorrow?'

'Really.'

'It seems an odd decision, to be leaving just when everyone else is arriving. Lady Tredegar came in yesterday for her annual cure, and she's a notable hostess, besides being an intimate friend of Mama's. I wish you might stay – there will be all sorts of parties and balls and routs.'

This was more hopeful. 'We are wanted at home,' she said. 'Sophie in particular is much missed by her family. And we have stayed, in any case, longer than was first planned.'

'Not long enough for some of us, however,' he said. 'What shall I do for company?'

'But you will be going soon yourself, I imagine,' Rosamund countered. 'You really cannot pretend any longer that there is anything wrong with your arm. Sophie tells me you and Mr Hawker were playing tennis yesterday, and you beat him soundly.'

'That's true. Tennis is not Hawker's game, of course ... But I'm staying now chiefly for Mama's sake – she dreads going back to Grasscroft alone.'

'Will not you be going with her?'

'I go to Cheetham Hill to supervise my building project. I want to have my house finished this summer. I may find time to take her down to London in October, however, though I dare say I shall not be able to stay above a few days. If I do come, shall I see you there?'

He smiled into her eyes, and she felt the familiar weakness creeping over her limbs. Yet his words had proved him indifferent to her. He liked her, but meant nothing serious by his attentions, or he could not have spoken so lightly, or regarded their separation as so little important. He would not rescue her from her fate – and in truth, she wondered whether she would have wanted him to. He attracted her very much, but she doubted whether she could live happily in such a place as Manchester, or with a person so single-mindedly attached to the processes of steam mechanism.

'I am sure you will,' she said, with a bright smile. 'I am sure to be a great deal in London this autumn. I expect soon to be married, you know.'

Did his eyes become watchful for an instant? 'To Chelmsford?' he asked abruptly.

'Yes.'

'Ah!' The music was silenced, and they were alone together in one of those cessations of time which he seemed to be able to conjure about them. She felt her skin ripple like the fur of a stroked cat under the touch of his eyes. 'Then we shall certainly meet again,' he said. Then, 'I like Chelmsford very much, and you will do him a great deal of good.' The music had come back, loud and suddenly jarring. Surely one of the fiddles was out of tune? She watched his lips moving, and forced herself to understand what he was saying. 'He needs firm handling – he is not strong-willed like you and me. I suppose with a mother like his, he could hardly have developed independent options. I don't envy you your mother-in-law. But you will see her off. I don't believe she's a match for you, Lady Rosamund!'

Rosamund shifted uncomfortably in her seat as she remembered it all. She had to struggle with the feeling that she had made a fool of herself in Scarborough, though she told herself again and again that to an outsider's eyes she had simply enjoyed an agreeable seaside flirtation with a handsome young man. Yet inwardly it felt as though she had asked and been rejected, and that was not a pleasant sensation. Her pride had been touched, and needed restoring. It was as well,

109

perhaps, that she was going back to Wolvercote and out of the public eye.

Lucy always stopped in Grantham on her journeys to and from Yorkshire, at the George, a large, busy, dull and respectable house. It was evidently where Parslow expected Rosamund to stay, too, to judge by his anticipatory movements as they rattled over the cobbles of the town. Here was an opportunity to assert herself, to shew that, young as she was, she was the captain of her own ship.

'We'll take a change here, Parslow, and go on to Stamford,' she said loftily as they pulled under the red-brick arch into the yard.

'Stamford, my lady?'

'Yes. The Angel. See to it, will you?'

Parslow was too good a servant to argue with her, or even to display surprise, but Rosamund could sense his disapproval, and was satisfied. She didn't know the Angel, of course, but she had heard of it as a smart and fashionable place – much more in her style, she thought, than the ponderous old George. Parslow climbed down from the carriage to pay the boys and order the change. The new team was led out and poled up, and in five minutes they were on their way again. It was an easy triumph.

But as soon as they pulled out onto the road south Rosamund regretted it. It was another twenty miles to Stamford, and she was already stiff and weary from travelling, and growing hungry. She had just let herself in for another hour-and-a-half on the road at least, and by the time they arrived it would be very late. The servants said nothing, of course, but Rosamund felt bad about them, too. *Do right by your servants, and they'll serve you well* was one of her mother's dictums, and most of her mother's servants had been with her for twenty years.

The flat countryside reeled by monotonously, and Moss fell asleep with her head against the corner squab. Rosamund glanced at her, and then caught Parlow's eye. 'I'm sorry,' she said meekly.

Parslow's lips curved slightly into the ghost of a smile. 'For what?' the smile seemed to say. The low sunset light shewed up a line of bristles above his top lip and around the edge of his jaw, grown since that morning's shave. They were grey

110

like frost; but above his lean cheeks, over his cheekbones, were the places where no whiskers grew, and there the brown skin was smooth, almost shiny. She suddenly had an intense and almost embarrassing sense of him as a person, as a man, together with the more familiar feeling of old affection. He sat very still, with the restfulness about him of the man who lives with horses – restful but alert, ready at any moment to cope, to care for, to be kind. His hat was on his knees, and his quiet hands rested on top of it. But she didn't want to look at his hands: she thought it might be too personal.

Moss sighed and settled in her sleep. Suddenly Rosamund said, 'Parslow, do you think I should marry Lord Chelmsford? I think he's certain to ask me when I get back.'

'I think it very likely, my lady,' he said, pitching his voice low, as she had, not to wake the maid. 'He and his mother and sister will be among the guests at Wolvercote.' Rosamund raised an eyebrow. 'I saw the list when Mr Hicks was consulting me about stabling for the guests' horses.'

'Ha! Well, theirs won't take up much room, unless Lady Barbara has decided to set up her carriage at last – and frankly, I'd give you better odds on the end of the world arriving tomorrow.'

'I believe they are coming by post-chaise, my lady,' he affirmed.

Rosamund met his amused eye. 'Well, then? Do you think I should accept him? And don't say "It's not for me to say, my lady", because I've asked you, and you've more sense in your little finger than most people have in their whole heads.'

He regarded her in smiling silence for a moment, and she thought he was going to refuse. But he said, very quietly, 'In confidence, then, my lady?'

'In confidence.'

'No, I don't think you should.'

As soon as she heard it, she realised she had expected him to say yes, and it surprised her into wondering why. Had she expected him to say yes because she had wanted him to? Ah yes, but why was that?

'Why?' she asked him bluntly.

'Because you're not in love with him.'

'Oh!' That was a leveller. It was surely ancient writ in the servants' hall that she had been in love with Marcus Morland

111

for ever. Besides, 'That's heresy, Parslow. What was love to do with it? You should be advising me to make a good marriage to a wealthy, titled man of good character.'

His eyes were too intelligent. 'If that was the advice you needed, my lady, you wouldn't have had to ask me. You know those things already. And if you were anyone else – if you were your sister, or any of your cousins – it's what I'd have told you.'

'Well, what then?'

'You're very like your mother, my lady,' Parslow said gently, 'and I wouldn't like to see you unhappy, as I've seen her in the past. Look, now, she'd never have married Lord Theakston if he'd offered for her years ago, because he wouldn't have been what the world sees as a "good" match, but he's the very person, if you'll forgive me, to make her happy.'

'He does make her happy,' Rosamund said. 'But don't you think that Lord Chelmsford will make me happy?'

He paused for a very long time, and watching his eyes, she saw that he was thinking a great many things that he was not going to say aloud. She wished she knew what they were. And then she thought that perhaps it would not be comfortable to hear them.

'I think Lord Chelmsford is still a fairy-tale figure to you, like a hero out of a schoolroom story-book,' was what he did say, which was uncanny, for it was what she had thought herself once before. She remembered a conversation she had had with Tantony about heroes, and how he had said that Hektor of Troy was his model. Dear, lovely man that he was, it was like him to choose Hektor rather than Achilles! Oh Tantony, how can you be dead? How can there just be no more you, ever?

'No, Parslow,' she said sadly, 'he's real to me now. That's the problem. I see him just as he is.'

He digested this, and then he said, 'He will never see you just as you are, my lady. I think you may find that very tiresome at last.'

She smiled faintly. 'You think I'm a horse that needs managing.'

'I will always serve you, my lady, to the best of my ability,' he said.

112

Moss stirred, half-woke, smacking her lips a little, and then settled her head back into the corner. The other two waited in silence until her breathing steadied again, their eyes on each other, their thoughts probably not far apart.

'Do you have a name?' Rosamund said at last. 'Apart from Parslow, I mean?'

'My given name is John, my lady,' he said neutrally. A neutral name, too, she thought. She tried it against him for size in her head, and after a repetition or two, she found she didn't mind it.

'John,' she said at last. 'How strange that I never knew it before.'

'I hardly ever think of myself by it,' he said, and it was the nearest thing to a confidence she had ever had from him.

The Angel at Stamford was crowded, but in a very different way from the George at Grantham.

'Rackety,' Moss said with a disapproving sniff. In view of the number of gigs and tilburies pulled up in the street before it, and the shocking number of low collars to be seen going in and out of the entrance, Rosamund was half-inclined to agree, but she had burned her boats behind her, and it was out of the question to go on further tonight.

'Don't be so particular,' she reproved. 'If I can put up with it, so can you. Parslow, go speak for rooms. We'll wait in the chaise until you come back.'

He was gone some time, and Rosamund guessed he had had trouble before he spoke. 'I've secured a bedchamber for you, my lady, but I cannot get a private parlour. The place is full to overflowing.'

Rosamund frowned. 'What about Moss? And what about you?'

'There is another lady staying here, my lady, whose abigail is willing to share her room with Moss, if you have no objection. There is a truckle bed,' he added for Moss's benefit, 'and the room is quite large enough for two.'

'If Moss doesn't mind it, I don't,' Rosamund said, wanting only to get out of the carriage now. She felt that if she didn't straighten her knees soon, she would simply die of sitting. 'But what about you?'

'I shall do very well, my lady,' he said cryptically.

113

She narrowed her eyes. 'Amongst the horses, I suppose?'

He almost smiled. 'Not quite, my lady – the hay-loft. I had sooner that,' he added as she opened her mouth to protest, 'than share a room with someone's valet.'

'Yet you are willing to suggest Moss shares with someone's abigail?'

'Abigails do not smoke tuppenny cigars in bed, my lady,' he said with spare humour. 'If you would care to step down ...'

The bedchamber proved to be decent, but small, and in the absence of a private parlour, Rosamund was obliged to take her dinner in the coffee-room along with the other guests and travellers. Moss had to accompany her, and grumbled a good deal, but though Rosamund felt she ought to pretend it was an imposition, she was really rather excited about it. It promised a little whiff of real life in her normally rose-strewn existence. One never knew who one might meet. A surprise encounter might change one's whole life, as it usually did in three-volume novels.

The landlord seemed flustered by her arrival, and would by no means allow her to sit at the common board. If she would wait just a moment, my lady, he would make a booth available to her; and he waved his hands agitatedly before dashing off through the haze of smoke that obscured the room. Rosamund stood in the doorway, looking with what she hoped was an expression of sophisticated amusement at the scene.

Around the common board – a long table down the centre of the room – guests and travellers, mostly young men and middle-aged couples, sat elbow to elbow, helping themselves and occasionally each other to the dishes laid out there. There was an enormous roasted turkey, a ham, a beefsteak pie three feet across with oysters and onions in its gravy, a smoking cauldron of what looked like pea soup, a gigantic duff sticky with raisins, a tongue in aspic, and a dish of stewed leeks which everyone kept missing because it was right in the middle and hidden from view unless you were standing up.

The potmen and maids kept running back and forth to the table with baskets of bread and pots of coffee and more and more ale, in between serving the people sitting in the booths with their more private dinners, and seeing to the needs of a noisy group on benches and stools in a semicircle before the fire. It was these latter who were accounting for most of the internal fog. They seemed to be drinking tankards of hot brandy punch and mulled ale with their pipes and cigars, and had drawn their circle so closely round the fire it had starved and grown sulky. Every now and then one of them would notice and throw something else on it, and poke it or kick it for encouragement, which made it belch another cloud of smoke to add to the tobacco fumes.

Moss drew her attention with a nudge to the activities of the landlord, who had approached two young men in one of the booths, and after a brief parley was escorting them to the common board and exhorting those already around it to 'hitch up a bit if you please, ladies and gents – they're only little 'uns'. To the vacated booth he then invited Rosamund with a bow and crook of the finger, brushing the crumbs off the table with the corner of his apron as he did so.

'That isn't right – to throw those two gentlemen out on our account,' Rosamund muttered to Moss.

'Oh, don't say so, my lady!' Moss said in alarm. 'I expect they were quite willing – besides, there's nothing else for it.'

'Well, I shall thank them, at least,' Rosamund said determinedly, and stepping past the bowing landlord she approached the two young men, just getting comfortable on their bench, and said, 'It is very kind of you indeed to make room for me. I hope you are not inconvenienced by it?'

Her approach threw everything into confusion. The young men, decent-looking clerkly types, both went scarlet, and attempted to rise politely to their feet, a difficult task in the confined space, and made more hazardous by the fact that one of them had just put his hat back on his head, chiefly because there was nowhere else to put it. On being addressed by a lady – and a beautiful young lady in a silk gown, at that – he naturally tried to sweep it off again, and caught his next neighbour in the ear with his elbow. The close proximity of the diners to each other sent the accidental shove running as though down a row of dominoes, and a man who had just spotted the dish of leeks and had risen to a half-way crouch to reach for it, was caught off balance and put his hand down straight through the pastry of his portion of beefsteak pie and shot a hot oyster into his wife's lap.

'Oh no, ma'am. It's our pleasure, ma'am,' the young men

stammered. 'Couldn't expect you to sit at this table, ma'am.'

'It's very kind, all the same,' Rosamund said. Keeping her eyes turned resolutely from the chaos further down the table, and biting the inside of her cheeks, she bowed her head to them graciously and allowed Moss and the landlord to hustle her into the booth. There she was able to put her handkerchief over her face until she had recovered.

'Now then, my lady,' Moss said, torn between disapproval and the desire to giggle herself.

'This is better than the stuffy old George,' Rosamund said at last, drying her eyes.

'I don't know, my lady,' Moss said doubtfully nodding towards the group round the fire. 'There's some very rough-looking types over there.'

'Nonsense. They're not rough, only loud.'

'It's the same thing, my lady. A man as talks that loud will be acting rough the next minute. I don't like it, my lady, and that's a fact. There's not a single gentleman in sight.'

'Pho! You're too nice. It's an adventure: don't be so cow-hearted.'

But before they had been served even with the soup, Moss's fears were realised. A man appeared at the end of their booth, removed his hat, swaying slightly, and bowed unsteadily. His head and face were pale and chubby and the one as innocent of hair as the other, which made him look both funny and sinister. His clothes were an over-bright, cheap and exaggerated version of a Dandy's, and he obviously took himself very seriously as a Bond Street buck, for his neckcloth must have taken half an hour to perfect, and his corset must have been causing him acute suffering. He had plainly been indulging himself already that evening: his eyes were clouded, and as he spoke his breath whistled past them like a gale from an empty brandy-cask.

'Good evening, ladies! Two lovely ladies, all alone? That won't do! Robinson's my name. May I have the honour of making your acquaintance, and buying you dinner? Anything you like – champagne, anything! Nothing but the best for two lovely ladies.'

Little round Judy Moss leapt like a terrier to her mistress's defence. 'You may not! Take your hat and your silly face out of here, and don't dare to address her ladyship in that manner!'

116

'Her ladyship, is it?' he said in slurred accents. 'Well, I'm dying to be her ladyship's servant – and yours, ma'am, I assure you! No offence intended.'

'You're as drunk as a brewer's horse!' cried Moss furiously. 'Go back to the tap-room where you belong – and if you can't tell a lady's maid from a lady, you'd better stay there!'

Mr Robinson seemed to find in these repulsive words only food for debate. He leaned his fists on the table to support himself and began deliberately, 'Now s'interesting you should say that, because I knew a horse once –'

At that moment another figure appeared behind him, a large hand attached itself to his collar, and he was lifted in a most surprising manner clear through the air and away from the table in mid-sentence.

'Not now, cully,' the newcomer said firmly. 'You're in no state to know anything – your brains resemble a dish of crambo at this moment, and I strongly recommend you go back to your friends and crawl back inside that brandy-bottle, where it's safe.'

The landlord appeared, tutting and flapping and spilling over with apologies, to finish the job of removal. Mr Robinson, apparently unaware that he had offended, was walked away and disappeared through the coffee-room door, still talking, with one proprietorial hand gripping his collar and another the seat of his pants to help him along.

And now the rescuer turned back to address the rescuee.

'My dear Lady Rosamund, what can you be doing in such a place as this? No, no, you must not answer, for it's none of my business! But if you will do me the great honour of taking dinner with me, I can protect you from any further nuisance of that sort a great deal more effectively than your maid – courageous though she is.'

Rosamund shook her head – not in refusal, but in wonder. So much, she thought, for meeting the stranger who would change her life!

'I should be glad of your company, and I'm sure Moss will be glad to be released,' she said. 'Pray, do sit down, Mr Hawker; and tell me, what on earth is crambo?'

It was an adventure, all the same – the first time she had ever had dinner alone with a man, and in an inn, to boot! It was a pity in a way that it was only Mr Hawker, in whom she had no interest; but on the other hand it was perhaps better to be with someone she didn't need to impress, with whom she could be comfortable. It gave her a light-headed feeling of being off the leash – she could say and do anything tonight, and it wouldn't count in everyday life. It was fen-larks, as they used to say as children when they crossed their fingers during chasing-games.

As a substitute for Moss, he was in all ways superior. And he was handsome, there was no doubt about it – if you liked that kind of dark, Byronic good looks. She need not be ashamed of being seen with him.

'So, Lady Rosamund, are you having enough of an adventure?' he said when the soup had been removed. 'I presume it was on your command that you put up here instead of at the George in Grantham?'

'Why should you have expected me to stay at the George?'

'It's where your mother always stays.' He laughed at her expression. 'Come now, don't look so surprised! Your mother is a public figure, and particularly well known on this road. Did you think you moved in a cloak of invisibility, you and your family?'

She frowned a little. 'I don't think I like that. Do you mean whatever I do, I am spied upon?'

'Hardly that. But you are not *incognita*, you know. I was told you were here five minutes after you stepped across the threshold.'

'So your being on hand to rescue me was not a coincidence?' He bowed. 'And what about Scarborough? Was our first meeting on the sands there arranged, too?'

'Did you suspect it was? You are a very noticing young woman, Lady Rosamund. Very well, I engineered the meeting; but I did go to Scarborough at Farraline's request, and he was there for his convalescence.'

'Why Scarborough?'

'Because it was the nearest seaside place that I thought would be tolerable. It was *à peine* that I persuaded him to leave his mills at all, you know, and I'd never have got him any further away than that.'

She was not quite satisfied with the explanation, but could hardly call him a liar when they were about to have dinner together, so she left the point and said instead, 'And why did you – engineer the meeting, as you say?'

He raised an eyebrow. 'Did I need a reason? My dear ma'am, two beautiful, vivacious young women, two unatt-ached and lonely men – is that not reason enough?'

'Oh stuff! You don't need to gammon me, Mr Hawker. What was the real reason?'

He laughed, and she noticed how very white his teeth were in his dark face. It made him look rather vulpine – but attrac-tive, in a dangerous sort of way. 'Such devastating honesty! You are like your mother in that, Lady Rosamund. Very well, I arranged the meeting for Farraline's sake. He needs capital to invest in his mills, and his brother is not willing to give him any. Where should a young man turn for capital? He can either borrow it, or marry it, and marrying it is a great deal more sensible.'

'Yes – because he never needs to pay it back,' Rosamund said drily. 'But he can only do that once, remember.'

'He needs only to do it once, if he does it properly.'

'Quite. So Sophie would not have done for him at all,' she concluded.

'How so? Is not Miss Morland an heiress, too?'

'Hardly. Your information is a little faulty, sir,' Rosamund said with amusement. 'What made you think she was?'

He looked at her for a moment thoughtfully. 'She is your aunt and uncle's eldest child, is she not? And the Morland property is not entailed.'

'The Morland estate will go to her brother Nicholas,' Rosa-mund said. 'Indeed, you may believe me. It is a fact.'

He heard the triumph in her voice, and chuckled. 'But you are mistaken – that was not why I paid her attention. As far as my supposition of her wealth goes, I thought on that account that she might do for Farraline, but I had no ambi-tions there myself. I chose her company because I liked her; because she reminded me of Fanny. Only in her looks, of course – she is nothing like her in character.'

'Nothing,' Rosamund agreed.

'Fanny was an original – unique.' He sighed faintly. 'There will never be anyone like her.'

'Come, Mr Hawker, have you not found a replacement already?' Rosamund said boldly. 'Lady Annabel is unique enough, is she not?'

'Ah, you know about that, do you? Farraline has a long tongue. But what a thing to talk to you of! What could he be about?'

Rosamund blushed. 'Neither he nor you seem to feel it necessary to talk to me of conventional things. It is very shocking.'

'But pleasant? After so much bland, sweet food, the palate craves spice and vinegar, doesn't it? Shall I continue to be shockingly frank?'

'Please do,' Rosamund said, still feeling her cheeks warm. Thank heaven there was no-one she knew to see her. But it was an adventure, wasn't it?

'Very well,' he smiled. 'Then I shall tell you that you are wrong about Bel. She is not, and never could be, a substitute for Fanny – for me or, I imagine, for anyone else. Yes, I see in your eyes that you have cause to doubt it. But you need never be jealous of Bel, I assure you.'

'Since we are being frank – I imagine you know that Marcus Morland made a fool of himself over her.'

'And you hold it against him – and against her. Well, that is very understandable. But I think I may explain it in a way that will take the sting out of it. You see, there are two ways in which a man can love a woman. Bel accounts for one sort. She attracts very strongly. She has a particular sort of excitement which is hard to resist – and with such a women as Bel,' he added with a shrug, 'there is no need to resist. It is all very simple – you hunger, you eat, and there's an end.'

There was no chance, Rosamund thought, of her blush's subsiding while this topic of conversation persisted. Yet it was fascinating. It was something she wanted to understand, and it was unlikely anyone else would ever try to explain it to her. 'Did you not – eat Fanny?'

He grinned at her phrasing. 'I loved Fanny. Yes, I ate her – I could never get enough of her! But there was something else, too. When you love a woman, you want to possess her entirely, to keep her to yourself so that no-one else can ever have any part of her. Mine, Fanny was mine, and I'd have killed any man who offered her the least insult!' He pulled himself up, seeming surprised by his own vehemence, and went on in his usual mild and cynical tone. 'One does not feel that way about such as Bel de Ladon, *voilà tout.*'

Rosamund shook her head doubtfully. 'But Marcus – Marcus wanted to marry her. He didn't just want to eat her – and he wanted to kill people who insulted her.'

He shrugged. 'You must forgive him for that – he was very young and inexperienced, and he mistook – for a very little while – what he was feeling. He knew nothing of women, you see. He had come from a protected background, straight out of the schoolroom and into the army. That, I grant you,' he said with a grin as though she had interjected, 'is enough to pitchfork some young men headfirst into experience, but Marcus is not like that. He's one of those shy, serious, good-hearted men who regards women as rare and delicate creatures from another species – goddesses to be worshipped. He would find it very difficult to think badly of Bel until she forced him to – which in the end, she did.'

'Yes, she did,' Rosamund remembered.

'She got bored with him,' Hawker explained simply. 'Later, of course, she wanted him back, but it was too late. Men like Marcus trust for a long time and against all the odds, but once they stop, they never forgive. Now I – I can forgive anyone anything, any number of times. But then, you see,' he added with charming frankness, 'I don't really care about any of them.'

'Except Fanny.'

'Excepting always Fanny. That was my once-for-all weakness. So you see you may trust what I tell you – I have no need or desire to tell you anything but the truth.'

'I don't quite understand,' Rosamund said slowly, 'why you are telling me any of this. It is kind of you to educate me, but why should you bother to be kind, if you don't want anything of me?'

He laughed aloud, making one or two heads turn. 'Well, I have certainly convinced you of my utter selfishness, haven't I? But I'll tell you – I like you, Lady Rosamund. You remind me of your mother, and I like her very much. She and your stepfather were very kind to me and Fanny in Vienna, and I don't forget kindness. And I like Marcus, too. He is good, and good people fascinate and rather puzzle me, for there are so few of them. And finally, I don't like Bel de Ladon. Yes, I eat her up, but I don't like her – she's bad and destructive, and I don't want her to have the satisfaction of having destroyed you and your Marcus. He truly loves you, and I think, because of her, you don't believe it. So here is my good deed for the day – perhaps for the rest of my life! – to persuade you to forgive him for making a cake of himself in Brussels. Every man is allowed to do that once in his life, you know: it is traditional.'

Rosamund listened to all this in silence, her thoughts tumbling as she tried to absorb it all and make sense of it. She felt confused, almost dizzied by the amount of new information that needed to be fitted into the spaces of her mind. The large, simple shapes that people had had for her from childhood upwards were changing, growing blurred and complicated, and she was not sure she liked it.

She looked directly into his eyes. 'You wouldn't want to marry me, would you?'

'Not for any consideration,' he said solemnly. 'You may trust me absolutely, my child. I am fifteen, sixteen years older than you, and though I am an expensive man, I have at present other ways to keep myself less troublesome than marrying twenty thousand pounds attached to a passionate young woman. You would tire me out! I don't say,' he added thoughtfully, 'that in five years or so, as a married woman, you might not have attractions; but for the moment you are quite safe from me.'

She coloured indignantly. 'If I were a married woman, you would be quite safe from me!'

He smiled lazily. 'That is exactly how you should think, and just what I would have expected from you. And to convince you further of the purity of my intentions, I shall make a point of calling on your mother when I get back to London to explain how it is that I have dined alone with you here, so that she won't hear it from someone else and draw the wrong conclusions.'

'Thank you,' Rosamund said, though rather absently. He had given her too much else to think about to have time to worry about her reputation.

122

Héloïse and John Anstey were taking a walk together around the moat. The sky above was clear blue, the sunshine hot – it was like a different world from the grey, wet one they had grown used to.

'Ah, this is good, this is peaceful,' Lord Anstey said, looking around him. 'It's good to get away from my problems for a little while.'

'Poor John,' Héloïse said. 'Was it very bad?'

'Not as bad as it might have been, but bad enough. And we got the bodies up – that was one blessing! I remember back in '74 we had a collapse at Tunstall where we lost forty people, and we never recovered them. We just had to close off that part of the mine in the end. I was only a child at the time, of course, but I remember my father coming in exhausted night after night and telling my mother about it. I heard him say once that the thing that puzzled him was that the survivors seemed to mind more about the bodies not being brought up than about the actual deaths: and do you know, it's still the same? The lower orders are extraordinary.'

'I suppose they accept that death can come at any time,' Héloïse offered, 'but the funeral is their comfort.'

'Yes, I suppose so. Well, there'll be a funeral this time, all right. I shall pay for it myself, of course.'

'How many people died?'

'Two men, three women and four children. And one of the women was with child. Bad enough, in all conscience.' He sighed. 'But it's the men's own fault, you know. They won't prop up properly as they go along, so we're bound to get these collapses.'

'But why won't they? It seems extraordinary that they risk their lives unnecessarily.'

'They say it takes too much time. While they're propping up, they're not actually getting coal, and so not actually earning any money. They're paid by what they get out, you understand; so they take short cuts, and leave things undone. I suppose they think the risk is worth it.'

'No-one ever thinks an accident will happen to him,' Héloïse said.

'True. And then, you know, sometimes they leave a column of coal as the prop, and at the last minute greed overcomes them and they don't want to leave it behind. So they take the chance the roof will hold without it. I understand that's what happened in this case. With the price of coal so low at the moment, they have to get out more each day to make the same money. And there was the coal prop, all nice and ready to hand, better than clearing a new gallery – so they thought.'

They walked on a moment in silence. Then Héloïse said, 'I don't like to think of the women and children working underground.'

Anstey shrugged. 'It isn't what anyone likes to think about. They're a dreadful sight, you know, those women – naked to the waist and dragging a tub along by a belt and chain. Especially when they're with child. We had a woman last month gave birth underground on one of the ledges – brought the baby up hidden in her apron, afraid she'd be turned off if anyone knew. It died though. Probably a blessing in disguise: it wouldn't have been much of a life for it, in the mines. They go down sometimes as young as four. We don't encourage it, but the parents insist.'

'But how frightened the little ones must be, going down into the dark!'

'Only at first. They soon get used to it – the women too. Someone must draw for the men; and if the children didn't work the traps, everyone would suffocate.'

'Couldn't men do those things?'

He shook his head. 'It isn't like that. The men who cut the coal want their women and children to work with them, to make up the family's wages. Usually the miner himself compounds for the whole family to work – you can't take him on without taking his drawer and his little stackers and trappers as well.'

'Yes, I see,' Héloïse said hesitantly. 'It's like the weavers, with their wives spinning for them, and the children scribbling and piecing and threading.'

124

'Precisely. And you know yourself that weavers' children begin work at four years old, or even younger.'

'But it is different, going down the mines from working in your own home.'

'No-one makes them do it. Every day there are queues of them at the office, begging for work – men, women and children – far more than I can employ, with trade so slack just now. And look,' he went on, though she had not interrupted, 'someone must employ them, or how would they live? I know there are people nowadays agitating for laws to be passed to prevent women and children working down the mines, but I can't see the justification for interfering with people's freedom like that. Besides, it's a dangerous precedent to set, giving the Government that kind of power. You see where it got the French! No, no, let people alone to choose their own way of life, say I. It's no bed of roses for the men underground, either, you know; but it's not for me to tell people they may not sell their labour how and where they wish.'

Héloïse nodded, seeing the sense of it. 'Yes, that's true. It is what Edward was saying the other day – that freedom is worth a little inconvenience. But death is rather more of an inconvenience than most people would bargain for.'

'Sometimes that's what it costs.'

They turned the corner of the house. The moat was full almost to overflowing, and the sunlight was dancing on the water and throwing a shifting pattern of light on the wall of the house. This was the kitchen wall. Héloïse glanced up automatically at the black stain on the brickwork high up, where the chimney had caught fire last year. It was a gigantic, mediaeval chimney, rising twenty feet above the roof, and so wide that the sweep didn't need to send a boy up – he could climb up it himself quite easily. It should never have caught fire in a thousand years, and investigation proved that it had only done so because it had not been swept in nine years: every time the sweep came, Monsieur Barnard had told him it was not convenient to be letting the kitchen fire out that day.

A little further along was the swan-window, low down near the water's surface, with the iron bell-chain hanging down beside it. The water level was so high, the swans no longer had to reach up for the ring of the chain to pull it.

'If it rains any more, the water will come in through the swan-window, and we shall have the kitchen flooded,' Héloïse remarked. 'It happened once before, I believe, when there had been a very hard winter, and the snow all melted at once. I read it in the Household Book.'

'Good lord, is that still going? It must make fascinating reading! You ought to write a history of Morland Place, you know, Héloïse.'

'I?'

'You're the obvious person. You've had all that practice writing your *History of the Revolution*.'

'Which I have never yet finished,' Héloïse pointed out.

'You will one day, and then you can begin on Morland Place. Meanwhile, you should start to take notes. Not everything gets put into the Household Book, does it? It would be a pity if some of the incidents were forgotten.'

'It would all be bad news now, I'm afraid,' she sighed. 'The hay-harvest is ruined, and the wheat is still green in the fields – I don't believe it will ripen at all. And in spite of all this rain, the fish have not done well. You would think, wouldn't you, that they at least would have been happy? But I've never seen so few carp in the ponds as this year.'

He smiled sympathetically. 'Everyone has troubles. We shall none of us be sorry to see the back of 1816. But never mind – there's consolation in this wonderful sunshine, even if it doesn't last long.' He looked around him and sighed with pleasure. 'God, how I love this place! I spent so much time here as a child, it was like a second home to me. I was always happy at Morland Place. It seems to have a very special atmosphere about it – safe and unchanging.'

'That's what Father Sparrow says. He says he can't remember ever living anywhere else, now.'

Anstey looked at her curiously. 'Ah yes, your wandering priest! James tells me you mean to take Nicholas out of school and have him educated at home again. Is that true?'

'But of course! That is what Father Moineau is for. It will be better for Benedict to have his brother at home with him, to set an example; and there is no point in paying school fees for what is to be had at home. Even we,' she added, 'need to save money where we can.'

'But Héloïse, is it safe? I mean, what do you really know

126

about this man? He just turned up, out of the blue, practically a vagrant – and a Frenchman too –'

'We are no longer at war with France,' she said quietly.

He reddened with embarrassment. 'I'm sorry, I didn't mean to be insulting. But you know there are different kinds of Frenchmen. You and your kind fled France when the Jacobins took over.'

'Well, so did Father Moineau also. He is *Old French*, John. He calls himself a citizen of the world, now. As to what I know about him – he has not been with us long, but I know him inside and out, as well as I know myself. Would I entrust my precious children to him, if I did not?'

'True enough. Well, God knows, if you are satisfied, I should be – it's none of my business.'

'Ah, but I hope it soon will be,' Héloïse said with a smile. 'It is what I wanted to talk to you about, John – why I asked you to walk with me.'

'And I thought it was just for the pleasure of my company.'

'Your company is always a pleasure to me,' she said gravely 'but conversation flows better for some subject matter. Now, dear John, I must tell you straight away that I want you to send Henry to us, and let him be educated with my boys by Father Moineau. Nicholas loves Henry dearly, and will miss him very much when he leaves school; and it is not good for little boys to be without others of their own age.'

'Then don't take him away from school,' Anstey said simply.

Héloïse frowned. 'The school is very well, but they do not learn much there. Only Latin and Greek, and mathematics once a week. It is too narrow – even James agrees. We wish them to study other things as well – history and philosophy and astronomy, and more of mathematics, and French and Italian besides. A gentleman,' she pronounced firmly, 'should be able to speak and read French and Italian, and know the main works of literature well enough to discuss them.'

'And you think your priest will be able to teach your boys all those things?'

'*Bien sûr*. And as it can matter not at all to him whether he teaches two boys or three, and as Nicholas would be lonely without Henry, it is sensible for Henry to share the lessons. Now is it not?'

He looked a little uncomfortable. 'You're very persuasive, but –'

'But what? What do you fear?'

'I'm afraid your priest might take the opportunity to stuff Henry's head with papist ideas. I'm sorry, Héloïse, I don't mean to offend, but you know we are not of that persuasion.'

She smiled. 'I'm not offended. And I promise you there will be no conversion. Why, Father Moineau even carries out a modified form of service in our chapel to suit our Morland Place peculiarities. He is no bigot, and no missionary, and I swear to you that he shall not attempt to change Henry – other than by the shining example of his goodness. There now, what do you say?' He still hesitated, and she added cunningly, 'You might send Aglaea too. It will be good for the boys to have a female's gentle influence on them.'

'No, no,' he said hastily, 'Louisa would never part with her "baby". You know how women are over their last-born. Well, of course you do – I'm being unusually clumsy today, aren't I?'

Héloïse smiled. 'Dear John, send Henry to us, and I shall forgive you everything. Come, what is there to fear? You said yourself that you were always happy at Morland Place – would you deny Henry the same happiness? And if you are not satisfied with his progress, you can always take him away again.'

'I'll have to talk to Louisa about it –'

'Consult your wife? What a modern man you are! James would simply tell me his decision,' she said demurely.

Anstey laughed aloud, 'James command you? That will be the day!'

The short period of sunshine in mid-August was too late and too little to help the harvests. It did, however, give a pleasant journey home from Eton for Lord Aylesbury and his two companions, especially since Lady Theakston had had the foresight to send an open carriage for them, instead of the respectable-but-dull travelling chaise.

'I say, Peg, this is something like!' Maurice Hampton exclaimed as they bowled along the excellent new surface of the Windsor-to-Oxford pike. The speed of the four high-fed bays, put along by a professional hand, obliged him now and then to make a grab for his best beaver lid, which in conformity to college fashion was tall enough to provide plenty of wind-resistance.

'Your mama must be a trump card – a bran-new barouche, and four prime 'uns to go!'

'Oh yes,' said Aylesbury. 'Mama knows what's what when it comes to a turn-out, don't she, Tough?'

Thomas Weston brought his thoughts back from a distance and grinned agreement. 'Better than Stevenson's pater's gig, ain't it?'

Hampton giggled. 'Poor old Stevenson! He looked blue as megrim when he saw us driving off in style. Good thing we were driving off, too, or he'd have found some excuse to give us toco! Let's just hope he's forgotten about it by next half.'

'He won't be there next half,' Weston said. 'Didn't you hear? His governor's taking him away – putting him into the family business.'

'By Jupiter! Poor old Stevenson a sugar-merchant!' Hampton said, struck by the awfulness of this fate even to pity the house bully who had made his life miserable for the first month of his school life. Hampton was a small, pale, delicate-looking boy, further cursed with a slight stammer, which had earned him the nickname of 'Polly', and brought all manner of persecution on him – until Weston had taken him under his wing.

Though only a month older than Hampton, Weston had already earned himself a reputation, and the right to be left alone by the bigger boys. He had performed the various feats of hardihood – and of fool-hardiness – beloved of schoolboys with the required mixture of courage and stoicism. He had risked his limbs climbing the flagpole to hang a cap on the top. He had courted pneumonia breaking ice to swim in the depths of winter. He had 'hunted the squirrel' in a hired gig along the Ascot pike, broken bounds at the risk of a flogging to go to the races, and drunk brandy punch at every inn within running distance. He had endured being tossed in a blanket, and used as a bride in Gretna Green races by seniors, fagged for them without complaint and with just sufficient energy, and taken sundry beatings without blinking or shedding a tear.

So much did many boys; but Weston had displayed a

certain cool detachment all his own, a disregard of his personal safety and comfort and, more, of other boys' ridicule, which had earned him the admiring but puzzled sobriquet of Old Tough. All little boys at some time or other cry out 'I don't care!' as the final defiance when faced with extreme adversity; but there was a general feeling in the school that Tough Weston really didn't care.

He was regarded by his fellow students as a 'rum 'un'. He was older by far than his years and knew things he shouldn't have known; he went his own way and stood the nonsense unflinchingly if it led him into trouble. He had a way of laughing at the wrong things which made some boys suspect him of being 'satirical'. He was a promising batsman, but admitted preferring reading a book to playing cricket. He had a taste in wine beyond his years, and it was rumoured amongst the seniors that this handsome, well-grown boy had already had a man's experience with the daughter of the landlord of The Crown at Clewer.

He had arrived at school in the company of Roland, Lord Aylesbury, a gangling, solemn, shy boy whose unnatural application to his studies had earned him the nickname of 'Peg', and Weston had early let it be known that whoever insulted Peg Aylesbury insulted him, too. By the time Hampton joined them and was assigned to the same house, it had not been necessary for Weston to do more than indicate that Hampton was under his protection for all but the worst bullies to leave him alone.

As they drew nearer to Wolvercote Polly grew more talkative and excited, while Peg grew quieter with apprehension. He was dreading the homecoming because he would be obliged to meet people and play the lord. The banner would be raised on the flagpole to indicate that the master was at home, and the tenants would all come visiting to pay their respects; Mama's friends would arrive and he'd be expected to take the head of the table at dinner and talk and be charming. This was a terrifying prospect to Aylesbury. He had spent years under the charge of an over-strict tutor, who had oppressed and beaten him unmercifully, and stripped him of his self-confidence.

Weston knew what was troubling him. In the same position, he could have carried it off without effort, and wouldn't have cared whether he did or didn't. But poor Aylesbury was terrified of failing, of disappointing his mother, of making a fool of himself, and would therefore, probably, do all three.

As they clattered past Walton Manor, Weston said, 'I wish you wouldn't worry so, Peg. Worry don't help – in fact, it makes it worse.'

'I know,' he said miserably. 'But if only they wouldn't make such a fuss. If only Papa hadn't hung up his tile. If only someone else could do it.'

'If only the Trojan horse had foaled, hunters today would cost less to feed,' Weston countered.

'I say, what's the trouble?' Hampton asked, suddenly aware that his was not the prevailing mood. 'You fellows are looking uncommon grim.'

'Peg don't like being Earl,' Weston explained. 'He's going to have to receive guests and generally do the pretty, and he don't like it above half.'

'Don't blame him,' Hampton said promptly. 'If anything should happen to my uncle Ballincrea, I'd be in the same boat. It'd be me for the ermine and the nine silver balls, and there'd go all the fun and gig. It could happen any time.' He shuddered. 'This business of titles is all gammon, ain't it?'

'You won't think so one day,' said Weston.

'No, but really, Tough,' Aylesbury said earnestly, 'if it's true that – you know – what you told me that time – it might just as well have been you, mightn't it? Which just shews you.'

'Shews you what?'

'Well, that it makes no difference, really.'

Weston shook his head at him sadly. 'Cabbage for brains!' he said. 'The whole point is that it isn't me. That's the difference that makes the difference. You're an earl, and I'm the illegitimate son of a sea-captain.'

'Yes, but –'

'Tush, Peg. Mum's the word.'

'Oh, it's all right, Polly knows about it. I told him last half.'

'You did, did you?'

'It's all right,' Aylesbury said, suddenly nervous, for Tough could give you such a cold look when he was annoyed. 'I swore him to secrecy.'

'Oh, *that's* what you're talking about!' Hampton cried, suddenly enlightened. 'Yes, it's quite all right, Tough. I'd

131

never tell a soul, honestly. And I think it's a splendid secret! Her ladyship's a trump – a real out-and-outer!'

'You two are a pair of clowns,' Weston said with patient humour. 'It don't make a shred of difference, can't you get that into your thick heads? We're still just what we always were.'

'Yes, very well for you,' Aylesbury said earnestly, 'but it does make a difference to me, Tough. It means you're my real, true brother, and that's everything.'

'I should say so!' Hampton breathed. 'I wish you were mine, too!'

'I was always worried what would happen when we finished school and you went off into the world,' Aylesbury went on, 'and I had to stay behind to be the earl. But now I know you'll always be my brother, so it's all right, isn't it?'

Weston looked at him with affection and faint irritation, but was saved from answering this unanswerable question by a loud halloo, accompanied by the sound of hooves. They all looked round to see a female in a dark-blue habit, sidesaddle upon a black horse, cantering down on them, and leading an unridden bay by the bridle.

'Is that your mama?' Hampton asked in awe as the barouche drew up and the rider came flying towards them across the Port Meadow.

'Of course not,' Weston said before Aylesbury could speak. He would have known his mother at any distance, in any light, and upon any horse. 'It's her horse – Hotspur – but it's Lady Rosamund riding.'

A moment later they could see that he was right. Rosamund pulled up at the last moment beside the carriage in a trampling swirl of horses, Hotspur digging clods out of the turf while the led horse went back on his haunches in a way that would have unseated any lesser rider.

'Ah, there you are, Aylesbury! Hello, young Hampton! Hello Tommy! I meant to catch you before you got this far, but I couldn't get this fellow over the brook. His name's Thunder – handsome, isn't he?' The led horse, thus addressed, tugged once more at the reins, and finding himself securely held, consented to put all four feet back on the ground and stand quietly.

'He's very nice,' Aylesbury said shyly. His tall sister always

132

made him feel small and young and useless, though in truth she had never been other than kind to him. But she was so bold, and so full of energy, and nothing ever seemed to embarrass or upset her. 'Are you having a nice ride?'

She grinned at him. 'Enjoying the last of my freedom, before the party arrives. Your mama and sister are here already, Hampton, but the difficult ones don't come until tomorrow.'

'How do you like Hotspur?' Weston asked. He did not share the family's passion for horses, seeing them only as a means of transport; but there was no doubt that Rosamund looked magnificent on horseback, and he knew Lady Theakston wouldn't have allowed anyone else to ride her black gelding.

'Oh, he and I are old friends,' she said, leaning forward to pat the warm black neck. 'And Thunder is for you, Aylesbury – a present from Mama. She and I picked him out ourselves, and I've been riding him for the last two days to work him in for you. So down with you, and try him out.'

'What – now?'

'Of course, now. Come, foolish, it's the perfect opportunity, with no-one but me to see you! We'll ride back the long way. The boys won't mind being left alone – will you? He's a beauty – a real gentleman – and if you get to know him now, it'll give you confidence when the party arrives.'

Aylesbury saw nothing but kindness in his sister's eyes – no desire to trick or humiliate – and a glance at Weston confirmed his approval. It did seem a good plan; and the bay horse, he thought with rising spirits, looked splendid.

'Well, if you don't mind, then, Polly?'

'N't'all. Wish I could join you,' Hampton said politely.

'Good fellow,' Rosamund said cheerfully. 'Come on, then, Aylesbury. Can you get up all right? He's a tall one. Don't forget to check your girth. I thought we'd go across at Fiddler's Island and round by Binsey and Godstow. Mama's spoiling to have another of her point-to-points while the company's here, and it will give you a chance to see the ground. Not that any of us will have a chance against her Magnus Apollo – that horse has wings in his feet!'

Aylesbury was up, and felt the horse eager but responsive beneath him, and his heart lifted as it always did when he was on horseback. Horses didn't laugh at you or make you feel small. He waved cheerfully to his friends in the barouche, and turned the bay after the trim figure of his sister, thinking with faint surprise that it was a very good notion of hers, and very kind indeed of her to think of it.

They had had their gallop, and were breathing the horses beside the abbey ruins, watching the fast, grey-brown water of the Isis run down just under the bank.

'Two weeks ago the Meadow was flooded,' Rosamund remarked idly. 'There's never been such a summer for rain. So tell me, what do you think of Thunder?'

'He's beautiful. I can't wait to hunt him.'

'I'm glad you like him. Don't forget to tell Mama so when we get in, and thank her. It was she who decided you should have a horse of your own.'

'Mama? Oh, but –'

'You mustn't be such a quaking aspen. Mama isn't a dragon, and she'll be much less sharp with you if you'll only face her and speak out boldly.'

'I couldn't,' he said, shrinking.

'You *can*. It's the same with everyone. You just have to stand up straight and speak firmly, and everyone will be as kind as Christmas to you. But it annoys people when you whisper and mumble and look frightened.'

'Yes, I know,' he said humbly. 'I see how it is with Tough – Thomas, I mean. Everyone likes him, because he ain't afraid. But what do you do if you *are*?'

Rosamund shrugged. 'I suppose – pretend. That's what I'd do. You're the earl, and you're going to have to face up to public life sooner or later. You might as well get used to it, Roly. There's no getting out of it.'

'All very well for you – you've never been afraid in your life.'

She looked at him thoughtfully. 'I've had to face up to unpleasant things. Last year in Brussels – you can't imagine how horrible it was, the men coming in with smashed legs and bellies torn open, and –' She stopped. 'But when I thought of what Mama was having to face, what she was having to *do* – well, I made myself go on, so as not to let her down.'

'I always let her down,' Aylesbury said with a moan.

'You mustn't. And I'll tell you how to go on. When I got a

134

really terrible wound in front of me to dress, one that made me feel sick and faint, I managed by thinking of it as separate from the person. Not a wounded soldier, but just a leg, all on its own, with no person attached. And I'd think, well, here's some blood that needs wiping away, and here's a splinter that needs removing, just as if it was – I don't know – a piece of carpentry, or some other job like that to be done.'

Aylesbury looked at her helplessly, and she went on, 'So you see, when you have to face up to some terrible dowager – all purple turban and diamonds the size of pigeons' eggs – just break her down into little pieces. Here's a mouth that's asked a question, and there's an ear that I've got to speak into, and there's a gown I have to admire without laughing –'

He grinned reluctantly. 'Maybe I could,' he said.

'Of course you could. Just don't think of them as people. And I'll tell you something else I've learned, Aylesbury – when they talk to you, they don't really think of you as a person, either. All you've got to do is memorise the things each set of people expects you to say, and say them. They won't care if you mean them or not. They don't really want to know what you think. They just want to hear the right things said at the right time.'

'But how will I know what's the right thing?'

'I'll help you. And I expect Tommy knows a lot of them. He was going around drawing-rooms with Mama when you and I were still in the nursery.'

'Yes,' Aylesbury said slowly, feeling more comfortable. 'I do thank you, Rosy. It's very kind of you to take all this trouble with me. But how do you know all these things? You suddenly seem very grown up and wise.'

'Oh, when a man knows he's to be hanged in a fortnight, it concentrates his mind wonderfully, you know,' she said casually. 'Come on, they're rested now. Let's have one last gallop to the park gates.'

At his mother's request, Weston entered her dressing-room and found her alone, sitting before the mirror. She turned, and her face lit at the sight of him.

'My dear boy!' She held out her arms, and he went to her to be embraced.

'Well, Mother?'

'You can't think how good it is to hear you call me that! Sit down, my darling, sit here.' She moved over so that he could share with her the long stool in front of the dressing-table. He sat, and picked up a small pot she had been using and examined it.

'Rowland's Essence of Magnolia – for a glowing, delicate complexion,' he read. 'What's this? Mother, have you taken to using cosmetic lotions? I'm shocked! Does Lord Theakston know?'

'Don't tease me,' she said. 'It's Theakston's own suggestion – my skin gets so dry when I'm out riding all day that it's sometimes quite uncomfortable. It's medicinal, you see – not cosmetic.'

Weston put the jar down and smiled at her. 'I didn't think it could be to make you more beautiful. You're already as beautiful as an angel – any more'd be unfair.'

'Such nonsense! You're getting to be an accomplished flatterer,' she said, pleased in spite of herself. 'Oh, but I've missed you, Tom! Tell me, how do you go on at Eton? Are you happy there? Have you made many friends?'

'I do well enough, Mother. Hampton's settled down, and his stutter's almost gone. I think he'll do very well, next half.'

'And Aylesbury?'

'He's begun to make friends amongst the seniors, which is a good thing. It isn't right that he should be with me and Hampton all the time. It makes the other senior men think he's a muff.' He caught her involuntary expression, and said sternly, 'You don't give him credit, Mother. There's a lot of good about him. You'll see, once he's got over his shyness.'

Lucy stirred restlessly. 'But why does he always appear such a stammering ninny in front of me? When I asked him how he liked the horse this evening, for instance –'

'Because he's frightened of you. If only you could be gentler with him –'

'If he weren't so frightened of me, I could be kinder to him,' she countered. 'But it irritates me when he starts like a deer every time I speak to him.' She sighed. 'I know it's unfair, Tom, but I just can't love him as I do you.'

'Yet he's my brother,' Thomas said simply. 'My father's son. If you love me for my father's sake, why not Aylesbury?'

'I don't know,' she said helplessly. 'I think sometimes

perhaps I shouldn't have told you that. It seems to make things more complicated.'

'You had to tell me,' he said. 'You can't keep secrets from me.'

'No,' she agreed, looking with renewed and astonished love at his calm, intelligent face. He was not like a child, at moments like these, but a companion; but then he had been her shadow since he was four years old. 'Does Aylesbury know – about his real father?'

'No,' he lied easily. 'But in any case, what's a "real" father? Lord Aylesbury accepted him, so he was his father in every possible way that mattered. For the rest –' He shrugged, and then seeing her grave expression, grinned and said, 'He's the earl and I'm the captain's son, and we both know who has the best of it!'

She laughed with a sudden release of tension. 'But you haven't told me how *you* are getting on at Eton,' she said. 'Do you like it?'

'Yes,' he said, though without great enthusiasm. 'It's pretty country, and some of the other boys are jolly. But the rules and traditions are so foolish, it's hard sometimes to make myself remember them.'

'That's heresy,' Lucy said. 'Traditions are sacred, and the rules –' She hesitated, not knowing, of course, what they might be. 'Well, what would the place be without rules? You have to learn to obey, my darling. We all need to understand discipline.'

'Yes, I know that,' he began, and wondered whether he could explain to her how it seemed to him that there was no good reason for any one rule rather than another; that they could have been taught discipline just as well sitting at their desks with pen and paper, writing it down like a mathematical theory. The strange rituals, the beatings, the bullyings, the fagging and flogging, the bounds and out-of-bounds, the where-you-might-wear-a-hat, the what-you-might-eat and where-you-might-walk, all seemed to him as arbitrary and therefore pointless as a pattern of raindrops in the dust. He conformed to it all because his mother wanted him to succeed in that strange world, and he wanted to please her, but as to its having any *intrinsic* value, his native intellect denied it utterly.

137

He contemplated for a moment trying to tell her all that; but then, looking at her adored face, he saw the anxious look in her eyes, and noticed for the first time the faint hatching of fine lines around them. He realised that she was not the other half of his soul, and though he loved her and knew she loved him, there were ways in which they were different. She was of a different generation: she probably wouldn't understand.

So he said, 'I do all the things I'm supposed to do. I like it there, Mother, but I'd sooner be at home with you.'

The anxious look disappeared. She opened her mouth to speak, but was prevented by a scratching on the door, which opened to admit the polite head of Lord Theakston.

'May I?'

'Yes, come in, Danby.'

The body, in a handsome maroon silk dressing-gown, followed the head. Theakston looked expectantly from one to the other, and then said, 'Well, is it done? Have you told him, my love?'

Lucy smiled at her husband. 'Not yet, I haven't had the chance. But now you're here, I think you should do it.'

'Oh, no, surely it would come better from you?'

'I insist, Danby. You're the head of the family now.'

Thomas looked from one to the other. 'Is something in the wind, sir?'

Lord Theakston, unexpectedly shy, stood before Weston, tried out his hands in his pockets and then behind his back, cleared his throat a couple of times, and plunged in. 'The thing is, Thomas, that I felt – well, your mother and I felt – that your position was rather anomalous. Perhaps a trifle uncomfortable for you at times.'

'Sir?'

'You know – being with your brother and mother and sister, and having to pretend not to be related. And then again, I wondered if you might sometimes worry about your future. I know you'll have your father's money, but it isn't a large fortune, and you have no official family. No-one to fall back on, so to speak.'

'No, sir,' Thomas said, still mystified.

'So your mother and I felt that it would make things easier all round – make the situation tidier, if you like –'

'It was Theakston thought of it,' Lucy interrupted. 'I'm

ashamed to say it didn't occur to me, though as soon as he said it, of course, I agreed entirely. Tom, with your approval, Theakston would like to adopt you as his son. Legally, you know – all the papers. And then we'll really be your parents. You'll inherit anything Theakston has to leave, and Aylesbury will be your brother, and you'll be able to call me Mama in public –'

'And me Sir, of course,' Danby finished with a glimmering eye.

'What do you think, Tom? Does it please you?'

He looked from one to the other, for once in his life at a loss for words. He was, after all, in spite of his precocity, not yet quite thirteen. 'Yes,' he said at last. 'Very much.' He looked at Danby. 'Thank you, sir.'

Danby beamed at him shyly. 'Very fond of you, my boy – and I've known you all your life. Almost feel as though you *were* my son.'

'I'll try not to let you down, sir,' Thomas said in a subdued voice. He dared not look at his mother.

'You won't,' Danby said quietly. This thoughtful boy with Lucy's face and Weston's eyes was everything he'd have wanted in a child. He had loved Lucy all his life, and if he couldn't have a child of his own out of her, he'd settle for Weston's boy. He had liked and admired Weston, and he owed him a great debt: if Weston hadn't died at Trafalgar, he would have been the one to win Lucy when her widowhood left her free. Danby wouldn't have stood a chance while Weston lived; the least he could do was to take care of his son.

'Then it's agreed,' Lucy said. 'We'll announce it at dinner tomorrow, and Beguid shall draw up the papers at once. And as soon as it's all settled, we'll have a grand party to celebrate. Oh, I am so glad you thought of it, Danby! It's the best thing that's ever happened!'

She looked from her husband to her son with a glorious smile of satisfaction, and all the softness of fulfilled love; and they both thought she had never looked more beautiful.

Rosamund and Marcus, dressed for riding, clattered down the wide oak staircase. It led to what had been the entrance hall of the original, Tudor building, but since the entire house had been turned around by the eighteenth-century additions, the

Oak Hall with its broad panelling and exquisite lacework carving was now at the back, and merely a convenient short-cut to the stableyard.

'So what do you think of this scheme of your step-papa's, to adopt Tom Weston?' Marcus asked her.

'I think it's splendid – don't you? And it will make everything much easier for us all.' She glanced at him. 'I suppose you must know that he's Mama's son?'

'I imagine that's the best-known secret in London,' Marcus said with a smile.

'Hmph. Well, she and the Captain did live together quite openly, so I suppose everyone guesses. However, I call Tommy a regular little trump, and I think it's first-rate.'

'It will certainly –' They went out into the courtyard, and Marcus stopped dead at the sight of the two horses waiting for them, being held by a pair of grooms. 'I say, Rosy, that's Magnus Apollo, isn't it?'

'Of course,' Rosamund said, gathering up the fullness of her skirt and stepping up onto the mounting-block.

'But you can't mean to ride him, surely?' Marcus said in alarm. Rosamund was taller than her mother, but Magnus still made her look slight and fragile. 'Does your mother know?'

She laughed at that. 'Of course she does, simpleton. Do you think I'd dare take him otherwise? Mother trusts me with him.' She put her foot in the stirrup and stepped up, and the big bay waltzed forward and back against the groom's restraining hand as her weight came onto the saddle.

'But he's too big and strong for you,' Marcus objected.

'Pho! Don't talk nonsense,' she said as she settled her skirts. 'Do you think Mother would let me ride him if there were the least danger? Hurry up, Marcus, do, or I'll go without you.'

He hurried, swinging himself up onto the decent-looking hack which had been provided for him, as he had no horses of his own to bring. Her last answer hadn't reassured him at all, since he knew that Lady Theakston trusted Rosamund not to hurt her horse, rather than not to hurt herself. But he was beginning to learn that there was no future in arguing with Rosamund; and he had graduated in holding his tongue from the very best of schools – his mother's.

They trotted out of the yard into the park. As soon as they got onto the turf, Magnus wanted to gallop, and began to fly-buck and canter on the spot. Rosamund held him, not in the least perturbed by his antics; but Marcus watched him flexing his jaw against the curb, and knew that she controlled him only because he was willing to be controlled. He was a big, strong horse, and if he decided to defy her, she would not have the strength to hold him – it was as simple as that.

After a few minutes he settled down into a high, springy trot which broke into a canter every few paces, but which was obviously more comfortable to sit than the fast trot Marcus's mount was forced to adopt in order to keep up. It made it difficult to hold a conversation: he was aware that no man looked his best posting along at double time like a monkey on a stick. He wished he had suggested a walk instead of a ride; but a walk would not have carried them so certainly away from everyone else and into privacy.

'Is your mother really going to hold a point-to-point?' he asked after a moment, looking for a neutral subject.

'Of course. She wants Aylesbury to have a chance to shine, and though he's very shy with people, he isn't at all a bad rider. What do you think of his new horse?'

'A very useful type,' Marcus said. 'And I should think it'll do well over country – nice quarters.' He smiled at her with some relief. 'I didn't understand that the point-to-point was for Aylesbury's sake. I was afraid – but of course, he wouldn't stand a chance of winning if your mother rode against him.'

'Oh, Mother will ride, all right,' Rosamund said casually, shattering his hopes. 'She's been longing to race Magnus ever since she got him, though of course she wouldn't do it in public. But here on our own land, against only family and close friends, Papa Danby says it will be quite all right.'

Marcus looked grave. 'Is that the advice he's given her? I can hardly believe it. Surely Lord Theakston doesn't believe that sort of thing is acceptable?'

Rosamund looked at him in surprise. 'Now what? What are you talking about, Marcus? Who is there to object?'

'Well, my mother says –'

Rosamund's expression soured. 'Oh, your mother! I might have guessed. What precisely is her objection, pray?'

'It isn't only her opinion, you know,' he said defensively.

141

'There will be plenty of people who will say it's *mauvais ton*.'

'Well we don't care for them, do we?' Rosamund said unkindly. 'We Morland women have always done pretty much as we please, and I believe we can be trusted to draw the line between what's proper and what isn't for ourselves – don't you?'

He read between her lines with alarm. 'You don't mean – oh Rosy, you aren't going to ride in this race yourself?'

'Of course I am. Mother's going to let me have Hotspur for the day, and I shall give a good account of myself, I promise you.'

'Oh Rosy, please, please don't! It's bad enough –'

He cut himself off abruptly, and her brows snapped together. 'What's bad enough?'

He looked as though he wished he'd bitten out his tongue before starting this. 'Nothing. Nothing at all.'

'No, come on, out with it. What has your mother been saying about me now? Don't you think I've noticed her frosty looks? She was almost shattering glasses with them at dinner last night. You'd better tell, Marcus, and get it over with. I've a right to know, haven't I?'

'She said –' He swallowed nervously. 'She was unhappy to learn that you had dined alone at an inn with a man of unsavoury reputation. Now I told her it was all nonsense,' he went on hastily, 'and that you'd never do such a thing in a thousand years –'

'I certainly wouldn't!' Rosamund had begun to laugh.

'And I said she shouldn't listen to gossip, but she said she had it from an impeccable source, and – oh Rosy, please don't laugh!'

'I can't help it,' she said. 'Marcus, you're such a fool! Why don't you tell her to mind her knitting? Or alternatively, tell me that you can no longer associate with a woman of impaired reputation? But do one thing or the other! If you go on straddling two horses like this, you'll give yourself nothing but pain.'

'It isn't true, then?'

'That's for you to decide. You miss the point.'

She closed her lips firmly, and they rode on in silence for a while, Rosamund still struggling with amusement, though there was a hint of hurt in it; Marcus struggling with far weightier adjustments.

'Rosamund, I do love you very much,' he began at last.

'You've a curious way of showing it.'

'What do you mean?'

'You're strangely willing to believe the worst of me, on the flimsiest of evidence.'

'But I'm not! I didn't! I told Mama –!'

'I'm not interested in her opinion, Marcus. I don't behave as I do in order to please her or offend her; and I wish you would decide for yourself what *you* mind, and stick to that. And now I'm going to have a gallop, because otherwise I think I may very well say something I shall regret.'

'But Rosamund –!'

She was gone. She had no need to spur Magnus on, only to yield with her hands, and he sprang away like a stag. Marcus was half-thrilled, half-appalled by the animal's speed. His own mount was jogging and tugging, not wanting to be left behind, and he let it go, and leaning forward urged it on in pursuit. There wasn't the slightest chance of drawing level with Magnus Apollo, but he felt he must at least keep the big horse in sight.

They galloped across open parkland, and after the first mad dash, Magnus settled into a ground-eating hunting stride which left Marcus's horse gradually further behind. Marcus kept his eyes fixed on the slim, straight back ahead of him, still anxious, though glad to see how secure she looked in the saddle.

Now they came to widely scattered trees, and beyond them was the reflected shine of the river which divided Wolvercote Park from Pixey Mead. Rosamund turned Magnus southward to gallop parallel with the river, and Marcus took the opportunity to cut a corner and catch up with her a little. After a little less than half a mile they began to run out of parkland as they came up to the mill. Marcus thought Rosamund would turn again to continue round the perimeter of the park, but instead she drove straight on, plainly heading for the open spaces of the common beyond the mill.

'Rosy, turn back!' he shouted. He didn't want to race on like this, with nothing to address himself to but her back. He wanted a pleasant ride side by side, with the chance to talk to her properly and privately. 'Turn back!' he shouted again, thinking she hadn't heard.

She flung a glance at him over her shoulder, and then he

saw her push Magnus on. She had misunderstood his intention, thought he was trying to stop her for her own safety. Exasperated, he shouted, 'No, Rosy!' and simply made things worse.

Magnus hopped over the backwater – the mill reservoir – like a contemptuous cat, cantered five paces along the bank beside the wheel, sprang over the narrow part of the race, and was then divided from the common by nothing but the end of the mill-cottage garden and the two hedges that bounded it. The hedges were not high, and the garden there came down to a point where it used up an odd piece of land between the river and the lane; but still it made a broad and awkward jump, especially since there was only a short run-up for the horses – only a couple of strides.

One, two, and Magnus went up into the air like a Congreve rocket, almost vertically, cleared both hedges with his forelegs, and brushed through with a snapping of small twigs with his hind legs. Marcus was even then gathering his own horse and driving it forward – feeling its reluctance but having no choice but to follow – when he heard Rosamund's cry of dismay and saw her leave the saddle and fly off sideways, starfished against the grey sky, and fall out of sight.

Marcus was right on top of the hedge: no way to go but forwards. 'Go on!' he roared at his horse, thumping its sides as it quivered on the brink of refusal. His determination was enough to make it jump, a rather clumsy lurch which carried it through rather than over both hedges to land with a stumble on the turf beyond. He dragged it to a halt and was out of the saddle even as he took in the scene – a ring of brown cows looking very surprised, Magnus standing, his eyes wide and his head up, and Rosamund lying on the grass, a sprawled blue figure against the green, horribly still.

'Oh God,' Marcus cried, staggering towards her, his legs suddenly weak, towing his horse behind him from a horseman's instinct never to let go of the reins. She was dead, his mind told him with hideous cold certainty. Her neck was broken, she was dead, his mother's worst prophecies had come true. 'She'll break her neck one day, careering about the countryside in that hoydenish fashion.' In that instant he knew both how much he loved Rosamund, and how much he hated his mother.

144

And then he saw that the reason Magnus was still standing there was that Rosamund, from that same horseman's instinct, had kept hold of the reins when she fell; as the horse pulled at them uncomfortably, she groaned and sat up. Marcus flung himself down on his knees beside her on the grass. She was laughing and moaning all at once, rubbing her side with her free hand and trying to catch her breath.

'Rosamund! Oh God! Are you all right?'

'Ooh!' she groaned, but it was rueful rather than agonised. 'That was stupid! Oh dear, I do ache!'

'You're hurt! Keep still – you've broken your ribs!'

'Not my ribs, but my vanity's bruised. It's all right, Marcus, I'm not hurt – I've just had the breath knocked out of me. My own fault – I should have known there wasn't room for a third stride there, for a horse of his size.'

'What?' Marcus said, bewildered.

'He took off before I was ready and I lost my balance, that's all. My fault entirely. Hotspur does it so neatly, but of course Magnus is nearly two hands bigger.' Magnus lowered his head and blew in her hair, and then began calmly to graze, while Rosamund, slipping the reins over her arm, brushed at the grass and dried cow-dung decorating her habit. 'Look at the state of me!'

Marcus felt as though he had stepped up a step that wasn't there. He sat down with a jolt on the grass, waited an instant for his insides to resume their accustomed positions, and then said as steadily as he could, 'I thought you were killed.'

She glanced up from her brushing with an innocent, amused and affectionate look. 'What, from falling off a horse? Don't be silly.'

As a remark, it was the essence of her. Suddenly it was all too much for him. He began to laugh. 'Oh Rosy, Rosy! Oh, that is so like you! Oh my dear little cousin, I do love you so!'

She grinned impishly. 'Come, that's better. You never used to be so solemn and pompous, when I was a little girl in plaits and you were my great hero.'

'I know. I don't know what's happened to me lately. I seem to have lost my lightness of touch.'

'I expect it was the war and everything,' she said kindly. 'But you'll have to get used to things like this if you mean to marry me. Not that I mean to tumble off horses every day of the week, of course, but I shan't stop doing things just because there's a risk –'

'What did you say?'

'I said I don't intend to fall off once a day, just to let you think you're a better rider than me,' she said mischievously. 'It's too undignified, for one thing, and it's ruinous to one's clothes.'

He captured her hand and her attention. 'Rosy, *will* you marry me?'

She was quiet suddenly, looking into his face with a thoughtful gaze that made him feel very exposed. He wished he knew what that long, searching look meant. He wished he could be worthy of her. If she would marry him, he damn' well meant to try to be. He closed his other hand about hers, too. 'Rosy? Will you?'

'I was right, wasn't I?' she said. 'You did intend to ask me?'

'Yes. That's why I suggested the ride – but there wasn't really an opportunity to –'

Her hand tightened. 'I know, I made it too uncomfortable for you. I behave badly sometimes,' she sighed. 'I'm sorry.'

'No, no, it was my fault,' he said. 'I was being such a wet Monday. You were very patient with me, considering how I was abusing you.'

A faint smile came into her eyes. 'Marcus, I won't marry your mother. You do understand that?'

His own answered it. 'I won't ask you to. But you will marry me?'

It wasn't much of a hesitation, but it was agonising to him. 'Yes,' she said. 'I will marry you.'

He closed his eyes with relief. 'Thank you,' he sighed.

'But it's the devil of a place to choose to propose to me,' she grumbled.

BOOK TWO

Acts of God

Now, 'tis our boast that we can quell
The wildest passions in their rage,
Can their destructive force repel,
And their impetuous wrath assuage.

George Crabbe: *Late Wisdom*

CHAPTER EIGHT

'The glass is dropping,' Edward said, standing up from the breakfast table. 'I think we're in for some bad weather.'

'But it's been so mild,' James said, engaged with a pork chop. This was the last of the pig they had killed for Christmas – and a good pig it had been, fed on parsnips and windfall apples, to make the meat sweet and tender.

'Too mild,' Edward said shortly. 'Unseasonable for January. We were bound to pay for it sooner or later.'

'What a Methodist you'd have made,' James said. 'Never happy unless things are going badly.'

Edward ignored this. 'I'm going to get the merinos in off the North Field and put them in the Fellbrook close. I want to keep my eye on them, and if there's hard weather to come, I don't want to find myself cut off from them.'

'Just as you please, old fellow,' James said, absorbing the last of the chop and the front page of the newspaper at the same time. Edward paused and frowned at him. 'What *is* that you're reading?'

James looked up at last, grinning. 'It's this new radical sheet everyone's getting so excited about – *Black Dwarf*. Provides a great deal of unintentional amusement.'

'Oh, Tuppenny Trash, is it?' said Miss Rosedale with interest. 'I've heard about it, of course, but I've never seen one.'

'How can a newspaper cost only tuppence?' Héloïse asked, buttering a bun. 'I thought that the Stamp Duty alone was fourpence?'

'It is; but this man Cobbett, who used to put out the *Political Register*, found a way round it – made it smaller, so that it fell under the heading of pamphlet instead of newspaper. There's no stamp duty on pamphlets, you see. And then, of course, the other reformists followed suit. What's the name of the *Black Dwarf* man?'

'Wooler,' James said. 'He has a tongue like a cat o' nine tails, and some of the things he says are so outrageous –'

'You shouldn't bring that sort of seditious rubbish into the house, Jamie,' Edward said, feeling the point was in danger of being missed. 'It's disgusting. And suppose the servants see it? Do you want to encourage treason and revolution in our own home?'

'Oh come –!' James protested.

'I mean it. Don't you know how dangerous the times are? The country's in ferment. Everywhere you look the lower orders are meeting together in large numbers and talking sedition.'

'Is it not better for them to talk than to act?' said Father Moineau.

'Talking leads to acting,' Edward said shortly.

'Gammon!' from James.

'Gammon, is it?' Edward turned on him hotly. 'What about Spa Fields, only a month ago? Or have you conveniently forgotten that?'

'Oh, that was just Orator Hunt,' James began uncomfortably. 'He was only spouting his franchise nonsense.'

'Wearing a Cap of Liberty and waving the Tricolor. And the second of his meetings turned into a march on the Tower. That's exactly how the French Revolution started, with the storming of the Bastille. An army marched through the streets of London – shops were looted – a man was killed – what more do you want? We've got to stamp out this nonsense before it goes any further. And I tell you something else,' he went on, silencing whatever James was about to say. 'There's something going on in the Hampden Clubs. I can't find out what it is, but they're seething like an ant's nest, and there's going to be trouble from them before we're much older.'

With that he turned and stumped out, and Tiger oozed out from under the table and padded after him.

'Oh dear, poor Edward,' Héloïse said anxiously. 'He does seem upset.'

'Pay no attention,' James said blithely. 'I never do. He's always fulminating about something.'

'But he looks so tired. He does too much. He is not a young man any more.'

'He always did too much. You'll never stop him. That's just

150

Ned, Marmoset. He likes to keep busy, that's all.'

'But now there's the worry about the reformists, too. I don't think he is looking well.'

'Old Ned's as strong as a horse,' James said, wiping his lips and standing up. He came round the table to kiss his wife. 'If you want to worry about anyone, worry about me. I've got a youngster to back this morning, and from the look in his eye, he's going to give me trouble.'

'Oh, be careful, James,' she said at once, and he grinned. 'Now *that's* better.'

Father Moineau got up too, and went off to collect his pupils from the nursery, and Sophie went away to write a letter to Rosamund, with whom she kept up a regular correspondence, leaving Héloïse and Miss Rosedale alone at the table.

After a moment, Miss Rosedale cleared her throat and said, 'I'm glad to have a moment in private with you, ma'am. There's something I want to speak to you about – a delicate matter.'

Héloïse looked blank, unable to imagine what matter of delicacy there could be between them. 'Is something wrong?'

'No – well, yes, in a way. It has been on my mind for some time, and I'm afraid it may have been on yours, too, without your knowing quite how to broach it.' Héloïse looked more than ever mystified, and Miss Rosedale plunged on, an uncharacteristic blush colouring her sensible cheeks. 'The fact is that I think it's time – and past time – that I thought about looking for another position.'

'You mean you want to leave us?' A more flattering dismay no governess could have hoped to see on her employer's face. 'But – but I thought you were happy here. I thought you liked us.'

Miss Rosedale smiled ruefully. 'I am. I do. Good Lord, no-one could have met with more kindness than I have at Morland Place. But Mathilde is married, and Sophie is "out", and the boys have Father Moineau. There's nothing for me to do here any more.'

'But you do so much for me,' Héloïse said, and stopped, and began again, tentatively. 'Perhaps – if it is a matter of your salary, I think we could manage a small increase –'

Now Miss Rosedale laughed aloud. 'Oh ma'am! It isn't

that! Quite the opposite – I can't justify the salary you pay me now. I'm not earning my keep, and I feel guilty about it. And knowing you, I'm afraid you are thinking the same thing, but are too kind to say so straight out.'

Héloïse looked relieved. 'If *that* is all your trouble ... Let us be quite frank with each other: do you want to leave? Would you be happier in another position?'

'No,' she said hesitantly. 'No, I don't want to go. I've come to regard this as my home. But –'

'There is no "but". Dear Rosey, I could not do without you, and nor could Sophie, and I don't want you to go. Please stay! In a little while, if you'll be patient, I expect there will be babies again. Sophie will marry one day, and perhaps she will send her sons to you. And Mathilde may not want her children taught by a stranger. And then when the boys grow up and marry –'

'Dear ma'am, you don't need to offer me any other inducement to stay, than to say you want me! I'm not a young woman, and uprooting myself at this time of my life was not something I looked forward to.'

Héloïse sighed with satisfaction and stood up. 'Then that's settled. You will stay, please, and regard this as your home. And don't frighten me again in that way.'

'I won't, I promise,' Miss Rosedale said. She managed to wait until Héloïse had left the room before rummaging in her sleeve for her big white handkerchief. Seldom could an educationist have had less to cry about, she knew, which made the lump in her throat doubly hard to swallow.

That Edward's prediction of a storm was right was apparent to everyone by the middle of the day. The barometer went on falling, through *Rain* and *Much Rain* to the Stygian depths of *Stormy*. Clouds crept up silently like assassins from the south-west and gathered in a dark and threatening mass. The swans disappeared off the moat, and the chickens went to roost at noon, huddling in the hen-house as though it were night time. Indeed, it began to get dark at about two o'clock, and the trees, which had been eerily still all day, began to whisper intermittently of impending trouble.

The brooding atmosphere made Héloïse nervous, and she was glad as the premature darkness thickened and the wind began to get up, to have all her family safe indoors. Edward and James were the last, coming in together from the yard, having checked that the horses were settled and that their half-doors were shut and bolted.

'It's going to blow some,' James said, rubbing his hands before the hall fire. Tiger nudged him out of the way and gazed into the flames, reflecting them in his strange yellow eyes. 'Do you think we ought to have the shutters put up, Ned?'

'Might as well,' Edward said. 'Better safe than sorry. I'll tell Ottershaw.'

'Did you get the sheep in?' Héloïse asked.

'Yes. They know there's a bad one coming,' he said. 'We hardly needed dogs. As soon as we opened the gate they came streaming through and made for the close of their own accord.'

'Strange how animals know, isn't it? The horses are restless, too,' James said. 'I've warned the grooms at Twelvetrees to stay alert. It only takes the crash of a tile coming off the roof, or something blowing over, to set them all panicking.' He looked around, at a loss for a moment. 'What time will dinner be?'

'At five o'clock, as always,' Héloïse said. 'We didn't look to have you all at home an hour before time.'

'No matter. I'll go and have a game of merels with Benedict until the dressing-bell. That boy is getting uncannily good at it.'

'They are still at their lessons. They don't finish until five.'

'We'll make today a special day,' James said, heading for the stairs.

The wind went on rising. After dinner, James went out to check on the horses again, and came back to report that it was now blowing a gale. 'A real sou'wester. It was quite hard getting across the yard. But all's peaceful inside the stables – like a haven, when you come in out of the wind. I've set two lads to refilling the hay-nets. The horses will be happy enough as long as they've got something to chew. Oh,' he laughed, 'and I counted eleven cats in there! Trust them to know a warm, safe place. There was one actually sitting on Victor's back, couched down on his loins with its paws tucked in and its ears at half-mast!'

153

They gathered around the drawing-room fire for the evening. It burned brightly with a red heart and white-gold flames too hot to allow the logs to spit and crack as they usually did. The wind crooned around the side of the house, making the drawing-room shutters creak and click as they worked against their fastenings, and moaned in the chimney with a strangely human voice.

'I love that sound,' Sophie said, looking up for a moment from her sewing. 'It makes indoors feel so warm and safe.'

'It is strange that there is no rain, though,' Héloïse said, holding up the baby-dress she was smocking for Mathilde's expected baby, to see if the pleating was even. The baby was due at any time, now – James's first grandchild. 'I wonder if it will be a girl or a boy,' she murmured.

'Boy, of course,' James said.

'It's hard to think of Mathilde being a mother,' Sophie said.

Héloïse smiled. 'Harder for me than for you. To me she is still the little girl I brought up.'

Hardest of all for me, Edward thought, but he said nothing. He looked at the baby-dress and then away again. The wind rose a pitch, and Tiger, lying flat out, belly to the fire, lifted his head for a moment as if he had heard a distant voice. 'There'll be some branches down tomorrow,' Edward said to change the subject. 'Plenty of clearing-up to do – as if we weren't busy enough already. Well,' he stood up, 'I think I shall go on up to bed. Good night, everyone.'

A murmured chorus answered him, and Héloïse looked up and smiled as he passed her chair. A little later, she too got up. 'I've done enough for tonight. My eyes are not what they were for this small stitchery. I think I shall go to the chapel one last time before bed.'

Their night candles were all assembled ready on the pier table outside the drawing-room door. Héloïse took hers up and lit it from the common candle, and walked down the little passage past the steward's room door to the chapel. Inside all was dark except for the distant red glow of the sanctuary-lamp. She closed the door behind her and walked forward down the aisle. Her shadow jumped away from her and flung itself upwards across the walls as her candle flame wavered. The windows must not fit quite tightly, she thought. The air should have been still, but there was quite a bit of movement.

In here, in the big silence of the high-roofed space, the sound of the wind was much more in evidence, and she knew a moment of anxiety as she realised how much it had risen even since dinner. It hooned about the walls with a wild glee, and battered intermittently against the roof as though it were trying to break in. She wondered about the tall east window above the altar – that would make a fine mess if it fell in. But it was on the leeward side of the house, and it had stood up to storms before. Indeed, all the house had. Whatever might happen outside, here they were safe. Sanctuary, she thought: these walls kept out the wild wind as the church in its spiritual sense kept out the storm of chaos which was Evil.

She turned aside into the smaller space of the Lady Chapel, all in darkness, except where an occasional glint hinted at a gold picture-frame or the rim of a brass fitting. The candle-light flowed like pale water before her, lapping up over the white lace-edged cloth of the altar to the foot of the ancient wooden statue of the Virgin. It stood between two silver candlesticks, prettily wrought in silver. On an impulse, she decided to light the candles from her own. Standing close up to the altar, she could smell through the hot wax the resinous perfume of the sprays of pine in the vases, and see the glassy glint of the dark holly-leaves. No flowers for the Lady in this dead heart of January; but the pine was sweet, and the holly was decorative, studded with bright berries – red beads like drops of blood.

The second candle took, and the flame bloomed and steadied. 'There,' she said aloud, and stepped back to look at the effect. The wind rose for an instant, and one of the roof-beams, settling, made a cracking sound like a rifle-shot, which made her jump; and at the same time something far away in the house fell over with a clatter. 'Foolish,' she chided herself, clasping her hands and pressing them against her breast-bone to quiet the flutter of her heart. She would say one prayer, and then go to bed. She knelt on the step, and looked up at the altar.

How strange, she thought. The statue of the Lady, lit from both sides by the candles, seemed to quiver in the moving light. The robes were painted blue, but the delicate hands were gold, as was the face, whose features had grown blurred with great age. Whatever the intention of the original carver, it was now a soft, sweet face, with a gentle, almost sad expression; and as Héloïse gazed at it, it seemed almost as though it were weeping. Of course, she told herself, while her fascinated eyes never left the statue, it was only the way the light caught the imperfections in the gilding, but it did look, just for a moment, as though there were tiny sparkling tears moving on the gold cheeks.

And then there was another gust outside, and the flames ducked sideways for an instant and then brightened. The illusion was gone. The wind moaned and banged outside the house like a restless lunatic looking for a way in. Héloïse crossed herself, said her prayer, then rose and blew out the candles, and hastened up to bed and the warm shelter of James's arms.

She woke in the pitch darkness of the curtained bed with the suddenness of one called. What was it? She lay still for a moment, holding her breath while she listened and assembled the information from her senses. James asleep beside her, on his side, turned away from her, his breathing steady and quiet. Beyond the bed-curtains the house, all in stillness, everyone asleep and in their beds. Beyond the house – ah, there was calm! The mad riot of the wind had stopped. Was that what had wakened her? The eye of the storm must be passing over them. It was the cessation of sound which had drawn her up from sleep.

She breathed again, turned onto her back, and listened to the quietness. Of course, no house was ever completely silent, especially an old house like this, whose timber bones creaked and settled with a sound like a ship at sea. The bracket clock over the fireplace ticked slowly, and after a moment, she heard the rattle of raindrops on the window-pane – as characteristic, instantly recognisable a sound as the clicking of a dog's nails on a wooden floor, or the sound of a chess-piece being replaced on the board, or the summer sound of a ball hitting a cricket bat. Comforting, familiar sounds. Rain at last – or perhaps it had been raining for some time, but the wind-noise had been too great to hear it.

And speaking of wind – here it came again, the low hooning of the body of it against the walls, and the high whine of it over the lightning-rod which was on the chapel roof not far above her window. Yes, she thought, now you couldn't hear the rain any more. She sighed and turned back onto her side to sleep again, and James stirred at the same moment, half-waking and turning towards her.

And then the wind rose suddenly, wildly, its voice climbing to a demented shriek, startling her so that she clutched at James, waking him fully.

'What is it?' he muttered. The wind howled and battered at the house so that it almost seemed to shake. The elemental fury was frightening. Héloïse pressed against James. It was only a storm, she told herself; but the screaming of the wind made it seem horribly purposeful, as though some great, black being outside were trying to crack open their citadel to get at them.

And then there was the most tremendous, terrifying crash. Héloïse cried out.

James sat bolt upright. 'God! What is it?' he cried.

'James!'

It was like an earthquake. It was a huge, shattering crash, followed by a prolonged rumbling. The floor under them shook. The bedroom door flew open and crashed back against the wall, the bed-curtains sucked inwards, there were thuds and the tinkling of glass as objects fell from surfaces around the room.

'Get out! Get out!' James shouted. 'The house is coming down.'

'Dear God, protect us,' Héloïse gasped, struggling with the bedclothes and the curtains. It was dark – no moon, no stars. Something dreadful had happened beyond their bedchamber, the wind had got in, the lunatic was in the house, and they couldn't see. Her babies, she must get to her babies. And Sophie. Sobbing with fright and frustration, Héloïse managed to fling off the covers, shoved aside the hampering curtains, groped instinctively for the candle and the tinder-box, almost shrieked as James's hand fastened round her wrist.

'Put this on,' he said. Her robe was thrust into her hand. Beyond their room someone screamed and kept on screaming, not a shriek of pain but a howl of fear. No, it was not quite dark – through the open door the glimmer from the night-light in the hallway, miraculously still alight, gave the edge of things. Thank God, thank God! James in his nightgown was a pale shape flickering towards the door. Héloïse, still struggling into her robe, flung herself after him, terrified of being left alone.

Outside the air was choking with dust, there was something gritty underfoot, there was too much wind, and a strong, pungent smell of soot. Had the kitchen chimney caught fire again? The screamer's screams choked off into a gurgling sob. Someone shouted something. Sophie was beside her suddenly, her hand icy on Héloïse's wrist. 'What's happened? Oh Maman, is the house falling down? Are we going to die?'

Héloïse couldn't answer. There were more voices and shouting, and someone had a light. It flickered and bounced, illuminating the strange fog in the air. Down the passage past the long saloon, there was a knot of people jammed together where it turned the corner towards the nursery. There was Miss Rosedale, her face turned towards Héloïse, drawn with horror.

'My boys!' Héloïse cried out. Her feet felt like lead; she wanted to run but it was as if she were struggling up a steep hill with the wind pushing her back.

'They're all right.' Had Miss Rosedale really said that? Héloïse couldn't be sure. It was she who had the light – a chimney-lamp she had always kept by her in case the children ever wanted her in the night.

'Rosey?' Héloïse said, tasting soot.

'The boys are all right.'

Héloïse could hear Sophie's breath sobbing with fright. There was Father Moineau now, shoving people back from him, making a space. He turned towards James, his hands stretched straight out in front of him as though he were drowning and reaching for a rope. The wind gusted again, and there was another crash, making several people cry out. Father Moineau seemed to be trying to speak, but no words would come. His face was white like a clown's, and Héloïse realised belatedly that it was covered with plaster-dust.

'Get everyone downstairs into the hall.' The priest's words came at last. As James reached him he seized both his hands so hard that Héloïse saw James wince. Instinctively she thrust Sophie behind her as she reached them too. She saw James jolt as though he had been struck by a bolt of electricity, and at the same moment, looking past the priest, she saw what James saw, and her mind rejected it.

The North Bedroom – Edward's room – simply wasn't there any more. The outer wall had gone, and the floor was splintered and broken as though a giant fist had smashed through it from below, leaving jagged ends of floor-board sticking up. The wind was rioting triumphantly through the room, snatching at the torn ends of wallpaper, and even as Héloïse took her one, horrified, disbelieving look, a pencil rolled across what was left of the floor and leapt wildly out into the darkness.

'Get everyone downstairs into the hall. God knows how much more will come down.'

It was still the same sentence. She had seen it all in the space of that one sentence. The wind had brought down the sixty-foot kitchen chimney, ripping away the side of the house as it went, a horror of violation beyond comprehension.

'Does anyone sleep above?' Father Moineau was asking.

'No,' James said. 'I don't think so.' It was only a storage attic above Ned's room. Ned –?

'We must take a roll call when we get downstairs. But first –'

'Where's Ned?' James said at the same moment.

Father Moineau didn't answer. He was thrusting them away from the violated room. It contained no bed now. Héloïse saw that not all the whiteness of his face was plaster.

It was like being shut inside the imagination of a lunatic, Héloïse thought. It would have been impossible for any sane person to have imagined the devastation, the destruction, the mess, the rubble and chaos; or the suspension of time which made that night seem so endless in its horror.

In the comparative safety of the Great Hall they got all the servants together, some weeping and sobbing, some chattering hysterically, others white-faced and silent with shock; and Héloïse, as the crowd of them milled purposelessly in the flickering light, tried to check faces, to see if anyone was missing.

The nursery-maids were there with the children wrapped in blankets. Nicky and Bendy were heavy-eyed and bemused from sleep, not yet understanding what had happened. Sophie and Miss Rosedale took charge of them, and the rest of the women. How was it Sophie was suddenly so grown-up, so capable and calm? Her room was next to Edward's – the shock ought to have been worst for her.

Edward! The most urgent thing was to find him, and then to check on the extent of the damage. Héloïse, without knowing quite how she began, found herself lighting lamps: candles would be no use in that wind. Moineau was gathering the men together – ah, thank God for him now! James and Durban, his man, had disappeared into the shadows of the ruins of the kitchen to make sure there was no danger of fire. Héloïse wondered briefly about the horses, remembering James's words about the crash of a tile setting them into a panic. But there were grooms there, who slept above the stable. It was foolish to be thinking about horses, except of course that she was thinking about them so as not to think about –

– about Edward. He jumped into her mind, the stored picture of him saying goodnight and going off to bed. To bed. There was no bed in the room. She had a sickening and involuntary vision of him and the bed sliding out into the blackness. It was the worst nightmare of childhood. The last, best safety of bed, the one place which from infancy you knew was inviolable: pull the covers over your head to keep away the bad things. Safe in bed. No bed in the room. Edward –

Moineau was leading the men out. The wind was too strong to open the great door, so they were going out through the buttery. Ottershaw, strange in a plaid dressing-gown instead of his black coat, was holding the door and counting the men through, checking who was there. A good man, Ottershaw. He caught her eye over the heads, and instantly she thought of Barnard. She hadn't seen her cook anywhere. She mouthed the name at Ottershaw, and he jerked his head towards the kitchen. Yes, of course, he would have gone there straight away, to his beloved kitchen. But it might be dangerous. James should make him come back.

James and Durban were returning, dishevelled and blackened from the dust and soot, followed by Barnard, who was wrapping a cloth around a cut on his hand. James came to her and took her hands. He meant to reassure her, but he could not have known, she thought, what his face was expressing.

'Keep everyone here. I don't think any more will come down, but I can't be sure. There's no danger of fire, but the debris has fallen in the moat; and I'm afraid there may be flooding. I'm going out now to look for Ned.'

'Oh God, James –'

'Pray, Marmoset,' he said starkly. 'Pray as you've never prayed in your life before.'

Then he was gone, and Durban – and even Barnard, too. Miss Rosedale and Mrs Thomson had got everyone to keep still at last, and were checking who was present. Sophie had got one of the housemaids to make up the fire, and was organising the nursery-maids into making beds for the boys on the two Louis Quinze sofas which stood on either side. They were too hard and slippery for beds, but it was natural to want to have the children go back to sleep. And it gave Sophie something to do. There was nothing for Héloïse to do but wait; and to pray of course – except that her mind seemed numb, and she could not shape the inner phrases. Dear God, was as far as she could get. Over and over again. Dear God . . .

Dawn in January is laggard, and never later than when most longed for. The wind, having done its worst, eased and died down, but the cold rain streamed from clouds which obscured the moonlight that was needed so much. The men came in at last in the grey light of approaching dawn, soaked through – both from the rain, and from the waters of the moat. They came in muddy, dishevelled, dirty, with bleeding hands and broken nails from scrabbling through the rubble. They came with noses and lips blue and numb, and fingers stiff and swollen from the icy water. They came in carrying Edward on a makeshift litter fashioned out of timbers and coats.

James reached Héloïse first. 'He's alive,' he said in answer to the question in her face. 'But –' He shook his head several times, slowly, as though his senses were fuddled. His hair was plastered down with water to his scalp and there was a long scratch across one cheek. 'He'd been thrown almost clear, otherwise we wouldn't have found him so soon. But there was still a lot of stuff on top of him. Father Moineau thinks –' Again the shaking of the head.

'Go to the fire, James,' Héloïse said. 'You're wet through.' She caught the priest's eye over his shoulder. 'Father

Moineau and I will take care of Edward.'

James gave her a dazed look, as though he had not understood her. 'We couldn't find the dog,' he said in a small, clear voice. 'Tiger always slept beside his bed, but we couldn't find him.'

'We must send someone for the physician at once,' Héloïse said. 'Stephen, where's Stephen?'

'Here, my lady.'

'Are you fit to go?'

'Yes, my lady.' He turned away without further words. A good man too, Stephen. Sam and William were setting the litter down across two chairs, as close to the fire as possible. Edward's face was a mask of blood, his nightshirt dark and soaked with mud and blood and water. Héloïse felt herself begin to tremble at the sight of him, at the extent of the ruin. What to do? Where to begin? It was Brussels all over again, except this was Edward, dear, good Edward, her brother.

And James was bending over him, wiping the blood tenderly from his face with the torn end of his sleeve. He looked up at Héloïse. He was trembling with exhaustion, but he seemed beyond noticing even that. 'We couldn't find the dog,' he said again. 'I wanted to go on looking, but they wouldn't let me. We have to go back and find him. Ned will never forgive me if we don't find Tiger.'

Tears were running down his face as well as rain-water, but he didn't seem to be aware of it. Horses sometimes died when they got to that pitch of exhaustion and shock, she thought. She ached to comfort him, but was afraid to touch him, in case it was the one last thing that was too much.

Miss Rosedale was there at Héloïse's shoulder, calm and strong, directing the servants and smoothing small problems, to remove one burden from her mistress. So glad now, Héloïse thought, that she hadn't gone away. What would I do without Rosey? And now that Edward – no, unthinkable thought.

They did what little they could for Edward, cutting away the shreds of his nightshirt, washing off the blood and mud, drying him, trying to keep him warm. It all had to be done without moving him. His visible injuries, strangely, were not so very serious: a long, shallow gash across the scalp, numerous minor abrasions, a deep cut on one shin, a broken collar bone and several broken ribs.

'But there may be internal injuries,' said Moineau. There must be, said the tone of his voice.

Héloïse looked at Edward's white, still face. He had not stirred since they brought him in. His breathing was faint and shallow, his pulse weak. He was still with them, still fastened to the earth, but by such a fragile thread. 'It is very bad, isn't it?' she said quietly.

Moineau didn't speak, but he nodded.

'It's a miracle he's still alive,' Héloïse said after a moment. The dislocation of shock, and the strangeness of everything, was making it difficult for her to realise that this was not a dream, that this really was Edward lying here, that in a moment she would not blink and find everything back to normal. Random violence had broken open their lives and looted them, as a fox raids a nest, breaking eggs, crunching up nestlings. How could they have been so always vulnerable, and not known it? It was unreal, unbelievable.

'There's nothing more we can do now,' Moineau said at last, as if to himself. 'Just try to keep him warm.'

James came back from having, at Héloïse's insistence, dried and dressed himself. 'How is he?'

She hesitated, hating the naked hope in his voice.

Moineau answered. 'It's not good. He's very pale. He may have internal injuries, in which case –'

James made a surprising, hoarse sound, and dropped to his knees beside the litter. 'What shall we do if he dies?' he cried helplessly. 'What shall we do?' Héloïse went to him, put her hands on his shoulders, and he covered them with his own hands, gasping as he tried not to sob. 'God, don't let him die!'

'I'm praying, James,' she said.

'Yes, yes, keep praying. Oh God, he mustn't die!' He rocked a little on his knees, holding on to Héloïse's hands, and staring and staring at the wax-white face as though he might will it back to life and strength. 'He's only fifty-five. It isn't old really, is it? We're a long-lived family. Papa lived to his seventies, and Mama to her sixties. He's too young to die.'

He knows he's going to die, Héloïse thought, holding him tighter. She hadn't really believed it until that moment. James began to cry. 'If only we'd found Tiger,' he sobbed.

*

He died just before the doctor arrived, without regaining consciousness. Between one faint breath drawn, and the place where the next should have been, lay death, unseen, unmeasurable, inexplicable. How can it be like that? Héloïse wondered, as she had wondered before. For the whole human space and solidity and reality of a person simply to cease to be, in so little a time – and irreversibly – was incomprehensible, and unfair, oh unfair!

Exhaustion and shock, in a strange way, enabled them to go on. There was so much to be done, so much clearing up to do, massive repairs to be made to the fabric, real and spiritual, of their lives. They would feel it later, Héloïse thought. For now they were numbed to the pain, all of them, even James, who when the physician confirmed that Edward was dead, simply got up without a word and went away to carry on with what had to be done.

The wind had died down completely, leaving a grey, cold day with a steady rain falling out of a sky as blank as a white eye. First the animals must be seen to – always the animals first – and then the damage inspected. With Durban by his side, James stood out in the rain by the orchard wall and looked at the ruin of his home. He could see how the towering kitchen chimney had gone, collapsing outwards and ripping a bottle-shaped section of wall away. It had fallen almost in one piece, and the upper section lay like a red snake across the grass, the flaunching and pots lying shattered in the debris of part of the orchard wall.

But in its falling it had also torn away the side of the North Bedroom, and the floor beams which were so solidly set into the thickness of the wall. The kitchen had originally, in mediaeval times, reached all the way up to the roof: the other floors had been put in later, when people had ceased to sleep in communal rooms and wanted separate chambers. Edward's room had once been part of the great kitchen. It was as if the chimney had tried to claim back its own.

Oh, but the damage was so terrible, the mess so unspeakable, that he did not know where to begin. The exposed innards of the house – the bedroom and the kitchen – were pathetic and horrible; pieces of furniture seen from where they should never have been seen cried mutely for decent burial. There were bricks and rubble and tiles and wood scattered over such a vast area, half-filling the moat, whose waters were beginning to spread outwards over the bank in default of their usual channel; between the orchard and the moat what had been a smooth grassy walk was a trampled, muddy morass. They would never be able to clear it up, never. Weary and frightened, he thought they should just go away, all of them, evacuate the house and leave it as it was, go and live somewhere else and forget about Morland Place. It could never be the same again. Let it stand ruined as a mute memorial to Ned.

The thought caught him unawares, and despair filled him. He couldn't be dead, not old Ned, reliable, hard-working, always-there Edward; his mother's 'best of sons'; the quiet one, the eldest. They couldn't manage without him. *He* couldn't manage without him. Inside he cried out, like a child wanting things to be put right. Give him back! It isn't fair! Oh God, he wanted Ned back! He wanted to tell him how much he had always loved him, and relied on him, and how little he could contemplate coping with the future without him.

Durban was there beside him, did not quite touch his arm, but the gesture was implicit in his stance. 'What was made can be mended, sir,' he said quietly. He had understood James's despair at the enormity of the ruin, but not what the loss of Edward was already meaning.

'You'd better go and fetch John Skelwith here,' James heard himself say. His voice surprised him by its steadiness. 'He can advise us whether it's safe. I dare say there'll be some shoring-up to do. And he can start making arrangements for the repair and rebuilding. Ask him to come at once, if you please.'

'Yes, sir.' Durban went, leaving James standing alone in the rain. The sound, at least, was comforting, as it pattered and dripped. It had a mesmeric quality. How easy it would be, he thought, to lie down here on the wet grass and never get up again, just close his eyes and wait for death to come. But he couldn't. Always before there had been Edward to leave things to, Edward to see things got done. Papa had died, and Mama had died, but there had still been Edward, and all the responsibilities James had shirked all his life had devolved onto those sturdy, uncomplaining shoulders. Ned would never neglect a duty, however tiresome, never put his own comfort first. He had accused Ned in his heart before now of not really loving Morland Place as he, James, loved it. But who was it who had kept and cared for and defended it? Who had performed the full and thankless tasks, who had carried the final burden of responsibility?

'Oh Ned,' he said aloud, 'I never thanked you. I'm so sorry.' And he turned his face up to the rain and cried – humble tears, for the brother he had never appreciated, until it was too late.

John Skelwith arrived without Durban. He rode over to James and slid weakly from his horse's back, and stared at the ruined house, stunned and disbelieving.

'It's incredible. The chimney – the whole wall. It ought to have stood for ever. God, I can't believe it! How did it happen?'

James blinked at him through the rain. 'Didn't Durban tell you?'

'Durban? I haven't seen Durban. What happened, sir?'

'If you didn't see Durban, what are you doing here?' James asked, bewildered in his turn.

Skelwith shook his head as if to clear his senses. 'I came to ask her ladyship to come back with me. Mathilde went into labour this morning. Isn't it wonderful, sir? I'm frightened almost to death about it, but the midwife says she'll be all right, and that nothing will happen for hours yet, so I took the chance to slip out, but I daren't stay long. I wanted to let you know myself, and I know Mathilde would like her ladyship to be there. I thought she would want to – but of course, I never expected this! I suppose she won't want to leave at a time like this.'

It had to be done, though perhaps not as brutally as James did it. 'My brother is dead,' he said.

Skelwith didn't take it in. 'Dead? Who –? How –?'

'That,' James said, nodding towards the disembowelled chamber, 'was his bedroom.'

Skelwith's face screwed up with pain. 'Oh dear God!' he whimpered. 'Oh no, it can't be true!'

'It's true,' James said flatly. 'We found him under the rubble.' He tried and failed to elaborate, and then made a casting-away gesture with his hand. 'I sent Durban for you in

166

your professional capacity. The house needs to be made safe, and then of course it must be rebuilt. I want you to send your men along as soon as possible to begin repairs.'

Skelwith stared at him as if he could not believe what he was hearing. 'How can you –' he began; but he was not a stupid man, and he quickly saw how it was that James could. He pulled himself together. 'Yes, of course,' he said. 'You'll want tarpaulins over the gaps, and everything shored up. I'll send my men out straight away, with my best foreman. And now, if you'll forgive me, I must get back to my wife. Will you –' He swallowed. 'Will you say what's proper to her ladyship? And tell her about Mathilde? I'll call again as soon as I can, and –'

He stopped again. James's white, blank face was so hard to address. 'Sir,' he said, 'I am so shocked, and so sorry. I wish there were anything to be said at such a moment.' He hesitated, and then held out his hand. James looked at it as though he did not know what it was; and then he looked at Skelwith's face, and a bewildered look came into his eyes, and a living pain instead of the blankness. His mouth quivered, and then with a blind, clumsy movement they put their arms round each other. Skelwith was the taller man. His arms were round James's shoulders, and he stared over his bent head towards the gaping, wounded house.

His throat tightened and his eyes filled with tears. 'Oh Father,' he said.

CHAPTER NINE

Edward's funeral took place a week later. In that time, the builders had done a great deal: fixed tarpaulins, shored up the outer walls, and tidied the rubble into heaps. With its wounds decently bandaged, the house did not look quite so bad. Inside, the door to the North Bedroom had been nailed up, to prevent anyone from wandering in there by accident. Everything rescuable had been brought out of the rubble of the kitchen, and a temporary theatre of operations had been set up for Barnard in the servants' hall, including a cooking-stove, whose fumes were conducted away by an ingenious series of flues which emptied into the Red Room's chimney.

Life could go on; life did go on, and the shock of losing Edward was in some ways blunted by the disruption to routine caused by the storm-damage. They had not yet had time fully to miss him in their normal daily round, since everything was topsy-turvy, and no-one was in his accustomed place anyway.

'I keep thinking my uncle's just stepped out of the room for a moment,' Sophie said once during that week. 'I expect him to come back in at any moment.'

'Yes, I know,' Héloïse said. She felt just the same. It was different when Fanny died, though she had been ripped out of life just as violently. But there had never been any doubt that Fanny was missing – the silence told you so. Quiet Edward, camouflaged against his background so that he seemed like part of the house, was different. It felt as though he *must* be there, somewhere – if not in the drawing-room, in the steward's room; if not in the house, then somewhere about the fields.

They knew – James in particular knew – that they had so far come across only the tip of the mountain of tasks he used to do, the decisions he used to make, the questions he used to answer; but already things were piling up. There would have to be a reckoning, Héloïse thought, and a redivision of his responsibilities. But for the moment they were all simply struggling from day to day through the unfamiliar landscape of shock. After the funeral, she thought, then they would have to come to terms with it all.

Lucy came up from London with her husband, Rosamund and the boys for the funeral of her brother. Their other surviving sibling, Harry, was at sea, somewhere in the West Indies. Neither of them had seen him for so long, he was more remote to them than Edward.

Lucy and James embraced. 'Now there's only the two of us,' she said. She reached back to arms' length to look at him. This falling from the branch business, she thought, made you realise how the years were passing. She was thirty-nine now, though she found it hard to believe most of the time, but James would be fifty this year. 'We should see more of each other,' she said. 'Families ought to stay together.'

He saw through her words, and smiled. 'Dear, tactless Lucy,' he said. 'I may be down to be the next to go, but I'm not going to pop off for a good few years yet.'

She didn't smile. 'I mean it, Jamie. What have any of us got but each other? Yet we rarely meet.'

He kissed her cheek – something he had hardly ever done in his life before. 'We'll make a point of it, from now on,' he said. He glanced towards her husband, standing watching them, his polite face unfathomable as usual. 'What a civilising effect you've had on this wild girl, Danby. There was a time when all she wanted was adventure.'

'That was never *all* I wanted,' she said briskly, pulling away from him, and looking around. 'The damage looked appalling from the outside, but in here you'd hardly know. Thank God it wasn't worse, I suppose.' She may have been fooling herself, but she didn't deceive anyone else for a moment. As she looked around her, all those gathered in the hallway could see the lost soul inside her, which was asking for reassurance from the walls and furnishings, familiar since childhood.

The chapel was crowded the next day – family, friends and neighbours, servants and tenants filling the seats and aisles and spilling out into the hall. Héloïse regretted again that there were no flowers, no flowers in January for Edward, to say goodbye to a dear friend and brother. She had done her best with greenery, and perhaps, after all, evergreens were the most fitting tribute to his particular qualities.

Evergreens and candles: it was like Christmas over again. She wished she could feel the rejoicing a good Christian ought that a soul was going home to God, but it had been too sudden and violent and shocking, and she was going to miss him too much. The best she could manage was a gladness for the gift of his life, for the good that he had been, and for the love he had generated, which was represented by the number of people who crowded into the chapel for his sake. He was not a man people had spoken of loving, but here they all were all the same, missing and needing him.

Here was his family – James, Sophie, Nicholas and Benedict; Lucy and Danby, Rosamund, Roland and Thomas; and John Skelwith, his secret nephew. Mathilde was still in childbed, of course, having been delivered safely of a girl on the morning after the storm. They had not told her at first about Edward's death, for fear of what the shock might do to her, so soon after giving birth. Héloïse had visited her yesterday for the first time, to see the new infant, and to break the news herself.

It had been a great shock, greater than Héloïse expected. Mathilde had wanted urgently to get up, to come to the funeral today, and with difficulty Héloïse had persuaded her that it was too soon. She had half expected her to appear all the same, but evidently John had managed to convince her that it would not be good for her in her condition. Mathilde, Héloïse knew, had been particularly fond of Edward, and they had been very close in the days before John Skelwith came on the scene.

It was a good thing, really, that she had the new baby to occupy her, and to give her an object of tenderness and concern which would blunt the loss of Edward. They had called the baby Mary, after John's mother. Héloïse supposed it was inevitable. Mary was a good saint's name, anyway; and she was glad it had been a daughter. Somehow that was easier to bear than a son. She thought Edward would have been glad, too.

The Ansteys were there, John and Louisa and their children, and the Pobgees and Micklethwaites, the Keatings and Shawes and Somerses. Henry Bayliss, the newspaper proprietor, and his brother the physician were there, and Havergill from the hospital, and Dykes the banker, and the Applebys, and Colonel Brunton the magistrate – friends from Edward's club, and colleagues from the various public committees he had sat on from time to time in his crowded life.

The tenants were there, and the spinners and weavers and outworkers, and the Governor of the hospital and the headmaster of the school, with an offering from all the boys. The sphere of his influence had been enormous. There was so much a man in his position could do for good or ill, so many lives he affected. There were a great many people with cause to thank God for Edward Morland, for his industry and energy, for his integrity.

Father Moineau conducted the service so beautifully and so movingly that it was impossible for any listener not to weep; and that, Héloïse thought, was as it should be. The tribute of tears was the good man's mead. Edward's coffin was lowered into the vault – where less than two years ago they had buried Fanny and her stillborn child – and the stone was replaced. And then the ceremony was over.

Later, when the guests had gone away, the vault was reopened, and a second, smaller coffin was lowered to be placed next to the first. It was not something that the family would speak of to outsiders, for there were some who might think it inappropriate or pagan, or even blasphemous; but for those who had loved him and known him best, it seemed right and comfortable that Edward should be buried with his good dog to sleep beside him in death, as he always had in life.

Mr Cripps, the assistant manager of Harding and Howell's, opened the door with a profound bow, and a deferential murmur of 'Good morning, your ladyship!'

Rosamund, buttoning her glove, was about to pass out into Pall Mall but drew back with a breath of annoyance. It had begun to rain since she came in. It looked as though it would only be an April shower, but she was wearing a new hat of her own design of which she was particularly proud, and a wetting would ruin it. It was a close-fitting cap of pale green damask, stiffened with ribs of darker green velvet, with an

171

edging of tiny artificial flowers which framed her face, and topped with a large silk rose. Even a spot of rain would be disastrous.

'Your ladyship's carriage –?' Cripps murmured enquiringly.

'Is to meet me in Bond Street,' she said shortly.

'You should have brought an umbrella, my lady,' Moss said, which was dangerously close to 'I told you so', particularly as she knew her lady hated carrying the wretched things.

Rosamund frowned. 'I suppose I must wait until it stops,' she said.

'I should be happy to summon you a hackney, your ladyship,' Cripps began, but a gentleman passing by in the street had turned his head at the sound of Rosamund's voice, and came across to her, smiling from the shelter of a very large, black umbrella like a young tent in mourning.

'Why, Lady Rosamund! What a pleasant surprise.'

'Why, Mr Hawker!' she replied in kind. 'You do seem to appear at the most opportune moments.'

'How kind of you to think so. I was just cursing the rain, but now I see it was a gift from the beneficent gods.' He gave her a comprehensive and admiring look from her confection of a hat to her green morocco boots which made her blush with its frankness. 'It would be a great pity to spoil such an enchanting *ensemble*. Please allow me to be of service to you. I am completely at liberty, and this is, as you see, a very large umbrella. Where do you wish to go?'

'Chelmsford House is only a step down the road, my lady,' Moss piped up daringly from the rear.

Rosamund refused even to hear her. 'I have an errand for my mother at Martin's in King Street, and then I am bound for Bond Street, where my carriage is to collect me in an hour.'

'Excellent,' said Hawker. 'Then will you take my arm, ma'am?'

Rosamund stepped out and under the umbrella, leaving Moss to follow and get wet, which was her punishment for daring to suggest Rosamund subject herself to Chelmsford House and her future mother-in-law on a morning when she meant to be free and enjoy herself.

'I suppose you must be very busy, shopping for your

172

'wedding-clothes?' Hawker said conversationally. 'I believe June is the month to be honoured, is it not?'

'You know about it, then?' Rosamund said, not very surprised.

'Nothing else is talked of in the best circles,' he assured her solemnly.

'Yes, we are to marry in June. It was to have been February, but we had to put it off, you know, because of my uncle's death.'

'I heard about that. It was very shocking,' he said gravely.

Rosamund raised her brows. '*You* say so? I understood you were at outs with my uncle Ned, even more than with my uncle James.'

Hawker shrugged. 'One does not generally wish death on people, simply because one has quarrelled with them.'

'I believe you are growing mellow with age, Mr Hawker.'

He ignored the mockery. 'And it is shocking to think of that noble old house in ruins.'

'Hmph. Well, your information is at fault there. It was only one wall and a chimney that came down – bad enough, of course, and then poor Uncle Ned – however, I don't wish to talk about that, even if it is a rainy day.'

'Quite. Life must go on. And June is a better month for a wedding, anyway. But, tell me, I'm curious, what changed your mind?'

'Changed my mind?'

'The last time we spoke, you were doubtful about accepting Chelmsford.'

'Oh.' She glanced at him. 'It was you, partly. And a sort of resignation to fate. And hearing myself giving advice to my brother Aylesbury about doing his duty.'

'Duty?'

'Something I imagine you know little about,' she said teasingly. 'But it has given a great deal of pleasure to a great many people, so I am satisfied.'

'Even to Lady Barbara?'

'She wasn't best pleased at first – but then she discovered that my "twenty thousand pounds" is actually a good sixty, so she determined to overcome her dislike of me for her dear son's sake. At least,' she added with a grimace, 'Chelmsford House is big enough to hold us all without a squeeze. With a little management, I may avoid meeting her more than once or twice a week.'

'You mean to live in London, then?'

'For the moment. Lady Barbara's anxious for Marcus to be purchasing a country property – the family seat, you know – but Mama agrees with me that there's no point until an heir is on the way, and that,' she lowered her voice, though Moss was a good distance behind them, 'I can assure you will not be for a long time, if I can help it.'

Hawker restrained himself nobly from any of the rejoinders he might have made. He said evenly, 'London is more agreeable for a young couple. And I suppose you can continue to go down to Wolvercote when you feel in need of country air.'

'Yes. In fact, there is another plan afoot, which makes it foolish to be buying an estate. Mama and Papa Danby plan to take my brothers on a Grand Tour. They feel it would be better for Aylesbury than the university, and since Mama has never travelled abroad except to Vienna and Brussels, Papa Danby wants to shew her all the splendours of Europe.'

'What an excellent idea,' Hawker said. 'How long do they plan to be travelling?'

'Two or three years; and while they're gone, they want Marcus and me to take care of things, so we shall have the run of Wolvercote whenever we want it. And,' she added with a grin, 'of Mama's horses. It breaks her heart to leave them behind, even with me and Parslow to take care of them.'

'Parslow?'

'Yes, I thought it would surprise you. It certainly surprised Papa Danby! I don't think she's ever been parted from him since he first came to her, and that must be twenty years ago. But she decided the horses needed him more than she did. It was an agonising decision!'

'Yes, I can imagine. Your mother riding or driving in the Park, with Parslow in attendance, was one of the great sights of the Season – like Mr Brummell strolling down Bond Street. Ah, those golden times seem to be over, don't they?'

'One of the things Mama's looking forward to is to visiting Mr Brummell when they get to Calais. She doesn't forget old friends. She wrote to tell him what she planned, and asked if she should bring him anything from home. He asked her for a jar of snuff from Fribourg and Treyer, and a box of good

English writing-paper – so that he could "nourish friendship and his nose at the same time". Doesn't that sound like him?'

'I dare say she will take many other things as well. She is the most generous of creatures.'

Rosamund looked at him askance. 'You seem determined to praise everyone this morning. But tell me, sir, what are you doing here anyway? In England, I mean. I thought you had some diplomatic post or other in Vienna.'

'I have been loaned by Castlereagh to Sidmouth, on account of my special experience in Manchester, so I expect to be in England for some time – probably until the situation is resolved.'

'Situation? What situation?'

'My dear Lady Rosamund, the State of Alarm! You surely can't be unaware of it, even if you are on the brink of getting married.'

'Oh – that!'

'Yes, that, as you so eloquently put it! Spa Fields in December – the Hampden Clubs' delegates' meeting in January – the Regent's coach attacked in February – Habeas Corpus suspended on March the 3rd – the Seditious Meetings Act passed on the 29th! You must have noticed that England is seething with discontent, riot and conspiracy – that it is on the brink of a revolution as bloody and convulsive as that of 1789?'

'Not precisely. It's only reformist nonsense, isn't it?' Rosamund said with a natural female contempt for anything to do with politics.

Hawker threw back his head and laughed. 'Would that women had the ruling of the world!'

'It would go on a lot better, I assure you,' she said firmly.

'It would,' he agreed. 'But what on earth would men do with themselves all the time?'

'Well, not march about the country with petitions, like those wretched Blanketeers, at all events.'

'Oh, you did hear about that, then? And wretched they were, too, the poor hungry dupes. But it was a clever notion,' he said thoughtfully. 'If it had come off, there's no knowing how far it might have gone. We got the ringleaders – Bagguley and Drummond – but I wouldn't be surprised if there hadn't been a better brain than either of theirs behind it.'

175

'Why? What was so clever about it?'

'Well, to begin with, the marchers were to set off in groups of ten: there's no law to prevent small parties of unarmed men walking to London, whereas a larger number would have caused instant alarm. Then they were to keep on the move, so that they could not be charged with obstruction, and to carry their own blanket and provisions, so that they could not be charged with vagrancy. It was well planned. They started with a public meeting in St Peter's Fields – in Manchester, you know. A peaceful meeting – and when they were ordered to disperse by the magistrates, they did so at once, because it was exactly what they wanted to do. Clever, don't you think?'

'I suppose so,' she said blankly.

'And their petitions made no political demands, which might have laid them open to charges of sedition – only a request to the Prince Regent to remedy the wretched plight of the cotton trade. There was nothing they could be charged with, nothing at all. In fact when the Yeomanry took up a couple of hundred of them outside Stockport, the magistrates couldn't think what to do with them, and simply had to send them home. But if it had come off,' he went on gravely, 'what then, eh? Six, seven hundred men, converging on the Capital, gathering support as they went ... the six hundred peaceful marchers growing into an army ... the impetus building ... They might have taken London. Oh, it was a famous clever scheme. We had a near miss of it, I can tell you.'

Rosamund looked sobered. 'I thought it was all nonsense,' she said apologetically. 'I mean, what can people like that want with the franchise? That's what this man Hunt and his friends are demanding, isn't it? That every man should have the vote? Weavers and dyers and chimney-sweeps and coachmen and all.'

'Yes, that's right. Every man.'

'Even if they don't own any land. It's the sheerest folly. And what do they want it for? What good do they suppose it will do them?'

'Oh, the weavers and dyers and the rest of them don't really want it. What they want is quite simple – more money in their pockets, more bread in their mouths. It all stems from hunger with them, you know. But there are those who have persuaded them that if they have the vote, all else will naturally follow. Don't ask me how.' He shrugged. 'Only an idiot or a madman would suppose that the Government can do anything about such natural phenomena as famine and plenty.'

'But what do these others want? The ones who are persuading them?'

'Interest,' said Hawker simply. 'To have your own Member of Parliament, to see that your Interest succeeds over the next man's – that's what's at the bottom of it all.'

'Yes,' Rosamund said thoughtfully, 'your friend Mr Farraline said something of the sort. He wants a special assembly for mill-owners.'

'I can only apologise for him. He's unsound on the subject of mills, but otherwise, you know, he's quite a decent fellow. Except that he does seem to spend a distressing amount of time talking to handsome young women about politics! His time might be so much better employed.'

He grinned his vulpine grin at her, and she smiled dutifully at his self-mockery. Then the grin disappeared. 'So you are to be wed in June,' he said speculatively. 'I wish it might be sooner.'

She eyed him cautiously, not understanding his new drift; and then remembered his words about her being interesting to him as a married woman, and blushed.

'Why do you say that?'

'Because, my dear Lady Rosamund, I should not like you to be disappointed. These disturbances are not over, you know. Sidmouth has been gathering reports from various sources for some time, and they all point towards a general uprising, beginning in the north, this summer – we believe at the end of May. I should not like to think your wedding might have to be postponed a second time.'

She stopped and looked at him for a long moment, hardly knowing what to think. Was he serious? Was he teasing? An *uprising*? What had he said earlier – a revolution as bloody as that of 1789? Her common sense protested. This was England. Such things did not, could not happen here. Of course, there had been that Spa Fields business, and food riots and machine-smashing last autumn and winter in various remote places. But a regular, organised revolution? It was not likely. The English lower orders were not oppressed like French peasants or Russian serfs; they weren't tortured or imprisoned or subjected to the arbitrary whims of feudal overlords. How could revolution benefit them? It wouldn't make a bad harvest good, or open closed factories and mines to give them jobs.

'No,' she said at last. 'I don't believe it.'

He had watched all the workings of her mind with a sympathetic smile, and now he laughed. 'Good! That's the stuff that has made England great! And in response, I promise you that we shall do our best to avert it, or at least contain it. I think we might do that. After all, only one of the Blanketeers actually reached London; and we can always hope that it will rain on the day. There's nothing so damping to revolutionary ardour as a good cold downpour.'

She laughed too. 'Now I know you're funning!'

'But I assure you! If only France had had our English weather, their revolution might never have happened. A wet summer or two might have kept old Louis XVI on his throne.'

Héloïse drove herself back from the village, where she had been distributing advice and help to what had become the usual number of families in want. She remembered John Anstey saying that they would be glad to say goodbye to 1816: for her, 1817 was already giving as much trouble.

Yet there was comfort in nature: today was the first really spring-like day, when the mildness of the air matched the tender colour of the sky. The black thorn hedges that marked the track and sheltered it from the prevailing wind were beginning to be blurred with the surprising, bright green of new shoots; and under them the primroses were opening amongst their clusters of oval leaves, like pale eggs in frilled, green nests.

In the fields beyond the hedges the sheep were grazing intently on the delicious new grass; and the early lambs, instead of huddling together for warmth, were stretched out on their sides like small fallen clouds to enjoy the sunshine. The renewal of growing things every year was like a renewal of hope. However hard the winter had been, it was always possible to go on.

She came to the bend of the track, where the clump of twisted trees hid the view beyond. She slowed the ponies for the turn, and as they rounded it, she stopped them, as she had got in the habit of doing lately, for the first view of the house. It was still a shock, every time, for her mental eye carried a picture of Morland Place that only years would eradicate; and it was reality, fitting so ill against that image, that her mind wanted to reject. The house looked so lopsided without its chimney; and its outline was foiled and cluttered by the ugly scaffolding, and by the piles of rubble and building materials on what had been open greensward.

Even so, it was better than it had been, presenting at least the hint of order being imposed upon chaos; and it was the chaos, almost more than anything, which had been so hard to bear. She didn't think she would ever be able to forget the heartbreaking, defeating mess in what had been the kitchen, for instance. Plaster-dust and soot covered every surface, drifting in choking clouds, cloaking the catastrophic piles of rubble, stones, crumbled mortar, tiles, moss, dead leaves, twigs, twisted pieces of lead, pot-shards, broken glass, metal and splintered wood. The night before the disaster, the room had been left scoured and cleaned to perfection as usual, every shining pan and spoon hung in its accustomed place, the stone floor washed spotless, the tables scrubbed white. Héloïse would never forget her cook, Monsieur Barnard, standing there the next day, staring at it all, his face blank and white, too utterly shocked even for tears.

John Skelwith had said that the chimney must have been fatally weakened by the fire a year ago, which had been a particularly bad one, and had spread to the chimney of the North Bedroom, which was in fact a subsidiary flue of the main kitchen chimney. Héloïse had hastily denied it, and John, probably understanding her concern, had not repeated the suggestion.

Yet Barnard was not a stupid man: probably he had thought of the same thing himself. He had borne his exile in his 'field-kitchen', as James called it, meekly at first, managing somehow to feed the family and the servants under very difficult circumstances. The estate outworkers had taken the house-servants home to dinner with them on a rotation basis to ease the strain, and kind neighbours had sent up pies and hams and other useful supplies in the most generous manner. But Barnard's temper had been more than usually erratic of late, probably because he blamed himself for the whole terrible incident.

'But you know, in any case,' Skelwith had said, 'that chimney was much too high. You don't need a chimney of those proportions nowadays. You could look upon it as a sort of blessing in disguise: now you can have the whole kitchen rebuilt and made beautifully modern and convenient.'

He didn't mean to be tactless; but even leaving aside the death of Edward, and acquainted as she was with the coy nature of the average blessing, Héloïse felt that this one was masking itself unusually well. A large part of the chimney had fallen into the moat, not only blocking it, but, it was discovered, damaging the retaining wall below water-level. Water had started to leak into the cellars; half the moat had had to be sealed off and drained for repairs to be carried out.

Because that was the more urgent work, the rebuilding had to take second place. Héloïse sighed. It seemed that for months now, their mouths and hair had been filled with grit and dust, their hands and clothes permanently dirty, without any progress having been made towards ending the situation. And washing was such a problem, even though the kennelman spent every spare moment boiling up hot water in the coppers in which he cooked the hounds' pudding. It was time and past time for the great annual cleaning, but though Héloïse's housewifely soul yearned for it as a dying man for water, it would clearly have been as nonsensical as impossible to attempt anything of the sort in the present conditions.

A flicker of movement caught her eye and she turned her head to see that a robin had flown down onto the curve of the dashboard, and was eyeing her speculatively, a green caterpillar dangling from its beak. He must be feeding his mate as she sat on their eggs, she thought. She smiled, and the robin was gone; but it had reminded her of spring again. Regeneration, renewal, hope. Whatever was made could be mended – that was a saying in these parts.

And the tragedy had not been entirely unproductive of good. It had changed James, for instance, in a way that could only be for the good of them all. She had known him for twenty-four years, since he was a young man, and there had always been a vein of restlessness and discontent about him. It was that which had led him into all the mistakes he had made, had caused him to do things that hurt not only him, but all those around him, and had shadowed even his happy times. She had never had any idea why he was the way he was; she supposed it was the way the Creator had chosen to make him, but it had always saddened her.

Yet since the death of Edward, it seemed to have disappeared. She sensed it; she knew it in some atavistic way that had nothing to do with intellect. It was as though a lingering infection that had gone on half-healing and breaking out again, year after year, was suddenly, miraculously gone. James, who had always idled and pleasured and fretted his way through his life, was now heartbreakingly busy from morning till night, shouldering the tasks and responsibilities which had been his brother's in addition to his own, and it had been the making of him. The discontent and destructive self-criticism were gone; he was simply too tired at the end of the day for reflection or analysis. If it existed at all, *that* was John Skelwith's true 'blessing in disguise'.

The estate people knew it, too. At first they had come reluctantly, calling him by the cadet title of *Maister James*, and referring wistfully to what Maister Morland had always done about this, what he had always said about that; and looking mulish at any proposal not hallowed by centuries of use. But as James had taken up the slack, they had seen, with surprise in some cases, that this small and handsome man – the popular one of the family, the 'best horseman in the Ridings' and 'a devil wi' the ladies' as he had always been known – was big enough to fill Edward Morland's shoes. Now they called him simply *Maister*, the title of honour, and they came to him willingly, with that sturdy, judicious respectfulness which made the English lower orders so different from the peasantry of other countries.

She had never been the Mistress of Morland Place in the same complete sense that Jemima had been. She hadn't the education or the intellect, for one thing, and though she loved it as dearly as anyone could, she had not, after all, been born or brought up there. She was the guardian of its spirit, that was all. She had never been able to take the material decisions about it – that had been left to Edward. Now James had taken over that role from Edward, and he had usurped a little of her function too. Well, she was happy that it should be so.

She thought that if Jemima could have seen what James was now becoming, she would have been happy to leave everything in his hands.

The ponies were growing restless, and she shook the reins and sent them on down the gentle slope towards the house.

As she entered the hall, Ottershaw came from his pantry to take her hat and gloves from her, and she asked, 'Where is your master?'

'He's in the steward's room, my lady. He did ask if you would step in to see him on your return.'

'Very well,' she said happily, for it exactly coincided with her own wishes. 'Has Monsieur Barnard begun the paupers' soup for this week yet?'

'I believe not, my lady.'

'I think we shall need more – another gallon, perhaps. There are two more families gone onto relief. I shall come and speak to him later; and Mrs Thomson shall tell us what roots can be spared.'

'Very good, my lady.'

She crossed the two halls and opened the steward's room door, and stood for an instant looking with content at her husband. His head was bent over the accounts, and the slanting sunlight from the window picked out the sheen of grey hairs over the fox-brown. There was a stack of ledgers to either side of him, and he had ink on his fingers and his cuff. The end of the bar of light fell across the floor to touch the rim of the basket by the hearth, in which a brindled hound-whelp was sleeping in the absolute manner of puppies, too deeply to have heard her come in. Its name was Kai, and it was one of Tiger's great-grandchildren. A smile touched her lips. Soon, she thought, he would take to wearing shapeless brown coats, and drinking beer for breakfast instead of coffee.

He became aware of her at last, glanced up for an instant distractedly, and then down again, saying, 'Ah, there you are, Marmoset. I wanted to speak to you.'

'So I understand,' she said, crossing the room. 'But first, my James –' She leaned over to kiss his brow, the only part she could reach, and he grunted an acknowledgement. The smile deepened. 'The grunt is all very well,' she said reasonably, 'but though I know you work very hard, I do not wish you to become any more like a steward interviewing an under-gardener.'

'Eh?' he looked up, startled.

'That's better,' she said, and cupped his face with her hands and kissed him again, this time on the lips. They smiled under hers, and his inky hands came up to hold her. 'Hmm,' she said a little breathlessly as she straightened up, 'you must be the only thing in the house that does not taste of plaster dust. What did you want me for, my love?'

'Do you need me to tell you that?' he said, smiling at her in a way that took her back ten years to the eve of their marriage. He got up and pulled a chair across for her to sit beside him.

'Well – but in particular?'

'In particular, I wanted to talk to you about the financial situation. I'm afraid things are not going very well for us at present.'

'Explain,' she said, settling herself and resting her forearms on the edge of the table. They distracted James briefly: her wrists were so tiny they made him think for an instant of the impossible fragility of robins' legs. But his business was important. He restrained himself from gathering her passionately into his arms, and explained.

The long French wars had been profitable for the Morlands. To begin with, there had been the extra demand for their horses: war is wasteful of horseflesh, and a contract with the Inspector General for three- and four-year-old remounts had proved highly lucrative. Then there was the contract with the Navy for wheat with which to make the sailor's 'hard tack'. Demand for corn was so enormous, and the price of wheat so high, that Edward had considered it worthwhile buying up all the extra land he could, to bring under cultivation. Land prices were very steep during the war but loans were easy to come by, and the estate's income was high enough for the interest repayments to be hardly noticeable.

But with the outbreak of peace, all that had changed. No more cavalry remounts; no more Victualling Yard corn. Suddenly everyone was poor – nobody was buying new hunters or riding horses; they were making do with two carriage horses instead of four. The price of wheat fell, and though the operation of the Corn Laws meant it was still too high for the unemployed to be able to buy bread, it was too low for the farmers to make a profit on all the extra land they had put under cultivation. Income disappeared – but outgoings still had to be met. Now the interest on those loans seemed appallingly high.

To add to that, last year had been disastrous, with the terrible wet spring taking its toll of the sheep – foot-rot, swayback, husk, staggers, broken limbs – and the lambing losses had been dreadful, in both ewes and lambs. Sheep, hardy creatures in many ways, proved curiously vulnerable to prolonged wet weather. And then the ruined harvests had left them without enough corn to sell, or enough hay to feed the beasts through the winter without buying in.

Héloïse listened, and looked obediently where his finger pointed. 'I don't really understand the figures,' she said, 'but I see there are a lot of minus signs. Are things very bad?'

'Yes,' he said. He looked up from the books and held her eyes. 'I've been keeping it from you, seeing you had so much else to worry about; but after all, Morland Place is yours, and you have a right to know. Things are very bad indeed.'

She frowned. 'But we've always been so comfortable. Perhaps if we retrench a little –'

'In normal times that might have been the answer. But it's income we need, real money to pay the interest on these loans.'

'Can't we sell the land again?' she asked.

'It wouldn't help. When we bought the extra land, farms were going for anything up to forty-five years' purchase. Now the price has dropped to fifteen, sometimes less. We wouldn't make enough from the sale even to pay back the capital; but we have to go on paying the interest. While our incomes have fallen, all our outgoings have increased. Taxes, for instance – they fall most heavily on us landowners. There's the land tax to begin with; and then the county rate has gone up sevenfold in the last ten years, and the poor rate has quadrupled. There's the highways tax, tax on farm horses, tax on harness – and our tenants owing God knows how much in unpaid rents. And if we throw them off the land for debt, what then? They'll just become an extra burden on the parish, which *we'll* have to pay for.'

184

'I had no idea it was as bad as this,' she said. 'No wonder poor Edward was so worried.'

'And now there are the repairs to the house to pay for. God knows where we'll get the money for that, and we can hardly expect John Skelwith to wait for ever.'

'We might sell the plate and jewellery,' she said doubtfully.

'It may come to that, though I should dislike it very much.' He frowned, tapping the open page with the end of the ruler. 'Economies alone won't do it – though there's enough room for them. In the kitchen for instance – either our servants are living as high as coach-horses, or there must be tremendous wastage.'

'Oh, no, nothing is wasted,' she said quickly. 'All that is left is made into parcels every day, for the poor at the gate.'

'The poor at the gate!' He smiled reluctantly at the expression. 'We're not a monastery, my love, to be giving food away like that. And in such quantities!'

'There are a great many to feed,' she said. 'Some are our own people who are old or out of work, and others are poor beggars passing through. We cannot turn them away unfed. Besides,' she added, remembering her order about the soup and refusing to feel guilty, 'if we do not feed them at the gate, they will come on the parish, so it will be the same thing.'

'Charity begins at home,' James said. 'Or it ought to.'

The kitchen 'left-overs', and the parcels of food that were carried out to cottages where there was sickness or want, were not the only drain on the household, as he very well knew. Morland Place leaked like a sieve. There was the school and the hospital, both of which had been endowed by long-ago Morlands, and which therefore felt obliged to apply first to Morland Place when extra funds were needed for repairs or equipment or special occasions. The Founder's Feast, for instance, at St Edward's School, was no longer a matter of a hundred penny buns to distribute to the pupils; and there was the annual prize-giving, and scholarships for especially able boys who were brought to Morland attention as worthy cases.

And what about the small army of Morland Place pensioners – former employees, who all seemed to enjoy an extraordinary longevity, and who seemed to live in houses needing constant repair? Even here in this house there were elderly servants who did virtually nothing for their wages, but who ate heartily three times a day none the less.

'Well, my James, I will try to find some way to *faire les économies*; but you said that would not be enough.'

'No. As I said, we need income. I think it's time to find out what is happening with the other half of your estate: the Hobsbawn Inheritance. I know things are bad in the manufactories these days, too – I suppose they could hardly be worse. But if your mills cannot turn in an income, perhaps they might at least be sold for enough capital to pay for the repairs to the house. Or perhaps we might be able to sell the machinery and rent out the mill-buildings as warehouses. At all events, it would be better than selling the family plate, or than selling land at a loss. What do you think, my love?'

She thought many things quite quickly – of old Mr Hobsbawn and his lifetime's devotion to his business; of Jasper Hobsbawn's blazing eyes as he gave her the mills so that they might not be destroyed by the costs of litigation; of all Fanny's scheming and burning ambition. If it were true that Fanny's journeying to Manchester so late in pregnancy had caused her miscarriage and stillbirth, it could be said that she had given her life in order to possess the Hobsbawn Inheritance.

So many people had wanted those mills so badly; but Héloïse did not hesitate for more than a second. 'I think you are quite right, *mon âme*,' she said. 'We shall sell them, if you think it necessary.'

CHAPTER TEN

Stainton was a small estate in the Chilterns, brought into the possession of the Marquesses of Penrith by an heiress of two hundred years before. It had served sometimes as a dower and sometimes as a cadet home, but in the last hundred years the house had more often stood empty but for a caretaker.

It was a small manor house in the black-and-white Tudor style, full of dark panelling, beamed ceilings, and cavernous fireplaces which smoked more than they warmed. Though perhaps beautiful in its way – the School of the Picturesque would have admired its crooked roof and the wavy, greenish glass in its diamond-paned windows – it was uncomfortable and badly positioned to modern ideas.

It was set in a damp, green place in a wooded fold of the hill – a small pocket of a clearing, carved out of the primaeval woodland. It was on low ground, and the tall trees grew close up to it, so that even the immense height of its chimneys was not enough to make the fires draw properly when the wind was in three of its four quarters. Little would grow in the garden except ferns and laurels. Moss flourished on its north-facing walls, and the narrow brick paths around the house were slippery with it.

The approach to Stainton Manor was through winding, sunken lanes. Black tree roots writhed in the steep banks, and the trees grew high above the traveller's head. In summer it was a cool and sweet-scented approach. A dappled light filtered through the canopy to touch the remote, pale flowers of the woodland: the delicate white stars of sweet woodruff and the faint, greenish lace of angelica. The air was damp and rich with leaf-mould, the woods silent but for the secretive rustle of birds foraging through the leaf-litter, the liquid cooing of wood pigeons, and always, somewhere, the sound of water.

But in the winter the trees stood naked and black. The rain

no longer pattered, but dripped sullenly from bare twigs, and the deep lanes were scoured ever deeper between the high slippery banks. Came the time when the depth of mud made them impassable to wheeled traffic, and Stainton was cut off from the outside world, except for those hardy enough to struggle through on horseback. Then the black-and-white house in its green and secret place brooded undisturbed through the chills and fogs of winter, the smoke trickling reluctantly from its chimneys to cling like rags to the bare tree-tops above the roof.

Here lived Flaminia, Lucy's elder daughter and Rosamund's sister, and now wife of Lord Harvey Sale, who was heir presumptive to the Penrith title. One day in May, 1817, she was taking her walk in the garden with her cousin Polly Haworth, who had lived with her since her marriage. Flaminia's ideas of exercise were never very energetic. Polly might well have put on a stouter pair of shoes and taken a walk through the woods, but Flaminia had decided that the paths would be too muddy, and that two turns of the garden would suffice.

It was a warm day, but there was no sunshine. The sun was hidden behind a hazy sky which was curiously colourless: greyish-white, hanging low and blank over the green, still world. Shut in by the hills here, there was hardly ever any sound, only the endless drip and trickle of water, and the sense of green things growing all around – like a murmured conversation just below the level of conscious hearing.

Polly felt her nerves strung out almost to snapping-point. She hated the monotony of these warm blank days, when there was nothing to mark out one hour from the next: no rain, no wind, no sight of the sun, not even the changing shape of a shadow. Such days seemed to reflect the monotony of her life. She would have welcomed a raging tempest or a blistering drought – anything to relieve the endless tedium of her situation.

Flaminia never seemed to mind the weather. 'I think May is the best month, don't you?' she said placidly, pausing at the junction of two paths to look up at the trees. Her pale, plump face was serene.

Polly envied her the ability not to think. 'You said the same thing yesterday,' she said, trying not to sound irritable.

'Did I? Well, I like all the pretty little leaves that you get in May. The big dark-green leaves that come later shut out the sun too much.'

'They're the same leaves, Minnie – just grown up, that's all.' In spite of her effort, Polly's voice took on an edge.

Minnie didn't notice it. 'To be sure, that's what I meant. I like them when they're young and soft, and they have that pink bit, like fur, around the bottom. So pretty! It reminds me of poor Loppy. I wish Loppy hadn't died. He had such beautiful furry ears. And the sweet little kitten died, too. It's such a shame.'

Polly shivered involuntarily. The fact of the matter was that Flaminia's succession of sweet, furry little pets had all died, and Polly was sure it was because Stainton was so low and damp. Yet Minnie seemed quite content to live here, even through the long winter months when they never saw a soul but the servants, and the occasional carrier who struggled through for the sake of the higher price Stainton paid – of necessity – for most goods.

Winter or summer, Flaminia's days were much alike. She interviewed her housekeeper in the morning – a process which would have taken Polly half an hour, but which for Minnie, with her slow speech and inability to make a decision, could go on for an hour and a half. Then she sat in the morning-room, dressed to receive callers until it was time to take a nuncheon.

After that she would take her walk, in the garden or the woods if it were fair, in the gallery or simply round and round the drawing-room if the weather were foul. Then she played with her children for an hour – the twins, Mary and Elizabeth, were rising two now – which brought her to the hour for dressing for dinner. After dinner she sat and sewed until it was time for bed.

The unvarying similarity of her days didn't seem to trouble her. Polly had once said, rather unkindly, that Minnie had the sheep's capacity for being perpetually surprised by the same things. The smallest occurrence – a sunny day, the arrival of a letter, a squirrel running across the garden path – seemed enough to engage her interest and secure her contentment.

For Polly, however, the monotony grew ever harder to bear

189

as she imagined her youth and beauty fading, and wondered what the future held for her. Would she go on like this for ever, trapped in this place, dependent on poor dull Minnie for companionship; without occupation except to listen to her cousin's platitudes with patience, without diversion except for books and the occasional solitary walk in the woods?

She looked with loathing at the black-and-white house in its lush, green setting, and felt frustration tighten inside her. Shut in by the trees and the hills and the low empty sky, there was nothing to see, nothing to do; no sound or movement, only silent things growing, inch by inch, year by year, imperceptibly.

There was no colour anywhere: everything was green and black and white. Black timbers, black as tree-trunks in the rain, white plaster, pale as rot, steep green fields and trees rising to the white sky. Oh God, she thought, for some other colour! Something scarlet, or blue, or yellow – anything to give relief to the eye! But the only rose that managed to survive in this dark garden was a white rambler on an ancient, age-blackened stem. There were green ferns against the blackened fencing, black-green moss over the path, dim white saxifrage flowers growing in the wall, and the green and white of lily-of-the-valley under the black shadow of the trees.

Four years they had lived here, but never in such isolation as they had known this last year. The master of the house, whose brief and sudden visits Minnie looked forward to with such placid joy, had scarcely troubled them since Christmas. He had been down once for a week in February, and for three days just after Easter, each time arriving unannounced and leaving without explanation. And even while he was at Stainton, he seemed uneasy, nervous and fidgety as a horse smelling lightning, scowling at the servants, snapping at his wife and refusing so much as to look at his daughters.

As to the neighbours, it was almost as if they had been warned off. There had never been many visitors to the old manor, but even the few who had called regularly before out of politeness had not been near them for months. Boredom and isolation were driving Polly to desperation. It was so unfair! Her beauty, her intellect, her talents were all to waste away unused, simply because she had no portion; while

Minnie, who had neither beauty nor intelligence, had married straight from the schoolroom because of her large dowry. And not only that, but she had married –

'I wish I had a little dog,' Minnie said, as she had said almost every day since the last kitten died. 'Shouldn't you like a little dog, Polly? A spaniel would be nice, with long ears and a long tail, and lovely soft fur.'

'Dogs don't have fur, they have hair,' Polly snapped.

'That's right,' Minnie agreed. 'But it's soft and silky, like fur.'

Polly restrained herself. 'There's no reason why you shouldn't have a dog if you want one,' she said. As long as it wasn't black and white, she added inwardly.

'I should have to ask Harvey,' Minnie said. 'I'll ask him next time he comes.'

'You don't have to ask Harvey. Just ask Tompkins to get you one. No-one can prevent you from having a pet dog if you want one. You can buy it out of your pin-money.'

'Oh no, I couldn't do that, not without asking Harvey.' Flaminia was definite on that point as on few others.

'Write to him, then. There's no knowing when he'll visit next.'

But Minnie never wrote letters. The last time she had taken a pen in her hand was in the schoolroom, to write an exercise for Miss Trotton. 'He'll come, sometime this summer. I'll ask him then. There's no hurry.'

Polly clenched her fists in her lap. 'Minnie, why don't you ever get bored? Don't you ever feel you want to just –' She was going to say 'scream and break things', but a glance at Minnie's expression, her round brown eyes only mildly surprised, made her stop. 'Don't you ever want a change of scene?' she asked instead, in a defeated voice.

'It's nice here. Why should I want a change?'

'What's nice about it? Why do you like it here?'

Minnie struggled with unaccustomed analysis. 'It's my home.'

'But do you like it better than being at home with your mama, in Grosvenor Street?'

'Oh, yes. I have my own house and servants here, and I can order whatever I like for dinner,' Minnie said.

'But in Grosvenor Street there were always people coming

191

and going. There was always company. Here you don't see anyone.'

'I don't like lots of people. They make me feel awkward, and I never know what to say. I have enough company here. There's Mrs Tompkins, and Hill, and the dear babies to play with. And you, of course. I shouldn't like it if you weren't here. And then,' she added, the summit to her worldly joy, 'there's Harvey's visits to look forward to.'

'Yes,' Polly said dully, 'I see. I can see now how it is for you.'

Minnie was not very noticing in general, but where she loved, she was solicitous, and she did love Polly truly. It had come to her notice over the last few exchanges that all was not quite well with her dazzling cousin.

'Aren't you happy, dearest Polly? I thought you liked it here too.'

'Whatever made you think that?' Polly said bitterly, before she could stop herself. It was not fair to take things out on Minnie – but then, who else was there to strike out at?

Minnie's damp hand crept into hers, and she scanned Polly's lovely face with a growing anxiety. 'You wouldn't go away, would you? You wouldn't leave me? I couldn't bear it if you left me.'

'Oh Minnie!'

'You said you'd stay with me always. You remember, before I got married? You said you'd stay with me.'

'Yes. I remember. But I never thought –' She stopped abruptly.

Minnie struggled with the unaccustomed burden of thought. 'I'll do anything you like – give you anything I've got. I want you to be happy too. Only you mustn't leave me, Polly! Please say you won't.'

Polly stared at her, frustrated, exasperated, and yet with pity. Since Minnie was born, she had felt the burden of her on her soul. At first it had been with pleasure – Minnie as a baby was her living doll, to be played with and dressed and carried about. And when a little older, Minnie had trotted at her heels, a faithful and adoring lieutenant, a flattering audience, a staunch supporter.

Once she had enjoyed having someone for whom she was always right; and it was not Minnie's fault if she now found it

192

irritating. She had accepted the adulation, and now she had to pay the price. Minnie depended on her absolutely: it would break her heart if Polly were to leave her.

'Of course I'll stay with you,' she said quietly. 'In any case, where else could I go?'

That point seemed to comfort Minnie. 'Yes, that's right,' she said, her worried frown fading. 'You haven't anywhere else to go now, except back to Mama, and she'll be going away after Rosamund's wedding.'

Aunt Lucy would not have taken her back, in any case, Polly knew: she had shrugged Polly off, with an allowance, to be Flaminia's companion. Grandmama was long dead, and Morland Place now belonged to Uncle James. She had no home unless it was Stainton. Unless she followed her sister Africa's example and went to live on board her father's ship in St Helena, there was nowhere else in the world Polly could go. She was trapped, trapped in this damp green monotonous place until the moss grew over her, too, and obliterated her like a tombstone in a churchyard.

'It will be nice to go to London again, won't it?' Minnie said, wandering off down another avenue. 'Rosamund's wedding will be every bit as grand as mine was; and we'll see Mama and Lord Theakston again, and Roland, and cousin Marcus and Barbarina.'

This was a better line of thought. Polly was glad to encourage it. 'Have you decided whether or not to have a new gown for the wedding?'

'No, I haven't. I was thinking of wearing my pomona green, because I've only worn it once, but Hill says that green is bad luck at weddings. But there's my rose-coloured poplin, which is nice, only it might be too heavy if the day should be hot. What do you think?'

'I think you should have a new gown. You haven't anything that's just right.'

'Do you think so? But a new gown, which I might not wear again this year – perhaps it might be too extravagant?'

'You want to be fine, don't you? And there will always be opportunities to wear it.'

'Well, I'll ask Harvey when he comes what he thinks,' Flaminia said inevitably. 'Harvey will know what to do.'

When he comes, Polly thought. *If he comes.* She was not

even convinced in her own mind that he would appear to take them to the wedding. She began to have the superstitious dread that she would never leave this place again, that she and Minnie would be left here to rot in solitude for ever.

But he came the next day, unexpectedly as always, arriving just before the dressing-bell, which meant that dinner had to be put back an hour to allow the cook to raise the meal Minnie had ordered onto a higher plane suitable for the master of the house.

During that hour, Lord Harvey avoided the happy smiles and clinging hands of his wife, seeming not even to hear her tempting offer of a trip to the nursery to look at his daughters, and shut himself in the library with a pile of correspondence and his valet, Benson, who acted upon occasion as his secretary. When the dressing-bell sounded, he went straight to his bedroom, and emerged only when it was time to take his place at the dinner-table.

Minnie beamed at him from the foot of the table. She was wearing a twilled silk gown of leaf-green – a colour she was under the misapprehension was a favourite of her husband's – and her emeralds, which had been a wedding present from the old Marquess. Her hair was elaborately curled and decorated with jewels and feathers by her maid, Hill, who though surly and sour was an excellent coiffeuse. With her plump, pale face and reddish hair Minnie would never be a beauty, but her happiness at the moment gave her a glow which made her almost pretty, had anyone been in a way to notice.

Between them, in solitary state on the long side of the table, Polly sat in an evening gown of white jaconet shot with silver, with a flounced hem and ruffled bodice and sleeves, and her mother's pearls around her long white throat. With her porcelain skin, glossy black hair and perfect features, she looked like the effigy of a goddess, beautiful in an almost inhuman way.

What smiles she could spare from her husband, Minnie directed towards Polly. 'Doesn't she look beautiful, Harvey?' she said at last. 'I think Polly is the most beautiful person I've ever seen.'

Harvey looked up from his plate, and turned his gaze slowly to the right. 'Yes,' he said. 'I believe you're right.'

Minnie beamed at having her opinion agreed with. 'I take pleasure in looking at her, always.'

Polly's eyes of sudden blue were fixed on him, shining and opaque as sapphires, so intensely blue it was hard to believe they had anything to do with the action of seeing. They seemed to exist for no purpose other than their blueness.

'It's so nice to have you here,' Minnie said next. 'The two people I love best in the world here together – and the dear babies, of course. It's so pleasant to have one's family around one, don't you think? Will you be staying long? Perhaps you could stay until we all go to London.'

'Go to London?' Harvey said vaguely. His eyes were fixed on Polly, as though mesmerised by her beauty, and he seemed hardly to have heard Minnie's prattle. 'Who's going to London?'

'For Rosamund's wedding,' Minnie said, her pleasure clouded by no apprehension. 'We're all invited. It's to be in the Abbey, don't you remember? Just like ours was, only in June, which is a better month for a wedding, really, for everyone will still be in Town.'

'Rosamund's wedding?' Harvey said, turning to her at last. 'Oh, yes, I suppose so.'

'It would be very nice,' Minnie went on, with hope undiminished by experience, 'if you would stay until then. It's so long since you had a good, long stay. We could invite the Longcrofts to dine with us,' she added enticingly, 'and then you could have a hand of whist afterwards.'

He frowned. 'Oh, no, no, I can't stay. I shall only be here a day or two at the most. I have pressing business to attend to.'

Disappointment clouded Minnie's eyes, but she said meekly, 'Of course. I understand. Your business must come first.'

'Indeed it must,' he said with an attempt at heartiness, 'or how shall I pay for your expensive tastes?'

'Oh dear, I'm sure I didn't mean to be expensive. Have I been more so than usual? I'm sure I don't recollect ordering anything out of the ordinary.'

'I was joking you, Flaminia,' Harvey said quickly. 'Don't upset yourself.'

'Well, you shall see my account books after dinner, and then you can tell me if there's anything I should not have ordered. I don't wish to be a drain on you.'

'I was only funning,' Harvey said again, and then, seeing Minnie's anxious-to-please, uncomprehending expression, he said, 'I shall look at your books with pleasure, my dear, if I have time, and I'm sure I'll find everything in order.'

Minnie beamed again. 'I hope so. And I needn't have a new gown, you know – my poplin will do very well,' she said, to her husband's mystification; and then she asked him if the dinner was to his taste, and so the conversation ground on as the meal was consumed.

Afterwards, Minnie and Polly withdrew to the drawing-room, leaving Harvey at the cleared table in possession of the port and humidor. He didn't normally stay long if there was no company, only long enough to smoke a cigar; then he would come to the drawing-room and ask Polly to play and sing to him, or engage her in a game of picquet or chess. Minnie would sit happily with her sewing, lifting her head between stitches to look at them contentedly, or offer some remark about the twins' progress or the next day's programme.

Tonight, however, he did not come. After some time, Polly stood up and excused herself. 'I shall go and get myself a book to read,' she said in automatic explanation. Minnie always wanted to know where she was if she left the room even for an instant.

The book-room was at the other end of the house from the drawing-room, and the way to it was along a dark, panelled passage, hazardous with the antlers of stuffed deer's heads and ancient pikes and halberds nailed up for decoration. The gloomy glint of glazed eyes followed her, watching from the petrified forest of branched horn as she stepped silently along the drugget. The door to the dining-room was partly open, letting a sliver of light and the smell of cigar-smoke into the passage. Polly walked past it without glancing in, pausing only at the branch of the passage to pick up a candle before passing on and entering the book-room.

It was cold in there, and as in any room in that house when the fire was out, it smelled of dampness, a mushroomy smell of disuse and mouldering books. She lit enough of the candles in the wall-sconces to see her way, and then carried her candle over to the first of the bookcases which lined the walls and held it up to illuminate the gilded bindings. She passed her eyes along the rows without being able even to take in the titles, far less choose something to read: her mind was far away, her senses attuned to another part of the house.

When the door opened softly, she knew who it was. This, of all rooms in the house, was one that Minnie would never enter of her own accord. The hair rose on the back of her neck, as though an icy draught had touched it. She turned and watched him walk across the room to her, allowed him to take the candle from her impassive fingers and put it down. She lifted her eyes to his without protest, and only shuddered when he took her in his arms and buried his face in the hollow of her neck.

'Oh God! My love, my darling!' he groaned, muffled by her flesh.

She said nothing, feeling as though everything in her had been numbed by the creeping dampness of this house; unable to react or resist, she submitted to the growing frenzy of his embrace, her eyes fixed unseeing on the shadows over his shoulder. He nuzzled her neck and ear and cheek, and sought her lips, and then she shuddered, responding at last, helplessly, as he held her face in both his hands and kissed and kissed her, pressing his body against hers avidly.

At last, though, she dragged her mouth away from his, and turned her face away, pushing him back from her.

'Don't, Harvey. No more,' she said.

He stared at her a little wildly, still panting from the violence of his passion. 'What is it? Why do you push me away every time? God, Polly, don't you know what I'm feeling, how much I need you? Don't you feel anything for me?'

'You know what I feel,' she said in a low, pained voice.

'I thought I did,' he said harshly. 'Now I begin to wonder if I was right. I thought you loved me –'

'I do love you,' she said, adding unhappily, 'God help me.'

'Well, then,' he began eagerly, reaching for her. 'If you love me, why won't you –?'

'No,' she said, pushing his hands away. 'Oh God, this is an intolerable situation!'

'Yes, it is,' he agreed bitterly.

'No, not in the way you mean. We can't go on like this. We must stop, before it's too late.'

'Stop what? There's nothing to stop!' he snapped cruelly, and then instantly relented. 'Oh Polly, my own darling, why won't you let me love you? Would it be so wrong?'

'You know it would. You are a married man –'

'Married against my will!'

It was a thing he often said, and it always angered her. He had been a grown man with a small but independent income when he had taken Minnie instead of her to wife. The situation had been far more his to control than it had ever been hers. In his position, she felt, she would not so tamely have submitted to his father's and elder brother's will; in his position, she would have fought for her love. Yet now he seemed to look to her to make things right – or as right as they ever could be.

But that sort of 'right' was wrong as far as she was concerned. No matter how she struggled, no matter which way she turned, it was still wrong.

'Nevertheless,' she said, 'you have a wife –'

'To the Devil with her!' he cried, shocking her. 'I don't care – I feel nothing for her. You know that. I care only for you. Oh Polly, come away with me – let me live with you! I must have you – it's driving me to distraction!' He gathered her again in his arms, and she struggled, but without great determination. She ached for him, too, yearned for love, for his arms and his lips, longed to be swept away heedlessly by passion, so that she no longer heard that nagging voice of conscience. She wanted happiness. Why should she be denied it?

'Why must you torture me?' she moaned between his frantic kisses. 'Harvey, Harvey!'

He felt her desire, believed himself to be winning. He released her mouth and imprinted his kisses on her white neck and the upper curve of her breasts. 'You torture yourself,' he murmured. 'Don't hold back from me. It's what we both want. Let me take you away from here. I'll take care of you, I swear it. You shall have whatever you want. Only let me love you. I'll give you your own place, clothes, servants, a carriage – everything you could want –'

'Except my peace of mind,' she said, putting him from her gently, but so firmly that he dropped his arms and stood looking at her, puzzled and afraid.

'Does it give you so much peace now?'

She looked away from him with a sigh. 'No,' she said into the shadows of the room.

'Then give in to me. Let me make you happy. Let me make *us* happy. You know that I could. You were my lover once – or have you managed to forget that?'

'No, I haven't forgotten. It tortures me to remember, but I do. I was weak, I did wrong, and I'm being punished for it. But you, Harvey –' She turned to face him, looking up at him with wide, opaque eyes. 'Don't you remember the promise you made me – that if I would only stay, you would never ask anything of me?'

'Yes, I remember,' he said desperately. 'But I didn't know what I was saying. How could I have promised anything so impossible to perform? You know how much I love you – want you – need you! How long must I wait for you? How long can a man wait?'

'For ever, if need be.'

'But I love you, only you! I'll divorce her – or let her divorce me, it makes no difference. She'll be well taken care of –'

'We would be outcasts.'

'We could go abroad to live.'

'But still we couldn't marry. It's no use, Harvey. You have a wife, and while she lives you can never have another.' There was a silence. He seemed to have no answer for that. Polly resumed, her voice weary with the impossibility of it all. 'But anyway, I promised her I wouldn't leave her. And what about the children?'

He clenched his fists. 'Oh don't! Don't go on! The children! Useless brats, my brother calls them, because they're girls – but he hasn't seen them. So small and soft, so pretty – God, how they tear at my heart! If only they were yours, Polly, yours and mine –'

'Don't,' she said. In her heart she added, they could have been, if you had only stood firm. 'It's useless to talk like that.'

'But you don't know what it's like to be trapped by a woman you never cared for, and two useless brats. I want you, Polly! I must have you! If you keep denying me, you'll drive me to madness.'

'Don't talk like that.'

'I mean it! I'm close to it now. Why do you think I've stayed away so much? Because I'm afraid if I see you like this and can't have you I'll do something desperate.' He clenched his teeth, and his eyes were bright and unseeing. 'What have I got to lose?' he went on, almost to himself. 'Sometimes, by God, I feel as though I could –'

'Sshh!' Polly said suddenly, staring towards the door.

'What is it?' The silence was profound, not even a ticking clock in the book-room to disturb it. He left her side and went silently to the door. It was not completely closed, and he snatched the handle and flung it open. Nothing. A dark and empty passage mocked his melodrama. He walked back to Polly's side, but the interruption had broken the mood. His anger had dissipated. He seemed now only weary.

'There's no-one there.' He took her hands, and spoke quietly, without force, like a rational man. 'Polly, do you tell me that you will never do what I ask – never love me again?'

It was harder for her to resist his sadness than his passion. 'I do love you,' she said, 'but I can't do what you ask. I can't be your wife, and I won't be your mistress.'

'Why not? Who would it hurt?'

'Me. Myself. I do enough wrong in loving you in my heart, but I can't seem to change that. I won't shame myself and break Minnie's heart. And now I'm going back to the drawing-room. She must be wondering where I am.'

She drew her hands out from his, and turned away, leaving him there in the half-lit room, feeling his unhappiness like a weight on the back of her neck, and her own like a cold stone inside her. Who would it hurt, indeed? Who cared for her or her reputation? It would be easier, so much easier to give in to him, as she had that one time, when she had spent three days with him in London, in the anonymous lodging in Bab Mae's Street.

But then, it had not been so easy, had it? Long in the planning, long in the aftermath; and the three days themselves, though burning in her memory for the consummation of their passion, had been as full of misery as of love. The secrecy, the shabbiness, the sense of degradation, the fear of being discovered, the sneaking about in disguise like a thief, hiding from all eyes – these had clouded the joy she ought to have felt at being at last in Harvey's arms.

And then afterwards, when she had returned to Stainton, there had followed weeks of unhappiness and guilt: missing him so dreadfully, worrying about what the consequences might be; having to sustain a lie, having to bear Minnie's joy at having her back again; hating Minnie, and hating herself for hating. No, giving in would not really be easier than resisting. She wanted most of all to run away, to escape from both of them with their stifling, ennervating demands, but she couldn't even do that, having given her word to both of them to stay. She was trapped in a situation only partly of her own making, and she could see no way out of it. She must simply endure, and hope that somehow, somehow it would be resolved.

As she walked through the drawing-room door, she realised that she had forgotten to bring a book, and cursed her unreadiness. She was not cut out to be a conspirator. Minnie would be sure to notice – interested as she was in every tiny thing Polly did or said. But even as she began framing an excuse in her head, she saw that there was no need – Flaminia was not there. Her chair was empty, her embroidery-frame was pushed aside, and only the innocent, crackling fire greeted her as she entered.

Polly went to her own chair and sat down, staring blankly at the flames, trying not to think. A moment later Harvey came in, trying for insouciance, his expression composed for the domestic tableau he expected. His surprise was almost comic.

'Where is she?'

'I don't know. The room was empty when I came in.'

'You don't suppose –? No, what am I thinking! She would have no reason to go to the book-room.'

Polly's face paled. She hadn't thought of that. 'You mean the noise I heard?'

'*Thought* you heard. There was no-one there, I tell you.' Wanting it to be so made it so for him. How comfortable to be able to live in such a world of your own making! 'Come, sit and play to me. She'll be back in a moment, depend on it.'

Better to have something to occupy her hands and at least part of her mind. Polly sat at the piano, opened a piece of music at random, and began to play, quite unaware of what it was. Harvey took a seat by the fire and opened the newspaper he had brought with him. It was to this peaceful scene that Flaminia returned a while later. Polly's hands suspended themselves above the keys.

'Oh, don't stop, I like that song,' Minnie said as she walked through the door. 'What is it?'

Polly had to look at the music to answer. 'The Ash Grove,' she said. She really shouldn't stare at Minnie, especially as she saw out of the corner of her eye that Harvey was staring too. Did Minnie look paler than usual? Was there something strange about her expression? She did not smile. Was she avoiding their eyes? Hard to tell, when they were avoiding hers.

But no, Polly thought, pushing away guilty fear, Minnie would be incapable of dissembling. She was simply not intelligent enough to hide her emotions, to pretend to be feeling something she was not. If she really had overheard something, they would have known it at once. Polly dragged her eyes back to the music and began to play again.

'Where were you?' Harvey asked after a moment, in an elaborately casual voice. It sounded so unnatural to Polly that she stumbled over a chord, and then flinched at her own stupidity.

'I went up to see the babies,' Minnie said, returning to her seat by the fire. 'You were both gone so long, and I – I just wanted to see them.'

She took up her needle again and began to sew, and Harvey stared at the top of her bent head, deep in furious speculation, while Polly played to the bottom of the page and then began again at the top, completely unaware of what she was doing.

Héloïse had never been to Manchester before, so her first sight of it was quite a surprise. Even from a distance it was surrounded by a pall of dark smoke.

'Oh dear, it does look so very dirty,' she said to Sophie. 'But I suppose it means that the manufactories are working, for which one ought to be grateful.'

Jasper Hobsbawn said the same thing when he met them at the door of Hobsbawn House. 'It would be a sad thing for Manchester if the air were clear and pure. I love that smell of smoke – it means all is well.'

'And is it?' Héloïse asked quickly.

'Better than it was,' he said. 'There are signs that trade is reviving at last – but we'll talk about that later. You must be tired from your long drive, and chilled. Even though it's May, one gets cold sitting still. Will you come to the fire and take some refreshment first, or would you like to go to your rooms?'

'To the fire, by all means,' Héloïse said. 'And I should be glad of some tea – would not you, Sophie my love?'

'Yes, please.'

'Tea, then, please, Richards,' Jasper said to the waiting servant, and led the way across the hall to the stairs. 'Your ladyship – Miss Morland – shall I lead the way? There's a good fire in the morning-room. It's more pleasant than the formal drawing-room, I think – though of course you must arrange everything to your own taste now you're here. Much of the house is shut up, but I've had the dining-parlour and morning-room aired for you, as well as your bedrooms. There's only a small staff here, but the housekeeper is very good, and the cook comes with her recommendation.'

'You are not living here, then?' Sophie asked in surprise, as they mounted the stairs.

'Oh no. I live out at Brindle. This house belongs to your mother, of course, like everything else.'

'Well, but I always thought that you would live here, Mr Hobsbawn,' Héloïse said with a smile. 'I'm sorry if I did not make that clear. It is a pity to leave the house empty.'

Jasper looked embarrassed. 'Oh, I use it now and then, if I am in this part of town for any reason, but I'm used to Brindle, and it's handy for the mills. Since I'm not married and never entertain, I have no need of an establishment. This house is very grand, but rather gloomy when you're alone, I find.'

He opened the morning-room door, and stepped back for them to enter.

'Oh!' Sophie cried in involuntary surprise. 'Look at the elephants!' There were two carved in ivory ornamenting the chimney-shelf, a large mahogany one in the corner with a torchère emerging from its back, another in ebony supporting a round brass table-top, and one at either end of one of the sofas, forming its arms.

'Yes, there are rather a lot of them,' Jasper said, his eyes on her face rather than the room. 'The whole house is furnished very much in the taste of thirty years ago – elephants and blackamoors and palm-trees, and all the gilding and lacquering and ornamentation of the period. There's a Chinese bedroom that would very much surprise you, I think – the canopy is shaped like a pagoda, and hung with hundreds of little ivory bells.'

'Oh, that must be pretty,' Sophie said.

'Yes, I suppose it is,' he said, gesturing them towards the fire. 'I like things plainer myself, but it's amusing in its way. I'd be happy to shew you over the house some time, if you'd like it.'

Héloïse, engaged in warming her hands, was struck by the tone of his voice and glanced towards him, to see his face illuminated by a smile as he looked at Sophie. Why, he is not so very plain after all, she thought. She had only met him once before, when he came to Morland Place in the year '15 to discuss the future of the mills, and stayed for three days. She had formed a favourable impression of him then, as an intelligent, sincere, if rather serious man. She had enjoyed his company, but had not thought of him as attractive until now.

'Although perhaps you would prefer to explore it on your own,' he was saying to Sophie now. 'It isn't so large a house as to require a guide, after all.'

He was plainly 'remembering his place' and 'not putting himself forward'. Héloïse felt very sensitive about his situation – cousin to the former owner, almost the owner of everything himself, and now reduced to the position of paid employee, feeling that he had to be deferential to the usurper of his kingdom. It was this difference, she guessed, which had prevented him from making use of Hobsbawn House, rather than its location or inconvenience.

So she said quickly, 'Who should know it better than you, Mr Hobsbawn? We should like very much for you to shew us round, if you have the time – *n'est-ce pas*, Sophie?'

'Yes, indeed, Maman,' Sophie said, looking at her feet, but out of shyness rather than reluctance. She liked Mr Hobsbawn, but he did stare at her rather.

'And around Manchester, too,' Héloïse went on. 'I have no acquaintance here, so I hope you will not abandon us in the evenings, or we shall find ourselves dining alone every day.'

He actually laughed at that. 'I'm sure that will not be the case, ma'am. Once it's known that you're here, there will be a stream of callers and invitations. All of Manchester society will want to pay its respects to you. But I assure you that I'm at your service, day or night, in whatever capacity you choose. Please command me, ma'am – and you too, of course, Miss Morland.'

The next day, after breakfast, the carriage took them to the mills, where they were met in the courtyard by Jasper. It was not yet eleven o'clock when they arrived, but Jasper had done half a day's work already.

'I like to be here most days when the hands arrive. It encourages them to know that I work the same hours as them,' he explained.

Héloïse thought this an odd precept. Surely it was more important to keep a proper distance from your servants and employees, so that they respected you? Obedience depended on respect, and how would an underling respect you if he thought you were no different from him? But she had not come here to debate his philosophy with him. That could wait until a more social occasion.

'Are the gates kept locked all the time?' she asked. They had had to be unlocked and opened for the carriage by a gate-keeper with a key large enough to have belonged to a castle keep.

'Oh yes, except at the beginning and end of shift.'

'Is it to keep out the Luddites?'

Jasper smiled. 'It's not for keeping people out, but for keeping them in. The gates are shut on the last strike of six in the morning, and any of the hands who arrive after that are fined for being late.'

'It makes it rather like a prison, though, doesn't it?' Sophie said, looking around with distaste at the grimy, soot-streaked buildings under a sky obscured by clouds of sulphurous smoke.

'Oh yes. Some of the Irish call the mills "the lock-ups". But punctuality doesn't come naturally to them, especially when they've worked at home before, able to start and stop as they please. If we didn't lock them in, they'd be wandering off after an hour or two, and that would never do. The machines don't stop, you see – they have to be tended all the time. That's what the hands have to learn: to work to the rhythm of the machines, and at their pace.'

'I see,' said Sophie, though she didn't really, never having seen a machine in operation.

'Well, now, I must shew you round,' Jasper resumed. He turned to look up at the building Sophie was staring at. 'This is what we call Number Two Mill. The old Number One is that building over there, and the red brick structure you can see at the end of it is what used to be the 'prentice house. Of course we don't use 'prentices now – it's all free labour.'

'Is that a good thing?' Héloïse asked. 'I know we used to send you pauper children as apprentices. It seemed a good idea to train them to do a useful job, so that they could support themselves honestly.'

Jasper answered evenly, though his expression was veiled. 'It might have been a good idea, but it never really worked. This is a much better system. The overseers didn't like working the pauper children, and having to beat them to keep them at their tasks. Now it's their own parents who work them, and take responsibility for discipline and so on. A man has the right to chastise his own child, hasn't he?'

'Are there many children here?'

'About sixty – that's children under sixteen. And we have forty-nine women and unmarried girls, and twenty-eight adult males, not counting the overseers.'

'So few men?' Héloïse said in surprise.

'They're the skilled spinners and engineers. The women and children do all the other jobs. They take better to the discipline. Well, shall we go in? I think I can promise you a sight you will never forget.'

Half an hour later, he was helping Sophie to a chair in his office, and hovering anxiously while Héloïse applied her vinaigrette to her fainting daughter's nose.

'Some wine,' Jasper suggested anxiously. 'Shall I fetch some wine for her? Shall I send someone for a physician? Perhaps she is ill.'

'No, I don't think so,' Héloïse said calmly. 'She will be better by and by. It was very hot in the spinning-rooms.'

206

'Yes, it has to be kept hot so that the threads don't break, but of course we get used to it and stop noticing how airless it is. Oh dear, I am so sorry! I wouldn't have had this happen for the world.'

Sophie was beginning to revive, enough to push the smelling-bottle away and struggle to sit up.

'I'm all right now, Maman.'

'Very well, but just sit quietly for a moment, *chérie.*'

A few moments more, and Sophie was well enough to feel embarrassed. 'I'm sorry to make such a nuisance of myself –'

'Oh! Good Lord, no, no nuisance at all,' Jasper said at once, reddening. 'The heat can be overpowering.'

'It wasn't the heat. It was the noise and the machines and – and everything,' Sophie said lamely.

There were beads of perspiration on her face, but they were nothing to do with the heat of the factory, nor even its airlessness and strange smells. It was the machines themselves that had affected her. Room after room of them, roaring, grinding, thumping, throbbing, moving their inhuman arms with such inhuman regularity, as though invested with some ghastly purpose of their own. And amongst them the workers had seemed dwarfed, frail creatures enslaved by the machines, scurrying like ants to tend their abominable needs and meet their endless demands.

Man had made the machine, she knew that as a fact – but to be inside a manufactory at work was to feel that it was the machine that ruled. It had taken over from its human sponsors, and could not now be governed. A sense of unstoppable power that threatened to blot out humanity had battered at her sensibilities and brought her to the edge of fainting.

Jasper looked as though he understood a little of what she was feeling. 'It can be overwhelming, the first time you see them in action,' he nodded sympathetically. 'And yet, it's wonderful, too, when you think what they can do! Such an abundance can be made, where there was scarcity before; so many goods –'

'The children,' Sophie said suddenly out of her own thoughts, interrupting him, 'were so small. When I saw the little ones crawling under those great iron things, I was so frightened. I thought of my little brother Benedict –'

'Oh, but those children were not so young as Benedict, my

love,' Héloïse said. 'Consider that poor peoples' children are always smaller.'

'We don't like to take them under ten years old,' Jasper said. 'Indeed, I would never do so, except that sometimes the spinner insists on having his whole family with him, including a younger child.'

'Ah, then it is just like the mines,' Héloïse said. 'Lord Anstey was telling me the same thing about the mines.'

'I wouldn't know about that, ma'am. But some mills take them as young as seven, and I would like to see the practice made an end of. Little ones under ten are simply too young to understand the work, the conditions are too harsh for them, and the hours too long. So I told the Committee last year – Sir Robert Peel's Committee. Sir Robert is hoping to put the Ten Hours Bill before the House next year, as you probably know –'

'Yes, Mr Hobsbawn, and I should very much like to discuss it with you,' Héloïse said gently, 'but I think perhaps another time. I would like to take Miss Morland home now.'

'Oh, of course – I'm so sorry. Thoughtless of me! How do you feel now, Miss Morland?'

'Better, thank you. But I should be glad to go home.'

'I'll pass the word for your carriage at once.'

'I shall leave the window down a little as we drive, Sophie, and that will revive you. Mr Hobsbawn, may we trespass further on your time, and ask you to dine with us today? Then perhaps after dinner we could discuss the mills in more detail?'

'But of course, ma'am. And thank you – I shall be delighted to dine.'

The journey back to Hobsbawn House gave Sophie much to reflect on: the manufactory, with its locked gates and the inhuman demands of the machines to begin with. The work, indeed, was not so very hard, even she could see that – most of the labour about a farm was harder, and much more dangerous and disagreeable. And the heat inside the mill would not be so unpleasant as the crippling cold endured by field-workers in winter. And for the children, the kind of work they were doing was much what they would have been doing for their parents at home anyway.

But it was the unnaturalness, the ceaseless rhythm of the power-gigs, their massive, thoughtless regularity which she believed would be hard to bear. She could not endure it for half an hour: what must it be like to have to work there for twelve or thirteen hours a day with no rest or respite? A man digging in a field might stop for a moment to ease his back, to exchange a word with his neighbour, to watch a flight of birds pass overhead; but in the manufactory there was no stopping while the machines ran.

And when the work was done, the hands emerged not into the genial greenness of nature, but into grim, grey streets, with the sky shut out by towering mills, and obscured by bitter smoke and drizzling soot. No pleasant stream to gaze at, or to fish in, but the stinking River Irwell, sluggish with refuse, effluvia, and the foul-smelling residues pumped out from the dye-works and tanneries along its banks. No cottage to go home to, with its own scrap of garden to grow beans and cabbages in, but a dark room in one of those filthy tenements they were passing, so meanly built that a man standing amongst the offal and rubbish in the middle of the street could have touched the houses to either side by stretching out his hands, and could have looked into the first-floor windows only by reaching up on tip-toe.

She remembered Mr Farraline talking about the mills, his enthusiasm, almost rapture over the machines, and she wondered how he could feel like that about them. It was perhaps different for Mr Hobsbawn, she thought, for she knew he had been born to it, had begun working in the mills himself (*fancy!*) when he was eight years old, so it was all the life he knew. The machines were very clever inventions, she saw that, but how anyone who, like Mr Farraline, had the choice, could want to be around them when they were in operation was more than she could understand.

The carriage passed from the hideous environs of the Irwell and the mills, through streets growing gradually wider and more handsome, with public buildings any town would be proud of, and grand houses belonging to wealthy people, and pulled at last into the sweep of Hobsbawn House.

'How are you feeling now, my Sophie?' Héloïse asked as they entered the hall. She turned to survey her daughter's pale face, wondering whether it had been a good idea after all to bring her. She had wanted to give her a change of scene, and had hoped that the more varied social life of the town might bring her out of herself. Sophie had been mourning Larosse for two years now, and at her age that was long enough. It was time for her to fall in love again, and get married. But she had not expected Sophie to be so affected by the mills, and she had plainly been brooding on the journey back here.

'I'm quite all right, Maman,' Sophie said at once, and smiled at her mother's anxious look. 'I didn't care very much for the machines, that was all.'

'Hmm. Well, the air was very foul, too. You must take a turn around the garden, *ma mie*, to refresh yourself. Ah, but look how many cards have been left! Mr Hobsbawn was right about that, at least. We must ask him who these people are, and make up a dinner party. And we must ask him when the Assembly nights are, too. I wish you to have some dancing while you are here. And perhaps there may be a theatre, or a concert-hall.'

'You don't need to worry about me, Maman,' Sophie began. 'I'm quite –'

There she stopped. As she spoke she had been watching her mother sort through the cards which had been left on the hall table by the morning's callers, and amongst the large number of ladies' cards, some accompanied by eldest-daughter cards with a top corner turned down, there was one which by its size and shape stood out as a gentleman's.

Héloïse, quite naturally, was attracted to it as well. She drew it out and placed it on the top of the pile.

The Hon Jesmond Farraline was printed across the centre, with the address underneath, *Batchworth House, Cheetham Hill*. And under that, written in a bold hand and blue-black ink, *With compliments*.

'He compliments us, how nice,' Héloïse said, smiling. 'This is the gentleman you met in Scarborough, with the mother?'

'Yes, Maman,' said Sophie. 'I had forgotten he lives in Manchester.'

'So he does. And he calls very promptly. That is polite. And without the mother. It must be for your sake, Sophie, for he does not know me. Well, if he calls again, we shall be very glad to see him, shan't we?'

'Yes, Maman,' said Sophie.

CHAPTER ELEVEN

'Sell them? Sell the mills?' Jasper cried in tones of horror. Then he took a pull at his reins. 'Well, ma'am, it must be as you wish, since they belong to you, but if you would allow me to advise you –?'

'That is why I am here, Mr Hobsbawn – to consult you and ask your advice. I will be frank with you. Things are not going well for us at Morland Place. It is the same everywhere, I think.'

'So I understand. The ending of the war –'

'It is strange, is it not? We all longed so for peace, and now it has come, nothing seems to go right. How can that be? Why is it that suddenly no-one has any money?'

Jasper smiled. 'I believe that's more than you or I could ever understand, ma'am. Or any man. Wealth seems to ebb and flow about the world like the tides, but the how and the why are beyond knowing.'

'We can only know the effects,' Héloïse agreed. 'And one of the effects is that we need money at Morland Place to pay the interest on borrowings made during the war.'

'You thought you might raise that money by selling the mills?'

'My husband suggested it, and since he cannot leave Morland Place at the moment, I came instead to consult you. The mills have not been doing well lately, have they?'

'No, not since the end of the war. Armies use up a great many cotton goods, you see, and we in England were supplying not only our own army but those of our allies as well.' He gave her a small, quirky smile. 'You may not believe it, ma'am, but at one time we were supplying Boney's army too!'

'No! Surely not?'

'It's true. I've seen bills to prove it. Back in the year seven,

211

the French army were wearing uniforms made from English cloth.'

'*Ciel*! That passes belief.' Héloïse shook her head.

'War is madness,' Jasper said. 'But it also means trade. And with the coming of peace, the orders fell off, and so we had closures and bankruptcies and part-time working, and all the other ills which have brought us low.'

'But still you do not recommend selling the mills?'

'No, ma'am, I don't – and not only because it would cost me my livelihood.'

Héloïse was embarrassed by the mention. It was something which James, in his large way, had omitted to take into account, but she had already been considering ways in which Jasper Hobsbawn might be compensated if it were to come to that.

'As to that –' she began, but Jasper shook his head, asking to be allowed to continue.

'My reasons for advising against selling are several. Firstly, there are signs, good signs, that trade is beginning to pick up. I have never believed, like some of my colleagues, that things will never get better. Manufacturers have short memories, you know. They forget that we have gone through bad patches before. I believe that in the long run our business cannot fail. People must always be clothed; and machines are not a passing fancy – they are here to stay. In the future there will be more and more of them, capable of doing more and more different tasks – not just spinning, but every other process of manufacture, from the raw cotton to the finished cloth.'

Héloïse smiled at his enthusiasm. 'Only so far? You do not, then, predict a machine for cutting out and sewing up?'

'Well, perhaps not that! But at all events, I believe business will improve – and soon. We're already getting more orders than we did six months ago. The worst is over, and I think by the end of the year we will be back to normal working.'

'I see. Very well, but you spoke of reasons, in the plural?'

'I did. Secondly, Hobsbawn Mills are in better shape than any of their rivals to benefit from the good times, and to withstand the bad times. My late cousin was a sharp man, clever and far-sighted in business. He built and stocked the mills from profits of previous ventures, without having to borrow a penny, so we have no investors to answer to, and no interest payments to meet – and I think you know, ma'am, how important that is at the moment.'

'Yes,' said Héloïse.

'When trade is bad, we can simply close down part of the operation, and when it improves we re-open, knowing there are no heavy outgoings which have to be met willy-nilly. None of the other mills is in that strong position.'

'I see. And thirdly?'

'We already have the capacity to expand once trade is back to normal, as it must be sooner or later – and I think sooner. Number Three Mill stands ready, with most of the equipment already in place, to begin power-weaving our own yarn as soon as the demand is sufficient.'

'Power-weaving? I thought that was impossible?'

'In the wool trade, yes. Woollen threads are not strong enough to withstand the force of a machine. But Mr Hobsbawn believed, and I believe, that one day power looms for cotton will be the rule rather than the exception. The looms he bought and installed are of the earliest type and rather crude, it's true. We've had problems with them – I won't trouble you with the details – and we really need an engineer to design us something better. But for the moment, we own one of the few steam-operated weaving sheds in Manchester, and once all the spinning-mills are back in operation, not all the hand-loom weavers in the country can keep up with demand. It would be a great pity, don't you think, to abandon that position?'

'You do not weave at the moment?'

'No, ma'am. The weaving-shed has been idle since 1813, but the capacity is there, ready to use. If you sell the mills – if you can find someone willing to buy them – you will have a sum of money in hand with which to pay off immediate debts. The price you'd get for them would not be what they are really worth, in my opinion. When prices are low, that is the time to buy, not to sell – you see that?'

'Yes, I see,' Héloïse said doubtfully.

'But if you keep the mills, you will have an asset which costs you virtually nothing to keep, but which will one day be of enormous value, and bring you such an income as you can have no idea of at the present!'

'In your opinion.'

Jasper's eyes had kindled with enthusiasm, but now the light died. 'Yes, ma'am, in my opinion. You are free, of course, to seek advice from any other source.'

She smiled encouragingly. 'I shall do so. But thank you for yours, Mr Hobsbawn. I shall consider what you have told me. And I shall do nothing, I assure you, without consulting you further.'

One of the people who had left cards on Hobsbawn House was Mrs Pendlebury, an ample widow of means, who regarded herself as a leader of Manchester Society. She had been well acquainted with the Hobsbawns over a number of years, her husband having partnered old Mr Hobsbawn in many a business deal. When Fanny had paid her visits to Manchester before her marriage, Mrs Pendlebury had acted as chaperone to her – as far as Fanny would permit it – and had taken her about in company with her two daughters-at-home, Prudence and Agnes.

The younger of these, Agnes, was now married, but Mrs Pendlebury had not succeeded in finding a mate for Prudence, and had lately reached the point of accepting that she never would. Prudence was a tall, thin, pale, serious young woman of twenty-four. She had never been much interested in dancing and flirting, and it was generally assumed that she would remain daughter-at-home, and ultimately act as housekeeper to her brother Fred when Mrs Pendlebury finally shuffled off the mortal coil.

Fred was now twenty-six, also tall, but stout and florid and extremely well pleased with himself. He had inherited his father's fortune and business at an early age, but left them to his mother to control. Being at one remove from the origins of his fortune, he regarded business as vulgar, and his purpose was to have as much enjoyment and as little exertion as were compatible with each other. He liked lying late in bed, eating and drinking, gaming if it were for small stakes, riding about in carriages, and strolling along the fashionable thoroughfares exquisitely dressed so that the young women might have the pleasure of admiring him.

Mrs Pendlebury had no anxieties about Fred's continuing in the bachelor state. She agreed with his own opinion, that he was the most eligible *parti* in Manchester, and she had not yet seen the young woman who was good enough for him. She would have got Fanny Morland for him if she could, though Fanny's subsequent behaviour made her glad she had not, for it would not do for her darling Fred to be shackled to such an unprincipled creature as Miss Morland turned out to be. Still, the Hobsbawn Mills were a delightful property – to say nothing of the legendary Morland Place – and the arrival of Sophie with Lady Morland aroused all Mrs Pendlebury's maternal instincts again.

To be sure, Miss Sophie was not a beauty: she was small and thin, and her complexion had no brilliance. Had it not been for her eyes and her teeth one might even have called her *plain*. But she was a well principled, pretty-behaved girl – and above all, she seemed gentle and meek. Mrs Pendlebury had no idea of retiring to a dower establishment when Fred did finally bring home a wife, so it was important that the future Mrs Fred should be governable, and not wish to rule the roast in Mrs Pendlebury's place.

The visit was said not to be intended for a long one, so Mrs Pendlebury had to move fast. The earliest possible leaving of cards, the earliest possible formal call, the most rapid advance of intimacy was called for. At first all seemed to go well – Héloïse was anxious to secure society and companionship for Sophie, and though she found Mrs Pendlebury bombastic and overbearing, there was no doubt that she was respectable, and knew everyone.

The fly in the ointment from Mrs Pendlebury's point of view was that though Sophie and Prudence took to each other with quite surprising rapidity, no spark whatever was kindled between her and Fred.

'But, Mama,' he protested when she took him to task, 'she's hardly more than a child. What interest could such a little schoolroom miss have for me?'

'She's no child,' Mrs Pendlebury snapped. 'For goodness' sake, Fred, have a little sense! She's nineteen years old –'

'Well she doesn't look it,' he snapped back sulkily. 'A skinny little dowd, no style, no face, no figure, and what –'

'She's niece to Lady Theakston, she had her come-out in Brussels, and the Duke of Wellington was a guest at her ball, that's what! She was betrothed within weeks of her *début*, and

215

if he hadn't been killed at Waterloo she wouldn't be single now. And don't talk nonsense about style, which you know nothing about – Lady Morland dresses her just as she ought, considering her late misfortune. All you need to remember is that she's to inherit the Hobsbawn Mills, and Morland Place too, for all we know.'

'I thought there was a son?'

'Two sons. But Miss Sophie is the eldest, and Morland Place is not entailed: it's Lady Morland's to leave as she pleases. So you see, my darling,' Mrs Pendlebury put on a coaxing voice, 'she'd be an excellent match for you, and she's a very sweet girl indeed. Prudence dotes on her already.'

'Well, let Prudence marry her then,' said Fred cleverly. '*I* don't want such an ugly little black thing!'

Mrs Pendlebury's mouth became grim. 'I tell you what, Fred Pendlebury, Jack Withington's been talking of trying for her, and if you don't do as I say and make up to the girl, he'll snatch her away from under your nose, and then you'll be the laughing-stock, after I've taken such pains to give you the start of him. So now!'

'Jack's my particular friend. He wouldn't do that,' said Fred, but her words had given him pause. There was no doubt that Jack was more popular with the ladies, and though they had been friends all their lives, there was a certain rivalry between them which was not always entirely friendly. If Jack was indeed thinking of Miss Morland, it was perhaps time that Fred had a closer look at her, to see if he was missing something.

In the meantime, the object of this speculation had gone out in the carriage with Prudence Pendlebury to visit her sister Agnes, now Mrs Percy Droylsden – a lively, snub-nosed creature, full of fun and gossip, who enjoyed every minute of her freedom as a young matron. She examined Sophie in a delightfully frank way, admired her pelisse and hat, and surveyed her countenance thoroughly.

'You are very like your sister Fanny, you know,' she concluded cheerfully. 'Don't you think so, Pru?'

'Not very,' said Prudence shortly. 'You do chatter so, Annie.'

'Oh but she is! About the eyes, you know, and the mouth.

There is a certain something of Fanny there.'

'I am not pretty as Fanny was,' Sophie said with a faint smile. 'But I loved her dearly.'

'Well so did I,' Agnes declared, 'and I don't care what Mama says. I remember the very day she met Mr Hawker, here in Manchester – don't you, Pru? She was with us in the carriage, and he rode up and touched his cap to us. He was the handsomest, grandest fellow in the world. I don't wonder she wanted to marry him! I would have. And I don't believe for a moment it was the case that she had to –'

'*Annie!*' Miss Pendlebury was shocked and scarlet.

Agnes clapped her hand over her mouth. 'Oh my tongue!' she said. 'I do beg your pardon, dear Miss Morland! You must ignore almost everything I say. Percy says I'm a dreadful prattle-box, but I don't mean any harm, you know. Well, you have caused a stir in Manchester all right! I can't tell you the parties that are being planned for your sake.'

'For my sake?' Sophie said, puzzled.

'Oh yes! Why, every mother with an unmarried son is already sending to the printers for her invitations. I dare say the mantuamakers will make you their patron saint after this, for every party means a dozen new dresses in this town, especially as it's said your gowns come straight from Paris!'

'They don't. And why should anyone want to marry me?' Sophie asked, perplexed.

'Ignore her,' Prudence advised firmly. 'Annie, do try for a little conduct, even though you're a married woman.'

'Oh, you are excessively modest, Miss Morland!' said Agnes, ignoring her sister. 'But I do beg you will not be tempted to marry my brother Fred. He is the dullest creature in the world, and cares about nothing but his dinner and his neck-cloths! Now I think, upon the whole, that you ought to marry Mr Farraline, for he's excessively handsome, and so romantic – unless you don't care for fair hair, of course? I prefer a dark man myself, but one has to make sacrifices in the line of duty, and I'd overlook a great deal for the sake of his lovely Grecian profile.'

Sophie smiled at her nonsense. 'Thank you, but Mr Farraline is not likely to give me the opportunity to accept or reject him.'

'But you do know him?' Agnes seemed disappointed. 'That

217

wasn't just a hum? Everyone says he called on you at Hobsbawn House.'

Sophie was conscious of blushing. 'Yes, he did call twice, and left cards, but unfortunately we were out both times.'

'I knew it! And he means to have you to dinner – or his mother does, I forget what Lizzie Ardwick said precisely.'

'I know nothing of that. I met him and his mother in Scarborough last year, when I was there with my cousin, but I assure you he is not interested in me in the slightest.'

'Oh well, never mind. Perhaps he might come round to it – and as long as you don't marry Fred – though I should dearly love you as a sister, you sweet thing! But however –'

The door was opened at that moment, and the butler announced Miss Withington and Mr Jack Withington. In the moment before they followed their names into the room, Agnes just had time to exclaim under her breath to her sister, 'Well, of all the impudence! That's just like Jack Withington, to use Libertine to scrape an acquaintance with Miss Morland!'

And Miss Pendlebury replied in a fierce whisper, 'Albertine! Her name is Albertine! One day you'll forget and say it in front of her!'

Sophie suppressed a smile at the exchange, and then brother and sister were upon them. Miss Withington was a small, plump young woman between Agnes and Prudence in age. Her brother Jack was a contemporary and friend of both Fred Pendlebury and Percy Droylsden; a big man, handsome in a coarse-featured, outdoor way. He had a hunting-field voice, a boisterous manner and an all-appraising eye.

'Well, Annie !' he exclaimed as he came in. 'Albertine was wild to visit you this morning, so I thought I'd come along and see how you were. Is Percy keeping you in ribbons and things? Oh yes, I see he is. Is that a new chiffonier? Thought so! How d'e do, Miss Pendlebury? No need to ask how you are – you're looking exceedingly handsome, as always! That's a killing smart hat, I must say.'

These pleasantries were thrown out broadcast to the sisters, but his glistening eye was roving all the time towards Sophie. Miss Withington had crossed the room to make her own quiet greetings and sit down on the sofa next to Prudence, and since Jack was still standing expectantly, staring at

Sophie, Agnes was obliged to make the introduction.

'Miss Morland, may I present our particular friend Miss Withington? And her brother Jack, who is a friend of my husband's.'

Miss Withington exchanged a civil nod with Sophie, but her brother bounced across the room to take Sophie's hand almost before she had offered it and bowed over it with a flourish that made her wriggle. 'Miss Morland, how do you do? I've heard so much about you. I must confess Albertine and I have been dying to meet you ever since we knew you were in Manchester. We knew your sister Fanny, you know. She was one of Albertine's dearest friends. They were quite inseparable, you know.'

Albertine looked at her feet and grew pink, as Agnes and Prudence exchanged a glance of indignation at this appropriation. Jack Withington took the seat nearest Sophie and as he drew breath to begin a new gambit, Prudence spoke up in a chillingly clear voice to fill the gap and prevent him.

'Do you go to the Benevolent Society meeting tomorrow, Albertine? I must tell you, Miss Morland,' turning to Sophie before Albertine could answer, 'that we have a very active society here in Manchester. There are so many sad cases needing our help, and Miss Withington and I do all we can. I do think it is up to us to lead the way. People look to those of our rank in society for an example, and I'm always sorry I can't interest Agnes in our activities.'

'Oh, I have enough to do,' Agnes, said lightly. 'I leave all that sort of thing to you, Pru. Besides, you know it annoys Mama.'

'It doesn't annoy her. She used to think I ought to spend my time in other ways –'

'Yes, buying clothes and getting beaux!' said the irrepressible Agnes.

'– but she has changed her opinion now,' Miss Pendlebury finished with dignity.

'What is the Benevolent Society?' Sophie asked, feeling something was expected of her.

'It's for the betterment of the condition of mill-workers,' Prudence said, watching Jack Withington out of the corner of her eye and keeping the ball determinedly in the air. 'Some of them are in the most appalling ignorance and want, and all of them are in need of guidance.'

'Do you know, there is not so much as a single Sunday school for their children? And the parents as often as not don't attend a church service from one year's end to the next,' Albertine added in shocked tones.

Jack did his best to intercept. 'I'm sure Miss Morland ain't interested in your philanthropist nonsense, Alba – are you, Miss Morland? It's all such stuff, you know! A young female wants to dance and enjoy herself, I know. Do you care for dancing, Miss Morland? You wouldn't want to be about sick people, I know!'

'I visit the poor and sick at home with my mother some-times,' Sophie said, disliking his rough manners and his bulging eyes. 'But they are our own people, of course. I have no general mission amongst the needy.'

'Ah, but here they will be your people too, many of them,' Prudence said quickly. 'Hobsbawn Mills employ some four hundred hands, I believe, and the conditions in which they live – well, they must be seen to be believed.'

'I saw something of it on the way back from the mills on our first day here,' Sophie said, remembering the squalid alleys and tenements that had so shocked her.

'You've been to the mills?' Prudence said in surprise.

'There, I told you she was like Fanny,' Agnes said.

'I have, but I should not care to go again,' Sophie said.

'Quite right. That's no place for a lady,' Jack put in eagerly. 'A lady should be –'

'I disliked the machines very much. But I am interested in the plight of the hands. Do tell me more,' Sophie said quickly.

Prudence exchanged a look with Albertine. 'We should be happy to – and to enlist your support for our little society. There are too few people willing to commit their time and energies. Perhaps you would like to come to our meeting tomorrow, in the Ardwick Hall? And if it would interest you, I could take you to see some of the conditions for yourself.'

'Oh Pru, Miss Morland won't want to go trailing through those horrible places,' Agnes said. 'She's only here for a short visit.'

'Yes, that's true,' Sophie said, 'but I think I should see for myself, even if only once, if they are, as you say, our people.'

'We'd be delighted to take you,' Prudence said. 'Wouldn't we, Albertine?'

'Yes, of course. This afternoon, if you like. And if you would care to come to the meeting tomorrow –'

'Well, it's no wonder you two never caught yourselves husbands,' Jack Withington said in disgust, 'the dismal things you do! Don't you go, Miss Morland! It's nothing but dirt and smells and horridness – and philanthropy is a lot of nonsense anyway. There've always been poor people, and there always will be. There's nothing anyone can do about it.'

'Thank you,' Sophie said to Prudence, ignoring him with an effort. 'I shall go with you with great pleasure.'

'Don't count on that,' was Withington's final effort.

Héloïse was fully engaged in trying to understand the financial workings of the mills, in gathering opinions as to their possible future, in replying to invitations, and in trying to arrange a dinner at Hobsbawn House. She was glad, therefore, that Sophie had found herself an unexceptionable companion in Miss Pendlebury, and happy to have her entertain herself in Miss Pendlebury's company during the daytime.

She was a little distracted when Sophie asked permission for her outing, or she might have enquired more closely into the details. As it was she said, 'You want visit the poor? Well, *ma chère*, if it will interest you. But who goes with you?'

'Miss Pendlebury and Miss Withington.'

'No older person?'

'They are both older people, Maman.'

Héloïse smiled at Sophie's idea of age; but when you're nineteen, twenty-five seems a lifetime away. 'Nevertheless,' she said, 'it is not what I like, unmarried girls going about alone together.'

'Oh, but they do it all the time, Maman, and it's quite respectable, I assure you!' Sophie said earnestly. 'They go in Mrs Pendlebury's carriage, with her coachman and footman to take care of them, and everyone knows about it, and no-one objects, because it is philanthropy, you see. You wouldn't prevent me from visiting the poor at home, would you?'

Héloïse looked at her with curiosity. 'Does it mean so much to you to go, my Sophie? Well, I would not wish to prevent you from doing good where you can, but this is Manchester, not Morland Place, and what is right for Miss Pendlebury may not be right for you. You shall go, but Alice must go with you, and stay with you the whole time. Will that suit?'

'Yes, Maman. Thank you. And I'll tell you all about it afterwards.'

'Yes, *ma mie*,' Héloïse said distractedly, returning to the report she had been reading. 'I'm sure you will.'

It did not turn out at all the way Sophie expected. To begin with, she was sure they did not visit the worst places, though whether that was because of her presence or not she could not tell. Some of the things they saw were distressing enough, to be sure, but the streets were nowhere near as bad as those she had seen from the carriage in the close vicinity of the mills.

The reaction of her companions to the situations they encountered was very different. Miss Withington's eyes filled with tears a great deal; she said 'Poor creature' and 'Poor dear soul' very often, and sighed, and looked grave; and her advice to the sufferers was usually to read their Bible, say their prayers, and try to attend church more regularly. She parted with all the small change out of her reticule in various doles, but she avoided actually touching anyone or anything in the poor houses they visited.

Miss Pendlebury said a great deal less and never looked in the least sentimental, but she was much more practical, and so was her advice. She, too, advocated the Good Book and regular Communion, but she also had useful information to give on cleanliness and medical matters, and knew how to make soup out of almost nothing. Oddly, though, Sophie saw that Miss Withington was obviously much the better liked of the two. The poor people appreciated it much more when she sighed and said of some screaming infant that it was angelic and the image of its father, than when Miss Pendlebury pressed its swollen belly and pronounced the colic, and actually produced gripe-water from her basket to dose it with.

Alice plainly disapproved of the whole outing, and remained as far outside each house they visited as was possible while still keeping Sophie in her sight. But Sophie reflected that there was nothing she would have to report to Héloïse of a nature to make her ban further visits, if Sophie wished to go again.

Sophie was not yet sure on that point. She felt that

they might have been more useful elsewhere, and that she was being protected from the harsh realities of the mill-hands' lives; but it was at least better than sitting at home and sewing all day, and she suspected that was why Miss Withington associated herself with it. The usual preoccupations of unmarried females – clothes and appearances and dancing-partners – were all very well when there was an imminent prospect of *getting* married; but when you were too old, like Miss Withington and Miss Pendlebury, or had had your heart broken, like Sophie, they lost their savour. Sophie still liked to dance and go to parties, but it was not enough to fill a life. A useful interest would make the days pass more quickly.

At last Miss Withington said, 'We ought to take Miss Morland to the mission, to meet some of the others. It will give her a better idea of our work, don't you think, Prudence dear?'

Miss Pendlebury didn't look as though she thoroughly agreed, but she asked, 'Are you tired, Miss Morland?'

'No. Well, perhaps a little. What is this mission you are speaking of?'

'The St Anthony Mission, in Steyne Street. It's where our Benevolent Society was born, and we have a small meeting-place there, where our members can collect pamphlets and ask advice of the missionary in residence, and rest or shelter if they need to.'

'And take tea,' Miss Withington said in a dry voice. 'There is always a kettle on the hob, you know. Should you not like a dish of tea, Miss Morland? It has been a hot afternoon, and you must be very tired.'

'Well –'

'It isn't far from here. Shall we, Prudence?'

'Yes, very well,' said Miss Pendlebury, evidently bowing to the inevitable. 'I suppose Miss Morland ought to see it.'

Steyne Street was a narrow street in a shabby but respectable part of town, the sort of area where poor artisans and printers and 'prentices lived. The carriage stopped in front of what had once been a shop, but now sported gay dimity curtains and the words 'St Anthony's Mission' painted in black and gold across the window. The newly-painted door was hospitably open, and as they descended from the carriage

223

a decent-looking woman of the tradesman class came out, and nodded to them respectfully before walking away down the street.

'One of our worthy helpers,' said Miss Withington. 'We try to interest women of that order in our work. They can be very useful.' It was she who was taking the lead now, where it had been Miss Pendlebury who commanded when they were amongst the paupers. 'This is our little refuge, Miss Morland. Don't you like it? It used to be such a shabby place, no comforts at all, but now it is quite a home from home, as you'll see.'

They went in, and Sophie saw quite quickly. What had been the main area of the shop had been transformed into a sort of public parlour, with comfortable chairs and sofas arranged around the room, and a round table in the centre on which reposed a bowl of roses and several stacks of pamphlets. There was a pleasant hum of talk and the tinkle of spoons against cups, for a number of smartly-dressed ladies of various ages were sitting about the room chatting and drinking tea. Now and then a neat woman in an apron came through from another room at the back, which Sophie guessed housed a kitchen, bringing more tea and collecting empty cups.

Miss Withington was greeted with cries of affectionate enquiry from all round the room, and plunged at once into the social embrace of this cosy enclave; Miss Pendlebury, standing beside Sophie in the doorway, said sourly, 'Well, Miss Morland, now you see what our Benevolent Society really stands for. I think three quarters of our members have never seen anything closer to poverty than this room.'

Before Sophie could reply, a voice behind them said, 'Too harsh, Miss Pendlebury! Everyone has not your dedication. We must allow them their little rewards, and coax them gradually to more exertion.'

Both young women turned, and Sophie found herself looking up at a tall, cadaverously-thin man with badger-grey hair, and dark eyes as ferally-bright as a wild cat's.

Miss Pendlebury's cheeks had more colour than Sophie had ever seen in them. 'Miss Morland,' she said, 'may I present to you Father Rathbone, the missionary in residence and founder of our society. He has been struggling with poverty and disease in these streets for more years than he cares to remember.'

'Very many more,' Rathbone said. He smiled a smile of piercing sweetness at Miss Pendlebury, and then looked down into Sophie's eyes. 'Miss Morland of Morland Place?'

'I – yes – that is, my mother is –' Sophie said, confused by his burning gaze. His eyes seemed to look right through her and into the most secret places of her soul. She felt weak and confused as though he meant to devour her, as a stoat does a rabbit after first mesmerising it.

'Yes, I had heard that Lady Morland was visiting Manchester. I am honoured to make your acquaintance, Miss Morland. I knew your chaplain, Father Aislaby – we went through seminary together.'

'He left us,' Sophie said abruptly.

'Yes, I know. He was called to India, to save the heathens. He wanted me to go with him, and once I might have, but I hadn't finished my work here. Somehow I think I never shall.'

'The poor you have always with you,' Miss Pendlebury said, and Rathbone turned his burning eyes on her, much to Sophie's relief. She didn't like him – he made her feel unfinished, awkward, exposed. There was something almost frightening about him. Miss Pendlebury, on the other hand, plainly did not feel that way. She seemed to want his eyes on her, as though she liked being mesmerised.

'That's true,' he answered her. 'And too many people take it as an excuse to do nothing. Unlike you, Miss Pendlebury. I wish there were more like you. Did you go and see old Phillips today?'

'Yes. His lungs are no better, I'm afraid.'

'And never will be while he lives in that place. And did you see Wellings?'

'No. I did not take Miss Morland to *that* part of town.' It was only a slight emphasis, but enough to tell Sophie that she had been spared the worst. She felt a brief surge of annoyance, but then dismissed it as foolish. She ought instead to feel grateful to Miss Pendlebury for her considerateness.

'There are a number of cases I wished to consult you about,' Rathbone said, holding Miss Pendlebury's gaze, 'but they must wait. I will not interrupt your conversation any further.'

Sophie said quickly, 'I beg you will not hold back on my account. I shall be quite happy to sit quietly over there and read your pamphlets while you conduct your business. Pray, Miss Pendlebury, don't worry about me for another moment.'

She stepped away from them hastily and, avoiding the trap of Miss Withington, who was deep in conversation on the other side of the room with a group of friends, she went to the table and picked up a pamphlet, which she discovered was on the subject of the virtues of cleanliness. She remained standing, reading it with enough attention to allow Miss Pendlebury her moments of communion with her strange priest, but still keeping an eye on her so as to be ready to leave whenever she should have finished.

They were standing just inside the door, and had to move aside a little every time someone came in or out, which was inconveniently often, but they seemed too closely involved with each other to think of removing to a more comfortable place. And then a man came in whose eyes went straight to Sophie as though she had been the only person in the room, and she looked up in surprise, and felt her cheeks colouring. It was Jasper Hobsbawn.

He came over to her, his face so grave that she thought at first he disapproved of her presence; but when he reached her and she looked up at him she saw that the expression of his eyes was warm. 'Why, Miss Morland,' he said, 'what a surprise to find you here. But let me see,' glancing round him briefly, 'you came with Miss Pendlebury, of course.'

'Yes,' said Sophie. 'And Miss Withington.'

'Miss Pendlebury is well known in philanthropic circles. She does a great deal of good,' said Jasper. He did not mention Miss Withington at all, she noticed. 'I hope she hasn't proposed taking you on her visits.'

'Why do you hope that?'

'Because there are some parts of town – around Water Street and Long Millergate and Grey's Court – which it would not be at all suitable for you to visit.'

She was puzzled, and a little annoyed. 'What can it be that Miss Pendlebury might properly visit, but I might not?'

He looked a little agitated. 'There are sights there, Miss Morland, which – well, you are a gently-bred young lady, and –'

'Miss Pendlebury is also a gentlewoman.'

'Of course, of course! I didn't mean to suggest – but she is a great deal older than you, and used to such things. While you –'

'I visit the sick and poor at home, Mr Hobsbawn,' Sophie said firmly. 'And I was in Brussels after the battle of Waterloo. I'm sure I saw worse things there than Manchester has to shew me. Besides –' She stopped, not wanting to be rude to him.

He looked at her for a moment with tightly-closed lips; and then he let out his breath in a shaky laugh. 'Besides, it's none of my business,' he finished for her. 'You're right, of course. It was just that I wanted, foolishly, to protect you from the unpleasantnesses of life. I should like to be able to make sure that only beauty and kindness ever impinged on you. But,' he went on hastily, 'I dare say you would not thank me for it, and find it boring in the extreme.'

He had spoken the words with such gentleness and sincerity that Sophie felt touched and glad and agitated, all at once. *Wanted to protect her? To secure for her beauty and kindness?* These were strangely tender sentiments from a man who was almost a stranger. She smiled up at him shyly.

'Oh no! That is – not boring, perhaps, but – we must be useful where we can, mustn't we?'

'We must,' he said, still looking at her as if he were having quite a different conversation with her from the one she was having with him.

'And the little I have seen, from the carriage window, suggests there's a great deal that needs to be done.'

'Yes, there is.'

'Are you interested in philanthropy, Mr Hobsbawn?' she asked in desperation.

'Yes,' he said, and pulled himself together with an obvious effort. 'Yes, I am. Or rather, I'm interested in the plight of the mill-hands, and how to improve their lot. It's a matter of the greatest importance to me.'

'Then won't you take me seriously, and tell me about your ideas?' She looked directly into his eyes, surprising him with her frankness.

'I do take you seriously, Miss Morland,' he said gravely. 'And of course I will tell you my ideas, if you think they'll interest you. I'd like nothing better.'

Sophie and Héloïse dined alone that evening. They ate in silence at first, both deep in their own thoughts. Sophie had arrived home so late that there had been no time for Héloïse to ask her about her day before they went up to dress.

'Maman,' Sophie said at last, abruptly, 'are you really going to sell the mills?'

'I don't know yet,' Héloïse answered, coming back from a reverie about Morland Place and James. 'That is what I've been discussing with Mr Hobsbawn. It's a question of money, you see. Why do you ask?'

'Well, I was thinking – I was wondering if it might be possible to keep them, and run them in a better way – a way that was more pleasant for the mill-hands themselves, I mean.'

'More pleasant for them? What can you mean, my Sophie? What could be pleasant about a manufactory?'

'Well, that's just it, you see. There are so many things that could be improved. Not only just the hours and the wages, but the care of the children, and the houses they live in –'

'Sophie, what *are* you talking about?'

Sophie took a deep breath. 'Have you ever heard of Mr Owen? Mr Owen of New Lanark?'

'New Lanark mill? Yes, the name is familiar, but I can't quite think what –'

'Mr Owen's Plan, Maman. An entirely new idea for the running of mills and the organising of the mill-workers. Mr Owen has it all worked out, and Mr Hobsbawn says it really works, that the people are happier and healthier and that they work harder, too, so that Mr Owen makes more profit.'

'Mr Hobsbawn? Our Mr Hobsbawn?'

'Yes, Maman. I met him today at the mission, and –'

'What mission? Sophie, tell me slowly from the beginning, or I shall go distracted.'

Sophie told her of her day's activities, and of her meeting with Jasper, and of what he had told her of the Owen Plan. Robert Owen had taken over the New Lanark mill as manager in 1798, and finding the condition of the work-force pitiful, had undertaken a radical and vigorous campaign of improvement. The hours of work were reduced so that the hands were not exhausted at the end of the day. A school was provided which all children under ten were forced to attend – they were not allowed inside the mills. Children between ten and sixteen had to attend for two hours a day, and on Sunday. The adult hands were taught and encouraged to keep their homes and themselves clean, to embrace sobriety and honesty, and to attend lessons and lectures at the school in their free time. And dancing and music and other cultural activities were provided which the hands were obliged to attend.

The result, according to Owen, was that the hands worked harder, made fewer mistakes, and produced more, and better quality, goods. The mill made more profit, and it was possible to increase wages, so that the hands could buy more food and were thus healthier and stronger and again worked harder.

'Mr Owen says that he has proved a healthy individual produces more goods than one permanently on the brink of exhaustion. He believes that as you take care of the wooden and metal parts of the machinery in the mill, you have to take care of the living parts, too,' Sophie pronounced, repeating what Jasper had told her.

'What a disgusting idea,' Héloïse said, surprising her daughter out of her enthusiasm. 'Living parts of a machine? These are not pieces of machinery, these are human beings, possessed of a soul, and responsible to God for themselves. They are not to be denigrated, reduced to the status of spindles or wheels, to be oiled and fuelled for a mill-master's profit!'

'Oh, no, of course not,' Sophie stammered. 'I'm sure he didn't mean that, Maman. Perhaps I haven't explained it properly. You see –'

'Yes, I do see. I understand very well, and I do not at all agree, my Sophie. People cannot be bullied into virtue, or planned into honesty and industry. This "scheme" is all very well, but people are what they are, and they are placed in that condition of society which pleases God. He has His plan for all of us, from the highest to the lowest, and it is not for Mr Owen to try to change it.'

Sophie was distressed. 'Oh, please, Maman, don't be angry. I'm sure I have not explained properly. Please wait until you hear Mr Hobsbawn tell it before you condemn it.'

'My love, why is it so important to you? Very well, I shall

say no more about it. But you know we have been talking about selling the mills because we need money. How can it help us to cut the hours of work? We would surely lose money that way. And as for building a school, look how much St Edward's costs the estate every year. In any case, it's well enough for house-servants to be able to read and write, but how could it help mill-hands? How would they ever be able to afford books, or have time to read them? It would only make them unhappy.'

Sophie bit her lip. 'I don't know. I suppose you're right, Maman,' she sighed. 'Only it did sound very good when Mr Hobsbawn said it.'

CHAPTER TWELVE

Great was the excitement in Manchester's best houses when the invitations arrived to a rout at Batchworth House. It seemed that Agnes was right – though the house was Jesmond Farraline's home, the invitations came from Lady Batchworth, who was evidently playing the hostess in order to allow her son to entertain respectably; and the fact that she was giving her specific countenance to the occasion gave rise to all manner of rumour and speculation.

Farraline was, after all, of marriageable age and unmarried: what could it mean, other than that the dowager meant to parade the eligible young ladies of the country before her son for him to make his choice in comfort? Some older gentlemen with no interest to pursue might use such disparaging terms as 'cattle-market' and 'Tattersalls come to Manchester', but the young ladies themselves had no objection to being paraded, and on the whole the mamas were all for it. Farraline might only be a second son, but he was the second son of an earl with an ancient name, a country seat and some extremely profitable mills.

His brother, the present earl, was known to be a hot-headed young blood with an excellent chance of breaking his neck before he ever got round to begetting an heir; and if by some unlucky chance he did survive long enough to cut Farraline out of the succession – well, there was his mother's fortune unaccounted for, and all money must be left somewhere, after all. Besides, the spinning-mills were not part of the entail, and it was well known that Kit Batchworth loathed anything to do with manufacturing. What could be more equitable and altogether *likely* than that he should give them to the brother who put so much of his time and energy into the running of them?

Thus ran many a line of reasoning on the great evening, as

231

papas forced themselves grumbling into the black silk small-clothes and hose which seemed to get unaccountably tighter year by year, while mamas opened the boxes newly delivered from the bank to inspect the family diamonds with the fondness engendered by absence. Meanwhile, in the inferior bedrooms, the Misses Jane and Georgiana and Augusta were being hooked and buttoned into their new gowns from Madame Renée's, with no thought further than that Jesmond Farraline was an Honourable, and the most handsome and romantic man in the world.

'Mr Farraline said that he had the house built to be convenient for the mills,' Sophie said in wonder as the carriage took them ever further from the heart of Manchester.

'I suppose it depends on your definition of convenient,' Héloïse said, holding on to the strap as they lurched over the ruts. Plainly the landlords around Cheetham Hill were not as passionate about road maintenance as Edward Morland had always been. 'The mill-masters of old may have built their houses overlooking their mills, but no-one who had the choice would wish to live near the Irwell now, would they?'

Sophie agreed, remembering the mean and crowded streets she had glimpsed from the carriage that day. There had not yet been an opportunity for Maman to hear from Mr Hobsbawn's lips his ideas for bettering the lot of the mill-hands. Sophie had been again to the mission, this time in the company of Agnes Droylsden, who had nothing to do that day. By a wonderful chance, Sophie had encountered Mr Hobsbawn there a second time. He had been deep in a discussion with Father Rathbone, but had broken off with flattering promptness when she came in, and seemed eager to engage her in conversation.

On that occasion he had told her his idea for pulling down the old tenements that were crowded between the mills, and building new ones along rational lines, with a pump and privy for every ten families. They would be let to the hands for a small rent for as long as they remained in employment at Hobsbawn Mills. The hands would be obliged to keep them clean and decent, with regular visits by an inspector from the mill, and fines – to be taken from their wages – for any dirt or damage or disorder that was discovered.

It sounded very sensible to Sophie at the time, but when

she had left his company and went over it in her mind, she decided against repeating it to Maman, remembering her statement that people could not be bullied into virtue, or planned into honesty. Sophie had the feeling that Maman would regard the cleanliness inspectors as an attempt to do just that. But Mr Hobsbawn's words had renewed in her a desire to visit the worse areas of the town, and to see for herself the extent of the problem.

She found herself envying the freedom of Agnes Droylsden – even of Miss Pendlebury, who, having reached an age where no-one any longer expected her to marry, might do things and visit places that Sophie might not. It might even be worthwhile marrying, she thought, to acquire that freedom – provided one could marry a person who would not object to benevolent activities. It was a year since her conversation with Rosamund about the horrors of marriage, and she felt she had grown up a lot in that time. One could surely put up with a husband's attentions, if they weren't too frequent, and if, as Rosamund had said, one liked him sufficiently. After all, many women did – Agnes Droylsden for one. Sophie didn't think Maman would approve of all of Agnes's conversation: she was certainly very indiscreet, but Sophie had gathered quite a lot from her in a sidelong way that no-one else would have thought to tell her.

Still, thoughts of marriage were all academic, since it seemed unlikely to her that anyone would ever offer for her – in spite of Agnes's mysterious hints on the subject. No, she must simply wait until age released her from the maiden's bondage, like Miss Pendlebury ...

The carriage pulled into the sweep, and they saw the new and handsome façade of Batchworth House, which had an abundance of large, clear windows, and a great deal of wrought-iron about it. In a few moments they had shed their mantles and were walking up the stairs to be received by the dowager and her son. Lady Batchworth was frighteningly splendid in puce satin and diamonds, but perfectly affable, greeting Sophie kindly and asking after her cousin, and telling Héloïse how pleased she was to meet her at last.

'We have so much in common,' she said, making Héloïse blink a little with surprise, and went on to explain, 'An old name and estate, linked to the new wealth of manufacturing.

233

I do feel we old families ought to look after each others' interests, don't you?'

'But of course,' Héloïse murmured, puzzled.

'And the fact that our estates are on opposite sides of the Pennines must not be allowed to prevent us from becoming very good friends, dear Lady Morland. I quite dote on your daughter already, and I know you and I will have a great deal to talk about.'

Héloïse managed to say what was necessary. Meanwhile Sophie was rediscovering how handsome and charming Mr Farraline really was, being warmly claimed as an old acquaintance, and being engaged to eat supper with him. As they passed on to allow the next comers to be greeted, Héloïse looked at Sophie with new eyes.

'Things must have stood very differently between you and Mr Farraline from what I believed, *chérie*,' she said.

Sophie looked pink. 'He is very agreeable, but I am sure he was never interested in me in *that* way, Maman. How could he be?'

Héloïse smiled. 'No use to ask a mother that, my Sophie. I should always rather ask how anyone could *not* be. But I cannot otherwise account for Lady Batchworth's friendliness. *Voyons*, she has nothing to gain from me.'

'Perhaps she just likes you,' Sophie said teasingly. 'I should always ask how anyone could not.'

Héloïse smiled and they passed into the first reception room. At once it became plain to her that something was going on that she had not been aware of, for they were quickly surrounded by young men, and mothers of young men, occasionally thrusting daughters forward as the excuse to scrape acquaintance. Sophie was plainly the centre of attraction in the room, and even allowing for a mother's partiality, it did seem a little odd. As her own attention was engaged by the matrons, Héloïse watched Sophie being surrounded by the sons, and gradually disappearing into a jostling throng of them which increased by the minute.

There was Mr Pendlebury, red-faced with the constriction of his stock and sporting a gold-embroidered waistcoat which tinkled with dangling fobs and seals, bowing over Sophie's hand and smirking with the confidence of prior acquaintance. There was Mr Jack Withington, bulging in his clothes as though he might split the seams with the very next flexing of a muscle, and attempting quite blatantly to elbow every other male aside.

There were the Ardwick twins, Richard and Robert, known to their friends as Voice and Echo, and Mr Philip Spicer the attorney's son, and Mr Adrian Worsley, who fancied himself a poet and wore a soft collar and a pained expression. There were three unmarried Audenshaw boys who were as like as three blonde peas in a pod and had five identical blonde sisters to match, and the younger Droylsden who played the violin *à merveille.*

If it had been a ball, Sophie would have been engaged for the whole evening within five minutes of arriving. No normal young woman in a new gown could object to being the centre of so much flattering attention, but still Sophie turned with relief when she saw Mr Hobsbawn, who had just arrived, standing apart and watching her unsmilingly. The young men's noise and nonsense had become a little wearying. She was not accustomed to it, and as soon as she saw Jasper, she realised how much better she would enjoy a rational conversation with someone who was not trying to impress her and outdo his fellows in outrageous compliments.

'Miss Morland,' he said when she turned aside from them to greet him. 'It's kind of you to spare me a moment, when I see your attention has so many claims on it.'

'I'm glad to see you, Mr Hobsbawn,' she said, offering her hand. 'I didn't know you'd be here.'

He merely touched the ends of her fingers, his face still grave. 'I was a little surprised to be asked. I am acquainted with Farraline through our common interest in the mills, but we have never met socially.'

Sophie retrieved her unwanted hand, cocking her head at him, wonderingly. He sounded stern, even angry about something. Now why? Did he think her frivolous? Did he disapprove of all social events, or only of this one – and if so, why had he come?

'Everyone seems to be here,' she said, since she had to say something.

It seemed to be the wrong thing. 'Yes, I suppose if they have got so far down the list, they may well have come to me,' he said bitterly.

235

She put her hand out impulsively. 'Please forgive me! I didn't mean it like that at all. I was so glad when you came in and I thought I should have someone agreeable to talk to after all.'

He softened a little. 'Don't you find *them* agreeable? I should have thought any young woman would like to be flirted with by so many young men.'

Ah, that was it, Sophie thought. He believed her to have been flirting, and disapproved of it. What a strictly moral man he was! But she hastened to reassure him. 'They were noisy and tiresome, but they meant no harm – like puppies playing, you know.'

He smiled at her suddenly. 'Puppies,' he said, as though the word pleased him. When he smiled, his eyes lit up in a way that made her feel very strange – humble and glad at the same time. His eyes could be as bright as Father Rathbone's, but with such a different light – a light that blessed and strengthened, rather than devoured and ennervated. 'Should you like to take a turn about the room, Miss Morland? It will take you out of their range for a while, and give you a little peace.'

He offered his arm, and she laid her hand on it without hesitation. 'Thank you, you are very kind.'

'No, I'm not,' he said seriously. 'At the moment I'm being entirely selfish.'

It was some time later when Jesmond Farraline came up to them. 'Now really, Hobsbawn, I can't let you monopolise Miss Morland like this. It's too bad of you. Miss Morland, I know you are simply too polite to tell this fellow to be off, but with every man in the room dying to make love to you as well –'

'Oh, but he was not,' Sophie said innocently. 'We were talking about manufactories.'

Farraline laughed. 'Were you, indeed? What a sad dog you are, Hobsbawn! Can't you find any better topic of conversation than that when you're with a beautiful young woman?'

'It was what you talked to me about when we were in Scarborough,' Sophie said.

'Did I? I must have been mad. But I claim the privilege of an old friend, Miss Morland, to ask your forgiveness.'

'But it's what I like. I'm interested in manufactories, espe-

236

cially now I've been to visit Hobsbawn Mills.'

'Have you, indeed? Then you must come and see Ordsall Mills, too. They knock all other mills into a cocked hat, I assure you. Shall I arrange a visit for you?'

'Oh – well, thank you – but –' Sophie was embarrassed.

'Miss Morland found the noise of the machines distressing,' Jasper put in. 'I don't think she'd care to repeat the experience. What we've been discussing is the welfare of the mill-workers.'

A faint expression of distaste crossed Farraline's features. 'Now don't tell me you're an Owenite, Hobsbawn! I had thought better of your intelligence until now.'

It had not escaped Sophie's notice from the beginning that there was a faint air of hostility between the two men, which she had not been able to account for; but now Farraline's rudeness was overt, and she was shocked.

Jasper, however, leapt to the fray with energy. 'It surely cannot have escaped even your notice that the mill-workers' condition is pitiful, and that something must be done about it.'

'Certainly something must be done about it. We must get our interest represented in Parliament, which is exactly what I have been trying to do these two years. I was saying to Sir Robert Peel only the other day –'

'Precisely,' Hobsbawn interrupted hotly. 'Sir Robert is to present the Ten Hours Bill to Parliament next year, and then we shall see –'

'Oh, that! That's the biggest piece of nonsense –! How the deuce are we to make a profit, tell me that?'

'But Owen has shewn how it can be done. He told the Committee last year that he'd reduced the hours and still produced more goods.'

'And as I remember, the Committee didn't believe a word of it. They were quite adamant that it's not possible to produce more goods from a spinning-machine without either speeding up the machine or running it for longer.'

'I don't care what they *believed* – he shewed it for a fact!'

'But in any case, the Bill is wrong in principle, which I should have thought you of all people would see,' said Farraline sharply.

'Why is it wrong?' Sophie asked. The effect on both men

237

was almost comical – they had both evidently forgotten her presence in the heat of their quarrel. Jasper reddened and pressed his lips together, and Farraline looked embarrassed.

'I do beg your pardon, Miss Morland,' he said. 'It was inexcusably rude of us to argue in front of you.'

'Oh, but please, Mr Farraline, now that you have, won't you please explain? Because you said that you wanted to be represented in Parliament in order to help the mill-workers.'

Farraline glanced doubtfully at Hobsbawn, who merely turned his eyes away, and then he said, 'Well, ma'am, the Bill Sir Robert Peel wants to introduce is intended to forbid the employment of children under ten years old in cotton mills.'

'And to limit the hours of children over ten to ten a day,' Jasper added.

'Just so. But I believe – most of us believe – that this is not a legitimate area for Government interference. The ills that beset factory-hands are not susceptible of improvement by legislation. Who are we to tell parents they may not put their children into employment, if they wish? A parent must know better what's right and good for his own child than a body of men far away in London who have never seen the child, the parent or the work-place.'

It all sounded very reasonable to Sophie, spoken in Farraline's measured and cultured tones. 'But what did you want Parliament to do, then?' she asked.

'To remove the Corn Laws, and allow the price of wheat to fall, instead of keeping it unnaturally high to please the farmers and landowners.'

Jasper could restrain himself no longer. 'That's all very well, Farraline, but when you've seen, as I have, little children of seven, eight and nine working thirteen hours a day until they are too exhausted to stand, seen them crippled by it, dying of it –'

'I've seen those sights, just as you have,' Farraline snapped, 'but your way is wrong, wrong, wrong! In this kind of case, when Government interferes, it always makes things worse, not better. A Government's business is to raise taxes for the defence of the realm, and to enact such laws as enable us to trade profitably with the rest of the world – and nothing more. Good God, man, we want less regulation, not more!'

'There are some human activities that need regulation. We

238

can't always do exactly as we like.'

'Do you want to license the Government to interfere in any aspect of our lives it pleases? Interference, despotism, tyranny – that was what we fought against with the French for twenty years! People know their own interests best. Leave them alone, and they'll find the answer to their problems sooner or later, without interference from politicians and soldiers and government spies.'

'That's all very well, when you're talking about healthy, able people, with enough strength at the end of the day to think about their problems. But when they're exhausted, weak and undernourished –'

'That's why we've got to abolish the Corn Laws! Cheap corn, cheap bread, that's the way to help the mill-hands. We must have the freedom to make our mills successful, so that we can offer the lower orders employment. They must be free to exchange their labour for wages. And bread must be cheap enough for them to afford it. Freedom, not interference, is the way forward! Then they won't need this philanthropist nonsense.'

'You wouldn't call it nonsense if you were one of them. Sometimes we have to interfere to protect people who can't protect themselves – like the children –'

'They have their parents to protect them. If you get this piece of legislation enacted, what then? The parents will be in the factories, working, and the children will be outside, doing what? Who's going to look after them, make sure they don't get into trouble? You're going to break up the families, don't you see that? At the moment children work with their parents, as they always have, under their care and supervision; but break up that arrangement, and you break up the family, and then the whole country will go to ruin. The children will turn from idleness to vice, and a whole generation will be lost.'

Jasper shook his head. 'You don't understand. Reducing the children's hours is only the first step. Of course it won't do to leave them idle and roaming the streets. They must be provided with schools and forced to attend while their parents are working –'

'Oh, you really are an Owenite, aren't you!' Farraline laughed, breaking the tension. 'And then it will be an academy for the adults, and drilling and dancing in the evenings, and lectures on temperance, until the poor devils can't call their souls their own. Well, it may be your idea of Utopia, but it's not mine – nor of the hands themselves, I suspect, though I dare say no-one will ask them. Well, Miss Morland, you have been bored long enough by this talk, and since Hobsbawn and I shall never agree, I shall take myself off and leave you in peace. Don't forget you are pledged to take your supper with me – and I promise you we shall talk of anything but manufactories!'

With a charming smile for her and a graceful bow to both of them, he went away, leaving Sophie thoughtful. Jasper watched her face for a moment, and then said, 'Well, Miss Morland, what did you think? Did he convince you that he's right and I'm wrong?'

'I don't know,' Sophie said uneasily. 'What he says sounds right, and very convincing; but all the same, I can't quite see how these poor people are going to be able to help themselves, not if they are in such very bad case to begin with.'

Triumph shone in Jasper's eyes, but wisely he didn't press it further. 'There you have the nub of it, I'm sure,' was all he said, before changing the subject. 'What a pleasant party this is, don't you think? I believe there's to be music later – I saw Miss Pendlebury's maid putting her music on the pianoforte. I suppose you couldn't be prevailed upon to play for us too?'

Sophie began to suspect him of teasing her. 'But you heard me play at Morland Place, Mr Hobsbawn, so you must know I'm a very poor performer.'

'No, I assure you, I enjoyed every minute of your playing when I had the honour of hearing you at home. It gave me much more pleasure than any public concert I've been to.'

Searching his face, she saw that he was quite sincere, which left her to wonder whether he had no taste in music, which would be sad, or a failing memory, which would be alarming. At all events there was no arguing against such gallantry, so she allowed the undeserved compliment to stand, and made a comment instead about the size and brilliance of the room, which he could have no difficulty in agreeing with.

The first of the proposals of marriage came the next day, taking Sophie completely by surprise. It was only the second she had received in her life, and would have been as unwelcome as unexpected if she had taken it seriously. Jack Withington cornered her in the foyer of the concert-hall and obliged her to hear him, and she was so sure she could not have borne to be Mrs Jack Withington that she refused him without even considering referring the matter to her mother.

Jack took his rejection philosophically. 'It's just as well, perhaps. There's no knowing if we should have agreed; but I wanted to be sure of getting in before Fred Pendlebury.'

'I'm quite sure Mr Pendlebury has no intention of making me an offer,' Sophie said in surprise.

Withington laughed. 'I'm quite sure he will! Lord, if he wasn't such a slow-top he'd have spoken by now – and when he does, Miss Morland, I'd be obliged if you'd tell him that I asked you first. Only he might not believe it from me, you see.'

'I'll be sure to mention it,' Sophie said gravely. 'He can hardly doubt my word.'

'Most obligin' of you,' Withington said, looking at her with new respect. 'I say, I suppose you're quite sure?'

'Quite sure. But I'm very much obliged to you for your good opinion.'

'Oh, n't'all! Alba said you wouldn't have me, though how the deuce she knows anything –! But however, Mama was all for it, so I thought if it must be done, I might as well get my word in quickly. I say, was I the first?'

'You were – I imagine by a very long margin.'

Withington looked pleased. 'Well, that's all right then! Here's your mama looking for you, so I'll wish you goodnight, Miss Morland. Shall you be at the Audenshaws' tomorrow?'

The Audenshaws' ball was one of a flood of invitations loosed by the Batchworth rout. Sophie was in the happy position for a young woman of nineteen of having no free evening for the rest of her stay in Manchester, and of discovering her wardrobe inadequate to the demands upon it.

'You must have some new gowns,' Héloïse pronounced, at which Sophie looked worried.

'But I had a new one for Mr Farraline's rout, Maman, and I know we are short of money.'

'Things are not so bad that we cannot afford a few yards of

241

muslin, my Sophie. You've hardly had anything new for a whole year, and it will be worth it if –' She had been going to say, if it gets you a good husband, but she changed it at the last moment to, 'if it gives you pleasure.' She knew that Sophie was tender on the subject; but she was beginning to think that if this stay in Manchester, with all its opportunities, did not produce a mate for Sophie, she might well stay single all her life. She would not meet anyone at Morland Place, and there was no-one in York who interested her.

Things looked very promising so far. For some reason, Sophie was plainly being pursued by a number of young men. She never lacked a partner at any dance, and when she went out in the carriage of Miss Pendlebury or Miss Withington or Mrs Droylsden, they were stopped every few yards by a gentleman on horseback or strolling, eager to pay his compliments. Héloïse thought that perhaps it was Mr Farraline's interest in Sophie which had sparked it all off. He was very attentive, called or left his card most days, secured the first dance for every ball, was always the first to the door of their box in the interval at the theatre, and neglected his mills to take Sophie driving in his curricle along the permitted thoroughfares.

Héloïse had to conclude from this public preference that he meant to make her an offer, and she hoped very much that Sophie would like him well enough to accept him. There is a certain amount of worldly ambition in every mother, at least to the extent that while she would not have her daughter marry a man she did not like, she would sooner see her in love with an eligible man than a poor nobody. Héloïse liked Farraline, found him charming, intelligent, and gentle, and thought that if he really did prefer Sophie, he would make her an excellent husband. It must be a disinterested liking on his part, since Sophie was neither a beauty nor an heiress, which was the more to his credit. As brother to an earl he might have almost anyone he wanted.

Another good effect of all this, from Héloïse's point of view, was that Sophie was too much engaged to have time for philanthropy. Héloïse would never try to prevent her daughter from doing something which she believed it her Christian duty to do, but she couldn't help being glad that Sophie was driving in a carriage along fashionable boulevards, nicely dressed and accompanied by the daughters of respectable, wealthy families, rather than risking her health and sensibilities amongst the stinking, fever-haunted slums of Water Street and Millergate, trying to help people who – from Héloïse's own experience – rarely allowed themselves to be helped.

It meant that Héloïse was free to concentrate on what she had to do without worrying about Sophie's welfare. She wanted to clear everything up quickly so that she could get back to Morland Place. She was missing James dreadfully, and not all the loving letters in the world – James was a good correspondent when he put his mind to it – could make up for having to sleep night after night without his arms around her.

Mr Pendlebury proposed, at great length, by letter. The missive arrived at breakfast-time by the hand of a Pendlebury servant, and provided Héloïse with much secret amusement over the coffee cups.

'Well, my love, what do you think of his offer?' she asked as soon as she was able to control her voice.

Sophie looked at her mother doubtfully. 'Well, I suppose it is very obliging of him, but – it isn't a very sensible letter, is it?'

They met each other's eyes, and dissolved into laughter.

'At least it leaves you in no doubt,' Héloïse said, drying her eyes. 'He asks you six times, in six different sets of words. I conclude, then, that you mean to refuse him.'

'Oh yes – if you please, Maman. I don't like him, or Mrs Pendlebury, though Prudence and Agnes are both the dearest people.'

'God forbid you should marry anyone you don't like, *ma mie*,' Héloïse said. 'It is a little strange, don't you think? He says quite clearly that he makes his offer with his mother's approval, but from what little I know of her, I would have expected Mrs Pendlebury to be consumed with ambition. I would not have thought you a rich enough prize to tempt her.'

'Perhaps he persuaded her to agree – oh dear! But that would mean he really did care for me, which would be shocking.'

'Have you any idea of it?'

243

'None. I never thought of it. He asks me to dance every time, but then so do they all.'

'Yes, they do, don't they?' Héloïse said thoughtfully. 'Well, don't worry. This letter doesn't sound love-lorn to me. You shall write your reply after breakfast, and that will be the end of that. Where do you go this morning?'

'To the Exchange, with Agnes and her brother. And this afternoon Mr Farraline calls for me in his curricle. He said he'd teach me to drive a pair.'

'That will put your father's nose out of joint,' Héloïse smiled.

Sophie thought Mr Henry Droylsden, brother of Agnes's husband, was the most pleasant of the young men she had met, apart from Mr Farraline. He was good-natured, quieter and more thoughtful than his peers, and had read a great deal more. This was perhaps partly because he was slightly lame, relic of a childhood disease which had laid him up for several years when other boys were playing cricket and falling out of trees.

When Sophie joined him and Agnes in Agnes's smart new barouche, he greeted her with a friendly smile, and took the pull-down seat facing her, fixing his eyes on her face with quiet intensity as Agnes plunged instantly into full flow.

'What a love of a hat! Sophie dear, you do manage to look so very striking with so little in the way of decoration! I wish I had your knack. It would take me ten feathers and a dozen spangled ribbons to make my head as interesting as yours. Now tell us at once, has Fred put the question? Harry says he was saying last night he meant to do it today, and Percy's groom told my maid that he'd seen Fred go out on horseback early this morning, so it must have been something important because normally he never gets up before noon, does he, Harry?'

'Not unless there's an earthquake,' Henry said in his droll way. 'That's why he don't hunt, you know – foxes have a frightful habit of leaping out of bed at dawn.'

'So did he call, dearest Sophie? And what did he say? I depend on you to tell me *everything*, because Prudence is far too discreet, and will only tell me to mind my own business, which is nonsense, because it is my business if my own brother proposes to my best friend. So tell, please – every detail.'

'I don't know if I ought –' Sophie began, upon which Henry gave a shout, and Agnes clapped her hands together in glee.

'He did call, then! You were right, Hal!'

'No, he didn't call,' Sophie said. 'He sent a letter –'

Again she was interrupted, this time by laughter. 'A letter? Oh the dull dog!' Henry crowed.

'No, really! Oh Sophie, I ought to apologise for the honour of my family! But what did it say? Have you it with you? Oh I die to read it! I'll bet Mama wrote most of it for him, though.' Her smile was replaced suddenly with a look of anxiety. 'You did refuse him?'

'Yes, I did.'

'Thank God!' Agnes said, fanning herself with exaggerated relief. 'Much as I long to have you as a sister – but as to that, you know there's more than one way to skin a mule. What do you say, now, to Harry?'

Sophie met Mr Henry Droylsden's eyes involuntarily, and then lowered hers with a deep blush. 'Please, Agnes,' she began in a muted protest.

'Annie, you go too far,' Henry put in sternly.

But Agnes was irrepressible. 'No, but seriously! Now, Harry, do be quiet, and let me put your case for you, because you know I'll do it better than you. I'm a female myself, and know how to put these things. Sophie, attend! Here is my dear brother-in-law, the nicest, most sensible man in the world, and the next best tempered after my own Percy, whom I wouldn't part with for the world. Now Harry is a handsome boy, speaks pretty, plays the violin like an angel, and rides like a perfect fiend, and Papa Droylsden will come down handsome with a settlement when he marries, if you care for that sort of thing.'

'Annie, you're outrageous!'

'But you see she doesn't say no – do you, Sophie? Oh you shy thing, all I can see is the tip of your ear, and that's as red as a rose! But don't you think Harry's nice? I do – and I can tell you that he's mad in love with you, and only wants a little encouragement to speak for himself!'

'Oh please,' Sophie managed to say in protest, but Mrs

245

Droylsden chose mischievously to misinterpret it.

'There, Hal, you see, she wants you to make love to her. Now don't sit there like a perfect stock – here's your chance to close the deal, as Papa Droylsden says. Miss Morland, he's every inch the gentleman, and has no bad habits in or out of the house. As to his lameness, why it's only a trifle –'

Sophie looked up, alarmed, saying, 'Oh no, please, I would not – I never for a moment –' She met Henry's eyes, and saw that he was perfectly comfortable, smiling at his sister's nonsense without embarrassment, and with a kind look for Sophie in her confusion.

'I beg you will not let my wicked sister upset you, Miss Morland. No, Annie, not another word! You need pay no attention to anything she says, I assure you. If you really have refused Fred Pendlebury, I shall make my own declaration in the proper form and –' with a stern glance at Agnes – 'at a moment of my choosing.'

Sophie was distressed. 'But I don't want to marry anyone,' she blurted foolishly.

Agnes looked concerned. 'What, no-one at all? Was your heart really broke, then, when your betrothed was killed at Waterloo? Albertine told me the story, but I thought that was her romance and nonsense.'

'Annie, you're being impertinent,' Henry said quietly. 'You're upsetting Miss Morland.'

'Am I? Oh dear, I didn't mean to,' she said contritely. 'Please forgive me, dearest Sophie. You know what a chatter-head I am. I don't mean anything by it. You shan't marry if you don't want to,' she added comfortingly, which made Sophie smile in spite of her shaken sensibilities.

'Thank you,' she said.

'All the same,' Agnes went on, irrepressibly, 'I'll wager you take the divine Mr Farraline in the end, for who could refuse him – even though Harry is probably nicer – and you can't want to end up an old maid like poor Prudence. And now I really won't say another word.'

At the Exchange they were met by Mr Percy Droylsden, who had abandoned his room at his father's bank for the much more pleasant occupation of walking with his pretty wife amongst the stalls of ribbons and fans and gloves and stock-

246

ings. Henry offered Sophie his arm, and they strolled happily along the rows, pausing every few yards to examine the goods or chat with their acquaintance.

It was soon evident that Fred Pendlebury's proposal was known all over Manchester, and the news of his rejection spread outwards from the Droylsden party like ripples from a stone. Sophie had the embarrassment of listening to her affairs being talked about with an almost childlike lack of inhibition.

'It's my belief he knew she'd say no – otherwise why did he ride off this morning?'

'Where did he go? Does anyone know?'

'Oh yes, he went over to his aunt's at Broughton Park. Philip Spicer saw him. He's trying to sell a horse to his cousin.'

'What, that black gelding with the iron mouth? It's only fit for the knacker's yard!'

'Never mind the horse – that was just an excuse, don't you see?'

'But if Miss Morland had taken him, he wouldn't have been there to receive her acceptance.'

'Well, precisely. So it must mean he knew she'd say no.'

'Nonsense! Fred Pendlebury's so conceited he'd never believe anyone would refuse him. He'll ask you again, Miss Morland, depend on it.'

'Have you heard Jack Withington's saying he asked her first?'

'Is he? Did he, Miss Morland?'

'You did well to refuse him, Miss Morland. He's got the worst seat on a horse of anyone I've ever seen.'

'Now Farraline's a first-rate man over the sticks. You never see his horses lathered up at the end of the day, like Withington's.'

'But Farraline don't ride more than eleven stone. Withington must come in at sixteen, without the saddle!'

'Still, you'd do better to take Farraline, Miss Morland ...'

It was with enormous relief that Sophie saw Mr Hobsbawn coming towards her. The Exchange was a large building, and built on the corner of Market Street and Cross Street, two main thoroughfares, with lanes running along the other two of its sides. It was therefore frequently used as a short-cut

247

between streets – one of the reasons it was said that if one walked about the Exchange for long enough, one would eventually meet everyone one knew.

Sophie hadn't seen him since the rout at Batchworth House. She had been out on the occasions he had called on her mother on business, and she had not been to the mission, or had time to pursue her desire to visit the tenements. Seeing him again, she realised how much she had missed him, and wished fervently for a long, sensible, and quiet conversation with him, instead of having this swell of frantic chatter all around her.

'Oh, Mr Hobsbawn!' she greeted him gladly.

'Miss Morland.' His face was grave. 'I hope you're enjoying your stay in Manchester? I think you must be – whenever I see you, you are at the centre of a crowd.'

'Am I? But you haven't seen me since the Batchworth rout.'

'Not so, ma'am. I've seen you several times, though I don't suppose you've seen me. I was never able to get close enough to you to pay my compliments.'

He was offended, she thought – but about what? They had been on such good terms at the rout, when she had last seen him. 'I'm afraid I've been out when you've called at Hobsbawn House,' she began tentatively.

He gave a tight smile. 'At your time of life, it's to be expected that you would be much engaged.'

'And I haven't visited the mission –'

'I'm sure no-one looked to see you there. You are very young, Miss Morland, and it's right that you should enjoy yourself. Pleasure must take preference over more serious considerations.'

'You're angry with me,' she said in a small voice. 'I am so sorry if I've offended you.'

His eyes widened, and he looked at her for a long moment, a strange look, full of trouble. Then he said, more gently, 'I'm not angry with you. I have no right. Indeed, I –' He stopped, and then resumed hastily, 'I have the warmest regard for you Miss Morland. I'm sincerely glad you're happy.'

He seemed about to leave her and walk on, but she stopped him with a slight gesture.

'I would still very much like to see the tenements you spoke of,' she said shyly, 'so that I could understand your plans for them.'

He hesitated, looking at her doubtfully, like a child who had too many times been given a bitter black pill concealed in a sweetmeat. 'If you really wish to –'

'Yes, really.'

'I have a little time this afternoon; or I could possibly make myself free tomorrow morning, if it would suit you –?'

Sophie was embarrassed. 'I'm sorry, I'm engaged this afternoon to drive out with Mr Farraline, and tomorrow morning –'

He bowed stiffly, his eyes veiled again. 'I quite understand. Another time, perhaps. Your servant, Miss Morland.'

And then he really was gone, leaving Sophie feeling dissatisfied and uneasy, as though there were some misunderstanding she had not managed to put right; though she couldn't quite think what it could be.

CHAPTER THIRTEEN

The first hint that anything was wrong came a day or two later when Héloïse and Sophie were at the theatre, sharing the box of Lady Batchworth and Mr Farraline. During the interval, Mr Farraline took Sophie for a walk around the corridors, leaving Héloïse to talk to the dowager, and to return the nods of acquaintances in other parts of the auditorium.

'Why, there's Lady Grey,' Héloïse said suddenly, seeing that impoverished viscount's wife in a box on the other side, her feathers brushing those of Mrs Pendlebury, with whom she was deep in conversation.

'Ah, the titled friend the Pendlebury woman boasts of!' Lady Batchworth said, lifting her lorgnon. 'Which is she? Do you know her?'

'She's a neighbour of ours in York. Some of her daughters were intimates of my stepdaughter, Fanny.'

'*Some* of her daughters? How many has she?'

'Seven – and no sons.'

'Unfortunate in the extreme. Are they handsome?' Héloïse hesitated, and Lady Batchworth went on, 'I understand. Not handsome. One must hope they have large portions.'

'I'm afraid Lord Grey's estate is rather encumbered.'

Lady Batchworth nodded. 'She will never get them off her hands, then. A girl must have either beauty or a fortune. Name alone is nothing.'

A puzzled question hovered on Héloïse's lips, and died there. She saw quite plainly that Lady Grey had seen her, and that she and Mrs Pendlebury were discussing her, for the heads were nodding vigorously while the eyes bored into her across the auditorium. Héloïse bowed civilly, and Lady Grey returned it slightly, but Mrs Pendlebury did not acknowledge her, which was strange, considering how effusive she had been until now. But perhaps, Héloïse thought, Lady Grey was

250

to usurp her position as favourite. If so, she was welcome to it.

Meanwhile Sophie's grand promenade with Mr Farraline had been interrupted by Mrs Percy Droylsden, who hailed her from her husband's arm and said cheerfully, 'Well, now, Miss Morland, your nose is to be put out of joint! Do you know who has arrived today? Mama's friend Lady Grey from York! And she's brought one of the Miss Greys with her – you know, the one with the squint. I forget her name.'

'Roxane?'

'That's right. There, I knew you'd know them! I told Percy ... Well, I've just seen her in the upper foyer making languishing eyes at my brother Fred – Miss Grey, I mean, not her mother – so it's plain as glass she's come to try to cut you out with him!'

'Come on, Annie. You talk too much,' said her husband genially. 'Servant, Miss Morland – sir.' With a civil nod to both of them, he dragged Agnes away.

'You'd better hurry if you want to change your mind, Sophie!' she called over her shoulder with an impish grin.

'Who is Lady Grey?' Farraline asked Sophie. 'Should one know her?'

'She's the wife of Viscount Grey, who has an estate near ours,' Sophie said. 'She was a Miss Parr before she married, so she's very proud; but she gets cross because none of her daughters is married. Your friend Mr Hawker would tell you about them – he had to dance with several of them at a ball at our house once.'

'Including the one with the squint?' Farraline asked, raising his brows in astonishment.

'I don't know,' Sophie said. 'I was too young to be at the ball.'

'And did Mr Pendlebury really have the impudence to make you an offer?'

'Was it impudence? I felt as though I *ought* to feel obliged to him.'

Farraline laughed. 'You have a cruel and subtle tongue, Miss Morland. Yes, it was impudence for a mere builder's son to address you, and if you have any more impudence of that sort from any of these creatures, I hope you will allow me, as an old friend, to send them about their business!'

Sophie blushed and looked at her feet, for really, his

attentions were growing very particular; and though there could be few young women with a more modest view of their charms to be noticed, even she was beginning to think that he meant, sooner or later, to make her an offer.

Later, when the play was over, they were all walking down the wide staircase towards the lower foyer when the odd thing happened. A little of knot of people was standing at the foot of the stairs, evidently waiting for carriages to arrive. They were talking amongst themselves, and Héloïse saw the long purple feathers of Mrs Pendlebury's head-dress wagging in the centre, with Lady Grey, like a wraith in voluminous grey gauze, Miss Roxane Grey in pink silk, and Mr Fred Pendlebury in a dazzling waistcoat, close beside her.

Suddenly Mrs Pendlebury turned and saw Héloïse, and tossing her head she turned abruptly away, hustling her party before her towards the door. It was the most obvious and shocking 'cut'. The group she had broken open with her departure stood as they had been scattered, looking awkward, embarrassed, or self-righteous according to character. One or two looked at Héloïse and quickly away again; others avoided her eyes altogether, pretending to be fastening a glove or looking in a reticule.

Such a thing had never happened to Héloïse before and it was upsetting, however little, at bottom, she cared for Mrs Pendlebury's opinion. She wondered what on earth it was all about, was angry, amused, and hurt by turns. Sophie, beside her, was scarlet-cheeked and bright-eyed with indignation; Farraline looked grimly amused; Lady Batchworth appeared not to have noticed anything. The crowds parted before them like the Red Sea, and they found themselves first out in the porch, with Farraline beckoning up his coachman and a space around them like quarantine.

No-one mentioned the circumstance on the short journey back to Hobsbawn House, where they were put down with cheerful farewells before the Batchworth carriage drove away. Héloïse and Sophie went inside to the waiting supper of hot soup and patties, and found other things to talk about until they went up to their beds.

They didn't have long to wait to find out why they had been snubbed. The following morning, shortly after breakfast, when Héloïse was preparing to leave for an appointment

252

with the attorney, Mrs Percy Droylsden and Miss Pendlebury were announced.

Héloïse glanced at Sophie. 'They're sure to be calling for you, my love, so if you don't mind, I won't wait, or I shall be late. Richards, shew the visitors up to Miss Morland, but don't mention that I am at home. I'll slip down when they are safely in here.'

'Very good, my lady.'

A few moments later Agnes and Prudence came in, Agnes looking excited and Prudence grave.

'Oh, dear Sophie, what fun!' were Agnes's opening words as she hurried across the room to kiss Sophie's cheek. 'I've come to tell you the news – but first, do tell, is it true that Mama cut you and your mama at the theatre last night?'

Sophie nodded, a little taken aback.

'Annie!' said Miss Pendlebury. 'It's not a matter for levity. Miss Morland, I was shocked beyond measure when I heard of my mother's inexcusable rudeness. I know I owe her a daughter's loyalty, but there are times when the demands of simple justice supercede that.'

Sophie invited them to sit down. 'It was more surprising than shocking,' she said. 'Maman and I have no idea what we've done to offend your mother.'

'You've done nothing, nothing at all,' Prudence began indignantly, but Agnes broke in, unable to restrain herself.

'It's the greatest joke! You can't imagine, Sophie – when Percy told me I almost died of laughing! He had it from Harry, who had it from Fred, for of course Fred would never come and tell me himself, knowing how I love you. But he's afraid he will be the laughing-stock now, only as I said to Pru, he's more likely to make a sport of himself with his behaviour *now* than anything he did before.'

'But what is it? What's happened?' Sophie asked.

'It's all Lady Grey's fault, as I suppose you've guessed,' Agnes said. 'Of course, Mama provoked her, boasting to her that Fred was all but engaged to marry you – oh yes, I know you refused him, but he meant to ask you again, and he never believed for an instant that you'd reject him at last. Only of course Lady Grey had come with the express purpose of getting Fred to take Squintabella off her hands –'

'Annie, don't talk so shocking. You make everything worse

by your immoderate language,' Prudence intervened. 'The fact is, Miss Morland, that Lady Grey probably did have some idea in her mind that Fred might marry Roxane, because she and Mama were such old friends; and out of jealousy, or to protect her own interests, she told Mama – she told her –'

Prudence evidently had difficulty in getting beyond this point. Sophie said, 'If some slander has been spoken about me, I wish you will tell me, so that I can refute it. I shall not blame *you*, I assure you. I know you would not do such a thing.'

'There, Pru, I told you not to worry. You see what a good creature she is! I told her, Sophie, that we should come and tell you at once, because it was only fair, and what any friend would do.'

'What did Lady Grey say about me?'

Even Agnes looked a little pink as she tackled the subject. 'She said – she said that though you are the eldest child, you were born – well, before your mama and papa were married.'

Sophie said nothing, but her eyes were very bright. Agnes coughed and continued more confidently. 'She said because of that you won't inherit the Morland fortune – it all goes to your brother. And not only that, she said the mills are not to go to you either. In fact she said that you're not a great heiress at all, that you'll have nothing but a few thousand pounds from your mama.'

Sophie looked bewildered. 'But I never said that I *was* a great heiress. Why should anyone think it?'

Agnes had recovered her spirits. 'But that's the fun of it, don't you see? When you came here with your mama to look at the mills, everyone assumed you were to inherit them – otherwise why had you come? And then when Mr Farraline paid attention to you, it seemed to confirm it, for everyone knows he needs a rich wife. So the story went from mouth to mouth, with your fortune increasing all the time, until everyone was convinced you were the greatest catch of the season! When Mama found out the truth, she was furious, thinking you'd tried to trap Fred under false pretences. That's why she cut you – and now she's telling everyone you're an imposter – you and your mama.'

Sophie stared in amazement and distress. 'But I never

pretended to anyone I was an heiress – and nor did Maman. We would not do such a thing. And if anyone had asked me, I'd have told them the truth.'

'But of course no-one would ever ask you,' Miss Pendlebury said seriously. 'They have only themselves to blame for the mistake. I'm shocked beyond mention at Mama's behaviour. Not only is she guilty of appalling rudeness, but she's exposing herself in the most humiliating manner, which will reflect on all of us. To reveal so openly that the only reason she courted you and your good mama was for your supposed fortune –!'

'Oh, but it's such a good joke, don't you think, Sophie dear? Yes, I know it's shocking and very bad, but only think, all those young idiots hanging round you, and their mamas whipping them on to propose to you! And Fred writing that comical letter too! I'll bet he wishes he may sink through the earth now!'

Sophie was deep in thought. 'So they all thought I was wealthy, and *that* was why ... All the attention, being asked to dance, and everything, only for the sake of an inheritance, and not for me at all.'

'Oh poor Sophie!' Agnes cried, jumping up to sit beside her and put an arm round her shoulders. 'Never mind it! You know we love you, Pru and I! And Percy says you're a little trump, and Harry thinks you're a very sweet girl! Anyone who matters loves you just as they always did! As for the others – they're not worth a plucked hen.'

'You may comfort yourself,' Prudence said seriously, 'on your own conduct, which has been impeccable throughout. There can be few girls whose heads would have been as little turned by so much attention as yours was. Indeed, you have nothing to reproach yourself with; it is my mother who should be ashamed, as I am ashamed of her.'

'Thank you,' Sophie managed to say. 'You're very kind.' She was thinking now of Mr Farraline, and wondering whether he, too, thought her an heiress. But his acquaintance with her had predated this visit, so surely he might be relied on? And yet even in Scarborough she supposed he might have been under a misapprehension. Perhaps that was why he talked to her in the beginning about mills, thinking she had mills of her own to join to his.

Agnes had caught up with the same thought. 'I say, I wonder if Lady Batchworth is another like Mama? Does Mr Farraline know the truth, Sophie? It would be a terrible shame to lose him as a suitor, just when everyone's saying he's bound to speak soon!'

'Oh Annie, do hush,' Prudence said. 'We came to ask you, Miss Morland, if you would come for a drive with us this morning in the barouche? If you don't wish to, we shall quite understand, but it would shew people that you don't care about the talk, and that we don't heed it. And in the afternoon, if you'd like, we could go and visit some of the mill-hands who are sick and unemployed.'

'I wouldn't call that much of a treat,' Agnes said, 'but Pru really thought you'd like it, and I'm willing to come along with you as chaperone, so that your mama won't worry.'

'Thank you, I should like it very much. I accept both your invitations,' Sophie said.

Thanks to Prudence, her thoughts had taken a happier turn: even if all her suitors had been pursuing her for an imaginary fortune, Mr Hobsbawn had always known that she was not an heiress. What liking he had shewn for her must, therefore, have been genuine.

The drive was a revelation to Sophie. On Agnes's insistence, she put on her very smartest bonnet and pelisse, and in the open barouche they drove slowly along all the main thoroughfares, ending up at the Exchange for some trifling purchases of fringe and needles for Agnes and a pair of gloves for Prudence. They were thus exposed to the view of almost every person of fashion in Manchester.

It was plain that tongues had been busy, and that society was already dividing into camps. The Pendleburyites comprised those like the Spicers who toadied to Mrs Pendlebury or depended on her patronage for their place in society; and those like the Ardwicks whose daughters had been neglected at balls for Sophie's sake, and who were now resentful that such a little black monkey of a person could have given herself such airs. These were joined by some of the young men who felt they had been lured into making cakes of themselves, and hadn't the self-possession to admit the mistake was their own. All of this camp believed quite firmly that Sophie and her mother had deliberately set out to deceive Manchester in order to get Sophie a husband.

The Morlandites comprised those who disliked Mrs Pendlebury and were glad to see her discomfited, the particular friends of the Droylsdens, and those whose loyalties were to neither family, but who liked a good joke, especially at someone else's expense. Both the drive and the stroll through the Exchange were marked by pointed displays of friendliness and hostility, the battle-lines drawing themselves up with such readiness that Sophie was half-inclined to believe it really had nothing to do with her, and that they had only been waiting for an excuse to go to war. She wished she had Agnes's robust self-confidence so that she could see some humour in the situation. From her heart she pitied Miss Pendlebury, who was evidently much distressed at her own position, finding herself obliged to side against her own mother, with whom she still lived and on whom she was entirely financially dependent.

When Agnes felt they had displayed themselves enough, they drove back to Hobsbawn House to refresh themselves with a nuncheon before going out again. In the morning-room they found Héloïse, returned from her visit to the attorney, and reading a letter which had been delivered by hand while they were out.

Agnes and Prudence, in their different ways, repeated to Héloïse the explanations and assurances they had made to Sophie, and Sophie told her mother of the morning's experiences.

'Oh dear, my poor little one!' Héloïse said with dismay. 'What a horrid thing to happen! I thought people were looking at me strangely this morning as I walked along Pall Mall. It is all such nonsense – but how cruel to take it out on you, my Sophie. As if anyone could suppose you were capable of such a deception.'

'It will all be forgotten soon enough, ma'am,' Prudence said. 'I am sorry and ashamed that my own family should have been at the bottom of it, but these things blow over very quickly, as I'm sure you know.'

Héloïse looked at her thoughtfully. 'Yes, you are right. I'm afraid it is you, Miss Pendlebury, who will suffer most from this. I am very grateful to you for standing by my Sophie so bravely. I know what it must cost you.'

Miss Pendlebury's mouth tightened. 'Thank you, ma'am. But I shall weather the storm. I'm afraid this is only the latest instance of a growing rift between my mother and me. We have differing views on so many things.'

Héloïse became aware of the letter she was holding. 'This becomes much clearer now,' she said wryly, holding it up. 'I had been puzzling over this letter – it is from Lady Batchworth, Sophie, very formal and correct, saying that sudden urgent business calls her away. She departs at once, and will therefore not be able to give herself the pleasure of calling on us to say goodbye. I suppose she has gone back to Grasscroft, now there is no prize to be won here.'

'And Mr Farraline?' Sophie asked in a subdued voice.

Héloïse reached out to touch her hand comfortingly. 'Yes, Mr Farraline too. Oh my Sophie, I'm so sorry. It is a hateful thing to happen.'

'It doesn't matter, Maman,' Sophie said.

Miss Pendlebury said, 'I'm surprised at Mr Farraline's taking this action, ma'am. I had thought better of his judgement than to expose himself to the charge of being a fortune-hunter.'

Héloïse shrugged. 'I suppose his means are not enough to take a wife wherever he will. He is a younger son, after all.'

'Well I think he's behaved most shocking,' Agnes said stoutly, 'and I shall tell everyone who asks that I think nothing to him.'

'He has to return to Manchester sooner or later,' Miss Pendlebury said thoughtfully. 'I wonder that he should risk his reputation like this.'

'Perhaps his mother insisted,' Héloïse said. 'Or perhaps he felt it was the kindest thing by Sophie, as he had raised so many expectations, to remove himself entirely and at once – the clean cut. Yes, on the whole, I think that is the most likely explanation. We should think well of people as long as we can.'

'Even of that horrid Lady Grey?' Agnes demanded.

Héloïse's expression hardened. 'She did not, after all, tell anything but the truth,' she said quietly. 'And now, let us dismiss this whole foolish matter from our minds. Sophie, my love, ring the bell, and let us have a nuncheon. What do you all do this afternoon?'

'Agnes and I mean to take Sophie with us on a benevolent mission, if you please, Lady Morland,' said Miss Pendlebury.

Héloïse smiled. 'Yes, of course – there is nothing better suited to restoring one's peace of mind than to see how much worse other people's problems are.'

'And as I shall be there to chaperone them,' Agnes said importantly, 'you need not worry about them, ma'am.'

Héloïse managed not to laugh, but she could not quite suppress a smile. 'I'm sure both will be safe in your hands,' she said. 'Young ladies, you must be sure to do just as Mrs Droylsden says.'

If the benevolent visiting were meant to be healing to Sophie, it was by way of a cauterisation, she thought, for this time she was taken to what surely must be the worst part of Manchester. Her respect for Miss Pendlebury increased enormously when she saw how unflinchingly she faced sights and smells which would make most women faint away. Agnes turned pale and grew very quiet, and anything that could silence her chatter must be very bad indeed. Prudence tried to prevent her companions from going in to some of the dwellings, but they were both determined to be resolute – Sophie because she wanted to be useful, and Agnes because she felt she must look after Sophie.

Water Street ran parallel with the River Irwell all the way from the new Salford bridge to St Mary's Gate, giving access to the mills and manufactories which lined the river. Leading off Water Street to both sides, crammed into the spaces between the tall, black mills and the belching chimneys, were the lanes and courts and entries where the mill-hands lived in the worst of squalor.

The tenements were old buildings, built of bug-infested lath and crumbling plaster, and divided and subdivided into ever smaller rooms and ever more teeming tenancies. The proximity to the mills meant that they were in perpetual half-darkness. A constant fog of smoke shut out the sun and choked the lungs, while a drizzle of soot blackened the buildings and further obscured the small, dim windowpanes.

In some courts it would have been possible for tenants of houses on either side to have joined hands by leaning out of their windows, had the windows been capable of being opened. In most there was an open kennel running down the centre, which was frequently so choked with offal and rubbish that the other effluvia overflowed and trickled into the basements. A common dunghill was the playground to such children as were not yet in employment; dogs truffled in the kennels for the tastier morsels, occasionally breaking off to bark at the rats, which were large enough and bold enough to challenge them for the rubbish in daylight. Sophie wondered where the residents got their water from, and supposed it must be a long way off. She hoped they did not draw it from the river: she never saw a single pump.

Even Miss Pendlebury would not venture into the basements, though she had heard of them from Father Rathbone and told her companions in a few terse words of the conditions there. The basement areas of most of the old houses were divided into several rooms, the inner ones opening off the outer ones and having no window or ventilation. In pitch darkness, therefore, the poorest or unluckiest lived eight or more to a room whose floor was always wet, and frequently flooded with the seepage from the kennels. Mattresses had to be raised off the floor on wooden pallets. There was no means of washing or cooking, and those who lived there rarely had any possessions beyond the mattress and perhaps a blanket. When they laid down and died – which many of them did – it was sometimes days in that Stygian darkness before their death was discovered. Yet such was the demand for accommodation, that almost as soon as a corpse was removed from a bed, its place was taken by a living body.

These things Sophie did not see, but what she saw was hard enough to bear. They visited Brooke's Entry, and went from room to room, advising, comforting where they could, and treating such ailments as were within their capability. Infections were frequent in those filthy conditions – indeed, Sophie wondered how any wound ever healed, when the people were so poorly nourished. Most of the children and many of the old people had rat-bites about them; lung infections, sore eyes, dysentery and scurvy were present everywhere; deformities of all sorts, missing limbs and ugly scars.

Sophie admired the spirit with which Miss Pendlebury, even when faced with the most pitiful and hopeless victims of sickness and misfortune, continued to recommend prayer, regular devotions, and church attendance along with whatever physical remedies she advocated. Sophie's own faith was strong, but she found it hard to speak of God's benevolence to those whose lives seemed rather a curse on them than any kind of divine gift.

'You must guard against despair, Sophie,' Prudence said to her briskly when they left these scenes of misery at last, and drove back to the mission to report to Father Rathbone and refresh their spirits after their labours. 'It is the easiest thing in the world when faced with such sights to lose one's own inner convictions; but we owe it to these people to fight against such feelings. God *is* good; there is hope for every creature, and redemption is sure for those who bear their sufferings patiently, and continue to love Him in their hearts. That is what we can give these people, more surely than food or clothes or medicine, and it is what is most important. Many of them will die untimely; most, perhaps all, of them will suffer; and without Faith, it is all in vain.'

'Yes, you're right, of course,' Sophie said. 'I do see that; and I will do my best.'

'I know you will,' Miss Pendlebury said with a rare smile. 'Remember that if we do not believe in God's goodness, there is no reason for us to try to help these people at all. Annie, are you all right? You're very quiet.'

'Oh, I shall be well enough,' Agnes said queasily, 'when I've got the stink of those places out of my head. Sophie dear, have you any lavender-water about you? I sprinkled all of mine in that first place we went to. Ah, thank you, that's better. I feel as if I shall never be free of the smell! I wonder you can bear it, Pru, and go back as often as you do.'

'Someone must do it,' Prudence said simply.

'Well, but why you, at all events? It's no task for a woman – or at least, not for a gentlewoman.'

'God takes no account of rank or sex,' Prudence said. 'He sees only our Christian hearts.'

'I don't see how you can always be so sure what God's thinking,' Agnes complained, her spirits reviving now they had left the black places behind. 'You always say He thinks this and thinks that, but who tells you so? In any case, it seems to me that if God wants these people to be helped, He might just as well not strike them down with disease and poverty in the first place. That would save everyone a great deal of unpleasantness.'

'Oh Annie!' Prudence exclaimed in exasperation, but a smile tugged at her lips all the same. It was impossible ever to be really angry with such a simple cheerful creature as her sister.

The mission seemed a haven of cleanliness and comfort after the tenements, and two or three cups of hot, fragrant tea were enough to restore Sophie to her normal spirits. The arrival of Father Rathbone took Prudence away from them for a long, private consultation, presumably about the afternoon's activities. Sophie and Agnes remained on their sofa, chatting in a comfortable way, and by unspoken agreement avoiding the subjects of poverty and disease.

Some time later, while Prudence was still in conference with the priest, the door to the street opened and Jasper Hobsbawn came in. Sophie started and blushed, and wondered at the strange coincidence by which she met him here every time she came. His eyes came straight to her, as if he had known she would be there, and he acknowledged her across the room with a bow of the head, but then turned aside to speak to Rathbone. Sophie ceased to hear anything Agnes said. Her eyes were fixed on the group on the other side of the room. She saw Rathbone speak, and then Prudence, and the eyes of all three turn towards her and Agnes. Mr Hobsbawn said something, and Prudence spoke again.

And then he was coming across the room towards her. Sophie lifted her eyes to his face cautiously, wondering what sort of greeting she would get from him, whether friendly or distant, approving or disapproving. His mood in her company had been so unpredictable in the past.

'How do you do, Mr Hobsbawn,' she said when he was still a pace or two off, to get it over with.

He didn't smile, but his expression was kindly, at least, and not disapproving.

'Miss Morland. I'm glad to see you. And Mrs Droylsden – how do you do, ma'am?'

'Good day to you, Mr Hobsbawn! We're feeling much better now, thank you, after some reviving tea. For really, you know, we've been through the mill today, haven't we, Sophie?'

Sophie smiled at the joke, but Mr Hobsbawn didn't seem to have been attending, for he said, 'Have you, ma'am? Which mill would that be?'

Agnes rolled her eyes at Sophie, and said, 'We've been to Brooke's Entry with Prudence, as I dare say she was telling you – and a very horrid place it is. I hope you will persuade Sophie never to go there again. It's all very well for Prudence, who's a grown woman and as strong as a horse, but Sophie's so young and pretty, she oughtn't to risk her health and complexion in those filthy courts. Don't you agree, Mr Hobsbawn?'

Mr Hobsbawn's eyes had been on Sophie's face all through this speech, so he had had ample opportunity to assess the state of her complexion and to judge if there had been any loss of bloom.

But he didn't directly answer Agnes. Instead he said gently, 'So, you have seen the tenements. I think they will have been worse than you expected.'

'They were – but why should you think so?' Sophie said.

'Because I should not like to think any gently-born woman could imagine such squalor until she had seen it for herself.'

'You're quite right, Mr Hobsbawn,' Agnes answered for Sophie. 'Pru had told me something of it, but nothing near the truth. I can't imagine why people go on living in such places. For myself, I'd sooner lie under a hedge or in an open field than in one of those courts.'

Again Mr Hobsbawn didn't directly reply to her comment. Still looking at Sophie, he said, 'And now you've seen the worst, have you resolved like a sensible person never to go near such places again?'

'Oh no,' said Sophie quickly. 'I was shocked, and I must confess I felt depressed when we came away; but most of all, I felt pity for those poor people. Miss Pendlebury warned me against feelings of despair, and I'm sure she is right. I feel very strongly that I want to do something to help, only I cannot immediately see what it should be. Everything is so very bad, that I don't know what I could do that would be useful.'

Jasper's eyes kindled through this speech. Now he smiled at her warmly and said, 'I honour you! And I could shew you, if you would allow me. It does seem beyond hope at first, I

263

know, but there is so much that can be done to help, and to change things. Most of all, I wish you could persuade your mother to think like you. In her position, she has the power to make the greatest possible difference to the lives of those people. If only you could draw her into our schemes –'

Our schemes! Sophie glowed inwardly at the words – never had he seemed so approving of her. But she was obliged to say, 'I'm afraid I have no influence with my mother.'

He looked faintly surprised. 'I'm sure you have,' he said, a contradiction which would have been rude if it had not been so obviously well meant.

'I've heard Maman talk disapprovingly about "interference", and I don't think she would care for your schemes. She doesn't like Mr Owen, you know, because he is an atheist.'

'Oh, but my schemes are not quite like Mr Owen's! I am not entirely convinced that everything he believes is right. If I could explain my ideas to her in the right sort of atmosphere – if you could just predispose her to listen sympathetically – I believe she would agree that there is nothing to object to in them.'

'But I don't even know whether she is going to keep the mills or sell them,' Sophie said sadly, reluctant to spoil the happy atmosphere between them. 'And then, you know, we shall be going away very soon. Our visit was not meant to be more than two weeks, and we have been here almost a month. Maman won't want to stay away from Morland Place any longer.'

Jasper looked very much taken aback. 'Going away,' he said, and then muttered, as though to himself, 'I should have realised – foolish of me.'

Agnes looked from his face to Sophie's with interest and a dawning understanding.

'I wish you need not go,' Hobsbawn said at last.

'I wish it too,' Sophie said sadly, 'but however, there's no helping it.'

He looked at her keenly, hesitated, and then said, 'I hope it is not because of – I have heard about the foolishness that has arisen over the matter of your supposed inheritance.'

Sophie lowered her eyes, embarrassed, not sure what it was proper to say on that head, especially in front of Agnes.

'And Mr Farraline has gone away as well, I understand,'

Jasper went on, scanning her face. 'That must have been distressing for you. I am sincerely sorry you should have been so much hurt, when everyone expected – when you must have expected –'

Sophie looked up. 'Oh no,' she said quickly. 'You are quite mistaken! Mr Farraline did not – that is, I was not hoping for an offer from him. Indeed, I rather dreaded that he might make me an offer, for I was not at all in love with him.'

'Not in love with him?' Jasper said wonderingly.

'No,' Sophie said, and a smile crept into her eyes. 'Nor with any of the others. It is shocking to have unkind things said about one, but on the whole I'm rather glad than sorry, not to have those young men crowding round me all the time. They were so very noisy and distracting.'

Mr Hobsbawn suddenly looked very much more cheerful. 'Mrs Droylsden,' he said, 'would you not say that is a remarkable preference for a young woman?'

'Yes, I would,' Agnes agreed vigorously. 'But then Sophie is not just in the usual style.'

Sophie returned to Hobsbawn House feeling much more at peace with the world than when she set out, though it would have puzzled her to say precisely why. On the journey back, she discussed with Prudence the cases they had seen that day, and made plans for further visits during the few days she had left.

'Oh I wish I did not have to go home,' she said more than once. 'There is so much to be done here.'

As the hour was growing late, the other two dropped her off at the house without coming in, promising to call again the next morning. Sophie ran upstairs to the morning-room and found her mother there, looking rather weary.

'Oh Maman, do we have to go back to Morland Place so soon?' she asked when she had told about her experiences that day.

'Do you like it here so much, then, my Sophie? I'm surprised,' Héloïse said. 'But I have to go back – I can't bear to be away from your Papa and the boys any longer. And you cannot stay here without me, ça se voit. It would not be proper.'

'What, even if Alice stayed with me?' Sophie asked, though without any real hope.

'Of course not. You are only nineteen, *chérie*. Think what people would say if you lived alone without a chaperone. It would be most improper. Not at all –'

'*Comme il faut*,' Sophie finished for her.

Héloïse smiled. 'I was going to say *bon ton*! But what a pity it is there has been this silly trouble, for I expect before it happened Mrs Pendlebury would have been happy to invite you to stay with her for a few weeks.'

'Yes, but then you know you wouldn't have been happy for me to stay,' Sophie said mischievously, 'because of all the foolish young men dangling after me. Now I am not regarded as a match, I am much safer here.'

'I'm glad you are able to laugh about it, my Sophie. But still, you cannot stay here alone, so there is no help for it.'

Sophie sighed. 'And if you sell the mills, we won't ever come again, will we? Do you mean to sell them, Maman?'

'I don't know. I must tell everything I have learned to your father, and then he will decide what is best to be done. It is not something I can decide alone.'

They went to the concert that evening, by invitation of the enormous Audenshaw family, who were numerous and wealthy enough not to need Mrs Pendlebury's approbation. Mrs Pendlebury was there, accompanied by Fred, Lady Grey and Miss Grey, and casting particularly dark and glowering looks across at the Audenshaw box, which the Audenshaws feigned not to notice. Sophie remarked that none of the Droylsdens was present, and that Miss Pendlebury was not in her mother's box. She hoped that her friends had taken no infection from the benevolent visiting.

The next morning explained all. The Droylsden barouche arrived very early, while Sophie and Héloïse were still at breakfast, and Agnes was announced alone.

'Oh, Lady Morland, I'm glad you're still here, for I particularly wanted to talk to you. I must tell you the news first – and very shocking it is, but really for the best all round, as I'm sure you'll agree! It's about Prudence –'

'Is she well?' Sophie asked quickly. 'I noticed she was not at the concert last night.'

'No, she was at my house. Oh such fun, you know! There was the most dreadful quarrel when I took her home, after leaving you here. Mama was there, and asked where we had

266

been, and when we told her she was so angry –'

'Should you be telling us this?' Héloïse interrupted uncomfortably.

'Oh yes, ma'am – you'll see why in a moment. Well, Mama was angry that Prudence had gone sick-visiting – though she's never forbidden her to do it, you know, so Pru didn't do anything wrong – and she said she'd never get a husband if she did such things, instead of making herself agreeable to the right people. So Prudence said – well, however, I won't tell you all the things that were said, for one way and another it wasn't agreeable in the least. But the end of it was that Prudence said she wouldn't give up doing what she felt she was called to do, and Mama said in that case she was no daughter of hers, and she could find herself another roof to live under.'

'Good heaven! She could not mean it!' Héloïse said, shocked.

'Lord, no ma'am! She'd have taken it back when she got over her temper. For all that she's never liked Prudence very much, she wouldn't cast her quite out of doors. But Pru didn't want her to take it back, and nor did I. I said at once that she could come and live with me, and Mama said she might do as she liked, and so it was settled.'

'Oh dear, but a family quarrel is so distressing,' Héloïse said.

'No-one will know about it,' Agnes said cheerfully. 'We'll put about that I invited Pru because I wanted company, and that's how it will be seen by the world.'

Héloïse doubted it, having regard to Agnes's volatile tongue and the general contagiousness of gossip, but made no comment on that.

'But won't your mother want her back as soon as she has – got over the shock?' she asked tactfully.

'Oh no! Mama's wanted Pru out of the house for years, and she'll only wonder why she never thought of it before. So everyone's happy you see.'

'Well, I'm glad of that,' Héloïse said, still doubtful.

'But now, ma'am, I came to beg a favour of you,' Agnes went on. 'I know that Sophie doesn't want to go home just yet, and I would dearly love to have her to stay with me. And so would Prudence – you know how she dotes on Sophie. So would you permit her to come to us when you go back to

Yorkshire? I'd take good care of her, you can be sure, and take her everywhere, so you needn't be afraid; and when it was time for her to come home, I'd send her in my own carriage, with my own maid and man, so that you needn't be at the trouble of fetching her.'

Héloïse hesitated, taken aback by the invitation. It was one thing to have considered leaving Sophie with Mrs Pendlebury, but Agnes was hardly a mature and responsible matron. Yet, on the other hand, though she was as dizzy a creature as ever drew breath, she was very kind-hearted and perfectly respectable. She looked at her daughter, and saw that Sophie was wearing her heart on her face. Why does she want so much to stay? Héloïse wondered uneasily. It could not be love, surely, for all her suitors had deserted her; and she had never shewn preference for any of them anyway. Could she still be counting on Farraline's preference? He must come back to Manchester to see to his mills sooner or later. Héloïse did not believe he would renew his attentions to her daughter; but if he did, he was a gentleman after all, and would never do anything exceptionable, even if Sophie were only chaperoned by Mrs Percy Droylsden.

'Do you really want to stay, my Sophie?' she asked at last.

'Oh yes, Maman, if you please!' Sophie said eagerly.

At least Prudence Pendlebury would be there too, Héloïse thought, and though she was unmarried, she had a great deal of common-sense, and a strong understanding of propriety. With Miss Pendlebury's guidance and good sense, Mrs Droylsden's chaperonage might do very well.

'Then I think you may,' she said; and while Agnes and Sophie were expressing their delight and satisfaction, she suddenly wondered about the 'quarrel' which had resulted in Prudence's taking up residence with her sister. Was it possible that Agnes had engineered it for this very reason? If so, it meant that Mrs Droylsden was much less dizzy than she seemed – which, of course, was all to the good.

CHAPTER FOURTEEN

England had its revolution in that summer of 1817, though few people knew about it at the time. And a very old-fashioned sort of revolution it was: an affair in the grand old style, of marching men, pikes and pitchforks, shouts and running footsteps and flaring torches in the dead of night.

Rosamund heard about it from Fitzherbert Hawker, who had called to pay his respects to Lucy and Danby, but found her alone at Upper Grosvenor Street. She was writing letters of acknowledgement for wedding-presents, which were arriving daily in a growing flood.

'Mama and Papa Danby are gone to Carlton House,' she said. 'Do sit down and talk to me. You can't think how dull this task is! I shall be glad to be prevented from going on with it for half an hour.'

So he told her about the Pentrich Revolution, which was all that remained of the rising in the north the Home Office had so long expected. The leader was Jeremiah Brandreth, who had been suspected of fomenting other troubles in Nottingham; but he was no reformist. As he sat in the White Horse in Pentrich with a map spread before him, he did not talk of franchise, manhood suffrage or annual parliaments. He was only an unemployed stockinger, and his purpose in wanting to overthrow the Government was simple, romantic and impractical. His dreams and promises were all of beef and bread and free rum, of a hundred golden guineas for each man who followed him to the storming of Nottingham Castle, of the band of music which would welcome them there, and the pleasure-trip up the River Trent that would follow.

'It's almost pitiful,' Hawker said. 'He believed all he had to do was to overthrow the Government by force, and food and drink and pleasure would automatically follow. As though the Ministers of the Crown were holding down the lid on some bottomless cornucopia which would otherwise spill over into the hands of the poor! He kept talking about setting up a provisional government, and it turns out he thought it meant a government that would distribute provisions.'

This man Brandreth, who called himself the Nottingham Captain, led his rebellion from a remote village in the foothills of the Peak District. It was to open with an attack on a local ironworks, for it was rumoured that a disaffected worker had been secretly manufacturing ammunition, and they hoped to seize it for their own use. During the night Brandreth's council of war scoured the area, stirring farmers and labourers out of their beds and herding them along the tracks and over the commons to form a motley army, which marched off through the dark, and drew up at last in the first light of June the 10th before the gates of the Butterley Foundry.

What was to have been the Battle of Butterley proved a severe anticlimax. The manager of the ironworks, appearing at the gates, refused to shew the slightest fear of the ragged assembly. Calmly he advised them to go home before they did something that would condemn them to the rope; and so resolute was his manner that many of the rebels, who hadn't much wanted to revolt in the first place, obeyed him. The rest turned away, muttering sulkily, and began the long tramp towards the Nottingham border.

'That was when the rain started,' Hawker said. 'I told you, didn't I, that our weather would always prove the death of revolution?'

Along the sunken Derbyshire lanes and past the deep cornfields, in the drenching rain, the army tramped in sullen silence. Soaked through, it grew more ragged by the minute, fraying at the edges as men slipped away through the hedges and across the fields to go home. Desperate to keep his band together, Brandreth told them that Nottingham Castle had already fallen, and even threatened to shoot deserters with his own hand; but when they reached Giltbrook Hill and found themselves facing the local magistrate, backed by a troop of Hussars, the reluctant rebels threw down their pikes and billhooks and fled for their lives.

Brandreth and forty-six others were taken up, and were imprisoned to await trial; and that was the end of the revolution.

'But did they really believe they could overthrow the Government?' Rosamund asked. 'Such a very small band?'

'They believed they were just part of a general rising – that the whole of the north was to rise up at once and converge on London, storm the Houses of Parliament, and seize the keys of the Tower. It's quite certain that there was some plan of the kind – it's been brewing up for the past year and more – but fortunately, owing to the action of certain agents of Lord Sidmouth, the rest of the would-be rebels were dissuaded from putting the plan into action. It's Brandreth's misfortune that he was stupid enough or passionate enough to go ahead with it.'

'What will happen to him?'

'There'll be a state trial, and he'll hang, along with a few of the other ringleaders – enough to make an example. Probably some of the others will be transported or imprisoned, and the rest will be let off with a caution. The heartening thing is how few of the rebels stuck it out to the end, and how quickly they ran when faced with even a small band of soldiers. But it's shocking that it happened at all, of course, and we're not out of the woods yet – there's still a great deal of disaffection all over the country. However, the good thing is that it's brought me to London to report, and given me the pleasure of seeing you again – and of being able to assure you that your wedding won't have to be postponed after all.'

'I never thought it would be,' Rosamund said.

Hawker cocked his head. 'Do I hear a note of regret, Lady Rosamund?'

'Certainly not,' she said firmly, though she coloured a little. 'I am not being married against my will, you know. I'm looking forward to it very much.'

'To the wedding, I don't doubt – everyone loves a wedding,' he said provokingly. 'But what about afterwards? And does Lady Barbara still mean to live with you?'

Rosamund gave him a clear look. 'You needn't worry about that. At the moment I am hamstrung by my single condition, but once I am married – well, I mean to be mistress in my own house, I promise you.'

'Brava! I wish you a happy adjustment – and I look forward with relish to hearing all about it. It should be a bonny fight! Cribb and Molyneaux all over again.'

'Oh you're impossible!' Rosamund said, trying not to laugh. 'I really should not listen – you say such improper things!'

He grinned. 'So I'm told. But I do sincerely wish you well, and I hope now we have the revolution out of the way that nothing more happens to put your wedding at hazard.'

'We have had bad news lately,' Rosamund said. 'It won't postpone the wedding, but it means my sister, Lady Harvey Sale, won't be there. Mama had a letter: the babies – her twin daughters – have died.'

Hawker was instantly serious. 'I'm sorry to hear that. Is she very much upset?'

'Yes, it seems so. It was some kind of colic, you know – one of the usual infant ailments – but though they were so young, she was very fond of them, and it must have been distressing for her to see them suffer. Mama was of the opinion that as they were only girls, it didn't much matter, and I dare say Lord Harvey shares that view. But Minnie was adamant that she wouldn't come to the wedding, and that means that Polly won't either, of course.'

'Oh yes, the lovely Miss Haworth,' Hawker said thoughtfully. 'She still lives with your sister then? And they are fixed at Stainton? What a great pity that such a beauty should be walled up for ever in that remote place.'

'Yes, they don't see much company there. Minnie doesn't mind – she's never been at her best with strangers – but it must be dull for Polly.'

'You'll be in a position to help once you're married,' he pointed out. 'You can invite her to stay with you in London, and chaperone her to parties, as I imagine you'll be expected to do with your sister-in-law.'

'Yes,' Rosamund said, 'I could have her to stay, couldn't I? I suppose I'd have to ask Minnie, too. She'd never let Polly come without her. Still, Minnie's never any trouble. Poor soul, I hope she's not very unhappy about her babies.'

'Fortunately, babies are easy to come by,' Hawker said. 'And as Penrith plainly never means to marry, Sale will be sure to try again for a son to inherit the title. I think you may safely assume that your sister will be *enceinte* again by the end of the year.'

Polly Haworth, reaching the top of the stairs, saw the back of

Mrs Hill, Minnie's woman, disappearing down the main bedroom corridor. She called out to her, but to her surprise, Hill didn't stop.

'Hill, just a moment! I asked you where Lady Harvey is.'

Hill turned to look at her, a burning look of resentment which took Polly aback. 'That's for me to know, and you to find out,' she growled.

Polly flushed. 'If you are insolent, I shall have you dismissed.'

'Aye, I don't doubt you'd try,' Hill said. 'But I'll not leave my mistress until *she* tells me to, so you may do as you please.'

Polly was as much puzzled as angry. She had noticed that Hill had been growing ever more sour lately, and had sometimes intercepted dark and brooding glances from the woman, but until now Hill had never behaved other than with rigid correctness. Polly wondered if she was perhaps becoming unbalanced. It did sometimes happen with unmarried female servants of a certain age; and God knew, this place was enough to turn anyone's mind.

Discipline, however, must be maintained. 'I insist on your answering me civilly,' she said coldly.

'Insist all you like – I've got your measure, my fine lady! I know how you'd break my lady's heart if you could – you and that creature she calls a husband! And if it weren't that she loves you, for God knows what reason, I'd tell the world about it this very minute.' Polly stared, dumbfounded. 'Yes, you can put on airs and look at me how you like,' Hill went on fiercely, 'but when it comes down to it, what are you? A poor relation! You're no better than a servant. And you're worse than me, for I'd know better than to tamper with another woman's husband.'

Polly glared at her in dull rage, unable for a moment to speak. 'How dare you?' she gasped at last. 'Are you mad? Are you ill? How dare you say such things?'

'I've seen you and him together – whispering and pinching fingers! So don't play Madam Innocent with me. Aye, he'd like to be rid of her now he's got her money, I know! That's why he's paying all these visits, after neglecting her so long – plotting with you how to be rid of her!'

'You must be quite deranged,' Polly said, drawing herself

up with dignity. 'That's the kindest thing to think. But I warn you, if you repeat one word of this – this *babbling* to anyone –'

'I know how to keep my mouth shut,' Hill snapped, 'but it won't be for your sake! And if you want my mistress, you'll find her in the nursery, poor lamb, where I doubt even you'd have the heart to disturb her.'

She turned and stalked away, leaving Polly shaken. Was it possible Hill had really seen anything? They had been so careful, and their stolen moments – innocent enough in all truth! – had been snatched in the least frequented and most uncomfortable of places, the last places a servant would go. No, it was impossible Hill could know anything. She had made the accusation out of her own disturbed imagination, and had merely hit by accident on something that was almost true. She was mad, that was all.

All? It was a horrible thing to contemplate, being shut up in this house with a deranged serving-woman. With automatic tread, Polly went on up the stairs towards the nurseries on the top floor, right under the roof. She thought longingly of Harvey. It was true, as Hill said, that he had been paying more frequent visits to Stainton in the last six weeks, after having neglected them entirely for so long. Recently he had been coming down for a couple of days every week: he had been here only yesterday. Polly wondered whether it was because the babies had died – to comfort Minnie, perhaps. But no, his increased attentiveness had begun before their fatal attack of colic.

She reached the top of the stairs. Through a skylight in the roof she saw a square of blank, grey sky, from which a steady rain was falling. She could hear the warm drops drumming softly on the roof just above her head as she walked along the dusty drugget, and felt her muscles tense, and her hands grow damp. It had rained every day for weeks now, confining them indoors, and the tedium and frustration had grown in her to the point where they tipped over into a morbid terror.

For outside the wet, green world relished the rain. The grass grew lush and long, the trees shook their full-leafed heads softly, whispering together like conspirators. She began to feel that the growing things were creeping closer day by day to the isolated house. Stealthily, inch by inch, they were reclaiming the little space Stainton had stolen from them. She would wake one morning and find the trees pressing up against the windows, trying to get in. The moss would creep over her chamber floor, over her bed, over her face, smothering her, stifling her screams...

She shuddered, catching herself back with an effort from the brink. She must not allow her imagination to wander. Whatever the reason for Harvey's visits, Polly was deeply grateful for them, for without them, she felt she must have gone mad, shut in day after day with the ceaseless sound of the rain. It was no wonder that Minnie was brooding so over the death of her babies. While they lived that had been the only changing thing in her monotonous life. She had nothing else to think about, nothing to stimulate her senses.

Harvey was fatalistic about the babies. He had been upset when they died – far more than she would have expected. Polly had witnessed his reaction, and had been surprised at how white and silent he'd gone when the apothecary came downstairs to say they were dead at last, poor wailing things. But babies did die, as he said afterwards in a hard voice – that was a fact of life, as any sensible person must accept.

Polly entered the nursery – empty now of the bustle and to-and-froing that had always attended the short lives of Miss Mary and Miss Elizabeth – and found Minnie all alone, sitting on a hard chair between the two empty cradles. The air was warm and stuffy up here under the roof-tiles, and quite still. It smelled dusty, and the silence was somehow emphasised by the close but muffled drumming of the rain above them. Minnie sat quite still, her hands in her lap, staring at the floor between her feet. She was very pale, and despite the best attentions of Hill, she managed somehow to give the impression of being slightly unkempt, as if she no longer cared about her appearance.

Polly felt a vast pity for her, tinged, albeit unwillingly, with irritation. It was somehow typical of Minnie that she should be so utterly cast down by the loss of her daughters. It was true what Harvey said – babies died all the time, and you knew with each one that there was a good chance it would not survive to its fourth year. Minnie had had two miscarriages before the birth of the twins: she knew the odds against them. Why then did she creep away and hide up here like this? Why

275

had she refused to go to Rosamund's wedding? Why had she become so listless and disinclined for any occupation that she seemed hardly ever to move at all?

'Minnie, what are you doing here?' Polly asked now – quite gently, but Minnie startled all the same, and looked up quickly with an expression almost of fear. She scanned Polly's face, and the doorway behind her, with one quick look, and then looked down again. Polly saw her mouth tremble, and a glistening of tears under her eyelashes, but she didn't speak.

'You really shouldn't keep coming up here all alone like this,' Polly went on reasonably. 'It doesn't help to brood over things. If you'd only find something to do, turn your mind away from it, you'd be over it in no time.'

'Please, Polly, go away.' Minnie spoke so quietly that Polly could only just catch the words. They were an indication of how far from her usual frame of mind Minnie was: she had always wanted to tie Polly to her side, not send her away – uneasy if Polly left the room even for a minute.

'Come downstairs,' Polly coaxed gently. 'Come down and take up your sewing again. Or I'll play cards with you, if you like, or read to you. Don't sit here all alone and brood. It only upsets you more.'

But Minnie looked up at her, a look of sadness and longing and reproach and apprehension that struck Polly to the heart. 'Please go away,' she said again. 'I want you to leave me alone.'

Polly hesitated, looking at the top of her cousin's head, wondering what more she could do or say. But Minnie sat on the small, hard chair as though planted, and Polly knew how stubborn she could be if ever she did make up her mind to something. There seemed to be nothing to do but to leave her as requested.

But Polly puzzled as she went away. Was there more to Minnie's withdrawal than grief over her lost babies? Was it possible that Hill had said something to her of her mad suspicions? No, surely that was impossible! Minnie would have said something – she had no notion of concealment, and had often in the past repeated things, to a general embarrassment, which anyone with more wit would have known were never meant to be repeated.

Polly longed, suddenly and fiercely, for Harvey; for a resolution to this frightful situation, for an end to the boredom, monotony, imprisonment – for escape! For the first time she thought seriously about escape. It was obvious that Harvey would never be able to save her from the situation which he had created in the first place; but if Minnie's clinging dependency were at last lessening, perhaps there might be another way.

Perhaps, she thought, clenching her fists against her breast in an unconscious gesture, she might simply go away on her own, leave them both. In some distant part of the country, she might find some way to support herself, as a governess or a lady's maid perhaps. It would mean poverty, discomfort, obscurity – all the things she had always dreaded for herself; but for the first time those things seemed less frightful than the continuation of her present dependency. Here, for all her material comfort, she seemed to be losing control of her very soul. Away from here, there might be, even in poverty, a way of becoming at last her own woman.

Rosamund went to her wedding in a calmer state of mind than most brides of her age. Indeed, Docwra, who had been sent by Lucy to dress her in case she needed reassurance, advice or encouragement, had nothing to do in those departments. Docwra was old-fashioned enough to have wanted to see her charge weep a little or turn pale and tremble, but Rosamund merely inspected her reflection in the dressing-table glass and said that she had no need of the spanish-paper Docwra had brought with her.

'It will be hot enough in the carriage, I'm sure, to give me the colour of a lobster. I'll rather need whitening than rouging.'

'You won't need either, my lady,' Docwra said, rallying. 'You'll look beautiful, and a lucky man he is to be receiving *you* at the altar.'

'Well, I am marrying my childhood sweetheart after all,' Rosamund said. 'I should think most people would say I'm the lucky one.'

Docwra couldn't tell from Rosamund's face whether she meant it, or was joking, and found it safer to say nothing. Instead she commented on her work as she arranged Rosamund's hair.

'A blessing it is that you're marrying in June, when the roses are at their best. There's nothing like roses for dressing up a head, though once you're married it'll be diamonds and pearls, o' course, you being a countess. Outrank your mother, you will, had you thought about that? She'll have to stand if you come into the room at a public function, and you'll go in to dinner before her.'

'What a thought!' Rosamund laughed. 'I hope *that* never happens. I must avoid public functions that she attends.'

'T'won't be your choice,' Dowcra began, but Rosamund interrupted, 'As to diamonds and pearls – have you seen the Chelmsford jewels?'

'I have. I was at Chelmsford House with her ladyship the day they was brought from the bank, and Hawkins let me have a look at them before he took them down to the strongroom. There's not much of them, compared with what her ladyship had when she married your late father, but they're good stones, the way you won't be shamed.'

'There's a lovely tiara of rose diamonds,' Rosamund said 'and a really pretty necklace of large half-pearls set about with rubies, and some other things I shan't mind wearing. Usually family jewels are so ugly and old-fashioned.'

'I expect they were made for Mrs Firth when she was married to the sixth earl. She was so young and pretty then, I remember hearing he had a lot of the family stuff made over for her, though she never cared much for grand occasions. Ah, there was a lot of jealous talk when the earl married her, her only being a soldier's daughter –'

'I'll bet Lady Barbara had something to say about it,' Rosamund said grimly.

Docwra quite properly ignored that. 'But they were very happy together, and she gave him a son just as she should, and all in all she was as good a countess as any that's been born to the rank. It's not so very old a title, but there's been some fine people who've been Countess of Chelmsford – your own grandmother, her ladyship's mother, amongst 'em.'

Rosamund raised her eyebrows. 'Grandmama? Really? I never knew that.'

'That's right. It was before she married your grandfather, and there was no children of the marriage, so I suppose it never got talked of. The earl died young, and the title went to his brother, and your grandmother went back to Morland Place and married her cousin. Still and all, she was Countess of Chelmsford all right, so you can hold your head up in the title and think of her.'

'She died when I was a baby. I never knew her,' Rosamund said. 'I wish I had.'

Docwra smiled at Rosamund's reflection in the glass, and rested her hand softly on the crown of burnished hair. 'She'd have loved you, my lady, no doubt about it. It was she that named you Rose of the World the day you was born, and if she saw you now she'd say you've grown up as beautiful as your name.'

'Thank you, Docwra,' Rosamund said solemnly. 'You're an atrocious liar, for I'm plain as a stick and always have been, but I know you mean it from kindness. And now, if you've finished with my head, hadn't we better be putting on the gown? It's after half past eleven.'

Docwra gave a shriek. 'Lord bless us! We'll be late. Where's that girl? Moss! Come in here, and don't be mooning about like a sick spaniel! Fetch her ladyship's wedding gown over, and mind you don't crumple it.'

The gown was of very fine white muslin over a stiffened pale pink silk slip. The waist was very high, as the fashion was, and the hem very wide, deeply flounced and ruffled with pink and white silk festoons of ruched ribbon, gathered up to clusters of pink silk roses with seed-pearls at their hearts. The same ruched ribbon decorated the low neckline of the bodice, but there the gathers were pinned with real roses. There were knots of ribbon on the puffed muslin sleeves, and her hair was dressed with more roses and ribbons, and short pink and white plumes held by clips set with pink freshwater pearls.

When Docwra and Moss had hooked her up and twitched the dress into position, Rosamund looked at herself doubtfully in the long cheval glass. She had grown up through a period in which women's gowns were classically plain and unadorned, and in any case had spent most of her life dressed in riding habits. The fashion for trimming and flounces had only come in in the last year or so, and she had never seen herself in anything so elaborate and frilly, and doubted whether it suited her.

Still, she thought, with an inward sigh, if the thing had to

279

be done, it might as well be done properly. Docwra slipped a gold filagree necklace – a present from the bridegroom – around her throat and fastened it behind, and then she was finished. As she turned away from the glass, there was a tapping at the door.

'Now what –?' Docwra began disapprovingly, and jerked her head at Moss.

The maid went across and opened it a crack, murmured something, glanced back over her shoulder at her mistress and said, 'It's Parslow, my lady.'

Rosamund nodded. Moss opened the door fully, and Parslow stood there on the threshold, smartly dressed in bran-new livery with a wedding-favour on the collar, his hat respectfully in his hand and his hair neatly pomaded down.

Before he could speak, Docwra hurried forward and said disapprovingly, 'Yes, yes, her ladyship's ready. There was no need for you to come hurrying her. Sure an' nothing's going to happen until she gets there anyway.'

Rosamund caught his eye over Docwra's fat shoulder. 'All right, Docwra,' she intervened. 'You and Moss can go and get ready. I shall come down in a moment or two. Go on, now, or you'll be late.'

The maids departed reluctantly, and she was left facing Parslow, across the room in which she had slept as a maiden for the last time last night. Tonight there would be the goose-feather bed and the new-wedded lord. What did Parslow think of it all, she wondered? She had not forgotten that his advice had been that she refuse Marcus.

Parslow's face was impassive as usual, but his eyes were bright with some unaccustomed emotion. 'My lady,' he said, on a faintly interrogative note.

'Well,' she said nervously, holding her hands out a little from her side in the manner of a child in a party-frock, 'will I do?'

His eyes never strayed from her face, and if that was not a smile on his lips, it was the next thing to it. 'You're beautiful, my lady,' he said softly.

Not her gown, but her! Her cheeks grew warm. The word 'gammon' sprang to her lips and died there, and she felt instead a piercing desire to burst into tears and fling herself into his arms. She suppressed it, drew a deep breath, and said,

'You came to tell me the carriage is here, I suppose?'

'Yes, my lady. And also – if you'll allow me –' He hesitated, seeming for once unsure of himself. 'I hope you won't consider it a liberty –'

'What is it?' Rosamund asked. 'It's all right, you can be frank with me.'

'Oh no, my lady. It's just that – I have something I wanted to give you, if you'd permit me?'

He reached into his waistcoat pocket, and drew out a very small paper parcel. She received it from him in silence, opened it, and found inside, in all the niceness of jeweller's packing, a tiny silver horseshoe.

'It's to bring you luck, my lady,' he said quietly as she looked at it in silence. 'And to remember the day. I hope you'll forgive my presumption.'

'Oh Parslow!' She touched it with one finger as it lay there on the palm of her other hand, and then looked up at him. 'Thank you. I shall never part with it. Oh Parslow –' Her eyes were dangerously bright, and he had half an idea she was going to step forward and kiss him. She half-thought so herself.

'No, no, my lady,' he said gently. 'All's well. The carriage is downstairs now, and his lordship's waiting for you.'

She bit her lip and nodded, and he stepped aside to allow her through the door. She picked up her gloves and started forward. Then in the doorway she stopped, inches from him, and said, 'I hope you don't feel bad about it? I'm a different person now, I think. I believe this marriage is the right thing for me. Marcus is – Lord Chelmsford and I will be happy together.'

'Yes, my lady,' he said, to all or any of it. She looked at him a moment longer, and received in return his steadiest look, which made no judgements, only promised always to be there, and always to care for her; and then she went past him and started down the stairs.

At the foot, Lord Theakston was waiting, elegant and slim and as neat as a pin, smiling up at her, ready to take her to the Abbey and give her away. I'm lucky, Rosamund thought suddenly, to have so many loving people about me; and the image came unbidden into her mind of her sister Flaminia, shut away at Stainton mourning the loss of her twin

281

daughters. Poor Minnie, she thought with the generosity of happiness. As soon as the honeymoon's over and Marcus and I are settled, I'll go down and visit her, and try to persuade her to come and stay for a while. So resolving, she pulled on her long pink kid gloves. Parslow's horseshoe remained in her right hand inside the glove, and the feeling of it pressing against her palm was comfortable and reassuring.

The bad thing about a wedding at the Abbey, Rosamund thought – generalising wildly as she drove away after the ceremony in the same carriage, but this time with Marcus beside her instead of Lord Theakston – is that you don't feel at all married afterwards. If we'd married in the little church at Wolvercote, for instance, or in the chapel at Morland Place ...

It had been a very grand occasion, though, she had to concede, and Marcus had looked quite splendid – divinely fair, tall, handsome and lightly flushed with emotion, his well-proportioned and soldierly figure exquisitely dressed by the same tailor who had enjoyed Beau Brummell's patronage. He was Prince Florizel incarnate as he stood at the altar, and Rosamund had imagined, wryly, the sighing and fluttering amongst the young female element of the spectators as he passed for ever beyond their grasp.

The Abbey had been far fuller than for Flaminia's wedding, for that had been in wartime when a great many people were overseas; and also the Chelmsford connections were more numerous than the Sales'. Now they were to return to Chelmsford House for a banquet seating a hundred people, with the Prince Regent as guest-of-honour; after which there was to be a reception for everyone else, followed by a ball, and fireworks to finish.

All in all, she thought, glancing sideways at her husband from under her eyelashes, this was likely to be the last time she was alone with him for quite some time. Married life, and getting to know him, would have to wait for a more private time – and she was not sorry, she thought, suddenly jittery, to have it put off. The wedding ring seemed to throb unnaturally on her left hand inside her glove, like the threat of an infection.

But Parslow's charm nestled warmly in her right palm, as

his words nestled in her mind. *No, no, my lady. All's well.* She didn't know how her mother was going to manage without him, especially abroad, but she was heartily glad he was staying with her. It would make the transition from Lady Rosamund Chetwyn to Lady Chelmsford less of a shock to have the familiar faces of Moss and Parslow around her.

For it was bound to be a shock, she knew that – however sensible she was going to be about it, and whatever she had said to Sophie. There would be a great many things to get used to, and some of them, she thought with a sigh, would not be pleasant.

Marcus heard the sigh, and turned his head to look at her. 'Tired?' he asked. 'It was rather a long business, wasn't it?'

'I'm a little tired, perhaps,' she said. 'And a thousand pins are sticking into my head.'

He smiled. 'But you look very beautiful. I could hardly believe it when I saw you coming towards me on Lord Theakston's arm –'

'Thank you!'

'Oh lord! I didn't mean it like that! I think you're beautiful anyway, you know that, but I'd never seen you dressed in anything so – well –'

Rosamund laughed. 'I think you'd better stop before you make it worse. You don't have to be polite to me, you know – I'm just your little cousin Rosy.'

He took her hand, startling her a little, and pressed it, his fingers finding the hardness of the ring through her glove. 'Not any more. You're my darling wife now – and I mean to make sure you never forget it. My lovely Rosamund! I shall never, never let you out of my sight from now on!'

Oh dear, thought Rosamund, how different such things sound in real life from when one reads them in a two-volume novel! Shall I ever learn to like them, or will I always simply put up with them, out of politeness?

'That might be rather inconvenient,' she managed to say, quite politely, she thought, when the words that were really struggling for expression were 'Don't be such an ass'.

Fourteen hours later the wedding was really, finally over, and Rosamund really was tired, so tired that she couldn't walk a straight line along the passage to the large bedchamber,

283

known as the Countess's Room, which had been prepared for her wedding-night. That was Lady Barbara's order, and Rosamund hoped it was the last instruction she would give as lady of this particular house. The Countess's Room was a cavernous apartment, draughty and uncomfortable, and the last place anyone would ever choose to sleep. Tomorrow, Rosamund thought determinedly, she would have a small, snug room allocated to her – and preferably as far away from Lady Barbara's as possible.

For tonight, though, she must put up with it, and be thankful that it was not the State Bedroom, which was even bigger and draughtier; and that there was not, in any case, much of the night left to pass there. Since leaving the Abbey she had smiled, shaken hands, given and received kisses, eaten, drunk, talked, danced, talked again, eaten again, danced again, and finally watched the fireworks and partaken of the last supper and champagne toast, and it was now two o'clock in the morning. She had hardly sat down since dinner. Her feet were hot and swollen, her back was aching, her head was throbbing with noise and reeling with champagne and tiredness, and her body felt as though she had been beaten all over.

It was fortunate, really, that this was not to be a night of love, the fulfilment of all her maiden dreams, for she was hardly in a condition to have enjoyed it. She thought suddenly of Philip Tantony, and imagined what her wedding would have been like had she married him. Not in the Abbey, that was for sure; and without the Prince Regent's portly blessing on the occasion. A small and quiet affair, she supposed it would have been – in the church at Wolvercote, perhaps, with the tenants drawing the carriage back to the house by hand. A neat wedding-breakfast, a few kisses and tears, and then she and Tantony alone together and embarking on an adventure which would have been –

She stopped herself with a jerk from drifting off into a waking dream. Tantony was dead, two years in his grave. Her future lay with Marcus, by her own choice, and she must make the best of it, which included, she supposed, this Night of Nights. It would simply not do to be thinking of another man when Marcus arrived. He deserved her loyalty at least. She must try to remember what it had felt like when she hero-worshipped him, when she used to sneak out from the nursery or schoolroom to sit on the stairs in the hope of catching a glimpse of him arriving or leaving, when every word that fell from his lips was precious and important.

Moss was waiting in the bedchamber, sitting on a chair half-asleep, and roused herself, shivering, as Rosamund came in. Rosamund looked around her grimly. Lady Barbara could not have chosen better if she had wanted to lay a blight on her son's wedding-night. The large number of finest wax candles which had been lit were too few to relieve the gloom of this enormous room, or to brighten the sombre colours of its ancient decoration and hangings. Despite the fire burning under the marble caryatids, swags of flowers and cornucopiae of the fireplace, the air was cold and stale; and the gigantic bed on its dais under a fifteen-foot-high canopy looked more like a catafalque than a nuptial couch.

Fortunately Moss was too cold and sleepy to want to chat, and undressed her mistress and helped her into her night-gown without comment, unpinned and brushed her hair in silence, and only when she had helped her between the sheets found anything to say.

'Goodnight, my lady. It was the best wedding ever, my lady – everyone said so.'

'Thank you, Judy,' Rosamund said, feeling a surge of affection. 'I hope you got some good things to eat and drink?'

'Oh yes, my lady, thank you. Mr Hawkins gave orders that all of us servants was to have a special supper, with cider to drink your health, and his lordship's, my lady, which we did with a three-times-three, and very hearty.'

'Most kind of you,' Rosamund said, stifling a yawn. Oh, to have undisturbed sleep to look forward to now! She envied her maid, who had no further duties to perform until the morning. 'Goodnight then.'

'Goodnight, my lady. And – thank you for keeping me on as your maid, my lady. I'm so grateful, my lady, and I promise I'll serve you faithfully to the –'

'Yes, I'm sure you will,' Rosamund cut her short. 'That's all right. Go away now, Moss, and snuff the candles as you go out.'

A few moments later she was alone in the huge bed, with only her bedside candle flickering away bravely in the cavernous darkness, waiting for her new-wedded lord. Despite her weariness, the situation seemed so ludicrous that she had a strong desire to giggle, which increased inconveniently when the door opened several miles away at the other end of the room and a halo of candlelight appeared and began to move towards her, with a dim white shape behind it. Marcus in his nightgown! Oh lord, she had never thought of that! She'd never seen him in his nightgown before, of course, and the idea of it was causing gusts of embarrassed mirth to rush up inside her.

Here he was, coming round to the empty side of the bed, putting down his candle, revealing himself in white nightgown, a dark-red silk dressing-gown draped over his shoulders, and a large night-cap with a long tail and tassel hanging down like a bell-rope, just begging to be pulled. And if I pulled it, she thought, whimpering inwardly, would his head swing back and forth and ring like a church-bell? If I pulled it hard enough, perhaps it might just fall off with a thud and roll away across the floor like a bowling-ball. She squeezed her eyes tightly closed and clenched her fists under the covers in an attempt to keep herself quiet.

'Rosamund? Are you awake?' he whispered anxiously.

'Yes,' she gasped, but dared not attempt a longer sentence. She knew he was looking at her, but she couldn't open her eyes. He would have to go on thinking she was desperately shy.

There was a rustling sound, and then the mattress moved as he got into bed beside her. In fact, Marcus didn't think her desperately shy – he thought her desperately afraid, as his next words proved.

'Don't be frightened,' he said tenderly. He was leaning over her, and she smelled the sweetness of much wine on his breath as it brushed her face. His voice sounded different, too. She supposed that after so many toasts, he must be a little foxed. 'I know it's all strange for you, but I'll be very gentle,' he went on. 'And we've all the time in the world. No need to rush. We'll just take our time.'

Another rustling and heaving interlude, as he stretched over to put out his candle, and then lay down, and turned on his side towards her. She waited, but nothing more happened, no further sounds or movements, only the steady sound of

Marcus breathing beside her. She opened her eyes just a crack. Her candle was still alight, its dim glow fluttering over the curtains and canopy above her. Then Marcus made a small, choking sound, like someone snorting with suppressed laughter. Glad surprise made her eyes fly open. Did he find the whole thing irresistibly funny, too? If so, their relationship might get off to a very good start after all, in this burlesque of a bed.

She turned her head on the pillow. His fair, handsome face, flushed of cheek and moist of eyelid like that of a healthy child, was a few inches from her, and he was fast asleep. So much for her fears and her struggles! So much for maiden terrors and old wives' tales! The long day, the dancing and the wine had acted upon him like a charm. He had not been laughing, in fact, but snoring.

CHAPTER FIFTEEN

The next day, Lucy, Danby and the boys set off from Upper Grosvenor Street on their Grand Tour.

'The house already seems so quiet without you,' Lucy said to Rosamund in unusually benign mood, 'that I'm glad we're going straight away. Now, you understand all the arrangements?'

'Yes, Mama,' said Rosamund. Beyond her mother's bedroom window it was a warm and overcast day, almost airless, and combined with excitements of the day before and the shortness of the night, it made her feel remote and light-headed.

Lucy was looking about the room as she talked, to be sure she had left nothing she might need. She was wearing a smart travelling-dress of smoke-blue trimmed with black silk corded ribbon, and a small carriage hat perched at a jaunty angle on her pale curly crop. She had always been a striking dresser. Rosamund's first-day dress of twilled grey sarsenet was her mother's choice, and the awareness of that made Rosamund realise that she was going to miss her in so many ways. Who would have thought, a few years ago, that that would ever be the case?

'Beguid will settle all the household bills for here and Wolvercote,' Lucy went on, 'and the servants' wages, of course. Both houses will be kept staffed, so don't be afraid to use them. The servants will be better for being given something to do. Just look upon the houses as your own, and use them whenever and however you wish.'

'Yes, Mama,' Rosamund said patiently. This had all been gone through already.

'And if you have any problems that Beguid can't answer, go to Mr Hoare at the bank. He will send on letters to us as well – oh, unless you want to contact me urgently, in which case you had better ask Mr Rothschild to send by his courier.

He will always do that as a favour to me, and he will know where I am. And as to the horses –'

'Yes, Mama,' Rosamund said with a small smile. 'I'm sure you've told Parslow everything that needs to be said about the horses.'

Lucy stopped and looked at her daughter's face closely. It was paler than usual, which made the freckles more noticeable. 'Well,' she said hesitantly, 'so you are a married woman at last.' There were many things she wanted to ask, but she had no habit of confidence from which to start. Rosamund was annoyed to feel herself blushing. 'Is everything all right? You look tired.'

'It was a long day yesterday,' Rosamund said defensively, wishing those keen eyes would stop scanning her face so searchingly.

'Are you happy?' Lucy asked bluntly. 'It was what you wanted, wasn't it?'

'It was what I wanted,' Rosamund said.

Lucy looked as though that were not quite answer enough. 'Hmm,' she said thoughtfully. 'Well, I hope it answers. You are a sensible girl, you will find out for yourself how to manage things. One word of warning – don't let Lady Barbara interfere between you and your servants. And if you have any trouble with her, ask the Prince's advice. He's been managing not to be bothered by people for years.'

Of all her mother's advice, Rosamund thought, that was the least practical. 'Yes, Mama,' she said, smiling, and on an impulse reached over to kiss the lean cheek.

Lucy looked surprised and pleased. 'I almost wish you were coming with us,' she said gruffly, pulling out her handkerchief from her sleeve and pretending to blow her nose. 'Come, we'd better go down. They'll be waiting for us.'

They were all gathered in the hallway to say their goodbyes, with the servants, moist-eyed, hovering in the background.

'Goodbye, Papa Danby,' Rosamund whispered in his ear as she was enfolded in a warm hug. His slim body was as hard as seasoned leather to her arms, and his fair whiskers tickled her ear.

'I'll miss you, my dear girl,' he murmured in reply, and then put her back to smile at her fondly. 'I'll bring you back something from Italy,' he promised.

'Just yourselves will be enough.'

There was her brother Thomas, grave and capable, and Roland, stooping and shy, and – surprising her all over again – her new-wedded lord shaking them by the hand and giving them elder-brotherly advice, as to the manner born, and a purse each for buying little luxuries. That was good of him! In a dream Rosamund said goodbye to Docwra, who never missed an opportunity to have a good cry, and exchanged a friendly nod with Papa Danby's man Bird, looking unfamiliar in a bran-new gentleman's gentleman's suit, which his ex-Hussar vanity had had made a little too tight in the leg.

The travellers were going out into the street now, where the carriage waited for them, a new berlin especially made for the trip, fitted out with a number of special features and luxuries of Lord Theakston's own design. At a pinch, failing an inn, they might all live in this carriage. Four job horses were poled up, and Rosamund saw Parslow give them a quick, sharp look-over to be sure they were good enough to bring his mistress to Dover and the packet. If they had not been, would he have prevented her from leaving, she wondered? Still in her dream-like state, she watched him looking at her mother, and almost felt the sharpening of his love and anxiety as Lucy went away from him, out of reach of his care and experience. He had never been parted from her for more than a few days since he first joined her service, and he trusted no other driver or horseman to look after her.

But then she turned back. There in the street, in front of everyone, Lucy, Lady Theakston, turned from the open door of the carriage and walked back to where Parslow was standing on the steps, and held out her hand. The world, Rosamund thought, might well have held its breath. Parslow seemed to hesitate before taking it, as if he wondered if she might regret the solecism of the public gesture later; but then her small, strong hand was engulfed by his large, hard one.

'Take care of everything for me. I entrust everything to you,' she said. Her voice sounded light and clear on the damp, grey air. He bent his head a little to her, as if in submission to her will, but it was only to look at her – she was much smaller than him.

'Yes, my lady,' was all he said. But then Rosamund saw –

or thought she saw – or at any rate afterwards remembered
that she saw – him put his other hand for an instant over her
mother's. Just for an instant the tableau was frozen thus; man
and mistress looked at each other in a moment of perfect
communion, and he said, 'God bless you.'

Then all was movement again, and sound. The travellers
climbed into the coach, the doors were closed, the coachman
cracked his whip, and everyone waved and shouted as the
berlin drew away, waved and shouted until it disappeared
round the corner in to St James's Square and out of sight.

As they turned to go back indoors, Rosamund found her
hand was somehow being held by her husband's. She looked
at the linked hands in surprise, not having noticed it happen,
and then, doubtfully, up at him.

'So now our married life really begins,' he said with a
smile. 'Until this moment, I think you still felt more like Lady
Theakston's daughter than Lord Chelmsford's wife. But now
she's gone and there's only me. You'll have to begin to depend
on me from now on.'

It was a pretty speech, and well meant, but out of the
corner of her eye she could see Parslow purposely not over-
hearing. *Mother's proxy* she thought. *She hasn't really gone.*
And if it came to it, she would always sooner entrust a
problem to Parslow than to the unknown quantity of Marcus.

In another way, however, it was that evening that her
married life began, and she knew well beforehand that there
would be no escaping it this time. After all the excitement and
strain of the wedding, everyone was tired, and there was
perfectly good reason for Lady Barbara to suggest, with the
confidence of a tsar that her suggestion would carry the
weight of law, that they should all go early to bed.

Rosamund remembered too late that she had given no
orders about a change of bedroom, nor indeed had had the
opportunity to discuss it with Marcus. So it was back to the
Countess's Room and the catafalque. Moss prepared her and
put her to bed, and there, without the benefit of so much as a
glass of champagne, she sat up against the pillows to await
her fate.

Marcus came in at last, just as he had the night before,
with his dressing-gown over his shoulders, hanging a little

crookedly so that it made her think of a cavalryman's pelisse. That was a good line of thought, reminding her that he had been the brave soldier she had waved off to war from the nursery window. He was still the same Marcus, and he should not be made to suffer because she was not the same Rosamund.

'Are you tired, my love?' he asked her as he put down the candle on the bedside, and shrugged off the dressing-gown. He looked so strange in his nightgown. It was a pity, she thought, that men couldn't wear some kind of trousers to bed, so that they looked more familiar, more like their daytime selves. It all added to her sense of dreamlike unreality.

'A little,' she said. Just as they say only the tip of any iceberg emerges from the water, so only a small part of what she was thinking was actually voiced. 'Reaction to all the excitement, I expect.'

'Yesterday must have been a great strain on you,' he said, lifting the covers to slide himself in beside her. 'You were the centre of all eyes, much more than I was, and you must have been aware of it.' As she was still sitting up, he too sat up solemnly, his hands folded on top of the sheet. 'It's a pity we couldn't have had a small, private wedding of our own, first. It would have been nice to go to the Abbey for the public ceremony having been married a few weeks first. Then I could have given you a husband's support through it all.'

What an odd thing to say, she thought – but it was kindly meant. And what a strange man he was, after all – for most people, such splendour and glory and publicity were proofs of status and very precious. But she understood what he meant, hearing the words under his words. 'You still don't really want to be Earl of Chelmsford, do you?'

He shook his head. 'I never did. I'm not cut out for it. I'm just a simple soldier, and I'd rather have married you in a tent somewhere, with the regimental chaplain presiding, and the men giving us three-times-three and throwing their shakoes in the air.'

Rosamund wrinkled her nose. 'Sounds damp and muddy to me.'

He didn't seem to hear her. 'It was Bobbie's title, and he was the man for it,' he went on quietly. 'I still think of him, throwing his life away to rescue me. He'll always be the earl, in my mind.'

'Well, since he made the sacrifice,' Rosamund said, 'you had better make sure it wasn't in vain, and do his job for him as best you can.'

'Yes,' Marcus said, and then his smile flashed out. 'And being earl has won me *you* – that's the greatest blessing. So I can't repine, can I? I'd never have had you otherwise.'

Rosamund couldn't think of anything to say to that, so instead she slithered down from sitting to lying, and was about to say let's go to sleep, when she remembered that there were other things to be done yet, and that her change of position must look like invitation to Marcus. Indeed, his smile disappeared, and he looked suddenly serious and intent, like a man in church about to take the sacrament. She didn't want to look at him looking like that, so she closed her eyes, and a moment later she felt him lean across her to put out her candle too.

That was better. Safe in the darkness, she opened her eyes again, and waited, lying on her back, for the worst. She knew about it in theory, but hadn't worked out the detail in her own mind – hadn't particularly wanted to. She had seen horses and other animals doing it, but knew, of course, that human beings did it lying down and in bed, so it couldn't be quite the same, could it? She wished she knew what she was supposed to do, or even, at least, if she was supposed to do anything. It made her feel so helpless to have to rely entirely on someone else's knowledge and experience, and helplessness always made her angry. It seemed so unfair: there was nothing else one ever did in life where one hadn't the slightest idea of the correct procedure, where one wasn't instructed beforehand on the proper mode of conduct. When she had been presented at Court, she had been schooled carefully in every word and gesture, and wasn't this, in its way, just as important?

Marcus moved, and she felt a quick spasm of fear. Now it was happening. He was making furtive, jerky movements just beside her; then she felt his hand on her midriff over her nightgown, and stiffened automatically.

He felt her tension. 'Don't be afraid,' he whispered. 'I'll try not to hurt you.'

Try? she wondered uneasily. That was not very reassuring. He ran his hand over her belly as if stroking a horse's rump, and then began to pull up her nightgown from the hem. It came up at the front all right, but soon got caught underneath her at the back. Now do I help him, or would that be unseemly? she wondered helplessly. Do I pretend I don't know what he's trying to do? He tugged at it, and she decided in the end that not to help might seem like resistance to the whole idea, and she had no desire to delay matters needlessly. So she lifted her weight slightly and with the hand furthest away from him, as discreetly as possible, freed the hitch.

When her nightgown was up as far as her waist, there was a pause, and then he loomed over her, jostled for space with his knees between hers, and then was lying on top of her, the warm, naked front of his body against the warm naked front of hers. A number of thoughts went through her over-active mind: *ah, so that's what he was doing before – pulling up his own nightgown*; and *goodness, how hot his skin is, and how smooth*; and *what an extraordinary business this is – animals manage it much better.*

Then his hand fumbled between them, and a shock of realisation went through her like a bolt of electricity, and she thought, *Not really? Not like that?*

'Oh my darling, my darling,' Marcus murmured in what sounded like ecstasy.

And then it really was happening. It did hurt quite a bit, but not unbearably, and it was all over quite quickly, and in silence except for Marcus's gasping breaths. When his movements stopped, she lay still for quite a while with his weight on top of her, wondering if that were all there would ever be to it, and if she would ever get to like it, and if it would have been different with someone else.

She remembered, guiltily, the excitement she had felt once in Philip Tantony's arms, how she had longed to be closer and closer to him, without knowing how such a thing could be possible. *Would she have felt differently if it had been Tantony in bed with her just now?* Well, she would never know now. Her life was with Marcus, and if there were any pleasure to be had from this strange business, it must be with him she found it.

The worst thing was being intelligent enough to wonder about things you could never know the answers to. She wished she could have gone to her marriage bed with a

294

stupidity to match her ignorance, and the comfortable lack of curiosity of a cow or a horse.

The Aylesbury summer fair was the biggest event of the year, and emptied the villages for miles around. It was a hiring fair, an agricultural fair, and sheer lighthearted entertainment all in one. It had all the usual stalls and shows, jugglers and fire-eaters, boxing-booths and fortune-tellers and freaks, archery competitions and bowling for a pig; any number of delicious things to eat and drink, the taverns open until far into the night, and dancing under the stars if the weather were fine.

It was customary for big households to allow their servants the day off for it, and even to provide a cart or brake to trans-port them – which made attendance all the more universal, for who would want to stay at home without servants?

It seemed that Lady Harvey Sale would.

'Oh don't say that, Minnie,' Polly cried. 'You must go! It's the greatest fun – don't you remember from last year? We'll walk about and look at the shows and have dinner –'

'I don't want to go,' Minnie said quietly.

Polly looked despairing. If Minnie didn't go, she would not be able to, and she couldn't bear to miss it. The one chance she had of getting out of this house, and seeing a little life and liveliness and cheerfulness – the thought of missing it was an agony.

'But you must! You can't stay shut up here for ever, it isn't good for you. It would do you so much good to have a change of scene. It would take your mind off things. You've been brooding too much – Harvey, speak to her.'

'Why don't you want to go, love?' he asked quietly. 'You know I've come down specially to take you.'

'Have you?' she said, looking at him blankly for a moment, and then away again. 'Well I don't want to, that's all.'

'But Minnie –!'

'Leave her alone,' Harvey said suddenly. 'If she doesn't want to, that's all there is to it.'

Polly drew breath to protest, but let it out without speaking. Beneath her piercing disappointment was a sense almost of panic. She really felt that she might go mad if she didn't get away from this place – yet what could she do? She was helpless, dependent on other peoples' wills. 'Very well,' she said at last, and her voice quivered perilously. 'If that's your decision.'

Minnie looked up from her perpetual study of her hands in her lap, and her eyes had that same blank, impenetrable look. 'You needn't miss it. Harvey can take you. I don't mind.'

Polly was bewildered. 'But the servants will be going. You can't stay here on your own. Or do you mean to stop them going?'

'Of course not. I shall be quite all right. You go with Harvey,' Minnie said.

'I can't leave you here alone,' Polly said uncertainly.

'I don't want you,' Minnie replied, and suddenly stood up, seeming agitated. 'I wish you would leave me alone! Always telling me what I can and can't do. I'm not a child, I can choose for myself.'

'Of course you can,' Harvey said soothingly. 'And if you want to stay here by yourself, you shall.'

'But Harvey –' Polly began, but he silenced her with a look.

Minnie hesitated a moment. Then, 'Very well,' she said, and went out.

'It's all right. What harm do you think can come to her, here in her own home?' Harvey said when he and Polly were alone.

'But it isn't right that she should be completely unattended.'

'If it's what she wants, why shouldn't she? Besides, there'll probably be someone about. I don't expect all the servants will want to go.'

'They will – you don't know! It's the greatest day in the year for them – and God knows,' she added bitterly, 'there's little enough fun for anyone in this place.'

'Any more objections,' Harvey said with a smile, 'and I shall think you don't want to come to the fair with me. It's the perfect opportunity to spend the whole day together – and with Minnie's blessing! What could be better?'

Polly still felt uneasy. 'It's not right,' she said, but with less conviction; and then, 'She'll probably change her mind when the moment comes. She's never been entirely alone since the day she was born. She'll change her mind.'

*

296

'Oh my lady, I wish you'd change your mind,' said Hill. She stared anxiously at her mistress, who was sitting in the big chair in her bedchamber, staring out of the window. It was a warm, overcast day, but for once the blind grey-white sky was high enough not to threaten rain. 'You'd enjoy it, I'm sure you would. Look, there might even be some sunshine later.'

'I don't want to go,' Minnie said again, as if that was all there was to it.

'Then let me stay with you. I don't want to go either.'

For once Minnie shewed a flash of spirit. 'You'll do as you're told.' Then she seemed to regret it. 'Please, Hill, just leave me alone.'

A scratching at the door prevented Hill from arguing further. It opened to reveal the under-housemaid in her best mantle and bonnet.

'Yes, Betsy?'

'If you please, my lady, the brake's here, and they're waiting for Mrs Hill.'

'Very well. Off you go, Hill. I hope you have a pleasant day.'

Hill looked as though there were many more things she wanted to say, but in the presence of Betsy she could not descend so far. She gave her mistress one last, keen look, bowed her head, and went.

Half an hour later, Harvey came in, leaving the door open behind him. Beyond it the house was already unnaturally quiet: even well-trained servants make a background of sound in a house, simply by being there.

'Are you sure you don't want to change your mind?' he said without preamble. 'There's going to be a troupe of acrobats, and a man with a tame lion. He puts his head in the lion's mouth, and the lion never offers to bite him. You've never seen a lion before, have you?' he coaxed.

Minnie went on looking out of the window, seeming hardly to know he was there.

'You don't really want to stay here all alone, do you? You'll want your dinner, and there'll be no-one to get it for you. You don't want to go hungry all day, I'm sure. Come with us, and we'll have dinner at the Crown, and you can order anything you like – sweet ginger pudding, and ratafia cream –'

She looked at him now, a sad and stern look, as though his

last words had provoked her. 'I'm not a child,' she said.

'No,' he agreed. 'But you're my wife.'

'Oh, you remember that, do you?'

'Minnie, what is it?' he said suddenly. 'Is it just losing the babies? I'm sorry about them too, but we can have more children –'

'Oh you liar,' she said softly, but with deadly force. 'I know what you thought about them, and what you think about them dying, and what you think about me. I don't want your lying promises. Just leave me alone. Go to the fair, and let me be.'

She turned her face from him, and he hesitated a moment, and then shrugged.

'So be it. It's your decision. Sulk here alone, if that's what you want.' And he went away and left her.

Polly didn't enjoy the fair as much as she wanted to. It was wonderful to get away from Stainton, to get out from under those crowding trees, to leave the wet greenness behind and enter a town again. She feasted her eyes on the cobbles underfoot and grey stone buildings to either side, and the delicious colours of bunting and stalls and fête-day clothes everywhere. It was wonderful to have people around, and noise and bustle, dogs barking and whistles blowing and traders shouting their wares, spectators talking and laughing and calling to each other and cramming their mouths with sweetmeats and hot pasties and baked apples.

But she suffered from a nagging sense of guilt over leaving Minnie alone to brood in her misery – even though, as Harvey rightly pointed out, Polly's staying at the house wouldn't have altered the brooding and miserable parts of it. And Harvey himself was in a strange temper, not fit to enjoy himself to the full. He seemed nervous, almost irritable, his mood changing rapidly; silent and withdrawn one moment, laughing too loudly the next. Several times he snapped at Polly, seeming almost to want to pick a quarrel with her, and when she challenged him with it, he laughed at the notion in a brittle manner and avoided her eyes.

Altogether, there was no day-long delight in being in his company to compensate for the feeling that she shouldn't have come in the first place. She began to feel very tired, and

298

pushing through the crowds from one stall to the next began to seem like too much effort for too little reward.

'Can't we sit down somewhere?' she asked at last.

'Are you hungry yet?' he asked. 'We could go and have dinner. It's early, but it might be as well to eat before everyone else. The decent places will be very crowded later.'

'Yes, all right, let's do that,' Polly said. Anything to be able to sit down.

'Come on then. I've booked a private parlour at the Crown.'

When they arrived at the large, handsomely-appointed inn, there seemed no surprise on the part of the landlord that they were so early, nor any delay in putting a meal before them.

'I ordered the food when I booked the room,' Harvey said in reply to Polly's question. 'I thought it would be as well. I hope you like what I've chosen?'

'It all looks very nice,' she said vaguely.

'Yes, very well, you may go,' Harvey said to the servant who was hovering, waiting for them to take their seats. 'We can wait on ourselves, thank you. And I'm perfectly capable of pouring the wine.'

When they were alone, Harvey seemed to recover his normal spirits, and became very chatty and gay, plying her with food and wine and so obviously trying to amuse her that she felt obliged to make the effort and be amused. The wine stimulated her, and she ate with a good appetite. The food in turn made her thirsty, and she emptied her glass, which Harvey quickly refilled. Soon she was responding to his chat, even laughing at his little jokes; and the part of her mind that wondered how she could, and offered her the image of Minnie sitting alone in her room and staring out of the window, shrank to a small and distant voice which it was quite possible to ignore.

It was when he started to talk about the future that she was brought back to earth.

'Don't, Harvey,' she said. 'Don't talk like that. We don't have any future together. You know that as well as I do, and I hate to hear you pretending.'

He grew suddenly serious, reaching across the table. 'I won't let you say that,' he said, pressing her hand painfully. 'My God! How can you even contemplate the future if you don't think we'll be together? I tell you, I can't.'

'You're hurting me,' she said, with a sigh of pain, but he didn't seem to hear her.

'If I can't have you, then there's nothing to live for. I will have you – I don't care what it takes.'

'I can't –'

'*Don't*! I tell you, Polly, I'm at the end of my tether! I've done my duty, I've done everything that was asked of me, and where has it got me? Well, I'm not going to take any more of it. Things have got to change, and they've got to change now, soon, or I shall do something desperate. You and I will have to – Polly? What is it? What's the matter?'

'I don't know,' she muttered thickly. She looked at her hand, gripped by his so tightly that her fingers had gone white, yet she no longer felt the pain. Her hand seemed small and far off, growing more distant all the time. He was receding too, and his voice boomed strangely, near and far away, like the sound of the sea in a cave.

'Are you all right? You've turned so pale,' she heard him say through the fog.

'I feel –' she began, and then swayed in her chair. 'Dizzy.' Too much wine, she thought. I'm not used to it.

'– too much wine,' he was saying. He let go her hand and came round the table, put his arm round her to support her, while he reached beyond her for the bell. She lolled against him, feeling so tired and strange, longing to lie down so that things would keep still and stop swinging round her like bells in a steeple, ringing in her head along with the sea booming in the cave ...

A servant came in, tiny and far-away, and there were hurried exclamations and explanations and after a long and confused time Polly discovered she was lying on a bed, and a maid she had never seen before was pulling a counterpane over her.

'... sleep, miss. You'll feel much better ...' her voice came and went. Polly sighed, and slept.

She dreamed she was falling, and woke with a jerk of her limbs; woke to confusion, not knowing where she was. Her head ached and she had a foul taste in her mouth, but worse than either was a nameless feeling of dread which filled her.

She sat up in bed and stared wildly round her at the walls and the furniture as though willing them to yield answers. Where was she? What had happened?

'Help me,' she whispered to the empty air. Memory seeped slowly back. She was at an inn. She was – in Aylesbury, yes. She had come here for the fair with – with Harvey! Yes, now she knew. Where was Harvey? How long had she been asleep? She must have had too much wine. She remembered feeling dizzy, and then – and then nothing, until she woke here.

Oh, but her head ached, and she was tortured with thirst. She must call for someone. She reached over for the bell-rope, and the movement made her dizzy again, but she got hold of it in clumsy fingers, pulled it hard and long, and then subsided against the pillows, breathing hard.

The door opened and a chambermaid came in. She looked vaguely familiar.

'You rang, miss? How are you feeling now? Proper poorly you looked before. I said to Mr Collins –'

'Where is Lord Harvey Sale?' Polly croaked.

'His lordship stepped out, miss, quite a while ago. He said you was to rest here quietly till he came back for you. I don't think he 'spected you to wake up so soon. You looked like you was out for the count, miss, begging your pardon.'

'Stepped out where? Did he say where he was going?'

'Not in my hearing, miss. I 'spect he went to see the fair – it's a rare good one this year, miss. What a crying shame you should miss it. Should you like anything, miss? A cup of tea, perhaps?'

'Yes, tea,' Polly said eagerly. Her tongue was sticking to the roof of her mouth.

'Very good, miss,' said the maid kindly. 'I'll bring some up right away, and some hot water – I 'spect you'd like to wash your face after being asleep. Makes you feel all sticky, don't it, miss, sleeping in the daytime?'

'Thank you,' Polly said. The feeling of dread was still there, but it had shrunk to the back of her mind. In the foreground was the urgent desire to quench her thirst and to urinate. 'How long have I been asleep?' she asked as the maid reached the door.

'Near four hours, miss,' the maid said cheerfully. 'Lord, you went out like you'd been poll-axed!'

Half an hour later, Polly had washed, straightened her hair and clothing, and drunk two dishes of tea, and was waiting, with increasing anxiety, for Harvey to return for her. Where on earth could he be? Why had he not waited at the inn? How could he leave her like that, so that she woke alone amongst strangers?

At last her restlessness drove her from the bedchamber and downstairs. The coffee room was as full as the tap room, and very noisy, and she had no idea where the private parlour was that they had used, or whether it would still be empty; so she walked along the passage and out to the front of the inn. There was a bench there which, for a wonder, was empty. She sat down with her back to the inn wall and watched the world going past.

The fair was obviously still in full swing, and gathering momentum in the sunset glare towards its evening excitements. The feeling of unreality left by having slept in the daytime, and so unexpectedly, was increased by the passing crowds of strangers in holiday mood. They all seemed to be oddly dressed; and wasn't there more than the usual proportion of deformed or pox-scarred people amongst them? A one-eyed man seemed to leer at her from under his hat as he passed, arm-in-arm with a man who hopped briskly on his one leg, a wooden crutch under his other arm painted red and white in stripes, like a barber's pole. A grotesquely fat woman in a purple pelisse coming the other way had an extraordinary shock of white hair, and her face was smeared with blood. Polly shrank back on the bench as the woman shrieked aloud; but no, she was shrieking with laughter, and the blood all over her mouth and chin was nothing but the sauce from some kind of pie she had been eating. She crammed the last of it into her open shrieking mouth, and wiped the red off her chin with her fingers as she passed.

Polly felt the dampness of her palms and armpits, and struggled to shake off the feeling that she was still asleep and dreaming. Oh, where was he? Why did he not come? She longed to see a face she knew. She longed to go home, to get away from the bedlam of this bizarre stream of misfits.

And then he was there, hurrying through the crowds from the direction of the square towards the inn, not having seen her yet. His face was set grimly, and he thrust people aside unseeingly as he approached, as a man might thrust through bracken.

She rose to her feet. 'Harvey!'

He stopped dead and jerked backwards slightly, his eyes opening wide, as though some unseen assailant had punched him hard just over the heart.

'Polly!'

'Harvey, what is it? What's happened?'

He came on, beginning to smile, holding out his hands. 'Nothing, nothing. I wasn't expecting to see you there, that's all. Are you all right? How are you feeling now?'

'But Harvey, are *you* all right?'

'You startled me a little, that's all.'

'But you're as white as a sheet.'

'Nonsense! I expect it's just the light. Are you better now?' he hurried on, 'Because we really ought to be going home. I don't want to drive back through the dark, and in any case, it isn't right to leave Minnie any longer, even if it was her own choice.'

'Yes, yes, let's go home. I don't like it here. The people all look strange and I feel as though something bad is going to happen.'

He took her hand gently and turned her towards the door of the inn. 'That, my darling,' he smiled, 'is a very common symptom of the aftermath of too much to drink. If you had been born a boy instead of a girl, you'd be familiar with it from many a carouse with your peers at Eton and Oxford! In its extreme form, it can bring the crawling horrors right up to the foot of your bed.'

'Oh, don't!' she shuddered. 'Don't talk of it! Is that really all it was, Harvey, just the wine?'

'What else? You're not accustomed to it, my love, that's all. I should have been more careful about refilling your glass — my fault entirely. You may blame and scold me as much as you please: I deserve it.'

He found the landlord and settled the bill and sent for his tilbury to be brought round, and then Polly was sitting up beside him as he cracked his whip and sent the horse forward. Once they were clear of the crowds, he put it into a fast trot, and they bowled homewards through the fading light.

The air was warm and full of insects, and though Polly

might well have dozed through the journey home, she was kept awake by moths striking her face softly, and small flies getting into her mouth. Soon the town was left behind, and the fields and hedges took over, and then the fields grew steeper and the trees began, and they were driving back into the green and alien heart in whose chamber she had survived for so many months, hearing nothing but its beating and the whisper of its unquenchable life.

'Harvey,' she said suddenly as the banks reared up to either side of her, and the canopy closed overhead into a green tunnel, 'I can't go on like this much longer. Living here, I mean. It's killing me. I must get away, one way or another.'

He had been silent all the journey so far, crouching a little forward, seeming intent on driving to an inch, getting the best speed out of his horse without foundering it. Now as she spoke he answered at once, almost as though his words were part of her sentence, without inflection, and without looking at her.

'Yes, my darling, you shall. Soon. Be patient a little longer, only a little longer.'

And there was Stainton Manor, its chimneys first amongst the tree tops, and then a glimpse of black and white, and a spark of gold from a window-pane throwing back a last ray of sun. Polly felt an increase of dread, or gloom; a sense of re-entering a prison. When she was at the inn, she had wanted to go home, but this was not home, was it? This was her cage. Then they were upon it, suddenly, as they rounded a bend.

Harvey stopped the horse at the front gate. 'Jump down, darling. You can go in this way, while I take the horse round the back.'

She obeyed him, lifting her skirt clear of the slimy moss on the front path and walking carefully towards the oaken door as the horse's steps diminished round the corner. The door was not locked. She pushed it open and went in, smelling the dusty, disused scent of her prison, the churchlike odour of dry rot and beeswax and old tapestries. The air was still, and neither warm nor cold, as though it existed in a place outside the real world where such concepts had no meaning. It was quiet, with the quiet of emptiness. The servants were not back yet.

Ahead of her the corridor disappeared into shadows. Suddenly she couldn't bear it. She had to get outside again, she had to get to Harvey, not to be alone here. She hurried forward, almost running, turning aside from the way that led into the heart of the house, and down the passage to the side door. Oh, but it was shut, she couldn't get it open! She fumbled, panicking, with the unfamiliar latch – an affair of black metal levers and counterpoises, big enough for a church. Her hands were cold and damp and slipped on the metal ring as she twisted and jerked at it uselessly. The house would not let her go, she thought despairingly. She would never get out! And then there was a click, and lightly and easily as a fingertip touch the levers engaged and the great bolt slid up and the door swung inward towards her.

Out into the open air she staggered: cooler, moss-scented, bat-flickering twilight air. Somewhere a wood-pigeon cooed liquidly. All was well. Why had she been so afraid? Dragging in her breath, trying to calm her foolish, panicking heart, she turned towards the back of the house, following the path round its perimeter, intending to go to the stableyard behind to find Harvey.

But she found him before that. As she turned the corner she saw him a little way ahead of her, hunkered down on the path, crouching over something that looked like a bundle of clothing.

'Harvey!' she called gladly, and then, on a questioning note, 'Harvey?'

He looked up, and his face seemed strangely out of shape, as though he had been made of soft wax, and his features had sagged and spread.

'Don't come any closer,' he said.

'What is it?' She heard her own voice sounding much higher than usual, very small and very frightened. But what was she frightened of? What was there to fear in a bundle of clothes, a woman's dress and shawl ...? 'Harvey, what's happened?'

'Would to God the servants were here! All there is is old Makepeace in the stables, God damn it, and he's over sixty. Well, he'll have to do. Polly, go to the stables and find Makepeace and make him understand. He's to take my horse and go as fast as he can for Dr Tibbs. Tell him not to stop for anything.'

Polly stood frozen where he had stopped her, trying to

understand what had happened with a mind which was refusing to understand, while the rest of her trembled with foreknowledge. She couldn't move or speak, but she could hear, and she heard noises from the stableyard which must be the servants' brake come back from the fair; and she could see, too, that long before the generality of passengers could have had time to alight, one person had come running through the wicket between the big brown backs of the coach-houses. The person came running before she could have known that there was anything to come running for, and saw and understood everything while she was still many paces off.

'My lady! My lady! Oh God, what's happened? What have you done to her?'

Harvey turned his head towards Hill as she came running, stumbling in her haste, her shawl slipping off backwards, and he lifted one hand slightly, as though he thought she might strike him.

'Oh my God, you've killed her! You murderer, you've killed her!' Hill shrieked.

And then Polly understood with all her mind, and all its capacity for horror, why amongst the bundle of clothes on the path there was a wig the same colour as Minnie's hair, and why there seemed also to be a face, just like Minnie's face, except that one side of it was very white, as white as china, and the other side was smeared and wet with red sauce.

BOOK THREE

Acts of Love

O deck her forth with thy fair fingers; pour
Thy soft kisses on her bosom; and put
Thy golden crown upon her languish'd head,
Whose modest tresses are bound up for thee.

William Blake: *To Spring*

CHAPTER SIXTEEN

Mathilde and John Skelwith were dining at Morland Place.

'It's wonderful how Monsieur Barnard manages to produce such delicious dishes under the circumstances,' Mathilde said appreciatively as Father Moineau helped her to the mackerel pie. 'This smells wonderful – what is the sauce?'

'Fennel and gooseberry,' Héloïse said. 'It's one of the old receipts out of the Household Book, but of course Barnard has put his own gloss on it.'

'And are those baked apples? Such heaven! Ours aren't ready yet; and when they are, our cook won't bake them a tenth as well as Barnard does. And when you consider the difficulties he faces –'

'Only he would consider them difficulties,' Moineau said with a smile.

'But Barnard simply pines for his open fire with all its inconvenience,' Héloïse added.

'Yes, that's true. Imagine, John, what our cook would say if we expected him to cook on an open fire!'

'I beg your pardon, my love – I wasn't attending.' John Skelwith turned to her from his conversation with James at the other end of the table.

'We were talking of cooking-stoves, and how Monsieur Barnard manages. How long will it be, do you think, before he has his kitchen back?'

'Not a tactful question, in front of her ladyship!' Skelwith said. 'I know it must seem that it's taking far too long.'

'We should not have given the job to you if we did not trust you,' Héloïse said reassuringly; but gave herself away by adding, 'I suppose it won't be finished soon?'

'It's so hard to get decent timber these days,' Skelwith said, 'and bricks are not what they were, either. But the main difficulty is with the foundations, as I expect you know by now. Either those mediaeval builders knew a thing or two that we've forgotten, or else Morland Place has stood up all these years by chance.'

'Oh, don't say that,' Héloïse said with a shudder. 'I still dream sometimes –' She stopped abruptly, and since nobody immediately spoke to rescue her, she said determinedly, 'What was it you were talking about when we interrupted with our domestic chatter?'

'Oliver the Spy, of course,' James said, smiling down the table at his wife. 'What else does anyone talk of these days?'

The Pentrich Rebellion had achieved more notoriety in the aftermath than in the act. Shortly after the arrests had been made, it became known that an agent who went under the name of 'Mr Oliver' had twice gone out incognito on a tour of the north, visiting Hampden Clubs and other centres of disaffection, and reporting back secretly to Lord Sidmouth at the Home Office.

It was claimed by the Government that it was largely because of the activities of Mr Oliver that the planned rebellion in the north had been confined to Pentrich. It was by his urging that the projected date of the rising had been put off twice, giving the participants time to grow nervous and have second thoughts; and giving him time to sew such doubts of the likely success of the venture that in the end all but Brandreth had given it up entirely.

The Opposition, however, had seized on the idea, and given it a twist to their own advantage. Mr Oliver was not an agent, they said, but an *agent provocateur*. He had not offered his services to gather information, but had been recruited and employed by Sidmouth as a spy; and far from having broken up the proposed rebellion, he had actually caused the sedition by stirring up men who would not otherwise have been stirred.

The Whig and Radical newspapers plunged in with delight, and soon 'Oliver the Spy' had been blown up from one rather shabby and inefficient informer, into a whole system and network of government agents, infiltrating every stratum of society and spying on honest, peaceful citizens with a view to perverting them to treason. It was outrageous, it was disgraceful, and above all it was un-English! Spying and informing and secrecy and knocks on the door in the middle of the night – that was the way Continental governments

310

went about things; that was how foreign powers oppressed their people. It was all of a piece with standing armies, paid police forces, and interference into mens' private lives, things a free nation like the English would not tolerate; and provocation to sedition was the last straw.

'I imagine that's the line the defence counsel means to take at the trials, isn't it?' Skelwith said. 'When are they to be, by the way?'

'In October, in Derby,' James replied. 'Well, if they do, it won't avail them. Provocation is no defence to treason.'

'Certainly not,' Héloïse agreed. 'It wouldn't matter whether Mr Oliver or Brandreth or anyone else tried to persuade them to rebel – they still should not have been persuaded.'

'But I thought – at least, didn't it say in the paper – that it wasn't a political rebellion at all?' Mathilde said. 'Didn't it say that they wanted bread, not the vote?'

'Yes, love,' Skelwith explained, 'but they still meant to overthrow the Government, pull down the Houses of Parliament, and seize the Tower, and that's a political action.'

'It was all part of the Reform movement,' James said, 'whether they knew it or not. Ned was quite right to condemn it. Such a lot of nonsense – and dangerous nonsense at that!'

'Pardon me,' said Moineau, 'but why is it nonsense? Could you perhaps explain why it is wrong for these men to want to be represented in Parliament?'

'But they *are* represented, that's the whole point,' James said impatiently. 'Each member of Parliament represents the interests of the entire people, not just of his constituents. Parliament isn't a congress of ambassadors from different sections with hostile interests, whatever the radicals might claim. It's a deliberative assembly with *one* interest, that of the nation as a whole – as they very well know.'

'But some of you have the power of choosing your member, and some of you do not,' Father Moineau said mildly. 'Is that not unfair?'

'Of course not. Representation has nothing to do with election. Every member represents everyone, whether he was directly chosen by them or not. Yes, very well, we choose a member, but once he's been chosen, he isn't the member for York or Exeter or wherever, he's simply a Member of

Parliament: a representative, not a delegate. Parliament is there to guard the interests, not to echo the will, of the people. It's a Trustee, just as the King is, and the Lords, and the Judges.'

'Yes, I see,' said Moineau. 'I think, though, that it might be too intellectual an answer to satisfy your weavers and spinners and orators. They will think it is a rationalisation of interest.'

'They may think as they please,' James said generously, 'as long as they act within the law. But if they choose riot and disorder, they will be punished under the law.'

'Poor things,' Mathilde said. 'I know they shouldn't have allowed themselves to be persuaded, but if they were hungry and couldn't afford to buy bread –'

'The harvest is good this year,' Moineau remarked. 'That should quiet the situation.'

'Yes, that's a point,' James said. 'Wheat has fallen to seventy-five shillings a quarter since June – that's a third less. I don't think we'll be getting any more marching and rick-burning this year.'

'Trade is picking up, too,' Skelwith said. 'The foreign markets are recovering, and orders for goods of all sorts are coming in. With plenty of work, and cheaper bread, the lower orders will have nothing to rebel about.'

'Is that true, James?' Héloïse asked. 'Are things better for the manufactories now?'

'Yes – Jasper Hobsbawn was right about that. He said trade would improve, and it has. I'm glad, now, that we didn't try to sell the mills back in June. We should get a much better price for them as things are.'

'But are you going to sell them at all?' Skelwith asked, just beating Héloïse to the question. 'Surely if they're beginning to do well, you'll want to keep them?'

'But who knows if the trend will last? It's too chancey – up one year and down the next.'

Skelwith smiled. 'What way of life isn't? What about the harvests, for instance? You don't sell the land because the harvest has been poor.'

'Owning land,' James said simply, 'is a different matter. That's life itself, not just a business.'

'Papa, if you do mean to keep the mills,' Sophie put in

312

eagerly, 'would you consider Mr Hobsbawn's plan about the tenements?'

'Now, Sophie, don't begin that again,' James said.

'But I only said *consider*,' Sophie said coaxingly. 'It couldn't hurt just to look at the plans, could it?'

'I must say, I'd be quite interested in seeing them myself,' Skelwith said.

'I'll bet you would,' James laughed. 'It would mean a great deal of work for you, wouldn't it, if we took it on?'

John Skelwith smiled. 'I should never press you in that direction, sir, as you must know very well. But there are other mill-masters in Manchester, and if trade does go on expanding, there'll be a need for new accommodation, irrespective of pulling down the old. People will always need somewhere to live, and the builder whose name is first known will be offered the contracts first.'

'But the houses must be built on the *rational* plan,' Sophie put in, seizing gladly on the unexpected appearance of an ally. 'I'm sure that if you only saw Mr Hobsbawn's plans ...'

Mathilde and Héloïse allowed the conversation to slip away from them. 'Sophie's become very interested in benevolent works, hasn't she?' Mathilde said. 'What's brought that on, I wonder? Is there a man in the case, Madame?'

Héloïse raised her brows. 'I suppose it's natural to think so. But Sophie always had a warm and generous heart.'

'Of course she has,' Mathilde smiled, 'but when a young woman suddenly develops an intense interest in something, one hasn't usually too far to look. I suppose it must be someone she met in Manchester?'

'I really don't know that there is anyone. Since she came home, she hasn't spoken of anyone except Jesmond Farraline, and I don't think he is particularly interested in philanthropic missions.'

'But I thought Mr Farraline was one of those who "cut" you?' Mathilde said. Héloïse had told her all about the unfortunate incident.

'He was, but it seems that when he returned to Manchester – after I'd left – he came to Sophie to apologise. Oh, not in so many words, of course, for that would have been disloyal, but he hinted that his mother had obliged him to leave with her,

313

and that nothing was further from his wishes than to insult Sophie.'

'That seems handsome enough. It sounds as though he is interested in her.'

'I'm not sure. From what she says, he did pay her attention, calling at the house quite often, and taking her driving, but always with Mrs Droylsden in attendance. I gather that he behaved very nicely: friendly and polite, but without any particularity that might arouse expectations.'

'Then you don't think he means to make her an offer?'

Héloïse shrugged. 'I don't see how he could. He is still a younger son.'

'Then I wonder why he troubled himself to heal the breach.'

'I think perhaps his pride was touched by being forced to behave like a fortune-hunter,' Héloïse said. 'He is after all an earl's son from an old family.'

Mathilde nodded. 'You may be right. Well, if that's all he means by it, I hope Sophie won't become too attached to him.'

'She doesn't seem to be,' Héloïse said, and there was a faint note of puzzlement in her voice. 'She finds him agreeable company, but I don't see any other symptoms there. I do wish for her sake that she might fall in love again – though not, of course, with someone who doesn't return her affections. I would sooner see her happily married than using herself up with benevolent acts.'

There was a pause, during which they could hear that the mill-talk was still going on at the other end of the table. Then Mathilde lowered her voice to ask, 'Have you heard any more about the situation at Stainton? It was such a dreadful thing! I was so shocked when John told me! He tried to break it gently, you know – he thinks I'm still in a delicate condition after Mary's birth – but I knew at once from his face that there had been a death.'

'I heard from Rosamund yesterday,' Héloïse said. 'All the burden fell on her shoulders, of course, since Lucy is away.'

'How awful for Lady Theakston, to hear news of that sort by letter, and at such a distance from home.'

'Yes,' said Héloïse. 'She will be dreadfully shocked. Rosamund sent word by Mr Rothschild's courier, but advises her

314

mother not to break off the tour, since there is nothing to be done. She has coped with everything very well, I think. She went down to Stainton straight away when she heard, and stayed there until after the funeral, and then took Polly back with her to London.'

'Polly was very shocked, I suppose? She and Lady Harvey were very close.'

'Yes, she's been very ill, Rosamund says. For a time they almost despaired of her, but she's recovering now – out of bed, at least, though still very low. But Stainton was not a healthy place, you know, and her health may well have been impaired before the accident. Rosamund thought that Harvey Sale would want to shut up the house, having such sad memories for him, but it seems he's been living there on and off since the accident, much as before.'

'I suppose it was an accident?' Mathilde said, a little carelessly, speaking her thoughts without properly considering their effect.

'Good God, Mathilde, what are you saying?' Héloïse said, low and shocked.

Mathilde coloured disastrously. 'Oh, Madame, I'm sorry! I didn't think – I didn't mean – I only wondered whether, having lost her daughters so recently –'

'Don't wonder,' Héloïse said sharply, glancing to either side to see they were not overheard; but the other conversation was still occupying all attentions but theirs. 'Poor Minnie was deeply grieved, but not deranged. Of course it was an accident. She was in the nursery which, being up under the roof, grew very stuffy on warm days, when the sun shone on the tiles. She must have opened the window to let in some air, and then, leaning out for some reason, lost her balance and fell.'

'Yes,' Mathilde said. 'I see.' She struggled with her curiosity for a moment, and lost. 'But what was she doing in the nursery? And why was she leaning out? She'd have to have leaned a long way, surely –?'

Héloïse grew angry. 'That is enough! I forbid you to speculate in that way, in this or any other house! Don't you know that is exactly how wicked rumours begin?'

'I'm sorry, Madame,' Mathilde said, lowering her eyes. Of course she had no wish to contribute to gossip, or to bring

315

shame on her cousin's memory. All the same, she couldn't help wondering – and the fact that Madame grew so angry could perhaps be an indication that she was not entirely sure about the matter either. It did have some strange elements to it, and it would be no more than natural to have doubts, however loyally suppressed.

The same doubts had occurred to Rosamund, who was perfectly certain they had occurred to Polly.

'Why else would she have been shocked almost to the losing of her reason?' she said to Marcus one day in the privacy of their carriage as they drove back from church.

'Why shouldn't it just have been perfectly normal grief? They had been as close as twins all their lives, after all,' Marcus said.

Rosamund shook her head. 'There was more than just grief there. Even Knighton shook his head over her, and you know he never exaggerates. He's the most level-headed of doctors. No, she had something on her mind – still has, for the matter of that. She's so silent and withdrawn. She's keeping something back, and I can't get it out of her.'

'Perhaps you shouldn't try. Perhaps if she's left alone, and not bothered –'

'It was Sir William who suggested she should be encouraged to talk, not me,' Rosamund said with faint affront. 'I'm not one to pry. He thinks she's brooding over something, and making it worse by going over and over it in her mind, without relief.'

'But what could she be brooding over, other than the sadness and shock of the accident?'

Rosamund took the plunge. 'I think she believes Minnie may have killed herself deliberately.' She saw from Marcus's face that the idea didn't strike him as immediately preposterous, and felt an inward sinking. Ever since the frightful suspicion had occurred to her, she had longed for someone to convince her it was ridiculous, unthinkable. *Felo de se* was both a crime and the gravest of sins. Suicides were not allowed to rest in hallowed ground, but were buried at a crossroads with a stake through the heart, and their souls were flung into the outer darkness for ever. That such a fate might await her own sister was too hideous to contemplate.

316

'Why should you think that?' Marcus asked at last, neutrally.

'There were odd things about it – the way she made sure to be left alone at home while everyone went to the fair, even refusing to allow Polly to stay with her. And she'd been spending hours every day sitting in that empty nursery all alone, brooding over her lost babies.'

'Precisely,' Marcus said bracingly. 'She was in the nursery just as she had been every day – nothing odd about that. It was a warm day: the sun came out in the afternoon. Surely it's most likely that she opened the window for air, just as they said, and fell by accident.'

'But Marcus,' she said anxiously, 'you've seen that window, how small it is, and how high off the floor. How could anyone fall out of it by accident?'

'Easily enough. It's a casement window, isn't it? Well, supposing it had swung completely outward, right back against the wall of the house? If she wanted to shut it again, she'd have to lean right out to catch hold of it. And then it would only need her foot to slip, or for her to lose her balance –'

Rosamund frowned. 'Oh, I wish you could convince me that was the case.'

'My darling, I shall. Look here, I just can't believe anyone who wanted to kill themselves would do it that way. The chances of being badly hurt rather than killed are far too great.'

'Yes, you're right,' Rosamund agreed hopefully. 'And Minnie was always very fond of her comfort, poor creature. Oh Marcus, it's frightful! My own sister – and Mama so far away! I feel so bad about it all. I meant to go down and see her, and make her come to London for a visit, only I kept putting it off. And now it's too late.'

'Darling –!' Marcus took her hand.

'Whether it was an accident or not, the fact is that she was very unhappy for a long time, and now she's dead, and I didn't lift a finger to help her.'

'You mustn't blame yourself. None of it was your fault. Things happen, that's all.'

'All very well for you to say that,' she said crossly, pulling her hand away. 'You've never been in the position. Your conscience is clear – you don't know what it's like.'

'Don't I?' he said gravely.

She looked at him in surprise. 'What do you mean? You don't mean Bobbie?'

'No, not Bobbie. That was his own choice. But there was a time in the Peninsula –' He sighed, and looked out of the window. 'I was out with a troop on reconnaissance, and I led them into an ambush. Two of them were killed. The rest of us managed to escape, and afterwards I was praised for my presence of mind in getting us away with so little loss. But I knew I was guilty. I should have known there'd be an ambush there – it was the perfect place for it. Only I was tired, and cold, and I had other things on my mind, and – well, I just didn't notice in time.'

'You never told me that before,' Rosamund said in a small voice.

He turned back to her, and shrugged. 'It never came up in conversation. And I try to forget it – that's what you should do.'

She looked at her husband with new interest. It was not the first time since their marriage that he had surprised her. She supposed that there were things going on in his mind that she was only now learning about as he grew slowly to trust her and to bring down the barriers that people always put up between themselves and the rest of the world.

She was not unhappy in her marriage. She had the establishment and the freedom she had contracted for, she had adjusted to the change of status more quickly than she had expected. She even enjoyed, in an amused way, being stood back for in doorways, taking precedence over women she had been obliged before to shew deference to, attending State functions – even being invited to the Prince's parties in her mother's place. She was slowly making Chelmsford House comfortable, and her allowance was more than generous. She had, as the saying was, her pennyworth for her penny.

As to the penny itself – the physical side of things, as she had expected, was not very troublesome. At present, and understandably, Marcus wanted to do it quite often, but it was not to be supposed that that state of affairs would last. And in any case, it was nothing much to put up with. It no longer hurt her, and it didn't take very long, and it seemed to make Marcus happy, all of which seemed a small price to pay for a contented husband.

She didn't mind chaperoning her sister-in-law, who, when away from her mother, was pleasant company in a mild and undemanding way; and it meant that she could continue to go to parties which she would not otherwise, as a matron, attend. The fly in the ointment, of course, was her mother-in-law, but even that in its way was beneficial, for without the pinpricks of irritation over Lady Barbara's interferences, she might almost have been in danger of being bored by the lack of friction in her life.

Except, of course, that there was Polly, sitting about the house like a sick shadow, and the terrible thought that poor Minnie might have been driven by misery and neglect to fling herself out of a window to her death. But no, as Marcus said, it was so unlikely. Minnie had always been so placid and insensible. Just possible, perhaps, to imagine her *in extremis* taking poison or drowning herself, but not clambering onto the windowsill, looking down at the path beneath, and –

She shuddered and stopped her thoughts short.

'Cold, my darling?' Marcus said. He was always sensitive to her least movement or change of mood. Had she been in love with him, it would have been her greatest delight to see how much he cared for her, how attuned he was to her slightest wish or need. As it was, she could see that there would soon come a time when she would have to find him something else to be interested in besides her, or she might find herself smothered to death by him.

She might encourage him to spend more time in the House; perhaps even persuade him to angle for a Government post. Yes, that would be both gentlemanly and time-consuming. Once let him get interested in politics, and he would disappear, like all the other men of his age and rank, into the clubs for six days out of seven, emerging only to accompany her to State functions and important parties, and she would be left alone to get on with her life in her own way.

It was a pity, she thought, that Mama and Papa Danby were to be away for such a long time, for their influence in the highest circles would have been enough to recommend Marcus to a suitable position in one of the ministries. However, they could still exercise their influence by letter, and Marcus, having been one of Wellington's staff officers, was not exactly unknown ...

Happily planning his political career, she managed for a time to forget the sad ghost of her sister, and the problem of her cousin.

The blow, when it fell, fell suddenly. Rosamund returned to Chelmsford House a day or two later in the company of Lady Barbara and Barbarina, with whom she had been making morning calls. They were met in the hall by the senior footman, Cowley, deputising for Hawkins on his day off.

'Lady Harvey Sale's waiting-woman is here, my lady,' Cowley said to Rosamund as he took her gloves. 'She asked for you –'

'A waiting-woman? Nonsense!' Lady Barbara intervened. 'Why is she still here? You should have sent her about her business, Cowley.'

'What did she want?' Rosamund asked, trying to ignore her mother-in-law.

'I suppose she's come looking for a place, or begging for money,' Lady Barbara sniffed. 'I know the sort only too well. But she'll get nothing from this house, if that's her game!'

'She didn't say what she wanted, my lady,' Cowley said, his eyes flickering from the young countess to the dowager and back. It was a foolish servant who would upset either of them. 'I told her you were out, and she asked to see Miss Haworth. So I asked Miss and she said to shew her up.'

'Where are they now?' Rosamund asked quickly, forestalling Lady Barbara's next tirade.

'In the Blue Saloon, my lady.'

'Very well. I'll go up,' Rosamund said, and ran quickly up the stairs before anything more could be said, leaving the wretched Cowley to Lady Barbara's mercies.

The Blue Saloon was the small, comfortable chamber the ladies of Chelmsford House had always used as their private sitting-room. There Rosamund found her cousin, looking pale and distraught, facing Mrs Hill, who stood before her not in the deferential attitude of a servant, but with a grim air of defiance which Rosamund immediately felt boded no good.

They both turned as she entered, and she went straight into the attack.

'Well, Hill,' she said briskly, 'what is it you want? You shouldn't be bothering Miss Haworth — she's far from well. And if it's money you're after, I may as well warn you right away —'

'It's not money I want, your ladyship, but justice,' Hill said, facing her boldly.

Your Ladyship, Rosamund noticed, not *my lady*. Hill had already taken on herself a mantle of equality. This was no servant come a-begging. 'Justice? What justice?' she said indifferently.

'Justice for my poor mistress! Justice and retribution by the law, which will surely be followed by justice in the next world,' Hill pronounced splendidly.

'I shan't listen to speeches,' Rosamund said sharply. 'Tell me what you want in simple language, or I shall have you shewn out right away.'

'Very well, your ladyship,' Hill said grimly, 'if plain speaking is what you want! My poor late mistress was hurried out of this life untimely, and I want her murderer brought to justice. So I came to you to ask for your help — you being her own sister — and Miss's, since she knows all about it.'

Rosamund stared at the lady's maid with incredulity and growing anger. 'Murderer? What the deuce are you talking about? My sister's death was accidental, as the whole world knows. What on earth could make you think she was murdered? You must have taken leave of your senses.'

'Not I,' said Hill firmly. 'I know the truth of it — aye, and Miss knows too, for all that she stands there like a stone image. You ask her, your ladyship — she'll tell you.'

Rosamund glanced briefly at Polly, who was gripping the back of the chair by which she was standing as though it alone were holding her upright. Why hadn't Polly summoned a footman to have this madwoman thrown out in the street?

'I shall ask Miss Haworth nothing. My sister fell by accident from the nursery window —'

'Accident?' Hill broke in, her face reddening. 'Was it an accident that she was all alone there that day, with no-one to care for her, not a single soul in the house but her? Was it an accident that the person who wished her out of the way made sure to be the first to come upon her poor broken body? Was it —'

'Wanted her out of the way?' Rosamund said. 'What are you saying? Who wanted her out of the way?'

'That wicked husband of hers, that's who! I warned her! I told her what he was, but she, poor precious innocent, with her forgiving heart, she would never believe any evil of him. But even I never thought he'd go so far as to – oh the wickedness! Otherwise I would never have left her, not if he was to have pulled me limb from limb!'

Rosamund saw that the woman was shaking all over, though whether from sorrow or anger it was impossible to say. She began to see, now, why Polly had let her remain here to rave – better that she should unburden herself here, in private, than be driven out resentful, perhaps to tell it to someone else who might believe it.

'You are quite mistaken,' Rosamund said, trying to speak quietly. 'I believe it is your love for your mistress that is speaking, but you must not repeat this wild accusation, or you will find yourself in grave trouble. Lord Harvey loved his wife dearly, and he –'

'He didn't love her,' Hill said, suddenly sounding quite calm. 'He never wanted to marry her in the first place. I heard him say so often enough. It was Miss he loved, and he wanted my mistress out of the way so he could marry her.'

In the shocked silence that followed, Polly looked up for the first time. She glanced at Rosamund, and Rosamund met her eye with a faintly questioning look. Harvey Sale had been Polly's beau before his arranged marriage with Minnie: Rosamund knew that, but it was not common knowledge. Was it possible that Hill had discovered it somehow, and had fuelled her fantasy with it? Or, on the other hand, was it possible that –? Polly looked down again, one bright spot of colour in each pale cheek.

Rosamund shut her mind to speculation, and concentrated on dealing with the problem immediately facing her.

'You had better tell me what you think you know, Hill, so that I can explain how you are mistaken. Speak quietly and do not exaggerate. Polly, if you wish to leave us –'

Polly shook her head briefly, without looking up.

'No, she had better stay and hear,' Hill said in a hard voice. 'She can tell you what I say is true. His lordship was mad for her, and she for him. Always meeting, they were, in secret,

322

talking and kissing and pinching fingers – oh, a pretty sight! But Miss wouldn't have him, him being a married man, so the only way out for him was to get rid of my poor mistress. I told her –'

'You told her that?' Polly looked up at Hill with horror.

'I told her everything,' Hill said defiantly, 'trying to warn her, but she wouldn't listen. Told me to hold my tongue. She wouldn't hear a word against either of you, and now it's too late. First he murdered the babies – poisoned them, poor little mites. Then he made sure my lady would be alone in the house, sent everybody to the Summer Fair, and went himself so no-one would suspect. But he came back in secret, came looking for her on purpose to do away with her – found her in the nursery where she sat every day, thinking about those poor blessed infants – and then –'

'Stop!' Rosamund's voice cracked. 'That's enough. You're wrong, quite wrong, in every respect. You must be mad even to have thought of such a thing! No, don't say another word! You will leave now, and I warn you very strongly against repeating these wild stories to anyone else –'

At that point the door opened, and Lady Barbara appeared, with Cowley behind her.

'My dear,' she addressed Rosamund, 'I'm sorry to say you really do not have the knack of dealing with servants. Here I find you still arguing with this creature, which is quite beneath you. You should have sent Cowley straight away to throw her out in the street.'

'Please, ma'am,' Rosamund said firmly, 'I must ask you not to intrude on this matter –'

But Lady Barbara had not heard a word. She stepped back and thrust Cowley past her with a little shove in the back. 'Do your duty now, Cowley – take the hussy away. And let me tell you, my woman,' she added sternly to Hill, 'that if you ever come here begging again, I shall have you taken up by the watch. Cowley, tell the other men that this baggage is not to be allowed through the front door on any pretext, and that if she is ever seen anywhere near the house, she's to be put in charge.'

'Baggage, is it?' Hill hissed in fury. 'You'll be sorry you insulted an honest woman –'

'Lady Barbara, I beg you not to interfere –' Rosamund cried.

'Don't stand there like a stock, Cowley,' Lady Barbara said impatiently. 'Do as I bid you and throw her out this instant.'

'Keep your hands off me,' Hill snapped as Cowley approached her reluctantly. 'I'm going, don't worry. But you'll be sorry, all of you. I see what it is now – you're protecting your own. Well, I'll take my story elsewhere. There's plenty around Stainton who know enough of the truth to help me find out the rest. You'll be hearing more of this, I promise you!'

And with that she stalked out, followed by Cowley, looking hang-dog. Lady Barbara remained champion of the field, and turned on her daughter-in-law triumphantly.

'There, you see – that's the way to do it. It's a great mistake, my dear Rosamund, to let servants argue with you. You will never manage them unless you keep them in their place.'

There was a great deal that Rosamund wanted to say, but for now she saw that Polly was close to fainting. 'Excuse me, ma'am,' she said firmly, 'but I must help Polly to her room. She's feeling unwell.'

'I'm not surprised,' Lady Barbara said, her voice following them as Rosamund supported Polly from the room, 'if she has to witness scenes like that. It's quite shocking to allow servants to take advantage in that way . . .'

In the privacy of Polly's room, Rosamund installed her in a chair, brought her some water, and offered her her smelling-bottle. In a few minutes she had recovered herself enough to thank her cousin in a thread of a voice.

Rosamund hesitated. 'Polly, I know you're not fully recovered yet, and this must have been a very shocking business, but if you feel you could talk about it, I think you ought to. It would be better to have it out in the open, don't you think?'

Polly looked at her with agonised eyes. 'You don't think – you can't believe Harvey could ever have done such a thing –!'

Rosamund sat down opposite her and looked at her steadily. 'Of course I don't. But it's plain to me that you've had something on your mind for a long time, and that it's making you sick. Now that Hill has opened up the subject of poor Minnie's death between us, why not tell me what it is that's worrying you so much?'

Polly shook her head, and looked away wretchedly. Rosamund watched her for a moment, and then said, 'Minnie was my sister, you know – my own sister. Don't you think I have a right to know, if there is something –'

'No!' Polly cried, startling Rosamund. 'There's nothing to know, nothing at all! Harvey was with me all day –'

She stopped short, catching her breath. Rosamund stared at her, unwelcome speculations arising in her mind.

'Were you lovers?' she asked at last, quietly.

Polly looked more miserable than Rosamund had ever seen her. 'Once,' she said, her voice hardly more than a whisper. 'Only once. But Minnie never knew about that, I swear it! No-one knew. We were so careful – it wasn't at Stainton – oh, I regretted it afterwards! It was a torment to me, but I was weak, weak –!'

'You love him?'

Polly nodded. 'Always. And he –' She stopped, swallowed, and resumed. 'He wanted me to go away with him. But how could I leave her? And anyway, we would have been outcasts. But he would never have – never have –'

'Of course not,' Rosamund said soberly. Dear God, she thought, what a torment they must have been to each other! And what price now, her suspicion that Minnie might have made an end of herself? If Hill really had told her all . . . Rosamund knew how much her sister had loved Polly, probably more even than she loved Harvey. Minnie killing herself in despair over the loss of her babies had seemed far-fetched to Rosamund, for after all, there could always have been more babies, and as long as she had Polly, she had everything to live for. But Minnie's was just that dogged, humble, unswerving sort of love that can make the supreme sacrifice. Once believing that she stood in the way of Polly's happiness with Harvey, she might – yes, it was horribly possible to imagine her doing it – remove herself from the path with a kind of insane but single-minded logic.

And was that, Rosamund asked herself, what Polly had been believing all this while? No wonder she had fretted herself almost to death. Hill's wild accusation of murder must have been almost a relief next to her own dreadful suspicions.

Rosamund offered her cousin her own former comfort. 'Even if Minnie did know anything about you and Harvey, I don't believe for a moment that her death was anything other than an accident. Even if she'd wanted to make away with herself, she would never have done it like that. Not Minnie.'

Polly hardly seemed to have heard her. 'Do you think – will that woman talk?' she asked faintly.

Rosamund frowned. 'I'm afraid my dear mother-in-law has made it rather more likely that she will. But I'm sure no-one will listen to her if she does. They'll put it down to insanity, which after all is what it is. Harvey was with you all day in Aylesbury.'

'Yes,' Polly said, looking at her with a dreadful fear in her eyes. 'Yes, he was. Except –'

'Except what?' Rosamund asked, startled.

'Except that I was asleep some of the time,' Polly whispered.

'Asleep?'

'For four hours, in a room at the Crown. And I don't know where he was.'

CHAPTER SEVENTEEN

The State Trials of the Pentrich rebels in October 1817 may have occupied the attention of the reformists and the radical press to the exclusion of all else, but in society at large there was only one topic of conversation: the arrest of Lord Harvey Sale for the murder of his wife and twin daughters. The news had so shocked his brother, the stout and rubicund Marquess of Penrith, that he had been taken with an apoplexy at his club and was not expected to live out the week.

'So then Harvey Sale will be a marquess and a murderer – and driven to it all for love of Polly Haworth. How romantic!' cried Miss Violet Edgecumbe, perched on a sofa in Lady Tewkesbury's saloon where she was paying a morning-visit on the countess's daughter, Lady Corinna Tulvey.

'Harvey Sale is such a handsome man, and so charming,' sighed Lady Corinna, who had had hopes of him before his marriage. 'I hate to think of him languishing in Aylesbury gaol like a common felon.'

'Murder is a common felony,' snapped Miss Lavinia Fauncett, who had once not been asked to dance by him at Almack's.

'Oh Lav, you're so hard!' cried Lady Corinna. 'Surely you don't think he's guilty? Poor Harvey Sale would never, never do such a thing. Poor Minnie Sale, and those poor dear little babies –!'

'Well, someone did, didn't they?' said Miss Fauncett. 'I was speaking to Julia Knaresborough yesterday –'

'Oh, have the Knaresboroughs come to Town? I thought they were quite fixed in the country,' said Miss Edgecumbe brightly.

'I haven't seen Julia since her wedding. Such a pretty wedding, too!' said Lady Corinna. 'I thought her wedding-gown was the sweetest –'

'Of course they've come up,' Miss Fauncett nipped this in the bud. 'Knaresborough is first cousin to the Sales, and now that Georgie Penrith is *hors de combat*, there's only him left on that side of the family. I suppose they've come to see what they can do to get Sale off. But Julia says it certainly wasn't an accident. I suppose they'll try to pass it off as suicide. That must be their best hope.'

Miss Edgecumbe's eyes opened wide. 'Oh no, how dreadful! Poor Lady Chelmsford, to have her sister set down as a suicide!'

'That would be just as bad as murder as far as the Morlands are concerned, wouldn't it?' said Lady Corinna. 'It would mean that Lady Harvey was driven to it by her husband's conduct with Polly Haworth.'

'Were they really – you know – all the time?' Miss Edgecumbe asked breathlessly. 'Ever since the marriage?'

Miss Fauncett was enjoying her position as Fount of Knowledge, and looked at her young acolyte witheringly. 'Of course not, Vi! That was the whole point – that she wouldn't, which drove him to despair.'

'Oh, like Anne Boleyn and Henry the Eighth!' said Miss Edgecumbe. 'I remember my governess telling me that story – quite thrilling!'

Miss Fauncett hesitated on the brink of repeating something she had overheard said by Lady Greyshott, but thought better of it in view of Miss Edgecumbe's extreme innocence. Helena Greyshott, another Sale cousin, had remarked privately to a friend, not realising Miss Fauncett was behind her, 'These virtuous women! They cause more trouble than all the rest of us put together. Why couldn't the silly little fool just follow her instincts, instead of acting a Cheltenham tragedy over it, like some early Christian martyr! Who the devil would have been any the worse – or any the wiser – for the loss of *her* virtue?'

'Really, you know, I never thought Miss Haworth so very handsome,' Lady Corinna was saying now. 'I came out in the same Season as her and her cousins, and I can remember she was never very much admired. She had good features, but no countenance, and no *brio*. She was reserved to the point of stupidity. All the men thought her very insipid.'

'Except Harvey Sale,' Miss Fauncett noted.

'But if he loved her so much,' Violet asked, 'why did he marry her cousin?'

'Oh Vi, don't be such a greenhead! Miss Haworth was a nobody, and she had no portion. It was all arranged by Lord Harvey's papa, the old marquess,' said Lady Corinna. 'He'd never have let Lord Harvey marry beneath him.'

'It must have been a thorn to Miss Haworth, all the same,' Miss Fauncett said thoughtfully. 'Flaminia Chetwyn was neither handsome nor clever, and yet she won Harvey Sale. And then for Miss Haworth to be obliged to dance attendance on her rival every day – she must have come close to hating her.'

Lady Corinna looked shocked. 'Oh Lavvy, what are you suggesting?'

'I'm not suggesting anything,' said Miss Fauncett blandly. 'But stand Polly Haworth and Harvey Sale side by side, and I know which I'd say was the more intelligent, and which had the most to gain by Lady Harvey's death.'

The silence which followed proved even to her that she had gone too far.

Marcus returned to Chelmsford House accompanied by Lord Anstey. It had been Parslow's private advice to Rosamund that Lord Anstey should be consulted, and she had immediately wondered why she hadn't thought of it herself. He had contacts throughout the Government at the highest level, and was liked by everyone; and as he regarded himself almost as a brother to Lady Theakston, there was no doubt of his will to help her daughter in this dreadful crisis.

He shook his head, however, as he followed Marcus into the Chinese drawing-room, where they usually sat in the evening. Lady Barbara was there with Barbarina, and she flung a question at him without even waiting for the formalities of greeting.

'Nothing, I'm afraid,' he said. 'Eldon says it's gone too far for him to interfere.'

'But he's Lord Chancellor!' Lady Barbara interrupted. 'Of course he can stop this nonsensical business! It must not come to a trial, at any cost. You can't have explained it to him properly.'

'Mama, Lord Anstey and I had a long talk with Lord Eldon,

329

and told him everything in detail,' Marcus said gently. 'He understands perfectly what the situation is, but he says that now the processes of law have been put into motion, he can't intervene –'

'Won't, you mean!'

'Yes, ma'am, if you wish,' Anstey said. 'The law must be seen to be impartial, or it will lose respect. Eldon is in the process of putting through an enormous programme of reform. He can't jeopardise that by impairing his own standing and integrity.'

'Then it must be stopped at some other point,' Lady Barbara said. 'The magistrate that this wretched serving-woman went to – surely he can be bought off?'

'Mama!' Marcus cried. 'You want to bribe a magistrate to corrupt the processes of law?'

'Oh, not with money, of course,' Lady Barbara said, unmoved by his outrage. 'That would soon get about, and then we should look nohow. No, no, I meant we should bring some other sort of pressure to bear on him. Who is the man? He's only a petty squire, after all, not a saint. He must have done something he'd sooner not have known, or want something we could get for him.'

John Anstey controlled his features with a valiant effort. 'I don't think that would at all be a wise action, Lady Barbara. It would be impossible to keep it secret, and once it was known we'd tried to stop the trial, it would be as good as admitting we believed Lord Harvey to be guilty.'

'Oh, why didn't the wretched man go abroad at once when his wife died,' Lady Barbara grumbled, 'and take that woman with him? That would have solved all the problems. But no, he had to hang around, waiting to be taken up like a common criminal –'

Marcus dug his nails into his palms and forced himself to speak calmly. 'Mama, I must beg you not to say things like that in front of Rosamund or Polly –'

'He's brought disgrace on us all,' Lady Barbara went on, ignoring him. 'Everyone's talking about us. I hardly know where to look when I go out in the carriage, with all the staring and whispering. Lady Tewkesbury was exceedingly unpleasant yesterday when I passed her in the Park. Yes, it's all very well for you, Marcus, to talk about ignoring it, but what about your sister? How is she to find a suitable match if everyone knows she's cousin to a murderer? Well, if Eldon's failed us, the Prince must do something, that's all. Rosamund must go to the Prince and use her mother's influence to have him call the whole thing off.'

Marcus cast a despairing look at Lord Anstey, who intervened gently. 'Eldon says that there's very little to worry about, Lady Barbara. He doesn't believe the evidence amounts to very much, and probably it won't go beyond the Assizes. But even if it did come to a trial, it would be in the House of Lords, of course, now that Sale has come into the title; and the Lords would be very unlikely to convict, especially in view of –'

'A trial in the House of Lords?' Lady Barbara cried, mottling with anger. 'No, that really is too much! The publicity – the notoriety! We should never hold up our heads again!'

'Far better, ma'am, surely, that Lord Harvey be tried and acquitted as innocent, than have people say for the rest of his life that he was too guilty to be brought to trial?'

But Lady Barbara plainly didn't agree. 'We shall be talked of whatever happens,' she snapped. 'You should never have married into that family, Marcus! I told you so again and again, but you wouldn't listen. There were any number of nice, respectable girls you could have had, but no, you would have Rosamund Chetwyn, in spite of –'

'Mama, don't go on, please!' Marcus said, embarrassed to have his mother expose herself in this way before a man he respected.

'Bad blood on both sides,' Lady Barbara flashed defiantly. 'Lady Theakston was always wild to fault, and look at her disgraceful liaison with that sea-captain, whatever his name was! And as to Lord Aylesbury, well! The talk there was about him and that –'

'Mama! Enough!' Marcus thundered, managing at last to silence his mother. Lord Anstey was white and tight-lipped, while Barbarina had begun to cry silently with distress and embarrassment. 'You forget yourself,' Marcus went on more quietly, but no less forcefully. 'We are all one family now. I forbid you to say such things, ever, to anyone.'

'*You* forbid?' Lady Barbara said, beside herself. 'You? How dare you? How dare you speak to me like that –'

The door opened, and Rosamund came in. She had been sitting with Polly upstairs, and had just been told that her husband and Lord Anstey had arrived.

'What news?' she asked eagerly as she entered, before she had time to notice the atmosphere. 'Oh Lord Anstey, have you had any luck?'

'The luck of this family ran out when my son married you!' Lady Barbara hissed, coming to her feet so suddenly that Rosamund instinctively took a step backwards. 'You're your mother's daughter, that's plain enough! But who was your father, answer me that? Barbarina, come!'

She stalked out, thrusting past Rosamund in the doorway, leaving her more bewildered than angry. Barbarina, still crying into her handkerchief, remained where she was. Rosamund looked from one face to another, and then went automatically to comfort her sister-in-law.

'What was all that about?' she asked, replacing Barbarina's flimsy handkerchief with a stouter, drier one, and stroking her hair away from her wet face. 'There, don't cry, Bab, no-one's going to shout at you any more.'

Marcus found his legs were trembling, and sat down abruptly opposite his wife and sister.

'Mama's a little upset,' he defended feebly.

'Eldon says there's no way of stopping the legal process,' Lord Anstey explained. 'But he doesn't believe the Grand Jury will return a true bill on the evidence we know about, so it will never come to trial.'

'Then what is your mama in such a taking for?' Rosamund asked, drying Barbarina's face like a brisk mother cat.

'She thinks that whatever happens, the notoriety will damage us,' Marcus explained unhappily.

'Well, there's nothing we can do about that, is there?' Rosamund said stoically. 'Better now, Bab? That's right, sit up straight and take deep breaths.'

'She thinks Harvey should have gone abroad and taken Polly with him,' Marcus said reluctantly.

Rosamund looked up. 'Good God, does she really think poor Harvey's guilty, then?' She looked from face to face, and her expression hardened. 'Do *you* think he's guilty?'

'No, of course not,' Lord Anstey said firmly. 'But she is

right in a way – there will always be those who think so, whatever the outcome.'

'Well, we don't care for them,' Rosamund said with equal firmness. 'They aren't the people who matter. As long as we present an unbroken front to the world – Marcus, you had better have another word with your mother.'

'Yes,' Marcus said unhappily. It wasn't so much the words he must have with her that he dreaded, but those she would have with him.

On the morning of the Assizes, Polly was in a state of collapse. The housemaid who had been maiding her sent for Rosamund, who came accompanied by Moss, and found her white and trembling, barely able to stand.

'Come, now, Polly, you must pull yourself together,' Rosamund said briskly, when she had sent the housemaid away. 'I shall lend you Moss to dress you and do your hair, but you must get up and try to be resolute.'

Polly looked at her despairingly, her teeth chattering. 'I can't,' she whispered. 'I'm so afraid.'

'Moss, where's that potion of yours? Ah! And are you sure that's how Docwra mixes it? Very well. Now, Polly, this will stiffen your spine and put some courage into you. Really, you are being very cow-hearted! Come now, drink it down.'

Polly drank the blood-red potion, gasped, coughed, and immediately looked a little less transparent.

'The trouble is that you've hardly eaten for days,' Rosamund went on briskly, as she and Moss helped Polly to her feet. 'You really are a fool. Don't you want to help Harvey?'

'Of course I do, but you don't understand –'

'Yes I do. It's very unpleasant to be called upon as a witness, to have to stand up in court, and talk about things you would sooner forget. But at least they've dropped that dreadful nonsense about the babies being poisoned. And you know what Lord Anstey told us Eldon said: once this is over, it will all be over, and Harvey will be a free man.'

'You *don't* understand,' Polly said bleakly. 'They'll ask me questions and – and I can't lie. I'll have to tell them everything.'

Rosamund looked alarmed. 'No you won't. You'll answer only what you're asked, and no more. You and Harvey went to the fair together at Minnie's own request. You came back together and found her lying dead on the path. And that will be that. I'm afraid,' she added gravely, 'that it may start up talk of suicide, but better that than murder. Come now, brace up, and let Moss dress you. I'll come back for you in half an hour.'

'Rosamund –!' Polly called her back as she was about to leave. 'Thank you, for being so kind to me. I can guess what people are saying about me.'

'No you can't,' Rosamund said briskly, hoping sincerely that Polly never found out what the Fauncett-Tewkesbury camp were saying. 'Don't worry, I'll be with you the whole time. It will be all right.'

Once outside the door, she allowed herself to sag a little. This business, she thought, had aged her ten years in as many weeks. And when it was over, she told herself grimly, she would get rid of Lady Barbara by hook or by crook. If it had not been for her interference, Rosamund might have kept Hill from voicing her suspicions publicly.

On Monday the 7th November, Brandreth and two other Pentrich rebels were hanged on the green in front of Derby gaol, before a huge crowd of spectators. The heads were afterwards severed from the bodies and displayed on poles, but the Prince Regent had graciously remitted the sentence of quartering that was customary in cases of High Treason. Twenty-three more rebels had been sentenced to imprisonment or transportation, and twenty others had been acquitted. It was generally held to be a very salutary lesson to any who felt they could bring down the Government by unlawful means.

In London, the event was washed into oblivion by the tide of shock and grief which followed the news that Princess Charlotte, the Regent's only daughter, and heir to the throne of England, had died the day before in childbed of a stillborn son, after eighteen months of happy marriage to Prince Leopold of Saxe-Coburg. The princess, pretty, intelligent, witty, and charming, had been the adored favourite not only of her father and grandparents, but of the whole country. People had looked to her to make England a better place when she succeeded her much hated father, and to save them from rule by any of his increasingly unpopular brothers. She was mourned deeply and sincerely by a shocked and bewildered populace.

But in the Chelmsford household, even that news was less shocking than the fact that the Grand Jury at Aylesbury Assizes had returned a true bill against Harvey Sale, Marquess of Penrith, for the murder of his wife.

'How did it happen?' Fitzherbert Hawker asked Rosamund gravely. 'There's been some mismanagement here, I'm sure.'

He had come looking for her at Chelmsford House, to find it under siege from crowds of gawpers and gossipers, and the family gone into hiding. He found her at last at her mother's house in Upper Grosvenor Street, preparing to go down into the country until the trial came on.

'When is the trial to be, anyway? I must be sure not to miss it.'

'It will probably be some time in January, when Parliament reassembles after the Christmas recess,' Rosamund said. 'But I doubt whether you'll be able to witness it – there'll be very little room in the spectators' gallery. Only very important people will be given tickets.'

'I am very important, didn't you know? I'm not so close to Sidmouth for nothing, you know.'

'You needn't sound as though the whole thing is a fairground show for your benefit,' Rosamund said. 'It's all very shocking and unpleasant.'

'Yes, I see that it is,' he said kindly. 'You look fagged to death, and no wonder – the whole burden must have fallen on you, if I know anything about those around you.'

'You're wrong – Lord Anstey has been wonderful, and Marcus is the greatest comfort to me.'

'I'm glad to hear it. Nevertheless, they don't feel it as you do, and if I speak lightly, it's not because it is a light matter, but because you must keep up your spirits, or your health will suffer.'

'I hardly know how to think about it, to say the truth. One part of me believes that the Lords will dismiss the whole thing with the contempt it deserves; but I still can't shake out a tiny seed of fear that it will end in tragedy. That doesn't bear contemplating.'

'Then don't!'

'It's so horrible and disgusting,' Rosamund added thoughtfully, 'and yet I suppose there's a comic side to it, if you look hard enough. All this fuss and parade, you know: a special committee of lords to present an address to the Prince, humbly requesting him to appoint a Lord High Steward for the occasion; another committee busy ordering the fitting out of the great hall, and working out a seating plan, and making up an invitation list for the spectators; every lord in the land brushing his robes or ordering new ones; and the newspapers in a perfect frenzy about the whole business – all because Lady Barbara needs must try to bully a servant, and not even one of her own servants at that!'

'Is that how it happened?' Hawker asked.

Rosamund told him of Hill's visit to Chelmsford House. 'She went away in a fury, determined to make it all public, and took her story to the local magistrate at Stainton. It happens that he's a strict moralist, disapproves of modern society and the antics of the *ton*, especially in regard to other people's wives and husbands, so he took more notice of her than anyone else might. He interviewed some of the other servants, and discovered that it wasn't only Hill who had noticed things.'

'Yes, servants always see everything. The wonder of it is that they don't talk more about what they do see.'

Rosamund looked tired. 'According to Polly, there wasn't much to see in this case: they only met secretly to talk. However, that was enough for the magistrate. He enquired in Aylesbury, where Polly and Harvey dined together at the Crown –'

'Oh, depravity!'

'Just so. But it might have ended there – the perfect alibi, you see – except that a pert little chambermaid happened to let out that "Miss had come over queer" during dinner and had been taken to a bedroom to recover, where she had fallen asleep for several hours. During that time, Harvey, naturally enough, left the inn.'

'Ah!'

'To look at the fair, of course. Well, he could hardly have sat by Polly's bedside all that time, could he? Anyway, Stainton's less than ten miles from Aylesbury. He could have been there and back in a couple of hours, and there were four hours unaccounted for. On the basis of that, and on the servants' evidence that Harvey and Polly had secret meetings, and that Harvey was in love with her and not with his wife, the jury – Methodists to a man – found a true bill, and the whole dreadful thing is to go to trial.'

'Where they will surely acquit him,' Hawker said comfortingly. 'I said there had been some mismanagement, and so there has been. This is no evidence at all, and it should never have gone beyond the magistrate's hearing. This has all been very trying for you, Lady Chelmsford, but take courage: it can't last much longer. Lord Harvey will go free, and you will soon be able to forget the whole sorry business.'

Rosamund didn't look comforted. 'The only good thing is that Polly wasn't called to give evidence at the Assizes, for she was in such a state of terror, the Lord knows what she might have said.'

'They were lovers, then?'

Rosamund met his eyes. 'Once, I believe – after which she told him she couldn't do such a thing again –'

'Thereby driving the poor man to desperation. Dear me!'

'It isn't a matter for levity.'

'No, no, of course not. I was merely anticipating what the prosecution might deduce. Well, Lady Chelmsford, the burden must not fall on you again. Miss Haworth must be carefully schooled before the trial, where she is bound to be called, as to what she must and must not say. Shepherd will appear for the Crown, of course – Sir Samuel Shepherd, the Attorney-General – which is a pity, for we could have done with him on our side. We must think who will be the best man to appear for the Defence. Denman is excellent, but perhaps he is not your man, after the Pentrich trials. There's Losh – Parke – Garvie – no, they won't do. Wait now, I have it – Sir Rigby Fielding is the one. You must have Fielding.'

'Is he good?'

'Very good, a most persuasive advocate. Would you like me to speak to him for you? We are acquainted.'

'I should be very grateful. You are kind.' She looked at him curiously. 'How do you come to know all these men of law?'

'Through the Pentrich trials, of course. It has all been the greatest fun imaginable! I'll tell you about it one day. Well now, I shall speak to Fielding for you, and you must not worry any more. You're going down to Wolvercote?'

'Yes, tomorrow. Lady Barbara and Barbarina left this morning, but I'm waiting for Marcus.'

'Very wise. You'll be able to keep yourselves private there, at the heart of your ancestral estate.'

'That's why we moved here from Chelmsford House, but it won't be long before the crowds find us again. We'll have Christmas at Wolvercote, and I'll try to get Polly out hunting, to take her mind off things. She really is in a pitiable state, poor creature, and no wonder.'

'None indeed,' Hawker agreed; but inwardly his thoughts were very much more in line with Helena Greyshott's on that subject. Rosamund, he felt, would never have got herself into such a situation. He was sure that active, decisive people caused far less trouble in the world than those who passively let troubles accumulate around them.

The trial in the House of Lords opened on the 20th of January, 1818: a day of pale, wintry sunshine, encouraging spectators to gather about the precincts of the Palace of Westminster in such numbers that a whole regiment of Hussars was called in to keep the crowds in check.

The sunshine filtered into the dark, wood-panelled hall through the high narrow windows, illuminating the mediaeval splendour of this most ancient of courts. At the stroke of eleven a fanfare sounded, and two by two, in their order, beginning with the youngest baron, the peers of the realm filed in. Robed in their crimson and ermine, attended by the Garter King-of-Arms and his heralds, they took their places on the benches down the sides of the chamber.

The gallery was packed with those influential enough to have acquired tickets, while the seats below the Bar of the House reserved for peeresses shewed not a single gap. Here Rosamund had her place, and knew herself to be an object of close scrutiny, in anticipation of which she had dressed herself in a style both sober and dashing: a smoky-blue pelisse with smart Hussar frogging and a sable collar, and a hat of the same shade, decorated with three curving black cocks' feathers and a cluster of jet beads like a bunch of luscious black grapes. From time to time Marcus looked up from his place amongst the earls and smiled at her, meaning to reassure her, but in reality reassuring himself that she was the bravest as well as the most beautiful of women.

Rosamund thought he looked very well in his robe and coronet. Her greatest trial was that since the peeresses' seats were for the daughters as well as the wives of peers, she was obliged to sit next to her mother-in-law, who was the daughter of the Duke of Watford, and who had declared that she would not dream of allowing Rosamund to face the ordeal unsupported. On Rosamund's other side, however, was Lady Tonbridge, who was a friend of her mother's and kindness itself, and beyond her the dashing Lady Greyshott, whom Rosamund had always admired for her flouting of convention. By turning her head that way, she managed to be comforted rather than undermined during the long wait before the Sergeant-at-Arms called for silence.

Now the peers were all seated, and the proceedings began at last, with the establishing of the court's authority. The Clerk of the Crown in Chancery knelt before the throne and presented the Commission under the Great Seal to the Lord High Steward, appointed *pro hac vice*, who was in fact Lord Eldon, the Lord Chancellor himself. The Commission was read out, and then the Garter King-of-Arms and the Gentleman Usher of the Black Rod knelt before the throne and handed the Lord High Steward his white staff of office – a staff which would be broken in half at the end of the proceedings to signify that its authority did not extend beyond this one occasion.

The Certiorari and Return were proclaimed, a long recitation at the end of which the indictment against Harvey Sale, Marquess of Penrith, brought wandering attentions sharply back to the present. Now they had come to the nub of it. Black Rod was sent to call the accused to the Bar, where he knelt before the Lord High Steward. Though no-one actually spoke in the gallery, there was a shifting and swaying all along the seats, and a whispering just below the level of sound, like a cornfield moving in a light breeze, at the appearance of the prisoner. Harvey Sale, dressed in a blue coat, buff small clothes and white stockings, was tall, handsome, and noble; but somehow fragile, bareheaded amongst the robed splendour of his peers. The black mourning-bands on his sleeves reminded everyone of the tragic circumstances of his appearance in the House today; and that innocent or guilty, his wife and children were dead; and his life in ruins.

The Lord High Steward indicated that the prisoner might rise, whereupon he was conducted to a stool placed within the Bar, and the charge was read to him: that the Most Honourable Harvey George Sale, Baron Lasonby, Earl of Wyndham, and Marquess of Penrith, a peer of England, on the twentieth day of August in the year of Our Lord eighteen hundred and seventeen in the parish of Stainton in the County of Buckinghamshire did kill and murder Lady Flaminia Sale.

To the charge, the accused pleaded Not Guilty in a firm but not defiant tone, and another inaudible sigh ran around the gallery.

'And how will you be tried?' the Lord High Steward enquired.

'By God and my peers,' said Penrith.

'God send your lordship a good deliverance,' said the Lord High Steward politely. The prisoner sat, and Sir Samuel Shepherd rose to make his opening speech and present the case for the Crown.

The first witness he called was Rebecca Hill, who gave a long account of the history of Sale's marriage, and of the relationships between him, his wife, and his wife's cousin. Other servants were called to testify that Lord Harvey Sale and Miss Haworth met in secret whenever his lordship visited Stainton, though none could say what the subject of their secret discussions might have been; and that his lordship was 'mad for her', and took every opportunity of being alone with her. And yet other servants were called upon to give their account of the day in question, how his lordship had arranged for them all to go to the fair in the brake, and how Mrs Hill had been that upset to be sent off, leaving her mistress all alone.

'Disgusting, is it all to be servants' tittle-tattle?' Lady Tonbridge said at last in an audible whisper, causing the Sergeant-at-Arms to look up at the gallery reprovingly.

Sir Rigby Fielding, however, agreed with her view when he visited Chelmsford House that evening, at the end of the first day.

'This case should never have been brought. The magistrate was an opinionated fool, the Grand Jury didn't know its business, and the bench should have directed it quite otherwise.

340

However, it can't be helped now, we shall have to see it through. But don't worry, Lady Chelmsford, we'll come out all right, we'll triumph.'

On the second day Sir Samuel called the doctor who had attended the twin girls in their last illness. He testified that Lady Flaminia had been deeply shocked and grieved, having been much attached to her babies. A picture was being painted of a simple, domesticated woman, prey to the machinations of two heartless lovers. It was a moving picture, Rosamund thought, but one that might easily backfire: a great many of the lords whose task it would be to make judgement must themselves have lovers as well as virtuous wives, without being in the slightest way inclined towards murder.

Then Polly Haworth was called. The spectators sat up straighter; all eyes were fixed on that pale, wraith-like figure, and the silence in the House was deafening.

'You were Lord Harvey Sale's lover, were you not?' Sir Samuel asked without preamble.

Polly swayed. 'No – no,' she whispered. Rosamund clenched her hands in her lap, and her nails dug into her palms. Don't ask her the wrong questions, she prayed; and towards Polly directed the urgent mental plea, don't say more than you have to.

'I suggest that is why you remained with Lady Harvey all those years: in order to indulge your criminal desire to be near Lord Harvey.'

'No. Not so. I was Lady Harvey's companion. We were brought up together. She asked me to stay with her.'

'Then how would you describe your relationship with Lord Harvey?' Sir Samuel asked sweetly. The trap yawned beneath Polly's feet.

'He was my cousin's husband,' she said at last, and there was muted laughter in the gallery.

'Do you mean that you had for him no more fondness than for any other cousin-by-marriage?'

Polly looked wretched. Her eyes were fixed on her interlocutor like a rabbit staring at a stoat. 'I loved him,' she said faintly.

'You were in love with him?' he pressed.

'Yes.'

There was a tense silence, and Rosamund held her breath,

wondering what the next devastating question would be; but then Sir Samuel invited Miss Haworth, in his most silky tones, to tell in her own words the events of that last day of Lady Harvey's life.

Polly began, falteringly, in a voice that barely carried to their lordships, far less the gallery, but she hadn't gone very far when Sir Samuel stopped her.

'Miss Haworth, you say that Lady Harvey urged you to go to the fair and leave her alone in the house. Was that not a very remarkable thing for her to have done?'

Polly did not know how to answer that.

'Why do you think she did that?'

'She had been very upset since the babies died. She never went out anywhere, or did anything.'

'She was shocked and grieved, we heard from Doctor Priddy. Would you agree with that?'

'Yes.'

'We heard yesterday from her maid that she was very much depressed after the death of her daughters. Would you agree with that?'

'Yes.'

'And yet you agreed to go away for the day and leave her alone in the house. Now is that not a very remarkable thing for *you* to have done?'

A mild upsurge amongst the spectators relieved Polly of the need to answer the question.

Sir Samuel resumed. 'What was Lord Harvey's attitude on this occasion? Surely he would not wish his grieving wife to be left alone in the house all day?'

'He tried to persuade her to come with us. But she was very stubborn when she wanted to be.'

'And did he try to persuade you to stay with her?'

Polly looked down at her hands. 'Lady Harvey wanted to be left alone. She said so many times.'

Sir Samuel passed on to their day at the Summer Fair. 'You stayed there all day with Lord Harvey?'

'Yes,' Polly said in a low voice.

'And was he with you all of the time?'

Rosamund saw the small figure of Polly seem to grow smaller, shrinking together with distress.

'Well, Miss Haworth? Was Lord Harvey with you for every

342

minute of that day in Aylesbury?'

'No,' Polly said, and it sounded like a sigh.

Under questioning she told of the dinner, her feeling faint, being helped to the bedchamber, waking to the presence of the chambermaid and being told she had been asleep for four hours.

'And where was Lord Harvey during that time while you were asleep?'

'I don't know,' Polly said unhappily.

'You don't know,' Sir Samuel said kindly. 'Well, of course you don't – it would not be reasonable to expect you to, would it?' A fluttering murmur through the House. 'And four hours is a long time. A man may go quite a long way in four hours, at four miles per hour on foot, or at *nine miles per hour on horseback.*'

Lord Eldon interposed at that point. 'Sir Samuel, this is not the moment for you to make observations of that sort. Kindly confine yourself to questioning the witness.'

Sir Samuel bowed and resumed, asked Polly when she next saw Lord Harvey, and she told in halting phrases about the journey back to Stainton, and the discovery of Flaminia's body. During the narration she grew gradually more halting, her voice weaker, her face paler, until at last she sank fainting to the ground, causing a sensation all around the House, which it took the Sergeant-at-Arms some time to quell.

When order was restored, and Miss Haworth was revived, and given water and a chair, Sir Samuel declined to ask any more questions, and Sir Rigby Fielding rose to his feet.

'Miss Haworth, you say that it was at Lady Harvey's insistence that you left her alone in the house. Did you, at the time, find this insistence surprising?'

'No.'

'Why not?'

'She had been spending most of her time alone – sitting alone in the nursery or in her room, staring at nothing. When I tried to coax her to do something, she would just send me away, asking to be left alone.'

'She sent you away – as she did on this occasion?'

'Yes.'

'And did Lord Harvey find it surprising that his wife should want to be left alone?'

343

'No, I don't think so.'

'You asked, in his presence, to be allowed to stay with Lady Harvey, and she begged you to leave her alone.'

'Yes.'

'And what did Lord Harvey say to that?'

'That she had a right to be alone if she wanted to.'

'Why do you think he said that?'

Polly's eyes strayed for the first time towards Harvey. 'He is a kind man. He hates to see anyone bullied, or forced to do things they don't want to do.'

'Thank you, Miss Haworth.'

A little later, Sir Samuel rose to his feet again. 'Miss Haworth, you say that Lord Harvey hates to see anyone bullied. Why is that? Was he, perhaps, himself the victim of bullying?'

'Oh – yes – I believe so. His father and his brother –'

'Yes, Miss Haworth? What did his father and his brother make him do?'

Polly had seen too late where these faltering footsteps led her. 'Nothing. I don't know.'

'Were you perhaps going to remind us that his father and brother forced him to marry against his will; to marry a suitable wife instead of the woman he loved – you, Miss Haworth?'

Sir Rigby and Lord Eldon objected to this very improper question almost simultaneously; but Miss Haworth would not have been able to answer in any case, for she was plainly close to collapse. The trial was adjourned for the second day.

Some of the third day's witnesses were very damaging. There was the waiter from the Crown Inn who testified that Lord Harvey had insisted on their being left alone to serve themselves, and the chambermaid who told how Polly Haworth had been taken ill very suddenly and then lost consciousness 'as though she'd been poll-axed'. There was the tap-room attendant who had seen Harvey Sale hurrying out of the inn immediately afterwards 'looking as grim as Old Harry'. There was the apothecary from Wendover who testified, apologetically, that he had sold Lord Harvey Sale a powerful sleeping-draught 'some time in early August'.

And then there was a witness Rosamund hadn't expected,

344

whose testimony came as an unpleasant shock. It was the ostler from a job-stables in Aylesbury, who swore that a man who looked just like the prisoner had hurried in to hire a riding-horse some time that afternoon, given his name as Mr Freeman – the name traditionally used by gentlemen wishing to be incognito – and since he was unknown at the stables, left a valuable gold fob-watch as surety against the return of the horse.

Sir Rigby rose each time to take the sting out of the evidence. The waiter was brought to admit that ladies and gentlemen dining in private parlours very often did want to be left alone together. The chambermaid acknowledged that Miss Haworth's breath was vinous, and that she might simply have taken too much to drink. The tap-room attendant's evidence was passed over as being of no possible importance. The apothecary, less apologetically, agreed that Lord Harvey was a gentleman of nervous, highly-strung disposition, and that he had made up sleeping-draughts for him on many other occasions, though not as strong as the last one.

The ostler, unfortunately, was a stubborn old man, and continued to assert that Mr Freeman and the prisoner were as like as two peas, and that if they weren't one and the same they must be twins. O' course it was the day of the Fair the stranger came in – he couldn't mistake that, now could he? As to the time, he couldn't exactly swear to it, but it was in the afternoon. He'd been left alone in the stables because all the younger men had gone off to the Fair, and left him to do all the work, which was just like them. The horse? Well, when it came back, it was sweating, like as if it had been ridden hard. No, not foundered, he wouldn't go so far as to say that, but tired-like. The stranger had paid him in silver, claimed his watch and gone away. He hadn't said nothing in a special way, not that he could remember. No, he'd never seen Lord Harvey before, but he'd heard of him all right – master of Stainton Manor, but wasn't hardly never there.

So the case for the Crown was brought to a close, and the House rose at the end of the third day.

At home that evening Marcus visited Rosamund in her bedroom.

'It's looking bad, isn't it?' she asked him in a small voice. 'That ostler –?'

345

'He's just a foolish, doddery old man looking for notoriety,' Marcus said comfortingly. 'I thought Sir Rigby brought that out famously.'

'All the same, Fielding didn't manage to make him change his mind, did he?'

'Don't worry, he'll demolish the whole shaky edifice tomorrow, you'll see. After all, what is the evidence? It doesn't amount to a handful of peas.' He looked at her searchingly. 'Darling, you aren't beginning to believe it, are you?'

'Of course not,' Rosamund said, unaware that she was frowning. 'But what *was* Harvey doing all that time, while Polly was asleep?'

'Looking round the fair, of course,' Marcus said, and decided to try shock tactics. 'Do you really imagine he hired a horse, rode back to Stainton, ran upstairs to the nursery, opened the window and pushed your sister out, and then rode back to Aylesbury as though nothing had happened?'

Rosamund paled as the images paraded before her imagination. 'Don't,' she whispered. 'Don't. It's too horrible.'

'Yes, exactly – it's too horrible. He would never have done such a thing, and you know it. What's more, the lords know it. They won't convict him on that sort of evidence.'

'Of course not. You're right,' said Rosamund, and then, surprising herself as much as Marcus, she burst into tears.

Marcus gathered her into his arms and held her, glad that she was crying at last; believing, as people do, that crying was somehow a good sign, and would make things better.

346

CHAPTER EIGHTEEN

Sir Rigby Fielding ended his closing speech in storming style.

'My lords, I do not say that the case for the Crown is not good enough – I say that it is no case at all. What does the evidence amount to? An old man claims that a stranger hired a horse from him. He believes the stranger was Lord Harvey Sale. This, his lordship denies absolutely. Which of them will you believe, my lords? The gentleman or the ostler?'

There was a ripple of laughter from the gallery. Sir Rigby paid it no heed, looking around the assembled peers with slow confidence.

'And will you, on this flimsiest of notions – the hiring of a horse by an unknown stranger – believe that the most honourable lord who stands before you now, bearing for all to see the outward signs of his tragic bereavement, did in such a cowardly and horrible way murder his grieving wife? No! I do not believe it is possible for any of you to stretch his credulity thus far.

'I said at the beginning that this case should never have been brought, and I am still of the same mind. But since it has been laid before you in all its inadequacy, and you have been obliged to consider it, there remains only for each of you in turn to stand, and lay his hand over his heart, and cry in a ringing tone, "Not guilty, upon mine honour!".'

The gallery burst into spontaneous applause which it took the Sergeant-at-Arms some time to quell. The Lord High Steward then summed up briefly, seeming to be tired of the whole thing – he was suffering from a particularly tiresome cold in the head – and the noble lords filed out as they had come in, two by two, to make their deliberations.

Marcus glanced up at Rosamund as he passed beneath her, and nodded slightly, and she smiled at him more buoyantly than on the previous days. It was easier to be confident today, since she was relieved of the presence of Lady Barbara, who had stayed at home pleading the headache.

Lady Tonbridge, who was occupying the seat next to Rosamund, leaned over and said, 'There, my dear, it's all over. Wasn't Sir Rigby splendid? Penrith will be free again within the hour, I warrant you.'

'Yes, ma'am, I'm sure of it,' Rosamund replied with automatic politeness. And yet, was she? She felt as though she would never be sure of anything again. Reality had been shewn to be so fragile, so easily mistaken, so easily disguised; and when you lifted the lid of anyone's life, did not the box contain as many troubles as Pandora's, all hidden from you before? For the five years of Minnie's marriage, Rosamund had had no idea of what had been going on between Polly and Harvey, and nor, it seemed, had anyone else. How was it possible, then, to be certain of anything in this case? She could not feel certain that the lords would acquit Harvey; and if they did not, he would hang, and what, then, would become of the rest of them?

The time seemed very long, and very full of doubtful and unhappy thoughts, before the lords returned to their places, and the Lord High Steward assumed his hat to address them.

'My lords, the question before your lordships is this: is the prisoner guilty of the felony whereof he stands accused, or not guilty? How say your lordships?'

The first lord stood up, turned to face the Lord High Steward, placed his right hand on his breast, and into the palpitating silence spoke the words: 'Not guilty, upon mine honour!'

A long sigh rustled round the gallery, a collective exhalation of relief. The first lord sat, the second rose, and so it went on, as one by one, in their appointed order, the lords stood to give their individual judgement, made upon their honour and not upon their oath: not guilty, not guilty, not guilty ...

The Hussars made an avenue through the surging tides of the crowd between the door of the King's Robing Room and the Chelmsford carriage, where Rosamund sat with the window up, waiting for her husband and her brother-in-law. Along this avenue at last Marcus came hurrying arm in arm with the Most Honourable the Marquess of Penrith, a free man at last, looking pale from his long confinement, and bewildered, but managing to smile a little to either side in response to the cheers of the crowd. Amongst the people, at least, Rosamund thought, it was a popular acquittal. They liked him because he was handsome.

The two men climbed into the carriage, the step was put up and the door closed firmly, and with four Hussars in front to clear a way and four behind to keep it open, the carriage moved off towards Pall Mall.

'Congratulations, Harvey,' Rosamund said; and yet it seemed a strange thing to say. Flaminia was dead – that was one unalterable fact.

Harvey looked dazed. 'Thank you,' he replied, as though he thought *that* was an odd thing to say, too. Yet conversation had to be made – life had to go on. 'It has been the strangest nightmare. I find it hard to believe it happened at all.'

'It's all over now, old fellow,' Marcus said bracingly. 'You must simply put it behind you and start a new life.'

Harvey shook his head. His face was gaunt in the wintry sunshine, and newly bare over the temples, and there were deep lines at his mouth corners which Rosamund had never noticed before. 'People will never forget,' he said.

When they reached home, it was a strange anticlimax to pass through the cheering crowds, past the smiling servants, and into the silent house. Barbarina was there to meet them, smiling shyly, but Lady Barbara did not appear, purportedly nursing her headache in her room, but in reality disapproving of the whole business, and believing that Harvey had brought disgrace on them all. Only Marcus knew that she had tried to prevent him from bringing Penrith back if the trial went his way.

'We don't want to be associated with him any further. Let him go to his own place.'

But Marcus had been adamant, for once overruling his mother determinedly. 'He hasn't a place in London, Mama. You can't let the poor fellow go to an hotel all alone after such an ordeal.'

Now in the hallway, Harvey looked round with the same, dazed air, and said, 'Where's Polly?'

'In her room,' Barbarina said. 'She was feeling faint, so I got Moss to put her to bed. She must know the verdict by now from the cheers outside, but I'll run up and tell her you're here.'

'Yes – thank you. I must see her,' Harvey said anxiously. 'She has suffered so much.'

'A glass of something first,' Marcus said, 'to put some warmth into you. You look as grey as a ghost. Bab, my dear, would you see if Polly is well enough for a visitor? And if so, tell her Harvey will come up in half an hour?'

In the drawing-room, Harvey drew shivering to the fire, and Marcus put a glass into his hands without comment, and waited until the glass was empty before speaking.

'Have you thought what you mean to do now?' he asked. 'You'll stay here tonight, of course, and for as long as you want. You must have business to conduct – you won't have seen a lawyer since you came into the title – so I expect you'll want to stay in London for the time being, won't you?'

Harvey nodded vaguely.

'If you prefer,' Rosamund said, 'you can use my mother's house. It's fully staffed, and smaller and more comfortable than this.'

'Thank you – you're very kind,' Harvey said. Marcus refilled his glass, and he gulped at it and then seemed to pull himself together. 'I suppose I will have to see George's man of business, and find out how things have been left. I don't even know what funeral directions were made for poor old George. I suppose they buried him in the family vault – I hope they did all properly. I shouldn't like to think anything was scanted or hurried over.'

'It was a rotten piece of luck, his dying like that,' Marcus said inadequately. But there was, after all, very little one could say to Penrith at the moment that would be either tactful or cheering. Marcus was beginning to learn the sad human truth, that grave personal misfortune is deeply embarrassing to one's friends.

Harvey said, 'We didn't see eye-to-eye on many subjects, but he wasn't a bad sort at bottom, and he was my brother. My only brother. Now I have no-one.' He sighed and emptied his glass. 'I shall have to go abroad,' he said. 'It would be intolerable to have people stare at me and whisper about me wherever I went.'

'Oh, I'm sure they won't,' Marcus said unconvincingly.

'They will,' Harvey said, and they both knew he was right. The lords may have acquitted him, but their ladies would not invite him to dine.

'It might be a good idea for you to travel for a while,' Rosamund said, 'just until it all blows over. And it can only do you good to get away from the scenes that hold sad memories for you – see fresh sights, restore your spirits and so on.'

'Yes,' said Harvey. 'I shall go abroad, and take Polly with me. At least now I can marry her,' he said with a ghastly smile, 'and make things all right for her. That's the one good outcome of this business. There's no-one now who can stop me, no Papa or George to tell me she isn't good enough to be a marchioness.'

Marcus and Rosamund didn't speak. There seemed nothing that could be said in good taste at that point.

'I'd better go and see her,' Harvey said, putting down his glass. 'Poor creature, she's had the worst of it! But I'll make it up to her somehow, if it takes me the rest of my life.'

Polly was on the daybed in her room when Harvey came in, but when she saw him, she rose to her feet with a little cry, and managed to take one step before he covered the rest of the distance between them and took her in his arms.

'Oh God, Harvey, you're alive!' she cried incoherently as he crushed her against him.

'My darling! My own darling!' he murmured, his lips against her hair. For a long time all they could do was to hold each other, weak with relief. At last she pushed him feebly away, and he saw that she was fainting. He laid her gently down on the daybed, and knelt beside her, clasping one of her hands and chafing it gently while he gazed into her face, waiting for her to recover.

At last her eyes fluttered open. 'Harvey, is it true? Are you really here? I'm not dreaming?'

'No, my darling, you're not dreaming. It's all over now. I've come back to you, and nothing will ever part us again.' She said nothing, only stared at him in a troubled way, and he began to grow apprehensive. 'What is it, my love? Why do you look at me like that?'

'It's not over,' she said. 'It will never be over. People will never forget.'

351

'They will, they will. It will take time, that's all. We'll go abroad, travel for a few years, see all the sights of Europe together, and when we come back –'

'No!'

'No what, darling?'

'I'm not coming with you. All that's over, Harvey.'

'But what do you mean? I mean to marry you, Polly – to make you my wife, my marchioness. You didn't think I meant –?'

'I can't marry you, Harvey. I can't be with you ever again.'

He stared at her, astonished. 'You can't mean it. Why? Why not?'

'Don't you see, if we do that, people will think that you really did kill Minnie in order to marry me. They'll think I knew about it, too. It will never be over, the talk will never die. They'll go on believing we're murderers, and that we escaped justice. Only if we never see each other again will they come to believe you're innocent.'

'What are you talking about? This is madness!'

'No, no it's not. The lords acquitted you, but the drawing-rooms never will, as long as they see that there was a reason for you to be rid of her. But if we part, they will know it was all a mistake.'

'Polly, listen to me, you're upset, you don't know what you're saying!'

'I know well enough.' She pulled her hand away from him, her face set in lines of bitterness. 'I know what they've been saying about us. I've seen the looks. They know we were lovers. They know about our secret meetings. They know you wanted to marry me, that you regretted marrying Minnie. And they believe you killed her, and that I knew about it and condoned it. And if we marry, it will confirm our guilt in their eyes. We must part now, and never see each other again. It's the only way. We must live in purity from now on, and purge ourselves of this stain –'

He rocked back on his heels, staring at her with increasing perplexity as she spoke, and finally, at her last words, with a dawning horror.

'You think I did it,' he whispered, stopping her in mid-sentence. She stared back, her eyes dilating. 'You think I'm guilty. It's true, isn't it? You really believe I murdered her.'

She didn't answer, only stared at him, wide-eyed, like a cornered animal facing its death.

'Polly,' he cried suddenly, 'it's me, Harvey, don't you know me? Do you really think I could do such a thing? Do you think these hands –' he spread them before her, and she swayed backwards away from them – 'these hands that have caressed you could do murder?'

He reached out for her, and she shrank from him, shaking her head slowly.

'You never came,' she whispered suddenly. 'Week after week we never saw you – and then suddenly you were there all the time. And the babies died, and Minnie died, and now you're the marquess, and –'

'For God's sake,' he cried aloud, 'do you think I killed them all? Is that what you think?'

'I don't know,' she whispered. 'I don't know what I think any more. But, oh Harvey, where were you while I was asleep at the inn?'

He opened his mouth to answer her, and then seemed to see the hopelessness of the situation, and closed it again. He shook his head and stood up, and his eyes filled with tears as he looked at her one last time, and then turned away.

'I'll leave you then, if that's what you want,' he said, his voice muffled. He waited, but she didn't speak again, and he went to the door, let himself out, and closed it quietly behind him.

The Times carried the story of the acquittal in a report entitled *The Ostler or the Gentleman?*, and the very fact of the question-mark seemed to suggest that there was still a question mark over Penrith's innocence.

'It's intolerable,' Marcus fulminated. 'When a man is tried and acquitted – that, after all, was what the whole thing was for! And you remember how the crowds cheered –'

'Everyone loves a lord,' Rosamund said, 'as long as they're at a great enough distance from him. But I'm afraid he'll always be remembered as the lord who was tried for murdering his wife – not the lord who was found innocent.'

'Poor Harvey! He's lost everything. It isn't fair!'

'Yet he brought it all on himself,' Rosamund said. 'Too weak to insist on marrying Polly in the first place, and too

353

weak to leave her alone when he'd married Minnie. I wonder if that's why Polly's refusing to go away with him? Perhaps she's finally seen how weak he is, and fallen out of love with him.'

'Well, she was pretty weak, too,' Marcus said crossly. 'She should have repudiated him long before, and then all this might never have happened.'

'All what?' Rosamund asked him with grim significance. 'You mean he might never have murdered my sister?'

'God, no, of course –!' Marcus opened his eyes wide as he realised what his words had implied. 'Of course, you're right,' he said quietly. 'And he's right. There will always be a shadow over him. It would be better, perhaps, if he stayed abroad. He's rich enough now, at least, to live in style and comfort. But, oh Lord, what are we going to do with Polly?'

'Do with her?' Rosamund enquired, knowing exactly what he was going to say.

'Well, we can't keep her here. Mama don't like having her in the house as it is. And it isn't fair on Bab, either.'

'You want to send her away, do you? Perhaps you'd like to throw her out yourself?'

'Don't be unreasonable, love. I didn't mean that, but – well, it would be very awkward having her with us all the time. You know how unkind people can be.'

'People? Yes, your mother, for one. Can you give me any reason your mother's wishes and opinions should rule our lives? Can you give me a reason why she should live here with us at all?'

'She is my mother, for heaven's sake. And *she* didn't bring disgrace on the family,' Marcus said hotly.

'Polly's my cousin, and we were brought up together like sisters,' Rosamund said, in a hard, calm tone that was more chilling than anger. 'If Mother were here, she would feel herself responsible for Polly, and since she's not, I must take over that responsibility. And if you don't care to pay for her upkeep, I'll do so myself out of my own allowance.'

Marcus flushed at the last words. It was true that his mother had complained about the expense of keeping Polly almost as much as the shame, but she had done so only to him, and Rosamund couldn't possibly know about it.

'Don't be silly,' he said. 'I didn't mean to cast her off, as you very well know.'

354

'I know nothing,' Rosamund said turning away. 'Your mother seems to rule you just as much as before you were married. I wonder she took the trouble to make you propose to me.'

'There's no need for that!' Marcus began, hurt, but she turned on him swiftly.

'There's every need. I tell you this, Marcus, I won't have my every decision in this house questioned by her, and since I see no prospect of her changing her ways, you had better start thinking of a way to get her out of here and into her own establishment where she can do as she likes. In the mean time, since you feel it's a disgrace to have Polly in the house, I'll take her down to Wolvercote. She won't be any trouble – or expense – to you there.'

It was their first quarrel, and it upset Marcus a great deal more than Rosamund, for she was upset already on a far greater scale. She did carry out her scheme of taking Polly to Wolvercote, for when Harvey had left, there was nothing Polly wanted more than to get away from prying eyes and whispering tongues, and to return to what was, after all, her childhood home. The servants there had known her all her life, and would never think harshly of her, and she would have the whole of the park to wander in, with the sweetness of nature to restore her, and no strangers near.

For much the same reasons, Rosamund, having taken Polly to Wolvercote, stayed there, and for a week enjoyed the sensation of freedom from her mother-in-law's irksome restraint on her. But it didn't answer – Marcus had not married Rosamund to be apart from her, and was soon fretting to follow her into the country. At first Lady Barbara was for remaining in Town – company was a little thin, but there were many of her old friends who lived in London permanently, and it would not be long before the families started to return for the Season. But a few days sufficed to prove to her that the only thing anyone wanted to discuss with her was the Trial and Harvey Penrith's possible guilt. Soon she and Marcus and Barbarina were on their way to Wolvercote too, where Lady Barbara could comfort herself for the pain of having to share a roof with Polly Haworth by the gratifying knowledge that they were all living at Lady Theakston's expense.

That summer of 1818, England was treated to the diverting sight of the stout middle-aged sons of George III scrambling into marriage to secure the succession to the throne.

The death of Princess Charlotte had revealed in what a parlous state the succession lay. The King himself was an old man, now for many years hopelessly mad and shut away as a virtual prisoner at Windsor. He had done his duty by the throne, producing fifteen children by his queen, of whom seven sons and five daughters survived: but not one of these was under forty years of age, and with the death of Princess Charlotte, none of them had a single legitimate offspring to inherit the crown.

The Regent himself was fifty-five, and had separated from his legal wife, Princess Caroline, twenty years before, since when he had amused himself with a succession of mistresses all very much older than him. He was now grossly fat, and his health was impaired by the style of his living. Even if a way could be found to divorce him from Caroline, and to persuade him to remarry a woman young enough to conceive, it seemed unlikely that he would be able to father an heir.

The second in line, the Duke of York, was married to that 'pretty little Princess Fred' who had been Brummell's good friend and patroness. She lived in deep retirement at Oatlands surrounded by her pet animals, and had never produced a child. The third son, the Duke of Clarence, was fifty-two, and had been living for twenty years in quiet domesticity in a house at Bushey with his mistress – a retired actress named Mrs Jordan – and their ten illegitimate children.

The next son, Edward, Duke of Kent, had made his career in the army where he was renowned as a niggling despot and ferocious martinet, given to public executions and flogging men to death. He had never married, but lived in apparent content with his middle-aged Canadian mistress, Madame de St Laurent. The fifth son, Cumberland, was married to a twice-widowed princess and had no living child.

The Duke of Sussex had been married twice, and his first marriage had produced a son and a daughter, but since both marriages were contracted without the sovereign's permission, they were void under the terms of the Royal Marriages

Act, and the children were excluded from the succession. The Duke of Cambridge, the youngest of the princes at forty-three, lived mostly in Hanover in order to save money, and had never shewn any interest in women, not even having ever kept a mistress like his brothers.

Yet within a few months of the death of the Princess Charlotte, the three unmarried royal dukes had rushed helter-skelter into wedlock. Cambridge married the daughter of Frederick of Hesse-Cassel; Kent the thirty-year-old widowed Princess Victoire of Leiningen, who was the sister of the late Princess Charlotte's husband, and who had a son and daughter by her first marriage; and Clarence took the twenty-five-year-old Princess Adelaide of Saxe-Meiningen.

'We must simply hope the Clarences produce a child,' Marcus said one day in July as he read from the paper the account of the joint wedding ceremony at Kew Palace for the Kents and Clarences, 'for the notion of the Duke of Kent's offspring coming to the throne positively chills the blood. The man is quite mad, you know!'

'Really?' Rosamund enquired absently. She was trying to decipher a letter from her mother which, at some point on its long journey from Venice, had got wet, causing the ink to smear.

Marcus found this encouragement enough. 'Oh yes. When he was given command at Gibraltar in the year two, he instituted a positive reign of terror. There were such floggings and hangings and punishments that in the end the men grew desperate and there was a serious mutiny. The authorities had to remove him from command. If his blood is to produce the next heir to the throne, England will be lost indeed!'

'Poor Princess Charlotte was always fond of him,' Lady Barbara remarked stiffly. 'She called him her "favourite and beloved uncle". And my father used to say that he was not fairly treated by his parents.'

'Well, Mama, the Beau couldn't stand him at any price, and that's good enough for me,' said Marcus, to whom the Duke of Wellington was still the fount of all wisdom.

'The only thing I know about him is that he disapproves of docking horses,' said Rosamund, 'so I suppose he can't be all bad.'

'Trust you to know something like that!' Marcus said,

smiling. Lady Barbara looked as though she were thinking exactly the same thing, but with strong disapproval.

'Uncle Edward sold a horse to him once,' Rosamund explained. 'Still, if you're worried about blood-lines, we may have high hopes of the Duke of Clarence, mayn't we? He did have ten children by Mrs Jordan, after all.'

'Pity he couldn't have married her,' Marcus said.

'It's a great pity the Royal Marriages Act was ever passed at all,' Lady Barbara said vigorously. 'It meant that when the princes were young – and they were all handsome men – they simply ran wild in society, made love wherever they wanted, and then said they were very sorry they couldn't marry. It quite spoiled them. They'd have married respectably if it weren't for that.'

'The Duke of York married respectably,' Rosamund said provokingly, for the Duke had been a close friend of Lady Barbara's late husband, and she revelled in the high connection, 'and that didn't do any good. Look at that dreadful scandal about his mistress selling commissions. And then there was that business over his valet –'

Lady Barbara put her knife and fork down with a rap that almost broke the plate. 'I don't think we want that sort of talk at breakfast,' she said coldly, trying to stare Rosamund into a sense of shame. But Rosamund was close to breaking point, and she stared back with rising colour.

'I don't think I need you to tell me what I may and may not discuss at my own breakfast-table,' she said.

Lady Barbara gasped at the insolence. 'Your table? *Your* table?' Then she recollected the presence of her daughter, before whom some things ought not to be said. Polly was not present – she took breakfast on a tray in her own chamber. 'Barbarina, leave the room,' Lady Barbara snapped.

Barbarina was so used to her mother's ways that she rose to obey without hesitation, without even displaying any surprise. Rosamund glanced at her with rising annoyance.

'Don't go, Bab. You haven't finished your breakfast. Your mother can have nothing to say to me that you can't hear.'

'Oh no, really, I'd sooner –' Barbarina murmured, glancing anxiously at her mother.

'Leave us!' Lady Barbara snapped, and Bab scuttled away gratefully. When the door had closed behind her, Rosamund turned on her mother-in-law.

'And now you have bullied her yet again, ma'am, it's time for you to learn that you do not give the commands in this house – I do. I shall say who sits at the table, and what is discussed there.'

'Oh will you, indeed?' Lady Barbara flared. 'How dare you, you insolent sprite? Never in my life have I been spoken to in such a manner!'

'That's the pity of it. It might have taught you something,' Rosamund snapped.

'You would presume to teach me, would you? Let me tell you it's you who have things to learn – a little conduct, to begin with! And respect for your elders!'

'Respect!'

'Something your mother evidently forgot to teach you – one of the many things, I may say –'

'Before you insult my mother, you might remember that we're living in her house – and at her expense, which no doubt pleases you no end!'

'It doesn't please me at all. If it weren't for the complete lack of morality and conduct of your cousin – who was brought up by your mother, let's remember – we would not be forced to rusticate in order to avoid public scandal!'

'You're forgetting that Lord Penrith is *your* cousin!'

'Oh stop it, please!' Marcus cried at last, having watched the stones fly backwards and forwards long enough. 'I can't bear it. Mama, Ros, please don't quarrel like this!'

Lady Barbara turned an outraged face to him. 'Quarrel? It is beneath my dignity to quarrel, and especially with my own daughter-in-law.'

'There will be no quarrelling,' Rosamund said, striving for equal dignity, 'if your mother learns that I intend to be mistress in my own house.'

Lady Barbara's head snapped round to her. 'Let me remind you whose son you have married! I am senior to you in years, consequence and sense, and my son will not see me slighted or insulted by a chit of a girl who vowed not so long ago to *obey* him! Marcus, I think your wife needs a few words from you on how to behave herself.'

Marcus looked from her to Rosamund, a picture of misery and indecision. 'Oh Ros, darling, please –'

Rosamund stood up, trembling with all the things she wanted to say, and dared not. 'You side with her, as always,' was all she did say. 'I told you when you proposed to me that I wouldn't marry your mother. I think you must have forgotten what your answer was on that occasion.'

And with that she turned and went out, leaving Marcus to answer his mother's inevitable next question as best he could. That, she thought furiously as she closed the door on them, could be his punishment for being so weak. Looking for comfort, she headed automatically for the stables and the large and soothing presence of the horses. Perhaps she would take Magnus Apollo out for a gallop and let the thunder of his hooves drive the restless rage out of her.

In the stables she found Parslow, just finishing grooming Magnus.

'He'll be ready for you in a moment or two, my lady,' Parslow said when he had returned her greeting. 'I just have to do his hooves.'

'Don't hurry,' Rosamund said, though Parslow shewed no sign of doing any such thing. She leaned on the pillar at the end of the stall and rested her chin on her hand. 'I don't mind waiting.'

Parslow drew up Magnus's near hind hoof between his legs and settled it comfortably against his thigh. He glanced up at Rosamund quickly, gauging her mood, and then said quietly, 'Adjustments always take time, my lady. And while they're going on, it always feels as if things will never be right again.'

'I don't know that they will,' she sighed. 'How can there be an adjustment? She won't ever change her ways. For things to be right again, it would mean my giving in to her all the time, and I don't call that an adjustment.'

'No point in riding through a bog if you can ride round it,' Parslow said, scraping the sole of the hoof clean and delicately probing the frog with his hoof-pick. 'You know the Duke always said you should get over heavy ground as lightly as possible.'

'The Duke didn't have Lady Barbara for a mother-in-law. If only she'd leave and set up home on her own! But she'll never do that while she's comfortable with us.'

Parslow set down Magnus's near hind and straightened up, looked at his young mistress thoughtfully, and then, leaning on the shiny bay rump beside him, said, 'Have you ever seen a fox get rid of its fleas, my lady?'

Rosamund burst out laughing, making Magnus turn his head to look at her in surprise. 'Better not let anyone hear you liken her ladyship to fleas! Tell me, then, what a fox does.'

'It finds a scrap of sheep's wool, my lady. It holds it in its teeth, goes to the river, and starts to walk into the water backwards.'

'Backwards?'

'And very slowly. Of course, feeling the cold water come through the pelt, the fleas move away from it. They scurry ahead of the water up the fox's body, over its head, and finally, when there's nowhere else to go, they climb onto the sheep's wool. And when the fox is completely submerged, all but the tip of its muzzle, it lets go the fleece, and the fleas go sailing off down the river.'

'Parslow, that's the biggest horse-story I've ever heard! How do you expect to get to heaven if you tell such terrible whiskers?'

Parslow smiled enigmatically. 'They say the fox is a wily beast.'

Rosamund pondered. 'But look here, I've already moved down here to Wolvercote, and she's still with us.'

'Perhaps you have to get further into the water, my lady.'

'Move again? But where? Deeper into the country, I suppose, and further from London.'

'Race week is not so long away, my lady. Your predecessor often used to have parties at Shawes for race week.'

Rosamund's face lit up. 'Yorkshire! Of course! I was forgetting we owned Shawes too! Parslow, you wily old fox, I do believe you've hit on it! Lady Barbara hates Yorkshire.'

'Yes, my lady – and if you make sure she knows you're taking Miss Haworth with you, it will give her ladyship a very good excuse not to accompany you.'

'Lord yes, Polly! I'd forgotten. It would do Polly good to go to Yorkshire, and especially to Morland Place. She'd have the chance to see that the rest of the world has other things to think about than her disgrace. Parslow, you're a wonder. Why didn't I think of it myself?'

'You've had a great deal on your mind, my lady,' Parslow

said kindly. She met his eyes and saw the real sympathy there, which brought a few foolish tears to her own. She blinked them away determinedly.

'Don't encourage me to be weak. Poor Minnie! I was no comfort to her when she was alive, and I forget her just as easily as everyone else now she's dead.'

'Not quite as easily, my lady. Would you like to take Magnus out now? He needs a good gallop to settle him down.'

'You mean *I* do. Yes, I'll take him out – and you had better come with me on Hotspur, for I shan't have time to exercise him today, with all the plans I have to make.'

'Very good, my lady.'

'And Parslow – thank you for suggesting the plan.'

He permitted himself a small smile. 'I love Yorkshire as much as her ladyship hates it, my lady.'

So it was that Rosamund was present at Morland Place for the unveiling ceremony of the new kitchen chimney.

'And really, you know,' said Mathilde proudly, 'John has done wonderfully well to finish it in only eighteen months. It was a dreadful mess. You simply can't imagine.'

'The upper floors aren't finished yet,' Héloïse explained to Rosamund. 'The north bedroom hasn't either a floor or a ceiling, but that will be attended to in time. The most important thing was to get poor Barnard back into his kitchen.'

'He and John have been poring over plans for weeks now,' Mathilde said. 'At least there won't be any doubt that it will be exactly the way he wants it.'

'Complete with open fire and roasting-spit,' Héloïse said with a smile. 'Barnard is no reformist in the kitchen. Ah, here they come now. Have you your tinder-box, James?'

'Here, my love, and ready,' James said appearing in the hall with John Skelwith, Marcus, Father Moineau and the boys, and the cook. There was Miss Rosedale, too, with Polly – they had been having long conversations together ever since the Chelmsford party's arrival at Shawes – and between them, holding a hand each, was Mathilde's daughter Mary. She was eighteen months old, an enterprising young scamp with round, brown eyes and fox-brown hair and a smile that was uncannily like James's when she wanted to please.

Behind them the servants crowded into the hall, eager for the moment that would signal a return to normality and comfort. The family moved into the kitchen passage, and there was the red curtain John Skelwith had hung over the kitchen door so that they could have a proper unveiling. James took the cord in his hand, and then looked about the group.

'Who shall have the honour? Rosamund, my dear, as our most distinguished guest –?'

Rosamund shrank back. 'No, no, Polly should do it,' she said quickly. 'Mama says my grandmother always called her the senior grandchild. She takes precedence over me in family matters.'

Polly looked at her with a wry smile, and said, 'Thank you. I should be honoured – but shall we let little Mary do it? A new generation for the new kitchen.'

'Yes, that's right and good,' Héloïse said warmly, looking at Polly approvingly. The fall of the old chimney had caused Edward's death, but as he died, so Mary had been born. Life out of death, renewal, the natural cycle. Let them always look forward, not back. 'Mary shall pull the cord.'

Lifted up in her father's arms, Mary Skelwith – with no clear idea of what it all meant, other than that she was the centre of attention, which in her mind was right and proper – grasped the cord in her fat little fist and pulled. The red curtain fell away, and through the doorway – the door having been fixed back for the purpose – they looked into the new kitchen and at the fireplace straight ahead of them.

'*Tiens*!' said Héloïse, and turned to look at her sheepishly-smiling cook. 'It was all done to your specific instructions, was it?'

'Wonders will never cease,' James said profoundly. They all streamed into the kitchen, where under the arch of the new chimney was no open grate, no roasting spit, trivets, jacks and pulleys – but a large, glossy, gleaming new Rumford cooking-stove.

They crowded forward, examining and exclaiming over the arrangements. Everything was as modern and convenient as could be, right down to a new copper with its own fire and separate flue for heating bath-water.

'No more succession of heavy kettles, and maids scalding

themselves, and putting the fire out,' James marvelled when it was demonstrated to him how the hot water poured out of a tap on the side of the copper.

'Everyone could bath at the same time. And you could have the bath as full as you liked,' Mathilde said. 'This is something I should dearly like at home, John. John?'

John Skelwith was demonstrating the wonders of the stove to Marcus and Miss Rosedale. 'There are five ovens, you see, of varying size and heat, and the plates on the top are for simmering or boiling or frying – whatever you please. The bread oven is separate, of course, although you can bake in these two ovens as well if you need to. And if you want to roast in the old fashioned way, over an open fire, you just lift this lid –' he did so with a flourish, 'and fit the uprights into these holes here and here, and there's your spit!'

'Oh, the swan window,' Mathilde exclaimed to Héloïse. 'I'm so glad you had it put back. The poor swans must have been so confused all these months.'

'It will take time for them to remember the old routine, I expect,' Héloïse said. 'James, had we not better get on with lighting the fire? Barnard will want to start cooking.'

'Yes, of course. I have my tinder-box here. Barnard, come forward, that's right. Take the taper and be ready.'

In a moment he had struck the spark and lit the tinder. Barnard lit the taper from it, and under Skelwith's guidance knelt down and touched the flame to the paper laid ready in the fire-box of the new stove. The paper bloomed into flame, and in a moment or two the kindling was crackling vigorously, and the first plume of smoke was passing invisibly up the flue into the new chimney. Having seen that it had caught properly, Barnard closed the fire door, stood up, and with an unexpected grin, took a deep and theatrical bow to the cheers and applause of the watching family and servants.

Later the family gathered in the dining-room to take a celebratory luncheon of cold foods, while Barnard got on with christening his stove, and the servants with restoring order to the servants' hall.

'I wish Sophie had been here to see it,' Héloïse said, a little wistfully. 'Barnard was always such a favourite of hers.'

'Will she be back for race week, aunt?' Rosamund asked. 'I haven't seen her for such a long time.'

'I don't quite know,' Héloïse said. 'Mrs Droylsden asked her to stay for the summer, but no date was set for her return. I suppose she will come back for race week – it would be a shame for her to miss it.'

'On the other hand,' said Miss Rosedale drily, 'if she's enjoying herself so much in Manchester, she may not want to leave.'

'What does she do there that's so much fun?' Rosamund wanted to know. 'I suppose it's quite a lively town?'

Mathilde answered for Héloïse. 'They say so, but I don't think that's what Sophie goes for – is it, Madame? She spends her time with her friends going amongst the poor people and doing good works.'

Rosamund raised her brows. 'What an odd choice,' she said, and catching Marcus's eye, saw him frown and shake his head slightly – thinking, no doubt, that there must have been some mismanagement for things to come to such a pass. 'Is she happy, ma'am?'

'I believe so,' Héloïse said, understanding pretty well what she was being asked. 'She wanted most urgently to go, or I should not have let her, for I do miss her very much, and if it were just balls and assemblies, she could have them here in York as well as in Manchester. But she's very interested in the welfare of the mill-workers – especially since we've now decided we shan't be selling the mills.'

'Oh, I didn't know you'd thought of doing so,' said Rosamund.

'They weren't doing well, and we needed capital,' James explained, 'but now trade has improved, and they're working at full capacity, we're glad we kept them. And we're to start mechanical weaving next year, if all goes to plan. That's where the new plans come in.'

'New plans?' Rosamund and Marcus asked simultaneously.

'When we open the new factory, we'll be employing another three hundred people,' James said, 'and they'll need somewhere to live. So John here is to build us some special housing on the empty plot right next to the factory, and we'll rent it out to the employees for a nominal sum.'

'Ah, yes, I see,' said Rosamund. 'You'll have extra control over them that way. If they misbehave, they'll not only lose their job but their home as well.'

Héloïse blinked. 'I don't think that was exactly what we had in mind. It was really more for their welfare. Mr Hobsbawn believes that happy, healthy individuals work harder and better than sick, unhappy ones.'

James grinned at her. 'It may not have been in your mind, my love, but I have to confess it crossed mine all right!'

'Mr Hobsbawn?' Rosamund said. 'That would be the cousin who was expected to inherit everything, would it?'

'Yes, that's right. He's our mill-manager,' James said.

'He's something of a philanthropist, too,' Héloïse said. 'These plans for rational housing for the mill-hands are only the beginning of his ideas. I can't say that I would go all the way with him, but Sophie seems to agree with much of what he says.'

'Does she?' said Rosamund thoughtfully.

'Well, I suppose we must allow that she has seen the conditions they live in, and we haven't,' Héloïse said bravely. 'All the same –'

'All the same,' Marcus said, 'that's the way it's always been, and that's the way it will always be. It's as difficult to elevate the poor as it is to depress the rich by anything we do.'

'Exactly so,' said Héloïse. 'I'm never sure how far we ought to interfere. Is it God's will that they should suffer, or that we should exert ourselves? It has me in a puzzle. What do you think, Father?'

Father Moineau looked up from the creamed chicken patties which had been occupying his attention to the exclusion of all else. A serious question had obviously been asked him which demanded a considered answer. He swallowed the present mouthful of delicately-spiced chicken, cream sauce and crisp golden pastry, remembering nothing about the question but that there had been an 'or' in the middle of it. But he had his reputation for wisdom to maintain.

'A little of both, I should imagine,' he said confidently.

CHAPTER NINETEEN

John Anstey returned to Yorkshire and the bosom of his family in time for race week, and paid a call on Rosamund at Shawes.

'And very fine you look in this setting, too,' he said, as she received him in the green drawing-room. 'Being a countess suits you.'

'Thank you,' said Rosamund. 'I must thank you, too, for all your help during the trial.'

'It was little enough I did – I wish it had been more. But of course there was nothing much to *be* done.'

'Your support was everything, and your great kindness –'

'Tush! No need for that. How is Polly, by the by? How does she take it?'

'She seems to have revived since she's been here. I think getting away has done her good. Even though we saw little company at Wolvercote, I think she still felt the scandal hung around her. Up here people have other things to think about.'

'Hmm,' Anstey said thoughtfully. 'I wonder, then – perhaps she might make her home up here permanently? What are her plans, do you know?'

'I don't think she has any,' Rosamund said with a short, revealing sigh. 'She seems to go from day to day in a daze. It's a year now since Minnie died, but she doesn't seem much better than during the first weeks.'

'There's no reason, at least, why she should continue to be a burden on you.'

'Oh, but she isn't,' Rosamund said in surprise.

'I didn't mean financially,' Anstey said. 'Besides, as far as that goes, I know your mother would want you to take responsibility in her absence. I meant a burden on your spirits. You're looking fagged and drawn, my dear. It's all been too much for you, young as you are, and just starting out in life. If you will permit me, I'll consult your aunt and

367

uncle about it. If Polly likes it, I'm sure they'll say there's no reason why she shouldn't make her home with them.'

'At Morland Place?'

'It was where she was born, after all, and where she lived while her mother was alive.'

Some of the shadow went from Rosamund's eyes. She had been finding the responsibility of Polly's endless misery very wearying. 'If it could be arranged, I think it would be the best thing for her. One could never be really unhappy at Morland Place, could one? But it must only be if it really is no trouble to anyone. You won't press my aunt and uncle if they aren't completely willing?'

'I promise you I won't.' Anstey surveyed her face. 'I think you're looking better already. Is your sister-in-law not with you?'

'No, she's in London with her mother. Lady Barbara didn't care to come to Yorkshire, and she wouldn't let Bab go without her. But Bab is no trouble to me, I assure you,' she anticipated his concern. 'I'm only sorry she can't be here to enjoy the fun.'

It was not Barbarina he was worried about, but he said no more, resolving instead when he was in London to keep a closer eye on Lucy's daughter. Now he said cheerfully, 'Race week this year is going to be the best ever. I've never seen so many fine horses. It's going to be hard to know which to fancy.'

Rosamund smiled. 'And there are more balls and routs and assemblies than I can believe. It's a pity we came so much at the last minute. Next year, I'm resolved we shall have one here at Shawes, and outshine them all!'

'Brava! A ball at Shawes would be a splendid thing indeed! I don't remember when the last one was. You will be doing everyone a service if you set yourself to becoming a great *entertaining* countess, my dear. There's been too little of that since the end of the war.'

'Yes, they've been difficult years, haven't they? Well, perhaps the hard times are behind us now.'

'Let's hope so. And now, I'm charged by Louisa to ask if you will honour us by coming to dinner with us at Lendal House, and if it pleases you, to name the day which would be most convenient to you. Any day will suit us except next

Tuesday, when we are engaged away. What do you say? Just a comfortable family dinner, and a few friends. We don't live in a grand way, as I expect you know.'

Anstey scanned her face as he made the invitation, and was glad to see her looking less tense and unhappy than when he had arrived. It had been a great deal for such a young woman to bear, he thought, even – or perhaps especially – such a brave young woman. And after her experiences in Belgium, too. He would make·sure the family dinner was as informal as possible, and that the children played some silly games afterwards that everyone could join in. It struck him that Rosamund needed to romp a little, as he would have expected her husband to know. But then husbands and wives did sometimes lose touch with each other. More importantly he would talk to James and Héloïse about Polly. That was something real and practical he could do to help her.

Rosamund's drawn and fatigued looks were not all due to the strain of the past year: there was quite another reason, which she could not divulge to anyone, least of all to kind Lord Anstey. Along with all her other worries had been the growing suspicion that she might be with child. Her flux, which had always arrived with clockwork regularity, was late.

For the first few days she had told herself that it was nothing to worry about, that it was late only because she was not quite well, a little fatigued and pulled; but by the time it was two weeks late, she began to fear the worst. She had no desire to be pregnant: the idea both frightened and dismayed her. Already her freedom – the freedom for which she had married Marcus in the first place – was curtailed by the disapproving presence of her mother-in-law. If she were with child, it would disappear entirely. She would not be able to ride for a whole year, or travel, or dance, or do anything energetic; and for the last months of the pregnancy she would scarcely be allowed to stir out of the doors, for heavily pregnant women were not expected to go into company.

Then there would be the childbirth itself, a prospect she retreated from even mentally. To go through that all alone – her mother, even Docwra far away, and none but strangers to attend her! She might die – she knew the chances. Only last year the Princess Charlotte had died in childbed after hours of the most terrible torture, she who might have been supposed to have the very best of care and attention that rank or money could acquire.

And afterwards, if she survived, as the mother of a child she would be expected to behave with dignity, forswear youthful pleasures, and shew a maternal interest in the brat. Every time she met another woman, whether in a drawing-room, a ballroom, at the dining-table or in the Park, they would talk to her about babies, nurses, colic and teething – all the tedious things she had heard other women talking about for years.

There was nothing about the business to like, in fact. She supposed that, as her duty to Marcus, she must try to give him an heir eventually – but oh, please God, not yet! She was too young, she had not finished enjoying herself – oh please, not yet!

It was Moss, of course, who discovered her trouble – no-one else was in a position to find out the truth so soon. Knowing her lady's rhythms as well as her lady, she probably suspected as soon as Rosamund did, and had Rosamund appeared pleased she would not have dreamed of saying anything until Rosamund told her. As it was, Moss watched her growing more tense and anxious day by day, which didn't seem natural in a young woman just a year wed; and so, out of concern and affection, she took a chance and mentioned it.

While she was brushing Rosamund's hair one morning, she said very casually, 'If I don't mistake, my lady, it seems to me a visitor we were expecting hasn't arrived on time.'

Rosamund looked up and met her eyes in the glass. Moss was shocked at how unhappy she looked. If *she* were married to his lordship, she'd be as pleased as punch to be in the family way, and not call it a bit too soon, either. But her lady looked at her with haunted eyes, and said, 'You've noticed, then. Do you think it means anything?'

'Well, my lady, with some people, I'd say it was too early to be sure; but our visitor's always been so punctual, like. I think,' she added with a last, vain hope that Rosamund might be pleased, 'you might flatter yourself, my lady, and say it was so. Just between ourselves, of course.'

The hope proved how vain it was. 'Flatter myself? Don't talk such faddle!'

'Why, sure, my lady, you want to have a baby?'

'Of course not. I can't think of anything I want less,' Rosamund snapped. 'Oh damn, damn, why did this have to happen?'

Hiding her own distress at this revelation, Moss tried to comfort her mistress. 'Well, my lady, we can't be sure yet, can we? It's early days.'

'You were just telling me I might flatter myself,' Rosamund said bitterly. 'And you're quite right, of course – I've always been regular. Oh lord, what did I do to deserve this?'

Moss went on brushing and arranging the coppery hair, and said no more for the moment. She hoped her lady would become reconciled to the idea; would begin to be pleased, in fact, in the normal, expected way. But each day saw her looking more haggard and unhappy, and Moss realised that it wouldn't do.

Coming to her on the first day in Yorkshire to wake her up, she said, 'Can I speak to you, my lady?'

'Yes, of course,' Rosamund said absently. 'What about?'

'About – you know what, my lady. What hasn't happened that you wish had happened.'

'Oh that! Yes – what about it? You haven't told anyone, have you?' she added in alarm.

'Of course not, my lady,' Moss said, accepting that young ladies did say irrational things at times. 'Who would I tell? No, I was thinking, my lady, that if you really didn't want – I mean, it isn't sure, yet, is it? And you'd have to promise never to tell your mother or Mrs Docwra about it, for they'd be mortal angry – but sometimes there are things that can be done.'

'Done?' Rosamund looked a little pale. 'What things? You mean –'

'It can be encouraged to happen – what hasn't happened. You know. But you mustn't say I told you so, my lady, please!'

'I see,' Rosamund said slowly. 'Well, of course I wouldn't tell anyone. But what would I have to do?'

'There are several things you could try. A really long ride is the first, lots of galloping and jumping, as much as you can manage. And then as soon as you come in, a long sit in a hot bath.'

'Yes,' said Rosamund slowly, 'I see. Of course, no-one would think anything of my going riding, would they?'

'No, my lady, that's what I thought.'

'And here at Shawes they have that lovely bath-house, which it would be natural for me to want to try out. Well, and that would do the trick, would it?'

'It's not sure, my lady, but it often does. Only – don't you think you ought to speak to his lordship first?'

'Good God, no!' Rosamund said, horrified. 'That's the last thing! Very well, Judy, I'll try it. I'll go out for a long gallop today. I wish my own horses were here. I suppose they must still be somewhere around Grantham. I shall have to borrow a horse from Morland Place. Put out my habit, and when you go downstairs, send word – no, wait a minute, I'd better write a note. Bring me paper and pen, will you? Now I come to think of it, it's probably better that Parslow isn't here, anyway. He has an uncomfortable way of knowing things.'

'Yes, my lady,' said Moss blankly. How could Parslow, a bachelor, know anything about the internal workings of a lady, she thought? The idea was preposterous.

But three days of hard riding and hot bathing had not done the trick. Even Marcus now noticed Rosamund was looking pulled, and what with the hard riding, he put two and two together and assumed she was trying to take her mind off the troubles of the past year with physical exercise. Trying to be tactful, he asked her quite mildly not to overtire herself.

'I won't risk asking you to be careful, after you bit my head off the last time,' he smiled, 'but remember we can stay here as long as you like. You don't have to try out all the horses in the first few days, you know.'

'Don't fuss me, Marcus,' was all his lady vouchsafed by way of answer.

'I won't, love, but you are looking awfully tired.'

'Stuff! I'm perfectly all right,' Rosamund said, looking far from all right.

'You don't want to knock yourself up before Parslow arrives with Magnus, and not be able to enjoy him, do you?' Marcus said cunningly.

'I'm as strong as a horse,' she said vigorously, 'and I have enough of being told what I may and may not do in London. Don't you begin on that here.'

Marcus felt it wiser to leave it there. When she was alone again, Rosamund sent for Moss.

'It's not working,' she said desperately. 'We've got to do something. Isn't there something else to try?'

'Yes, my lady,' said Moss, putting her doubts behind her. It surely could not be worse for her lady than worrying so much.

That day, whenever she could be sure of not being discovered, Rosamund jumped down off things – chairs, stools, benches, boxes – landing as heavily as she could; and that night as she prepared for bed, Moss brought her a bitter concoction to drink, which she said was made from periwinkle, broom, juniper, elder and foxglove. It looked brown and cloudy, and tasted disgusting.

'I hope I've got it right, my lady,' Moss said anxiously. 'I was told *what* to use, but not how much of each thing, so I had to guess.'

'I hope so too. I also hope you haven't poisoned me,' Rosamund said as she handed back the empty cup.

Half an hour later, she was suffering from an acute stomach-ache. She lay hunched up in her bed, her knees drawn up, sweating a little, groaning softly, and deeply thankful that Marcus had not chosen this night to sleep with her. After a while she began to be afraid that she might really have been poisoned, and wondered whether she ought to call for help; but then it would all come out about the tisane, and she didn't want that. Fortunately the stomach pains began to wear off shortly afterwards, and she fell at last into an exhausted sleep.

When she woke in the morning, she found that either the jumping or the herbal potion had worked: she was bleeding. A wave of enormous relief washed over her, making her feel quite weak, and when Moss came in she told her the news in a voice high with euphoria.

'Yes, my lady? I'm very glad for you, my lady,' Moss said in a voice brimming with gloom.

'You don't sound it,' Rosamund said. Of course, servants always wanted their mistresses to be having babies – and all very well for them! she thought savagely. But Moss's lack of enthusiasm had punctured the balloon of her relief. As she washed and dressed, her gladness seeped slowly away, to be replaced with a sense of anticlimax, and, oddly, disappointment. She shook that away, angry with herself, and reminded herself of the horrible fate she had avoided.

But as the day wore on, she began to feel guilty and depressed. If Marcus knew, how upset, how angry he would be! He, of course, would love her to have his child. Well, he was not the one who had to go through with it. All the same, she felt she had cheated him, done something dishonest by him. And what of her mother? If her mother ever found out, she would be horrified, Rosamund was sure. It was a bad thing to do, wasn't it? Unnatural – a sin, even.

Oh damn those feelings! Out with those thoughts! It was done now, and that was that, and having taken the decision and gone through with it, it was foolish beyond permission to agonise over it. Besides, it might have happened anyway. The things she had done might have had nothing to do with it. She was only a few weeks late. She might not have been with child at all.

And then, ever the realist, she told herself that she had better hope it was Moss's remedies that had done the trick, or what would she do next time it happened? But a further conversation with her maid told her that it might not have to come to that another time. Moss told her that there were times when a woman was more likely to conceive than others, and if she avoided her husband's embraces at those times, she might manage very well without ever falling pregnant.

'Why, my lady, there are fashionable ladies in London – you'd know which ones better than me, I dare say – who don't have babies, and never even have to go riding, if you understand me.'

'I understand you very well,' Rosamund said with a grimace; and then, not to be ungracious, 'Thank you, Judy. I do appreciate your help, and I'll buy you something nice next time I go into York.'

'Thank you, my lady. There's no need – but thank you.'

'By the way –' Rosamund called her maid back from the door, 'where did you find out these things?'

'When we were in Brussels, my lady. Some of those foreign maids were real knowing creatures – and my, how they liked to talk!'

In Brussels, yes – it fitted, Rosamund thought as Moss went out. She looked at her pale reflection in the glass, and felt a hundred years old. She wondered which ladies of her acquaintance had maids with that sort of knowledge. None in London that she could believe it of – except perhaps Lady Greyshott, who was reputed to have had a great many lovers, but had only had the two children. In Brussels, of course, the presence of the Allied Army had attracted a much more dashing set. Amongst them, Marcus's Lady Annabel, for one, must have known what was what, she was sure. Yes, Lady Annabel would surely, in her long and dishonourable career, have had to have recourse to jumping.

When John Anstey raised the question, Héloïse expressed herself more than willing to offer Polly a home at Morland Place.

'I know what it is to be homeless, and unhappy, and afraid,' she said to James when they were alone together. 'I only don't know why I didn't think of it before. Since Lucy is abroad, this is the obvious place for Polly to live.'

'I'd have thought that with Rosamund was the obvious place,' James said, 'but however, I don't mean to put objects in the way. If she'd be happier here, I have nothing to say against it. There's plenty of room in the house, and she's so quiet, I dare say we'd never even notice her.'

'Much too quiet,' Héloïse said. 'She's like a person newly bereaved. I wonder if there is something more troubling her that we don't know about.'

'She seems to have taken to Miss Rosedale,' said James. 'Perhaps she could talk to her and find out.'

'Yes, of course. What a good idea! When I think how dear Rosey did such wonders with Fanny – though the cases were quite different of course – she must be the very person to get Polly to confide in her.'

'I'm sure Rosey would relish the task. You know she feels she hasn't enough to do to earn her salary. If she can help that poor tormented young woman, she will have earned it ten times over.'

The Morland box in the grandstand was crowded on the opening day of the meeting, for the Ansteys traditionally shared it on that occasion, and various friends were walking up all day to sit for a while and chat, to take a glass of champagne, or share a cigar and some inside information.

'Put your money on The Dook,' James advised everyone cheerfully. 'It's the best advice I can give you.'

'But the odds are so short. Seven to four on is the best I can get,' Lord Anstey complained.

'That's because he's going to win,' James said simply. 'Would I offer you a loser? I brought that colt up by hand, I know him.'

'I'd sooner you offered me an outsider.'

'Put Louisa's money on him, then – she won't care about the odds, she'll simply enjoy seeing him romp home!'

Father Moineau leaned across. 'Be advised, sir, that Mr Morland's money is entirely elsewhere! A very pretty horse by the name of Turkish Princess, I believe –'

'Treachery!' James cried in mock wrath. 'That's the last time I discuss horses in the confessional!'

'Would I break the confessional, sir?' Moineau said, pretending outrage. 'No, I was standing beside you when you placed the bet, don't you remember?'

'Oh you villain, James,' Anstey grinned. 'Turkish Princess, eh? Chubb's new filly! And what were her odds – a little longer than seven to four on, I imagine?'

'A hundred to one,' James said with a shrug. 'Well, there's no point in betting on the favourite, is there? And I reared Princess by hand as well – sold her to Chubb last month. She's a scud, and has a heart like a house!'

'Yes, I see – this way you're covered. If The Dook wins, you have the prize money, and if Princess wins, you have the betting money –'

'And either way it's a Morland horse, so we get the fame!'

'And how much did you put on Turkish Princess, may one ask?'

James dropped a wink. 'A hundred. But for God's sake, don't tell Héloïse! Oh Lord, I wish Ned were here!' he sighed. 'It just doesn't seem the same without him.'

'Don't tell me what?' Héloïse asked, joining them with Polly and Miss Rosedale.

'Nothing, my love. Well, Polly, have you chosen your horse yet?'

'Not yet, uncle. Aunt Héloïse has just invited me to make my home at Morland Place.'

'Ah, yes, good. And have you accepted?'

'It is most awfully good of you, sir, but I'm afraid I would be a burden to you.'

'Of course you wouldn't,' Héloïse said. 'Family is never a burden. And if you feel you must have something useful to do, you can always help Miss Rosedale – she has so much to do, it is hard for her to get through it all.'

'Yes, that's right,' Miss Rosedale said without blinking. 'I should be glad of a hand now and then.'

'Well, in that case, if you're sure –' said Polly doubtfully.

'It must be as *you* choose, my dear,' James said. 'If you feel you would be happy here, we would like to have you.'

'And it would be lovely for Sophie to have a companion,' Héloïse added.

'If she ever comes back from Manchester,' James added drily. 'Our daughter seems to have lost her heart to those dirty old mills. To miss race week, of all things!'

'She will be back soon,' Héloïse said soothingly. 'You know she never cared for horses as Fanny did. She takes after me, I'm afraid, rather than you, my James. But I know you're a fine horsewoman, Polly – isn't she, James?'

'She should be – she had the best teacher! So is it settled then? Are you to come and live with us?'

'If you please, uncle,' Polly said, looking happy in a bewildered sort of way. 'I should like it very much. But I must speak to Rosamund first. She's been so kind to me, I couldn't arrange anything without consulting her.'

'We'll ask her now, shall we?' Miss Rosedale said. 'No time like the present.'

'She's gone with Mathilde and John to look at the horses,' Héloïse said.

'Well, I feel like stretching my legs,' said Miss Rosedale. 'Will you walk with me, Polly?'

'Yes – gladly.'

Rosamund had indeed gone to the collecting-ring with Mathilde and John, but had managed to lose them in the press of people when she got there. She had accepted their invitation to get away from Marcus, who was being solicitous; but Mathilde had been talking almost without drawing breath about her Expectations, which had been confirmed only that morning to a sufficient degree to make the news public.

John listened with complacency as his wife talked about the date the new child was expected, and how they hoped it would be a boy this time so that John would have a son to carry on his business after him, but how they would be quite content if it were another girl, for Mary was such a model child, and it would be nice for her to have a sister to play with, and how they were going to tell Mary about the news and how they thought she would take it, and how John wanted to engage an accoucheur this time, but Mathilde was doubtful whether the expense was warranted . . .

And so on, and so on. It was exactly what Rosamund had dreaded she would be exposed to once she was a mother herself, and here she was suffering it anyway, which was ironic, considering her own recent activities. Quite apart from being boring, she found it unexpectedly upsetting. There was still a residual trace of guilt in her mind which Mathilde's chatter stirred up; and worst of all was that Mathilde was obviously blissfully happy to be with child, and John was almost equally so. They kept giving each other glances of tenderness and contentment which irritated Rosamund so much that she led them into the thick of the crowd gathered around the ring, and then allowed two very large gentlemen with cigars to come between her and them and cut her off from them.

It was perfectly easy then to slip through the press to the other side of the ring, where she could look at the horses in peace. What a comfort horses were! she thought. So beautiful, so elegant, with their glossy coats and slender legs and bright, kind eyes; so simple and uncomplicated in their loves and their requirements. The Morland colt, The Dook, went past with his head up and his ears pricked, extremely full of himself, and giving a little fly-buck every now and then simply to show off. It was obvious that he liked the crowd: being hand-reared, he had never known anything but affectionate attention from human beings, and regarded them as his natural subjects. Oh, she thought, sighing, to be a horse!

'My thoughts exactly,' said a voice close beside her. 'Too handsome by half, and knows it.'

Her heart thumped irrationally as she looked up into Jesmond Farraline's beautiful face. 'Yes, it's what people have said about me, more times than I can count,' he went on, his eyes laughing into hers. 'Come, now, Lady Chelmsford, wasn't that what you were about to say? You may speak the truth to me – we have a pact, don't you remember?'

'What are you doing here?' was what she did eventually say.

'I'm trying to pick the winner, of course, though I'm afraid it's all too obvious, and the odds will not be worth placing a bet for. You Morlands breed lovely animals, don't you? Lovely, handsome, and full of spirit.'

His voice was caressive, and he was looking at her in that way that made the world stand still around them. She knew perfectly well that when he said 'lovely animals', he was no longer talking about the horses. It was outrageous for a man to call a woman an animal, and yet it was strangely exciting, and in a curious way – just at the moment – true. They were male and female animal, standing alone together in an otherwise empty world, like Adam and Eve, just that instant created and knowing nothing yet but that they existed. She had a brief, alarming vision of herself as naked as a horse turned out in a field, and as free. God, that life could ever be that simple!

'The Dook will certainly win,' she said, iceberg-like. 'My uncle James says so, and he should know. But what I meant was, how can you leave your mills to be here? Don't they require constant attention?'

'Just at the moment, everything is going so well that I am able to leave them for a much-needed holiday. We are working at full capacity, orders are coming in fast, and my manager and overseers have only to keep the wheels turning. I found myself suddenly *de trop*, and recollecting it was race week, thought I would take time for a little recreation. How splendid to find you here, though!'

'Have you seen my cousin Sophie in Manchester?' she asked abruptly.

'Yes, I have. I see her quite often. She is staying with Mrs Percy Droylsden again, and thank God for it!'

'Why?'

'Because Mrs Droylsden makes her go into society, to dances and concerts and assemblies. Otherwise she would spend all her time grubbing about in the tenements helping sick mill-hands. Your cousin is a young woman with a

379

passionate need to love, and at the moment, no-one is making use of it. So she wastes herself on philanthropy.'

'So much concern for her well being, Mr Farraline? What is it to you whether she wastes her love?'

He smiled, quite unprovoked. 'She is my friend's sister-in-law. Fitz cares about her, and so must I. In any case, am I such a block, am I so insensate and selfish that I can't care for what is worth caring about? Miss Morland is a lovely young woman, as I have cause to know. She and I have become great friends.'

'Friends? Can a man and a woman be friends?'

'What a bitter question! Of course they can – and if you can ask it, you must need a friend very badly. Well, here I am – make use of me. And, yes – for I see the question in your doubting eyes – I did know you were here. Your cousin Sophie told me she had had a letter from you from Yorkshire. She sends her love and everything appropriate.'

'Is she happy? She tells me nothing in her letters about herself.'

'She is on the verge of being happy,' Farraline said. 'I am doing what I can to advance her cause.'

'You? What can you do for her? Are you intending to make her an offer?'

He laughed. 'That would not advance her happiness, I assure you. I am in no position to take a wife without a large dowry. Oh, there was a time when she was my object, I admit. That was why Fitz introduced me to her in the first place –'

'What?' Rosamund looked scandalised.

'Yes – didn't you know? I thought he must have told you that, or that you would have guessed it.'

'Not precisely,' she said grimly. 'I suspected it at first, but Sophie is not an heiress. Then Mr Hawker revealed to me that he had thought she would inherit Morland Place. But I always thought it was for himself that he intended her, not for you.'

'It was not Morland Place, but the mills I was after,' Farraline said frankly. 'They would have fitted very nicely with mine – and I had every hope that if I married the Hobsbawn mills, Kit would give me the Ordsall mills for my own.'

'Oh you villain! How can you confess to me so calmly that

380

you had such dastardly plans towards my cousin? Don't you know I love her?'

He raised his brows. 'Why do you call it dastardly? I meant to make her an honourable proposal, to marry her and dedicate myself to making her happy – indeed, I always meant to make her happy! I would not do less for any woman I married. Pride alone would require it, leaving aside any question of affection.'

'Worse and worse! What false coin you would have offered!'

He looked offended. 'I'm not so despicable a match, am I? I may only be the brother of an earl, but my blood is good. And if Kit should die without an heir –'

'That is not likely.'

'Never mind. Even at the beginning, my plan was not dishonourable. And when I came to know her, I began truly to esteem her. Why, otherwise, would I have gone against my mother's wishes, and made myself her friend after Manchester discovered she was not an heiress? Why would I have been advancing her cause all this summer?'

'You still haven't told me what *that* means.'

He smiled enigmatically. 'She hasn't told you, then? Well, I had better not go into details. Suffice to say she is in love with someone, and unsure of a return. My plan is to pay her attention so that the other party will notice her many attractions, and perhaps grow jealous enough to try to cut me out with her.'

Rosamund looked suspicious. 'I'm not sure I believe you. Who is this other person?'

'I think I had better let her tell you that in her own time. And now we have talked enough about your cousin. Let's talk about you instead. Ah, there's that look coming into your eyes again. My dear Lady Chelmsford, in the last few minutes, while we were talking, you were neither bored nor unhappy; but you have been both, haven't you? And now you are thinking of your troubles again.'

Rosamund didn't answer. It was true that she had forgotten everything for a while, but that only made it worse when she remembered again.

'You're looking unwell, too. Won't you tell me what's wrong?'

381

Under cover of the crowd, he took her hand, and pressed it warmly. She looked up into his face, and saw there such kind and above all *personal* interest that for a wild moment she felt that she could tell him anything, even about the jumping off chairs. She wanted to tell him everything, to confide all her foolish troubles to him, to be folded in his arms and made happy, to be crushed against him and –

Good God, what was she thinking? She surprised herself in the middle of the thought, and felt her cheeks burn with shame at where it had been leading her. 'No,' she said abruptly. 'I can't.'

He smiled then, as if he had heard everything that had gone through her mind. 'You can. You can tell me anything – don't you remember our pact? – and I will never pretend to be shocked or even surprised by what you say. Listen to me: I know some of what has been happening to you, and I can guess more. You need someone to talk to. You can talk to me. Indeed, you will talk to me, I promise you that.'

'I'm a married woman,' she said, not quite sure what she meant by it. He seemed to understand, though.

'You can talk to me about that, too. And I shall dedicate myself, while I'm here, to distracting you from your troubles, as I did just now. A respite is better than nothing, isn't it?'

'How long will you be here?' she asked.

'Just for the racing, I'm afraid. But afterwards – London is not impossibly far away. One must visit London quite often, you know, on business, and the coaches are so fast nowadays. I shall see you in London, and there one may be much more anonymous than in a small community like this.'

'Or like Manchester,' she said dazedly. Was he saying what she thought he was saying? And was it possible that she was not finding the idea shocking? What was happening to her? His blue eyes seemed to pour light into hers, dazzling her as if she were staring up into the brightest part of the summer sky. She was trembling lightly all over with the urgent desire to touch him. She had never felt like this before. It was as though she were sickening for a fever.

And then they were interrupted.

'Oh, there you are!' said Marcus, his head appearing in a gap in the crowd behind Farraline. 'Miss Rosedale and Polly are looking for you.'

Rosamund dragged her attention away from Farraline, and looked towards her husband as he got his shoulder between two obtruding bodies and squeezed himself through into their space.

'What were you –? Oh! Farraline!' Marcus looked taken aback. 'I didn't recognise you from the back.' He looked from one to the other, and there was a small pulse of awkward silence. 'I haven't seen you for a long time. How's the arm?'

Farraline answered smoothly. 'First rate, thank you, Chelmsford. Nothing more than the occasional twinge in wet weather.'

'Well, we all get that, don't we?' Marcus said brightly. 'The war left none of us quite sound.'

'Congratulations on your marriage, by the way,' Farraline said. 'You're a fortunate man.'

'Yes, I know it,' Marcus said, his eyes going from face to face again. 'I didn't know you and Rosamund were acquainted.'

'We met two years ago in Scarborough,' Farraline said in an unhelpfully neutral tone.

'When I was staying there with Sophie,' Rosamund added impatiently, seeing Marcus's blank look. 'You remember, Marcus.'

'Yes, I remember. Well, well. And are you staying for the whole week?'

'Yes indeed. I'm staying with the Howicks – do you know them? Piers Howick and I were at school together.'

'Excellent. Well, we must get together while you're here – talk over old times. Peninsula days, and so on.'

'That would be delightful,' Farraline said gravely.

Marcus glanced at Rosamund. 'We'd better be rejoining our party now. Come, Ros. Goodday, Farraline.'

He took her elbow and pushed her gently, and it annoyed her. Removing her arm from his grasp quite firmly she extended her hand to Farraline and smiled her most charming smile at him. 'Goodbye, Mr Farraline. I hope we meet again soon.'

His eyes gleamed with amusement as he bent over her hand politely. 'I'm quite sure we shall, Lady Chelmsford. I have been invited to dinner at Morland Place tomorrow after the racing. Lady Morland is eager for news of her daughter.'

She laughed. 'Unscrupulous! You knew that all along!'

'Indeed, ma'am,' he bowed his head. 'Make sure of your ground as you go, that's the rule in dangerous country! And so it is quite certainly *au revoir* and not *adieu*, you see.'

Marcus hurried her away, and when they were out of the crowd he said in a disapproving voice, 'You seem to know Farraline very well.'

'What does that mean?' she counter-attacked at once.

'Only that you spoke to him in a very familiar way. I don't think you ought to – it might be misunderstood.'

'Oh?' she said frigidly, raising her brows at him. 'By whom, pray?'

He looked embarrassed. 'Well, not by me, of course –'

'There was no-one else present.'

'But I mean another time – if you meet him in company – well, Ros, I only mean you should be careful what you say, how you behave in public. People love to talk, as you know very well.'

'Do you think I need to be told how to behave?' she asked, whipping up her anger. 'I wonder why you married me, then, for I am exactly what I always was.'

'I love you just as you are,' he said desperately, beginning to feel he was being driven towards a trap. 'It isn't me, but others –'

'Others?'

'Well, Mama says –' he began fatally, and she swung round on him so fast that he flinched away from her.

'Your mother says a great deal one way and another! I'm obliged to put up with her when she's with us, but I'm damned if I'll have her quoted at me when I manage to get away from her for a few days!'

'What do you mean?' He began to redden.

'Exactly what I say. And I tell you what, Marcus, I won't put up with her much longer, with her interfering and criticising and spying on me –'

'How dare you accuse Mama of spying?' He lost his temper at last.

'Because she does. I don't want her living with us any longer, that's all!'

'It's not your decision to make! She doesn't live with us, she lives with *me*, in *my* house, at *my* expense, just as you do, may I remind you! And it might behove you to remember also that I've allowed your cousin to live with us for a whole year, and you never heard me complain about that!'

'Polly's no trouble. She doesn't interfere –'

'My mother does not interfere! She gives you the benefit of her experience, and very good of her it is to take the trouble! A lot of mothers wouldn't, especially when you're so rude and ungrateful.'

'Ungrateful!' Rosamund said with a sarcastic laugh.

'Why, she's been kind and attentive to you all along, taken you to places, introduced you into company, given you her countenance –'

'Thank you, I think my credit is good enough without that! And as for introducing me into company, my mother did that for me long ago!'

Marcus opened his mouth to make a sharp retort about *her* mother, and suddenly stopped himself, staring at her with rapidly cooling anger. What on earth were they quarrelling about? It wasn't his mother, that was for sure. 'Ros, don't,' he said. 'Please.'

She looked at him suspiciously, and with hostility, like a wild colt eyeing the carrot that was always accompanied by a rope.

'What's wrong?' he asked her gently. 'You haven't been yourself for weeks now.'

She stared at him in silence, but she had no temptation to tell him everything. He was too much a part of what was wrong, too mixed up with feelings of guilt and frustration; he was her victim as much as she was his, and there was nothing she could say to him about that. That she had stepped voluntarily into his cage did not make the longing to escape any less; and the feelings of fondness and affection she certainly had for him were too much overpowered just then by the simple desire to get away from him.

'Nothing's wrong,' she said. 'I'm sorry I spoke as I did. Let's go back and join the party. The first race will be starting soon.' She forced herself to smile, and put her arm through his; and when Marcus smiled back, followed her cue, and talked about the race, she thought she had placated him.

But Marcus knew the sound and look of a door closing as well as any man; and though he was at bottom a simple soul, he loved her too much not to be able to act at least as well as that.

CHAPTER TWENTY

Polly was walking through the Italian garden with Father Moineau. It was a mild day with a smell of woodsmoke in the air, and the sunshine was vague and pleasant like an absent-minded caress. It said a great deal for Polly's recovery that she had voluntarily entered the Italian garden, and was actually enjoying walking between the tall, darkly formal hedges which closed in the view on all sides. The green of them was almost black in the shadows, and against them the marble statues stood out dead white like bleached bones.

'Aunt Héloïse tells me that any number of previous owners of Morland Place have meant to change this garden. The intention is recorded again and again in the Household Book, but somehow no-one ever gets round to it.'

'Yes, that's right. I've been reading it too,' said Father Moineau. He looked around him appreciatively. 'I'm glad they did not dig this up, after their various passing fashions. There's something timeless about it. When I walk here, I can almost feel the hot, southern sun, and smell that particular smell of aromatic plants ...'

He drifted off for a moment, and then came back to say, 'It's a wonderful document, the Household Book. Have you read it?' Polly shook her head. 'Oh you should, you should. All of history is there, if you know how to read between the lines. I have been trying to persuade her ladyship to write a history of Morland Place – and I'm not the first to suggest it – but she says she has not the time, and I suppose she is right.'

'She's busy every hour of the day,' Polly agreed. 'I feel I ought to do more to help, but whenever I offer, it always seems everything has just that minute been done.'

Moineau smiled sidelong at her. 'She wishes you to have a long holiday, and grow well and strong.'

'But I haven't been ill.'

'Indeed you have. But I think you are getting better.'

They stepped through the last section of hedge and came out onto the bank of the moat. Polly looked up in affection at the old rosy brick of the house, its every imperfection and irregularity thrown into sharp relief by the westering of the sun.

'It's this place,' she said simply. 'There's something healing about it.'

'It's a good place,' Father Moineau said. 'I said so when I first came here. But it's a kind of goodness which is going out of the world, and the world will be the poorer for it.'

'What do you mean?' Polly asked. They turned their backs to the sun and walked along the bank towards the Long Walk.

'There's an order here,' Moineau said. 'Each person knows his place, and is comfortable in it; each place has its privileges and its responsibilities. It creates a stillness.'

'Yes,' said Polly.

'Outside, the world has grown restless. It craves change, movement, novelty – all the time something new, something different. It is the fault of the Revolution, at least in part.'

'Because people stepped out of their place?'

'Yes; and because men permitted themselves to do things they knew were wrong, believing that they did them to achieve a good end, and that they could cease to do them when the end was achieved.' He sighed. 'But of course, it does not happen that way.'

He paused for so long that Polly felt he needed prompting. 'How does it happen, then?'

He looked at her rather curiously, as though he had been thinking about something else, and had only just noticed she was there. 'We humans have constructed walls around us, of laws and customs and interdicts – which are necessary, because in our cleverness we are very dangerous creatures. We have not the simplicity of the animals to keep us true. The effect of all these rules is to restrain us – perhaps, you know, as we restrain lunatics,' he added with a smile, 'so that they shan't hurt us or themselves.'

She returned the smile faintly: she had an idea where this was leading.

'Yes, we are very like lunatics, we clever animals,' he continued, evidently struck with the idea.

'Full of sound and fury, signifying nothing,' Polly murmured.

'*Bien sûr*,' he agreed vaguely. He had not read Shakespeare. 'But when we are restrained, when we grow quiet, into that quietness creeps another sound, something we cannot hear when we go rushing and bellowing about: we hear the voice of God, telling us how to make sense of things, telling us if we have got things right. In our madness, we cannot hear it; and without it, there is no end to our madness. It is – how do you call it –?' He made a gesture with both hands.

'A vicious circle?' Polly said.

He nodded. 'Here, at Morland Place, there is the stillness. But in the restless world outside there is no chance for that voice to be heard, and so people do things they know are wrong, and having done them, tell themselves they were not so bad after all. It is bad fruit, which makes you sick in a particular way – it makes you want more.' He paused, and then felt his way back to where he had started. 'So it was with the Revolution. Every bad thing that was done made the next worse thing not only easier, but inevitable.'

'Yes,' said Polly. 'I see that.'

He nodded to her. 'You cannot do evil that good may come, for only evil comes of evil – that is the way of things.'

They turned the corner of the house onto the Long Walk. At the far end the swans were couched on the grass, preening. They turned their heads to look at the humans for a moment, then went back to the much more fascinating question of the state of their plumage, magnificent in their self-possession.

'Then what will become of the world?' Polly asked. 'Is there no way back?'

'The way back is as you have found. Just to stop, and be still, to listen and be healed.'

'But I didn't do evil that good might come.'

'Didn't you?' He cocked his head at her, enquiring as a bird.

She stared back, wide-eyed. 'Yes,' she said reluctantly, 'I suppose – in a way. But it wasn't entirely my fault.'

He ignored that. 'It made you sick, did it not?'

'It wasn't only that, it was – wondering – not knowing –' She stopped, and then went on in a painful burst, 'Father Moineau, can I tell you? I can't tell anyone else.'

388

'Of course you can,' he said, nodding pleasantly, a small, round, brown man, as little threatening as a tame sparrow. And so it was to him, and not to Miss Rosedale, that Polly finally poured out her trouble.

She told him of her long captivity at Stainton, and of Minnie's death, and of the terrible suspicion that had haunted her ever since that perhaps after all Harvey had killed Minnie, in order to be free to marry her.

'And what made you think that he did this terrible thing?' Father Moineau asked at last.

'Oh, many things – little things, but together –' She rubbed a hand over her face. 'The fact that the babies fell sick just after he arrived, when they'd always been perfectly healthy. And suddenly he was spending so much time with us when he'd stayed away before. Then what happened to me in the inn – feeling dizzy and falling asleep so suddenly, as if I'd been drugged. And afterwards, when he came back for me, he seemed so strange, nervous and excited.' She stared wide-eyed at nothing, remembering. 'He drove home fast, talking all the while. That wasn't like him. And the things he said – I didn't tell anyone, I didn't dare – but he said that something would happen soon so that we could be together, that it had to happen or his life would not be worth living. And after-wards I started to think – I didn't want to believe, but I couldn't seem to help it. So you see –?' She faltered and stopped.

'Yes, I see. But those things you have told me were not why you believed,' Moineau said seriously.

'Not?' Polly looked bewildered.

'No, *ma chère*. Suspicion is a sickness which does not depend on any evidence for its existence. It is a monster which gets into your head and eats everything it finds there, no matter what it is, and grows stronger on it.'

'But where did the monster come from?'

'You made it yourself, out of your own sense of wrong-doing. You bred your own sickness. You will be well when you cast out your sin.'

'I did cast it out. We – Harvey and I – I was not sinning any more,' Polly protested. He gave her the sidelong look which invited her to answer her own questions. 'You mean – just being there? But I couldn't have left! Minnie needed me,

389

she couldn't do without me. I wanted to go, but they wouldn't let me!' Again the look. Protest weakened. 'I don't see what else I could have done.'

'When you do see, you will be well,' he said simply.

'Then what must I do?' she asked fretfully. It was answers she wanted, not riddles.

'Stay here,' he said comfortably. 'Be still, be quiet, listen for the voice of God. You don't have to go to Him – He will come to you, if you are still enough. That is where that big, restless world outside mistakes: always seeking movement, change – activity. It is not necessary to *do*, only to *be*.'

'I don't understand,' Polly said resentfully.

'But you will. We will talk again, *ma petite*, many times. I enjoy your mind so much.' He looked at her downcast face. 'Don't be discouraged. Nothing worthwhile is ever easy,' said Father Moineau, and he smiled. 'That is what I tell my boys every day.'

Héloïse came into the drawing-room and found Sophie sitting at the pianoforte, idly touching the keys. She checked the cheerful greeting that rose to her lips when she realised that Sophie was not aware of her presence, that she was, indeed, very far away. She seemed to be pressing the keys at random, but after a moment Héloïse discerned that though there were long gaps between the notes, they actually formed the tune of *La Bayadère*, a soldier's song which had been all the go in Brussels when the Allied Army gathered there before Waterloo.

Héloïse was filled with a rush of tender concern towards her daughter. That was the song which Major Larosse had sung to her: it seemed her poor little Sophie was still mourning him, after all this time! And she had believed and hoped – hoped so much! – that Sophie was over him at last, that she had recovered from her loss, and had begun to look forward rather than backward.

The two long holidays she had spent in Manchester Héloïse had believed were symptoms of that recovery. It was true that since she came back this last time, Sophie had been rather quiet and thoughtful, but it had not seemed an unhappy thoughtfulness. Héloïse was angry with herself that she could have mistaken, blamed herself for not taking more time to see that Sophie really was happy. She had been so busy – as always, so busy! – and Sophie had seemed contented enough, especially now that she had Polly as a companion close to her own age.

Héloïse looked searchingly at her daughter, sitting at the pianoforte, her head bent a little over the keyboard so that her long side-curls fell forward. Her slender hands moved lightly, barely touching the keys, her long dark eyelashes drooped, shielding her eyes. Héloïse realised with sudden shock that Sophie was not a child any more. The full, childish curve of her cheek was gone, and her profile revealed the more angular planes of adulthood. She was twenty years old, a grown woman, with a grown woman's feelings and secrets and desires. Héloïse realised she had no idea what Sophie might be thinking, and it was a lonely realisation, a cold touch of encroaching age. You gave life to your children, and they were part of you, sustaining you by their existence, she thought; until the day came when you realised they had become quite separate, and then they took life from you.

'Why Sophie,' she said quietly, 'you are in an absolute reverie!'

Sophie looked up, turned her head quickly towards her mother, and a rosy blush coloured her cheeks. 'Oh, Maman,' she said, and in that moment Héloïse saw, with a mixture of relief and wistfulness, that she had not been sitting in a daze of reflective sorrow, but had been thinking about something essentially pleasurable. No woman who had ever been in love could mistake that blush and that particular smile. Sophie had been thinking about a man – about her Beloved Object, in fact.

Ah, very well, thought Héloïse, but who could that be? I should have spent the summer in Manchester with you, my Sophie! Why had his name not cropped up in conversation? A woman in love usually managed to bring the Beloved Object's name into every second or third sentence, but when Sophie talked of Manchester she talked of nothing but the plans for the betterment of the mill-workers' lot.

Perhaps it was someone Unsuitable, that Sophie dared not talk about. Pray God that was not it! If he were only poor, that wouldn't matter – she and James could always make a settlement on Sophie, or find some way of promoting him –

as long as he was Suitable ...

'Well, *chérie*,' she said at the end of this long but extremely rapid series of thoughts, 'there will be no time for sitting and dreaming next week, when our guests arrive for Christmas. I'm glad Mathilde and John are going to stay with us. I know we see them tolerably often, but it will be lovely to have a baby in the house again.'

'Yes, and Mary is such a little love!' Sophie said. She had always loved babies, ever since she had claimed Aunt Lucy's Thomas as her own, all those years ago in the little house in Coxwold. 'All the maids are in ecstasies about it already. I don't think Mathilde will be allowed so much as to hold her baby as long as they're here.'

'And how nice that Mr Hobsbawn is going to spare us a few days, too,' Héloïse went on innocently. 'You will be glad to hear news of all your friends in Manchester.'

'I don't suppose for a moment he will have anything to tell me about them,' Sophie smiled. 'Except perhaps for Prudence, I'm sure he never sees any of them. He cares for nothing but the mills, you know. But it doesn't matter, Maman: Agnes writes to me now and then – though I wish it were more often,' she added. 'She writes good letters – she notices everything, and knows just what will interest and amuse me.'

'You're lucky to have such a correspondent,' Héloïse said, and tried another tack. 'Does she ever mention Mr Farraline? I had a long talk with him when he came to dine with us, and shared our box at the races. He's a nice man, I think – and he spoke so pleasantly of you. It was such a pity you weren't here at the same time.'

'I was sorry to miss race week,' Sophie said lightly, 'but there was so much doing in Manchester. Agnes mentions Mr Farraline from time to time, but I don't think they go to many of the same parties.'

'Is he above her touch, then?'

'Oh, no I don't think so. It isn't that, it's just that he and Mr Droylsden don't have the same friends.'

She spoke with pleasant indifference, and Héloïse thought she did not seem much interested in Mr Farraline; and yet, if he did not share a circle of friends with the Droylsdens, how did he come to see so much of Sophie when she was in Manchester, unless he deliberately sought her out? The conversation had got her nowhere. She was no wiser about Sophie's inner thoughts, and it occurred to her, a little uncomfortably, that perhaps she was not meant to be.

Later on that same day, but on the other side of the Pennines, Jasper Hobsbawn and Jesmond Farraline came face to face in the ante-room of the Exchange Hall, where there had just been a meeting on the need for factory legislation. Hobsbawn's views on the subject were diametrically opposite to Farraline's, but that did not seem sufficient reason for the hostility with which he stared at him, especially as Farraline was favouring him with a very friendly smile.

'Well, Hobsbawn, things seem to be going your way at last, don't they?' Farraline said cheerfully. 'It looks very much as though Sir Robert is going to get his ten-hours act through Parliament at the next attempt.'

'Why should you think that?' Hobsbawn said resentfully. 'Your people threw it out this year, and no doubt they'll do it again next year.'

'My people?' Farraline looked quizzical.

'The Lords,' said Hobsbawn tersely.

'My dear fellow, you mistake! The brother of an earl is a commoner. As witness the appalling state of my hands.' He spread them ruefully, and Jasper saw the grimy stain along the side of the forefinger and under the thumbnail familiar to him from his own hands. It took days of scrubbing to remove that particular kind of black machine grease. 'One of our engines was overheating today, and somehow I just can't leave well alone,' Farraline said. 'But these are hardly lord's hands, you will admit.'

Hobsbawn felt uncomfortably as though he had been shewn up in an ungracious light. He changed tack. 'All the same, I know you are against Peel's act –'

'Of course I am: any sensible man would be. Is it right, I ask you, that Parliament should have the power to interfere between parent and child? Or between master and man? It sets a dangerous precedent, Hobsbawn, and I do wonder if you and your friends have properly thought what it may lead to. Once you have opened Pandora's box, you will never be able to close it again.'

'I only know that I'm sick of seeing children being beaten

393

to keep them awake at the end of the day, and falling down from exhaustion outside the factory gates, too tired to walk home – too tired, some of them, even to eat their supper,' Hobsbawn said hotly.

'Ah yes, you are a romantic, my dear fellow, but not a visionary. It explains a great many things. Still, I greatly fear that the age of romance is just beginning, and that Sir Robert's ill-conceived act will go through – something we will all have to pay for at a later date.'

'If you think the act so ill-conceived, I don't know why you came here tonight,' Hobsbawn said, finding himself being led unwillingly ever further down the paths of ungraciousness. Why could he never be civil to this man, who, after all, was never less than civil to him?

'I came to see you, as a matter of fact. There is something I want to talk to you about – a matter of some delicacy.'

Hobsbawn stared. 'I can't think of anything you and I can have to discuss of a delicate nature.'

'What about Miss Morland's future?' Farraline enquired smoothly.

Hobsbawn began to redden. 'Look here –' he began.

Farraline held up his hand. 'Please, don't ride grub before you know what I'm going to say! Sentences that begin "look here" so often lead to disaster. Won't you come with me next door to my club, and take a glass of wine with me? I can't think of anything I've done to incur your enmity, except for disagreeing with your views, and surely a man may do that in a civilised society?'

Jasper drew a deep breath, pushed his resentful feelings down as far as they would go, and managed to accept the invitation with a fair approximation of civility. Farraline talked lightly of the weather and a play he had seen recently during the few minutes it took to reach the smoking-room of his club, relieving Jasper of the need to say more than yes and no.

When they were comfortably seated with a decanter between them, Farraline fell silent for a moment, turning his glass in his fingers and watching the light gleam in the ruby-coloured depths of the wine. Jasper took the opportunity to survey the handsome, elegant man opposite him, and his sustaining resentment drained away, leaving him with nothing but the stark realisation that there was no field in which he could compete with Jesmond Farraline. Farraline was ten years younger and four inches taller. His blood was at least half-blue, his features pure Grecian, his manners charming, his wit ready, his address engaging. In comparison, Jasper felt himself to be meagre, pallid, undersized, dull and surly. No woman in her senses would prefer him. He was defeated before he began.

'Well,' he said upon this conclusion, drawing a resigned breath, 'what did you want to talk to me about?'

Farraline regarded him thoughtfully. 'It is, as I said, a matter of some delicacy. It's hard for me to know where to begin, because it involves my making some assumptions which are going to make me sound like a coxcomb. But to begin with I want to assure you that I bear you no ill-will – on the contrary, I wish you nothing but good.'

Jasper looked at him warily. 'You said something about Miss Morland.'

'Yes. Yes, I did. Hobsbawn, you will perhaps have noticed my friendship with Miss Morland?'

'I have,' Jasper said shortly.

'You may, then, have noticed that I have made very sure not to do anything to compromise her in any way. I have met her always in the company of a respectable chaperone, and preferably in a large group. I wished to be sure no-one could have any reason to talk about her. I felt she had had enough of notoriety – none of it her fault, I hasten to add.'

So that was it, Jasper thought with dull resentment. 'I can guess what you're going to say –'

'No you can't, old fellow, I assure you!'

' – and I have to tell you you're quite mistaken! Good God, do you think I would do anything to harm her reputation? I would never – never –!' He choked on his emotion.

'Yes, I know you would never,' Farraline said hastily, 'and that's precisely why –'

It was no use. Hobsbawn wasn't listening. 'I have never been alone with Miss Morland, and although I know the presence of those poor unfortunates we visit is not precisely what the world regards as respectable chaperonage, yet I would have thought the occasion itself must have saved her from any unworthy suspicion –'

Farraline sighed and interrupted. 'If she could hear you now, the poor dear creature would shake her head and give you up for lost.'

Jasper glared. 'If you mean Miss Morland –'

'Of course I do!'

'Then you may be about to make her an offer, Farraline, but until you are officially engaged to her, I'd be obliged if you would not refer to her in those disrespectful terms, and save me from the trouble of knocking you down!'

Farraline burst out laughing. 'Hobsbawn, you are a true Gothic! Positively mediaeval! I really can't imagine why Miss Morland prefers you to any other man, but since she does –'

'What do you say?'

'Oh yes – that's what I've been trying with all delicacy to tell you this half-hour, but it seems I'd have done better to put it more bluntly. Miss Morland is in love with you,' he enunciated clearly, 'and since I hold her in great – and completely respectful – affection, I want to know what you mean to do about it. For I warn you, if you go on breaking her poor heart like this, I shall very likely have to call you out.'

Jasper could find nothing to say. He stared at Farraline as though he had been poll-axed. At last he managed to whisper, 'You are making sport of me.'

Farraline became serious. 'No, I'm not. And to do away with your next objection, I do know whereof I'm talking. I have a tolerably large experience of women's ways, and I have taken pains to get to know Miss Morland. Why do you think she has developed this extraordinary interest in the Benevolent Society? Why do you think she spends her summers in Manchester? Why has she persuaded her parents to endorse your extraordinary building-scheme? My dear fellow, anyone less wilfully blind than you would have seen how she looks at you.'

'But – but – how could she love me?'

'A question I've often asked myself,' Farraline said lightly, 'especially since I was forced to come to the galling conclusion that she prefers you to me. But if you doubt it, ask yourself where she was in August, during race-week, when her parents confidently expected her back home at Morland Place, and when I had taken great pains to let her know that I would be in York. Was she not toiling amongst the tenements in your company, and poring over plans for rational dwellings with you, under the chaperonage of Mrs Droylsden, who must have the patience of a saint, by the by –'

'Good God,' said Jasper. A flood of images rushed through his mind, and some of them, given this flattering new interpretation, filled him with a wild and heady hope. 'Can it be – are you sure?'

'Quite sure.'

'But – but why are you telling me this?'

'I've already told you – because I am very fond of Miss Morland. And I have an odd sort of liking for you, too. And most of all, I hate waste, and it is such a waste of two perfectly good people to be going on like this. So now, what are you going to do about it?'

Jasper was looking at some inner, and sunlit landscape. 'I've been invited to Morland Place for the Christmas celebrations,' he murmured happily.

'Excellent. An ideal opportunity,' said Farraline bracingly. 'You can choose your moment to speak.'

The sun went in. 'But suppose you're wrong?' Jasper said.

Farraline sighed. 'Suppose it if you must. But need I remind you of the old adage about faint hearts and fair maidens? Good God, man, what have you to lose? And what to gain?'

Jasper straightened his shoulders with decision. 'You're right. I'll do it! I can hardly believe – but I suppose you are in a position to know. I do thank you, Farraline. This is behaving like a friend indeed. I beg your pardon for all my rudeness to you. It was because –'

'I perfectly understand,' Farraline grinned. 'I'd have hated me too, if I were you. Let me fill your glass, and we'll drink a toast – to the lovely Miss Morland, and to your success.'

'If I win her, I'll make her happy, I swear it,' said Jasper earnestly. 'I would die to make her happy!'

'If you'll take a word of advice, Hobsbawn, much better live to do it,' said Farraline.

It was unfortunate that Jasper had so many days and so many miles between his meeting with Jesmond Farraline in Manchester and his arrival at Morland Place. It gave him time and space in which to think of all the objections there were against him as a potential husband of the angelic Sophie Morland. Not least amongst them was his lack of fortune, and the fact that he was merely manager of the mills her mother owned. He knew that Lady Morland liked him – in her generous way she had made that quite plain – but she was hardly likely to think him a suitable guardian of her only daughter's happiness.

By the time he reached Morland Place, he had almost decided not to speak. The difficulties in the way were enormous. He only had Farraline's word for it that Sophie cared for him. How could he find out if that were true without declaring himself to her? And how could he declare himself to her without first discovering if there were any chance at all of her parents' accepting his suit? And how could he speak to her parents without first knowing whether she cared for him or not . . ?

But his reception was everything that was kind. When he alighted from the mail at the Hare and Heather, a carriage was waiting there to convey him to Morland Place, though he had been perfectly prepared to walk. When he entered the great hall a while later, there was the cheering sight of an enormous fire under the huge chimney with a living heathrug of dogs toasting their bellies before it. Branches of evergreen decorated the walls, their aromatic scent vying on the air with the hot smell of cinnamon and mince pies.

He began to feel a sense of impending comfort and well-being that was almost intoxicating. His life had always been one of urgent imperatives, amongst which his own comfort had rarely figured. He hardly knew what to do with the pleasure of it when Lady Morland came into the hall in person to greet him, and shook his hand so heartily, and said in such a believable tone of voice that she was glad to see him.

She conducted him to the drawing-room, and there a comfortable crowd was gathered – James Morland, Mr and Mrs John Skelwith, Father Moineau playing chess with the beautiful Miss Haworth, Miss Rosedale playing spillikins on the floor with the little boys and being much hampered by the dog Kai, who would try to join in, but whose paws were not designed for the business.

But for Jasper there was only one face turned in his direction as he entered the room. Sophie was kneeling on the rug by the hearth playing with baby Mary. She looked up at him from a tumble of curls, fragile bare arms touched with fire-light, white muslin gown turned rosy by it. She looked up with shining eyes, and lips parted in a smile, and such a delicate, such an encouraging blush colouring her cheeks. He felt that it might almost have been worth dying there and then of happiness, except that for the first time in his life, he thought that there might possibly be even more happiness to come.

On the following day everyone dressed up warmly to go up to Ten Thorn Copse to bring home the yule-log – a delightfully pagan ceremony involving much hilarity and singing, and which Father Moineau seemed to find perfectly in keeping with his priestly status. He and Polly stumped along side by side, and noting their cheerful conversation, Héloïse said to Miss Rosedale, 'What is it that they talk about all the time?'

'Philosophy, I think,' Miss Rosedale replied. 'And religion. And such related subjects.'

'But that sounds so dull. Would that make Polly smile so?'

'Polly is a very unusual young woman. It's a pity really she couldn't have been a man. There are so few opportunities for a woman to use her intellect.'

'I suppose so,' Héloïse said without resentment. 'I don't really know, for I never had one. But I'm glad she is happier. I hoped she might make a friend of you, dear Rosey, but as long as she confides in someone, I don't much mind who it is.'

'I don't think she rates my intellect very highly,' Miss Rose-dale smiled, 'ever since she discovered I have never read Spinoza. Benedict, no! The ice isn't thick enough yet! You'll go through!' She rushed off to rescue her boys from their own daring.

James came up beside Héloïse and tucked her hand through her arm. 'What do you think of that, over there?' he said, nodding to where Jasper and Sophie were walking a little apart. 'Can you guess what they're talking about?'

'It is no guess,' Héloïse laughed. 'Mill-workers, to be sure. Look how absorbed Mr Hobsbawn is!'

'Not at all,' James said triumphantly. 'Sophie's telling him the history of our Christmas traditions. From the bemused expression on his face, you'd think she was a mermaid singing to him! It must be the first time in years he's thought about anything but machines and cotton.'

'Poor young man,' Héloïse said, her ready sympathy aroused. 'He's had such a very *uncomfortable* life! We must make sure he has a good holiday while he is here. I shall tell Sophie not to talk about the building scheme at all for the whole week.'

It was growing very cold, and in the copse there was a great deal of stamping of feet and rubbing of hands as everyone stood round Father Moineau. He blessed the log, which had been cut back in October under James's direction, and had been drying ever since. Then the ropes were fixed, James, Nicholas and John – who were taking the first turn – took up the strain, and a great cheer went up as they began to drag it home. Benedict jumped up and down, shrieking with excitement, and the dogs rushed round in maddened circles, jabbing their wet noses into hands and faces in lieu of barking.

In the van of the procession, Father Moineau drew a small flask out of his pocket, unscrewed the top, and handed it to Polly.

'I think it is going to snow,' he said. 'You look cold – try some of this. It will warm you up.'

Polly's eyes widened. 'Ardent spirits?' she said. 'I've never had anything like that before. Are priests allowed –?'

'*Pourquoi non?*' Moineau's eyes twinkled. 'It is part of God's good harvest. Regard it as medicinal, if you like.'

She sipped, and choked, and then looked surprised. 'It does feel warm once it's inside,' she said.

Sophie came up alongside her. 'What's that, Polly?'

'I'm not sure, but it's very warming,' Polly said, and with a glance at Moineau, passing the flask to her. 'Try some.'

'Good God, Father, what are you giving the young ladies?' Jasper protested, joining them in time to see Sophie repeat the action of sipping and choking.

'Medicine,' said Polly. 'A remedy against the cold.'

'It's horrid!' Sophie laughed, handing the flask back to Father Moineau. 'Oh, I do hope it snows for Christmas Eve! It looks so lovely when it's all fresh and crisp! Do let's sing the yule-log song now – Polly, you start us off. You have the truest voice. You remember the words? Mr Hobsbawn, come and take a turn on the ropes! Everyone has to take a turn, you know, for good luck.'

Polly began obligingly to sing as Sophie ran off to beg a turn at the ropes. Jasper hesitated, watching her, feeling awkward and self-conscious, too old and ungainly, surely, to run after her.

Father Moineau, observing him with sympathy, passed the flask across to him and said in a voice meant only for Jasper to hear, 'I think you'd better have a little of this yourself. It takes much courage to woo a young woman.'

Jasper looked at him, startled, and then, seeing nothing but kindness in the priest's eyes, smiled, and accepted the offer. 'Thank you,' he said, and hurried off after Sophie.

When everyone had had their turn, the servants took over the real work of dragging the log home, and the family turned their energies to singing. The sky was closed and pearly overhead, the light strange and greenish, the world very still. As they reached the top of the slope down to the house the first snowflakes began to drift down. Walking a little behind the main group now, Sophie turned her face up, and forgetting her womanly dignity, tried to catch them on her tongue as she had as a child, just as Nicky and Bendy were doing.

'They look black when you look up at them,' she remarked wonderingly to Jasper, who was still at her side. 'How they come rushing down! Whirling madly. It makes you quite dizzy!'

He couldn't spare the attention to look up – he was too absorbed in gazing at her face, the brightness of her cheeks in the cold air, the vigour of the dark curls thrusting out from under her bonnet, the thickness of the eyelashes fluttering defensively against the satin touch of snowflakes. Staring up into the sky did make a person dizzy: a few steps more, and Sophie stumbled, and Jasper was there to catch hold of her. It wasn't much of a stumble – she wouldn't have fallen – but she didn't seem to mind the touch of his hands at all, or to wish him to remove them. She looked directly into his eyes, began to say something – thank you, perhaps – and then blushed vividly.

Jasper's remaining self-possession fled.

'Oh Sophie,' he blurted out like an idiotic schoolboy, 'I do love you so much!'

An expression came into her eyes that he would have died to witness, had it been necessary, which, miraculously, it seemed it was not. 'I love you too,' she whispered; shy, but so eager, as though she had wanted a long time to say it.

They stopped still and stared at each other through the increasing snow. The singing of the rest of the party, drawing steadily away from them down the slope, was already muffled on the thick, white air.

'Do you? Do you really?' he said wonderingly. 'I never would have believed ... I'm not anyone, you see. I'm not handsome or rich or –'

He stopped himself from going on, seeing that she was only looking at him with that same expression, saying nothing, waiting for him to stop behaving like a half-wit. The snow-flakes were settling on her hair, on her face, too, as it was turned up to look at him. He removed one tenderly from the tip of her nose. 'Sophie, if your parents will allow, will you marry me?'

'Yes,' she said. Just that – but at the same moment she put both her gloved hands into his, a gesture of such willingness and trust that he needed no other words.

'Sophie,' he said idiotically, and then realising that it was becoming difficult to see her, he drew her hand through his arm and said, 'We'd better get indoors before we get lost in a blizzard. Come, my love.'

Sophie allowed him to hurry her down towards the house, her hand safe in the crook of his arm, her feet some inches above the ground, not in the least worried about blizzards. She thought she had never heard three more beautiful words in her life than those last three.

Jasper Hobsbawn had delivered his speech, the verbal equivalent of a Congreve rocket as far as James and Héloïse were concerned.

'I know I should have spoken to you first, before I said anything to Sophie – Miss Morland – your daughter. I fully intended to, but I was just – well, overcome. It all came out before I could stop myself.

'Of course you will want time to consider, I understand that,' he went on rather unhappily when neither of them spoke. 'I'll leave you now and – and await your decision.'

'Er – yes, very well, Hobsbawn,' James said faintly. 'Thank you. Yes, we'll certainly – er – consider everything you've said.'

Jasper withdrew, and James turned his stunned eyes on his wife. 'Well, that caps the globe!' he exclaimed, reverting in his amazement to his childhood vocabulary. 'Had you any idea of this?'

'No, not the least – though I suppose now I think of it, I ought to have realised. I have been very stupid, I'm afraid, but I thought things were quite otherwise.'

'I suppose he couldn't be mistaken?' James said hopefully. 'About Sophie's feelings, I mean?'

'Oh James! Do you suppose that shy man would have put himself through such agony if he weren't sure? You see how little he values himself –'

'Well, I agree with him there,' James said vigorously. 'He's hardly what I'd consider a suitable match!'

Héloïse looked anxious. 'You don't mean to refuse permission, do you?'

James frowned. 'I collect you think I should say yes? Don't you think we ought at least discuss it?'

'Oh yes, I suppose we should, but James, if Sophie loves him, how can we say no?'

'Now don't start that again,' James said angrily. 'We had all that nonsense with Fanny and Hawker, all that talk about love, and look where that led!'

'But the cases are quite different. Fanny was so very young, and headstrong –'

'Sophie may not be headstrong, but she's still only a child. She knows nothing about life.'

'She's not a child any more, my James,' Héloïse said sadly. 'She's twenty years old, and a grown woman. She has been in love before, and lost her lover in the cruellest way. I do not think she is likely to be deceived about her feelings now. And besides, you know, what is there to attract about Mr Hobsbawn if she does not truly love him? He is not a glamorous figure who has dazzled her, as you thought Mr Hawker did Fanny.'

'I still say a young woman of twenty doesn't know what's good for her. She can't begin to understand the dangers of life. It's a father's duty to protect her interests – as I would

403

have done for Fanny, if I'd been allowed!'

'James, what happened to Fanny was just bad luck,' Héloïse said quietly. 'It had nothing to do with Mr Hawker. It would have happened whoever she married.'

James stared at her a moment longer, and then his resistance crumpled. He sat down, looking miserable and old.

'I just don't want her marrying the wrong man and being unhappy. Look at him! He's not the man you would have picked for her, is he? He's nobody. He's nothing.'

'He's the man she loves, my James, and Sophie's such a good girl, she would not choose badly. I know Mr Hobsbawn doesn't look like a fairy-tale prince,' she teased gently, 'but he's a good man, I truly believe.'

'He's dull,' James complained weakly. 'And plain.'

'No, I don't think so. I think he's only poor, and we can change that – we can make him not poor.'

'What do you mean? Give him money?'

'No, better than that.' She sat down beside him and took his hands. 'You know I have often worried about the unfairness of old Mr Hobsbawn's will? Well, Sophie will have a little money of her own from me anyway, but if she really wants to marry Jasper Hobsbawn, why should we not give her the mills as a wedding-present?'

'Give her the mills?'

'Yes, don't you see, it would be the answer to many things. You know Mr Hobsbawn will always care for them, and manage them well and faithfully, but this way they become his when he marries her, which is right and good. Oh, we can have the settlement drawn up any way you like, to protect her interests, and ours. But it will give her security and a place in society – and if we give them Hobsbawn House as well, she will have a fine home, too.'

'A fine home – on the other side of the Pennines!'

Héloïse shrugged. 'She would always have moved away, whoever she married. You could not wish to keep her at home all her life.'

He sighed. 'Why couldn't she marry some nice local boy, like Mathilde, and live close by?'

'Because she doesn't love some nice local boy,' Héloïse said. 'Come, now, James, what do you say? Is it not a good idea?'

'The mills are yours to do with as you wish,' he said sulkily.

'And Hobsbawn House too, if it comes to that.'

'Well, but the permission to marry is yours to give, *mon âme*. Why don't you have Sophie in and ask her? Perhaps she will be able to convince you that she has chosen a good man, who can make her happy.'

'I dare say she'll be able to wheedle me, as you do.' He smiled reluctantly, and drew her onto his lap. 'You like him, don't you, Marmoset?'

'Yes, I like him.'

'Enough to understand why she wants to marry him?'

'He would not have been my choice, for me or for her. But yes, I can see that he is a person one could love.'

James held her close, pressing his mouth against her hair and rocking her a little as he mused. Then he sighed.

'Very well, I'll let her persuade me. Shall we have her in, my love, to tell us all about his manifold perfections? And then if it's as you think, we might as well have him in, and get it over with.' Héloïse got up and went to ring the bell. James watched her cross the room with absent eyes. 'Hobsbawn!' he said, but without great heat. 'To think a daughter of mine should end up a Hobsbawn!'

CHAPTER TWENTY-ONE

The travelling-chaise that pulled up before the steps of Hobs-bawn House was new, dashing of design, and drawn by four horses, but the coat-of-arms painted on the panel was almost completely obscured by thick white dust. July 1819 was a hot month, following a dry spring, and the roads were fast, but very dusty.

The footman from the house hadn't even got as far as opening the chaise door when the lady of the house appeared on the steps behind him, her hands clasped excitedly at her breast and her face alight with eagerness. Only the awareness of her new dignity as a matron stopped her running down the steps and enveloping her cousin in a bear-hug as soon as she got out.

'Oh Rosamund! I'm so glad to see you!' Sophie cried. 'Oh do, *do* come in! How was your journey? Are you very tired?'

'Not the least bit in the world,' Rosamund said, shaking out the folds of her travelling-gown, and standing where she was to look up at Sophie. An irresistible smile spread over her face at the sight of that familiar small, thin figure – unchanged in any way, it seemed to her, except for the absurd lace-trimmed cap which now adorned the dark curls, and the attempt at dignity which was restraining her movements. To Rosamund, Sophie looked like a child playing at being grown up. But she was glad to see that Sophie also looked happy. There was an air of quiet content about her, as well as her present excitement.

To Sophie, Rosamund seemed very different. The romp of a débutante she had known in London and Brussels, who had become the smart but high-spirited girl of Scarborough, was now a cool and elegant young woman. Everything about her appearance spoke of wealth and high fashion. Sophie drank in every detail of the cambric carriage-dress – the hem was wider than any she had seen in Manchester, and there were three rows of ribbon trimming, not two. And that darling blue silk spencer, with puffed sleeves over long sleeves, and piped seams! Sophie had heard of piped seams, but hadn't seen any yet. And the high-crowned bonnet – Rosamund managed it so well, getting out of the carriage! And the marabou tippet and muff – marabou was wildly expensive, Sophie knew, and so impractical in its fragility that only an exceedingly leisured woman could afford to wear it.

More than just the clothes, Rosamund's whole air spoke of sophistication: the assurance of her manner, the way she was obviously perfectly at ease with her appearance, taking it for granted in a way that the lesser belles of Manchester never did. Why, if Miss Ardwick or any of the Audenshaw girls had had a marabou muff like that, they would have found some way of flourishing it to draw attention to it; but Rosamund was holding it carelessly in one hand down at her side, and as Moss came round from the other side of the carriage, she handed it to her without even looking at it.

And more than either her clothes or her manner, the evidence of the change in her was in her face. She looked more beautiful than before, in a cool, sculpted way: as a girl she had not been pretty, but as a woman she was handsome. Her expression was composed; her eyes curiously veiled, as though she were used to concealing her emotions; her mouth was a firm line, not precisely unhappy, but not relaxed. Sophie's pleasure in seeing her faltered as she watched Rosamund give directions to the footman about her luggage and the chaise, and handed him her purse to pay off the post-boys. Everything about Rosamund was elegant, composed, authoritative – and unapproachable. What had happened in the years since Scarborough to bring about this change?

But now Rosamund was coming up the steps at last, she was putting her gloved hands into Sophie's (such gloves! – pale blue suede with jet buttons – Agnes would die for them!) and she was smiling, a warm smile that lighted her eyes almost in the old way.

'And now that's done, my dear Sophie, and I have all my attention for you. Let me look at you. Oh, what a little matron you've become!' She laughed, stretching Sophie's hands out and looking her up and down. 'You look so very married! Tell me at once, are you happy?'

'Oh yes,' Sophie said. 'So very, very happy. I couldn't have believed this time last year that my life would have changed so much.'

Rosamund drew Sophie's hand through her arm and they walked indoors together. 'I'm sorry I couldn't come to your wedding, love.'

'Well, it was rather short notice,' Sophie agreed. 'But there didn't seem anything to wait for, once Maman and Papa had agreed, and the settlements had been drawn up.'

'I should think not, indeed. Anyway, it's better this way – we shall have much longer together. It must have been the prettiest ceremony, though. Much nicer in the chapel at Morland Place, I should think, than mine in Westminster Abbey. And you wore your mother's lace, that she wore for her wedding?'

'Yes. Fanny had it too, for her wedding. Poor Fanny! But I'm sure she and Mr Hawker really did love each other, just as Jasper and I do. I thought of Mr Hawker on the day, and of Mr –'

'Where is Jasper?' Rosamund interrupted, as Moss took her gloves and bonnet from her.

'Oh, he was so sorry he couldn't be here to meet you,' Sophie said, 'but he had to go to the mill – there was some trouble there with a machine running hot.'

'He still insists on doing everything himself, does he?' Rosamund said, seeming amused. 'You haven't trained him properly, Sophie. He's the master now, not the manager.'

Sophie blushed and looked away. 'He only supervises things. He just likes to make sure everything's done right.'

Rosamund linked arms with her again. 'I didn't mean to criticise. I was only teasing you. Come, shew me your wonderful new house. I've never been here before. Is it very magnificent?'

Sophie smiled a little uneasily. 'I don't know whether you'll think so. Maman thinks it's very funny – all the elephants and mandarins and sphinxes make her laugh – but I've grown so fond of them. I don't want to change anything.'

'Why should you? I should dearly like a house I could laugh at,' Rosamund said. Her tone was amused, but her mouth was hard. 'Oh, look at the little bells on that looking-glass! Is it all like that? Dear Sophie, you mustn't change a thing! Come, shew me everything at once, especially the elephants. I die for the elephants!'

'We'll start upstairs, then,' Sophie said, yielding to her

cousin's charm. 'Oh Rosamund, I'm glad you're here! What a pity Marcus couldn't come, though. You will miss him. I should hate to be away from Jasper for so long.'

'Don't think of it,' Rosamund said lightly. 'It's different for people like us. My lord and lady don't live in each other's pockets the way you and Jasper do – and a good thing too, for it wouldn't suit me at all. I need a long rein and light hands, love, and I've never been broken to harness.'

'Is he still in London?' Sophie asked. She found it hard to visualise what their lives must be like.

'In July? In this heat? No, he's travelling round the country, looking for an estate to buy. When Mother comes home next year, we won't be able to use Wolvercote as we do now.'

'But – shouldn't you be with him?'

'His mother is with him,' Rosamund said grimly. 'He can't have both of us at the same time.'

'Oh Ros!' Sophie's eyes brimmed with sympathy. 'But surely he can't choose a country seat without your seeing it too?'

'I don't mind in the least. It makes no difference to me where I live. No, really, I mean it. If I had one house, a small house, like yours, of course it would matter. But when you move from one great mansion with fifty bedrooms to another, they all seem very much alike.'

Sophie was not convinced. 'You love Wolvercote,' she pointed out.

'Yes, I suppose I do – but that's just sentiment, because I grew up there. Really, you mustn't worry about me on that score. I'm sure I shall like whatever Marcus chooses.'

She spoke so firmly that Sophie felt obliged to leave the subject, and took her instead to see the Chinese bedroom. When they had looked over the house, they returned to the morning-room, and the new butler, Wells, brought them a nuncheon. Sophie watched the cold meats, fruit and cake being laid out on the round table with anxious eyes, hoping that it would seem elegant and varied enough to Rosamund's sophisticated palate.

Rosamund's appetite, it seemed, had not changed along with everything else. She ate with a will, and praised what she ate.

'Tell me the London news,' Sophie begged. 'I want lots of

details to pass on to my new friends, so they can see how sophisticated I am!'

Rosamund laughed. 'Well, now, what can I tell you?' she said obligingly. 'Mrs Fitzherbert's in a froth because George Dawson wants to marry little Minney Seymour – you know, her ward?'

'Yes, I remember.'

'She's so determined he shan't – though he's a perfectly respectable young man: he was wounded at Waterloo, and Marcus says he had two horses killed under him. But Maria Fitzherbert thinks he won't do, so she's begged the Duke of York to have poor Dawson posted to the West Indies, where she hopes a fever will carry him off. And meanwhile she's carried Minney off to Paris to keep her out of the way. They're living in Alvanley's apartment there. Of course, Alvanley's as soft as butter, and he's promised Dawson to try and make it all right, both with the Duke and the Fitzherbert. He'll have his work cut out! No-one ever changed our Maria's mind about anything.'

'Did Lord Alvanley have any news of Mr Brummell?'

'Oh yes, he always stops in to see him as he passes through Calais. But did I not tell you in one of my letters that we saw Mr Brummell ourselves, in December?'

'Good heavens! No, you didn't.'

'He came over to London for a few days. It was all very dangerous, of course, for had he been recognised, he would have been taken up – and far from being able to pay off his English debts, he's now running up fresh ones in France, poor man! He was terribly disappointed that Mama was still abroad, but I let him have the run of her house in Upper Grosvenor Street – of course the servants there are absolutely to be trusted. I had to keep it from Marcus, though, for he can't keep any secrets from his mother, and she'd have had Mr Brummell arrested without a second thought –'

'Oh, surely not? He's never done her any harm.'

'You don't know her! But anyway, it all passed off very well, and he got safe away again. Poor man, he's changed so much! He's grown so thin, and so melancholy, though he tried to hide it, and chatted amusingly in his old way. But I suppose he couldn't be completely at ease, afraid of being arrested at any minute.'

'What did he come for, if it was so dangerous?'

'He said it was to buy snuff – you know how he is – but actually, I think it was to consult his attorney about his business affairs, in the hope that something might be done to clear his debts. However, I suppose the answer was no, since he went back, and we haven't heard any more.' She paused for a moment, and then went on with a smile, 'He complained very much about the gas-lamps along Pall Mall and around St James's. Very inconvenient, he said, for a gentleman *incog*. It's lucky he didn't go out in the daytime, or he might have caught sight of the Prince Regent. Since Prinny left off his stays, he can't get up on a horse any more, so he's taken to riding about in a gig, like a common cad. The sight might well have thrown Mr Brummel into a fit!'

'Oh Ros! Ought you to speak so about the Regent?'

'My dear Sophie, I'm very much kinder to him than most people! He's always been good to me, so I have a sort of affection for him; but he is behaving very badly over the Duke of Kent's daughter, who, after all, is a legitimate offspring, born to a perfectly respectable princess. You know the baby's three months old now, and he hasn't even announced her birth to the other European rulers as he ought?'

'It's such a pity the Clarences' baby died,' Sophie said. 'It would have pleased everyone if she'd lived. Everyone seems to like the Duke of Clarence.'

'Well there's every probability they'll have another – after all, the Duchess is only twenty-six, and the Duke has proved himself amply with Mrs Jordan.' Sophie blinked a little at Rosamund's directness. Rosamund went on, 'So all in all, there's little chance the Kent baby will succeed to the throne, but the Prince hates the Duke of Kent so much that I think he'd sooner strangle the little mite than acknowledge it. He wouldn't even let it have a proper State christening, you know – which annoyed Lady Barbara no end, for she was bound to have been invited to a public ceremony, and she loves anything of that sort.'

'So you didn't go either?'

'No-one did. On the Prince's orders it was a private ceremony at Kensington Palace. However Alvanley told me about it – he got it out of the Duke of York. Apparently, Kent wanted to call the baby *Victoire* – after its mother –

Georgina, Alexandrina – after the Tsar, who was godfather – *Charlotte, Augusta.* But apparently, right at the last minute, when Canterbury had the little brute actually dangling over the font, the Prince suddenly announced that they couldn't use the names Georgina, Charlotte or Augusta – all royal names, you see.'

'Oh dear, how very embarrassing!'

'Just so. There was a long silence. Kent went scarlet with fury, and apparently the Duchess was almost in tears. Then Canterbury asked the Prince terribly politely what they *might* call it, and the Prince said "Alexandrina". Well, of course just one name wouldn't do for Kent, so he asked the Prince if they could have Elizabeth as well. The Prince snapped "Certainly not!" – we had a queen regnant called Elizabeth, after all – and then he added that they could call it after its mother, but that the name couldn't precede the Tsar's name. So it ended up as Alexandrina Victoria; and the sooner the Clarences have another brat and put poor Prinny out of his misery, the better.'

'You tell it all so well,' Sophie sighed with satisfaction. 'I shall never be able to make it sound so diverting when I pass it on. Tell me more.'

Rosamund looked at her with amusement. 'I can't think of any more. Except that your Sir Robert Peel got his factory regulation act through Parliament at last, but I dare say you'll know more about that than I do. Is Jasper pleased about it?'

'Well, in some ways: he says it's a beginning. But they were all disappointed that it had so many modifications before it went through. The minimum age for children to be allowed to work in factories was put down to nine instead of ten; and the hours for children of nine to sixteen were only reduced to twelve a day instead of ten – which hardly makes any difference at all, for they work thirteen or fourteen hours now.'

'You're lucky to have got it through at all. There's a great deal of feeling in the clubs that the whole principle of trying to restrict free labour is wrong.'

Sophie sighed. 'Yes, I know; and when I hear the opponents arguing, what they say sounds so sensible! But then when I hear our side, that sounds sensible too. I really don't know what to think. However, Mr Farraline says the Act won't make any difference in the short term, because there was no provision made for inspectors to see that the rules are put into force, so in reality factory owners may go on doing just as they like. He says the only effect will be in the long term, as a bad precedent.'

'Do you see much of Mr Farraline?' Rosamund asked lightly.

'Not really, not now I'm married. It's only if I go to one of the meetings with Jasper. Mr Farraline's always there. I can't think why, since he disagrees with everything so entirely. I think he must do it to torment – he does have a very strange sense of humour, and says the oddest things, so that one never knows if he's serious or not. He's never anything but kind to me, however, and friendly to Jasper. When I think how we met him and Mr Hawker at Scarborough, I little thought how it would all turn out.' She looked at Rosamund as a thought struck her. 'He went to London in May, now I come to think of it – during that heat-wave, which we thought very odd of him. Did you happen to see anything of him?'

'No, I didn't *happen* to,' Rosamund said with a strange little smile. 'So tell me, dear Sophie, has it answered for you, being married? Are you happy? Does your Jasper make you happy?'

Sophie's face lit. 'Oh yes! Oh, so much, Ros! I never knew I could be so happy.'

'Didn't I tell you that you would marry for love? And I remember your telling me that you could never marry anyone but Major Larosse.'

'Yes, I did say so – and I believed it,' Sophie said. 'And in a strange way, I don't think I could have loved Jasper if it hadn't been for René. But he was a very different person. There was a sadness about him, even when he was happy – a part of him I couldn't reach. It isn't like that with Jasper. I think I am much happier with him than I could ever have been with René, even though part of me doesn't like to admit it.'

'And does Jasper love you as much as René did?'

'That's a strange question. I don't really know how much René loved me. I never had a chance to find out. But, oh Ros, Jasper loves me so much it frightens me sometimes! To be so adored – to be the object of such passion . . .'

Rosamund tried to imagine Jasper Hobsbawn in the throes

413

of passion, and failed. It just shewed, she thought, how limited was the human imagination; and how love could come in the strangest of guises.

Sophie was evidently building up to some personal revelation. Rosamund felt she could almost have dispensed with it, for the realisation that everything in Sophie's life was falling pleasantly into place, only emphasised that her own life had gone wrong, and that she didn't in the least know how to correct it. And yet she loved Sophie, and would not have turned away her confidence. Also, she thought wryly, there is always in women a deep-seated desire to know how other women's lives go on.

'Do you remember,' Sophie said tentatively, 'when we used to talk about such things, how I felt that I could never bear the intimate side of marriage with anyone but René?'

'Yes, I remember. You quite shrank from the idea. But it's not so bad, is it, once you get used to it?'

Sophie's eyes opened wide. 'Not so bad? But, Ros, it's wonderful! It's so extraordinary and exciting and – and *touching*, somehow. To be so close to him, to have no barriers between us, to feel how much he wants me! It's such a powerful, physical force, and yet so full of care and tenderness that it touches me unbearably. It makes me feel so proud, and yet almost as though I want to cry. Well, of course, you must know,' she added, a little embarrassed by her own vehemence. 'You're married too.'

'Yes, of course,' Rosamund said blankly.

'I think of the marriage vow – you know, when the man says "with my body, I thee worship". There is something – I don't mean to sound blasphemous, but it is so – something holy about it. When Jasper looks at me when we're –' a deep blush – 'when we're making love, and touches my face, as if I were something so precious –'

'Yes,' said Rosamund desperately. 'Yes, love, I'm very glad you're happy.'

It was so obviously an attempt to stop her that Sophie was afraid she had overstepped the mark and spoken too freely. 'I beg your pardon,' she said in a small, hurt voice. 'I wouldn't have mentioned such things to anyone but you, but I thought as we had been such friends, and – and – I thought it would be all right.'

414

'Oh Sophie, I'm sorry, I didn't mean to hurt you. Of course, I'm honoured that you confide in me. You can say anything to me, anything at all. It's just that – well, love, I suppose I'm jealous, in a way. I don't imagine many people's marriages are just like yours. That side of things – it's not always blissful, you know.'

Sophie looked distressed. 'Well, yes, I suppose I did know, but – you and Marcus, Ros? You love him so much. Surely it must be – well, all right?'

Rosamund felt such a sadness, though it was foolish to feel it in the face of Sophie's innocent happiness. Everything was so simple for Sophie: love and marriage, and now sexual pleasure, were all part of the same thing, indivisible, and Sophie could not imagine any of them existing separately from each other. Perhaps with one part of her brain she might acknowledge that in some cases it was so, but only in the same way that she acknowledged there was a place called Africa. It had no reality for her. She didn't really *believe* it. And loving her, Rosamund could not wish her to think any differently.

'Yes, of course it's all right,' she said, smiling reassuringly. 'I didn't mean otherwise. Only that – well, not until I'm as *good* as you, dearest Sophie, will I be able to be as *happy* as you. So now tell me,' she changed the subject brightly, 'what news from Morland Place? Have you seen Mathilde's new baby yet? Polly writes that they called it Harriet. What a pity they had another girl – I'm sure John must have wanted a boy.'

'Oh, no, they both adore her!' Sophie was successfully diverted. 'She's the sweetest little thing! Polly dotes on her, and I'm sure she spends as much time at Morland Place as at Skelwith House. I've only seen her once, when Jasper and I came back from our honeymoon – she was born while we were in Scarborough – but Mathilde writes me long letters about her, so I feel I know everything about her.'

Yes, I'll bet you do, Rosamund thought. She could imagine those letters, with all their endless, boring detail. Well, at least a letter could be ignored. Rosamund had learned all she ever wanted to know about Miss Harriet Skelwith at York races, long before the little brute was even born.

Sophie turned on the step and said again, 'Are you sure you

don't mind my leaving you? It does seem rude, when you've come so far to see me.'

'Of course I don't mind. Sophie, do stop being so polite! We have four whole weeks together, maybe more if Marcus doesn't press me to go back. I can certainly spare you two afternoons a week, especially in such a good cause.'

'You're sure you don't want to come with me?' Sophie said doubtfully.

Rosamund shuddered. 'I can think of few things I'd like less than to go visiting your dreadful tenements. I loathe bad smells and dirt and sickness.'

'But you were so wonderful in Brussels, after the battle, with the sick and wounded soldiers.'

'I can do it when I have to. That doesn't mean I like it – or that I'll do it except under extreme duress. No, no, my Sophie, you go and play loblolly boy to your heart's delight, and don't worry about me. I shall drive to the Exchange and waste my pin-money on ribbons and purses like a frivolous woman, and you may think me as decadent as you please.'

Sophie put her arms round her cousin in a swift, surprising hug. 'I *love* you,' she said fiercely, as if Rosamund needed defending. 'I just want you to enjoy yourself.'

'I shall, I promise you. Each to his own. Now *go*!'

Ten minutes later Rosamund was putting on her hat, and meeting Moss's eye in the glass, said, 'Is it all arranged?'

'Yes, my lady.'

Rosamund sighed. 'And you can take off that disapproving look. If you aren't happy in my service, you can always look for another place.'

She saw the hurt in Moss's eyes, and after a moment of inward resistance, said, 'I'm sorry, Judy. I didn't mean that. I'm grateful to you.'

'You don't need to be grateful to me, my lady,' Moss said, stiffly. 'You pay my wages to give me orders.'

'I don't pay you to love me, though, do I?' Rosamund said, smiling, though her eyes were strained.

Moss melted. 'Oh my lady, I only want you to be happy, that's all.'

'Then go on helping me. Yes, I know everything you think about this, and I don't want to hear it. We all have to take happiness where we can. There, will I do now, do you think?'

'You look beautiful, my lady,' Moss said fervently, and stepped forward to lift down Rosamund's veil for her. Then she went to the door and opened it, listened, and said, 'It's all quiet, my lady. The hackney'll be waiting at the second corner. You will be careful, won't you, my lady?'

'Of course I will. Thank you, Judy. And if anyone asks about me –'

'You went shopping, yes, my lady. Don't worry – I'll put 'em off.'

Ten minutes later a cab pulled into the sweep of a small, rather shabby house on the Bury road, and a veiled lady stepped down, paid the driver, knocked at the door, and was admitted by an unseen hand. Inside the hallway she lifted her veil and carefully removed her hat, looking round her to remark with faint distaste, 'What is this place? Is it yours?'

'No, it belongs to a friend. It was his mother's, but she died recently. Oh, nothing infectious, I promise you!'

'I didn't suppose it was. I was only wondering whether he was to be trusted. Does he know what you wanted to borrow it for?'

'He knows what. He doesn't know who, of course. And yes, he is entirely to be trusted. Don't worry, my darling, we're quite safe. And it's better than an inn, you must admit.'

Rosamund put down the hat, and let out a quivering sigh. 'Oh Jesmond!' she said.

'Yes, my dear love?' He gathered her into his arms, turned her face up to his, and began to kiss it, gently, all over – brow, eyes, nose, lips.

Rosamund had been going to say *why does life have to be so complicated*, but she suddenly realised she didn't want to ask that any more. His arms were strong around her, the familiar sweet smell of his skin was affecting her. She turned her mouth to intercept his, and kissed him, long and hungrily; and when they broke, she sighed again, but a different sigh this time.

'What have you prepared – a bedroom? Then let's go there, now.'

He raised an eyebrow. 'So hasty, Lady Chelmsford? Shouldn't you like some civilised conversation first? Or a dish of tea?'

She took his hand and led him firmly towards the stairs.

417

'Don't be a clown. And don't call me that, you know I hate it.'

'Very well, then, Lady Rosamund,' Farraline said, and suddenly scooped her up in his arms, making her shriek with surprise. 'I know my place. I shall ravish you first,' he laughed, 'and talk to you afterwards ...'

A long time afterwards they lay on the bed together, eating cherries. 'I'm glad you remembered the sheets this time,' Rosamund said idly, leaning up on one elbow and dropping the stones into the bowl. 'I shall never forget that dreadful inn where there were only blankets on the bed – and such blankets!'

'I know. Your tender patrician skin ought never to be touched by anything less than silk,' Farraline said. He leaned across and pushed the fiery mass of her hair away from one white shoulder, and kissed it. 'You look so magnificent when you're naked – like a beautiful wild cat, a glorious gold-striped tigress.' He kissed her neck and cheek, and she turned her lips briefly and received a kiss there, too, before going back to the cherries. 'I knew,' he went on, 'the first time I saw you, on the sands at Scarborough, that you would look wonderful sprawled naked across a bed.'

'Shocking!' she said, drawing a stalk out of her mouth. 'I was a pure young girl – how could you think such a thing?'

'Experience. I knew that very instant that one day there would be something wonderful between us.'

'Faddle. You were after Sophie – you told me so yourself.'

'Oh, to marry, yes. But you I wanted for quite other reasons.'

'One woman for one thing, and another for another. How horrid and practical you are, Mr Farraline.'

'Well, my love, I knew there was no chance in the world of my marrying you. You, an earl's daughter with fifty thousand pounds –'

'Sixty.'

'You see?'

She turned to look at him with veiled eyes. 'You'd have married me if you could?'

'Then, now, or at any time in the future,' he said, his blue eyes pouring into hers. 'Don't I tell you I love you, my tigress?'

She held his gaze for a moment, and then flung an arm over his shoulder and rolled onto her back, pulling him with her. 'Liar!' she said. 'You want me for this, don't you – only for this!' She pulled his head down to her breast. He took her right nipple gently between his teeth and she sighed and arched her body. 'Make love to me again,' she said. 'Jesmond, oh my dear Jes. Make love to me.'

He stretched over her, kissing her fervently, feeling her body reaching hungrily for his. 'Rosamund, my beautiful one,' he whispered fiercely. Their bodies met and coupled smoothly, knowing every movement in the elaborate dance, loving it, never able to have enough of it. 'I love you,' he said as passion mounted. His mouth against her ear, he said, 'I love you. I love you.'

She pressed against him in response. But when the last moment came, he dragged his head back from her, his teeth bared, his eyes screwed shut as though with pain, and in that moment Rosamund opened her eyes and looked up at him, as she always did, with a sad, lost look he never saw.

Afterwards they lay side by side, her hair tumbled over his shoulder, his fair face flushed, and looked at their reflection in the cheval glass opposite the end of the bed.

'We make such a handsome couple,' Rosamund said, watching her reflection smile back at her, glitteringly, like a tiger. 'Naked like this, like two lovely, innocent animals. What a pity no-one else ever sees us naked together. Can you imagine if we appeared at a public function, walking up the red-carpeted stairs, with my hand on your arm. How the old pussies would cry out and faint! It would be almost worth it, my Jes, just once, just to make them all sit up!'

'Shall we?' he said. 'I will if you will.' He watched her eyes in the glass. There was a seriousness under his lightness that she heard, and would not hear.

She dug her fingers into his thick, pale hair and tugged a little, warningly. 'No, not even once. On second thoughts, I want to keep you all to myself. I want no-one else to look at your lovely body.'

'I believe that's all you want me for,' he said lightly. 'Just my lovely body, nothing else.'

'Of course,' she said. 'What else?' She tugged the hair harder, shaking his head gently from side to side. 'What else are you good for, Jesmond Farraline, tell me that? Good to serve me, like the fine stallion you are. And after all, what more can you want?'

For once he ignored the warning in her hand and voice. 'Much more,' he said. 'I want much more. I want everything.' He reached up and unfurled her fingers, releasing his head; pulled away from her, jumped up onto his knees to face her, looking down into her face seriously. 'I want all of you, Ros. Don't you understand that yet? I love you –'

'You desire me,' she corrected flatly.

'Yes, of course I do! God, you're the most desirable woman that ever lived! I want you and want you all the time. But if it was only that – oh, I could resist that.' Seeing her faint, mocking smile he went on fiercely, 'And I would, too! Do you think I like deceiving Marcus?'

The smile disappeared. 'Don't talk to me about Marcus.'

'I like him. He's a fine man. I wouldn't do this to him if it was just a matter of – of passion.'

'Stop it.'

'But I love you, Rosamund, every part of you, your body and mind and soul –'

'My dear Jes,' she said in a hard voice that was holding back tears, 'I don't have a soul. I gave that up long ago.'

'Why can't you love me?' he cried wildly. 'I know that we can't marry. I know there can't be a divorce. But if you just loved me – if you just said that you loved me –!'

'Is that all you want? I love you – there, will that do?'

'No, not like that.' He ruffled his hair in frustration. 'You know very well what I mean.' He stared at her for a moment, and then leaned forward, stroked her cheek with one hand, kissed her brow and eyes tenderly. 'Dear love –'

'Don't,' she said in a small voice.

He gazed at her, his mouth quivering. 'You do love me. I don't believe it could be as good as this if you didn't love me. I don't believe you would go on seeing me like this. I know you love me – I feel it when I touch you, when I kiss you. If you would only let go, tell me how you feel, let me have your love completely while we're together. *That's* what I want. To have all of you, just while I can. Is that so much to ask?'

'Yes it is! It's entirely too much,' she said in a small, bitter voice. 'To give you *everything* – to give in to you completely –

and then to pull back, to drag myself away from you, to go back to that other world and behave as if nothing had happened? How can you ask that? You're mad, Jesmond Farraline, mad!'

'Rosamund, Ros, tell me you love me,' he whispered, kissing her. He pushed her back onto the pillows, and felt her body yielding to his. He caressed her. 'My lovely one, my queen. Tell me you love me.'

Her mouth snatched at his, her arms came round him to hold him close, crushing him against her with all her strength. And then he felt her withdrawing from him again. After a moment she pulled her mouth away, pushed him back from her.

'No, no,' she said, smiling tigerishly, 'you don't get a halter on me that easily. Love you, indeed, what nonsense!' She sat up, shaking her hair back, regarding him with cool, laughing eyes. 'You really are quite mad, you know. Any other man would be delighted to have a mistress who didn't make demands on him, but you – you're just perverse, I suppose.'

He struggled with the hurt, and with the desire to strike back as she had struck him; and when he had won the struggle, he looked at her seriously for a moment. 'Why, Rosamund?' he asked. 'No play-acting. Just for once, remembering our pact, tell me *why*?'

The veil lifted, the eyes widened, she looked at him with such sadness that he flinched from it, almost wishing he hadn't asked. He couldn't know that she was thinking of Sophie and Jasper, of Sophie and her in Brussels, and of how far their lives had moved apart, down such different roads, never to meet again.

'Rosamund?' he said. 'Why?'

'You were too late, Jes,' she said sadly. 'You should have been there before Waterloo. Now it's too late.'

Habit enabled them to resume their easiness with each other. He helped her dress, and then pinned up her hair, and she watched in the glass, smiling a little. 'You are suspiciously good at this,' she said. 'It speaks a very long and disgraceful experience, I'm afraid.'

'Plaiting horses,' he explained. 'I'd have thought, given your love of horses, you'd be better at it yourself.'

'I can do it on other people, not on myself,' she said.

He met her eyes. 'Shall we meet again?' he asked abruptly.

'What? Yes, of course. Sophie goes philanthropising every Tuesday and Thursday. If I don't come to you, I might have to go with her.'

'I thought perhaps, after what you said –'

'But I still fancy you, you know,' she said, and then, ruefully, seeing his expression, 'Jes, Jes, don't be sad, my dear. Let's enjoy what we have while we can.' He didn't answer her, and she went on, 'You've made such a difference to my life. When I met you at the York races last year, I was desperate. I'd been so unhappy – all the strain of Minnie's death, and that dreadful trial, and my marriage to Marcus and his mother. You've made it possible for me to bear it all. You've given me so much pleasure.'

'But it doesn't make you happy,' he said. 'I want to make you happy.'

She turned on the seat to look at him instead of his reflection, put her hands up to cup his beautiful face, smiled at him. 'You do make me happy! God, how can I tell you? You do! Without you I would shrivel up and die!'

He folded his hands over hers and leaned down and kissed her, and said no more, allowing her to think she had convinced him. She couldn't know, of course, of the lost look in her eyes, even while she was smiling.

Two days later Sophie and Jasper gave a very small dinner party in Rosamund's honour, the guests being Mr and Mrs Percy Droylsden, Mr Henry Droylsden, Miss Pendlebury, and Mr Jesmond Farraline.

'I couldn't help it, I was invited,' Jesmond whispered to Rosamund as he took her in to dinner on his arm.

'You could have refused,' she replied without moving her lips.

'I didn't want to,' he murmured indignantly. 'Are you going to be horrid to me? Because if so, I shall dedicate the evening to embarrassing you.'

She chewed her lip to repress a smirk. He would do it, too. He knew just how to bring her to the blush. 'I'll be nice,' she promised. 'But don't make me laugh.'

'I won't.'

He didn't – though as he was seated next to her, he spent quite a lot of the time covertly stroking her thigh – much to the amusement of Henry Droylsden, who was sitting opposite her and took a couple of kicks on the shins when things went too far and she tried to shake Jesmond off. Henry enjoyed the situation hugely, and felt Rosamund ought to have been grateful to Farraline for diverting her, for otherwise the dinner was as dull as a wet Monday, the talk never managing to stray far from the linked subjects of the depression in the cotton-trade and the revival of the reform movement.

After the brief upsurge in trade between 1817 and 1818, the market had become glutted, trade had fallen off, and the factories were idle again. In addition, since the harvest of 1818 had been a poor one, the price of bread had soared, and everything seemed to be back where it had been in 1816. At the beginning of the year the Government had eased its laws on public assemblies, in response to the long period of calm, and the reformist clubs had started up again, like weeds the more vigorous for having been cut back.

'We shall have trouble again soon, you mark my words,' said Mr Percy Droylsden, helping himself liberally to roast duck with cherries. 'The mill-workers are hungry, and Bamford and Cartwright and all these reformists will play on them for their own ends, just like before. Calling themselves Radicals now, whatever that's supposed to mean! You'll see all their claptrap appeals to sentiment coming out of the cupboard again. Out will come the Tricolor Flags and the Caps of Liberty –'

'And Orator Hunt's white top-hat,' Harry put in. 'Lord, how I longed to throw a stone at it when he held that meeting at St Peter's Field in January! What lad of spirit with a catapult could resist? I wonder what's happening to the youth of today.' He shook his head sadly.

'I think he's rather handsome,' said Agnes. 'I don't suppose he really means any harm. I expect he just likes to hear himself talk, like other men.'

'He's dangerous,' Percy said firmly, ignoring the barb. 'If I were Sidmouth I'd have gaoled him long ago.'

'No, no, he can't do that – it would be taking him far too seriously,' Farraline said. 'Hunt is a joke.'

'Wolseley got gaoled all right,' Percy pointed out, 'and he's one of us – a gentleman, I mean.'

'Ah, that's what happens when you take a joke too far – particularly when it isn't a very good joke to begin with. Don't you think so, Lady Chelmsford? May I help you to some of this galantine?'

'I know nothing about Wolseley,' Rosamund said, nodding consent to the galantine.

'And care less, as the saying is,' said Farraline.

'Sir Charles Wolseley is one of the new breed of gentleman-radicals,' Prudence explained.

'If that's not a contradiction in terms,' murmured Harry.

'He presided over a reformist meeting in Stockport last month,' Jasper took up the explanation. 'They held mock parliamentary elections, and elected him Representative for Birmingham. He was arrested afterwards and sentenced to eighteen months in prison for sedition.'

'I still think that seems awfully harsh,' Sophie said doubtfully. 'It doesn't sound as though they were doing any harm.'

'It isn't the harm it does, it's the harm it leads to,' Jasper said.

'Quite right. We've got to stamp these things out before they go too far,' said Percy. 'These people play on the feelings of the lower orders, whip them up into sedition, and before you know where you are, you've got revolution on your hands. The poor would never think of it for themselves – perfectly decent creatures, most of 'em, only just now there's not much work about, and bread is dear.'

'Quite. It's bread they want, not the vote,' said Farraline.

'I thought you were all for Parliamentary reform, Mr Farraline,' said Rosamund sweetly.

He lowered his eyelids to conceal a wicked gleam from all but her. 'I was not aware that I had ever disclosed my political opinions to you, Lady Chelmsford.'

'Whatever anyone's opinion about the question of reform,' Jasper said, 'none of us can have two views about the danger of a large public meeting here in Manchester. There are too many unemployed weavers already banding together and making demands, and the situation –'

'Don't you have a power-loom factory, Hobsbawn?' Farraline asked innocently. Rosamund kicked him reprovingly under the table.

'Yes, we have a weaving-shed, but we've never yet been able to bring it into full production, and now it's idle again.'

'Why is that?'

'Because just as we were starting to bring it into use, the orders began to fall off again, and there wouldn't have been enough work for the hand-weavers as well as my machines. Though now, of course, there isn't enough for the hand-weavers anyway.'

'You mean – you had orders, but you gave them to hand-loom weavers?' Farraline said, serious now. 'For God's sake, man, why? Why let expensive machinery stand idle – machinery that can do the job better, what's more?'

'I won't run machines while men starve,' Jasper said tautly. 'If they can't be complementary to each other –'

'That's madness,' Farraline said. 'Don't you see, the days of the hand-loom weaver are over, finished! Oh yes, I know there aren't enough power looms in the whole country at the moment when production is at peak, but there will be. The writing is on the wall for anyone to see. The future is with the machine. One day all the manufacturing processes will be done by machine. It's simply flying in the face of history to keep on employing hand-weavers at the expense of the machines. It's no kindness, believe me, to encourage them in their delusions. The time will come when they will have to find something else to do.'

'Well that time is not yet,' said Jasper stubbornly, 'and frankly, I don't believe that it will happen in your lifetime or mine, if it ever happens at all. There's no reason why we can't go on as we do –'

'It's as I said to you before,' Farraline said resignedly. 'You're a romantic, not a visionary. You see only what's under your nose.'

'Mr Farraline, won't you help Mrs Droylsden to some of the galantine,' Sophie said desperately, feeling her dinner party sliding towards disaster. Neither man heard her.

'I see no reason why progress can't go hand in hand with compassion,' Jasper said.

'Ah, as in Mr Owen's little kingdom, eh?'

'Never mind about Owen and your damned philanthropy,' said Percy Droylsden good-naturedly from the other end of the table, where he had missed a large part of the point, 'what

425

about this radical meeting they're going to call? That's what worries me.'

'What radical meeting?' Sophie asked, glad to have any diversion from the near-quarrel.

'Advertised in the *Observer* – what? – ten days ago. To be held on August the 9th, St Peter's Fields, the same sort of thing as that Stockport meeting, with the purpose of adopting Major Cartwright's plan of Parliamentary reform, and electing Henry Hunt as "representative" for Manchester.'

'No, no, that won't come off,' Farraline said. 'Since Wolseley's been imprisoned, they'll know it would be regarded as treasonable. Hunt won't risk it, not when he thinks things are going his way at last. That August the 9th meeting will be cancelled, I promise you.'

'I certainly hope you're right,' said Droylsden. 'This hot weather makes the lower orders fidgety, especially when they haven't enough to do to keep 'em out of mischief. A public meeting of any sort would be bound to lead to trouble.'

Agnes concealed a yawn behind her hand, and said, 'Have you been to our theatre yet, Lady Chelmsford? We saw a very good play last week, didn't we, Percy? What was it called?'

'Much Ado About Nothing, wasn't it?' Harry answered for his brother, and dropped the ghost of a wink across the table at Farraline.

CHAPTER TWENTY-TWO

The proposed reformist meeting for the 9th of August did not take place, but it was not cancelled. Instead it was postponed to the 16th of August, and a new notice in the *Manchester Observer* announced that its purpose would be 'to consider the propriety of adopting the most legal and effectual means of obtaining Reform of the Commons House of Parliament'.

'Mildness itself, you see. A most modest declaration of political intent. These people have learned something in the last four years,' Jesmond Farraline said to Rosamund as they lay on the bed together on a Thursday afternoon.

'I can't think why it interests you so much,' Rosamund said sleepily. It was another hot day outside, and love had made her drowsy.

'It's like a process of manufacturing,' he said. 'In goes the raw cotton, thump thump thump go the machines, and out at the other end comes the yarn. In this case, the raw material is the labouring poor, and the radical machine has processed it into a single political animal.'

'Oh gammon,' said Rosamund. 'You don't suppose any of those simpletons really knows what it's all about, do you? Political animal, nonsense! The lower orders are like sheep: you set one of them running in a certain direction, and they'll all follow – straight over a cliff, if that's what happens to be in the way.'

Farraline laughed. 'I won't argue with you – I'll just invite you to come with me tomorrow and see for yourself.'

'See what for myself?'

'The reformist meeting, of course. Listen, I didn't tell you, did I, that I rode out to Grasscroft yesterday?'

'Did you?'

'I had to see Kit on some business. I was quite late by the time I left to come home, but of course the evenings are light, and it was only just growing dusk when I got to Miles

Platting. There's a big, level piece of heath there where the road turns off towards Cheetham Hill – do you know it?'

'No.'

He continued in the face of her determined indifference. 'There was quite a crowd assembled there – a group of something like thirty or forty men of the labouring sort, and an even larger number of women and assorted children. The women and children were watching, and the men were – can you guess? – drilling.'

'Drilling?'

'Marching in step, turning, wheeling and halting – and doing it pretty well, too, considering what a motley bunch they were!'

'But – what on earth for?'

'I naturally wondered that myself. It occurred to me that a group of labouring men going through military manoeuvres, with no gentleman in sight to command them, was a pretty alarming sight, especially to a man who's spent his best years fighting the French. Puts one in mind of Paris and the Bastille.'

'Good God, yes! Were they armed?'

'No, not with so much as a stick. But still worrying, all the same. I pulled up just above them, and was wondering what was best to be done, when I realised that I knew the old fellow who was acting as drill-sergeant. He was one of our veterans in the Peninsula, and as stout and honest a fellow as you could wish to find. I'd been spotted by this time, so I rode across, hopped off my horse and gave it to a boy to hold, and went straight up to Old Drills and said, "Well now, Collins, what's going on here? Planning a revolution?"'

'Did he remember you?'

'Lord, yes. It was obvious there was nothing havey-cavey going on, for his face lit up at the sight of me. He halted his troops and came to attention and called me *Captain Farraline, sir* just as if we were back at Torres Verdras! Very flattered, he was, too, that I remembered him.'

'Of course he was,' Rosamund said, amused. 'So, what was he doing?'

'He said to me, "I'm licking 'em into shape, sir, just like we did them Portuguese dagoes, with a bit of the old close-order marching".' Farraline was a talented mimic. 'So naturally I asked him why-the-deuce, and he said, "Mr Hunt's instructions, sir. He wants everything to go like clockwork on Friday. He wants us to shew the authorities that labouring men know how to conduct themselves with order and propriety, sir."'

'Insolent man!'

'Who?' Farraline frowned, distracted.

'Hunt, of course. Go on – what did you say to that?'

'I asked him in a casual, roundabout sort of way if they were going to be armed for the meeting. Old Collins looks shocked at the notion. "Lord bless you, sir, no," says he. "We ain't an army, sir – just meaning to display cleanliness, sobriety and decorum, sir, like what Mr Hunt says. To come in our Sunday best, Mr Hunt says, and armed with nothing but clear consciences – ain't that so, lads?" And the lads all give a cheer, crowding up to me, you know, like dogs wanting to be petted.'

Rosamund nodded, enjoying it all.

'"And the lads asked me to help 'em out, sir," Collins goes on, "seeing as I know how it's done, on account of being with Old Hookey right through to Salamanca when I took my wound, sir." So then I asked him what the meeting was all about, and what it was they were hoping to gain. He opens his eyes very wide, as if I ought to know such a simple thing, and he says, "Why, sir, we want annual parliaments and universal suffrage, sir." Just like that. And the lads all give another great cheer.'

'What stuff,' Rosamund said. 'What on earth can people like that understand about universal suffrage?'

Farraline grinned. 'As little as ever, I imagine. But the impressive fact was that they all knew what it was they wanted, and wanted it badly enough to give up their free time to drilling, so as to impress the world with the seriousness of their purpose.'

'It's more likely to impress the world with the idea that they should be locked up and transported! Look what happened to the Pentrich rebels. The sight of a group of orderly, marching men would be enough to send any magistrate into strong hysterics.'

'No, no, you're too harsh! They won't be armed, you know – that isn't their intention at all. As you say, I doubt whether one in a hundred of them knows what they want the vote *for*, but the fact of the matter is that Hunt and Cartwright and the rest have managed to convince them that they ought to have it. So, shall you come with me tomorrow and see the fun? The meeting starts at eleven o'clock. I could come for you in my tilbury.'

'Not I, thank you. I think Agnes Droylsden probably has the truth about orator Hunt – that he simply likes the sound of his own voice! Besides, my time will be taken up by Sophie tomorrow morning. She always feels guilty about leaving me on Tuesday and Thursday afternoons, and tries to make it up to me the next day.'

'Oh well, if you're sure. I shall go along, anyway. It might be amusing.'

'Go with my blessing – and come and tell us about it afterwards.'

'Shall I?'

'Yes, do. You don't need my invitation – you know Sophie's always glad to see you.'

'And you?' Farraline said, rolling over to look down at her. 'Are you always glad to see me?'

She ran a long finger down the line of his jaw. 'Always, my Jes, my dear. Even though you are a torment to me.'

'How am I a torment to you?'

'Come closer,' she murmured, slipping her hand behind his neck and pulling, 'and I'll tell you.'

It was possible from the morning-room of Hobsbawn House, with the window open, to hear the distant murmur of the crowd in St Peter's Fields. Rosamund would have had no need to tell Sophie about the men drilling, even if there had been a way to do so without mentioning Jesmond, for hundreds of them came marching down the street right past the gate that very morning.

She and Sophie had been hanging out of the window watching them go past. It was a most extraordinary sight, the like of which had never been witnessed before anywhere in the country. Men, women and children, all dressed in their best, talking cheerfully, some of them singing, went marching past, armed with nothing but banners decorated with devices such as *Liberty* or *Unity and Strength* or *Suffrage Universal*. Never had a mob displayed such discipline and orderliness.

Never had a mob been drawn together from so many different interests. Coal-miners marched alongside farm-labourers, weavers kept step with cutlers, chimney-sweeps with water-carriers.

'They have nothing in common at all,' Sophie said wonderingly, 'except that they are all of the lower orders. How strange!'

They had no idea of the size of the crowd that was gathering on St Peter's Fields, for of course they must be converging from all directions, but judging by the number that went past Hobsbawn House, Rosamund guessed it would be several thousand. They also saw a troop of the 15th Hussars clatter past, wearing their Waterloo medals, and grinning broadly beneath their cavalry whiskers. Both young women stared after them eagerly, falling silent for a moment, wondering if they might recognise an old friend. Rosamund was reminded painfully of that other time they had hung out of a window watching the soldiers go past – a lifetime ago, it seemed, in Brussels. Ah, but those soldiers had not come marching back.

'Jasper says the magistrates have called on the Manchester and Salford Yeomanry to keep order,' Sophie said, and the tone of her voice revealed that she had been thinking of the same thing. 'But I suppose they will like to have a trained body on hand, in case of trouble. The Yeomanry are not very well drilled.'

'That's not quite what he said, is it?' Rosamund said, watching the last bobbing tails and swinging pelisses disappear. 'I happened to overhear him this morning – he said they are a joke, and not a very good one.'

Sophie smiled faintly. 'Do you think there will be trouble?' she asked in a small voice.

'Of course not,' Rosamund said. 'Why should there be? If they were worried about it, the magistrates could have arrested Henry Hunt at any time. The fact that they're allowing him to go ahead must mean they know it will be peaceful.'

'Oh, yes,' Sophie said, and added, 'Jasper means to be there, you see.'

'Not amongst the crowd?'

'Oh, no, at the tavern on the corner of Windmill Street.

431

He'll watch from a window. All the same –'

'Then there's nothing to worry about,' Rosamund said firmly. She wondered if Jes would meet up with Jasper. It would be a good way of ensuring he was invited back to Hobsbawn House to tell them all. On the other hand, knowing Jes, he was just as likely to want to mingle with the 'mobility' and be in the heart of it. Still, he was tall and strong, unlike Jasper; he would not get jostled by a crowd of labouring people, all of whom would be much shorter and more puny than he.

They heard the roar go up from the invisible crowd, which must signal the arrival of Orator Hunt on the field. Rosamund looked at Sophie and raised her brows. 'That,' she said, 'is a very large crowd indeed. I shouldn't wonder if there weren't ten thousand in it.'

The cheering went on for some time, and then faded away, leaving behind it the sound of 'God Save the King' being played slightly out of synchronisation by two bands. When that died away, there was silence as far as the women were concerned. Presumably Hunt had begun to speak: his voice alone would not carry to them here. They turned away, and Sophie shut the window.

They settled themselves with their work and their conversation, to pass the time until Jasper – and Rosamund hoped Jesmond – should come in to take a nuncheon with them. The time passed pleasantly, for they were always good company for each other, and they did not particularly notice any further sounds from outside, until suddenly Sophie interrupted Rosamund in the middle of a sentence, sitting up straight and saying, 'Listen!'

'What is it?'

'I thought I heard someone scream.'

They both listened tensely for a moment. There did seem to be some distant kind of clamour coming from outside, but it was impossible to make out what it was.

'They're just cheering,' Rosamund said after a moment.

But Sophie was looking pale. 'I don't think so,' she said. She put her work down and went quickly to the window, and threw it up. At once the hot, August air pushed its way in, carrying on it the sound of a large crowd in the distance, not cheering, but shouting.

'Something's happening,' Sophie said, her eyes wide. A splurge of sound, hoarse male voices, the shrill neigh of a horse, and then what was unmistakably a woman's scream.

'It's probably nothing,' Rosamund said. 'I expect someone got out of hand and they had to send in the troops.'

Down below them, beyond the sweep and the handsome iron gates, the dusty street was empty under the midday sun, mocking their fears with its blandness. But all the while the clamour in the distance was growing, still maddeningly indistinct, but now and then punctuated by a scream or a whinny. And then suddenly into the end of the street the crowd irrupted.

'God, what is it?' Sophie cried.

They came running down the street, men and women, some of them dragging children by the hand, some of them with torn clothes, some of them wounded; fleeing from God-knew-what terror, mouths open wide in one composite scream, dusty faces streaked with tears, with sweat, with trickling blood. They saw a man with one arm dangling, the sleeve slashed almost in half, pause for a moment, clinging to the gate with his good hand, turning his face this way and that in blank terror, before the crowd snatched him up and bore him away like a piece of paper down a storm-drain. They saw a woman clutching a child, its legs locked around her waist, stumble and fall forward, to be scooped back onto her feet by the men running either side of her.

They rushed past in a grey and brown and black flood, and in only a few minutes they were gone, leaving behind them a thick dust which hung on the air, and settled slowly over a scattered trail of debris – splintered poles, torn banners, and lost and trampled property. Rosamund and Sophie found themselves clutching each other's hands, with dry mouths and prickling eyes, staring down the street in the direction of St Peter's Fields, waiting for the next terrible thing to happen.

They hadn't long to wait. Soon into the street came three men, two of them supporting a third, who staggered between them as though drunk.

'It's Jasper!' Sophie's cry came out involuntarily as though she had been struck. Rosamund saw that it was so. The man on the left – smaller and slighter than the other two – was

Jasper Hobsbawn. The man on the right – good God! – was Fitzherbert Hawker. The man in the middle, she saw with a sickening sensation of falling, was Jesmond Farraline: he was hanging on their shoulders, his hands dangling limply, his feet stumbling, and his face was a mask of blood.

They were in the hall as the men came in through the door. Farraline seemed almost unconscious. Jasper was grey-faced and gasping for breath under his weight, and as he stepped into the hall, his foot caught on the door-mat and he stumbled, going down onto his knees, and depositing Farraline unceremoniously on the floor.

Before Sophie could speak or even think, Rosamund had gone past her, was down on her knees beside Farraline, and a single cry had escaped her.

'Jes! Oh Jes!'

Hawker glanced at her grimly, and then looked at Sophie. 'I'm sorry, Mrs Hobsbawn. We thought we'd better bring him home. We shall need hot water, and plenty of clean cloths.'

'I've already sent Wells for them,' Sophie said distractedly. 'I gave the order when we saw you coming. But what happened? We saw the crowd running past and – Jasper, are you hurt?'

Jasper was rapidly recovering, and was already getting up. 'No, love, just out of breath.'

'Explanations must wait,' Rosamund pronounced. After her one moment of weakness, she thrust shock aside and had been examining Farraline's face and head with fingers so sure that Hawker had simply left her to it. 'We must see to Jes first. We'd better get him upstairs – the morning-room sofa will do. Can you carry him?'

'I can, but I don't know about Hobsbawn,' said Hawker. 'He got rather crushed by the crowd. How are your ribs?'

'I'm all right – just bruised,' Jasper said tersely.

'Mr Hawker, you're the strongest,' Rosamund said, standing up. 'If you take his shoulders, Mr Hobsbawn and I will take a leg each. Sophie, do you run ahead and make the sofa ready. Lift him carefully – he's been hit on the head.'

'Yes, I know. I saw him go down – didn't see what it was,' said Hawker, and then saved his breath for the task.

Farraline was now unconscious, which was perhaps as well,

for he was a heavy man for three of them to move. The shuffling procession crossed the hall and started up the stairs, and Rosamund was glad to relinquish her share of support to Wells when he caught them up half-way up the flight. In a few minutes, however, they had the injured man on the sofa, and Rosamund, kneeling beside him, was gently cleaning the blood from his face and scalp.

'He will need a stitch in this,' she pronounced when she'd uncovered a gash down his cheek. 'Sophie, can you send someone for a doctor? Whoever is the nearest. Poor fellow, his beauty will be spoiled after this. I'm afraid it will leave a scar, though it's a nice clean wound. What did it?'

'Cavalry sabre,' Hawker said succinctly.

'Ah yes,' Rosamund said. 'I should have recognised the handiwork. His head seems to be intact, though, thank God. No fracture. Probably he's just fainted from the heat and the loss of blood.'

'It's always these great strong men who faint most easily,' Hawker said with a mocking grin. 'Hobsbawn, what about a glass of wine?'

'Oh, yes, of course – that will bring him round,' Jasper said, hastening to the side-table.

'I dare say it will, old fellow, but I was thinking of myself,' Hawker said pleasantly.

Rosamund glanced at him. 'Don't tease,' she said. 'They don't know your ways. Ah, good, he's coming round. It's all right, Jes, you're at Hobsbawn House. Don't try to move, my dear.'

Farraline groaned.

'Yes, love, you've taken a blow on the head, and your face is cut. Wait now, take a sip of this.' She supported his head while he tasted the wine, and then set it down again. 'Now just lie quietly, and try not to move. I'm going to hold the edges of this cut together until the surgeon gets here, and the stiller you keep, the less of a scar you will have at last.'

Sophie came back in. 'I've sent Scott to fetch Dr Halsey. Oh, thank you!' She received a glass of wine from Hawker. 'While we wait, won't someone please tell us what happened?'

'It was all the stupidest mistake,' Jasper said wearily. 'It should never have happened.'

'You're right,' said Hawker, 'and if that fool of a

435

magistrate, Hulton, had listened to me, it never would have. I told him to arrest Hunt before he ever reached the field – I even went to the trouble of getting an affidavit sworn out for him. But first he leaves it too late, and then when it was obvious things had got out of hand, he needs must send in the Yeomanry, who don't know the first thing about handling their horses in a crowd!'

Bit by bit, from Hawker and Hobsbawn alternately, the story was told. The cheer the women had heard had indeed been for Henry Hunt, who had arrived at the south end of the field in a barouche drawn by his supporters and decked with flags and ribbons. The crowd – which numbered by then more than fifty thousand, a multitude almost beyond imagination – had parted to form a lane from the barouche to the hustings, which were hung with flags and banners, and beside which the bands were playing a stirring march.

Henry Hunt in his white top hat stepped along this lane, which closed after him as the crowd surged forward, each man hoping to get close enough to hear the Orator for himself. There was, however, another lane, kept open by a double row of special constables, leading from the other side of the hustings to a house on the corner of Mount Street. In an upstairs room of this house, watching the proceedings from a window, was the principal magistrate Mr Hulton, and the magistrates of all the surrounding districts, along with the Deputy Constable, Mr Nadin, and two of the reeves. Down this lane, if it were to be deemed necessary, the Deputy Constable was to be despatched to arrest the Orator and bring him back to the magistrates.

Hunt had hardly begun speaking when Mr Hulton evidently decided that it would be better to arrest him. Mr Nadin, eyeing the size of crowd and the distance to the hustings and back, protested that he could not do so without military assistance. Mr Hulton then gave the order to send in the Yeomanry.

'God knows why!' Hawker interrupted Hobsbawn at that moment. 'Yeomen! Great stupid boobies of innkeepers and shopkeepers that they are! Ham-fisted to a man, puffed up with their own importance, and out to teach everyone else a lesson. The kind of cowards who turn bully as soon as you give them the least little shred of power over their neighbours.'

'I dare say Hulton thought it would be less inflammatory than sending in the Hussars,' Jasper said mildly.

'More fool him,' Hawker snapped. 'The Hussars were a disciplined force, with nothing to prove about themselves.'

'But what *happened*?' Sophie cried in frustration.

The Yeomanry charged onto the field, knocking down a woman and killing her child, and driving their way into the crowd in an attempt to reach the hustings, Jasper told them.

'Hunt said something and pointed at them, and the people nearest started cheering, and it was picked up all over the field. Meanwhile most of the Yeomanry had come to a halt because of the sheer density of the crowd. I dare say the people would have liked to get out of the way, but they simply couldn't move. One or two of the Yeomanry reached the hustings, and they hustled Hunt away, between the special constables and into the magistrate's house. The specials got themselves out of the way pretty quickly too, and that lane closed up, and there were the rest of the Yeomanry, scattered about singly or in small groups, completely hemmed in by the crowd, like little islands in a vast sea.'

Hawker took over the tale. 'The crowd was still fairly good-tempered, though they were jeering and laughing. Left alone, I dare say nothing much would have happened. With Hunt gone, the crowd would have started to drift away from the outside, and then the Yeomen could have dismounted and led their horses out. One or two might have been roughed up a little, but serve 'em right.

'But no, Hulton needs must get into a panic. He called to Colonel L'Estrange, who was commanding the Hussars, that the Yeomanry were being attacked and must be rescued, and gave him a direct order to go in and disperse the crowd, which L'Estrange couldn't disobey.'

'Ah,' Rosamund said, a soft sound of acknowledgement of disaster.

'They were ordered only to use the flat of the sword, but pushing their horses into that sort of crowd, there were bound to be accidents. Of course some people were trying to get away, and shoving one way, and others were trying to attack the Hussars and shoving the other way; and then people started screaming –'

The doctor arrived at that moment, and the narrative was

broken off, to the relief of all. Rosamund's fingers were growing numb, but Dr Halsey praised her foresight in holding the wound together, and told Farraline he would have her to thank if his scar were more dashing than disfiguring. He noted Farraline's pallor.

'I think you had better have a nip of brandy before I begin, young man. Probably lost a lot of blood. Blow on the head? I see, yes. We'll have a look then. Ah yes, a nasty contusion, but no fracture. Your diagnosis too, ma'am? And where did you read medicine, may one enquire? Waterloo! Plenty of cases there to study, I should think. So, no concussion in the case, would you agree? And brandy indicated? Just so. Then perhaps it would amuse you to assist me, ma'am, in my operation?'

Talking cheerfully he drove everyone but Rosamund away from the sofa and got out his suturing needles. Jasper was a little outraged at his asking Rosamund to do anything so unladylike as assist him, but seeing that neither Sophie nor Hawker felt it necessary to intervene, and knowing from Sophie a little of Rosamund's history, he held his tongue.

'Shocking business this, at St Peter's Fields,' the doctor said in a moment. He always made it a rule to talk while he stitched, to keep the patient's mind occupied, for it was a painful and protracted business. 'Not at all the thing to send the army in against an unarmed crowd. Still, if it saved a general riot, I suppose it was just as well. Can't have mobs roaming the streets, can we? This isn't Paris. Should never have allowed the meeting in the first place – crowd of that size, and none of 'em local people, you know. Come now, this is looking better! Another two and we shall be done. Bear up, young man. Sword cut, was it? I suppose you got caught up in it, eh? Just so. Curiosity killed the cat, so they say. There'll be many a yard of catgut used today by what I've seen. The place looks like a battlefield – quite frightful – littered with hats and shoes and broken staffs, and bodies everywhere –'

'Bodies?' said Sophie and Rosamund, almost simultaneously.

'Fifty dead, they're saying, and hundreds wounded – some with sabre cuts, others crushed and trampled. I must go back as soon as I've finished here. No fees to be had from those poor devils, of course, but one must do what one can.'

A silence followed his words, and then Jasper crossed the room swiftly to put his arm round Sophie and help her into a chair.

'There, that's done,' the doctor said, snipping the last stitch. 'You'll feel like the very devil in an hour's time, but I'll send my boy round with a draught for you, and come in and see you tomorrow. And now I must, as I said, go straight back to the Fields, if you'll forgive me, Mrs Hobsbawn.'

'Of course – thank you, Dr Halsey,' Sophie said faintly.

'I'll come with you,' Hawker said. 'I may be of some use. I'll come back later if I may,' he added with a glance between Sophie and Rosamund.

It was on Jasper's lips to say he would go too, but Sophie anticipated his intent, and looked at him so pathetically that he closed his mouth again, the words unsaid.

Sophie and Jasper insisted that Farraline remain at Hobsbawn House for a few days, and Farraline was only too glad to accept the invitation. The following day after breakfast Rosamund went up to see him in his chamber, and found him reading the newspaper which Jasper had left for him when he went out that morning.

'Eleven dead, and about four hundred wounded,' he told her. 'Of course, no-one can be sure of the exact number of wounded, since many of them will have gone home and treated themselves. The Massacre of Peterloo, they call it here.'

'Peterloo?'

'St Peter's Fields – Waterloo. An ignoble as opposed to a noble battle.'

'Still, hardly a massacre.'

'Eleven people dead, my love,' Farraline said gravely.

'Yes, but the deaths were purely accidental. Mr Hawker spoke to Joliffe of the 15th yesterday, and he said it was a tribute to the forbearance of his men that there weren't more injuries. However, the Whig press will have a wonderful time with it, I suppose. Sidmouth must act quickly to prevent them undermining confidence in the magistracy.'

'An excellent principle of Government, Lady Chelmsford – it doesn't matter too much whether what you do is right or wrong, as long as the people think it's right.'

'Never mind that,' she said sternly. 'You haven't told me

yet how you managed to get this perfectly hideous wound. Your face is twice its usual size today. It looks like something more usually found in a butcher's shop.'

'Thank you. You are most reassuring. Here I am, lying at death's door, my soul quaking at the thought of my disfigurement –'

She kissed the end of his nose. 'You will never be less than beautiful to me,' she said sweetly. 'But to it, Farraline! How did you get embroiled?'

'Like an idiot, trying to rescue a woman.'

'I knew there'd have to be a female in the case. Your appetites will be the ruin of you.'

'Not my appetites, but my idiot chivalry. I was quite safe in a doorway until I saw this particular female go down under one of the horses. She was in the way as it swung its rump, was knocked off her feet, and was in danger of being trampled. I shoved my way in to her, and in order to drag her up, put my hand out to grab hold of the horse's shabraque to steady myself. I got the Hussar's leg instead, and I suppose he thought I was trying to pull him down. He swiped at me, I ducked, and – that was that.'

'He tried to kill you?'

'Oh Lord, no, he meant to hit me with the flat, but it was a backhanded blow, you see. Simply bad luck. I don't know what hit me on the head, but down I went, and the rest is a blur. At some point I found I was being dragged out from the crush, and I suppose I have Fitz and old Hobsbawn to thank for my life.'

'Particularly Jasper Hobsbawn. *He* had no brief to save you, and has ended up with some very painful bruises. Poor Sophie was convinced she'd never see him again when we heard the noise of the riot.'

'Well, here we are, safe and sound, anyway, and it's all over now,' he said soothingly. 'Very much a storm in a teacup. I don't suppose anyone will think twice about it this time next week.'

Later in the day Mr Hawker came to visit his friend. When he left him he took himself to the morning-room to pay his respects to the ladies, and found Rosamund there alone, Sophie having been called away to attend to some minor domestic crisis.

440

'And what was your part in all this?' she asked him. 'I can't tell you how surprised I was when I saw you come down the street with the other two.'

'I don't know why you should have been surprised. You know about my special assignment with the Home Office.'

'Yes, of course. I didn't mean that precisely. I suppose Sidmouth sent you to keep an eye on Hunt?'

'Yes, amongst others. He's been alarmed at the upsurgence of activity in the Hampden Clubs this year; but what I've seen here is something quite new and much more worrying, something he hasn't at all bargained for.'

'What, a mob turning to violence? What's new about that?'

'No, you mistake me. I told you the violence was the merest and most stupid mistake. No, what was different was what happened beforehand – though I know I shall never be able to convince Sidmouth or any of the others of it. But Farraline understands.'

Rosamund frowned, trying to track down an elusive memory. 'Yes, I have it,' she said abruptly. 'I was trying to recall – Sophie said, when we watched the people going past to the meeting, that they had nothing in common. They were from all manner of different interests – farm-labourers side by side with mill-hands.'

'Yes, you are there!' He looked at her admiringly. 'What a pity, Lady Chelmsford, that you weren't born a boy! Yes, this mob was drawn together right across the traditional divisions of interest, and they were clamouring *peacefully, and within the law* for something they thought would be of benefit to them all. You simply don't expect co-operative effort like that from the lower orders. These were no starving farm-labourers burning ricks, no out-of-work weavers smashing looms. Always before, when the lower orders have protested, it has been in the mindless way of animals, undirected and futile violence. The sophistication of this latest meeting is what is so terrifying.'

'But they had sophisticated leaders,' Rosamund reminded him. 'They didn't think of it for themselves.'

'It doesn't matter. All risings have leaders more sophisticated than the mob; but they have never before managed to make the mob behave in a sophisticated way.' He shook his head. 'I think what we have seen here is an indication. A phase of our history is coming to an end.'

Rosamund looked at him doubtfully. 'Surely you exaggerate?'

He met her eyes. 'I think that the reform of Parliament they are clamouring for is bound to come, now that the Hunts and Cartwrights of this world have learned how to make a tool of the mobility. And that means the end of a thousand years of one system of government, and the beginning of – what? Something we cannot imagine, because it has never existed before. I don't know how that will change our lives, but I know that it *will* change them.'

She said nothing, still unsure of how seriously he meant her to take him. Then his expression changed, to one of mingled amusement, reproach and kindliness.

'And as for you, Lady Chelmsford – Rosamund, what the deuce are you doing?'

She was startled out of her self-possession. 'I – doing? Nothing. Why, what do you mean? I'm not doing anything.'

'Coming it too thick and rare, my child. I saw you yesterday fling yourself upon Farraline's lifeless body like Lady Anne in *Richard III*. And you forget that he and I are friends. He tells me everything.'

'When you bully him into it,' Rosamund said indignantly.

'Well, yes, that's what I meant, to be sure. But, seriously,' he reached out and took her hand, 'how can you have got yourself into this muddle? It's not what I hoped for you, not at all.'

'All very well shaking your head at me, but you yourself promised to try and seduce me once I was a married woman.'

'Did I? Oh villainous! But not so soon: you've only been married two years. And besides, I am not Farraline, or rather, he is not me. An affair with him is not to be taken lightly – and I see that you do not.'

She looked at him for a moment, remembering the dinner they had taken in the inn so long ago, and wishing they might be alone again like that, so that she could confide in him. And yet what would she tell him? Nothing, probably, that he didn't know for himself already. That bliss which Sophie had found in Jasper's arms, she had found in Farraline's: that was all. The touch of his hands translated her; with him she seemed to live with a greater intensity, as though every sense

442

were sharpened, every experience magnified. She remembered Hawker's telling her about his feelings for Fanny, how he said that he had *devoured her*. Well, she devoured Farraline, and there were only two paths she might follow from here – to go on doing it, or to give him up. Which would Hawker recommend? She couldn't guess – and she didn't much want to know.

'No. I suppose I don't,' she said at last. 'But if I am in a muddle, it's one of my own making, and no-one else's responsibility.'

Hurried footsteps were coming along the hall: they were about to be interrupted. Hawker pressed her hand briefly and withdrew his. 'Very well; but if you ever need a friend – and I'm persuaded you will, sooner or later – remember you can call on me at any time.'

The door opened, and Sophie appeared, her face wreathed in smiles and flushed with excitement.

'Oh Ros,' she cried, 'guess who's here?'

There was no need to guess, for as she spoke another figure appeared in the doorway behind her, dusty and rumpled as though from a long journey, his pale hair tousled, his rather protruberant eyes jumping straight to Rosamund and scanning her face with as much uncertainty as delight. Hawker was saddened, seeing how unsure Chelmsford was that his wife would welcome his arrival.

'Marcus!' she said. 'What are you doing here?' It was not precisely unwelcoming, but it was not rapturous either.

'I missed you,' he said, 'so I thought I'd come and see how you are. But what about this riot you've had in Manchester? I heard about it at the inn last night. Are you all right?'

'Of course. Don't I look all right?' Rosamund said. 'Mr Hawker will tell you about it. He knows everything that went on, and he'll explain what it all means, too. He sees it as a sign of the ending of civilisation.'

'How you do exaggerate, ma'am! Pay no attention, Chelmsford – your wife is in a mischievous mood. How are you?'

'How d'e do, Hawker,' Marcus said, still a little bewildered. 'I wasn't expecting to see you here.'

'Well I wasn't expecting to see you here,' Rosamund said. 'Have you abandoned your quest for a country seat?'

443

'Oh – no – not at all. In fact, we think we've found one. That was partly why I came to see you – to tell you all about it. Mama thinks it will do very well, and I'm sure you'll like it. When do you think you'll be able to come and see it?'

Hawker sighed and shook his head mentally at Chelmsford for being so dim-witted as to sound wistful at that point. Such pawkiness was not the way to handle a bold, high-spirited mare: naturally enough, sensing his timidity, she kicked out.

'If you and your mother have already decided on it, it won't signify whether I go and see it or not.' It was spoken quite pleasantly, with a smile, but none of the four people in the room had any doubt as to its real meaning.

Marcus flushed. 'Of course nothing has been decided,' he said quietly. 'How could it, without you?'

Sophie couldn't bear it any longer, and intervened. 'I hope you won't take Rosamund away immediately, cousin. I expected to have her for at least four weeks. Now you're here, I hope you will stay and let us shew you the pleasures of Manchester. It can't compare with London, of course, but we'll do everything we can to amuse you and make you comfortable.'

The real warmth of her invitation was balm to him. He turned to her and smiled uncertainly. 'I should like to stay very much, if it doesn't upset your arrangements. My mother and Bab have gone down to Brighton for a few weeks, so I'm quite at liberty.'

It was unfortunate in its phrasing, and Hawker flicked a glance at Rosamund, hoping she would resist the temptation to use it against him. But she, too, had noted the difference between Sophie's tone and her own, and did not desire to shew herself up any further.

'Yes, do stay, Marcus,' she said smoothly. 'You can have no idea how amusing Manchester can be. When all other entertainment fails, they put on a riot for our diversion! What a pity you didn't get here yesterday. It's all in this morning's *Observer*, however – let me get it for you.'

The paper was lying on the table under the window, and she crossed the room to fetch it. Her back was thus turned on Sophie and Marcus for a moment, but Hawker saw her face as she went past him. It was stony, and she was chewing her lip in vexation.

TWENTY-THREE

The incident on St Peter's Fields acquired more notoriety than any of them, except perhaps Mr Hawker, would have expected. The cynical title bestowed on it – The Massacre of Peterloo – excited popular imagination, and the Radicals soon enjoyed the support of the Opposition, who seized on it as a lively stick with which to beat the Government. Crude political cartoons appeared in the newspapers, and there was a great circulation of cheap and lurid engravings shewing cavalrymen with huge bristling whiskers and flashing swords trampling their horses over heaps of hapless men and women.

It proved, cried the Whigs, that the Government was with within ame-sace of imposing military rule on the once-free peoples of England. This claim, fortuitously, coincided with the arrival in England that autumn of the Duke of Wellington and the Army of Occupation, coming home from Europe at the end of their period of peace-keeping, which looked like a confirmation of the fell purpose.

The Government, however, held firm, regretted the sufferings incurred at Manchester, but praised the prompt, decisive and efficient measures taken by the magistrates for the restoration of public tranquillity. The alarm in Manchester gave rise to six bills for the preservation of order which were placed before Parliament in November. They were passed with general acclaim in December, being so obviously sensible that only determined opponents of the Government criticised them. They were to prohibit drilling; to restrict the right to bear arms; to regulate the right of public meeting; to simplify the procedure for bringing cases to trial; to allow magistrates to seize blasphemous or seditious literature; and to impose a stamp duty on all newspapers, periodicals and pamphlets – which would effectively eliminate the 'tuppenny trash' of the radical press.

Whether it was the effect of the Six Acts, or of the bitterly cold winter that followed, or of the revival of trade which gradually brought the manufactories back into full operation, there were no more general disturbances. There was one incident in February 1820, but it had the air of a left-over from other days, a curious relic, like the Pentrich rebellion, of a more violent past age.

It was the brain-child of one Arthur Thistlewood, who had been imprisoned after the Spa Fields troubles in the year sixteen, and was released from gaol just in time to hear about the Peterloo Massacre. Bent on avenging its victims, he met with a few of his friends in a loft above a stable in Cato Street, off the Edgware road, and plotted to overthrow the Government and seize London in the old manner, by blood and violence. They were to begin with the murder of the entire Cabinet, planning to burst in on a Cabinet meeting and cut up the members with butchers' knives. Then they would parade the heads through the streets on pikes to the Mansion House, and there install Arthur himself as First President of the Britannic Republic.

The plot was discovered, however, and Thistlewood and his conspirators were arrested before they had ever left Cato Street; and the incident caused almost as much amusement as outrage. Thistlewood was plainly quite mad; and Sidmouth's 'system' had averted the trouble most efficiently, with the aid of informers. It gave the Government, moreover, the opportunity to strike back at the Whigs through the radicals, whom they had so often supported.

Meanwhile, public attention was able, gratefully, to turn to the far more diverting subject of the Succession. In January 1820 there had been a double blow to the Royal Family. The Duke of Kent, the healthiest, most sober-living of the princes, had died suddenly on the 23rd, leaving his infant daughter Alexandrina fourth in line to the throne, after her uncles, the Prince of Wales, the Duke of York, and the Duke of Clarence – who was still without a legitimate heir.

Six days later the baby's proximity to the throne took an upward leap as death came at last to release the prisoner of Windsor: on the 29th, the mad old King, George III, went to meet his final reward. The Prince Regent became King George IV, and immediately fell desperately ill with pleurisy. The strain of his corpulence and his way of life had undermined his general health and stamina, and under this new attack his life was despaired of. If he died, York would become King, and then only the childless Clarence would stand between Princess 'Drina and the crown.

The new King, however, survived; and as soon as he was out of bed, the awareness of how close the nation had come to having one of the hated Kent blood on the throne prompted him to ask his ministers to start divorce proceedings on his behalf. His estranged wife, now calling herself Queen Caroline, had been living in voluntary exile in Italy for some years; if he were rid of her, he might marry again and possibly beget an heir.

Rosamund had a letter from her mother, delivered to her via Mr Hoare's bank, mentioning the subject.

'We met Princess Caroline lately – I hesitate to call her Queen yet. She has been in constant correspondence with Brougham, who, I dare say, hoped to ride to power on Princess Charlotte's back – once the Regent died – by reuniting mother and daughter. Now, of course, all that has changed. Caroline has become an embarrassment, and I half-wonder whether Brougham might be tempted to use her to blackmail Liverpool into giving him an office. These lawyers are up to all the tricks! She, of course, supposes that he will negotiate for her to return in time for the Coronation. We shall see.

'As far as a divorce goes, the investigation into her behaviour back in the year six was inconclusive, and I doubt very much whether the evidence will stand up any better now. You are in for some lively times if she is *not* persuaded to stay out of England, for the mob, for some reason, always liked her and considered her deeply wronged.

'I suppose the Coronation will be some time in 1821. As soon as I know the date of it, I shall make our plans for coming home. I had meant, as you know, to come back this spring, but Theakston has a great desire to shew me Portugal and Spain, and the scenes of his military triumphs, and the boys are wild for it. I must say I should like to see the Spanish horses, and perhaps buy a new team to bring back with me, if they are as good as they're supposed to be.

'If I do buy horses, you may be sure I shall not repeat the experience of crossing the Channel by steam-packet! It may be very quick, and the convenience of not having to rely on the wind I suppose is considerable, but you cannot conceive of the noise, to say nothing of the smell and the smuts and sparks! It would throw a sensitive horse into convulsions.

'By the way, we met Harvey Sale – or I suppose I should call him Penrith, now – in Venice during the Carnival. He did not seem to be enjoying himself very much, so we took him back to our palazzo where he spent almost the entire time playing cards and Speculation with the boys and refusing all invitations. I told him he had no talent for enjoying himself and ought to go back to England, but I'm afraid he took it as serious advice, and asked me if I thought the scandal would have died down by now. If he'd been of our generation, I'd have said yes, but you younger people are so much more censorious than we were. I wonder why that is? At any rate, I told him he had nothing to lose by going and finding out, and he seemed to take that to heart, so I dare say you'll have him amongst you again before long.'

Lord Penrith arrived in London in April 1820, secured himself a modest room at Limmers, and immediately sent his card round to Chelmsford House, where its arrival precipitated a new quarrel between Rosamund and Lady Barbara.

Lady Barbara's dissatisfaction with her daughter-in-law had increased year by year as she proved herself to be wanting in respect, gratitude, and frequently the merest common courtesy towards her elders. Rosamund's sins were many. She had been married almost three years now, and shewed no sign of producing the heir Marcus was entitled to expect. She seemed to delight in leading an independent – and expensive – life with her own circle of quite unsuitable friends, entertained them lavishly, and appeared to regard her husband's company as essential only at official or Court functions. Despite this, she seemed to have what Lady Barbara considered an undue – and unhealthy – influence over him. She had even somehow persuaded him last year not to buy the estate near Dorchester which Lady Barbara had gone to so much trouble to find for them.

Not only that, but she had failed to do anything for Barbarina, where any other young woman in Rosamund's situation, out of sheer gratitude and proper feeling, would long ago have found her a husband and relieved Lady Barbara of the expense of keeping her. Not only the expense, but the embarrassment: Barbarina was heading towards her twenty-fourth birthday, and was now plainly regarded as being upon the shelf.

Lady Barbara was inclined to believe that, far from helping to get Barbarina off, Rosamund had probably hampered her chances of making an eligible match. And if she had not actively hindered, she had certainly done so passively, by having a sister who had the bad taste to get herself murdered, and a brother-in-law with so little sense of propriety that he needs must get himself tried for the murder in the most public fashion.

The scandal of the trial rankled deeply in Lady Barbara's mind. She was sure no-one had forgotten it, and that Looks and Whispers followed her wherever she went. Of *course* all her efforts to shove Barbarina's boat off had met with failure: who in their right mind would want to ally themselves with a murderer's family? Thus when the Murderer himself reappeared on the scene, and had the audacity to send round his card, Lady Barbara was naturally incensed.

'You will, of course, ignore it,' she pronounced at once. 'No, wait, that is not emphatic enough! He should know exactly how much we deplore his lack of taste in returning to this country. I think you had best return the card to him, torn in two. That should be unmistakable, even to a man of no sensitivity.'

'I should think it would be unmistakable,' Rosamund said, half-amused, half-angry, 'if I were to do anything of the sort. But I am not so infatuated. I shall send him a civil note, asking him to call tomorrow.'

'Asking him to call?' Lady Barbara mottled alarmingly. 'Have you taken leave of your senses, child? You will do no such thing!'

'I beg your pardon, ma'am,' Rosamund said lazily, though her eyes were dangerous beneath her half-lowered lids, 'but I shall not expose myself to the charge of incivility towards my own brother-in-law – who is bearing, moreover, as you see from his message, a letter from my mother.'

'That's just his ruse, and if you haven't the wit to know it, it shews you still have need of my guidance, however much you flatter yourself that you are up to every rig.'

'I wouldn't care if it were a ruse,' Rosamund snapped. 'I

should still invite him to call.'

'Then it is as I feared – you are utterly lacking in conduct! But however much you may wish to ruin your own life, I shall not allow you to ruin those of my children. I forbid you to invite that man into this house, or to correspond with him in any way.'

Barbarina had already shrunk back into her chair, and now looked utterly miserable at being thus invoked. Marcus – fortunately or otherwise – was not present to hear his wife round on his mother.

'*You* forbid? You forget yourself, ma'am. You do not command in this house – I do. And as to ruining lives, I have no intention of allowing you to expose us all by your lack of judgement, your narrow-mindedness, and your petty malice.'

Barbarina made a soft sound like a moan, but it was instantly drowned by her mother's fury.

'How dare you speak to me like that? You call it lack of judgement to try to protect my maiden daughter from the corrupting influence of a known murderer –?'

'Known only to you, of course,' Rosamund blazed back. 'Everyone else in the world knows that he is innocent of any crime but misfortune – though I suppose that is a grave enough sin in your book!'

'So innocent that he stood public trial for his hideous crime –'

'The law of this land, ma'am, is that a man is innocent until proved guilty. Lord Penrith was innocent and proven innocent to the satisfaction of everyone but you!'

'Innocent? When he stood condemned by his own admitted behaviour with *that woman*? Or is adultery no crime in your book? Perhaps not – you are, after all, your mother's daughter!'

Rosamund's face tightened. 'And what does that mean?'

'You may interpret it as you please,' Lady Barbara said, scenting victory. 'But it seems to me that when a married woman goes off alone as you do, and refuses to say where she has been, she must have something to hide. Perhaps you should examine your conscience – and ask yourself why your husband prefers to dine at his club three days a week, rather than at his own table.'

Rosamund rose to her feet and drew herself up to her full

impressive height, like a goddess of Ancient Greece preparing to strike down a mortal with some kind of heavenly fire.

'You want to know where I go, do you, you impertinent woman?' she hissed. 'Well, I'll tell you –!'

But at that moment Barbarina stood up too – thin, pale and colourless, like grey rain against Rosamund's fire. 'Don't, Ros,' she said.

Her voice was light, always disregarded by her mother, but not, this time, by her sister-in-law. Rosamund looked round at her in surprise, and enquiringly, and Barbarina met her gaze steadily, albeit with an embarrassed blush. Rosamund's anger subsided as quickly as it had risen.

'You're right,' she said to Barbarina; and turning to Lady Barbara said calmly, 'I shall invite Lord Penrith to call. If you do not choose to meet him, you may absent yourself from the house. And there's an end.'

It was not the end, however. Rosamund sent a note asking Harvey to call; but Lady Barbara got to Marcus first. That evening he came to Rosamund before dinner, while she was still in her dressing-gown – a circumstance that made her feel vulnerable. He did not, nowadays, trouble her very often, but he had a wistful way of looking at her which made his not troubling her almost as troublesome.

Today, however, he had wound himself up to being stern.

'Ros, I wish you will not quarrel with Mama.'

'I, quarrel with her?'

'It behoves you to be respectful to your mother-in-law. She is, after all, your elder –'

'But not, I think, my better,' Rosamund said, keeping a rein on her temper. Three years of marriage had taught her that, at least – three years, and having Farraline, her warm and sustaining secret. He would be coming to London soon – in May – and she would see him again. Only a few more weeks to get through; she would not quarrel with Marcus now.

'Do you know what the quarrel was about?' she said mildly.

'Yes, about Penrith. I must say I wish he had never come back to London. His presence must be an embarrassment to everyone. At all events, he should not have offered to come to this house. Mama was quite right to ask you to refuse him.'

'*Ask* me? She ordered me,' Rosamund said, her tempo

451

quickening despite her resolve. 'But in any case, am I hearing you aright? I know your mother's least opinion is sacred to you, but you do not, surely, share in her perverse and wicked delusion that Harvey is a murderer?'

Marcus flushed. 'Of course not,' he said. 'He is, however, a self-acknowledged adulterer, and he should not on that account have presented himself to you as he did – particularly when my unmarried sister is still living in the house. It shews a want of delicacy on his part.'

Rosamund found herself remembering the words of her mother's letter: 'You younger people are so much more censorious than we were.' Not I, Mother, she said inwardly, though without pride or pleasure. No-one could judge a situation from the outside, but that is what everyone did – what everyone was obliged to do. She found she could think of nothing to say to Marcus in reply. This is 1820, she thought. The Regency is over, and we are all older and sadder, though perhaps no wiser.

'There's no need for him to call here,' Marcus said more gently, disarmed by her silence. 'It's a pity you've already responded to his card, but no matter – I shall do all that's necessary. Don't worry, I shall be perfectly civil. I'll send a note to him this evening, asking him to dine with me at my club tomorrow instead. That will cover our family obligations to him, without involving you or Bab – or Mama.'

Rosamund felt an extraordinary impulse of gratitude towards him for resolving a difficult situation with such delicacy – which was absurd since it was only his mother's interference which had caused the situation in the first place, and since the delicacy on his part was quite unnecessary. She reminded herself that he had once more sided with his mother against her, but even that didn't seem to whip up her anger as it should. She simply felt weary of the whole thing.

'Thank you,' she said at last.

The expression of her eyes, the tone of her voice, the whole of her posture, spoke such deep-seated unhappiness that he was filled with a fierce and protective tenderness towards her. She looked suddenly so soft and vulnerable – so womanly – so suddenly approachable, when normally she was strong and well-defended. He sat down on the stool next to her.

'Ros,' he said. She looked at him passively, but he couldn't

452

think how to go on. All he wanted to say was *I love you*, but he could not be quite sure, even now, that she wouldn't laugh at him for that. And yet, she was his wife – he ought to be able to reach her. Surprising himself with his own boldness, he put out a hand and touched her cheek, ran his fingers along her jaw, and then, when she didn't pull away, down her neck to her shoulder. Her dressing-gown was loose, and the tips of his fingers slid inside almost without his meaning to, at the hollow of her neck where the blood beat hot under the fragile bones.

'Ros,' he said again, and it sounded more like a question this time. He put his other hand out, cupped her face, leaned towards her. Her eyelids fluttered closed, but she made no other movement, towards or away from him. He could hear his own breathing now. He held her face in his hands, and her passivity was exciting him.

He touched his lips to hers, and they were soft, slightly parted. He felt that she was not altogether unwilling, and accustomed as he was to rejection, even so little encouragement was enough. He kissed her again, and let his right hand slide down inside her dressing-gown until it encountered the small, hot mound of her breast, and he felt her quiver. Love surged up in him, reinforcing desire.

'Ros,' he whispered, his mouth against her ear, 'my dear. Shall we?'

The dressing-bell had only just gone; it lacked almost an hour until the dinner bell, and her maid would not return until rung for. Still Rosamund said nothing; but when he got up and led her to the daybed across the room she went with him unresisting.

The Marquess of Penrith gazed at Héloïse hungrily across the section of the drawing-room which separated them.

'How is she? Is she well?' What he really wanted to ask was 'Does she ever talk about me?' but he hadn't quite worked up the courage for that.

Héloïse's reception of him had been everything that was kind, despite his arriving without warning, and calling her in from a crisis in the fowl-yard which would not be resolved without her. She pitied him very much, knowing how unforgiving the *ton* could be to those who drew notoriety to

453

themselves; and as to his act of adultery, how could she be the first to throw stones?

He had told her about his dinner with Marcus, and how he had been implicitly forbidden contact with the Chelmsford women-folk. Héloïse knew, as he did, that Marcus was a kind and sensible man, and not given to flying up into the boughs over nothing. If *he* could not find Penrith acceptable, what chance was there that anyone else in London would?

'So I decided to go home,' he had told Héloïse. 'Well, it was either that or to go abroad again, and you've no idea how hateful abroad is: full of foreigners and exiles. And the exiles are just the kind of loose screws one most wants to avoid – sharps and debauchees and bankrupts.'

Héloïse allowed this large condemnation to pass, and said instead, 'Home?'

'Back to Lasonby Hall – the family seat, near Penrith. I thought there, perhaps, they would not be so concerned about – about such matters. It's quite remote there.'

'Yes,' said Héloïse. 'And you would be lord of the manor – that is everything.'

He wasn't sure quite how she meant that, but there was nothing but kindness in her eyes. 'They would accord me the respect due to the family,' he said hesitantly. 'And I thought that if I dedicated myself to being a good landlord and a good master, I could at least win the love of my tenants and servants, even if –'

Even if that's the only kind of love I can ever have, was what he meant, but he didn't say it. But of course she knew exactly what he meant, as he could see from her expression. It was then, after a pause, that he blurted out his question about Polly.

'She is well,' Héloïse said. 'And she seems contented. When she came here first she was very shocked and distressed. Thin and pale, too. Now she has put on flesh, and there is colour in her cheeks – I think she has never looked better.' She smile deprecatingly. 'Our good Yorkshire air, and good Yorkshire food, have done the trick.'

He stared at her, as if trying to suck more sense out of her words than they would yield. 'I was very glad when Marcus told me she had come here. I thought it was exactly what she needed, and I'm so grateful to you for giving her a home. I did feel – responsible for her. I still do, though I suppose most people would think that was absurd, or impertinent in me.'

'Not at all,' Héloïse said. 'And I perfectly understand the necessity of your going abroad when you did –'

'She wouldn't come with me,' he said, anticipating some criticism. 'I asked her – begged her – but she refused. I asked her to marry me –'

'Ah,' said Héloïse unemphatically.

He looked at her questioningly. 'You think that was wrong of me?'

'Perhaps – a little tactless.'

'But what else could I do?' he asked, his voice rising a little with the unfairness of it all. 'If I hadn't asked her, she would have thought I was abandoning her, wouldn't she?'

Héloïse nodded. 'I didn't mean to suggest there was an alternative. Things have perhaps worked out as well as they could.'

He bit his lip. 'May I see her? Will you allow me to see her?'

Héloïse raised an eyebrow. 'Allow you to? How is it for me to forbid you? Polly is of good age – she may choose for herself.'

'*Will* she see me?' Harvey asked.

Héloïse hesitated. 'I don't know. But I think perhaps she should. Why don't you go out to her? She's walking in the rose garden with the little girls – my granddaughters. Their mother left them here while she made some calls. Polly is very fond of them. She loves children.'

'Yes,' said Harvey somewhat bleakly, and Héloïse felt she had not been tactful. But with a man who had suffered such things, there was very little that it was quite safe to say.

'I will ring for someone to take you to her,' she said.

It was a warm, still day, and within its retaining hedges the rose garden was full of fragrance and the sound of bees. Such a mass, such a dazzle of colours and scents was almost overpowering, almost more than the senses could bear. Harvey could hear the light, high sound of female voices somewhere in the heart of the garden, and dismissed the servant who had brought him.

'I'll find her myself from here, thank you.'

'Very good, my lord.'

455

Harvey followed the sound of the voices, stepping on the turf edging of the gravel paths so as not to be heard, passing from one section into another, past bed after bed of massed blooms, heady with scent on the moveless air, penetrating as if into the heart of a gigantic flower, rainbow coloured.

Through a last opening, and then there she was, sitting on a stone bench under a high hedge of white roses, whose blooms made a natural bower round her dark head. The cool simplicity of her was a refreshment after the exotic colours, slender in her dress of blue cambric, her hair knotted high, revealing her long white neck. He gazed at her hungrily, seeing how her beauty was undiminished. Indeed, as Héloïse had said, she looked better than he had ever remembered her. There was a light flush of colour in her cheeks, and a serenity in her expression that he had never seen before.

Two girl children were playing on the grass in front of her, and two nursery-maids were looking on, with the proud and restless look of those restraining themselves from removing their charges to the safety of their professional care. One of the maids looked round and saw him, and Polly, following her gaze, looked up and saw him too.

Her expression betrayed no emotion but surprise, and never had the brilliant opacity of her blue gaze been more frustrating to him. He started across the grass towards her, and the maids did what they had been longing to do, and snatched the children up into their arms.

Polly removed her gaze from him for a moment and said calmly, 'Yes, very well, you may take them away. Go along, Mary dear, with Harriet, and I shall come and see you later.'

The maids went away, with sidelong glances at Harvey as they passed him, and then he was alone with her at last. He stood before her like a schoolboy presenting himself for inspection, but more uncertain of himself than any schoolboy had ever been. Polly's composure was absolute. He hadn't the slightest idea what she was thinking or feeling, or whether his presence was welcome or unwelcome to her.

'Well, Harvey,' she said at last. 'What a surprise to see you here. I had no idea you were in England.'

'I arrived ten days ago. I stayed in London only just long enough to buy some new shirts and neck-cloths, and then

456

came north. You look well, Polly. Life here must agree with you.'

They were being heart-breakingly polite to each other.

'It does,' she said. 'And you – have you enjoyed your Grand Tour?'

'No, I hated every minute,' he said abruptly, breaking through it all. Uninvited, he sat down beside her. 'I hated being away from England, and I hated being away from you. Why wouldn't you come with me?'

'You know why.' She looked away across the garden, away from him. 'This is so unexpected, I hardly know what to say to you. Why didn't you write to say you were coming?'

'Because I thought –'

'Because you thought I might refuse to see you? Well, perhaps I would have,' she mused. 'Perhaps it's as well you didn't give me the choice.'

'But you don't know what I have to say to you.' She looked at him. It was hardly an encouraging look, but still he struggled on. 'I've decided not to live abroad any more. I'm going home, to Penrith, to live on the family estate, and I've come to ask if you will marry me and come with me. We can have a good life together at Lasonby Hall. No-one there will care about – you know – the trouble. We can put our past behind us, and start a new life. And eventually the fashionable people will forget about it too, and we'll be able to go back into society –'

'I don't care about society,' she said, interrupting him. 'I never did.'

He brightened. 'Nor do I, really, only it seemed unfair that you shouldn't have it. But I should be just as happy to stay up there all the time. The country is wonderful, and it has the best hunting of all, better than the Shires, if you don't care about fashion. Lasonby Hall is a little old-fashioned, but we can have it done up, or even rebuilt if you like. And as Marquess and Marchioness of –'

'Please don't go on,' she said. 'I can't marry you.'

'But –' He was visibly taken aback.

'I'm sorry, I didn't think you would take what I said for encouragement. I have no wish to hurt you. I hope you will be happy there. I think it's the best thing you could do, to go home; and one day, you'll meet someone else –'

There are few more irritating things that can be said to a lover. 'I don't want someone else. I want you. You're the only woman I've ever loved – you know that. How can you say such a thing to me?'

She bit her lip, her composure broken at last by his reproach. 'People change. Feelings change.'

'Mine haven't.'

'But mine have.'

He stared. 'You mean – you don't love me any more? Is that what you're saying?' She didn't reply, keeping her eyes away from him. Then his mouth turned down bitterly. 'You still think – you still believe – that I –'

She turned to him, her hand flew out. 'No, not that! Oh my dear, I was half mad with shock and fear at that time. I didn't know what I was saying. How could I ever really think that you – the most gentle of men, and loving, and kind –'

He seized the hand, pressed his lips to it. 'You do love me!' he said triumphantly between kisses. 'I knew you couldn't have changed. After all we've been through together – all the suffering – all the waiting! You will marry me – oh my love, say you will!'

'Please Harvey, don't.' She tried to pull her hand away, succeeding in freeing it from his kisses, though not from his grasp. 'I do still love you, of course I do,' she said with desperate calm, 'but not in the same way. Feelings *do* change, my dear. I believe yours have too.'

'No! Never! I love you! I want to marry you!'

'Yes,' she said sadly, 'but only, I suspect, because you still believe we are two exiles from society, clinging together in the face of a storm of reproach and unfair abuse. It's not like that any more. No, let me finish! I have been able to think about things very clearly and carefully since I've been here, and I've come to understand a great many things – about the world, about feelings – about ourselves. When you've had time to find yourself again, when you've settled in at Lasonby and discovered that you are loved by many, many people, you will find you feel quite differently about me. Yes, I do believe you will always love me, as I will always love you – but it is not the kind of love on which to build a marriage.' She smiled faintly. 'I would not make a very good marchioness. Your brother was right about that.'

458

'This is nonsense,' he said, half-angry, half-afraid. 'You still think that if we marry, people will believe I murdered Flaminia – that's it, isn't it?'

It might have been kinder to let him think so, but Polly resisted the lure of the easy solution. 'No. I don't want to marry you, that's all. Being here has changed me. I've come to understand myself much better, to discover strengths in myself I knew nothing about. I've never before had the chance to be what it was in me to be. Always I belonged to someone else – to my aunt, to Minnie – to you. Now I'm mine, only mine, and it feels so good, I don't want to give it up – even for you, my dear.'

He put her hand from him, and she saw he hadn't understood a word. 'There's someone else, isn't there? That's what you're trying to tell me. You've fallen in love with someone else.'

She gave up. 'Yes, if you like,' she said, looking away from him.

Harvey stood up. 'You should have said so at once,' he said with dignity. 'I wouldn't have pestered and embarrassed you like this if I'd realised –'

'Oh Harvey!'

'Dear Polly, I do most sincerely wish you well. Whoever he is, he isn't half good enough for you, and I hope he realises it, and dedicates his life to making you happy, as I wanted to do.'

She looked at him helplessly, and he took her hand again and kissed it, but lightly, in courtly farewell.

'I hope you know that you have in me a sincere friend, should you ever need one,' he said. 'Goodbye, dearest Polly. And, God bless you.'

She let him go. It was for the best, even though sadness for him and exasperation towards him were still mingled with an old affection that tugged at her like an importunate child. She had been in love with him all her adult life, and it was a hard thing to let him go thinking that she had stopped loving him and fallen in love with someone else. She sat in silence for some time, her head a little bent, deep in thought, while the warm, perfumed air exhaled its thousand summer scents, and bees came and went in the creamy hearts of the flowers that embowered her.

She had no idea how much time passed before she was disturbed by a movement, and looked up to see someone else coming into the garden. At the sight of him she smiled, and a look transfixing in its beauty came into her eyes, whose brilliant blue depths mysteriously lost their opacity at that moment.

'The children are hard at work on an exercise, and I thought I would take the chance to breathe fresh air,' said Father Moineau. 'I must not be more than ten minutes, however. Will you walk and talk with me? Or do I disturb you?'

'No, you aren't disturbing me,' Polly said. 'I should be happy to bear you company. And there is something in particular I'd like to talk to you about, if I may? Something that's just happened. May I tell you about it?'

'Tell away,' said Father Moineau, taking her hand and slipping it comfortably through his arm. 'You know that everything about your life interests me very much.'

Queen Caroline, on Brougham's advice, came back to England, and entered London in a kind of triumphal progress on June the 6th, passing through streets lined with cheering crowds. Such was her popularity that even the sentries on duty outside Carlton House saluted her, despite the fact that a bill was to be put through Parliament to dissolve the marriage and deprive her of her title. To support the bill, a new enquiry was to be opened into her conduct. Meanwhile, though it was plain that the King would like to be rid of her on any terms, it looked as though it might not be necessary for him to marry again after all, for a strong rumour was going about that the Duchess of Clarence was pregnant again.

Rosamund had little interest to spare for these fascinating matters. It had not so far been a good summer for her. Farraline had not come to London for his planned visit in May. Manufacturing trade was picking up all the time, and it seemed that things had reached just that pitch where his presence was essential in Manchester. A letter from him – he addressed the envelopes to Moss, who had developed quite a reputation amongst her fellow-servants – begged her pardon, and hoped to be able to get away later in the summer. Not even a promise, Rosamund thought, but only a perhaps – and no date to look forward to, to keep her from going frantic in her gilded cage.

And there was other trouble. Her moment of weakness in the dresing-room with Marcus must have caught her at a vulnerable time. Three weeks later she was sure that her flux was overdue, and after four weeks she was beginning to experience tenderness of the breasts and slight nausea in the mornings. With leaden spirits she went out for the long rides, and sought the privacy of remote parts of the house for her jumping activities. But the seed that Marcus had apparently planted proved difficult to dislodge, and when her own actions failed, Rosamund had to ask Moss for help. This time, however, Moss had been difficult to persuade.

'Oh my lady, isn't it time you settled down?' she said wheedlingly. And 'It does seem such a mortal shame, my lady, when his lordship would be so happy.'

'Don't be sentimental,' Rosamund snapped. 'I shall decide when it's time to settle down, as you put it – and it's certainly not now. Are you going to help me, or do I have to look elsewhere?'

'It isn't right. And it isn't good for you, my lady,' Moss said stubbornly. 'You might damage your health in more ways than you look for.'

The argument went on for several days, increasing Rosamund's anxiety all the time; but in the end, of course, Moss did help her. Then the maid was able to scold and fret and worry over her when the remedy proved to make her very ill indeed. While she was suffering, Marcus was white and silent with worry, Barbarina was stricken, and Lady Barbara was quietly hopeful that the way might be being paved at last for her to acquire the daughter-in-law she deserved.

Rosamund didn't help matters by refusing to have a doctor called in, and when Marcus, in desperation, sent for Sir William Knighton without Rosamund's permission, she refused absolutely even to speak to him, and obliged the long-suffering Moss to lock her bedroom door until she was assured that the King's physician had gone away.

Moss later relayed the news, which she had learned by a roundabout servant's route, that Sir William had explained Rosamund's behaviour to Marcus as female hysteria caused by childlessness, and advised him to do his duty by her and

461

get her pregnant as soon as possible. On hearing this, Rosamund went off into a fit of black laughter, which eventually changed to tears, and developed into a storm of weeping so violent that Moss was half-inclined to believe Sir William might have been right.

When Rosamund was out of bed again, Marcus shewed himself maddeningly attentive. He gave up going to his clubs, dined at home every day, and dedicated himself to driving Rosamund out in his curricle for exercise and trying to entertain her in the evenings. It was fortunate, she reflected ironically, that the fact of her recent illness made him tender about forcing himself on her, or he would have been in a fair way to fulfilling Sir William's orders before midsummer. As it was, she was able to go on quite successfully looking pale and weary at bedtime, enough to ensure she retired to her chamber alone.

It could not go on for ever, though, she knew; and already Marcus was shewing signs of restiveness. When she finally rebelled against the boredom of being driven round and round Rotten Row in his curricle and took herself off, alone except for Parslow, for a gallop in Richmond Park, he was so upset that he dared to remonstrate with her.

'You're still looking very pale and thin, my darling. I don't think you're well enough for such violent exercise.'

'Oh fiddle!' Rosamund snapped. 'If you must know, I'm pale through being shut indoors all those weeks, that's all. Don't fuss over me, Marcus. You know I hate it.'

'But Ros –' He bit his lip, evidently building up to some difficult exposition. 'Don't you ever wonder –? I mean, we've been married four years now, and you've never even –'

Rosamund's brows drew down sharply. 'Never even what?' she asked forbiddingly.

'Well, I mean, there's never been any sign of a child, has there? I can't help wondering if – well, if all this riding hasn't something to do with it? Mama says –'

'Oh yes – and what has your mother been so obliging as to say this time?'

He plunged on into danger. 'Well, she says that sometimes women who do a great deal of riding have difficulty in conceiving. She says if you would only give it up, you'd probably be with child within a few months.'

462

Rosamund felt an unwelcome pity for him, for if she knew Lady Barbara, that was not all she had said by a long chalk. Probably Marcus had been berated also for not insisting on his marital rights, and for not being firmer with his wife. Rosamund had no doubt at all that Lady Barbara had perfected some system of knowing exactly how often Marcus visited his wife's bedroom. The thought of that old witch lying there at night listening for the footfalls in the corridor made her hot and cold with anger.

'You may thank your mother from me, and tell her that when I want her opinion, I'll ask for it,' she said. 'And that if she doesn't restrain her impertinent curiosity about my private life, I shall be forced to take some action she won't at all enjoy!'

'Oh Ros, darling, don't be angry! She means it in the kindest possible way. She's only trying to help us. Don't you want us to have a child?' Marcus said anxiously.

'She isn't trying to help, she's trying to interfere,' Rosamund said, ignoring the rest of the sentence. 'She doesn't like to ride, so she thinks no-one else should. Well it happens that I do like to ride, and I shall go on doing it, when and where I please, and with or without your mother's precious permission.'

The summer was hot, and the great families were soon going out of Town, seeking the refreshment of their country seats. Lady Barbara revived the agitation for Marcus to purchase an estate, and suggested that they all four went on a protracted tour of the nearest counties to look for one. Rosamund refused, but said she was happy for Marcus and Bab to go with their mother, an invitation Lady Barbara would have accepted with alacrity. But Marcus said no, and said it firmly enough for his mother not to argue with him for once.

Rosamund was not happy about this. She had to stay in London until she had word from Farraline, and if he were to come down for a visit, it would be far better if the rest of the family were out of Town. Fortunately, as the sultry weather continued, Barbarina began to suffer from it and look really ill, and when Rosamund suggested impatiently that Lady Barbara should take her to Wolvercote, the dowager agreed.

That only left Marcus, who in spite of his new and maddening attentiveness towards her, was much easier to circumnavigate. Then just when London was beginning to be quite uncomfortable, making it difficult to justify remaining there, a spell of rain at the end of July cleared the air and brought in a period of cooler, more refreshing weather; and a letter came from Farraline to say he would be in London in the first week of August.

TWENTY-FOUR

Rosamund sat up in bed, her arms clasped around her knees, her hair falling like a cloak all around her. Jesmond lay on one elbow watching her, waiting for her to tell him what was wrong. They had made love as hungrily as always, but he had felt how different it was – that she had devoured him, like a starving man, in the knowledge that it would not be enough.

At last she said, 'Did you see Sophie before you left?'

'Yes, I dined with them on Thursday. She was looking well; and of course they're wildly happy. I suppose she will have told you about her Expectations?'

Rosamund looked up. 'Expectations?'

'They aren't making it public yet, but as I'm such a close friend, they let me in on the secret. I'm surprised she hasn't told you.'

Rosamund spoke absently, as though out of a dream. 'She writes regularly, once a week. Her letter isn't due until tomorrow.'

'Ah, that would account for it. I imagine it has only just been confirmed – the baby isn't due until March.' He saw the glitter of a tear on her thin cheek and sat up hastily. 'Ros – darling! What is it?'

She shook her head, swallowing hard, unwilling to cry even before him. He put his arms round her rigid shoulders and drew her against him. She pressed her mouth against his neck to stop it quivering, and he felt her drag in uneven breaths, where any other woman would have sobbed.

'My own love, tell me what's wrong,' he said gently. 'It's pointless to keep it from me. What's making you so unhappy?'

'Oh Jes!' she said, and made a shapeless sort of sound, swallowing tears. Then she said. 'It's just that – when I think of Sophie –'

'Yes, love?'

'We came out together. And our lives are so different.'

There was nothing he could say about that. He stroked her shaking shoulders. She went on, 'Now she's going to have a baby, and she's happy about it. It's like – like a practical joke on me by God.'

He could sense that it was going to come out now. He eased them both into a more comfortable position, and said, 'Tell me, darling.'

She told him. He listened gravely, holding her tightly, her head on his chest, his cheek against her hair. She was his most precious possession, and not his at all. He loved her so much he would die to save her the least pain, and yet there was nothing he could do, nothing, that did not hurt her.

When she stopped he was silent for a while. Then he said, 'You remember when we were at Hobsbawn House together, after that Peterloo business? And Fitz was there, too. He came up to talk to me privately, while I was still in bed.'

She lifted her head to look at him, and touched the scar on his cheek gently with a fingertip.

'He told me then,' he went on, 'that I should stop seeing you. He said it would only bring you trouble.'

'Yes, he tried to warn me off, too.'

He gave a shaky smile. 'We both took his advice to heart, didn't we?'

She ran her hand absently over his chest. 'I couldn't have parted with you then – or any time. It wasn't what I meant at the beginning – I don't suppose it was what you meant. It all began so lightly. But now – you're the only thing that makes any sense to me. Being with you is being alive. Everything else is just a play – and a burlesque at that.'

'Darling –'

'I never meant to do anything like this when I married Marcus. I meant to be so sensible and long-headed and unemotional – to make a good marriage, you know, and give up all thoughts of romantic love. I thought I could live without it. And though I was fond of Marcus, he didn't trouble me in that way. I'd been a little afraid of what being in bed with him would be like, but when it came to it, it wasn't like anything. How can it be so different with two different people?'

'I don't know what it's like with him,' he said with spare humour.

466

'No,' she said seriously. 'And this, you know – being with you – it ought to feel like a betrayal of him. I know it *is* a betrayal, but it doesn't feel like it. It feels like real life, and everything else is unreal, a dream. Perhaps that's why –' She stopped and frowned. He waited. 'Why I can't bear to have his baby. That would be a betrayal of us.'

'Oh my love, Fitz was right, you know. We ought to stop seeing each other. It can only get worse – harder to bear –'

She sat up suddenly, shaking her hair away as she turned to look at him.

'No,' she said sharply. 'I can't give you up. Don't say it.'

'It isn't that I want to –'

'Then don't even think it. I must have you. Oh my Jes, my dear friend, let's not talk about it any more. Let's just enjoy each other.'

While we can. Neither of them said it, but the words were there between them; and to drown out the sound of them, she threw herself down on him and kissed him passionately. He enfolded her, and they made love again, clinging to each other like two people drowning.

When she reached Chelmsford House again, it was to find the great hall full of pieces of luggage. Hawkins met her across them with an odd, warning look, and said, 'Lady Barbara has just arrived, my lady. She's in the blue saloon. She asked if you would go up and see her immediately you arrived, my lady.'

'Did she, indeed. Is Miss Morland here, too? I don't see her luggage.'

'No, my lady. Her ladyship came up alone.'

'His lordship is not back yet?'

'No, my lady.'

'Very well, I'll go up,' said Rosamund. She walked up the stairs wearily, girding herself for some unpleasantness. Lady Barbara would hardly have come all the way up from Wolvercote unless she meant to upset Rosamund pretty badly. Well, it couldn't last long, at any rate. Marcus should be back at any moment, and then she could scrape Lady Barbara off on him.

She entered the blue saloon, and found Lady Barbara standing before the hearth, still in her pelisse and hat, glaring at the door in preparatory rage. Her face was already mottled red – a bad sign, Rosamund thought – and her congested eyes seemed to bulge slightly.

'Well, ma'am,' Rosamund began coolly, but that was as far as she got.

'Where have you been?' the dowager demanded furiously.

Rosamund raised a brow. 'I beg your pardon? I don't think –'

'Don't trouble to lie to me, you hussy! I know exactly where you've been and what you've been doing!' Lady Barbara raged.

Rosamund's heart sank so fast it made her feel sick. It was as bad as could be. Still she said coldly, 'I wasn't going to lie to you. I was going to tell you to mind your own business.'

'How dare you? How dare you?' Lady Barbara didn't even seem to have heard her. She was so consumed with anger she walked about, little steps first in one direction, then the other, mangling her gloves between her hands. 'I would never have believed it, even of you, but now I see that it's all of a piece with the rest of your behaviour! Oh, you're your mother's daughter all right! Bad blood! Bad blood always comes out, yes, and yours is bad on both sides! I told him! I told him not to marry you. But even so, I never would have thought you would be so abandoned – so utterly wicked – so shameless!'

'I don't know what you're talking about,' Rosamund said.

The bulging eyes came round to her. 'How dare you? How dare you stand there and say that? Have you no shame? Have you no proper feeling at all? You've deceived your husband, besmirched our good name, betrayed your marriage bed, and you stand there, you bold-faced hussy, and give me the lie direct!' She took a step towards Rosamund, and Rosamund forced herself to stand her ground, though she was feeling more sick every moment. 'I saw you! *I saw you!* Yes, that takes you aback, doesn't it? You thought you could get away with your grubby little deceit, sneaking off like a thief to Kensington – Kensington of all places! You didn't think you'd be seen there by anyone who knew you. But I was going past in the carriage as you came out of the door! Yes, my fine lady, and I saw you getting into a common hackney – you, the Countess of Chelmsford in a common hackney! *And* I saw a man waving you goodbye from the door!'

468

She doesn't know, Rosamund thought, and the relief was as violent as the previous shock had been. She doesn't know who. She doesn't even, really, know what – I could have been going there for any number of reasons. She couldn't think at that moment of a single one, but it was enough to stiffen her jaw and her resolve.

'What I was doing is my business, and my business alone,' she said in a hard voice, 'and you had better be careful before you repeat your foul accusations. I've been patient with you for a long time, ma'am, but my patience is not endless. I will not be followed about and spied upon, by a woman with no more conduct than to interfere in what is not her business –!'

'Not my business?' Lady Barbara raged. 'When my own son's wife –'

'Hold your tongue!' Rosamund snapped, losing her temper. 'I've had enough of you and your nagging and spying and criticising! You may be able to bully your children, but you can't bully me, and if you say one word about this to anyone, I shall have you thrown out of the house – by the scruff of your neck, if need be! And don't think I wouldn't do it, for I would!'

No-one had ever spoken thus to Lady Barbara – or indeed to any other woman of her age and rank – and it silenced her, only because her rage was too great to allow of articulation. Her face darkened, her eyes bulged alarmingly, her hands lifted a little and drew up into claws, and a gobbling noise came from her part-open mouth. Knowing it was the only way she would ever get the last word, Rosamund took advantage of her mother-in-law's paralysis of rage to get out of the room, slamming the door behind her.

Then she ran, blindly, to the haven of her chamber. She sat down on her bed, clenching her hands between her knees, staring sightlessly before her, waiting for her pounding heart to slow down. The hollowness of shock filled her chest, her stomach knotted with nausea. Oh God, what a scene, what a frightful scene! And what more was to come? It might have got her out of the room, but her threat would not stop Lady Barbara from repeating everything to Marcus when he came in, and whether he believed it all or not, he was going to ask her what she had been doing in Kensington. What could she say? What excuse could she think up? She could say she had not been there, that Lady Barbara was mistaken – that might be the easiest thing – but whatever happened, she was going to have to lie to him, and she had never had to do that before. It was bad, it felt bad. She didn't want to do it, to look him straight in the eyes and lie to him. Yet, she sneered at herself, how was that any worse than what she had already done to him? Oh God, it was all as bad as it could be – and it was all Lady Barbara's fault. That wicked, evil, spying, prying old witch! How she hated her! How she would like to claw her to bits! If it hadn't been for her, her marriage with Marcus might have been all right – right enough for her never to have needed Jes at all. But Marcus would never blame his mother – of course not! It was Rosamund who was going to be branded the wicked one.

She lifted her head, listening. He was back already! She heard the voices, muffled, from the hall. She strained her ears, staring sightlessly ahead of her, trying to track his movements. Well, she must face up to the trouble now, whatever it was. On the bedside table, lying beside her book, was the silver horseshoe that Parslow had given her for luck on her wedding day. She had carried it with her all the time, until she began her affair with Jes. After that, she had left it at home, here, beside her bed, for some superstitious reason she had never analysed. What would Parslow say if he knew? Perhaps he did know. Parslow always knew everything. And if Marcus repudiated her, everyone would know. What would her mother say? She clenched her fists, waiting for the storm to break.

There was some kind of commotion going on – shouts and running footsteps. She distinguished Marcus's voice shouting for Hawkins – why on earth didn't he just ring the bell? She got up cautiously and went to the door, opened it a crack, tried to hear what was going on.

Footsteps coming along the corridor. She closed the door and went back quickly to the bed, looked round for something to be doing, but there was no need – no time. There was a scratching at the door, but it was flung open before she had a chance to speak. Moss was there, her eyes taking up most of her face.

'Oh my lady, come quickly, his lordship's calling for you!' she cried. 'It's her ladyship – she's had a seizure. They've sent

470

for the doctor, and his lordship's in such a state! Oh, please come quickly!'

With her hands in Marcus's – she would find bruises afterwards, he held them so tightly – she heard how he had gone upstairs to the blue saloon, and found his mother lying on the floor, unconscious. So she had never had the chance to say anything to Marcus, Rosamund thought, guiltily glad. She remembered that congested face as she had run out of the room. Lady Barbara's rage, thwarted of expression, must have overcome her. She must have fallen even as Rosamund left the room. Now the guilt had no gladness: if she had remained one moment more, she would have been there to help the old woman sooner.

She and Marcus sat on hard chairs outside the bedroom door while the doctor – not Knighton, there was no time, but a local man, Sir Paine Walters – examined her, with her maid and Moss in attendance. Rosamund was glad that Marcus didn't seem to want to talk. He was so shocked, he didn't seem to have any curiosity about what she had been doing in the blue saloon alone, still in her outdoor clothes, or whether Rosamund had seen or spoken to her.

The door of the room opened at last, and Marcus looked up, painful with hope, as Walters came out.

'How is she?'

Walters met his eyes kindly, and shook his head. Such a little, deadly movement. 'I'm sorry, Lord Chelmsford. I'm afraid there is little hope of recovery.'

'What is it? Is it her heart?'

'A stroke. She has not regained consciousness, and I would be raising your hopes irresponsibly if I were to tell you there was any likelihood that she will.'

Marcus made a hoarse sound, clutching Rosamund's hands more tightly. After a moment he said, 'Can I see her?'

'Yes, of course,' said Walters.

They went into the room. Lady Barbara's head on the pillow looked strangely shrunken with her hair covered by a nightcap. Her mouth was open, and she breathed through it stertorously, and her face was mottled. Her elderly maid, Ashby, was standing beside her weeping and wringing her hands, the tears rolling unselfconsciously down her wrinkled cheeks. There was one person, Rosamund thought remotely, who really loved the old termagant.

Marcus went to his mother, took up one of her limp hands, looked down helplessly at her. Then he looked at Ashby.

'Why did she come back?' he asked. 'Why did she come up from Wolvercote?'

Rosamund glanced at the maid under her eyelashes. How much did Ashby know? Even if she knew, would she tell, now that her mistress was at death's door? How vile, even at this moment, to have to think about self-preservation. She tried to find some pity in her for Lady Barbara, but could find only a closed-off, stony relief. Impending death had changed nothing – they were both still what they were.

Ashby, speaking unevenly through her tears, only said, 'It was the news, my lord – about the Duchess of York dying. My lady thought she should pay her respects to the Duke, seeing as they were such old friends. So she came up to Town. She never thought – none of us ever thought –'

'No, of course not,' Marcus said meaninglessly. There didn't seem to be anything else to say. They all stood around the bed, avoiding each other's eyes, listening to the rattling breaths, until at last the ghastly sounds stopped, to be succeeded by an even more ghastly silence. And then Marcus laid the white hand down gently on the sheet, and walked away without a word or a look to anyone.

The enquiry into the Queen's conduct opened on August the 17th amid enormous notoriety. The Duke of York, arriving at the House of Lords on the first day was greeted by a huge crowd yelling 'Long live Frederick the First!'

The King had probably never been so unpopular amongst the lower orders. He had discarded his old mistress, Lady Hertford, for a new one, Lady Conyngham, a very fat lady in her fifties who was referred to irreverently as The Vice Queen, but who was thoroughly occupying his attention. That, and the fact that the Duchess of Clarence was definitely pregnant again, meant that his interest in the enquiry was due more to the determination not to accord Caroline the titles and privileges of consort, rather than any real desire to remarry.

The mob, however, was firmly on the Queen's side, and

met and escorted her carriage with banners and cheers to and from the House of Lords every day, booing loudly when they passed Carlton House, which they called 'Nero's Palace'. The Archbishop of Canterbury had already said that it was a mistake to have begun the proceedings at all. Better, he said, that the bill should be thrown out, with the higher orders convinced she was guilty, than passed with the lower orders convinced she was innocent. And a little ditty went around the clubs:

> Gracious Queen, we thee implore
> To go away and sin no more;
> But, if that effort be too great,
> To go away at any rate.

The feeling in the Lords was that they would never get the bill past the Commons, and that they should not try. Once it was dropped, they predicted, the mob would lose interest in Caroline, and she could be bought off with a pension and a house, and got out of London before the Coronation, which was set for next year, July 1821.

These matters passed almost unnoticed at Chelmsford House, where the six weeks of deep mourning were succeeded by no lightening of spirits. My lord and lady received no callers, either separately or together, and refused all invitations. My lord shut himself away in his book-room all day. At first my lady went out alone, without ever saying where she was going, returning hours later looking exhausted and unhappy; but latterly she had shut herself away too, and saw no-one. Within the house, the atmosphere was so tense and unhappy that the servants crept around like whipped dogs and quarrelled with each other over trifles.

One day in late September, Rosamund went downstairs dressed for riding, and found Parslow waiting for her in the hall instead of outside with the horses. She raised her eyebrows enquiringly as she crossed the marble flags towards him. His face was impassive as always, but his eyes scanned her keenly, and she felt an apprehensive sinking of the heart.

'Well, what is it?' she said unencouragingly.

'My lady, may I speak to you in private?' he said.

She didn't reply at once, but returned his look evenly,

locking wills with his, though aware that she would never defeat him. Then she sighed and said, 'Very well, if you must,' and turned aside into the nearest room. It was called the Trophy Room, a small, grim apartment, the walls lined with glass cases of stuffed animals and birds. The small fireplace, in which no fire was ever lit, was surmounted by a moth-eaten stag's head with spreading antlers, and the furniture consisted of a round wooden table and two uncompromisingly hard chairs. It was used only as a waiting-room for the least favoured of callers, where they might feel uncomfortable until the butler came to send them away.

Here, under the gloomy stare of innumerable glass eyes, Rosamund turned to face her groom. 'Well? What have you to say to me?'

Parslow turned his hat round and round in his hands, a sign of his powerful emotions. 'You're not looking well, my lady,' he said at last.

She made an impatient gesture. 'Is that all? My health is not your concern. Come, I wish to go riding –'

'Yes, my lady, it is, begging your pardon,' Parslow cut in firmly. 'And I know why you want to go riding, and it's not right.'

'Not right?' she said incredulously. 'What are you talking about?'

Suddenly he straightened, putting his hat down on the table with the gesture of a man making himself ready for some task that would need both hands. 'It's not right, as you know very well,' he said sternly, no longer man to mistress, but more like father to daughter. 'All this galloping and jumping day after day – and it isn't the first time, neither! What would your mother say, my lady? And if she were here, you'd never have got away with it – she or Mrs Docwra would have noticed long ago.'

'Stop it!' Rosamund said, frightened of what he might say next. He took a step nearer, his face warm and human with concern – concern for her, and as things were, how could she bear that?

'Aye, you've been shockingly neglected – his lordship's late mother being what she was, and Judy Moss with no more sense that a martlet. And his lordship – well, he's young. But as for me – how am I ever to face her ladyship if this gets out?

I should have taken better care of you. I knew about Mr Farraline, of course –' Rosamund gave a little gasp at the name, and he looked slightly distracted, as though she had thrown an irrelevant question at him. 'Well, of course I did – but then I thought it was none of my business, and I couldn't have stopped you anyway. But *this* – oh my lady, it's not right, and you know it!'

'Stop,' Rosamund whispered, white as paper. 'No more. I can't stand it.' Her hands were trembling, and she folded them together deliberately to keep them still. 'How can you talk to me like that?' she said, but it was more perplexed than angry.

'I care about you,' he said, shocking her, for servants didn't say such things, *Parslow* didn't say such things, impassive and proper as he always was. The essential distance was always kept, must always be kept, or the world would crack like a china plate and the halves tumble away into the void.

But she looked into his eyes, and saw an ordinary middle-aged man, rather lined and weather-beaten, a man who would have made an admirable husband and father, whom in other circumstances most women would have found attractive. John, she thought fearfully, his name is John, and he cares about me because he loves my mother; and my mother loves him probably more than anyone in the world apart from Papa Danby. He once gave me a silver horseshoe for luck, and he knows everything about me – everything.

'You said I shouldn't marry his lordship,' she said faintly, 'and you were right, but for the wrong reasons.'

'I know,' he said gently, 'but now it's done, can't you make the best of it? Your mother would never have done – this.' He waved his hand vaguely to indicate the unspeakable.

'I'm not my mother,' she said. She pulled herself together, reaching for firm ground. 'Come, Parslow, it's not such a big thing,' she said with an uneasy smile. 'Lots of fashionable ladies do the same. Times are changing.'

He didn't answer, looking at her levelly, as if asking her to be her own interlocutor. There were moral questions here, as uncomfortable to live with as these Trophy Room chairs, and she didn't want them, not now.

'You are not to be my conscience,' she said, hardening herself. She put her head up. 'I wish to go riding now. If you will not come with me, I shall take one of the other grooms.'

He lowered his eyes then, and she thought she heard him sigh. 'No need for that, my lady.'

'Well,' she pressed her advantage, 'are you with me or against me?'

'I am yours to command, my lady,' he said, and turned away to open the door for her. She walked out past him, but felt no sense of triumph, only an uneasy relief.

Ironically, before they even reached Richmond Park, she knew from her physical sensations that this ride, at least, was no longer necessary. That relief, too, had its uneasy aspects. She rode home, and took herself up to her room, aching all over, weary with guilt.

A little later, Marcus came to her there. 'Ros, I want to talk to you,' he said.

You too? she thought grimly. His face was grave, marked with trouble; but she saw also a determination there, as though he had come to some difficult decision and was not to be deflected from it.

'Must it be now?' she asked. 'I'm very tired.'

'I see you are. And a little unwell, too.'

She didn't want his concern, and shrugged it off. 'It's nothing. Just the usual, woman's trouble.'

'Yes, I know,' he said. 'That's what I want to talk to you about.'

Fear sharpened inside her. She looked up quickly, not realising how much she was revealing in her haggard face. 'I don't know what you mean.'

'Yes you do,' he said gently, almost pityingly. 'We can't go on like this. Only look at you. You're making yourself ill.'

'I'm perfectly all right. It's just the first day, that's all. It's always bad the first day.'

'Oh Ros, how can you say that?' She met his eyes, struck by the tone of his voice, and saw them full of tears. It seared her, like a needle to the heart, and her lip quivered for a moment before she caught and stilled it. 'Do you think I'm a block, an insensate thing? I know what you've been doing. All these long gallops – I tried to tell you once before, but I spoke clumsily, and set your back up. But darling, it can't, it mustn't go on. You'll harm yourself, quite apart from –'

476

He stopped abruptly, biting his lip, and risking a glance at him she saw that he was struggling with an excess of emotions, hurt and anger and shock as well as concern for her, pain for her pain.

'Why, Ros?' he went on suddenly. 'You're my wife, God damn it!'

She flared. 'Do you think that gives you the right –'

'I'm not talking about rights. You married me of your own free will. I thought you cared for me. Why have you refused to bear my child?'

The words, spoken aloud at last, were shocking. They went through her like a bolt of electricity, snapping her head back, and the words jumped from her lips before she could stop them. 'It wasn't –'

Then she stopped herself, too late. Oh too late, then, to deny the whole thing, as she might have done, to laugh it off as his imagination, or mere chance. Too late to hold things together; too late to hold on to a little piece of solid ground on which she might stand and be safe at last. In the pause that followed she stared at him in white and desperate silence, and wished that he would kill her and have done with it. But people are never so merciful to each other, she thought.

At last he said, 'No, I suppose it wasn't. Stupid of me not to have thought of that.'

'Oh Marcus, no,' she said. She lifted a hand, wanting to touch him, but had just enough wit left to know that her touch would have been no comfort just then, but an insult.

He stared at his hands. 'I suppose it's Farraline.' She felt sick, her mouth was dry, she couldn't speak to say yes or no; but her silence was admission enough. 'I should have guessed. I thought when I saw you together – but then, it isn't something one would easily suspect.' A pause. 'He visits you – in London?'

Still she couldn't speak, only nodded, though his head was down, he could not have seen her. He turned his hands over, seeming to inspect them thoroughly. 'Why him, I wonder?' he said, trying to sound indifferent. 'Why did you prefer him to me? No, stupid question.' He shook it away. 'All the same, if you preferred him, why didn't you marry him? Or wasn't he rich enough for you?'

A vast, unwelcome pity filled her, not only for him, but for

477

herself, for *them*. 'It wasn't like that,' she said. 'I didn't care about him when I married you. I never meant to – it wasn't what I planned. You can't believe that. I never wanted to hurt you. It just happened.'

He looked up at last, and they faced the naked hurt in each other's eyes, and the tenderness; goodwill towards each other, and helplessness in the face of the situation.

'Oh Marcus,' she said, 'I'm so sorry.'

He swallowed with difficulty. 'I don't want to talk about it any more. I don't think I could bear it. But I love you, Ros. You're my wife. Can we put all this behind us and start again? I know things have been difficult for you, but now that – now that – Mama's not with us, maybe it will be easier.'

Tears welled up in her, closing her throat, at his generosity. He loved her so much that he was willing to offer up his mother's death to her, willing to forgo his rightful sorrow, along with his just anger. And yet, she thought helplessly, I can't lie to him; I can't make him promises I'm not capable of keeping.

'I don't think I can give him up,' she said.

'Ah,' he said. He looked at her for a long while, and she couldn't tell what he was thinking. Then he got up without another word, and walked away. She felt a coldness like the onset of death in the space he left. She didn't believe he would simply go away like that, and only when he reached the door did she speak.

'What shall we do?' she said desperately.

He paused, but didn't turn round. After a moment he said, 'Just go on, I suppose. What else is there to do?' His next words were so quiet she barely caught them. 'I do understand, you see: I can't give you up, either.'

And then he went, quietly, closing the door behind him as softly as though she were sleeping and he didn't want to wake her.

The Duchess of Clarence's baby was born on the 10th of December, a girl, but healthy; and when it was plain that she was going to live, she was Christened with the proper regal name of Elizabeth. When her father and two senior uncles were both dead, she would be Queen Elizabeth II – unless, of course, the Clarences went on to have a son. The Duke of

York had pronounced very firmly that he had no intention of remarrying. The future of Princess Elizabeth of Clarence was assured, and the country was safe from the Duchess of Kent's baby at last.

The bill against the Queen had been dropped, and in January 1821 she finally accepted a pension from the King of £50,000 a year, and a house in Hammersmith. She left London for her rural retreat, and was at once forgotten by the populace, to whom she was no longer a symbol of resistance to oppression, but a privileged pensioner.

Thus the problems of the succession seemed to have been solved. Trade continued to improve rapidly, the manufactories were once again working fulltime, and the armies of unemployed were being soaked up. The reformist disturbances had died out, and the peace that should have taken effect in 1815 seemed at last to have descended on England.

'I think the troubles really are over,' James said one day in February as he sat on the bed watching Héloïse help Alice pack her trunk. Durban was in the dressing-room attending to James's belongings, and would have looked very much askance had James been so wanton as to suggest helping him.

'I hope so,' Héloïse said, 'or we would not be going away from home together for the first time since – how many years is it?'

'Not since before Benedict was born,' James said. 'Not further than York, at any rate. Ah, but we've deserved this holiday! We've worked long and hard to reach this plateau.' He looked at his wife critically. 'And you're looking exhausted. You need a rest and a change of scene.'

She straightened up for a moment to smile at him. 'Not more than you, my James. You've worked harder than anyone.' She put out a hand to him, and he picked up her fingers and kissed them.

'I believe I've enjoyed it,' he admitted. 'It has been hard, and yet I feel more – more *myself*, if you understand me, than I ever have.'

She nodded, understanding perfectly. 'Can it really be four years since Edward died? How they've flown past!'

Kai, lying at James's feet, yawned hugely, and James reached down absently to scratch his ears. 'Yes, so many things have changed – and yet everything seems the same.'

'That's the great strength of home and family,' Héloïse said. 'The elements change, but the whole remains the same.'

'You sound like Father Sparrow,' James laughed. 'There's one thing that's different, you see – and yet I can't remember the time when he wasn't here. I suppose Aislaby wasn't a man you could get fond of.'

'I miss Miss Rosedale,' Héloïse confessed, 'but of course it is better for her to be where she can be useful. She did so hate having nothing to do to earn her keep – as she saw it. When Mathilde's new baby is born, there'll be three of them to exercise her talents on.'

'Yes, it looks as though the Skelwith nursery is set to go on expanding,' James said drily. 'John is certainly making me a grandfather with a vengeance!'

'And now our little Sophie is set to make me a grandmother, too,' Héloïse said. She stood still for a moment, a chemise forgotten, half-folded, between her hands, her eyes far away as she thought back through Sophie's life, all the way to her birth in the little house in Coxwold, when it had seemed as though that obscurity would be hers for her whole life.

How lucky she had been, Héloïse thought! To have her husband and her home and her three lovely children, and now a grandchild to come, and the love of so many people! She was so rich – and she could only offer up silent and humble thanks to God for it, for she knew she didn't in the least deserve to be rich when others were poor.

James saw the slight shadow cross her face, and misinterpreted it. 'Don't worry, she'll be all right,' he said. 'Women have babies all the time. And you'll be there to keep an eye on her.'

The shadow disappeared. '*We'll* be there,' she corrected. 'I can't tell you how much I'm looking forward to it – not least because I shall have you to myself, my James, instead of sharing you with Morland Place.'

He laughed and caught her round the waist to pull her against him. She bent her head to kiss him, while Alice, having grown accustomed to their shocking ways, stoically carried on with the packing.

'Here's something that hasn't changed,' James said softly, kissing her mouth several times, and the end of her nose for luck. 'How much I love you, my Marmoset.'

'I love you too, my James,' she said huskily. 'Everything's all right now, isn't it?' Then Kai, feeling left out, thrust his head between them, and whined, pawing at James's lap. They broke apart, and Héloïse went back to helping Alice. Durban came in with an enquiry about neck-cloths, and whether James wanted any books packing.

'There's another thing that hasn't changed,' James said when he had answered the queries, 'and I don't suppose it ever will.' Héloïse looked at him enquiringly. 'You haven't finished your History of the Revolution,' he grinned.

It was time for them to leave. The elderly travelling-chaise was harnessed up to four prime York bays. Morland bred and Morland trained, a living advertisement to the stud which James hoped might attract some orders while they were in Manchester. People had money to spare again, and when they had money to spare, they liked to buy fine horses.

The family assembled on the top step in the chilly February sunshine to say goodbye. Nicholas and Henry Anstey, at the age to be shy of kissing and displays of emotion, shoved their hands in their pockets and made foolish faces and jostled each other in a mock fight. Nicholas, whose voice was breaking, alternatively bellowed and squeaked, disconcerting his mother as much as himself, and sending Henry, who hadn't reached that stage yet, into fits of derisive giggles.

Benedict, who would have his ninth birthday while they were away, was becoming quite worryingly beautiful, and offered kisses to everyone with an expression of deceptive angelicacy. He had a talent for mischief second only to his talent for making people love him. He had lately been described by one of the tenants, with a mixture of admiration and despair, as 'A fiend in yooman shape, ma lady!'

Taking her farewell of Father Moineau, Héloïse took the opportunity to whisper to him, 'Barnard knows about the cake and the special dinner. You remember where his birthday gift is hidden? And you will let him off lessons for the day?'

Moineau smiled. 'Don't worry. I have it all in hand. And the occasion will be made very special, I promise you. A day he will never forget.'

'I hope that doesn't mean the neighbourhood will never forget it either!' Héloïse turned to Polly. 'Goodbye then, my dear Polly. We shall write to you as soon as ever there is news.'

Polly smiled and returned her kiss, and anticipated her next sentence. 'I'll look after everything for you – not that there will be much to do. You have everyone so well trained, I'm sure the house would run itself.'

'But there is always the unexpected,' Héloïse said, looking at her niece curiously. Polly had never looked more beautiful, but she seemed quite to have given up all thought of being married. Why would she not accept poor Penrith – who still, to Héloïse's knowledge, wrote to Polly regularly, and what would that be for but to renew his offers of marriage?

She would make a lovely marchioness, Héloïse thought, and better that than a nun, or next thing to a nun. Polly had become very devout of late, spent a great deal of time in the chapel and reading religious literature, and was taking instruction in the Roman Catholic faith from Father Moineau. There could be no truer Catholic than Héloïse, but she believed in worshipping through one's normal life, and she couldn't help regretting all that loveliness and passion being wasted on purely intellectual religion. And yet Polly did not look dried-up or thwarted: *au contraire*, she had about her the glow, the particular look of loveliness that Héloïse associated with fulfilled love. She looked the way Sophie had looked that Christmas after Jasper had proposed and been accepted.

Ah well, Héloïse sighed inwardly, it is not my business. 'I am glad you are here to take care of things,' she said aloud. 'I should not feel happy about going away for so long otherwise. But if there is anything that worries you, you know that Miss Rosedale is not far away. You can always ask her advice.'

Polly laughed. 'I expect she'll be here more often than not, bringing the little girls to visit. But I shouldn't dream of troubling her anyway. Father Moineau and I should be able to answer all questions between us.'

A few minutes later they were driving away, circling the yard before pulling out through the barbican and taking their last glimpse of the group on the steps. Moineau, Polly, Nicholas, Bendy: father, mother and two children, Héloïse found herself thinking rather randomly. Now why on earth did that come into my head?

★

Héloïse and Sophie were enjoying a *tête-à-tête*, comfortably alone by a roaring fire amongst the elephants in the morning-room. The menfolk were out: Jasper had taken James to see the weaving-shed, which had not been in operation the last time he visited Manchester, after which they were going to dine at Jasper's club and meet some of the other mill-masters. James had retained, on Héloïse's behalf, a fifteen per cent interest in the mills, for which he was extremely grateful now they were doing so well. The Morland Place debts were in a fair way to being paid off at last, with profits from the spinning operations alone.

'I always liked the elephants,' Sophie remarked, stitching the hem of a baby-dress, 'but now I like them even more. I don't feel so out of place when I'm amongst them.'

'I don't think you are so very big, *ma mie*,' Héloïse said judiciously, looking at her little dark daughter who seemed to be sharing the armchair opposite with a very large bundle of washing. 'It's only that you are small and slight, so it shews more on you.'

'I can't believe I shall ever be small and slight again,' Sophie said. 'Jasper shakes his head at me at night and sighs and blames himself for ruining my figure.'

Héloïse smiled. 'You are happy, aren't you?'

'Oh yes! So much, Maman! I think I love Jasper as much as you love Papa. And he is so good to me. He cares for me, you know. He can't bear the slightest thing to upset me. He is really just like the brave and gentle knight in the stories we used to read when I was little – and I'm the maiden he rescued from the dragon.'

The dragon, of course, being unhappiness, Héloïse thought. 'Well, that is everything I could have wanted for you, my Sophie,' she said.

Sophie looked up from her work, a little anxiously. 'Then you don't mind – I mean, about Jasper not being tall and handsome and rich and titled and all the other things mothers are supposed to want?'

'Of course not. I like your Jasper. I always liked him.' But there was, of course, always the tiniest wisp of a lie in it when she said that, for every mother wanted her cherished daughter to marry someone tall and handsome and rich and titled, however illogical she knew that wish was. It was just

483

the way God built mothers.

'I wish Rosamund were happier,' Sophie said thoughtfully, following a logical line of connection. 'Her letters are always full of news and chat, and she never quite says anything about it, but I can tell that she's not happy.'

'Still no sign of a child for her and Marcus?' Héloïse asked.

'No. And they've been married nearly four years.'

'Perhaps that's what ails her. A woman can never really be fulfilled until she bears her man a child.'

'I don't think Rosamund feels like that, though. She's never spoken about wanting a child. In fact, she talks very disparagingly about them – calls them "little brutes" and so on.'

'Covering up her feelings,' Héloïse said. 'I thought when she stayed with us that time, before you went to Scarborough, that she was a very private person, and very good at concealing what she felt and thought. And people like that often suffer the most, poor things.' She looked at Sophie's grave face, and added cheeringly, 'But her mother will be back soon, and that will help.'

Sophie looked brighter. 'Yes – I do think she has missed Aunt Lucy.'

'They were becoming real friends, weren't they? I could see it when they were in Brussels together. It is pleasant for a mother when her daughter grows up enough to be a friend.'

'Did I tell you what Ros is hoping to plan with Aunt Lucy when she gets back? A special celebration and house party at Chelmsford House for the Coronation! Everyone's to be invited – all the family, you and Papa and Polly and the boys, and Jasper and me, and all Marcus's relations, and all their friends. She says she wants to fill Chelmsford House to the rafters and have a party no-one will ever forget.' She folded her hands over her belly. 'I'm so glad the baby is going to get here in time for me to be able to go. I should hate to miss it.'

'It sounds almost too attractive. But two holidays in one year,' her mother said doubtfully. 'I'm not sure what your father will think! It was hard enough to persuade him to come away this once – he thinks the estate will go to rack without him. He's getting more like Uncle Ned every day.' There was a silence, and she glanced up at her daughter. 'Sophie? What is it, chérie?'

Sophie's eyes were filled with a mixture of alarm and

excitement. 'I don't know because I've never felt it before, but I think –' She broke off with a grunt and closed her eyes for a moment. 'I think,' she resumed more faintly, 'that the baby is coming now.'

James turned and put himself into his wife's arms, weak with relief.

'There, my James, I told you it would be all right,' she said; but her voice sounded strained. After eighteen hours of assuring James that first babies always took a long time to arrive, quite apart from coping with her own maternal fears, she was feeling drained.

'A girl,' Jasper said, and his face was so transformed with joy and wonder that Héloïse thought he looked almost handsome. 'I'm glad it's a girl!'

'I am too,' Héloïse said. 'I think you will be a good father to a daughter.'

'Girls are much more difficult than boys to bring up,' James said, giving his son-in-law a friendly, man-to-man look across Héloïse's shoulder. 'And then, just when all the difficulties are over, they get married and you have to part with them.'

Jasper grinned. 'If you want me to apologise for marrying Sophie, I'm afraid I can't oblige you. And I'm not prepared to give her back, either.'

James smiled back. 'I'll let you have a long lease on her. Well, can we go in and see her, and the baby?'

It was a shock to him, all the same, to see his little Sophie in bed, weary from her ordeal, and yet with that transfiguring smile he remembered from when Nicky and Bendy had been born. It was a shock to see the white bundle in Sophie's arms, and realise his little girl was now a mother herself. It was painful, most of all, to remember Fanny, who had been robbed of this moment of moments, along with all the rest of her life.

Héloïse and Jasper were on either side of the bed, kissing Sophie, exclaiming over the baby – which from where he stood, at the end of the bed, was just a white cocoon with a red face. He felt suddenly cold and frightened, haunted by his memories. He was cut off from the warm precincts of reality – something he hadn't felt for years now, not since the first weeks after Ned died. Since then, he seemed to have found his place in real life; it was bad, at such a moment especially, to lose the sense of it again.

Sophie looked at him down the length of the bed, and for a moment she was so like Fanny that it made him shiver.

'Papa,' she said, 'come and see her. Come and see the baby.'

They were all looking at him now, and he saw the quick flash of anxiety in Héloïse's eyes as she realised all was not well for him. Of course, she would always know how he was feeling, even if she didn't always know why. Well, he must do his duty, he mustn't upset Sophie. He went up to the bedhead, bent over and kissed her cheek, said something – in his daze he didn't know what. And Sophie was lifting the bundle up, she was saying, 'You must hold her, Papa. Take your granddaughter.'

He took the bundle; and it wasn't a bundle, of course, but a real, living, oh such a tiny baby! Straightening up with it, he looked down into the small, sleeping face. No, not sleeping. The eyes were shut, but the lips were moving, the eyebrows going up and down – she was throbbing with the force of the new life in her. Surely it was too powerful for her tiny body to contain. Some of it must spill off somewhere, he thought. Perhaps it was absorbed by everyone who held her for the first few hours – a kind of radiant halation, like the glow you sometimes saw round a star.

Sophie spoke again, sounding a little anxious, but mostly hopeful. 'We thought, if you didn't mind, Papa, that we'd call her Fanny.'

He felt a jolt of surprise – and yet, deep down, he wasn't surprised at all. It was what Héloïse was always telling him about the wheel turning: God's pattern was worked out, if you only gave it long enough. The baby lay pulsing with new life in his arms, and all that had ever been taken from him was being given back. God's grace on him, His mercy, undeserved and yet freely given. He was forgiven at last, ransomed, healed, restored. Absorbing the spilled radiance from his granddaughter's new life, he felt suddenly young, and full of laughter.

'Little Fanny Hobsbawn,' he said in wonder.

He laughed aloud, and the baby pursed her lips at him judiciously; and then he looked up at the others, and saw that they were laughing too.